THE KEYS TO PARADISE

Texas-born Robert E. Vardeman is the co-author of the bestselling THE WAR OF POWERS and THE WAR OF POWERS 2: ISTU AWAKENED. Of these two sagas the critics said:

'A dazzling new fantasy, glowing with barbaric energy.'

'Fast-paced and fun.'

'Realistic, adult and funny.'

Now he returns with an epic three-book fantasy quest presented here in one large volume. **The Keys To Paradise.**

The Gate of Paradise can only be opened with five golden keys. An unlikely group of people get together to find those keys and see what's on the other side of the Gate.

Giles Grimsmate, battle-toughened veteran of the two-decade-long Trans War. His home has long since broken up, and all he knows is the life of a soldier. Keja Tchurak, wiry, wily thief and seducer who doesn't like taking orders from anybody. And Petia Darya, a sleek, beautiful Trans — a human with residual feline characteristics left over from an ancient curse on the people.

Together they plot and plan, chase and challenge their way back and forth across the land and past innumerable obstacles in their search for the most coveted prize of all.

By Robert E. Vardeman with Victor Milan
and published by New English Library:

THE WAR OF POWERS
THE WAR OF POWERS 2: ISTU AWAKENED

THE KEYS TO PARADISE

Robert E. Vardeman

NEW ENGLISH LIBRARY

A New English Library Original Publication, 1986

Copyright © 1986 by Robert E. Vardeman

First NEL Paperback Edition July 1986
Second impression 1986

NEL Books are published by
New English Library,
Mill Road, Dutton Green,
Sevenoaks, Kent.
Editorial office: 47 Bedford Square, London WC1B 3DP

Typeset by Rowland Phototypesetting Ltd
Bury St Edmunds, Suffolk
Printed and bound by
Cox & Wyman Ltd, Reading

British Library C.I.P.

Vardeman, Robert E.
The keys to paradise.
I. Title
813'.54[F]   PS3572.A714

ISBN 0-450-01660-9

Book One

The Flame Key

To Anna

One

GILES GRIMSMATE hungrily tore a piece of coarse black bread from the round loaf in front of him. He used it to sop up the last of the salty fish stew from his wooden bowl. It had been a long while since he had found food this good — or surroundings so pleasant.

A young serving maid grinned at him as she removed his bowl and spoon. 'Lick the bowl?' the shapely brunette asked, her words falling like honey over Giles. He had been away from people far too long, he decided, when even a simple comment aroused him. Giles took a swipe at her behind as she turned away, but she dodged with practised skill and did a saucy dance step on her way back to the kitchen. The weather-battered man wiped his mouth on a many-times-patched sleeve that had seen better days — and worse, too. He couldn't remember when he had eaten such a good meal. And fish was far from his favourite food. There had been little else during the War, but it had filled his belly well enough while others starved. Giles took a slender white bone from the pouch at his side. He turned from the table and rested his back against the wall, putting his legs up along the bench. Contentedly, he surveyed the room as he picked his teeth.

The room in the Laughing Cod was warm and comfortable and gave a respite from sleeping under hedges that would only drip cold rain on him all night. Giles decided the presence of others gave him the tonic he needed. He'd been alone with only his thoughts for comfort more than he cared to remember these past twenty years.

The maid returned, running a wet rag across the table to

3

clean up spilled stew and breadcrumbs that had escaped his voracious appetite.

'A flagon of ale when you have a moment, please.'

'La de dah, isn't he the polite one?'

Giles saw that the small courtesy pleased her, however. She stopped her chores and scurried off to draw the ale, returning almost immediately.

'The ale goes on the bill,' he said, 'but this is for you.' He laid a coin on the table. She scooped it up; it disappeared into an apron pocket. Her smile warmed Giles more than the strong ale puddling in his stomach. He sighed. He was getting old — had grown old. And what did he have to show for it save scars and grey-shot black hair and memories?

Memories. Good. Bad. And even worse than bad.

Giles took another hefty drink from the pewter flagon and studied the maid. His wife had had a smile like that when he first met her. Red, full lips and white teeth and a smile that melted his soul. Giles drank heavily and remembered better days. Days when his two sons were born, days when Leorra was young and passionately supple in his arms, when he owned a plot of good, rich farmland and a horse and a cow, and rights to grazing outside the village.

That was all before the Trans War. For twenty long, bitter years he had fought in that accursed war. And what had it accomplished? A dead family. The wife he so loved killed in a raid on his village. His boys dead because the War had lasted too long, and they had grown to fighting size. Giles closed his eyes and felt the pulse thundering like war drums in his head. They had been sent off to the brutal eastern provinces where the fighting had been fiercest and had never returned. Word came eventually that they were buried somewhere near Gallania and that they had died honourably. After twenty years of senseless death, he remained unconvinced that any of it was honourable, the war, the raids, the battles, the killing.

Only the leaders had profited greatly from the Trans War. Playing on emotions and creating prejudices where none had existed before, they had prolonged the hostilities. Cleverly, they had manipulated the people, acquired territory, and avenged themselves on old enemies. But above all else, they had become richer and richer. What did they care that men and women had died, both Trans and humans?

The War had ground to a halt, both sides depleted of troops and heartsick of the killing and endless suffering. Mass desertion, the leaders had called it. Sanity was the only word appropriate. Still, the commanders had not protested. Their games of conquest and wealth-seeking only turned to different avenues.

Giles hoped that others found peace when they returned home. He certainly hadn't. He had found his plot and his house — devoid of everything that he had loved. He took another deep draught of the ale, but it did nothing to erase the pain felt from that homecoming.

The village elders were no longer elder. They were young upstarts with ideas contrary to his own. Oh, yes, they made room for the grizzled veteran on the governing council. They gave a small celebration in honour of his return and grudgingly moved in an extra seat for the council meetings. The meetings were filled with endless bickering over the most trivial of matters, accomplishing little more than making Giles angry. Soon, he stopped attending.

He didn't know the villagers any more. He couldn't make friends with them because few were his age, and fewer still had shared the constant hardships and the ineffable bonds of friendship forged by trooping.

Giles put away his toothpick and took out a plain, well-used darkwood pipe. He filled it carefully with tobacco shaved from a block. Clouds of noxious blue smoke enveloped him, and he stared into it, oblivious of the activity and conversation in the room.

Six months had proved to him that he could no longer call this village home. He had rolled up his blankets, made a small pack of his few belongings, had his boots repaired and left quietly. He imagined that the village sighed in relief when they found him gone.

Giles puffed deeply, the smoke filling tired lungs and bringing back a tantalising hint of youth. For just a moment, to be sure, but he felt it. The past months had been nothing but aimless wandering little better than staying in his village.

He walked, he rode, he travelled, and still memories of

Leorra haunted him. And the good life now gone because he had believed and fought for the War, and found only misery.

What had he accomplished? Early this afternoon he had come down into this delta town along the coast, Klepht, they called it. It seemed no better or worse than a dozen other seaports.

As he had ambled along the waterfront, Giles had been amused by the inn sign. The Laughing Cod, it proclaimed. The artist had portrayed the plump fish with its fins on its waist and a mouth open in what had to be a loud guffaw. Giles had entered only to have an ale, but it was such excellent ale that he had found himself taking a room for the night. He had a few coins jingling in his pouch and no schedule to keep. Why not enjoy a night at the inn, someone else's cooking, sleeping in a real bed, and maybe a moment's conversation? It had been too long since he had a decent travelling companion to argue with, to swap lies with, to depend on.

Giles puffed harder as the tobacco burned down to spent embers. Outside, the sun set and cast cool grey fingers of twilight through the cobbled streets of Klepht. The inn slowly filled with sailors and fishermen whose day of hard labour had ended.

Giles sat listening to the talk of nets and gear and the catch and cargo. He shared little with these men, but the dim reflections of their shared companionship proved better than being alone for still another night.

In a quiet moment, he signalled for another flagon. When the maid brought it he asked, 'Do they ever talk of anything but the sea?'

She ran her hand through the thick mat of her curly brown hair. 'No. But they'll slow down pretty quick and begin to dice. Do you have any skill?'

'Not much, but a spot of luck rides at my shoulder now and again,' Giles said. 'What's the game?'

'Anadromi. Do you know it?'

'Never heard of it.' Giles flexed arthritic fingers until they snapped as loud as a cannon shot. They felt up to a game of dice, as they had on many a night with his men during the War. 'I'm sure they'll teach you. Go easy or they'll have all your money. You won't be able to pay your bill, and I'll have to put up with you as scullery maid for the next week.'

'Is that so bad?'

'You'd look a perfect fright wearing a dress and apron,' the brunette said, white teeth gleaming.

'You've convinced me to be careful. My knees are not nearly as comely as yours.' He settled back and sipped his ale. Warm, dry, full, content, a bit of harmless flirting. All a man could ask for when his world had become a hollow shell.

The talk around Giles slowed, and the men of the sea quieted, contemplating their burning bowls and their memories.

At last, a stubby little man at a table raised his fist and waggled it back and forth. The serving maid nodded and took a leather cup from the shelf behind the serving counter. She brought it to the table and shook it several times before rolling six bone-white dice out on the table. She bent over to see what she had rolled.

'Not bad,' she said. 'Maybe I should play tonight.'

The stubby man grinned up at her. 'And who'd serve the ale?' he asked.

'Why, you would, of course.'

'Get yer out of here now,' the man said.

Giles knew this was another oft-repeated dialogue that had become a ritual, and once again he longed for the steady companionship of good friends.

The man dumped the dice back into the leather cup and rattled it twice. He rolled the dice out, looked at them and shook his head glumly. For a time, he seemed to be the only one in the room interested. He rolled them again and again, shaking his head and muttering every time he examined the results.

'You can't fool us, Niss. When you shake your head like that, everyone knows you're netting the big fish.' Chuckles rolled around the room.

'Just tryin' to warm them up a bit. Come along and help, Tal.'

Several men went to the table. Each took his turn at rolling the dice, warming the leather cup with their hands before each toss.

Giles left the warmth of his spot to wander over, standing back and watching the results of the rolls.

'Are you ready, lads? It's time to be serious.' The little man looked around the circle of men at the table. Then he glanced up at Giles. 'They hang back. What of you, stranger?'

'I don't know the game,' Giles said. 'Let me watch for a bit till I see what it's about. Maybe later.'

The man shrugged, going back to rattling the dice in what he hoped was an enticing fashion. He passed the cup to his left. The men rolled once around the table to see who would begin.

For half an hour, Giles only watched. It was not a game he had seen before, but it wasn't difficult to understand. It had to do with runs of numbers in ascending order and differed little from a game played in camps during his days of soldiering.

Two players lost consistently and bowed out of the game. Five men still sat at the table. Niss gestured to Giles and to the empty seats. Giles nodded and sat down.

For a time Giles' losses equalled his winnings. The game became more familiar; he decided there was little strategy to learn for Anadromi, unlike some he had played which involved multiple rolls and decisions of which die to leave and which to roll again.

A big, burly man had a good run of luck and reduced the players' ranks to only four. The pile of small coins slowly grew in front of Giles, but the gnarled seaman won consistently. On the next round Niss dropped out, sweeping his few remaining coins back into his pouch. 'The luck's not with me tonight,' he said. 'Mousie seems to have the most of it.'

Giles grinned at him. 'Maybe another night.'

'Aye, there's always another night.'

On the next round a young, round-faced, red-bearded man followed Niss' example.

Giles looked at the burly seaman. 'You ready to call it quits?' he asked.

'Not on your life,' Mousie growled. 'I'm looking to hook the big fish tonight. I'll take your money as well as the next man's.' He glowered at Giles.

Giles shrugged, picked up his coins and let them slip neatly from his thick fingers into a stack on the table. 'Your choice,' he said. 'Let 'em roll.'

Mousie shoved half of his coins into the centre of the table. Giles matched them. But luck was beginning to abandon the seaman. The dice rolled out and stopped. A triple six, a three, and a one. That was an excellent roll for many different games, but not this one. Giles' roll fared scarcely better, but it won the round.

The seaman shoved the rest of his stack out, and Giles matched it again. As winner of the previous round, he rolled first — a nearly perfect roll. Two, three, three, four, five, six. Giles felt no sense of triumph, only a quiet pleasure at the roll. He had outgrown youthful enthusiasm over such matters. 'You give up? It looks like a tough one to beat.' He passed the cup to Mousie.

Two fists enclosed the cup and shook it vigorously. The fisherman concentrated on the rattling dice, willing them to obey his mumbled commands. Giles relaxed, knowing full well that there was nothing he could do about six cubes of bone with black spots on them.

The men in the inn sensed the drama at the table and gathered to watch the roll. When the dice came spinning out of the cup and slid to a stop, a sigh passed through the crowd. Giles had won again.

Mousie stared around him as if he couldn't comprehend what had happened. He looked at the pile of coin in front of Giles. For a moment, he seemed about to fling himself over it.

'Let me see those bones.'

Silently, Giles passed him the leather cup. The man stared moodily into it, then upended it, spilling the dice out onto the table. One by one he picked them up, examining them as though he suspected that Giles had substituted for the real dice. Finally, he looked up at Giles. 'I want a chance to get me money back.'

'I gave you a chance to quit. Didn't you keep anything back?'

'No,' the man muttered.

'That's foolish. Then you've got nothing left to wager, have you?'

The sailor said nothing, staring off toward the fireplace. Making a hard decision, he tugged open the neck of his sailor's smock and pulled a string from around his neck. A key dangled from the string.

Mousie pulled the string over his head and handed it to Giles.

'I'll wager this against the whole pile,' he said.

Giles turned the key over in his hands. It appeared to be gold. The three teeth were square and the circular shank stretched nearly four inches, ending with a flat round circle. In the centre of the circle was a small, light green gemstone; peridot, Giles thought. Encircling the stone were finely etched runes.

'You're sure you want to wager this?' Giles asked.

Mousie nodded glumly.

'It looks valuable. Gold, isn't it?'

'Yes.'

'Where'd you get it?'

'A friend. He left it to me. We were shipmates once. He was killed in the War. He'd understand me wagering it.' Mousie snorted derisively. 'Old Pragg bet more'n this in his day. Best two out of three rolls?'

Giles turned the key over in his hands, thinking. He had won all the sailor's money, plus some from each of the other players. Now this man wanted a chance to win it all back. Luck was with Giles tonight and, for the most part, it was other men's money.

He nodded. 'Two out of three. Your key against my coin.'

Giles felt more alive than he had in weeks. 'Want to roll one die to see who goes first?'

Mousie won the roll of the single die and grinned as if he had already won. He dumped the six dice into the cup and shook it with confidence.

But it ended quickly. Giles won both rounds and pocketed the key.

The sailor stood up, knocking over the bench. 'You cheated me!' he yelled.

The room grew quiet. Mousie's work-roughened hands clenched at his sides. Giles stood quietly, pushing his pouch around to the back of his belt so that it wouldn't get in his way. As casual as the gesture was, it carried professionalism and deadly resignation with it. Giles' mind settled into fighting calm as he appraised his would-be foe.

He realised that the rest of the men in the room had backed off, watching silently.

'Easy, now, friend,' Giles said. 'I gave you the chance to quit twice. I asked if you were sure you wanted to bet.'

The man's face flamed. 'You cheated!' he roared.

'You can't cheat at this game,' Giles said. 'It's all luck. You checked the dice.'

A call came from the corner of the room. 'That's right, Mousie, you know you can't cheat in that game. The stranger won right squarely.'

'But it's not fair,' Mousie argued. 'He took all my money.'

'I didn't take it. You wagered it and lost,' Giles said.

The man shook his head, not wanting to believe what he had done.

'Come on, friend. Sit down and share a brandy, and we'll talk about it.' Giles raised his voice. 'Landlord, brandy here for me and my friend. Brandy for everyone!'

A cheer went up around the room. The landlord looked at Giles as if to reassure himself that the stranger meant it. Giles nodded. The expression on his face made the innkeeper blanch. He had seen veterans before, that look, the deadly quality that they carried with them wherever they went.

Mousie looked around him at the beaming faces. He didn't want to believe that his mates were abandoning him. Giles reached across the table and laid his hand on the other man's thick arm.

'Come. Sit down and have a brandy. We'll work something out. I don't want to take your last coin. I've been without a hope, much less a pair of coppers to rub together. I know what it's like.'

The man stared up at Giles to see if he was serious. The serving maid quietly set glasses of brandy on the table and scurried away. Mousie watched her go, a perplexed look on his dull face. Finally, with a sigh, he righted the bench and sat down. He picked up the glass of brandy and swallowed it in one gulp. Giles shoved the second glass over to him.

'Go ahead. She'll bring more. Drink it down, then we'll talk.'

The second brandy took two gulps. The crimson wrath had gone out of Mousie's face. Giles was certain that he no longer wanted to fight. He fingered the coin and key on the table.

'You shouldn't have continued to gamble until you lost everything. Excuse me for saying so, but that's a stupid thing to do.'

Chagrined, Mousie hung his head.

'I don't want you to go hungry before the next catch,' Giles said. 'I'm not giving it all back. After all, I did win fairly.' He let the coins riffle from his cupped, calloused fingers. 'Maybe next time you'll be more cautious. But probably not, eh?'

Mousie stared at Giles, then laughed. 'Probably not. This is not the first time.'

'I suspected so.' Giles shoved a stack of five coins over to Mousie. 'See if you can hang on to that for a week. Friends?'

Mousie stared bemusedly at the coins in front of him. He reached out and grasped Giles' hand. 'Friends,' he said.

Giles slipped the rest of the coins into his pouch and stood. 'I'll be back and drink with you later. I need to speak to the landlord.'

When he had finished assuring the landlord that he would stand brandy for all, and ale when that ran out, Giles retired to his seat by the fireplace. Stranger things had happened to him. While not afraid of the sailor, Giles was pleased that he had been able to placate Mousie. He wasn't sure that he could have bested the burly sailor, even knowing a thousand ways of fighting learned over a lifetime. Bumps and bruises were a thing of his past.

Giles reached into his pouch and pulled out the key. Leaning forward to catch the light from the fire, he examined it closely. It was gold, and the small peridot caught the dancing firelight and winked at him, as if sharing a wondrous secret.

The runic inscription ran in a tight circle around the small stone. Giles puzzled it out, rune by rune. 'The Key to Paradise,' it read. Giles frowned.

A man much older than Giles limped over to the table. He carried his tumbler of brandy with him.

'I came to thank you for the brandy, stranger. It warms these poor old bones. May I sit with you?'

Giles gestured to the empty bench opposite. He looked at the key again and started to place it back in his pouch.

The old man's wizened, blue-veined hand reached across the table. 'May I?' he asked.

Giles laid the key in the man's outstretched palm. After careful scrutiny, he returned the key to Giles. 'I thought so. The Key to Paradise.'

'So I read,' Giles said. 'What does it mean?'

'Don't you know?' The old man looked to see if Giles was poking fun at him.

'It means nothing to me.'

'I could tell you a story, but my throat's dry,' he said slyly, feigning a harsh cough. Giles raised his hand to the serving maid. He pointed at the old man's glass.

'Ah, you're a rare one, sir. Thankee. Now, the Key to Paradise. Somewhere out there is the Gate of Paradise, and if we can believe the tales, this key will unlock that gate. Now, what's behind the Gate . . . ah, the stories! Gold, jewels, beautiful women, power, wealth, your heart's desire! Nobody knows, but the stories say that it's everything you could ever want.'

'Do they? And just where is that Gate to Paradise?'

'Ah, there's the rub. Every story I've heard puts it in a different place. North, south, east, west, take your choice. Might be it's in all those places — or none.'

'Sounds like just another tall tale to me,' Giles said. 'Have you ever heard of anyone who actually saw the Gate?'

'No,' the old man admitted. 'But that fits the story, too. The story runs that you've got to have the key in your hand to actually see the Gate.'

Giles threw back his head and laughed.

'You laugh, sir. But people believe that story. I do. And here you are with the key in your hand. Best keep it safe — unless your charity extends to offering an old crippled man the key as a token.'

'I spent twenty years at the Wars. Promoted to sergeant and broken to the ranks three times. Through it all, I learned one lesson: be generous to beggars, but not too generous.' The grizzled veteran stood, saying, 'Your story is worth another brandy. But no more. I'm off for a drink with my erstwhile gambling partner, and then to bed. Thank you for your company. 'Come round tomorrow night and I'll buy you another.' He laid his hand on the old man's shoulder.

After a quick drink with Mousie, Giles nodded to the landlord and mounted the stairs to his room above.

The wind had blown the threatening storm clouds away, and Giles stood at his window for a brief while, looking down over the moonlit waterfront.

The night had been unexpectedly profitable, and had provided a moment's diversion in what had become a life of pointless drifting. Pointless. No home, nothing to tie him down. Giles rubbed his aching joints, wishing the storm would come and get it over. The threat of rain only protracted his pains. He stretched, yawned, thought on the fable the old man had told. Absurd maunderings, nothing more than superstition. Giles had heard it all before, in a dozen places, over the years.

And what if it were true? Riches to carry him into his old age, which wasn't so far off. He straightened his right arm, wincing as joints protested at even this small movement.

Giles kicked off his boots and lay down in the bed, pulling the covers over himself. The Gate of Paradise. Why not go looking for it? He had nowhere else to go or anything of a pressing nature. Why not wander with a purpose? But no hurry, no hurry.

Those were his last thoughts before his eyes closed for the night. By the time the rains pelted wet and cold against the window, Giles Grimsmate snored loudly, his dreams about Paradise.

Two

THE LEATHER Cup was deceptively quiet even though it stood just off Kelpht's main street. A few labourers from the shipyards stopped in to end their working day, but they lingered only long enough to drink a couple mugs of watery ale. One by one, they shouldered their tool bags and departed, worn men on their way home to families. Some would be met with love, others with the shrilling of wives and the snivelling of children. None noticed the small, dark, quick-gestured man lounging in one cobwebby corner of the tavern.

An oddly cheerless lot, Keja Tchurak thought, even for such an undistinguished delta town. Not for the first time, Keja cursed the treacherously unkind fate that had driven him from a comfortable berth and a willing woman and sent him fleeing, to hide from shadows, to jump at the slightest of sounds behind him. But such kept him free — and alive.

He cut a bite-sized morsel of beef from the greasy slab on the plate before him. It was awful, tasteless.

Keja leaned back, chewing thoughtfully. Rosaal had been quite a woman. Raven hair, long slender legs so willing to part for him, the sumptuous body of a courtesan. He stopped chewing as he remembered with real fondness their nights together. It had been a favour of the gods that her family had money, too. That she showed herself to be a bit on the dim-witted side rankled after a few passionate nights, though. Keja eventually had became sated enough to realise that her body and loving ways weren't everything.

Keja resumed chewing. The tough beef required many swallows of ale to get it down. The bread was little better, and it wasn't fresh. Yesterday's, probably. Keja hated inns where the owner took so little pride in what he served. No doubt this accounted for the other patrons simply swilling the pitiful ale and then leaving to go tup their mistresses or wives. That's what Keja would rather be doing than sitting in the Leather Cup, had he mistress or wife.

He looked around the nearly empty room. Not good. If the city guard came a'checking, he would stand out like a red silk bow on a swine's snout. He prayed for a quick change in the innkeeper's penurious policies, for good ale and food, for the room to fill up. Perhaps some locals would come in after their suppers and a lusty roll with their mistresses. That would make it easier to remain inconspicuous. If patrons didn't show up soon, Keja saw no choice but to retire to his dismal room upstairs.

He tried another bite of beef. As he feared, it had not improved. Keja waved to the serving wench to take it away. 'Bring me a couple of hard-boiled eggs,' he ordered imperiously. 'This beef is a disgrace even to the bottom of Klepht's sewer, if there is one.' He pointed to his cup. 'And another ale.'

The serving wench said nothing, accepting his order with ill-concealed bitterness. Keja watched her walk away with a grace no human shared. A Trans, and part cat. He hadn't seen many in Klepht. Keja eyed her critically and decided she'd be a pretty one if the landlord didn't keep her on the run so much. She was a bit dishevelled, her hair mussed, and a streak of soot ran across her forehead, probably from stoking the kitchen fire. But she was slender, with clean, sharp features, and that unmistakable feline quality in walk and gesture. Keja shivered a little when he saw her yellow eyes; definitely catlike, with vertical slit pupils — and predatory.

Keja wondered what it would be like with her, all night long, releasing those animal passions. He had heard tales of love-making with a Trans. Keja had to admit the idea excited him.

The cat Trans serving maid returned with his ale and two eggs rocking to and fro in a small wooden bowl. He picked up a speckled brown egg and rapped it against the side of the bowl. Egg white oozed out onto his fingers. He glanced up at her. Those fierce yellow cat eyes shone with defiance, daring him to complain again.

Keja shoved the bowl away, silently picked up his ale and carried it over to the fireplace, standing with his back to the flames. The young man felt nothing but disgust at the service, at Klepht, at everything. Under different circumstances he would have complained loud and long. Not now. He dared not. He peered across the room, trying to study the weather outside, but the windows were too dirty. It figured.

Keja needed to get away from this provincial jerkwater town, to keep on the move. At the moment, however, he needed rest. He had been hounded too long. This slovenly inn provided him a good enough respite; it was not the sort of place guards would expect an accomplished thief like the great Keja Tchurak to choose.

Keja's left arm still ached where one of Werlink l'Karm's personal guards had sliced it with a lucky thrust. Idly, he rubbed it. It hadn't hurt this badly in days. It must be turning to rain outside.

Keja smiled. Master thief that he was, he'd escaped, and with a tidy haul, too. But l'Karm didn't give up easily. The merchant's private guard had dogged Tchurak's steps at every turn, only overwhelming cleverness saving him on several occasions. But Keja had to admit that when they closed in on him along the River Kale, escape had come through pure luck. The story he had told the old fisherman about jilting a lover rang too true, but the fisherman being at the right place could only be called luck. Hiding under a wagonload of fish was not at all pleasant, but seemed like high times at Gresham's Fair in comparison with what the guard would have done to him.

And the haul stayed intact. A hefty bag of coin, some baubles he would sell off when he got to a bigger city, and the gold key. If he had thrown the guard off his trail, and it looked as if he had, he might follow up the chimerical story behind the key told him by loving Rosaal, lovely Rosaal.

His backside good and warm from the fire, Keja sighed at the memory of the fiery Rosaal gracing his bed, then wandered back to a bench near the corner. Locals drifted in, bringing with them gusts of fresh air from the windy weather outside.

Keja ordered another ale and watched the patrons playing a board game. They were a quiet lot, glum and dour. They played with too much seriousness for his taste.

He reached into his pouch and pulled out the golden key. His thoughts drifted far from booty or key. Unconsciously, Keja turned the key over and over in his hand.

'Bring more wood in from outside, and there's two hands up out there looking for their ale.' The landlord's loud, grating voice stirred instant dislike in Keja. He had heard that tone too many times when he had been down on his luck and actually doing menial tasks to survive. 'When you've done that, the baking pans haven't been washed from yesterday. And don't give me any of your dark looks, my Pet.'

'Don't call me Pet.' Keja looked from the Trans serving wench to the landlord. The way the light caught her face highlighted the cat-portion over the human. He wondered if she would rip out the insulting landlord's throat. If Keja had been in her place, he would have.

The landlord of the Leather Cup wiped greasy hands across the expanse of his apron and laughed. 'Don't we have our pride? Get on with you, don't stand idle.' He turned back to stir a pot of ill-smelling stew.

Petja Darya made an obscene gesture behind his back and stormed into the taproom to fill two cups for the thirsty patrons. She'd been working at the inn for a week and would stay only long enough to earn a few coins before moving on. Servitude did not suit her at all.

She carried the brimming cups across the room to the men who scowled at her. They were the same two who had harassed her all week. 'Filthy Trans bitch,' she heard one of them mutter as she turned away.

Petja felt the desire to turn and show them a bit of her cat nature, but she subdued her temper. She vowed to get her revenge, not only on them, but on the landlord, too. Soon.

Two more men came in and ordered, and for the next few minutes she busily fetched ale. By the time she had caught up with the orders, her anger only smouldered.

She brought wood in from outside until her arms ached, then set to washing the baking pans. She was interrupted from time to time with calls for more ale. The landlord was being his usual obsequious self to the customers, but drawing and

18

serving was beneath his dignity — which he let her know at every turn. Petia was kept busy between kitchen and the public room.

She wished that she were anywhere except here in Klepht. Petia had left Trois Havres in a hurry, her burglaries too careless. It was a case of overconfidence. If she had not seen the handbill seeking her arrest, she might now be working off seven years in the Duke's gold mines. Luck had come her way when she found a ship crossing the Everston Sea and a cargomaster willing to look the other way for a few coins to augment his paltry wages.

Escape had not been without other penalties. She had arrived in Bericlere with only a few coins to show for all the troubles besetting her. Petia stoically accepted that; it was part of her heritage. Trois Havres, her home and the home of many of the Trans, was pleasant enough, but had few opportunities for the ambitious. Petia almost sneered at the idea of ambition in a Trans.

For over two hundred years they had been scorned, reviled, made into little more than slaves by a sorceress far too quick with her curses. Cassia n'Kaan had turned the people of an entire continent into part human, part animal for a relatively minor offence. Petia often wondered if the broken trade treaty with Lord Lophar had, indeed, been the cause for so much misery for her and untold others turned into Trans. She guessed at more between sorceress and merchant-lord. It mattered little now. The sorceress had perished, and the Trans had slowly evolved, regressing to human form.

And she had been indentured and escaped, become a thief and escaped, and now Petia tried her hand at serving. From this she'd escape, too.

Petia held out her hand and sharp talons snapped out like the blade of a folding knife. The Trans became more human with every passing generation, but many traits remained. For that, Petia thanked gods living, dead, and to be.

Because of the partial humanity, Petia and others of her kind worked harder to prove themselves, to get ahead, to survive. That driving ambition had provided fuel for the Trans War. A demagogue with honeyed voice and inflammatory mind arose to condemn the Trans for economic setbacks. Even now, even after twenty years or more, Petia felt anger rising at Duke Pattch. His coin was not of gold, but of hatred.

For all those dying during twenty years of fighting, Pattch lived, as did the other lords who had seized the opportunity for aggression. It became expedient to correct disputed bound- aries, attack old enemies, and, if one were strong enough, to acquire new territory.

Twenty years of war had worsened the commoners' lot and bettered those in power. And throughout it all, the Trans still bore the brunt of it. Hatreds, illogical or not, festered and corrupted even the most decent of men. Few on either side escaped.

Petia Darya did not escape, nor did she want to. Especially with humans such as this foolish, fat landlord to fan the fires of her prejudices.

She finished the last baking pan and set it on the wooden rack to dry. As much as it rankled, Petia knew she must clean up after the patrons. They were little better than pigs — and she knew many pig Trans who were impeccably clean compared to the humans and the Leather Cup's landlord.

Petia poured cold water into a bucket and then added hot water from the stove. A brick of hard soap would help to cut the grease. She couldn't believe those tables. Had anyone ever cleaned them before her? Were all humans so compulsively dirty? Without realising it, she licked the back of her hand and drew it quickly across her face.

Petia started in the corner nearest the door. Several patrons had left, and those remaining clustered near the fire. She didn't blame them. It was draughty by the door, cold rain blowing in. The only thing she hated more than being dirty was being wet. Hot water, soap and hard work took off the top layer of rings from the beer mugs and grease from spilled stew. Petia worked slowly from table to table. Two more men left, leaving the door unlatched. It swung open in a gust of wind, and the landlord yelled at her to close it.

Petia obeyed, noticing the insolent man who had sent his beef back earlier in the evening. He silently moved closer to the fireplace but did not settle in with the rest of the group. From the corner of her eye, she saw he held an object in his hands, turning it over and over.

She moved closer, still cleaning the table tops. Curiosity got the better of Petia. She had to see the glittering object. Probably some insignificant memento of the war. A small knife, perhaps, or a coin. Something that occasionally reflected a golden glint of firelight.

The Trans woman couldn't get a clear view, no matter how she tried. Spying the empty ale mugs of the departed customers, she quietly walked past his table and gathered them up. Turning, she asked, 'More ale for you this evening, sir?'

He started, pulled from his reverie. 'What? Oh, yes, another.'

Petia smiled happily. She got a better look at the object. It was a key — of solid gold, if she was any judge.

As the ale gurgled from its barrel into the mug, Petia's mind churned with plans. That man was staying at the inn. His room could easily be reached from the roof. That room had a window that didn't stick, unlike some. She had opened it only that morning to let in fresh air while doing the upstairs cleaning.

The gold key might unlock a new future for her. If nothing else, it would get her away from the inn and the doltish landlord.

She hurried back to the table where the man stared into the ebbing fire. Petia set the frothing mug in front of him, getting a closer look at the key. Gold. Definitely. Thoughts of fencing it raced through her mind. She knew one contraband merchant over on the Street of Fins who had a reputation for being almost honest. Twenty percent of value? Could she barter for that much of the key's true value? More?

Petia took up her rag and continued scrubbing tables. For the first time in days she hummed tunelessly as she worked. With luck and a modicum of caution, the key would be hers this night, and by morning she would be gone.

Sleep came easily to Petia. Fatigued from the long day's work, she curled up on a straw mat near the fire in the kitchen, pulling the thin wool blanket up to her chin. She concentrated for a moment, then closed her eyes, confident of awakening in a few hours.

It lacked a few minutes of the second watch of the night when Petia awoke. She stretched luxuriously, catlike, loosening her limbs. Petia fashioned her hands into claws and smiled with satisfaction as her nails lengthened. There was some advantages to being a Trans, particularly a feline.

Petia tucked her bright red blouse inside her skirt, then hoisted the long, dark skirt above her knees. Taking hold of the front hem, she pulled it between her legs and tucked it into the back of the waist. This gave her freedom of movement and lessened the chances of getting caught on a protruding nail as she climbed.

Silently, she left the kitchen. For a moment she stood near the tap, eyes adjusting to the darkened inn room. Petia crossed the room to the outside door. She opened it noiselessly, slipped out, and faded into the darkness.

Reaching up to the small gable over the door, she found the bracing and swung herself up. She crouched on the roof, thankful that both wind and rain had quieted. She examined the roof for weak spots and loose tiles.

The cold night air cleared her head. Petia felt alive, in her element. The night sky her sole companion, an empty roof, a quest with a rich prize at its end, the chance to use her light-fingered skills once again set her pulse racing. This was what life was meant to be, not running to every ale-guzzling, dirty human's call.

Petia confidently traversed the sloping roof, angling up to the main ridge. Reaching it, she straddled it and caught her breath, listening for any sounds from the rooms beneath her feet.

Checking the downslope, she gauged the distance from the corner to the window of Keja's room. She hesitated, sinking into a dark shadow when she spotted the lantern of the night watch. The man checked the doors of businesses along his route and occasionally raised his lantern to peer down an alleyway. In less than a minute, he had passed on. Her sharp ears told of his steady progress away.

Moving more slowly now, Petia crept down the roof. Reaching the gutter, she lowered herself and peered over the edge. A smile darted across her lips. She had judged accurately. Less than a foot to her left opened the window of her prey.

She turned her body parallel with the roof edge and hooked her left knee and foot into the gutter. Reaching down, she grasped the window frame with clawlike fingernails. After a small prayer to Dismatis, protector of thieves, she exerted pressure upward. The window slid quietly open. She gripped the gutter and swung herself down to the sill and into the room.

Petia moved sideways from the window like the hunting cat that she was. Never show a silhouette, should the man awaken. Unless the man had rearranged things, she knew the furniture's placement.

Where would he hide the key? His pouch? Most men kept their smaller valuables there. In the subtle light, Petia made out his clothes tossed over the back of a wooden chair. She moved silently to the chair, feeling cautiously for the clothing. He had removed his shirt last and it was on top. She picked it up and placed it over her arm. Beneath were his trousers, but she found no belt.

A smart one. She replaced the clothes and moved to the chest along one wall. It was a low, flat-topped cabinet only two drawers high.

Carefully, she felt along the top. The belt! But no pouch. She ran her fingers down the front of the cabinet, feeling for the drawer pulls.

The top drawer slid open. Petia reached into it. Nothing. She closed it and reached for the handles of the second drawer. A snore came from the bed, followed almost immediately by a coughing spell. Petia stood motionless, crouched over the lower drawer. The coughing stopped, and Petia continued her search. The sleeping man moaned once, then his breathing became regular again.

Petia's heartbeat slowed, and she pulled the bottom drawer open. Nothing.

Cautious soul, this one, she thought. The pouch must rest under his pillow. That called for a great deal more stealth. She looked over to the bed. He slept, oblivious to her presence.

Petia made her way to the foot of the bed and stood looking down at him. Outside, the scudding night clouds cleared to send silvery moonlight flooding through the room. During the evening, she had been much more interested in the object in his hands than in what he looked like.

Not bad looking, she decided. For a human. But even in sleep, he had a demeanour which warned that he should not be taken casually. Petia wondered if he might not be Trans, also. She felt an oddly compelling kinship with him; his looks held the same intensity she carried within her breast.

She moved on light feet around the bed to be at his back. Searching under a sleeping person's pillow was a delicate operation. If he stirred, she might be able to hide beneath the bed until he again slept soundly. Better hiding under a bed than being in them, she had always told her fellow thieves. Especially with a smelly human, though Petia had to admit this one's odours pleased her.

Cautiously, she felt for the edge of the pillow. Her hand thinned as she slipped it underneath. Leather thongs brushed her deft fingertips. The pouch rested directly under the man's curly-haired head.

She pulled back to consider her next move. Petia yelped in surprise as the man grabbed her, exploded to his knees, and faced her.

'What have we here, my Trans beauty? Come to share the wondrous lover's bed, eh? You ought to have told me of your uncontrollable passion. I would have left the door unlatched and saved you the trouble of sneaking in through the window.'

'Let me go!' Petia tried to pull away, but Keja's strength was too much for her.

'Don't struggle, or I'll break your wrist,' he said. 'We don't want to wake all the rest in this miserable inn. Unless it is with the moans of our mutual rapture.'

'You impudent . . .' Petia started. She swallowed hard, realising the danger. She shook her head, deciding on another tack. 'Please, sir. Please don't wake them. I was only going to take a little money, not all, sir. Just enough to get away from this awful place.'

'An honest thief? Dare I admit having met one who tells the truth? No,' Keja said. 'It's too good to be true. You would have stolen the lot and left me with nothing. Not even a memory of a warmly glowing groin for my stay in this poxy inn. All we agree on is a desire to leave this blackroach-infested pit.'

'Yes,' Petia spat. 'I want to get away from a greasy inn with a greasy landlord.'

'A greasy landlord who will turn you over to the guard when I tell him his Trans serving wench is burgling the rooms of his patrons. He won't like that, I'm sure.'

'You wouldn't do that, sir.' Petia assumed her best fawning posture. Her mind estimated, judged, evaluated how difficult it would be to escape.

Keja's grip relaxed. 'No, I wouldn't do that,' he assured her. Petia was quick to slip her wrist free. She knelt back on her haunches, distancing herself from the man. There would be no theft of the key this night. If she could convince him that it was only a desperate need for money that had prompted her venture, she might get off free. Appeal to his obvious vanity. Promise, but never deliver. That looked the best course for her escape.

'There's another way besides theft, you know,' Keja said.

'What's that, sir?' Petia asked naïvely. Inwardly, she turned cold with the too-easy success. She had read this man right. For some reason, this bothered her.

'You can spend the night with me. In the morning, I'd see that you had enough to leave here and get far away.'

Insane light flashed in Petia's cat eyes. 'Damn you. I'll not give my body to anyone for money.' Emotions raged out of control, emotions betraying her true feelings. Even as she acted, Petia cursed herself for it. She had intended to play the man like a fish on a line. Instead, she had acted the fool. She raised her hands toward Keja's eyes and watched him edge back as her cat claws extended.

'You know full well there are laws against what you suggest. Trans and humans are not allowed to mix.' Petia knew this argument meant nothing — all too well she knew it.

Keja laughed. 'Foolish laws that have not stopped me before. Admit it, you have some measure of lust for me, don't you?' Keja eyed her critically. 'I do for you. You are comely. Together we can . . .'

Keja dodged back as Petia's claws flashed within a hair of his dark eyes. 'But if it goes against your grain, then I apologise. You miss the thrill of a lifetime, though.'

'I'll rip out your throat before you lay a hand on me.'

'It was only a suggestion, but a good one. I'll be gone tomorrow. Off to make my fortune, while you, my tawny one, will still be cleaning tables in the Leather Cup. Truly, I do pity you your fate. Dirty tables and never to have shared my bed.'

Keja clucked his tongue and shook his head in mock sadness.

Petia hissed. 'You jackal.' In one lithe movement, she was on her feet and backed towards the window. She held her hand ready should Keja drop his ironic pose. Petia was surprised, however, when he rose from the bed, extended his leg and literally swept the floor with his courtly bow.

'May you sleep as well as you can — without me,' he said. His smile almost made Petia return to wipe it from his lips. She forced down her anger, gripped the gutter, swung up to the roof.

She was more determined than ever that she would have that key. It would be little enough revenge on the smirking, self-confident human. She edged to the corner of the building and settled down as comfortably as she could. He'd not leave in the middle of the night without her knowing it. Perched like a gargoyle, Petia Darya watched through what remained of the night.

Three

PETIA SHIVERED. The night had passed slowly with no sign of movement from the inn. That jackal had probably gone back to sleep immediately. Still, it had been prudent of her to spend the night watching. It was better to take too much care than too little in the pursuit of such valuable booty.

The first pink and grey vestiges of false dawn appeared in the sky. Petia rose stiffly to her feet, joints aching from her night-long vigil. She flexed her knees and allowed the blood to circulate into cramped legs. She looked across the rooftops of Klepht. It wasn't a bad town, but not the town for her. Quiet, sleeping, even the night watch absent, the prejudices against her kind also slept. It would be only a few minutes before people and their hatreds began stirring, no better or worse than any other human town.

Petia stretched one last time, then she climbed across the inn's roof and dropped softly down from the entrance gable. She slipped through the front door, latched it securely so the landlord could not berate her, and walked silently to the kitchen.

She busied herself removing the ashes in the cooking stove and building a fresh fire. From the root cellar, she brought a sack of potatoes and began peeling them. By the time the landlord came downstairs, a neat pile of potatoes lay in a bowl upon the counter. He found nothing to complain about, but started to anyway. Something about the hot look Petia flashed him stayed the unwarranted criticism.

'Beginning to get the routine of it, eh?' He grumbled and waddled off to the taproom to draw his first ale of the day.

Nearly an hour passed before the inn's guests began arriving for breakfast. Petia was kept busy serving the plain breakfasts the morning cook made. Porridge, scrambled eggs, a mug of ale. And fresh bread this morning. Petia looked forward to her own breakfast after her night on the roof.

Keja Tchurak came down the stairs whistling softly. He warmed himself before the fireplace, then took a table. Petia brought him a small kettle of porridge and a jug of goat's milk.

'Good morning,' he said with a cheerfulness that rankled. 'A fine day blooming. Far better than the night. Rained a goodly bit, didn't it? Wouldn't have wanted to be out in all the . . . rain and wind. Not at all.' Petia glared at him.

'Nothing like a good night's sleep to make for a good start to the day,' he continued innocuously. 'Hope you found a soft bed. Mine was hard. All night long.'

Petia spun angrily and marched to the taproom to draw a mug of ale for him. His low chuckle mocked her all the way and firmed her resolve to separate this irritating man from his wealth.

When Keja had finished eating, he left the inn singing, off key, the chorus of a well-known sea ballad. A deaf woman would have heard the inn door slam behind him.

Petia found the landlord snoring behind a stack of crates in the storeroom, sleeping off his early morning ales. She threw down her apron and grabbed her shawl from a hook. As she hurried out of the kitchen door, she saw Keja cross the street, heading for the waterfront.

Petia ran on cat-light feet to the corner and peered around. Keja had put nearly half a street length between them. He walked purposefully, looking neither to the sides nor behind. It was not difficult to follow him unobserved.

At the docks, Petia watched as Keja talked briefly to a disreputable pair of lounging sailors. They pointed to a ship farther along the waterfront. Keja nodded and set off again.

By the time Petia found a safe spot to spy from, Keja had entered an impassioned discussion with the captain of a small coastal lugger. The captain leaned on the ship rail, punctuating his conversation by spitting over the side. Petia busied herself looking over the first boxes of fresh catch arranged alongside a warehouse opposite. Her sharp ears easily overheard the conversation.

'Neelarna, is it?' the captain said. 'Ah, there's been a goodly bit of unrest there. I'm not keen on making the trip without cargo. Waste of time. Dangerous.'

'How much?' Keja called up to him, knowing full well from his earlier talk with the sailors that Captain Jelk had a full hold bound for Neelarna. 'I'm willing to pay a fair rate. I don't care to be cheated, but I see your concern.'

'Well, now.' The captain spat again, then seemed to be doing sums in the clouds overhead. It was obviously hard work deciding by how much he could cheat Keja. He grinned and named a price ten times too high.

'Done,' Keja said. 'When can we sail? This afternoon?'

'In a hurry, are you?' The captain's grin broadened in pleasure with himself. He had accurately appraised this one's need to be free of Klepht.

'Right. I'm off to find the Gate of Paradise. Make my fortune and find a bevy of lovely damsels.' Keja did a fancy clog step.

'And I'm the ruler of the universe,' the captain said scornfully. He spat, the gobbet landing only a few inches from Keja's boots. 'Don't allow fools to ship aboard the Feral.'

'Or,' said Keja, 'a certain lord has taken a dislike to the attentions I so graciously lavished on his daughter.' The captain nodded solemnly. Keja laughed. 'Or maybe I just want to visit my grandmother. Take your pick, Captain.'

'Show me your money, and we'll sail on the afternoon tide,' the captain called down.

Petia frowned. Keja had sounded jocular when he mentioned the Gate of Paradise, but the gold key? The gold key to the Gate of Paradise? She had always thought it more than mere legend. This might be proof of her belief.

This was a goal worthy of Petia Darya's talents! Her mind worked furiously on the new problems involved with stealing the key. Aboard ship? impossible. Stowing away was out of the question. On land? Yes, to Neelarna. She'd arrive in Neelarna before Keja, travelling overland. She'd be waiting for him when he sailed in. He knew where the Gate stood — he had the key, after all. She would follow him, then steal the key!

Petia smiled wickedly and returned to the inn. The landlord still snored noisily where she had left him.

She grabbed a flour sack and stuffed it with a flitch of bacon, a joint of beef, some potatoes and a few loaves of bread. It took only a few moments to don travelling clothes, brown home-spun breeches and shirt, boots almost to the knee, a soft tam. She threw a cloak over all, buckled a short sword to her belt, slung the sack and said a heartfelt farewell to the Leather Cup. Petia reached the door, then paused. If she carried the brand of thief for stealing food, why not also for real theft? Petia went to the baking ovens and pulled out a loose brick near the floor. From the bag the landlord hid there, she emptied all twenty coins. It was more than he owed her, but far less than she deserved. Besides, he shouldn't have so carelessly let her sniff out where he stashed his money.

All continued going Petia's way. When the halfwit stableboy left for his morning ale, she slipped in and threw a bridle on a coastal marsh pony. He was an ugly animal, but she knew of no hardier breed of horse. She hoisted her pack onto his back, mounted and circled north around the city, then took the coast road heading east, riding as if all the hounds of Bericlere nipped at her heels.

Petra would be in Neelarna long before Keja Tchurak. The wind against her face pulled the laughter out and streamed it behind her as she rode.

The tide turned in late afternoon. Keja boarded the *Feral* a half hour before. The first mate showed him where to store his meagre belongings, and left Keja to watch the activities as he bellowed orders to the sailors. Hawsers were loosened and shipped, and the tide carried the lugger away from the dock. Sails unfurled. The ship turned easily in the light winds and warped out of harbour.

Keja leaned over the rail and squinted into the sea breeze. He felt as if a heavy weight had been lifted from his shoulders. The guards could seek him all they wanted now – in Klepht. As quickly as he considered the guards, so did his thoughts fleetingly touch on the Trans serving wench. Keja smiled and shook his head. Why had she followed him to the port? She was no informer for I'Karm. She looked like a thief to Keja, and he knew thieves.

Such a comely one. He felt a twinge of sorrow that she hadn't stowed away, that she had given up so easily on stealing the key in his pouch. Keja lightly brushed nimble fingertips over the leather pouch.

The Gate of Paradise. Such a high sounding thing, that. And he, Keja Tchurak, thief with no peer, would be the one to loot Paradise!

Once out into the Everston Sea, the lugger coasted slowly eastward, moving as the fitful winds dictated.

Night fell and lanterns were lit. The captain came up to Keja and asked, 'Share supper? Been a while since the *Feral* carried a passenger.'

'You mean one willing to pay such an exorbitant fare,' said Keja with no malice in his voice.

'Your tale must rank with the best,' said Captain Jelk. 'I am always interested – in the Gate of Paradise.'

Keja looked sharply at the captain, but the man only joked.

'I do feel a need for sustenance,' admitted Keja.

Captain Jelk kept up a desultory conversation about this piece of the coast and his trips along it throughout the meal. Keja tried to show interest, but he didn't really care – until the captain started on the tales he had heard of the Gate of Paradise.

'How's that again?' asked Keja.

'Mistress Mellon knows all about how it grants immortality,' Jelk said. He scowled darkly. 'You look truly interested in this.'

'I don't really seek the Gate. My business involves other matters in Neelarna,' Keja replied, trying to sound unconcerned. He knew he had failed from the way Jelk stared.

When they had eaten their fill and a sailor had removed their plates, Jelk brought out a bottle of brandy and two glasses. 'It'll help you sleep. Landlubbers have a time of it when they put to sea,' he said.

It was evident that the old fellow could put it away. The captain filled the glasses liberally. 'Drink up. There's more where this came from.' Jelk waved the bottle about, inviting Keja to help himself.

Keja noted that the captain had emptied his glass, while he had only taken a couple of swallows from his own. Jelk refilled his glass and sat back, staring out of the poop windows, watching the moonshine reflecting off the ship's phosphorescent wake.

Jelk sat back, his hooded eyes searching Keja's face for evidence that he was lying. He couldn't tell. 'Strange story, that,' he said.

'What?' Keja asked. 'The Gate of Paradise?' He regretted having mentioned it, even in jest. 'I don't really know much about it. I thought it was just a children's story.'

'The Gate,' said Jelk, scratching himself. 'The Gate to immortality opens with a lovely key.'

Keja sipped at his glass. He tipped the bottle, adding a few drops of the liquor to his own glass and filling the captain's. He had an idea that the old codger meant it to be the other way around, but had forgotten about it.

'I've never heard anything about a key,' Keja lied.

Jelk's tongue was numbed from too much brandy. 'Oh, yes.

Gold key,' he slurred. 'Valuable all by itself, so they say. Jewel in it. Some say green, some red.'

'It makes a good story,' Keja said. 'But only a child's tale.' He wanted to say nothing more to the captain. Keja knew a good way of ending the conversation, one that never failed. Keja yawned.

The yawn became contagious, as he'd known it would. Jelk yawned in response. 'Tale going round that the key's somewhere along the coast,' he said. 'Just a tale, I suppose. You don't have it, do you?'

'Me?' Keja put his hand to his chest in mock surprise. 'Never heard of the key until you told me. It's late for a landlubber like me, Captain Jelk. Thank you for your hospitality. Unless you can offer me a saucy wench for a passing diversion, I'll be off to bed.' He stood and drained the last of his glass.

The captain muttered something Keja did not catch. Keja stooped and left the cabin, glad to be away, glad to have gleaned some small information from the garrulous captain.

Mistress Mellon, eh? Perhaps she not only knew of the Gate of Paradise but was also a lovely young lass who sought a lover with his astounding abilities. Keja went to sleep, the thought warming him.

Toward the evening of the third day, dark clouds began to build in the west. The wind picked up, and the storm hit the following morning.

Keja stood on the deck watching waves twice as high as the *Feral* come crashing near the ship. He braced his legs and held tightly to a rope that ran from the mast. Fear rising, he watched the frantic activity of the sailors as they scurried across the deck, fastening down the hatches and removing loose gear. He muttered alternate curses and prayers for the sailors sent aloft to furl the sail – and heaved a sigh of relief that he knew nothing of such work and wouldn't be asked to help.

The captain roared at him, 'You're safest where you are, Tchurak. Hang on tight.'

'I don't intend to let go!' he shouted into the storm. Keja clung to the rope as wave after punishing wave swept over the deck. The ship lost steerage and wallowed dangerously in a trough. Jelk fought the wheel, willing the ship to head into the waves.

Salt water streaming down his face, Keja caught sight of a flapping overhead. For a moment he thought he imagined it. No sound came – then he realised the howling wind drowned out the whip-crack of the sail.

Drowned. The word rang like a death knell in his head. He closed his eyes, but the morbid fascination of the scene forced him to look aloft again. One end of the sail, improperly cleated, had worked loose. The yardarm yawed back and forth, the wind gnawing at it. Another wave hit Keja, lifting him into the air. When he regained his feet, the yardarm was dangling, flailing dangerously against the mast.

Keja barely heard Captain Jelk shouting for someone to climb the mast and cut it loose. No one moved. None was able in the fierce winds and hammering waves.

Jelk shouted to Keja, 'Take the wheel, man. Those bastards will have us all on the bottom of the sea.'

Keja tried to shake his head no, but unexpected courage drove him to Jelk's side. He grasped the wheel as if it were precious ivory.

'Just hang on and don't let go,' Jelk yelled in his ear. Then he vanished into the white veil of salty spray.

Keja clung to the spokes of a wheel intent on ripping itself free from his hands. His knuckles turned white with effort; his muscles strained just to hang on. Holding the wheel steady was almost impossible.

Keja's wiry muscles came to the end of their endurance. He closed his eyes and grunted, forcing every last ounce of strength he possessed into holding the wheel. The sudden release of pressure on the wheel took him by surprise; Keja slammed painfully to his knees. The wheel swung back and chucked him under the chin – but he hung on.

Only slowly did he realise that Jelk had returned. He looked up at the mast. The yardarm had been cut away. Keja ducked his head as a wave washed over the ship, but it was not as big as the previous one. Behind him the sky was becoming lighter, and clouds scudded away behind the ship. The storm lessened in severity as they skirted the edge. The enemy had gone.

'Stay here,' Jelk commanded.

'Of course, Captain,' Keja said. The wiry thief clung to the railing, unable to move. His legs had turned rubbery and refused to function. Jelk paraded around, shouting orders, getting the damaged yardarm lashed down. Finally returning to Keja, the captain glowered.

'Have to make for land. Put in if we're to get that yardarm back in place.'

'You have my permission,' Keja said. For an instant, he thought Jelk might toss him overboard for his impudence. 'Just a figure of speech,' he said hastily. Jelk still saw no humour in the comment.

With a temporary sail, Jelk worked the ship into a small cove along the coast and dropped anchor.

Keja regained the use of his legs and hurriedly went below while the crew started their repairs. The black looks shot in his direction told him that the superstitious sailors blamed him for their problems. Keja wasn't about to bandy words with them over the topic; all he wanted was a dry bunk and solid ground beneath his feet again. The sooner he left the *Feral*, the happier everyone would be.

He fell into his bunk, exhausted. With the first light, Keja was awakened by the rattling of the anchor chain. He heard the creaking of sails as the ship left the cove. He stirred, rolled over and tried to sleep again.

Almost immediately he heard the lookout cry, 'It's pirates, Cap'n!'

Keja's first panicked thought was to leap overboard and swim for shore. Control returned, and he chuckled ruefully. He couldn't swim.

As Keja came on deck, Jelk roared, 'Break out the weapons.' Keja's darting, ebony eyes caught sight of a ship's sail as it rounded the point of the cove. A pennon emblazoned with a black falcon flew from its mast. Keja watched the ship's progress with hypnotic interest. The tiny specks on the deck took on detail: armed men. Pirates. The ship came alongside.

Grappling hooks with bright silvered tips flashed in the morning light. The pirates pulled themselves up onto the railing ready to leap when the ships swung in unison.

Keja hung back and waited. He saw a sailor cut down by a boarding pirate. Another pirate prepared to leap between the two ships. Keja lunged and caught the sailor in mid-air. The impact of the falling corpse knocked Keja to the deck. He struggled to escape from under the pirate's body. Barely had Keja regained his feet when another man leaped to take his place.

Keja found himself forced backwards. His broken-toothed, insanely grinning opponent wielded his cutlass as if it were a toothpick. Brute force rather than any skill turned the tide against Keja. He backed away, parrying a sidewise sweep from the man. A shock ran through his wrist.

'Can't we discuss this at our leisure?' Keja asked. 'Surely there's nothing two intelligent men like ourselves can't work out?' He ducked under a slash designed to separate his head from his torso. 'I see one of us lacks even rudimentary intelligence.'

He backed away, avoiding the pirate's graceless swings. Keja stepped inside a wild sweep and sliced down the man's sword arm with his short knife. For a moment, a look of surprise crossed the pirate's face. Then he simply ignored the cut.

'No sense, no feeling. I ought to have realised.' Keja eluded another powerful slash and moved to his left as they came even with the afterdeck. He turned and ran toward the other railing, the pirate in pursuit. Leaping up onto the rail, he held a rope with one hand and turned to face his pursuer. The hulking pirate came at him with his weapon high, just as Keja had hoped. Keja judged carefully, then swung free, feet dangling over the sea. The pirate slashed, found empty air, carried through and fell over the rail. Keja swung back aboard, panting. The pirate had simply taken an unwanted bath; he would return.

The battle went against the crew of the *Feral*. The pirate leader and his men encircled Jelk and four others near the bow. The large number of dead and wounded men scattered about the deck had drained courage from the crew.

Keja let himself over the stern, feeling with his feet for the captain's cabin window. Locating it, he kicked it in. Below the window ran a small board serving as decorative trim. Keja let his feet down until he stood on it. He reached through the window, unlatched it, and dropped inside.

He moved quietly into the passage to the foot of the companionway. The hatch cover lay back, but the hatch doors obscured his view. He crept up a few stairs. The pirate leader stood with his back to the hatch, bellowing orders.

Keja moved to the top step, then, not pausing for second thoughts, burst through. He caught the pirate leader between the shoulder blades with the point of his sword. The thrust continued through the man's body. The pirate captain jerked, let out a liquid, gurgling noise and slumped to the deck.

Keja pulled his sword free, yelling, 'Fight, damn you! Or do you lack the balls? I have enough for all of you!' He threw himself against the pirates with reckless abandon, not caring about the cuts accumulating on his body.

For a heart-stopping instant, Jelk's crew simply stood and watched. Then they burst into action. The pirates, leaderless and faced with berserk tenacity, now fought only to regain their own ship. They backed to the rail, defending themselves. Keja was everywhere, shouting like a madman, assisting, aiming strokes at any pirate already engaged. He flew to the rail and cut the ropes holding the two ships together.

The ships began drifting apart.

'Begone, you swine!' shouted Keja, brandishing his sword. Blood dripped down his hand and trickled the length of his arm. Keja stopped and stared, trying to decide if the blood was his. It wasn't. Not all of it.

Reaction set in, and Keja sagged weakly against the rail. The only time he had felt worse was after the storm. Travelling to Neelarna by ship had not been one of his better ideas.

He stared in a daze as the pirates still on the *Feral* leaped overboard rather than trusting to their fate if they remained behind as captives.

Jelk wasted no time; he grabbed those of his crew who seemed least shaken, and set them to trimming the ship.

Keja expected some thanks for his part in fighting off the pirates. Instead, the mutterings which had been behind his back came out into the open.

'First he brings on the storm, then the pirates. The man is a jinxfish. We'd have been better off staying in Klepht.'

'Cap'n says the fish looks for the Gate of Paradise. By the

gods! No wonder we have poor luck. A man's supposed to live his life out, for good or bad.'

All the words were hot, bitter, against him. Keja was no fool. Before the crew had been sullen. Now they threatened.

Keja Tchurak had stayed alive by quick thinking and never looking back once a decision had been made. When Captain Jelk came by, Keja spun quickly, knife driven point-deep into the man's spine.

'What is this?' the captain cried.

'Be quiet,' Keja snarled. Over Jelk's shoulder, he yelled to the crew, 'Your captain will come to no harm if you follow my directions.'

For a moment, they hesitated. The grumbling became angry shouts. They advanced.

'Damn you all!' shouted Jelk. 'Do as he says or I'll have your ears nailed to the mizzenmast!'

With obvious reluctance, the crew put a boat over the side. Keja watched the captain climb down the rope ladder and sit at the oars, his spindly legs turning blue in the morning breeze. Keja jauntily waved goodbye to the crew and joined him.

'Row me ashore and you're free.'

Jelk wheezed as he pulled at the oars. 'What about the bonus you promised?' he asked between strokes.

'You're just lucky you don't have any gold on you for me to steal,' Keja said. 'Or do you? No? Then pull.' He tapped the captain's chest with his knife tip to emphasise the message.

Four

THE COAST road stretched nearly empty before Petia. Farmers bringing produce had entered Klepht hours ago and no other traveller ventured out this day. The ugly pony whinnied enthusiastically as he trotted along; the sense of freedom communicated to Petia, who felt cheerful for the first time in weeks. The outdoors appealed more to her than smoky, dirty human dwellings.

After a few miles, she found a trail following a watercourse that would bring her out on the clifftops above the coast. She dismounted and led the little pony.

Some distance behind her two men paused to fill their pipes and enjoy a leisurely smoke. 'Wouldn't have thought that she had so much spirit in her. Stole that pony just as easy as you please. Maybe we'll get a reward for bringing it back.'

The other glanced over the bowl of his pipe. 'Gonna have a little fun first, though, ain't we? I want that tawny body.' They chuckled, then continued following Petia.

At the top of the climb, Petia rested and let the pony breathe. She adjusted the load on its back, ran her fingers through its tangled forelock. Its shaggy coat was matted with mud and manure, offending her cat-clean nature. But there was little she could do at the moment if she wanted to make good time along the road to Neelarna. It wouldn't do for that gold key to arrive before she did.

She soon urged the pony on again, taking a rough track through a forest of scrubby, windblown trees. A shiver passed through her lithe body as she entered the miniature forest. The tree limbs, sculpted by the wind whipping over the cliff top, created a grotesquerie of patterns, casting their twisted shadows onto the ground and frightening her horse. Petia soothed the animal, cursing at its fright even as she enjoyed the bizarre shapes dancing about her.

The day passed in magnificent solitude, and well before dark she found a satisfactory place to make camp for the night. She gathered small chips of wood and shredded some bark, then took out her flint and steel. Soon, a small curl of smoke gave evidence of an ember underneath. She nurtured it with soft puffs of breath and allowed it to grow into a full-sized fire.

The joint of beef didn't have as much meat on it as she remembered, but there was enough for a sparse meal. She sharpened a green branch, impaled the meat and started it roasting. Petia leaned back, thinking as her supper cooked. Even if she didn't get the gold key – and she would! – simply being away from Klepht pleased her. She felt a part of this wilderness, not the city with its filthy humans and their prejudices.

Petia delicately nibbled at the rare meat and had to agree with Keja – it was tough and tasteless. She started to toss it away when the snap of a twig alerted her to the two men spying on her. Whether she tensed or they had already decided to attack, she didn't know. Petia tried to reach for her knife and make the motion seem natural. Her hand got only halfway to the weapon when an ear-splitting, 'Haieeee!' echoed through the forest and both men charged like wounded water buffalo.

She rose in one fluid motion and flung the beef joint at the nearest one. He flinched as it glanced off his cheek. This gave Petia time to draw the knife from the top of her boot. The men hesitated, their surprise attack failed.

'Don't be fearing us now, little one,' said the larger of the two. He kept his hands in front of him like a wrestler, groping, grabbing, never stopping for an instant.

Petia moved around the fire and leaped forward at the man. He lunged to meet her, his arms wide to wrap her in a bear hug. In one lithe movement, Petia sidestepped, flicked the knife to her right hand, slashed out. He screamed and threw calloused hands up to his eyes. Petia helped him along with a kick to his kneecap. He tripped and fell headlong into the fire. Petia watched it in slow motion – the man tumbling, landing in the fire, screaming, the flames licking at his clothing.

'Wol! Wol!' the other man cried, horrified at the sight of his friend ablaze. Petia drew her short sword and lunged. The point took him in the sternum. He put his hand to his chest and seemed fascinated by the blood seeping out between his clenched fingers.

'I'm dying,' he said, face ashen. He sat down heavily, trembling like a leaf in a high wind. Petia grabbed the boot of the man in the fire and pulled him out. She shook her few supplies from the flour sack and used it to beat out the flames on his coat and trousers. The man moaned constantly, his clothes still smouldering.

Petia propped him against a scrub tree nearby, lashing his hands to a low branch. 'No, no,' he moaned. 'Help me!'

'You'll get none from me,' Petia said bitterly. She stuffed her supplies back into the sack. 'You should never have attacked a Trans. But you humans are all alike, thinking you're so superior.'

She fastened the sack onto the pony, looking at the sky to see what illumination she might expect from the moon. 'I don't take such attacks lightly. I ought to hang you up, then do what a real Trans would do to you.'

'Wh-what's that?' The man's voice carried true terror.

'You'd be found naked, claw marks covering your chest and stomach. The tendons in the back of your legs would be severed and more than likely you'd be emasculated. See how lucky you are that I don't have the time to waste?'

'But you can't leave us here like this,' the man moaned.

'Can and will.' Petia wiped her weapons on some leaves and replaced them. 'Tell whoever finds you – if anyone does – what you were about. Don't lie to them.'

She clucked at the pony, and they moved off into the darkness, the man's shrieks following, growing weaker and weaker.

Smoke. Petia cursed. For two days she had ridden this track and now came evidence from a dozen different fires. She had hoped to avoid all further human contact after her encounter with the would-be rapists and robbers.

She sat on the cliff overlooking the encampment, watching

and thinking, and warmed herself in the sun. Above in the bright azure sky a hawk soared. Its screech warned her of the boy and girl climbing towards her.

Petia considered avoiding them, then decided that she ought to be the one in control. 'It's all right,' she called down to them. 'I won't hurt you.'

The little girl was shy, but the boy pretended to be brave. He came up to Petia. 'Who are you?' he demanded arrogantly.

'My name is Petia, a traveller to Neelarna. Who are you?'

'I'm Etter. That's Milla,' he pointed. 'She's my sister.'

'Are those your people?' Petia pointed to the smoke below.

'Aye. We're charcoalers.' Petia had already guessed as much from the black, grimy hands and faces. 'We come here every year,' the boy continued. 'Good wood.'

Petia nodded.

'Are you a Trans? We've got Trans in our camp,' the boy volunteered. 'Wanna come see?'

The girl stood and watched Petia silently, with nearly all of one small, grubby fist in her mouth.

'Yes, I'd like that.' Petia pulled up the pony's stake and tucked it in the sack. 'Lead the way,' she said.

The charcoalers' camp was much cleaner than Petia had expected. The camp perched at the edge of the 'good wood' forest. The columns of smoke she had seen came from the charcoal-producing fires tended by solemn adults. Of any other children, Petia saw no sign.

The children took Petia to their mother. She was a buxom woman who welcomed the Trans without a flicker. 'You'll stay the night with us?' she asked, and seemed to welcome it.

'If that's all right. I'd appreciate it,' Petia replied.

'The children are always dragging somebody back to our camp. We've become accustomed to it. We tend to spoil them. There's so few, you see.'

'I don't see many other children,' Petia said. 'What's become of them?'

The woman vented a sigh like a fumarole. 'This is a hard life,' she said, as if that explained all.

'No life is easy these days,' Petia pointed out.

'Many hound us,' the woman said, as if admitting to high crimes. 'They buy our charcoal but revile us as they do. The

41

young women find it easier in the cities and the young men, well, they prefer easier labours.'

Petia understood. The nomads were a dying breed.

She changed the topic. 'The children said there was another Trans in your camp.'

'They exaggerate. One travelled with us for a while last week. A truly awful person. Always barking and yapping like a dog.' Then, fearing she had insulted Petia, the woman added, 'Not that we minded. The company perked up our spirits and livened the fire tales.'

'A dog Trans?' Petia couldn't help but smile. 'I have little love for them myself.'

'No, I suppose not.' To her children, the woman called, 'Find your father and the others. Tell them I will throw away their supper unless they come immediately.'

The children rushed off, giggling and laughing, the only merriment in the camp. Slowly, a string of blackened men came in from the fires. One man grabbed the children by their collars and playfully dragged them off. When they returned, they were all as scrubbed clean as their natures allowed.

'Hard keeping them clean,' he said. 'No way to keep them as clean as the likes of you.' He eyed Petia critically, almost accusingly.

'It is dirty work,' Petia said, 'but necessary.'

'More should have that attitude.' They ate in silence, others coming and picking up plates of the almost tasteless stew the woman had prepared. After eating, the men fixed pipes and smoked, for the first time smiles coming to their faces.

'Tell us a story,' said Etter.

'Oh, yes, please do,' cried Milla, when the little girl saw Petia hesitate at the request.

'I'm not much of a storyteller,' Petia said, but she saw that the adults gathered around were just as eager. She had eaten their food; she ought to repay them in some fashion. This seemed an easy enough way to do so.

'Do you know how the Trans came to be?'

'Yes,' said Milla.

'Shut up,' her brother said. 'No, no we don't. Tell us!'

Petia almost laughed at the exchange. 'Well, it was over two hundred years ago. The story goes that Baron Lophar of Trois

Havres made an agreement with a sorceress.' Petia had heard the story so many times during her childhood in her own land that she remembered it almost word for word.

'The agreement between Lophar and the Sorceress Lady Cassia n'Kaan was an important one, one involving trade, treaties with other lands, contracts for shipbuilding, the transfer of livestock. Much money would be made.' Petia could see that she held everyone's attention, even the adults. She warmed to the telling.

'Lophar let greed get the better of him. He would have become immensely wealthy by the treaty. There was no need for deception and deviousness. But even so, Lophar sought benefits beyond the contract. It is said that in his private chambers he danced with glee and that his cackling laugh could be heard all the way to the harbour.

'What followed when the Lady Cassia learned of Lophar's treachery?' Petia's voiced lowered for dramatic effect. 'The Trans! Never had Lady Cassia been so outraged and, some say, hurt, for she loved Lophar. Not only was Lophar to suffer, but all his people.

'With a power that not even her sister sorceresses had suspected, Cassia n'Kaan changed the human population of Lophar's demesne – every man, woman, child – into beings which were part beast, part human. A wave of her hand, *pop*! and it was done. Nor was it a simple spell. Oh, no. Some became part cow, some part pig, some part horse, and even less common animals. And some, like me, became part cat.'

The children's eyes widened. Petia rushed on with the story.

'Ten generations have passed since the creation of the Trans. Gradually, most of the animal features have faded, becoming human features again. Perhaps the Lady Cassia planned it that way. But the personalities of us Trans are still marked by the animal.' Petia had them all leaning forward to hear her almost whispering voice. With a loud snarl and a hiss, she clawed at the air just inches in front of Etter's nose. The boy let out a yelp, then laughed when he saw it was only part of Petia's story.

'And that's my story,' she said with satisfaction.

Some of the men grunted their approval. 'Well told, stranger.'

'Do you ever get to Neelarna?' she asked, accepting a cup of

43

herb tea from Etter's mother. 'That's where I'm going, and it's a new city for me.'

'Sell charcoal there once a year,' said the children's father. 'Not a pleasant city, not for our kind.'

Petia read into that a veiled warning. If Neelarna was unpleasant for charcoalers, what would it be like for a Trans?

'Things are pretty unsettled there, we've heard.'

'I'm always careful,' Petia said, thinking about her fight with the men several days before. 'It's been a long time since I heard a story. Now it's your turn.'

'What would you like to hear?' asked Etter.

'Do you know the one about the Gate of Paradise and the golden key?' Petia asked guilelessly.

The simple request opened the floodgates of the charcoalers' tongues. What Petia got in the next half hour was a hodge-podge of all the stories about the Gate and the key. There were nearly as many versions as there were people around the fire. Sorting through it all, Petia decided that there was a Gate of Paradise somewhere, as she had always believed. Nobody knew the location, and a person with the gold key could unlock the Gate. And behind the Gate? Immortality, said some, others hotly insisted on love, immense wealth, jewels, slaves, finery, anything a heart valued.

'That makes a fine tale,' Petia said when the stories wound down. 'Has anyone seen the key or found the Gate?'

'No, but it's there. I know it is,' one lanky old charcoaler said. The others around the fire nodded in agreement.

'I doubt it very much,' Petia lied. 'It's just a good story, a tale that offers everyone in the world a chance for untold wealth – a hope and little more.'

'No, it's true,' another man cried. 'You just ask Mistress Mellon when you get to Neelarna. She'll tell you. She knows all about it. She told me the story, and she'd not lie!'

Again everyone nodded, as if Mistress Mellon were the final authority on key and Gate. Petia tried not to show her eagerness.

'Well, now,' she drawled. 'Who's this Mistress Mellon?'

'A wise one,' the woman seated across from Petia answered. 'She knows all the herbs, and how to heal, and many fine stories, and she can cast spells. You just go see her when you get to Neelarna. You ask her. She'll tell you. You tell her the Lowbend Forest charcoalers sent you.'

Everyone beamed at the recollection of Mistress Mellon, obviously a favourite of them all.

'How do I find this wonderful woman?' The irony was lost.

'The Cheese Ring, the Cheese Ring,' the children chanted.

'What?' Puzzlement showed on Petia's face.

'Outside the city walls. You just ask anyone for Mistress Mellon at the Cheese Ring. They'll know.'

Catlike, Petia only dozed all night long. Before any in the camp stirred, she rose and silently departed. Petia wanted no fuss at her leaving. As in many other ways, she shared this trait with her feline companions. Greet warmly, leave quickly.

As she rode, Petia watched the morning sun warm the vale. Dew glistened on the wildflowers, then soon dried. Wispy clouds disappeared like so many wraiths under the sun's rays, leaving behind bright blue sky. And high above, a hawk lazily circled, looking for his breakfast.

The morning wore on, and Petia realised that the hawk still wheeled above her. She dismounted to watch it. As the bird banked, jesses flashed in the sunlight, showing this to be a trained hawk and not a wild one.

The hawk folded its wings and swooped at her. It hurtled down, the wind whistling past it. Stunned, Petia backed into the side of the pony. The raptor continued its dive, and Petia saw that it hunted her with its slashing talons. She raised her hands and let claws inch out. A hiss escaped her lips as she readied for battle.

The bird opened its wings at the last instant, sensing the danger it courted. It zoomed over Petia's head. Baleful eyes glared at her, and behind that deadliness, an evil intelligence. It frightened her.

At times, with other animals, she achieved some tenuous empathic contact. With the hawk she failed totally. This worried Petia even more.

She kept her eye on the sky, but the hawk did not attack again. It circled continually, shaking Petia's nerves. When the trail joined the coast road and Petia turned eastward towards Neelarna, the hawk flew north and out of sight.

'Too high,' she protested. Petia stamped her foot and glared at the farmer. He sucked at his cheeks and nodded.

'Four coppers, then. For currying the beast and what feed I have. Not much around here.' The farmer told the truth on this count. Petia had decided to stable her pony outside Neelarna, where it would be cheaper. An owl-eyed urchin peered at her from the inside of the barn. Petia guessed the boy would get the job, and his father would keep the money.

'Done,' she said. 'Half now, half when I return.'

'Seems fair,' the farmer allowed. 'What's your business in the city?'

Petia tried to keep the tremor of eagerness from her voice when she answered. 'Looking for Mistress Mellon.'

'Oh.' The farmer spat. 'Another one lustin' for the damn aphrodisiacs, eh?'

'Could you help me? With directions to the Cheese Ring?'

The farmer's laconic instructions would serve her well, Petia decided. She nodded to him and set off, but she had gone only a few hundred yards when the clanking of metal on metal alerted her to danger. Petia dove for cover, hiding beside the dirt road, waiting.

'Looking for a damned Trans,' came the disgusted complaint. 'You'd think they'd find better things for us to do. What's she done, anyway?'

A tired voice came back. 'They don't ever tell us. All I know is we're lookin' for a cat Trans. Now shut up and march.'

Petia went cold inside. She didn't know if they were referring to her, but a gut instinct told her they were. Only when the soldiers had passed did Petia emerge from hiding. Fear added speed to her steps now.

Petia recognised the Cheese Ring instantly when she spied it. A circle of craggy, pale grey stones eroded into contorted arches and passageways provided protection for a small hut. Hesitantly, Petia entered the Ring, and, surrounded by the soft rock, felt increasingly uneasy at her unannounced intrusion. Swallowing hard, she went to the hut door and knocked.

'Come.' The command rang out, sharp, crystalline.

Petia stooped and entered. A small fire burned fitfully in a shallow, rock-lined pit. Lost in the swaying shadows was a heap of a woman. Her head wreathed with a shawl, the ends pulled across her face, only her eyes glinted in the faint firelight. Petia heard her sigh.

'Ah, the cat Trans for whom everyone searches. Are you a murderess, my child?'

Petia started. 'Is that what they're saying?'

'Two men slain on the clifftop outside Klepht. Lured them up there, did them in. A vicious crime.'

'That's a lie!' Petia denied hotly.

'I do not doubt that. You know men. They have to make you sound dangerous, capable of deceit, cunning. Otherwise, they seem the less for it.'

'They attacked me,' Petia said. 'The one might be dead, but the other was alive when I left him.'

'Dead now, but he accused you of his murder just before he died.' Cold eyes peered out at Petia. 'You're no casual murderess. It's not in your eyes. But they don't ask me, do they? Only for pains in their elbows and headaches and constipation and flatulence. Oh, yes. Something for infection, something for catarrh, something to harden their cocks, but never anything important. Now. Enough of that. What do you want, girl?'

'I travelled with the charcoalers who told of the Gate of Paradise. I didn't believe them, so they said to come and see you.'

'Don't lie to me, child, not to Mistress Mellon. You believed them. But they didn't know enough, isn't that right?' The old woman hunched forward to look keenly into Petia's eyes.

'Yes,' she said softly.

'That's better. Here's what I don't know. I tell everyone the same. Been doing it for years. Nobody's found it yet, far's I know. I don't know where the key is. I don't know what the treasures are. Might be wealth untold. Might be nothing. I don't know.

'Here's where I do know. The Gate is many miles north of here. A place called Hawk's Prairie. But I'll warn you. Many have come back and told me they couldn't find it.'

Mistress Mellon adjusted her shawl and lowered her head. 'Close the door firmly when you leave. It's going to be cold tonight.'

Petia had been dismissed.

Five

GILES GRIMSMATE leaned back, basking in the warm sun and watching the bustle along the waterfront. More days ought to be like this one, he decided. Nothing to do but feel lazy, no one to kill, no battles to fight, no forced marches. Almost of its own accord, his arthritic hand went to his pocket and pulled out the key.

Gold, no question of it. The soft metal yielded under his knife point. Virtually unalloyed gold. Three teeth, a slender shank, and the round, flat end with the peridot set in it. Runes, worn but still distinct, surrounded the small gem. Giles read them again. 'The Key to Paradise.'

He snorted. A pretty piece of jewellery, but he had a hard time believing the story the old man had told him last night. Still, he had little else to do than scent this spoor a while longer. He might as well stay in Klepht and talk to Mousie again to find out more about this mysterious key.

Towards sunset the air became chill. Giles returned to the Laughing Cod where the landlord greeted him, poured out an ale, and gestured over to the blazing fire.

The evening started much like the previous one, the only difference being less money for wagering in the dice game.

'Ale for all,' Giles cried. 'I still have a few coins left.' The inn's patrons gratefully accepted Giles' generosity.

Giles and the others talked until Mousie came in and took

some good-natured ribbing about his gambling. 'Next time, next time,' he retorted and made his way to Giles' table.

The serving maid brought him his ale. He nodded his thanks. 'You know what I heard today?' he said, his tone secretive.

'Can't imagine,' Giles replied.

'There was some fellow down on the docks seeking passage on a coaster. Said he was going looking for the Gate of Paradise. Wanted passage to Neelarna.'

'Why Neelarna?' Giles asked.

'Don't know.' Mousie pulled at his ale. 'Anybody who goes looking for the Gate of Paradise has to be slightly crazy, anyhow,' he said. 'Might as well look for the Gate of Hell while you're at it.'

'You don't believe the story, then?'

'Pure flotsam and jetsam.'

'What about the key?' Giles fingered the key in his pouch.

Mousie threw back his head and roared. 'Some rich man heard the story and said to himself, "Why don't I make a key like that? Then I can show it to my friends. It will give them a good laugh."'

'Where'd you say you got it?'

'Friend of mine left it to me. He was washed overboard during the battle of Hensaar during the Trans War. He left it in his belongings. It was booty from a raid on Glanport. Porgg didn't find it himself. He traded with another sailor for it.'

Giles dropped the key onto the table. Mousie picked it up and weighed it briefly. He handed it back. 'Probably about an ounce, ounce-and-a-half. When you get to a bigger town, take it to a goldsmith. Have him melt it down. That's about all it's good for, far as I'm concerned.'

Giles put the key away again. 'You're probably right.'

Later in the evening the old man came in, and Giles motioned him over. 'Care for a brandy?'

'Wouldn't mind,' he said, but his eyes glinted.

'I've been thinking about that story you told last night,' Giles said. 'Mousie doesn't think there is any such thing as the Gate. It sounds pretty fantastic to me, too.'

The old man sipped at his brandy and stared into the fire. 'Mebbe, mebbe not.'

They sipped in silence for a long while until the old man said, 'I been thinking about that key all day.'

Giles stirred himself and looked questioningly at the old codger. Perhaps he had decided to talk. Giles kept quiet.

'I heard another story about that gate. A long time ago. I'd almost forgotten it. Took all day just sittin' and thinkin' to dredge it up. That's what happens when you get old. Can't remember things. Still can't remember all of it.'

Giles didn't try to fill the silence. He'd let the old man tell it in his own time.

'Up north somewhere. Kalanak, that's where it was. I was just a youngster, out to make my fortune trapping. Chelta cat, you know. Beautiful furs.' He stopped again, reliving his days along the trap line.

A trapper from the east had come to try his hand at the chelta. He hadn't done well but was appreciated for the new stories he brought with him. This was the first mention any had heard of its location.

'Delek mentioned many places, trying to give us some familiar landmark to orient on. But none of us knew any of those places. We'd never travelled there. Weird names.

'But one stuck in my mind. He said that the Gate was at a place called Hawk's Prairie. Funny thing, though. I just remembered. He said he'd been to Hawk's Prairie and didn't see no Gate. But everybody in those parts swore that's where the Gate was.'

Giles sighed. Not much information for listening to the old man's rambles, but more than he had really expected. Perhaps he'd go to Hawk's Prairie. Or find the source of the key in Glanport.

The door burst open, startling Giles. With an instinct born of long years in military service, he slid what money he had off the table and into his pouch for a quick departure. It took only a sidelong glance to know that the captain of the city guard had made his grand, arrogant entrance. Four guardsmen fanned out behind the gaudily uniformed peacock. The captain postured for a moment, looking over the room. He knew most in the room, many by name, the rest by sight.

He nodded to the landlord.

'Looking for someone, Captain?' the landlord asked.

'Keja Tchurak, or so he calls himself.' He raised a quizzical eyebrow and gestured at Giles.

'Not the one you want, then. Name's Giles Grimsmate, or so he says,' the landlord replied.

'I'll speak to him anyway. Ale for my men.'

He strutted over to Giles' table. 'Mind if I sit down, stranger?' He pulled out a chair and sat before Giles could respond.

Giles felt everyone in the inn watching him. He crossed his ankles on the chair next to him. 'Evening, Colonel,' he said, deliberately overstating the man's rank. 'Something I can do for you?'

'Buy me a drink and tell me who you are.'

Giles lifted a finger to order. The landlord hastily brought the ale, happy that someone would pay for it. Too often the captain had lingered, the drinks coming from the landlord's meagre profits.

'My name's Giles Grimsmate, Colonel.' Giles studied the man, deciding what might impress the guardsman enough to make him leave. 'Veteran of twenty years in the War.'

'Show me your papers.' The officer drained the mug in one long, noisy gulp. Silently, Giles ordered another.

'Up in my room. Want me to get them? Discharge papers.'

'Not yet. Perhaps later,' the captain said. He lifted his refilled mug and drank. 'You wouldn't know Keja Tchurak, would you?' the captain asked. 'Or where he might be found?'

A voice called from across the room. 'There's a man named Tchurak staying at the Leather Cup, Captain.'

The officer turned to face the rest of the room. 'Do you take me for a fool? I know he was there. *Was* there. Where is he now?'

'What's he wanted for, Captain?' Little enough happened in Klepht. They all waited for the answer.

He raised his voice. 'Seems Tchurak stole a golden key from Werlink l'Karm, after laying in the arms of his daughter.' The captain waited for Giles to order still another mug of ale. Giles tired of this game, but he had played it before, in other towns, with petty officers bloated by self-importance. For the price of the ale, he avoided trouble. 'The merchant is less upset at his daughter's loose morals than the loss of the key. He's sent his

51

own private guard after the man. And offered a sizeable reward to any other who finds this Tchurak.'

At the mention of the golden key all eyes turned to Mousie, then to Giles. One started to indict Giles, only to receive a hard elbow in the ribs from the landlord; he had not forgotten who had bought most of the ale he had served – and who still owed for the night's drinking and the guard captain's share.

'Best be checking out other hiding places, men. Drink up.' The captain stood. He peered down, face twisting into a parody of a man deep in thought. 'You staying long?' he asked Giles.

'Be moving on soon enough. I've never been along the coast before. Plenty to see here.'

'Be wary, then. Stay out of trouble.'

The captain set his mug down, thrust out his chest, and led his men out of the inn.

A babble of voices broke out when the door closed. Giles sat back and listened to the ebb and flow of excitement. It would be prudent to leave Klepht. When wealthy merchants felt cheated, their anger knew no bounds. Whether he was this Keja Tchurak mattered little because Giles did hold a gold key. That seemed to be at the bottom of the matter and would undoubtedly cause endless trouble.

Inevitably someone would mention his key and he'd be questioned. Simply getting rid of it solved nothing, either, and Giles was damned if he'd give it back to Mousie. He had won fairly at the dice. A stranger could be thrown in gaol until the local magistrate was satisfied, which might be anything from a matter of hours to several weeks. Giles knew better ways of wasting time.

'I think I'll settle up now,' he told the landlord. 'I'll be leaving in the morning.'

The landlord looked into his grey, weary eyes. 'Yes, it might be best,' he said quietly. He gazed out around the room. Giles turned in time to see eyes looking everywhere but at him.

In public he had said morning; he left immediately. The pack felt good on his back and the bright moon promised easy travel. Giles took a side street to avoid passing the city guard's barracks.

The houses dwindled away as he hurried along, and Giles

soon saw the beginning of the track northward up the coast. Ahead, he sighted a man in a creaking mule cart.

Giles lengthened his stride and had gone only another hundred feet or so when two guardsmen stepped out from behind a large-boled tree beside the road.

'Halt.' The guard came toward Giles. 'Giles Grimsmate?'

Giles nodded.

'We've orders to search you for a golden key.'

'At your pleasure.' Giles gauged his chances of fighting free and saw no hope. He seethed as they spun him around and shoved him against the nepler tree, weight far forward. Giles stumbled, scraped his face against the rough bark as he fell to his knees. But as he moaned loudly, his thick fingers pulled out a tiny parcel and stashed it amid the thick roots. The guardsmen jerked him to his feet and forced him to lean against the tree.

The search was thorough, but it revealed no key.

'We're taking you back to the magistrate. The Captain has received reports that you have the key. You won it in a dice game last evening.'

'Yes, I did. I gave it away. I gave . . .'

'Don't bother. Tell your story to the magistrate.'

Giles shrugged, trying to remain calm. He really had nothing to worry about, yet he had seen too many injustices, both during the War and after, not to chafe at this 'official' theft. At worst, he would lose the key and spend a few days in gaol.

The magistrate's dwelling was near the centre of Klepht. Giles bit back an angry comment when he saw the pompous jackass – it had to be the guard captain's father or uncle. The family resemblance was far too great for mere chance.

'Why did you try to escape?' demanded the magistrate, without preamble.

'Escape?' said Giles, holding his temper in check. 'I was unaware of being officially detained.'

'An investigation of the first order is in progress. No one leaves Klepht. Especially those under suspicion.'

Giles said nothing. The magistrate hefted his kettle belly around and sat in the heavily padded chair behind his desk. Glaring at Giles accomplished nothing; Giles returned the stare with mirrorlike perfection.

'The key, man,' the magistrate said. 'Give me the key and you'll be released. That's all we want.'

Giles wondered at the size of the reward offered by the merchant. It had to be substantial – or might only be an excuse for petty extortion. Giles had spent twenty years of his life being robbed, risking his very existence for a pittance, and would take no more of it.

'I know nothing of any key belonging to this merchant,' he said. 'Now, may I depart? I feel the need of fresh air.'

The magistrate's face turned purple with anger. But through his incoherent sputterings, the guard managed to catch the drift. Giles found himself in gaol before the magistrate's colour returned to its normal florid hue.

It was a time of waiting. Giles had had plenty of practice during his war years. He lay on his matting and thought his own idle thoughts. In one week, the war of nerves ended with Giles the victor.

The magistrate seemed to have gained an extra twenty pounds in the brief week. Giles had lost half that eating the swill served in the Klepht gaol. The one thing that hadn't changed was the magistrate's attitude. He acted as if Giles had duped him when he loudly announced, 'I've received a description of this Tchurak fellow from Werlink l'Karm's men. You don't fit it.'

'No more than anyone else in Klepht. Tchurak is long gone. Eluding your crackbrained men must have been easy – you spend all your effort imprisoning innocent men,' Giles said.

The magistrate reddened. 'You'll do well to keep a civil tongue.'

'I take it ill when people deny me my freedom for no reason.' He snatched his papers from his table. 'I hope you get boils on your arse.'

Time lost, he thought, leaving the magistrate. That the man did not again imprison Giles told the old veteran of new tactics on the official's part – the battle still played out for the key.

That impressed Giles all the more. He had thought of the key as a diversion. Now it assumed a larger role in his life; if nothing else, keeping it from the magistrate and the merchant gave him a certain degree of pleasure.

Giles set off for the docks. Within a few minutes, he found a small fishing boat.

'Going north along the coast?' Giles yelled to the sailor on board. Giles looked back over his shoulder in time to see a man duck into a convenient doorway. As he suspected, a guardsman had followed him.

'What if I am?' came the reply.

'Thought you might take a passenger. For a fee, of course.' Giles saw the man's greedy eyes light up.

'Might. How far you want to go?'

'Glanport.'

'Not going that far. I can take you as far as Fleth. That's about half way. You can get another boat from there.'

'Done,' Giles said. 'When do you leave? I've got a small errand to run.'

'Half hour, no later. The tide's not waitin' this day, nor am I, even for a man as generous as you.'

'I'll be back.' Giles stepped onto the boat and slung his pack and roll into a corner. In seconds he was on his way again, fully aware of the city guard following half a street away.

He rapidly calculated the distance to where the key and his dice winnings were hidden. How much time dared he spend in losing the guard? He set off at a rapid pace, wondering at the guardsman's physical condition. If he were as good as even half the recruits Giles had trained, there'd be trouble.

After only one long block, Giles knew he'd have no trouble at all. He heard the guardsman gasping and wheezing loudly. Giles took a shortcut through the ostler's stable, ducked into an open warehouse, then doubled back and lost the guardsman sooner than he had anticipated. He shook his head at such inefficiency. With any luck – or even more stupidity on the magistrate's part – his brief and loud inquiry at the docks might be considered a diversion not worth even a single guardsman.

The sealskin pouch lay undisturbed among the roots of the huge nepler tree. He tucked the key and coins into his belt, smiling broadly.

'Now, to get back to the dock without being seen,' Giles said to himself. The embarrassed guard might well have spread the word by now.

With all the skill Giles had learned as a scout during the War, he returned to the waterfront. The fisherman squinted as he stepped aboard. 'Right on time. Thought I had myself a pack and roll.' He cast off, and they moved out into the harbour.

Giles sat at the stern, chuckling to himself. The fisherman worked at getting the boat on course and missed seeing the guard captain and four of his men jumping up and down, shouting insults and berating one another.

Glanport was much larger than Klepht. The people were busier, the inn not nearly so friendly. On the first night, Giles sat watching men silently drinking an ale brewed in the kidneys of an animal with gastric difficulties and pissed into clear glass bottles. A half bottle was all that Giles could tolerate.

He wasn't likely to get any information from this sullen group.

In the morning, alone in the inn, Giles questioned the landlord. 'Settle a wager for me, will you? A friend told me a tall tale about the Gate of Paradise and I . . .' The landlord snorted in derision and cut him off in mid-sentence.

'You don't look like one of them,' he said.

'One of them?' Giles asked.

'One of them crazy old religious folk. Thought they'd pretty much died out.'

Giles laid a coin on the counter. 'I'm not. But tell me about them anyway.'

The landlord had little to say, but Giles left the inn with nebulous directions for finding the temple.

By mid-afternoon Giles stood outside the Temple of Welcome and stared at it, shaking his head. It was run down, needed whitewashing, and certainly could have used a good sweep inside. A single candle glowed in front of the altar. It illuminated a large room, mostly empty. He saw where expensive pews had been removed and replaced by simple wooden chairs; even these had seen better days.

Giles peered down the centre aisle. As his eyes became

accustomed to the dim light, he made out the figure of a man sitting in the front row. The rattle of beads almost drowned out the litany.

He advanced slowly down the aisle, wanting neither to frighten the priest nor to disturb his prayers.

The priest heard him, however, and turned a worn but patient face to Giles. He fitted in well with his surroundings. 'The Temple of Welcome opens its doors to you. What may I do for you?'

'I need information. About the Gate of Paradise and the golden key opening it.'

'You are interested in converting, my son?'

'No!' Giles said, too sharply. His experiences with priests during the War had been such that he avoided them whenever possible.

'Ah.' The priest sighed. 'So few follow the Temple's faith these days. You want to know what many seek.' He sighed again, shaking his bald head. 'For us the Gate is metaphorical. The seeking is the thing. We strive for a right life, a purity of heart, the utmost faith in our single god, an all-encompassing love for our fellow beings. The Gate is the promise of a more fruitful life in the hereafter rather than the reward itself.'

Giles expected little other than blather from a priest. 'Have you scriptures?' he asked.

'There are no copies I can let any but a true believer take away, but if you would care to look at our Holy Book, you can read here.' The priest gestured for Giles to follow.

He led Giles past the altar to a small sacristy where sunlight filtered down from a high window. The priest removed a leather-bound book from a ragged case of brocade and laid it on a table. Giles scooted a stool over and perched on it.

'Treat it with care,' the priest requested, eyeing Giles.

'Have no worry on that score,' Giles assured him. The priest left silently, returning to his devotions.

Giles turned page after page until his eyes blurred. The text had been hand-scribed, sometimes illegibly, often faint with age. It was twilight when Giles came upon a cryptic passage buried in a parable concerning travellers on the way to a market town. He did not understand it at first, but Giles was intrigued by a description of an area much like one in which his troop had camped during his army days. He read it again, then sat back to envision that particular bivouac some eight years before.

Giles went back to the beginning of the passage, realisation dawning on him that within the context of the teachings of an early patriarch of this church, the parable could be interpreted as directions – perhaps to the Gate of Paradise.

'Those brandies proved beneficial. The old man wasn't so far off,' Giles muttered. 'Hawk's Prairie it is.'

Giles was straining to memorise the description when a loud noise from the nave interrupted him. Curious, he rose to investigate. In the church he saw no sign of movement, but his sharp ears detected someone attempting to move without being heard. Hand on sword, he entered the church to investigate.

Giles made his way to the front, then turned to a side room. The priest lay face down on the floor, a pool of blood expanding beneath him. Giles turned the man over and felt for some sign of life. None.

He sensed rather than saw someone behind him. The blow struck him on the side of the head. Darkness swallowed Giles as he slumped forward over the priest's corpse.

Six

KEJA TCHURAK stood on the sea strand, watching with some misgivings as Captain Jelk rowed back to the *Feral*. It had certainly been adventurous aboard the coast lugger. Storms and pirates. Keja snorted in disgust. He would have made better time if he had stolen a horse.

Keja climbed the twenty feet up the low sand dunes to the

road. Pausing before he scrambled over to the road, he heard the tramping of feet in cadence. Keja sank back into scrubby, bethorned undergrowth, waiting. He had taken the sea route to avoid such meetings. Too many wanted his head on a spike.

The marching soldiers came up to Keja's hiding place and moved past. Keja heard angry mutterings from the men. Soldiers were always grousing about something. He waited until they were well past, then cautiously moved onto the road. Keja let out a heartfelt laugh. He had the road to himself.

'I have fought jealous fathers and storms and pirates and sailors wanting to kill me, and tupped many a wench along the way, and I have arrived unscathed!' Keja laughed again. Even the long walk into Neelarna failed to dampen his spirits.

Neelarna proved a larger town than Keja had expected. Somewhere in this sprawling market town he would find the Mistress Mellon mentioned by Captain Jelk. From this sooth-sayer, it could only be a short distance to the Gate of Paradise. How else could it be when luck rode with him, as it did now? He took out the key stolen from Rosaal's father and let it gleam brightly in the sun.

'My key to a greedy heart's desire,' he proclaimed.

He became increasingly angry as the day wore on. None admitted knowing Mistress Mellon. Wherever he turned, he found only cold stares or occasionally an amused chuckle. These irritated the short-tempered thief more than anything else. Keja could have asked the city guard but discretion's voice whispered in his ear that this might court disaster. All his usual sources, the silversmiths, the carpet merchants, the chest makers, did not know or would not speak.

Keja thought to settle his growing disquiet with a cup of tea. Crouched against the wall near a street vendor, Keja warmed his hands on the mug and wondered what to do next.

'Give us a copper,' came the shrill command. Keja looked up over the rim of his mug. He saw what had to be three of the dirtiest street urchins in all the far-flung country of Bericlere.

'What do I get for my copper?' he asked.

The question took the three urchins aback. Usually they

grovelled after some small coin tossed in the dust at their feet, or were sworn at and chased off.

Keja grinned at their confusion. 'I need information. Where do I find Mistress Mellon?' Keja held back his thrill of triumph. These beggar children knew of the woman mentioned by the sea captain. He could see it in their faces.

The children looked from one to the other. 'Why?' asked the oldest and dirtiest of the trio.

Such boldness on their part startled him. 'There is a certain bit of . . . information I seek from her. You know her, don't you?' It was more statement than question.

'We know her. All the "dross" know her.'

Keja had not heard that term in many years. The truly poor, that layer of humanity below even the dregs of society were the dross. If Mistress Mellon catered to this class, he knew why those of higher social rank — even the lowly street vendors — refused to acknowledge her.

'It will cost you, and we make sure first that she wants to receive you. Wait here.'

The three disappeared before Keja could voice his objections. He bought another tea and waited for their return. At first content to watch the parade of citizens and foreigners who passed before him, he grew more and more restless during the hour before the three appeared as silently as they had slipped away.

The eldest one spoke, eyes darting as if he expected the city guard at any instant. 'Five coppers for the information, and you find your own way. This evening, after dark.' The boy sounded adamant, but the jut of his chin told the true tale. Keja did not haggle. He knew the signs. He counted the five coins into a grubby palm. The directions were specific and given quickly.

Another tugged at the largest one's sleeve and whispered. He nodded. To Keja, he said, 'Who do we tell her is coming?'

'The name would mean little to her. Just tell her "The Lover."'

Keja sat cross-legged before Mistress Mellon's fire, warming his hands against the evening's chill. But the hut was stuffy, a haze of blue smoke seeking vaporous egress and not finding it.

'A lover, eh?' the old woman said. 'You seek one of my potions to enhance your prowess?' Keja started to say that he did – the idea intrigued him – but he shook his head.

'I have no need of that.'

'Such a lover, then,' Mistress Mellon said sarcastically.

Keja ignored the implied insult. 'I seek more. I seek the Gate of Paradise.' The old woman's harsh, barking laugh irritated him. 'Do you find this so ludicrous?'

'You are the second seeking the Gate this week.'

Keja looked sharply at the shapeless bundle sitting in the dark.

'Two? Another besides myself? Who might that be?'

'I ask no names. A Trans woman, part cat. A beauty, she was.'

Keja sucked in his breath. The serving wench from the Leather Bottle! It must be! And he had thought she was only a simple sneak thief. His admiration for her mounted.

'If anyone is foolish enough to look for the Gate, I tell them what I know. There is more to it than just a gate.'

'I know.' Keja's hand went to his chest, reassuring himself at the feel of the key beneath his tunic.

'Ah, do you now, lover? You know all about the Gate except where it is, eh? For that you come to Mistress Mellon. Better you should take ship for the Gentian Coast and use your thievery on the wealthy there.'

'The stories say . . .'

'Yes, the stories tell of great wealth, jewels and gold, power, beautiful women and handsome men. All that is unattainable by most people, eh, lover? Don't the stories always hold out fine promises? Something to wish for, something to hope for. A magic gate for the "dross" to dream about. Are you a dreamer, lover? Or are you a doer?'

Keja glowered across the fire at the old woman. 'I see what I want, then I act.' He spat into the fire.

'Then go do, lover. Go use your clever fingers on the wealthy, eh? They will not miss it. Share some of it with the "dross". Ah, but I see that is not the answer you want.'

Mistress Mellon sighed. In a monotone, she gave Keja

Tchurak the same information given to Petia Darya only two days before. When she had finished, Keja began to fish in his pouch for some money to leave with her.

Mistress Mellon's voice crackled with sarcasm. 'No, lover. If you wish, give your money to the "dross". I have no need of it. I give this information to many. You're just another in a long line. Now go.'

Keja started to make a smart reply, but the old woman's manner had disarmed him. He obeyed without comment.

Near the Arlien Bridge, Keja Tchurak found a horse dealer. An hour had passed in haggling before Keja and the trader argued out a deal. The horse was a beauty, black and shining, standing just fifteen hands, strong and with the look of eagles in his eye. Keja managed to get the trader to throw in a saddle, but to the horse he said, 'Sorry, this is the best available,' then gave his eloquent shrug. The trader glared, but the horse seemed to accept his fate.

He arranged to collect horse and saddle later and set out to purchase supplies for the journey. Clothes first, he decided.

While Keja may have had an eye for horseflesh, his taste in clothing brought many unenlightened sniggers from both clerks and onlookers. The quality of cloth, its ability to wear well or to hide the stains of the road, never entered Keja's mind. What Keja purchased might have been useful for a social occasion and impressing the ladies.

'Perfect,' said the clothier, fighting to hold back his laughter. The brocade morning coat with crimson velvet collar tabs, carved bone buttons and gold piping better suited a courtier than a traveller. Keja did not notice.

'I like it,' he said, admiring his reflection in a full-length mirror. The haggling over price went quickly enough; the clothier whispered to his friends that he never thought to find anyone foolish enough to purchase it.

Keja didn't care. He liked the way the jacket hung. For him, the line was perfect.

He found the three urchins waiting for him near the inn. 'Give us a copper,' demanded the eldest.

'I gave you too much yesterday,' Keja replied. 'I'm down to

my last one.' He turned up his pouch and one small copper coin fell into his palm.

'Wouldn't have any hidden on you?' The youngest peered into Keja's face, searching for any sign that Keja lied. Then the youngling asked, 'You going to a masque in those funny clothes?'

The leader cuffed him. He was all business. 'We're selling information, important information.'

'Not a copper more.'

'Then it's your misfortune,' the urchin said. 'The information's valuable.' He turned to his companions. 'Come on.'

'Wait,' Keja said, sensing their gravity.

He pulled a pair of earrings from his pouch. 'These are from Lasrunal, famed for their artisans in enamelling. Would they be worth your information?'

The eldest held out his hand, and Keja dumped the earrings into it. The boy inspected them with an old-young experienced eye, then tucked them into his filthy, tattered sash.

'The guard's looking for you. A special guard belonging to some rich man has come here from Klepht.'

Keja was dismayed. He thought that he had evaded Werlink l'Karm's men. 'Where are they now?'

'Scattered throughout the town. They have split up, two of the city guard for every one of the specials. It will be difficult for you to avoid them.'

'Can you take these clothes and supplies and hide them for me?' He ducked into an alleyway and stripped off his flashy new clothing, then scribbled a note. 'And take this to the horse dealer by the Arlien Bridge. Bring horse and tack to me outside the city walls after dark. Will you do that?'

The boys looked from one to another.

'I'll have something to give you for your efforts,' Keja said. 'Just meet me with my things outside the north gate. At dusk.'

The boys nodded and disappeared.

Keja collected his few belongings from his room. Had it not been for his sword, he would not have bothered. At the door of the inn he hesitated, caution warning him to look before he walked out into the street.

Three guards trooped towards the inn. Keja turned and ran for the kitchen. A startled cook and serving maid started to protest, but he put a finger to his lips to silence them. He turned to leave, then came back.

'How can I depart without doing this?' he asked the serving maid. He kissed her on the lips, as if to seal them.

'Sir!' she protested – but not too much.

Laughing, Keja stepped into the alleyway behind the inn. For the moment he was free. He intended to stay that way.

At the end of the alley he paused, peering around the corner. He waited until the guards entered the inn, then sauntered into the street and headed away.

He turned a corner. Three more guards. They stood nonchalantly, but Keja knew this was deceptive. He backtracked to the next street, cut over three more, and found himself getting farther from the marketplace and the protection of numbers it offered.

Keja calmed himself and said, 'They are mere dolts. I am Keja Tchurak, thief without peer! I spit upon their boots!' The dramatic pose he assumed drew unwanted attention. Keja bowed. One or two hesitantly applauded, then moved on. Keja quickly joined the tiny knot moving away and eventually reached the market.

The marketplace was not nearly as crowded as Keja would have liked. He ducked under an awning, attracted by a young woman selling fruit. Her exotic, almond-shaped eyes dazzled him.

'I am captivated by your beauty, milady,' he said, playing to her vanity. She knew those bewitching eyes were her best feature, for she had outlined them in blue.

In spite of the guards so avidly seeking him, Keja found himself utterly fascinated by the woman. He stared at her eyes, blacker than olives and alluring. But her contemptuous smile froze him. She looked past him, signalling to three guards entering the small tent.

'Ah, my lovely darling, it has been so thrilling – and a night together might have been the stuff of legends.' He grabbed a shallow brass bowl filled with a delicate yellow fruit and flung it at the guards. One piece splattered in a guard's eye. The bowl hit another of the guards on the wrist, and he yelped in pain. The third leaped for Keja.

Keja ran towards the soldier. He held out his arms and

puckered up. 'A kiss, my lovely?' When the guard stopped in surprise and disgust at the offer, Keja grabbed the iron rod supporting the awning, swung up and lashed out with his feet. He caught the guard in the stomach; the man went down.

Keja's weight, however, proved too much for the rod. The awning collapsed and heavy cloth enveloped him. He groped and found the young woman. 'If only there were time,' he muttered as his arm circled her trim waist.

He struggled and found daylight. In an instant he was on his feet and fleeing across the marketplace. Ahead he saw a costermonger's cart and above it a beam projecting from the front of the building. Without breaking stride, he leaped to the front edge of the cart and then up to the beam. Keja used all his thief-sharpened strength to pull himself up. Looking back, Keja saw fish spilling all over the street. 'Fish before swine,' he sighed, seeing the guards slipping in the smelly mess. Then he grabbed the edge of the roof and pulled himself up.

He dashed across the rotted wood roof, praying that his feet wouldn't find a weak spot and go through. He jumped from building to building until he was well away from the market. The nimble thief found a secluded spot which could not be seen from the ground and rested.

His respite was brief – the guards had also taken to the roofs. No doubt the angry costermonger had told them where he had gone.

Keja got to his feet, ran up the nearest slope and topped the gable. Two guards came up the other side. Keja cursed so volubly that he nearly overbalanced and slid right down into their arms.

'Stop! That's him! Stop!' yelled one guardsman.

Keja had no intention of obeying. Quickly, he righted himself and agilely danced along the roof ridge. The guards now scrambled madly to get up to the gable.

'Good day,' he greeted them. The black looks might have frozen a lesser man. He waited until they had arrived puffing at the top of the pitch, then swooped down the roof, letting the momentum carry him up to the ridge of the next roof and over. Now the guards were all behind him again. He turned right and down the next valley. He was on the roof of a warehouse. A beam carrying pulley equipment projected out from the front

65

of the building. Grasping the edge of the roof, Keja let himself down carefully until his feet touched the solid beam.

'There he is.' Keja heard the shout from below. He craned around to see a man in the street pointing up at him.

He heard footsteps above him coming closer. Keja turned smoothly on the beam, and leaped to the ground fifteen feet below. He rolled nicely, came to his feet and took three quick steps toward the man who had betrayed him to the guard.

'May I one day have the opportunity to properly repay you,' Keja told him. The man's frightened expression began to fade. Keja smiled, then punched the man in the stomach.

Keja ran on down the street, turned left and crossed a small foot bridge. Ahead he saw a mill. He continued past, then ducked in alongside it, searching for a hiding place. The ground sloped away to a stream channelled past the mill to fuel the huge waterwheel. No place to hide.

Keja began to sweat, partly from his run, but mostly from growing fear. He had come too far to be caught now. He trotted downhill to the waterwheel, a huge spiderweb of a thing, but too open and airy for hiding. The guardsmen would be rounding the corner of the mill at any moment.

Keja sucked in a great lungful of air, then grabbed a spoke of the wheel as it came past him, clinging to it for dear life, letting it lift him forty feet into the air.

On either side of the great wheel a huge timber fork held the axle. The main stanchions extended beyond the axle, but not nearly to the top of wheel's arc. Keja uttered a quick prayer to Dismatis, who watched over thieves, waited until the spoke had carried him nearly to the top, then dropped the several feet to the top of the stanchion, praying again that it would not be too slippery. He hit perfectly, but the timbers were wet. Then Keja's feet slid off and he grabbed for the timbers with his arms. A drowning sailor couldn't cling any tighter to a mast.

Carefully, he pulled himself up until he crouched atop the cradle. He hoped that the wheel might disguise his silhouette. The soldiers came round the corner, searching along the edge of the stream and passing down the slope to the canal below the mill.

'Can't see him anywhere.'

'Maybe he went into the mill.'

They trooped back around the corner and were lost to Keja's view. He breathed a sigh of relief. If he weren't spotted, it might be a good idea to stay here until nearly dark. He turned carefully to find a more comfortable position, silently congratulating himself on eluding the doltish guards.

Keja stared across at the wooden building. A short, balding man stood in an open bay of the third level of the interior. He stared back at Keja, then lifted his finger to his lips. Keja awkwardly executed a bow in the man's direction. The man disappeared, returning a half hour later.

'Those filthy barstids 'ave gone,' the man called. 'And begone with ye!'

'How may I thank you?'

'You canna bring back my little ones they took from me. Now be off!'

Keja wondered at the man's story. Neelarna held much misery, and Keja wanted nothing more than to be away from it as quickly as possible.

With his eyes fixed on the moving spoke, Keja leaped across the open space. His timing was good, but the wet spoke caused him to slip off and tumble into the frothy water below.

The millrace ran swift and carried Keja a hundred feet to the canal before dumping him unceremoniously over the spill-way. Coming to the surface, Keja sputtered and panicked. Flailing wildly, he managed to find a tree branch. Using this for support, Keja paddled to the canal's edge. He pulled himself up and sat on the edge, shivering in the evening air and examining himself for bruises.

'I am going to *have* to learn to swim if this dunking continues. This is a day I have no wish to re-live,' he grumbled, shaking off the water like a half-drowned dog. 'Though the wench in the marketplace was a fine one,' Keja sighed. Too bad she had been so quick to signal the guard. A pity that even a lovely thing like that would do anything when tempted with foul reward monies.

He took a roundabout route to the northern edge of the town, twice avoiding patrols. Hiding in the shadows near the city wall, Keja waited until the guardsman left the gate to relieve himself. Quickly, he passed through the gate and outside the city of Neelarna.

The circuitous route had wasted most of the day, but Keja didn't mind. He was still free. Clouds obscured the moon and the sun had set some hours earlier. Where were those boys with his horse and supplies?

'Good sir,' came the soft cry. 'We have your belongings.'

'That's more like it,' Keja said. He stood and stared, anger rising when he saw not the beauty he had bought that morning, but a long-eared mule with a sack of oats thrown across its back.

'What's this?' Keja demanded. 'Where's my horse and supplies?'

'We sold them, for our fee. These will do as well.'

Keja pulled his sword. 'No, they won't do at all, my lad. On your life, they won't do.'

A line of men appeared from the shadows and encircled him. They outnumbered him and were no starved ragtag band – and they were confident.

'Why not take everything?' he asked, bewildered. The urchins were backed by fathers and uncles, probably Neelarna's thieves' ring. He knew the kind. Wasn't he a thief himself?

'Mistress Mellon takes pity on you,' the lad he had dealt with said. 'She says you have a good heart – and a purse too heavy.'

'No longer,' muttered Keja. He saw no way of remedying the sad malady.

A whistle came from the dark. 'Guards coming!' someone whispered.

The boy stepped forward and thrust another sack at Keja. Then they melted away into the darkness.

Keja peered into the sack and saw only tattered garments. His finery had vanished, along with the horse, the tack and all his belongings.

'One day, urchin, when you are rich, I shall return and rob you naked!'

The sound of approaching guards lent speed to Keja. He grabbed for the reins of the mule. If the guards pursued on horseback, he had no chance of escape.

The mule brayed and started off, much too slowly for Keja. The sounds of pursuit grew louder.

Seven

THE FARMER'S boy, gasping for breath, raced up the path to Petia.

'Whoa, slow down,' Petia said, putting out her arms to stop him.

The boy collapsed. He tried to get the words out. 'The house . . . surrounded . . . soldiers.'

Petia knelt down beside the boy. 'First catch your breath, then tell me.' Irrational fear seized her.

They'd caught up with her. Mistress Mellon had said the guards sought her for killing the two would-be rapists. Flee! Yes, she'd have to flee. Her only regret was having to leave the pony.

The boy's breathing eased. He looked up at Petia, tears and adoration in his eyes. He had never known a Trans before and thought Petia's cat-moves beautiful.

'My father,' he said. 'He warned 'em. Why did he do that?'

'Don't worry. Thank you for warning me.' She gave the boy a hug and he clung to her. Petia wanted to take him with her, but that would never work – for either of them.

'Do you know who they are?'

'Not regular guards. Those fancy black and silver uniforms, and they wear only a padded right glove. A . . . a crest unlike any I've seen before. I think they must be a private force.'

Petia tensed all over, stunned beyond words. These were not ordinary guardsmen. _He_ had found her. Her mouth as dry as cotton and her hands shaking, Petia fought to regain control. After all these years, it had to be _him_!

'Where are they?' she asked, her voice hardly more than a whisper.

'Hiding at the house,' the boy answered. 'A couple of them are inside, but several are outside waiting to grab you when you come back.'

'Where's my pony?'

'Down in the lower pasture. He can't get out.'

'Can they see him from the house?'

'No.'

'Can you get him for me? Without being seen?'

'I think so. If I can get out to the barn, I can sneak away without them seeing. I can get him out, I'm sure I can. And they'll never know. I can meet you down by the stream.'

Petia thought about it. 'All right, you do that. I'll wait until dark. If you run into any trouble, don't worry. I can take care of myself, and I'll be gone by morning.'

The boy looked up at her. His small face was serious. 'I'll get your pony, don't you worry.'

Petia gave him another hug. 'I'm counting on you,' she said. 'Now, it would be a good idea for me to find a place to hide until evening.'

The boy pointed over the hill. 'Follow downhill on the other side. You'll come to the stream. Go upstream a ways until you come to some big nelk trees. You can hide up in the branches like I do. Sometimes I spend all day there and nobody can find me. I'll see you this evening with your pony.' He turned and walked away, his shoulders back, head up, determination showing in every step.

Petia retraced her footsteps up the hill, then followed the boy's directions through the field. Upstream she found the big trees he had described. Petia looked around and saw no sign of pursuit. She crouched down like a cat, then jumped. Strong legs propelled her into the lowest branches. Stretching, arching her back, Petia found a comfortable resting place among the leafy branches.

She passed the afternoon dozing, resting, preparing herself for the flight that must come. The years. She had thought herself safe after all this time. A tear ran down her cheek. A quick move of her index finger snared the wayward droplet and flicked it away. Even after returning to Trois Havres for so many years before coming back to Bericlere, she had not set herself free of *him*. Petia wondered, no matter how far she ran, if she would ever be free of *him*.

She doubted it.

The boy arrived after supper, leading the pony by a rope.

'You're going to be in trouble for this, you know.' Petia was without a bridle, but the rope the boy had brought could be shaped into a hackamore.

'I don't think so. They're not so bright, and I've got a good story to tell. I'll be all right,' the boy said. Almost shyly, he asked, 'How about you? Where are you going now?'

'To that, I have no good answer. Just away, as fast as I can ride.' Petia heaved herself up onto the pony's back, stared down at the waif and almost broke her resolve not to ask him to accompany her.

She reached in her pouch and pulled out a crown. 'You hide this well until you're grown. Don't let your father have it. Keep it to remind you of me – and the bravery and loyalty shown me this day.' She handed the gold coin to the boy, ruffled his hair, and turned the pony. Petia looked back once; the boy waved.

She rode through the night, putting miles between herself and those seeking her. Petia walked the pony through the stream for a while so they wouldn't be able to follow his tracks, doubled back often, rode across rocky stretches, did whatever she could to throw off a tracker.

The thought of *what* might be following gave her the shakes. Involuntarily, she hissed and spat, her claws inching out. Petia tried to control herself, but *he* had always affected her thus. She tried not to push the pony, but fear made her apply her heels more than she would have done in other circumstances.

Two days later she trudged up the road leading to Becker Pass, a savage rock-cut through the Tomkos Mountain range. The sun burned her and made the pony lathery.

When the road levelled and they entered a high, cool, grassy mountain meadow, the pony's ears twitched.

'Plenty to eat here,' Petia murmured softly, scratching the animal's ears. 'Time for a rest, eh, Marram? Cool off a bit.' Somewhere along the way she had stopped addressing the pony as 'Your Ugliness' and had given him a name more to his

71

liking. Petia placed her hands on either side of the long, thin head and concentrated.

Vague stirrings only came to her. Empathic contact was tenuous at best, and Marram had tired quickly on the long road through Becker Pass. All the pony wanted was to graze and rest. She dropped the reins of the hackamore. The pony would not wander far. As he cropped the grass, Petia slipped off her boots and massaged her feet. Never would she get used to 'civilised' wear. The meadow grass was cool against them; wiggling cramped toes gave her a sample of Paradise.

The Gate of Paradise.

Petia almost purred at the thought. She had been thwarted in Neelarna by *him*. He had chased her away from the fool with the key to Paradise, but Petia saw other chances to steal the key. Whatever the arrogant man's name was – Keja Something-or-other – he had to get the same information concerning the Gate's location.

Their paths would cross again, and this time Petia would hold the key. She deserved it! Memory of all *he* had done to her convinced her of that. She would steal the key from Keja, elude *him* and walk in a land of splendour!

The pony's head came up and it looked back along the road, ears up and alert.

'What is it, Marram?' Petia let her cat senses emerge. Soft on the breeze came the voices of hounds on a trail.

'No!' She held back a sob and the fear driving it. She dared waste no time now. Not now! Petia quickly slipped her boots on and stood. She ran to the pony and grabbed its reins. The baying frightened her. She knew the sound all too well.

'I hate to do this to you,' Petia said, flinging herself onto the pony's back. With the reins in one hand, she whipped the pony into a gallop. His gait was uncomfortable and to an expert would have appeared unsightly, but it covered the ground rapidly.

Petia glanced back over her shoulder. Behind, she saw the pack of dogs running, heads low, muzzles to the spoor. Her spoor. Petia reached for her sword and pulled it free, urging the pony to even greater speed.

Those hellhounds were faster than Marram and gained rapidly. Petia angled for the edge of the meadow and an upward slope. She no longer hoped to outrace the hounds. All Petia sought was protection for her back, a mound of dirt or a standing stone.

No question remained about the pack now. Lurchers, intelligent dogs bred by the nomads, these belonged to Lord Ambrose, or more exactly, to his son, Segrinn.

He had found her again.

Ahead she saw a huge boulder left from the glacial age. She turned Marram toward it. The lurchers ceased their deep-throated growls and now ran silently to the kill. Petia wheeled the pony and slashed at the leader as they swept by. She missed but caught another with the sword tip, slashing its muscular shoulder.

Petia turned for the boulder and slipped down from the pony before the pack formed for its attack. She slapped Marram on the flank and sent him on. No sense in his getting hurt. The pony trotted to where the ground began to rise, leaped to a ledge a few feet higher than the meadow. Two lurchers followed him. Rearing on his haunches, he lashed out with powerful forefeet and caught a lurcher in the head with a hoof. The dog's skull cracked like a dropped ceramic pot. It tumbled, kicked feebly, then lay still.

Petia set her back to the stone and waited for the attack. 'Dogs, why do you attack me? What have I done to you?' she called out.

The lead dog stopped, tongue lolling and sides sleek with sweat. 'Trans bitch run away. Master wants. Orders run bitch down.' The voice was guttural and almost indecipherable.

'Your master is cruel!' Petia cried. 'Has he not whipped you?'

'Dog's life. Obey or be whipped. Gives us meat. Dry kennel. Bitches.' Cunning eyes sized up the woman. Tiny jerks of the head and a few sharp barks formed the other lurchers in an impenetrable ring around her.

Petia's mind whirled, trying to think what might dissuade the lurchers from continuing their attack. 'You can pretend that you chased me off and lost me.'

'Why?' The lurcher seemed genuinely puzzled.

'Because I'm going to kill some of you if you don't.'

'Cat bitch. Hate cats.' He leaped at her. The others followed.

Petia was nearly caught off guard. She stunned the attacking lurcher with a blow under the throat using her left arm and slashed the next hound across the flank. On her backswing, she sliced an ear from the third. This one, a lean, brown-spotted lurcher, fell back, howling piteously. The dogs backed off and regrouped. The solid boulder behind her kept the attack only from the front or side. If she confronted the dogs head on, she'd leave herself open from the rear.

Petia drew a breath and waited for the next attack.

'Ho, come away!'

He sat nonchalantly on his stallion, grinning down on her. 'Did you think we would forget about you so easily, my Trans beauty?'

Petia tilted her head proudly. 'I prayed for your death, Segrinn.'

'A noble's memory is long, especially for such a lovely indentured servant. You'll see that Lord Ambrose and his son –' Segrinn bowed mockingly from the saddle '– do not let runaways off so easily.'

'Ambrose couldn't care less, Segrinn. As I remember, my lord,' Petia said ironically, 'lust burned brightly in your eyes whenever I was near. You never quite caught me alone, did you? Is it that failure which makes me so important?'

Segrinn's black and silver uniformed men lowered their eyes. They knew too well the excesses of their lord. A dozen serving maids had swelled with bastard children in the past year.

'Bind her,' he ordered his troops. 'Her tongue is sharp, but the rest of her body is as curvaceous as ever. It will be a pleasure well worth the long hunt.'

Two men swung down from their mounts. Petia lunged, pinking one in the arm. The other grabbed her sword with the padded glove worn on his right hand, forcing her against the boulder. But the lurchers decided the matter. They rushed forward, snapping at Petia until she surrendered.

The men took her sword and bound her hands behind her.

Segrinn smiled wickedly down. 'Where's that bedamned pony she was riding? Never mind, let her walk. Keep a close eye on her. We don't want my beauty wandering off, do we? Certainly not before . . . my evening's diversion.'

He frowned at the dead lurcher and the other whimpering in pain. 'Kill that one. I can't stand the whining.' He turned his horse and looked around the meadow. 'There's one missing. Collar the rest. I don't want them disturbing my pleasures.'

'You'll never have any pleasure from me, Segrinn.' Petia hissed and spat.

'Certainly I will. Soon.'

He reached for the rope binding Petia and gave it a jerk, nearly pulling the cat Trans off her feet. 'Come along, my beauty.'

Petia stumbled after Segrinn's horse, trying to be defiant. But fear devoured her from the inside. *His* punishments were always cruel. And *he* had been thwarted for so long . . .

Eight

THE MORNING sun shone down from the high window, creating a shaft of light that seemed to come from the gods. Giles Grimsmate stirred, his head throbbing like a kettle drum at the Spring Fair. The last time he had felt this bad, he and four of his comrades had been on a week-long furlough in a Gentian Coast bawdy house.

Giles groaned loudly and shoved himself to hands and knees. The body of the old priest lay under him, long past the point of stiffening death; putrescence had set in.

Giles turned the priest gently. From his belly protruded a knife. Several tears in the robe indicated that he had been stabbed more than once.

'Why?' Giles said softly. Staring at the dead priest made him feel years older, weary. He blinked at the sunlight coming through a dirty pane and was reminded of the sacristy where he had examined the holy book.

'The book!' Giles got to shaky feet and stumbled through the nave to the sacristy and burst into the small room. On the table still rested the book – but with the page he had tried to memorise ripped out. Ragged edges greeted his fingers as he examined the holy book. Dizziness hit him again. He leaned forward, hands flat on the table until the giddiness passed.

'They won't get to the Gate before I do,' he said. He had no idea whom he referred to, but they wouldn't beat him to the Gate! Giles rubbed the large lump on his head and winced, then looked around the small room until he found a quill pen and a pot of light blue ink. He ripped several more of the pages out of the book and began scribbling down all he remembered of the tale from the missing page.

The lines of his crabbed handwriting were a pitifully inadequate reconstruction of what he knew had been on the missing page, but he didn't stop until he had filled the margins with as much as he could remember.

As he finished, Giles heard scuffling sounds from the church. He stuffed the pages into his tunic, not caring if the ink smeared or not. His sword came from its sheath in a movement made smooth by long years of practice.

'Who's there?' Giles called. Old habits returned to him, habits he had hoped to submerge in a more peaceful existence. Giles advanced on silent feet when no answer came to his challenge. A hulking man wrapped in a faded green cloak bent over the priest's body. His fingers lightly, almost lovingly brushed the hilt of the dagger in the old man's belly.

Giles crept forward, intent on sneaking up on this unknown visitor. The thought flashed through Giles' brain that this might be the murderer, returned for whatever reason. Perhaps the page hadn't contained all the information needed, and the killer sought more.

Giles came within striking distance when a short, stained wooden club smashed down on his wrist. His sword clattered to the floor. Giles swung around, but the club moved faster. It struck him on the forehead and drove him backwards. He smashed into the wall; the club landed hard on top of his head. Giles fell to the floor, more dazed than aware.

Giles tried to push himself away from the floor. The pain was excruciating. He got only as far as his elbows. Then he fainted.

A knocking inside his head sounded again; a tattoo on his ribs, adding more pain to that already in his body, made Giles wince and moan. The man thought he knew what it felt like to be locked in death's grip – how could it be worse than the way he felt?

He opened his eyes and croaked, 'Stop it!'

'On your feet, then.' The command was punctuated with another kick to the ribs.

'I would if I could. I've been clubbed.'

'Of course you have. I did it.'

A strong hand grabbed Giles by the arm and hoisted him to his feet. He was shoved and staggered across the floor to crash into the wall. The world still blurred around him, he sensed rather than saw that his captor had taken him back to the sacristy. Giles smashed hard into the table and collapsed across it. Gingerly, he reached for his head and felt the legions of lumps. When he took his hand away, he was not surprised to find blood from the new wounds on his fingers.

Those powerful hands straightened him up and spun him around. He faced a Glanport city guardsman decked out in a faded green cloak. Giles stood, weaving from side to side. He tried to will his legs to hold him and his eyes to focus. He leaned back against the table.

Some of the injury was real – the rest Giles feigned. Fingers blunted by arthritis worked to close the book of scriptures on the table behind him. He had already decided who would be the primary suspect in the priest's death: Giles Grimsmate.

'Here now, that's evidence against you,' the guard said, shoving him away from the book.

'Evidence?' Giles asked. 'What do you mean? It's just a book. I haven't stolen anything.'

Even as he spoke, Giles heard the rattle of parchment inside his tunic. Unfortunately, the guard's hearing proved equally as acute. He ripped open Giles' tunic and grabbed the sheets.

'Bejj, Koram!' the guardsman shouted. Two more guards entered the room. They looked at the first for orders.

'Take this man to the gaol and see that he's well secured. Charge him with murdering poor old Pater Daliferrian.'

The two men seized Giles by the arms. He tried to struggle but was still too weak.

'You're accusing me of the murder of that old priest? I found him dead. I got hit over the head, as any fool can see, and . . .'

'And thought to rob his church.' The guardsmen shook the pages so hard they snapped like the cracker on a whip. 'Get him out of here,' the guard said. 'And send someone to take care of the priest's body.'

Giles rubbed his arms and stamped his feet to ward off the penetrating cold. It did little good. He eventually collapsed onto the straw mat, shivering.

When a guard passed by in the corridor, Giles yelled out, 'A blanket, damn you. It's freezing in here.'

'It'll get colder,' the guard said, smirking. 'When you're hanged and buried.' He made a grotesque face and imitated a man being dropped through a hangman's trap, rope around the neck.

'Wasn't even this cold during the Pannatiree Campaign,' Giles grumbled.

The guard peered in at him, his expression altering. 'You fought at Pannatiree?'

'More's the pity, I did,' Giles said, sensing sympathy on the gaoler's part. The man was too young by far to have fought in one of the bloodiest battles of the Trans War. 'Fourteen months we marched and countermarched through snow and rain. Lost all but nine in my original company.'

'My father died at Pannatiree,' the guard said. 'So did my two uncles and my eldest brother.'

'More'n twenty-three thousand went with them,' Giles said grimly. Old memories were worse than the cold.

The gaoler left without another word, but about an hour later a blanket mysteriously appeared. Giles wrapped it around his quaking shoulders. It did little to fend off the dank cold, but for the first time Giles thought he might have a slim chance to convince them he was innocent of killing the priest.

Giles had no idea how long he spent in the cell. Without a window to see the passing days, he was effectively cut off from the world. Occasional meals came. He had no idea if he was being better fed than the others. He doubted it, but the guard did look in on him more frequently. Giles snorted. Probably to see if he had died yet.

But Giles Grimsmate wouldn't die. Not in a prison cell. He had lived through too much, seen too many bloody ways of dying, to succumb in a filthy gaol.

He slept, he awoke in cold sweats from evil dreams, he paced, he tried to exercise, but mostly he endured the boredom of his imprisonment. From time to time, he pulled out the gold key and examined it. The guards had somehow missed it when they searched him. How, he couldn't say.

Because of this one small lapse, the footloose wanderer was happy. That key – and what it promised – kept him sane and determined to win free of the cell.

The clank of metal weapons awoke Giles. The gaoler opened the squeaky, rusted door to his cell, and four other guardsmen dragged him to his feet. He looked questioningly at the gaoler.

'You're being taken before the magistrate,' the guard said. 'A word of advice. Don't antagonise him. He has a very quick temper.'

The four soldiers stared curiously at the gaoler. Giles took this to mean that such advice was seldom offered.

'Thanks,' was all he managed to say before being hustled along the littered corridor and up into the bright light of midday. Fresh air struck him like a fist. He sagged down, grateful for this hint that the world still existed, that he might again be a part of it.

They took him into a one-storey frame building not a hundred feet from the entrance to the gaol. Giles walked on unsteady legs, but he walked proudly. He stopped in front of the low railing that separated the prisoners from the magistrate and tried to evaluate his chances.

They didn't appear too good. The magistrate had the look about him of keeping 'score' of victims hanged – Giles wondered if he had been given a quota that had to be filled every month. He had heard of such in other towns governed by strict lords.

The white-haired magistrate looked up from his table. 'You smell, prisoner.'

'No doubt, Honoured One. I've not bathed since the guards-men tucked me away in your gaol.'

'Murderers deserve no better.' The words came with a hint of distaste.

'Am I already tried and convicted?' Giles asked.

The magistrate's pale eyes blazed. 'Don't be impudent.'

'I'm not trying to be,' Giles answered, holding down his own anger. 'Honoured One, I was set upon in the temple, came to with a bad cut on my head, a guard kicking me in the ribs, arrested, thrown into a cell, my wound not treated, and now I seem to have been convicted already, as you call me a murderer. Forgive me if you believe me to be impudent.'

The magistrate continued to look Giles directly in the eye. Giles met him stare for stare. This sort of silent contest had been played out before. Giles had stonily out-eyed many an officer in his days as a sergeant. Reluctantly, the magistrate broke eye contact and looked down at the papers before him, having met his match.

'I'm told that you were found robbing the Pater.'

'Correction, Honoured One.' Giles chose his words care-fully. The evidence against him was highly incriminating. 'I had been given permission to read from the book of scriptures. I was doing so when I heard a noise. I went to investigate and found the priest. Someone clubbed me. I staggered about in a daze. Perhaps in my confusion I put the pages into my tunic. You can see the severity of my injuries.'

To that the oozing wounds on his head bore full testimony. The magistrate made a face. 'That's festering,' he said in obvious distaste. He gestured to a bailiff sitting by the wall. 'Get a surgeon. I want that wound treated after we finish with this trial.

'Who struck you?' the magistrate asked. 'Other than the guardsman during your capture?'

'I have no idea,' Giles replied. 'I saw the priest, examined him and was struck from behind.'

'This seems to be a simple enough case. The Pater of the Temple of Welcome has been killed. You are found in the church, with pages ripped from the holy book. The story you tell is flimsy, and no one is likely to testify on your behalf.'

The magistrate peered at his papers, then quickly dashed off a few notes. Giles knew that he would be sentenced to die for the priest's murder and nothing could be done to change the magistrate's mind. Giles tensed aching muscles as he prepared to fight his way from the room, if he could.

The bailiff came in and hurried to the magistrate. They whispered for several minutes. The magistrate scowled, then dismissed the obsequious bailiff.

'I am now ready to pass judgement in this matter,' the magistrate said. He looked as if he had bitten into a persimmon; his cheeks collapsed, and he had to force out each word. Giles sensed the guards behind him moving to thwart any escape.

'Honoured One, I . . .'

'Silence!' The magistrate wrote another note on the page before him, then said, 'It is my considered opinion that you speak the truth, that you did not slay Pater Daliferrian of the Temple of Welcome, and that you are free to leave.' The magistrate glared at Giles, adding, 'Leave immediately.'

Giles was surprised. The guards behind him were flabbergasted. One even squawked in protest. The magistrate's cold glare silenced him.

Giles bowed his head slightly. 'Thank you, Honoured One, for your justice. Will I find my things still being cared for at the inn?'

'The gaoler, for whatever reason, has personally seen to it.' Am impatient gesture told Giles he had been dismissed – and with ill-grace. He started to ask the bailiff what message he had given the magistrate, but found the guardsmen more than a little anxious to see him away from their normally quiet township.

Giles found leaving Glanport easier than he had anticipated. The gaoler put him onto a good deal for a horse. While the animal had seen better days, Giles found himself liking the balky, bald-patched creature. He'd seen better days, himself.

The guardsmen accompanied him to the top of the hill overlooking the town. They said nothing, nor did Giles have much to say to them. The mystery of his sudden acquittal bore closer examination, but if such nosing about put him back in the gaol, he could live with his curiosity as he rode off in the fresh air and looked at the clouds drifting over the city. Being free again and cleared of charges made him into a new man.

He rode, a bawdy song on his lips and the golden Key to Paradise in his pouch.

Above him, a hawk trailing silvered jesses wheeled in the sky, watching.

Nine

PETIA DARYA lay bound outside the warming perimeter of the fire. Occasionally her stomach growled, but she was damned if she would beg. Propping herself up on one elbow, the Trans watched the men passing around a bag of wine. They had already eaten, more beastlike by far than any Trans she had ever known, even the porcine Trans. They tore chunks of meat from the bone with their teeth and dipped their hands in the stewpot to grab pieces of almost raw potato. Their behaviour offended her catlike sensibilities.

'Hungry, my beauty?' Petia glared up at the smirking Segrinn.

'I've brought you a plate of food, but I don't think I want to unbind you. I'll feed you.'

'I'd rather starve.' Petia spat at him and missed.

'You don't really mean that. There, your stomach's growling. Listen to it. Oh, you're hungry, all right. You're hungry for food – like I'm hungry for your body.'

'I'll kill you, Segrinn. You're a filthy swine. Your brain dangles between your legs.'

'You are right, my pet. There's so little else in the world to take pleasure in.'

He set the plate of food on the ground and reached for her. She hissed at him, teeth closing just a fraction of an inch from his outstretched hand.

'I'll not take you here,' he said softly, eyes gleaming lustfully. 'Between satin sheets, with a mattress that we can sink into as we fornicate. Not out here in the open with this offal looking on.' He gestured toward his soldiers, one of whom sang off key and too loudly in his drunkenness.

'We'll get you home,' Segrinn continued, 'give you a lovely perfumed bath and dress you in something more revealing than boots and homespun. It will be an occasion of splendour that I will remember for a lifetime. Your body next to mine, quivering with rapt passion. Much of the delight is in the anticipation, and I anticipate, oh yes, I anticipate!'

'You'll not have me. Ever. A knife in your heart is all you'll ever get from me.'

'We must keep up appearances, mustn't we? Eat. I won't have you fainting from weakness. Three days' travel brings us home. I really would like you to get there without dying of starvation.'

Taking a slice of meat on the end of his knife, he offered it to her. Petia turned her head aside. The aroma of the meat proved too enticing, and she reluctantly opened her mouth. She looked away as she chewed.

Segrinn said nothing as he fed his captive, but his hands lingered on parts of her body, touching lightly, obscenely. Petia felt sick to her stomach but endured. Soon, Segrinn would pay. How he would pay!

When she had finished, Segrinn stood. 'That's better. There's nothing worse in bed than a scrawny woman.' He turned and walked back to the fire. Petia spat on the ground behind him, hating herself as much as she hated him.

It was nearly three in the morning when Petia awoke. The fire still burned. The sentry tended it when he wasn't dozing. He sat on a small log, huddled against the cold at his back. He had wrapped himself in a blanket, and his head dropped forward, multiple chins resting on his chest.

Petia stretched her legs, willing the blood to circulate. She needed to relieve herself badly, but that would have to be done later. The cat Trans turned herself over, naturally as one does in sleep. She grunted once, then snored several times before letting her breathing resume normally. Through slitted eyelids she watched the sentry's head come up and look in her direction. He watched her until he decided that she really was asleep, then he yawned, stared at the fire and decided against making the effort to put on more wood. He nodded off again.

Petia stretched her fingers and felt the claws. Her slender body became thinner, sleeker. The ropes binding her slackened. She checked the dozing figure at the fire once more.

Petia wriggled downward until the ropes binding her arms to her sides slid over her head. Her wrists were still tied, but she could now move her arms. Inching back up until the rope was hidden by her body, she pulled the blanket over her.

For several minutes, she worked at them, perspiring from the effort. The ropes had been tied well. A sudden crackling noise startled her; the guard threw another piece of wood on the fire, but he was so sleepy he never looked in her direction.

Petia let out a tiny sigh of relief. Working faster now, she got one hand free. The other quickly followed.

Petia considered cutting the sentry's throat – and going on to slay Segrinn. Feline glee rose within her breast at the idea, but the need for retribution faded and caution asserted itself. One mistake and Segrinn would have her. This time, he'd not be so gentle. At the memory of what he had done before, the woman shuddered.

Escape. She crept off, cat quiet, to find her pony.

Keja Tchurak cursed constantly, becoming more inventive with every passing mile and every additional unsettling bounce from the lurching mule. Ragged clothes flapped around his wiry frame, his blanket roll looked like a picnic lunch for moths, the sack behind nearly empty when it ought to have held riches and all his fine clothing.

Keja's discouragement grew like a weed. True, he had accepted from l'Karm's guards, but the ignominy of having new clothes, horse, saddle, and supplies stolen, then being forced to wear the rags of a beggar and ride a mule overwhelmed him. Life was not treating Keja well.

For a week, he had let the bouncing mule abuse his backside. Laughed at and scorned, Keja had learned the beggar's trade quickly. Out on the road it did not appear to be a lucrative one – he saw little enough to even steal. In the cities, he had heard that some beggars grew wealthy and fat for their efforts, but Keja had gone hungry more than once. And sometimes he had eaten food not fit for pigs.

The mule stumbled once, then began to limp. Keja climbed down, circulation returning to his hindquarters in a painful rush.

'What ails you, you miserable creature?' The mule turned and one huge brown eye peered accusingly at Keja, as if this were all his fault.

Keja picked up the animal's left front leg and examined the hoof. A stone, With his knife, he removed it. 'C'mon, old thing. I'll give your back and my backside a rest. Over the next hill, they say. Just over the next hill, Hawk's Prairie. It's been over the next hill for three days now, eh? You wouldn't be leading me in circles, would you?'

Keja snorted in disgust. Talking to animals. He certainly had tumbled from a lofty pinnacle when his only company was a swaybacked mule.

He pulled on the rope and got the animal moving. Keja had got on all right with the mule, but it wasn't the same as the beautiful black that he should have been riding.

The mule continued to limp. Keja knew that he wouldn't be riding any more this day. Ahead he saw the road rising into a range of hills turned purple with haze. He was tired of the road, of working, of having to beg. Most of all he was tired of being misdirected by peasants too ignorant to learn even elementary geography.

And not a one of them had been the least bit comely – or even female, for all he could tell.

By afternoon, Keja had climbed into the hills. When the road crested, a vast plain stretched before him.

'Oh, blessed relief,' Keja said. 'Hawk's Prairie! It must be. But where lies the Gate of Paradise?' He nudged the mule and got only a wet snort for a reply. Keja chuckled, feeling happier than he had in weeks. The goal wasn't far off. It couldn't be now!

By evening, he rode onto the flat. A sense of mounting despair overwhelmed him. The plain stretched for miles, flat and seemingly empty. The soil was sandy and littered with small stones. A wispy brown grass grew in clumps, fighting for its life against a hostile environment. The mule bit off a mouthful and chewed patiently while Keja stared across untold miles of empty plain.

A stream ran down from the hills and tentatively skirted the edge of the barren plain. Seeing the cool water, Keja decided to camp for the night. Tomorrow would be soon enough to begin his search for the Gate of Paradise.

Two days of wandering Hawk's Prairie brought Keja close to the point of desperation. The prairie was huge, flat, monotonous, soul-defeating. He tied the mule's halter rope to a large rock and found himself another rock to sit on. He wiped the sweat from his face. He realised that his teeth were clenched in frustration.

'Where is it?' he demanded of the mule. 'It's not a myth. I'Karm is not the type to believe in fantasies – and Rosaal was convinced of the Gate's existence.'

At the mention of the lovely woman, Keja felt a twinge of irritation. While she had not been a mental giant, she had been skilled in ways pleasing to him. It had been too long since he had found any woman, skilled or not, and it rankled.

What disgusted him even more was that he had not been wandering aimlessly and still he had not discovered the Gate. He had carefully been quartering the plain.

Nothing. Not a trace. No sign, no matter how inconsequential. Maybe it was just a legend after all. Perhaps he had wasted his time. He took the key from inside his tunic and held it in his hand, reading the curlicue runes for the hundredth time.

Keja stared across the heat-shimmered plain. Opposite him the plain ended and the hills rose with the promise of coolness. He closed his eyes against the fierce, hammering sun. For a moment he thought he had seen the vague outline of an archway. But he had just passed by there. He opened his eyes and peered again across the all too empty space.

Behind the dancing curtain of heat, the image continued to waver.

Keja rose to his feet and took a few steps forward. The image of the arch did not change. Hope exploded in his chest. Not taking his eyes off the archway for fear it might prove to be a mirage and vanish if he looked away, Keja untied the mule. Pulling it behind him, he began to walk across the plain. With his free hand, he tucked the key back inside his tunic.

When he looked up again, the archway was gone.

'No!' he shouted. 'Come back, come back, dammit!' Keja halted. It had been a mirage. The few steps he had taken made the arch vanish, an image conjured by tired, watery eyes.

He took the key out again and looked at it. 'Maybe I should just melt it down, sell it for whatever I can get from a gold-smith.' It sounded more and more attractive to him. Keja did not like the burning heat under his bootsoles or attacking the top of his head.

He glanced up and saw the archway again. He frowned, concentrating on the image, and carefully stowed the key between his belt and tunic. The Gate disappeared, leaving only the plain and the hundred-foot-tall swirling column of a dust devil. Keja reached down and rested his fingers on the edge of the key.

The archway reappeared.

He located a landmark in the hills beyond that wouldn't vanish on him, then headed for it. His hope was renewed, but he had not found real faith as yet.

Halfway across he touched the key once again, afraid of a cruel hoax. The Gate wavered, clearer now. Keja whirled about in joy. He let out a loud laugh that eventually echoed back from the hills. The mule's ears pricked up at his master's antics.

'The Gate of Paradise! I've found it! I have!' Visions of lovely houris raced through his mind, courtesans serving him iced wines and popping succulent titbits into his waiting mouth, noble ladies with an intense yearning for all he had to offer.

'The Gate!'

Keja did not touch the key again until he reached the far side and tethered the mule to a scrubby tree. Closing his eyes and offering a small, heartfelt prayer, he pulled the key from his belt. He opened his eyes.

No Gate.

'Come back, Dismatis curse you, come back!' Keja lost control, pounding fists against scrubby trees and rocks and sand. He collapsed onto the ground, clenching the key in his fists. He passed beyond rage.

'What mad jester created this?' he asked, all emotion drained from him. 'I'd seduce his women, steal his valuables, rob him of life itself for this if I but knew his name!'

Keja staggered to his feet and turned to go back to his mule. The Gate stood magnificently, only fifty feet away. His jaw dropped.

He stared, transfixed. The afternoon sun blazed down on two immense white Gentian marble columns joined at the top with an ornate arch wrought of a delicately veined black stone and shot through with red. Keja walked to the Gate and touched one glossy, cool column.

'It wasn't a fool's chase. It was real!' He stood back and stared at the arch. Large runes across the top boldly proclaimed: 'The Gate of Paradise.' Puzzling out the smaller inscription required too much effort. Keja vowed to study it at length. Later.

Between the two columns stretched an iron gate decorated with complex, swirling branches and delicate leaves. At the centre where the two gates met and well within the reach of a person's grasp were five hasps, one above the other, each with a lock.

Keja looked at the key in his hand. 'The Gate of Paradise,' he whispered. He stepped forward and fitted the key into the bottom lock. He turned it, but it refused to budge. Keja pulled the key out and examined the lock closely. He saw no sign of weakening rust, and the internal mechanism had been cunningly concealed behind a thick plate.

'It bears closer examination,' he said, 'later.' Keja pulled the key from the lock and tried it in the next keyhole. His key failed to open the second lock, and the third. When he tried the fourth lock, almost in desperation, Keja felt the tumblers give and the shank of the lock fell away. Keja opened the hasp and let the opened lock dangle from the staple. The fifth lock would not open either.

Keja frowned, trying to understand the mind of whomever had constructed the Gate. Long ago he had discovered a thief's work became much easier if he placed himself in the victim's head and tried to *understand*.

Nothing came. 'Never mind,' he said aloud. 'I've found the Gate. Locks have never stopped me before.' Confidently, Keja rummaged in his pouch until he found a small ring of slender picks.

For the next half hour, Keja worked at picking the four locks not opened by his key. He used every pick on every lock without success. Frustrated, he began again, summoning skills taught him by the greatest thieves in all of Bericlere. Sweat beaded on his forehead and ran into his eyes. His face contorted in intense concentration. At times, his tongue would slip out from between his teeth and twist as if Keja thought this would add some extra dimension to the work at hand.

Again, he used all the picks against the four stubborn locks. Finally, he stepped back, gave the gate a good kick, and turned to stalk away.

'Not having any success?'

The man sat astride his horse, watching with quiet amusement.

Keja grabbed for his sword, then reason regained control. Without the key, Keja had been unable to see the Gate. The cool and collected rider could see nothing of the Gate. It had to work that way. Keja relaxed, his mind turning to the lie he would tell.

'Just angry because I have to cross this desolate plain,' Keja answered.

'Yes, I imagine so,' the stranger said. He looked across the flat, barren expanse. 'It is a wide one, all right. I see from your animal's tracks that you've just come from the other side of the hills. Now you have to go back, eh?'

'I do, if it's any matter to you.' Keja grabbed at the excuse.

'You couldn't get the other four locks open?'

'No, only the one.' It took only a second, then Keja blanched. He had answered the casual question without thinking and given away all! 'What locks?'

Giles Grimsmate quietly held up his gold key.

Keja's hand flashed to his side. The key still rested there, tucked firmly in his belt. 'Where did you get that?' he demanded.

'I might ask the same of you, except that I know about l'Karm. I had troubles of my own with his guard – they mistook me for you.' Giles dropped his reins and dismounted.

Keja watched as the older man walked to the Gate and fitted his key into the bottom lock. It would not open, nor did the next. The third lock snicked open easily. The fourth lock was hanging open. The topmost lock would not budge for Giles' key.

'This is something of a puzzle,' Giles said. 'We'll try again later. Dealing with magicks can be tricky – not something I cherish doing. It might be that they will only unlock at a certain time. I'm going to camp up there.' He waved up the hillside to a flat space shaded by stunted nepler trees. 'Care to join me?'

'I've nothing to offer for food,' Keja said.

'No matter. Come on.' Giles picked up the reins of his horse and started for the dubious shelter of the trees.

Keja watched him with a puzzled look. Then he untied his mule and followed.

Giles unsaddled his horse and handed the reins to Keja. 'Tether the animals while I gather firewood.'

'You trust me with your horse?' Keja asked, startled. The animal, as old and decrepit as it was, looked far better than his mule.

Giles laughed. 'No, not much. But you're not going any-where until the Gate is open. Nor am I. So a tiny bit of trust, maybe.'

Keja shook his head. 'You're a rare one.' He did as Giles asked and, soon enough, a wisp of smoke grew into flame, then bloomed into a welcome fire. The meal was not fancy, but to Keja it represented a banquet. When he had finished, Giles offered him a pipe. Keja waved it off. Giles filled it for himself and lay back on an elbow to enjoy the pungent tobacco mix.

'Were you here long before I arrived?' Giles asked between puffs.

'No.' Keja wondered how much the man knew and how much he ought to tell him. 'I found the Gate, unlocked the one lock and tried to pick the others. You certainly startled me.'

'You were concentrating so hard that you didn't hear me come up,' Giles said. 'You should have seen the look on your face.'

Keja bristled at this, then calmed. 'You obviously know where I got my key. How'd you come by yours?'

'Won it in a dice game. The sailor who wagered it didn't know anything about the Gate, but one man knew quite a bit about it. He told me the story in exchange for enough brandy to float a brigantine.'

Little by little, the two men relaxed. Talk became easier as Giles told of his time in the War and his restless need to wander. Keja warmed to the telling and regaled Giles with some of his more successful exploits.

Giles thought that perhaps he bragged too much. Still, this Keja Tchurak looked like a man who could handle himself in a spot of trouble. Giles knew Keja spoke the truth about being a thief; only a thief could be conned into trusting a street urchin. Giles had long ago learned that those capable of theft were the ones most easily robbed. They never thought it could happen to them – and so it did.

The moon rose, nearly full. Giles tapped the dottle from his pipe and unrolled his blankets. 'We'll see what the morning brings. Better luck, perhaps.'

'Hm?' Keja was deep in his own thoughts. 'Oh, yes. Good night.' He fetched his own ragged roll and stretched out near the fire. Soon both men were asleep.

Petia crept along the hillside's edge. She had left Marram tied to a tree downwind, over a mile distant. Petia had watched the two men for nearly five hours, trying to understand what had transpired between them.

It was a strange, bizarre ritual they went through. She watched the stranger guide his horse down the hillside and sit quietly watching whatever Keja was about. She was bemused when Keja drew back his foot and aimed a kick at empty air.

Whatever they did, they had finally given up and made camp. Petia chewed on dried meat from her pouch while she watched the men being domestic. When they were soundly asleep, she would act.

Keja still had the gold key. Petia had seen it glint in the sunlight. She was determined to have it. For all she had been through, it was small enough compensation.

The moonlight proved enough for her acute night vision to find a quiet path into the campsite. She squatted down and watched the two men's chests rise and fall. Both slept soundly. The fire burned lower and neither rose to tend it. That was a good sign.

In another half hour, Petia decided to make her move. She stealthily moved down the hill toward the men. The stranger slept on one side of the fire, Keja on the other. She went to Keja.

A loud snap made her jump. A limb, burned through, fell into the flames, scattering sparks into the velvet black of the night sky. Both men burst from their blankets and pinned her in seconds. Petia fought with all the skill imparted by her cat nature, but she was no match for such strong men.

Keja locked one of her arms behind her. Petia snarled in pain, then stopped fighting. He would relax; her chance for escape would come if she waited.

'Look who we have here.' Keja grinned at Petia.

Giles glanced at Keja. 'You know the Trans?'

'You've not met, have you? A serving maid from the Leather Cup in Klepht. She tried to steal the key from me once before. The gods alone know how she comes to be here.' Keja yawned. 'Let's tie her up and sort this out in the morning. I'm still tired from my trip. But do watch her. She's a tough one.'

Giles fetched rope from his pack. The two men tied Petia hand and foot and laid her none too gently near the fire. Keja slipped quickly back to sleep, but Giles lay awake watching. He wondered how this young Trans fitted into the adventure.

Ten

GILES GRIMSMATE came awake instantly, too many clues assailing his senses. He rolled over to check their prisoner. Gone. Giles jerked erect, grabbed at his weapons, and yelled at Keja, 'She's escaped!'

'Yes, I have.' Giles spun about, feet tangling in his blanket. Petia squatted on the opposite side of the fire. 'I thought I'd get us some breakfast. Porridge?'

Giles rolled out of his blankets and stood, running his fingers through his black, grey-shot hair. 'Bedamned,' he said. 'How did you get out of those ropes? I tie a fair knot, and those have held stronger ones than you.'

Petia smiled wickedly, teeth showing. 'It's a little trick of mine.' She walked over to Keja's sleeping figure and kicked him none too gently. 'Up, you lazy lout. The day's half gone.'

Keja groaned and blinked. He closed his eyes again and muttered, 'I was dreaming that the serving wench had got free.'

'Listen to him.' Petia returned to the fire and ladled porridge into bowls, handing one to Giles. 'I'm Petia Darya. And you?'

Giles admired her straightforwardness. 'Giles Grimsmate,' he replied. 'My pleasure. What were you looking for last night?'

'His key, of course,' she said. 'I've completely lost my touch, I think. That's the second time I've failed.'

Giles nodded. 'You just tackled a pair of men whose senses are extra sharp, honed by years of suspicion. Twenty years of the War did that to me. I don't know about Keja. Maybe thievery does that to you.'

'It does. But I'm obviously out of practice.'

Keja muttered and groaned for half an hour, prowling

around the campsite, bowl and spoon in hand. Finally, Giles tired of inaction and said, 'Let's try the keys again.'

'More than one?' Petia asked, her sharp eyes darting from one man to the other. Giles felt undercurrents of greed rising in her. If one key was valuable enough to chase after, two made the hunt twice as rewarding.

'We each have one.' Giles warily studied the Trans.

'Maybe I should have tried to steal yours instead.' She caught Giles' dark look. 'And maybe it's just as well I didn't.'

Giles headed toward the Gate, holding the glittering gold key between thumb and forefinger.

'How do you know where the Gate is?' Petia asked.

'You can't see it?' Giles held out his hand. 'Try the key.'

Petia daintily touched her finger to the key. The Gate suddenly shimmered below at the edge of the plain.

Keja came stumbling down the path behind them. 'Is it still there? It didn't go away, did it? I find it so tiring to deal with magicks of this order.'

Giles looked up to the heavens. 'Open your eyes, man. No, it didn't go away.' He walked to the Gate and inserted his key into the lowest lock. Trying each in turn, he found that his key once again opened only the third lock. 'Might require opening in a particular sequence,' he muttered.

Petia stood back to watch the seeming charade of Giles trying a different order in what she saw only as empty air. She became bored and wandered off. Keja sat on the ground, his head in his hand, still trying to wake up.

'Did you see that, Giles?' he yelled. 'She walked through that stone column.'

Giles looked up from his work. He saw Petia on the other side of the Gate. 'What's over there?' he yelled to her.

'You don't have to shout. I can hear you perfectly well, extraordinarily well, in fact. Nothing's over here, except the plain.' She turned and gestured behind her across the barren land.

'Come back here for a minute.'

Petia strolled back, walking 'through' the metal bars of the Gate, and stood at Giles' side.

'Great Ephrem! They're illusory,' Giles cried.

'What?'

'The gate, the columns, the entire Gate of Paradise. You walked away from me and *through* the stone columns. You've returned by walking *through* the bars.' A slow smile crossed Giles' face. 'We're home free.'

Giles briskly strode forward and smashed hard into the Gate. He reeled back and fell, while Petia walked forward and *through* the Gate, unimpeded.

Giles stared up, a foolish expression on his face. He looked from Petia to the key in his hand to the Gate.

'Mind explaining this?' asked Petia. 'Why did you fall?'

'I thought to simply walk through the Gate, as you just did. But while I hold the key, the Gate is solid, impassable.'

Petia rejoined him, sticking out her hand. 'Let me hold it.'

Reluctantly, Giles passed over the key. He rose; the Gate had vanished totally. When he walked forward, he felt only hot wind against his flesh. Giles looked back and saw Petia's expression – to her, as long as she held the key, he passed *through* the solid Gate.

'I thought it would work,' he said sadly. 'I thought I could enter, but when I hold the key, the Gate is impenetrable.'

'And,' cut in Keja, 'when you no longer hold the key, you can't see the Gate at all, so you can go through with no resistance.'

Giles took the key back from Petia, who surrendered it to him with obvious regret. He saw the light in her eyes die as the Gate vanished for her and reappeared to him. Giles went to the Gate, closed his eyes and stepped forward. He smashed into solid metal.

'You've already tried that,' pointed out Petia. 'Why did you do it again?'

'Something Keja said. I thought if I didn't see the Gate, but still held the key . . .' Giles' voice trailed off. It sounded lame, silly. Like so much else in his life, it hadn't worked out the way he'd intended.

'I'm going to make one more attempt to pick those locks,' Keja said. 'I've come too far and endured great hardships, to give up easily now. Besides, the challenge excites me.'

'A knothole excites you,' muttered Petia. Keja gave her a superior look, then set to work picking the locks.

Finally Keja gave up. 'I don't understand it at all. There's supposed to be immense wealth behind the Gate of Paradise. You don't suppose it's a false gate, do you?'

'No,' Giles said. 'The story of the Gate mentions only the one.'

Keja's head drooped. 'My bad luck with the locks is exceeded only by the dismal luck I've had recently with women and retaining my belongings.'

'The picks did nothing?' Giles eyed the Gate. No amount of explosive would budge it either, he guessed. Physical against magical proved an unequal match; the magicks usually triumphed.

'Not even a scratch,' Keja said. 'And it isn't my lack of ability. Those locks were not meant to be picked. Not even by the masters.'

'It's obvious then how to open the Gate.' Petia smiled sweetly at the two men staring at her.

As much as her superior nature in this irritated him, Giles liked the imp lurking in those eyes. 'All right, brilliant one. I knew you turned up for a purpose. Reveal all to your humble audience.'

'It's a plain as a hump on a lirjan. There are five locks and you've opened two of them with two keys. Somewhere there are three more keys.'

Giles said nothing, digesting Petia's words. He had felt alive in this quest. The tiredness descended upon him once more, making him into a man years older than his age.

'That ends it,' he said. 'We've only got two keys, and Keja hasn't been successful in picking the other locks, so we're out of luck.' He stared at the Gate of Paradise. 'It would have been the adventure of a lifetime,' he said softly.

'You don't suppose we could find the other three keys, do you?' Petia looked from Giles to Keja and back. 'You give up too easily.'

The men stared at her.

'Well, it is such a crazy idea? Find three keys and the fortune is ours.'

Giles gazed off toward the Gate. 'The idea is sound, but I have no hint where to go a'hunting for the other keys.'

'What do we have to lose?' the Trans insisted.

Keja looked up and scowled. 'You mean form a team to go

searching for them? Why should I become partners with a Trans who tried to steal my key from me, not once, but twice?'

'What bothers you most, Keja? The fact that I'm a Trans, or a female, or a cleverer thief than you?' Petia threw a clump of dirt at Keja. 'Back in Klepht it didn't matter that I was Trans.'

'No, it didn't,' Keja said, a slow smile crossing his lips. 'Still doesn't. But you are hardly the cleverer thief. Let me tell you of . . .'

Giles broke in. 'It hardly matters. None of us knows where to find – or steal – the other three keys. Even if we did, I can't say I trust either of you. In the army we executed thieves, and I did my share of that chore with a certain willingness.' Giles heaved a gusty sigh. 'And you two obviously don't trust each other. We wouldn't make a very successful team, it appears to me.'

'We might, once we got to know each other.' Petia's eyes glinted. 'You both smell nice. And I don't have anything better to do. There's a troop of guards after me claiming I killed a couple of men outside Klepht. It was self defence, I swear it was.' Neither Giles nor Keja much cared about this. They had experienced similar problems of their own. 'There's worse,' Petia went on. 'A despicable insect named Segrinn also follows me. I was indentured to his father, Lord Ambrose. I ran away to escape Segrinn's bed.'

'You do that a lot, don't you?' Keja asked.

'Never mind,' cut in Giles, irritated at all that had happened that day. 'What's the point to this, Petia?'

'I'll be frank. I wouldn't mind the protection you two could give me.'

She curled up, catlike, and watched their responses. Petia continued, 'Keja has guards after him, too. His key is stolen, if what I heard in Klepht was right.'

Giles nodded. 'They came into the Laughing Cod the night after I won the key. City guard and guards of someone named l'Karm.'

'They almost caught me in Neelarna,' Keja said morosely. 'I'm sure they're still after me. Sooner or later they'll pick up the trail.'

'And you, Giles?' Petia smiled sweetly. 'Who is after you?'

Giles picked up a stick and drew squares and circles in the

dirt at his feet. 'Demons,' he answered. Demons left over from a futile war, from killing too many men like himself, men foolishly loyal to self-serving commanders, from losing wife and sons, from knife-edged memories chasing him across the barren lands locked within his head.

Giles said, 'You know, I spent an afternoon in a temple in Glanport reading from a holy book.'

'Religion? You don't look the type.' Keja glared at him, as if expecting better.

'Listen.' The crack of Giles' command silenced the wiry thief. 'I sought clues to this gate. The Temple of Welcome is an old religion, dying. I skimmed their scriptures.

'At the beginning was a passage that mentioned keys. It wasn't what I sought so I skimmed on. Something about five tribes closely connected at the beginning of time. The five tribal leaders said the keys were given to them by the gods. Probably had the keys made and concocted the story. But it welded the tribes together into a true nation.'

'Politics and religion, always the perfect combination for keeping people in line,' grumbled Keja. Giles ignored him and went on with his tale.

'Their world grew cold and they had to move.'

'So Petia may well be right. Five keys. But we don't know where the other three are.'

Petia spoke so silently Giles almost missed her words.

'I think I know where another of the keys is.'

Giles motioned for her to continue.

'I come from Trois Havres, across the Everston Sea, on the continent of Milbante. Trois Havres are three rich coastal cities. Living somewhere inland is a sorceress – the Flame Sorceress. There are many stories about her, but one I remember from my childhood involves a gold key.'

Petia stopped.

Keja broke the silence. 'You're suggesting that we all go looking for the third key? Not this lad. Keja Tchurak is a loner. I work best alone – or perhaps with a willing woman beside me. In bed.' He glared at Giles and Petia, daring them to dispute his claims.

'For my part,' said Giles, 'I'm wandering nowhere in particular, but I don't need the sort of adventure you're suggesting.'

Petia shrugged. 'It was just a thought. A bit selfish on my part. I'd like to see my home again.'

'It would be a fantastic adventure, though, wouldn't it?' Keja mused. 'Just think – gather the five keys, open the Gate, rake in the immense wealth. What a great story to tell my grandchildren, of whom there will be legions.' He pursed his lips and lost himself in consideration of this wild scheme.

'Two thieves and an old warrior,' Giles said, 'off to seek their fortunes. It sounds like a tale told by a drunken sailor. Let me be honest with you. How could we ever trust each other?'

'Are you so pure, Giles?' asked Keja. 'Have you never stolen? Even a crumb or two when you were hungry?'

'That was different,' Giles said, on the defensive. 'My men starved and . . .'

'Aha, you admit it then. Theft is theft, my friend.' Keja smirked. 'Me. I'm for trying. Come with us, Giles. We need your experience – and you might make upright citizens of Petia and me. You've got nothing else to do, you admit that.'

Giles looked at the two. For all his jesting tone, Keja's eyes were sincere. Petia nodded solemnly.

'I will regret this. I know it.' He rose. 'Let's take one more look at the Gate.' He examined the archway once more.

'The Gate of Paradise,' in large runic letters blazed out at Giles. Then he worked to decipher the smaller, less distinct runes. They read: 'Only One May Enter.'

Short and direct, Giles thought, but cryptic. Did it mean that only one may enter at a time or that only one may ever enter? Giles decided to keep this small secret to himself.

'The journey might be worth it,' Giles said aloud. Petia and Keja came over.

'So we go to Trois Havres to find this Flame Sorceress?' asked Keja. 'Petia tells me she is reputed to be gorgeous, just the sort of woman who is irresistibly attracted to me.' Before Petia could say a word, Keja clamped one hand over his heart and cried, 'But I will forsake this sorceress if only you, my darling, will . . .'

'Enough of this,' cut in Giles. 'I have misgivings enough about my decision to join in this mad search for what might not exist.' He thought of the dead priest. The Pater had said the Temple of Welcome taught that the seeking was more important than the finding. Giles began to think such a teaching carried with it a kernel of truth. Again, with just the promise of a goal, no matter how tenuous, Giles felt himself coming alive and wanting to travel, to experience, to see again what the world had to offer.

Keys or not, entry through the Gate or not, he would seek. The finding might be nothing or it might represent more. Only the attempt would tell the truth.

Petia's head came up. 'Shh,' she said, putting her fingers to her lips. She listened intently.

'What is it?' asked Keja. 'Do you listen for the rapturous beating of my heart? With you so near, I can do nothing else but feel the heat, the excitement, the . . .'

'Keja!' Giles silenced the thief. 'Still your tongue and use your ears. Listen, man!'

'There it is again,' said Petia, her face set into a mask of fear. 'Segrinn's back on my trail.'

'What is it? What do you hear?' Giles asked.

'You don't hear it yet? No, you wouldn't. My hearing is superior because of my cat nature. Segrinn's lurchers bay, hot on my spoor. They're still distant. We'd better leave. Soon.'

Without questioning her further, Giles turned back up the trail to the camp. Keja and Petia followed. When they caught up with the grizzled old warrior, Giles had already kicked dirt on the fire. Petia threw her belongings into her sack and strapped it to Marram's back.

Giles glanced at Keja. 'Hurry, man. Lurchers are not respecters of life. Get a move on.'

'Do they truly send *lurchers* after her?' Keja asked. 'That seems dubious to me. They are expensive beasts, cantankerous. Their very nature, their intelligence, make them of questionable use.'

'If we are to find the keys, we must survive,' said Giles. 'And to survive means depending on one another. My ears cannot pick up the sounds like Petia's.' Giles left the rest of the sentence dangling. Keja understood. His senses weren't as acute as the Trans woman's, either.

'Mistake pulling out so precipitously,' he grumbled. Quickly, they packed and saddled the animals. Petia, impatient, was the first to swing up into her saddle.

Giles stood gazing around the campsite, wishing that they had time to obliterate all evidence that three people had camped here. Segrinn and his men might be put off their trail. Giles shook his head sadly, realising how wrong he was. Lurchers were not fooled easily.

'Did you check the locks?' he asked Keja.

'No, I didn't think to.'

'Start on up the trail into the hills. I'll catch up.' Giles kicked his ancient horse into a trot toward the Gate of Paradise, pulling his key free so that he could see. He cursed. The lock for Keja's key dangled open. Without dismounting, Giles reached over and snapped it closed. For good measure, he tried the other four locks. All secure.

The horse surprised him with the heart it displayed in its valiant uphill ride. He caught up with the other two sooner than he had anticipated. He slowed to a walk. 'Got your key?' he asked Keja. Giles saw that he would lend more than experience to this strange partnership; he would have to nursemaid the other two constantly or all their heads would be spitted and put out in the sun.

Keja patted his chest. Giles curtly acknowledged as the thief put the string with his key around his neck and tucked it into his tunic front.

'Trusting souls, aren't we? Shall we pick up the pace and see if we can put some distance between us and this Segrinn that Petia talks about with such loathing? I don't like him and I've never even seen him. At the moment, I don't like anyone who travels with a force of men. They are too likely to seek the reward on my head – or be the pawns of a jealous husband or father.'

Giles scowled. Keja appeared to enjoy this. Giles urged his mount to the front. 'I've been over this trail. Let me know if you can't keep up.' We must make a funny looking bunch, he thought. A horse, a marsh pony and a mule, a has-been warrior, a Trans woman and a thief dressed as a beggar.

Giles Grimsmate then thought only of eluding their pursuers. *Their* pursuers, he told himself, not just Petia's.

101

Segrinn sat astride his horse, directing his men. The lurchers milled about, yelping at the occasional scent of their quarry but confused by the other spoor mingling with that of the cat-woman.

'What's the matter with the dogs?' he shouted. 'Whip them into finding the trail.'

'They seem confused, Lord,' a soldier shouted back to him. 'There are footprints and hoofprints all around this area, ones not belonging to a Trans.'

Segrinn rode along the edge of the plain until he reached the place where many footprints and a set of hoofprints led across the ground. He guided his horse along the tracks until they came to the place where Petia, Giles, and Keja had attempted to unlock the Gate of Paradise.

'There's nothing here, you idiots. She laid a false trail to confuse us. It won't work with me!' Segrinn shouted. 'Scout around the area, then report what you find.'

The evidence of three people camping and remnants of a recent fire did little to improve Segrinn's mood. They had let the Trans woman get away when he thought they were close on her trail. Now the lurchers seemed confused. Where he expected to find one person, three now left their tracks.

'Chain the dogs. We'll camp here for the night. We can't be far behind the Trans now, no thanks to following the wrong trail for so long. She'll be mine yet.' Segrinn slid from his horse and paced back and forth, rubbing his hands together. 'Get a fire built. Start a meal. Must I tell you every move to make? Damn!'

Is Petia Darya worth this effort? Segrinn wondered. Scores of women on the estate would be happy to oblige even his most outrageous whim. But Segrinn refused to quit. The damned cat Trans had become an obsession.

Eleven

'THIS IS what I was looking for.' Giles reined in and waited for the others. Keja's mule balked obstinately, forcing Petia to ride in the rear where she occasionally whacked the animal in the hind quarters with the end of her hackamore rope.

The trail crested and gave the three a view down onto a stream. A narrow, rickety wooden bridge crossed the ribbon of swiftly running water before the trail wound uphill again.

'Any sound of the lurchers?' Giles asked.

Petis shook her head. 'Nothing at all today. You don't suppose we've lost them?'

'No, not likely. Just because you can't hear them doesn't mean they aren't back there, sniffing our trail.'

'Hadn't we better keep moving?' Keja asked. 'This miserable animal is holding us back. Curse you, you long-eared whoreson!' Keja thumped the mule squarely on the top of its head. The mule turned an accusing brown eye on him and stubbornly planted its feet, daring Keja to continue the abuse.

'Don't worry,' Giles said. 'I think we can throw them off for a bit by taking to the stream. It seems shallow enough this year. The bridge tells me that in the spring the water must run high.'

'How are we going to get down to it?' Petia asked, staring at the steep incline.

'The dogs would pick up on our scent immediately if we entered straightaway. We ought to take a chance and back-track a bit.'

Keja shook his head. 'I don't like heading back towards our pursuers. That sounds suicidal.'

'Trust me.' Giles grinned when he saw the sour look on Keja's face. None trusted any of the others – too much. 'Petia will hear those lurchers if they get near enough to matter. Since she can't right now, I'm sure we can go back a short way before we leave the trail. When he sees the stream, Segrinn will know we took to the water to hide our tracks. Our best chance is to confuse him for as long as possible, perhaps even duping him into either splitting his force or going in the wrong direction.'

Keja and Petia nodded. It made sense.

'Are we agreed, then? If we lead the animals, it will help. The trail is dusty and our tracks won't show well. And we can always pray for wind to further confuse the spoor. The dogs track by smell and should get thoroughly confused right about here.'

It felt good to be on the ground again. They stretched their legs, then tugged the animals around. The mule cooperated for a change. For a quarter of an hour, they retraced their tracks. Finally, Giles halted them.

'This looks like a good place for what I have in mind. Find some rags to tie around the animals' feet.'

Keja shook his head in mock horror. '"Trust me", he says. Now he wants me to take off what few clothes I have.' He plucked at the rags he wore. Giles and Petia laughed.

'Poor, abused Keja,' Petia said insincerely.

In a few minutes, Giles had the hooves of the three animals wrapped. He threw the remaining scraps to the others. 'Now do up your own feet. We'll lose them yet. A trick I learned while scouting during the War.'

With their feet bundled as if they were heading for the snow regions, they left the trail. They reached the top of a hill and zigzagged down the other side, finding the rockiest areas. This presented problems for the horses, but Keja's mule sure-footedly walked. Giles even thought he detected an air of arrogance and superiority in the beast, as if it said, 'What's wrong with you clumsy oafs?'

Silently, Giles pointed towards the stream. He was pleased when they reached its edge, leaving little sign of their passage along the hillside. The hoof coverings prevented the shod animals from leaving revealing nicks and scratches on the rock, and in the few places where dirt graced the hill, only amorphous prints marked their passage. The shallow stream had a gravel bed. Seeing this made Giles actually hope they would elude Segrinn and his lurchers. Giles and his companions would leave no trace at all now.

'Get ready for a long ride,' he told the others. 'Once we start, we stop for nothing.' Giles filled his leather water bag with the fresh water, then led his horse into the stream. He headed upstream; the others followed.

For nearly an hour, the stream remained shallow. Giles' hope that they'd escape Segrinn rose to impossible heights, only to be dashed when they came to a waterfall.

'Out,' Giles said. He failed to hide from the others his disgust at this sorry turn of events.

'What do we do now?' Keja asked, looking at the golden hills surrounding them and the deep notch through which the stream tumbled hundreds of feet to a pond below.

'Unless you can turn horses into fish, we climb.' Giles pointed up a narrow draw leading into the hills. He didn't have to point out that this might prove to be a box canyon that could cost them precious hours.

'My swimming abilities are minimal,' Keja said, then launched off on a spicy, outrageously exaggerated version of his sea trip from Klepht.

Giles let the small thief ramble on until he'd had enough. He cut him off with an abrupt gesture. 'If we're going to go after the key Petia told us about, we've got to get to the coast and find a ship. Perhaps the one on which you found such fine company.'

Keja sputtered and fell silent about his sea-going exploits.

'But the coast is back there.' Petia gestured the way they had come. 'How are we going to reach it if we're heading north?'

'The shortest distance between two points is not always a straight line. When you are fleeing, that is.' Giles constructed a map by stacking pebbles from the stream. 'There's a major road north of these hills. We can travel west along it, cross through Margaret Pass, and make our way back to Druse Hook. We should be able to catch a ship from there. Anyone got a better idea?'

Petia sat cross-legged, staring at the ground.

'Petia, do you see any problem?' Giles asked.

'What? I'm sorry, Giles. I wasn't paying attention. I've been thinking. I was eager to get away from Segrinn and needed your help. I didn't exactly lie to you about that, but I don't really know where the key is. I mean, it's somewhere near Trois Havres, but I don't know *exactly* where.'

'Now you tell us!' Keja exploded. 'Here we are, on our way to take ship across an odious amount of water, and all you wanted was for us to rescue you.'

'You're on the run, too. So you're not losing anything.'

'Silence, you two,' Giles bellowed. 'We're not going to get anywhere if we start fighting among ourselves. I don't blame Petia. Segrinn is someone we'd all like to avoid.'

'True, but . . .' started Keja. Giles cut him off again.

'I didn't say I'd search for the keys, either, if you think back over our conversation.'

'Well, are you or aren't you?' Keja asked. 'If you're not, we might as well split up this instant.'

'I've thought it over. I will. And I don't think it makes any difference whether Petia knows where the key is or not. She knows the general area. We'll just have to keep our ears open and see what happens when we reach Trois Havres. Meanwhile, her arguments about someone tracking you still hold. The men of this merchant l'Karm are going to find you sooner or later unless you leave Bericlere.'

'I suppose you're right,' Keja said with ill grace. 'Are we ready to move?'

Giles knew that the argument was over – this time. The old sergeant detected the seeds of other disagreements blooming, but they would be dealt with when only they blossomed. Later. They headed up the draw and into the hills.

For over a week they rode, north to the Margaret Road, west over the pass. Occasionally, Giles would leave them camped in the forest, ride into a town and purchase supplies to keep them going. Shopkeepers sometimes raised their eyebrows at the quantities he asked for, but his money silenced questions. Giles never volunteered any information.

When they had crossed the mountains and come down into the grasslands, Giles said, 'We near Druse Hook. Before we enter the city, we must be in full agreement.'

'We go on,' said Keja. 'The more I think about the Gate, the more I want to see what lies behind it.'

'He talks in his sleep about it,' Petia chided. 'The moans, the cries of thwarted passion! He calls out for blondes and red-heads and brunettes, women of all shades, to do his bidding.'

'There might be more on the other side of the Gate,' Keja said. Then he brightened. 'But if there isn't, I shall be well enough pleased!'

Druse Hook was a small port with a harbour situated inside a sandy hook continually deposited by the fierce action of wind and restless currents. Giles chose an inexpensive backstreet inn, but not before the innkeeper assured him that tubs of hot water came with the price of the rooms. Finding a ship across the Evester might be their prime consideration, but having a hot bath first wouldn't hurt. As Giles said, 'Prime and first are not always the same.' And clean clothes followed.

Much refreshed, Giles told Petia and Keja, 'I'll go to the harbour to see about our passage. The best thing you two can do is stay in your rooms. You are both being sought. Your likenesses may have been circulated by l'Karm or Segrinn.'

'I have an odd feeling,' Petia said, 'that Segrinn has caught up with me. I'm going out to check.'

'That's not a good idea, Petia. If Segrinn has followed us here – or decided we would eventually come here – you might be seen. He'd have his men out asking questions. You could endanger both Keja and me.'

'They won't see me. They'll see only . . . this.'

Giles and Keja watched silently as Petia's body became leaner and took on the characteristics of a cat. Giles blinked and rubbed his eyes when he saw Petia drop to all fours and stalk across the floor. Her hands became paws, her eyes narrowed and the irises grew even more vertically elliptical.

As quickly as the change had come, Petia stood in front of them, normal again.

Giles had seen similar legerdemain during the War. A Trans in his company had been able to assume – or make others think he had assumed – the shape of a snake. Such obvious differ-ences between Trans and human still left Giles uneasy.

'Don't do that again,' Keja said uneasily. The small thief

rubbed a nervous hand across his lips, then tried to hide his feelings.

'It bothers you, this little secret that we Trans have?' Petia asked, taking an impish delight in her display. 'I do it using my empathic powers – it is an illusion, partly giving what you want to see and partly hypnotic.'

'But your body doesn't really change?' asked Keja.

'I do have some slight ability to alter my form, thanks to Cassia n'Kaan's long-ago curse. But mostly it's the reading of emotions and . . . it's hard to describe. *Meshing* with them.'

'You're sure you'll be all right?'

'Oh, yes. I've done this often.' Petia headed for the door.

Outside the inn door, Giles watched uneasily as Petia once more became catlike and melted away down the street. She was flaunting her talents too openly, he thought. Anything unusual would be commented on in the coastal city. While Trans visitors were common enough, especially in seaports, Giles still worried.

Petia roamed the darkened streets of Druse Hook, revelling in the freedom of being away from Keja and Giles. While she thought they both smelled nice, Petia rebelled against the enforced nearness. Her nature required a certain distance that had been denied her while they rode the trail.

Now she ran wild, occasionally meeting a real cat and snarling at it, just to keep in practice. She listened intently at every street corner for the barking of the lurchers, and for an hour Petia quartered the upper town, prowling with no success. Distressed at not finding Segrinn, Petia finally stopped prowling and started thinking.

'Segrinn wouldn't stay at a cheap inn,' she said to an alley cat perched on a tall fence. The battered animal stared at her, no kinship between them. Petia ignored the fact that she had invaded the alley cat's territory and continued talking aloud. 'With his wealth, and especially after being on the road, he would go to the best inn in town. And just perhaps my hunch is wrong. Perhaps he's not here at all.'

The alley cat yowled. Petia hissed back but didn't accept the challenge. She rose and followed a side street toward the harbour. Less than two turnings later she heard the barking and followed the sound. Petia felt adrenaline rushing through her body as she neared the inn's courtyard. She hesitated, fearful, listening carefully as the dogs gave voice to their frustrations.

'The lurchers,' she hissed. There could be no question.

She moved forward on light feet and sat quietly at the foot of the entrance archway. Segrinn and his men had just arrived and were stabling their horses for the night. The dogs, tied to a wooden hitching rack, snapped and bawled.

Petia crept into the courtyard, crossing near the lurchers, but just beyond the reach of their leashes. The dogs yelped at her approach and gave tongue.

'Cat bitch,' the leader snarled. 'Kill cat bitch!'

A window on the second floor opened and someone shouted, 'For the gods' sakes, shut them hounds up.'

Segrinn and one of his men dashed out of the stable area, brandishing whips. They laid into the dogs, screaming obscenities at them and cutting at their flanks and hindquarters with the leather. Petia went through instinctual motions of cleaning nonexistent whiskers. Her purring message struck through the sound of swearing and whistling whips.

'Master!' cried the lead dog. 'Cat bitch! Aieeee!'

Segrinn laid into the beast. Petia watched, taking intense pleasure in the animal's pain.

Another of Segrinn's men came out of the stable. He saw her crouched in the corner of the courtyard. Emotions flowed, but Petia failed to control the man's hatred. She confused his mind enough to make him believe she was nothing more than a cat, but he still picked up a stone from the ground and sidearmed it at Petia. The stone hit where she had been and skimmed into the side of a lurcher, setting off another round of frenzied barking and even more frenzied whipping.

'What are you doing, you oaf?' Segrinn shouted.

'The cat, the cat,' the man faltered. 'That's what upset the dogs.'

Segrinn stared around the courtyard. There was no cat in sight.

Petia heard him shouting as she went over the courtyard wall. 'Wretch, if you've finished with the horses, get over here and help us settle down these miserable beasts.'

Not a bad evening's work, she thought. With a spring in her step that hadn't been present for too long, Petia returned to the inn.

'The *Marilla Le Bow* departs on the morning tide,' Giles was telling Keja as Petia slipped into the room. 'I've booked passage for the three of us. Ah, you're back, Petia. What news?'

Petia warmed herself before the small fireplace in Giles' room. Giles saw right away that she was pleased with herself.

'You found them?' Keja asked.

'Certainly did. I got even with the lurchers, too. When I left they were being whipped to ribbons.'

Giles looked disappointed. 'They're just doing what their nature requires, trying to please a master that's none too kind, from what you tell us.'

'I expected something else from you, Giles.' Petia defiantly held her head high.

Giles sighed. 'And I expected common sense from you. No sleeping in soft beds tonight, then.'

'Why not?' Keja cried. 'The serving wench in the tavern next door eyed me and I thought . . .'

'You think with your gonads,' snapped Petia, venting her ire on him.

'We leave,' Giles said firmly. 'There's too much risk staying here now. The lurchers know Petia is near. They'll be restless all night, and eventually Segrinn will listen to them. The best thing we can do is to board the ship tonight before Segrinn posts his lookouts on the streets.

'Gather your belongings. I've already sold the animals. An ostler will collect them from here in the morning.'

'Marram,' Petia muttered.

'The pony will be all right,' Giles said gently. He just hoped they would be, also.

The harbourmaster's crew pulled at their oars, and slowly the ship began to move up the inside of the hook towards the entrance to the harbour.

Petia tensed, leaning over the rail. 'Listen,' she said.

The sound of barking cut through the inshore breeze. Giles motioned Petia to stay where she was. He walked across the ship to the other rail. A heavy-set man rode his horse onto the wharf. He was accompanied by several other men on horseback and a pack of slender hounds. Segrinn.

Giles lurched, then grabbed the rail as the ship caught the first of the incoming waves at the harbour mouth. He couldn't resist. He waved.

The porcine innkeeper's huge belly rubbed the desk, and his jowls wobbled as he greeted them. Generations of evolution had brought the Trans closer to humans, but this man worked at being a pig.

'Welcome to our fair city of Sanjuste. Will you be staying long?'

Keja tried not to stare at the hundreds of Trans they had seen along the streets leading from the harbour. He'd seen Trans before, but never in such numbers.

'Couldn't we find a better inn than this one?' he complained, once they were in their room.

Giles' stare was cold. 'You paying?'

'Ah, well, there is that little matter, isn't there?' Keja maintained his aloofness. 'I've been meaning to ask a favour of you, Giles. I am so tired of these rags. The ladies ignore me, and I thought that maybe you could advance me a couple of crowns. For a suitable collection of clothing, so I won't disgrace you when we are seen together on the streets, of course.'

'Keja, they just don't make many like you. Thank the stars! I'm not giving you a bent copper. If you're half as clever with those fingers as you boast, put them to work. If thievery is your trade, then so be it. Until then, I will lend you some of my clothes.'

Giles spilled the contents of his pack onto the bed. He threw a shirt and trousers to Keja.

'But they'll hang on me,' Keja complained. 'I will look like a fool!'

'All right, give them back.'

Chagrined, Keja stripped off his beggar's shirt. Giles' shirt

111

fell over his head and hung loose about him. He stepped behind a modesty screen and changed into the borrowed trousers. They would have fallen off him had he not cinched the belt tightly.

Petia stifled a laugh when Keja came out from behind the screen.

'I look like a scarecrow,' Keja said.

'Indeed,' Giles agreed, 'but a clean one.' He hesitated at the door. 'Try to stay out of trouble, Keja.'

Keja listened as Giles' footsteps faded away down the stairs. 'Damn him.' He threw his rags in anger at the corner of the room. 'Where's he off to?'

'Off to learn what he can, just as I am.'

Keja watched Petia leave. He heaved a deep sigh and told himself, 'Let's see if those fingers are as nimble as they were in Klepht.' He flexed them. The crowds in Sanjuste would go home this day lighter in the pouch, if Keja Tchurak had anything to do with it.

Petia felt more comfortable than she had for some time. She was home again. Seeing so many Trans on the streets made her remember better days. She wandered through the market-place, smelling the smells, delighting in the colours, the movement, the voices of the vendors haggling with their customers. She saw Keja slipping through the crowd, his light fingers restlessly moving from pouch to pouch, but Petia didn't want to share her company with him.

She wandered to the river and squatted along its bank, watching the women below washing clothes. Fragments of their conversation floated up to her.

'The Lady Sorceress says that she will keep us close to her.'

'But the Flame is the thing, the Flame burns forever in the temple. When the Lady Sorceress is not there, the Flame keeps her in our hearts. She will deliver us of all our woes, and the Flame will make us strong and purify us.'

Petia moved down the bank to the riverside. She removed her boots and dabbled cramped feet in the water. The brief conversation surprised her. A cult had sprung up around the very Flame Sorceress for whom they searched. A new religion, a new development to tell the others.

Petia listened to the women while they wrung out the clothes and packed them into reed baskets for the trip home. They were so serious, so involved, so totally immersed in the Flame and its Lady Sorceress. Power, power gathering. She felt it like the gathering tension before a thunderstorm.

Twelve

DIMLY NEW, the largest of the three coastal towns comprising Trois Havres, teemed with excitement. The three felt it when they rode into town on the mounts acquired in Sanjuste. Giles reined in to let a small parade of cloaked and hooded penitents cross in front. They walked with heads down and feet shuffling, as if the weight of the world rested on their shoulders. But in spite of their gravity, Giles felt the tension as if it were a thing alive, groping with tentacles to pull in all and wrap them with its vitality.

'A curious place, this one,' commented Keja. His expression told more than his words. He was disgusted at so many decked out in religious garb. Monks seldom carried money with them, choosing to beg. How could he rob a beggar, much less a begging holy man?

'The religious fervour carries over, even here,' said Petia. 'We might not have to seek out the Flame Sorceress. She may come to us, if we wait.'

'They have the appearance of waiting for divine presence,' Giles said, looking around. 'The rumours in Sanjuste that this was the place were correct, it seems.'

'I'm hungry,' grumbled Keja. 'The ride was long and . . .'

113

'And you're always famished or in search of a willing woman,' finished Giles. 'The ride amounted to little more than an hour, but there's a likely looking spot.'

'I agree, I agree,' Keja said. The woman lounging outside the tavern caught his eye. If Giles hadn't led him past, Keja would have forgotten his hunger to spend a few minutes flirting with her. She seemed only too inclined.

'She'd just take your money and leave you high,' said Petia.

'No, no, you're wrong,' said Keja. 'She had the look of a seeker of wisdom about her. An intellectual wanting company to compare theories.'

'A whore seeking a midday tumble,' said Giles.

'You might be right, but still . . .'

The landlord stopped by their table and interrupted Keja. 'Have you come to visit the temple?'

'That we have,' Petia said quickly, before Keja could deny it.

'The town swells with people who have come from far and near to learn about the Confraternity of the Flame.'

'Actually, we are here on a matter of commerce,' Giles answered. 'But we will listen to what is being said. The people at home will be asking us about the Confraternity. We must be able to portray an accurate picture for them.'

'Yes, of course. And where is home?' the landlord asked.

Giles saw hopes of money in the landlord's eyes, full rooms at the inn when they reported back to their associates. 'Bericlere. We come from the city of Neelarna.'

The landlord's enthusiasm changed to disappointment. 'So far away. I hope your business is well transacted,' he said curtly and moved on.

'So, this new cult goes by the name of the Confraternity of the Flame,' Giles said in low tones. 'It bears investigating. We must listen carefully to the street talk, listen to the preachings. The Lady Sorceress, as you heard her called back in Sanjuste, Petia, seems to be the same one you told us of.'

'We'll soon see,' Petia replied. They wolfed their meal, eager to be on their way.

They had only been on the street for a few minutes when they saw people greeting each other with a sign made by extending the hand, palm forward and fingers up.

Keja watched with amused superiority. 'They speak in

riddles. This Confraternity is no more than any other mumbo-jumbo religion.'

They heard a maddening array of ritualistic slogans and catch-phrases. 'Beauty is flame.' 'Flame will rule the world.' 'Flame will burn out the ills of the world.' 'Flame destroys evil.'

In a few minutes they had heard enough.

'I don't understand it,' Keja said. 'Why do they all greet each other with those phrases?'

'It sets them apart, makes them different, part of a community,' Giles said. 'It's like a secret password that makes them feel special.'

'Sounds crazy to me,' Keja muttered.

Further on, they came to a temple set up hastily in a small warehouse. A hand-lettered sign had been tacked above the door proclaiming: The Temple of the Confraternity of the Flame.

'Doesn't look like much to me,' Keja said as they walked past. 'Certainly not worth robbing.'

Giles said nothing. This crude temple didn't seem to match the numbers of converts in the street. By the time the trio reached the centre of the town, however, they had passed five more temporary temples, and near the town square they found a new temple. It was nearly finished, but scaffolding still surrounded the exterior where the final touches were being completed on the intricate – and expensive – carved stone facade.

'We've misjudged,' Petia said. 'Obviously the Flame Sorceress has acquired a great following – and greater wealth.'

'It might be time for us to become proselytes,' Giles said. 'We need to find out more about her, to see if she has the key we seek.'

A Trans woman stepped up to Petia, thrusting a broadsheet at her. Petia glanced down at it, a drawing of a flame adorning the top of the sheet.

'Come to our evening service,' the woman said. 'Hear the good news of our redemption. Learn how we can help you better your life. See how you can find immediate happiness.'

Petia studied the woman's rapt, bovine face. It was intense, believing, dedicated to bringing others to the temple and its faith. Petia had never seen such mindless intensity in another person. It frightened her.

'What time?' she asked.

'Just after sunset. It is said that the Lady of the Flame will be visiting the temple soon, perhaps this evening.'

'Thank you. I'll attend,' Petia said.

The woman held up her hand in the gesture the others had used. 'The Flame be with you. You won't regret it. It will change your life.'

'Not likely,' Petia said to Giles and Keja, after the woman hurried on and was out of earshot.

'Have faith,' said Keja. 'They obviously do. Too much of it, for my taste.'

Petia bristled, even though she agreed with him. Admitting that to Keja rankled. 'You are too quick to condemn. If this Flame gives comfort, what is wrong with that? You can't know the suffering we Trans have gone through.'

'Enough,' said Giles, breaking up the incipient argument. 'Keja may not know, but I do. And we are here for other reasons, ones not fought out during the War.'

'Petia, go to the services this evening. They seem geared towards Trans, and you'd attract less attention than either Keja or I.'

'What do we do till then?' she asked.

'Wander,' answered Giles. 'Listen. Try to learn what we can. The more we know, the easier it will be to get the key.'

'If this Flame Sorceress even has it,' grumbled Keja, more to annoy Petia than anything else. She snorted and went off to stroll around the marketplace alone, lost in the remembrance of her childhood here.

Petia watched outside the temple, wondering if she ought to enter or not. The coolness of the city after sundown appealed to her more than the stuffy interior of a church. Still, Giles had made a good point about her being less conspicuous than either of the two men. The throng around her was composed almost entirely of Trans of every persuasion: cat, dog, pig, a few avian, and even an oultands elk. Petia reluctantly joined the flow when the summons bell rang three times. She was

116

swept through tall wooden doors carved with the depiction of a brazier from which flames leaped upward to a brilliant light emanating from a gate.

Petia didn't have a chance to examine the gate carving more closely, but it looked a great deal like the Gate of Paradise. Her heart began beating faster at the idea of the Flame cult being based on the Gate.

The Flame Sorceress might actually have the key! Petia would show that Keja Tchurak she could deliver!

Inside, Petia chose a seat near the back, so that she might observe and not have to be a part of the service. The temple filled rapidly until people crowded shoulder to shoulder in the aisles along the side walls. A buzz of conversation rose as all the Trans waited for the service to begin.

Petia studied the sanctuary area. She had had little experience of such things, but it certainly was plain. In the centre of a common table – altar? – rested an immense brazier, in which a flame burned. On either side stood large bouquets of freshly cut linn flowers. To the right of the altar was a plain lectern.

She waited impatiently, watching those about her curiously as they greeted each other without any hint of enjoyment. Their faces were set, deadly serious. What sort of religion had such fervour and yet no joy?

A deep chime rang twice, and the people concluded their conversations immediately and settled into their seats, expectant looks on their mesmerised faces. Petia leaned forward to better see the altar. Everyone else sat back, heads bowed.

A dog Trans entered the sanctuary through a side door. He wore a long, flowing, orange robe and carried a censer billowing clouds of smoke. Petia's sensitive nose twitched from the pungent smell of the incense. The Trans went to the altar and bowed to the flame. He slowly turned to the congregation and, holding the censer high, blew clouds of smoke in all directions. The people sighed and raised their heads once again.

A robed human man and a bird Trans woman entered, carrying a slim book. They bowed to the flame and took their places before the lectern. Without preamble, they began reciting a litany, alternating between the phrases. After each

117

phrase, the people in the assembly chanted back, 'Blessed be the Flame.'

Many around Petia closed their eyes, and some had a look of ecstasy on their faces. Petia felt a rising contempt for them, her feelings matching Keja's. She did not understand this charade, and it struck her as pointless, even degrading.

She grew increasingly impatient as the litany droned on. Finally, it ended with a prayer to the Flame, almost screamed by the congregation. After the echoes from the prayer faded away, the people on the altar departed. The assembly broke into a babble of conversation and the temple began to clear. Petia could not get out quickly enough. She brushed by the woman who had handed her the broadsheet earlier. 'I'm late,' she said. 'I must meet someone.'

'Come again to our wonderful service,' the woman called after her.

'It was awful,' Petia explained later that evening. 'The chanting went on and on. The only thing that might be useful was one line of the chant, something like "O seat of wisdom at Belissiam." Belissiam is north and west of here, and that may be where the Flame Sorceress resides.'

'That makes sense,' Giles replied. He worked to get his pipe lit. Sucking in the soothing smoke, he went on. 'From what I could learn, the cult started here in Dimly New. There is a large forest west of here in the direction of Belissiam.'

'Lesser Green,' said Petia.

'That's the name,' Giles went on. 'I watched scores of people leaving town in that direction. Some of the people seemed to have business that way, wagoners, woodcutters and the like. But there were others who walked with nothing but a sack over their backs.'

'Good, we'll go to Lesser Green and see what we can find,' Keja said. 'Never have I encountered a more boring city.'

'None of the women will have anything to do with you?'

'Saw none I'd have on a bet,' Keja said testily.

'They think you're a clown in a carnival, wearing those silly garments.' Keja reddened at the Trans' insult.

'These are the finest to be had. Can I help it if neither

118

Sanjuste nor Dimly New is at the forefront of fashion like Neelarna?' Keja calmed down, knowing Petia could needle him and he would still respond. 'I will be once more in the wilderness, happily, not that Dimly New is far removed.'

'I think it would be best if I went by myself,' Giles said. 'Disguised.'

'But I don't want to hang around in this town,' Keja pleaded. 'I don't have anything to do now that I have decent clothes again.'

'There's one thing you do pretty well, Keja. Visit the taverns and keep your ears open.' At this, the wiry thief smiled broadly. 'You'll likely hear talk about the cult, but it won't be the same talk that you would hear from members of the temple. I might also advise you to spend a little time at weapon practice. We don't know when we are likely to need skills that are probably a bit stale.'

The grin on Keja's face left as if a cloud had blotted out the sun. 'The right hand gives and the left hand takes away,' he said.

Giles rented horses and a wagon and left Dimly New disguised as a woodcutter. The wagon was empty and the horses handled well. He took the road west and soon came to a fork leading to Lesser Green. Here, he paused simply to enjoy the countryside. Giles had too seldom taken time to reflect on the beauty of the woods, the singing of birds, the gentle wafting scent of multicoloured flowers. They took away the blanket of weariness that had again descended upon the man.

'You're too old for this,' he told himself. 'But the reward!' The idea of entering the Gate of Paradise held him captive. 'Only One May Enter,' he said softly, 'and I will be that one.' Heartened by this thought and the fine day, he clucked his tongue and got the horses moving once more.

A mile further on, he pulled over to the side of the road to let an oncoming woodcutter's wagon pass.

'A good load you've got there,' Giles hailed him.

'Aye. I don't know how much longer we'll be able to cut in this forest, though.' The old gaffer seemed willing to sit and talk, giving his animals a rest.

'Why's that?' Giles asked. The old man had taken him at face value – a fellow woodcutter.

'Haven't ye noticed the strange goin's-on up in High Forest? Down here it's all right. But there's not much we can cut here worth the mention. Plenty of wood still up in the high forest, but there's people there keepin' me out. Don't know who they are, but they're armed – nasty whoresons they are, too. Best get careful-like when you go up there.'

'Can they do that?' Giles asked. 'It's open forest.'

'Don't know as they should, but they are. I'm not about to argue with a sword. They act like they's got the right, and I don't know no better. Turned me right around, they did, and chased me off. I got my load lower down. But if they keep us out, we'll have to go over to Nether Forest. I don't like that. It's a longer haul.'

'Who'd they say they were? Who owns that land?' Giles' curiosity was aroused.

'Didn't say. Just ran me off. Wouldn't take no argument. Like I say, you best be careful.'

'Thank you for the warning,' Giles said. He reached behind the wagonseat and handed two apples to the old wood-cutter. 'These will help your journey. Juicy and sweet, they are.'

The man accepted them with a nod, and clucked up his horses. Giles moved back onto the track and continued his journey.

Three more times he met people coming down through Lesser Green. The information he received from them matched that from the old man. By afternoon, Giles left the lower forest and entered High Forest. Mentally, he prepared himself to meet these sentries. He didn't have long to wait.

'No further, woodcutter.'

Giles pulled the horses to a stop. He put his finger to his forehead in a sloppy salute. 'Afternoon, yer honours,' he said.

Three men blocked the road. Two were middle-aged, but one was only a shiny-faced youngster. 'You can't go any further. This is now a private estate.'

'But I've always cut my wood here.' Giles pointed up into the forest. 'Up there, you see where that rock sticks out? Just below that.'

'Well, no more cuttin' allowed,' an older man said. 'Yer goin' to have to find another place.'

Giles shook his head in disbelief. He looked behind him, as if asking for help in setting these men straight. There was no help behind, and he began again. 'I don't understand. I cut wood here since I was a child, used to come with my da. Right up there.' He pointed again. 'I'll walk up and show you.' He began to climb down from his wagon.

One man lifted a staff. 'No, you don't. Just stay up there on your seat. There'll be no getting down. And no showin' us where you used to cut. No more cutting beyond this point. Do you understand?'

Giles stood on the floorboards in front of his seat. 'No, I don't understand. My da and me . . .'

'You told us. Now we're telling you. This is private land now. You can't come on it anymore. Now go back.'

Giles looked up at the men. 'But we can't cut down below. The trees need more growth.' Mentally, he thanked the man he had first met for that information. 'We'll have to go clear over to the Nether Forest.'

'That's your problem, 'init? Turn your wagon around and go on back down.'

'I'll get my fellows and we'll be back. Can't keep us out,' Giles threatened. 'What lord owns this land now?'

'Ain't no lord, mister,' the youngest spoke up.

'Hold your tongue, boy.'

Giles hid his grin by turning to adjust the sacking on the wooden wagon seat. He began to his team and wagon around for the trip back. 'You ain't heard the end of this,' he said.

Behind him he heard the young voice. 'May you keep the Flame.'

Certainly these were devotees of the Flame, so the headquarters of the Flame Sorceress were somewhere in the vicinity. He'd found out more than enough to justify fetching Keja and Petia from Dimly New.

The Flame Sorceress entered Dimly New as if she were a queen and the town part of her holdings. Two acolytes went before her, shouting, 'Make way for the Flame Sorceress. Make a path to the temple.' She bowed right and left as people parted for her, and others came running for a glimpse of the important personage.

Petia nudged Keja in the ribs and said, 'She is going to the temple. I'll follow.'

Keja said, 'What you want to do that for?'

'We need to learn everything we can about her, dolt. She has the key. Remember? And it might make the difference between living and dying. Or doesn't that interest you?'

'I suppose you're right. Indeed, I am interested in living. Go ahead, then. I'll visit another tavern, just as Giles ordered.'

'Lucky you,' Petia snapped.

The beginning of the service was similar to that of the previous evening; the long litany followed by the congregation's interminable responses. Just as Petia wondered if her legs would continue to hold her up, an orange-robed priest strode out, ringing a small bell. A hush fell.

'All worship the Flame Sorceress!' he called in a clear, resonant voice.

The woman swept into the sanctuary, made a perfunctory bow to the flame, and, ignoring the lectern, came to stand at the centre in front of the altar. She wore a carmine robe that fell to the floor. Around the hem, stitched golden flames licked upward. On the back was embroidered the symbol of the gate from which light emanated, the same as that carved on the temple doors. Hanging from a chain around her neck was a golden pendant shaped like a heart from which flames leaped.

The Flame Sorceress stood in splendour, arms held high, palms in, welcoming the glow of warmth and love from the assembly. When she began to speak, it seemed to Petia that she did not raise her voice, but it reached into the furthest corners of the temple with clarity and power and urgency.

'People of the Flame,' she addressed them. 'Are you people of the Flame?'

'Yes.' A mighty roar attested that they were.

A smile of inordinate beauty crossed the woman's face. Petia shivered a bit; the sorceress knew she held her worshippers in thrall.

'You are humble people, good people,' the sorceress said in a soft, beguiling voice. 'Your ills are not caused by bad crops or

122

poor trading or fish refusing to jump into your nets. No.' The hum passing through the crowd told Petia that each of the congregation listened and believed. '*They* are responsible for your woes, the starvation, the taxes. *They* rob you of your pitiful gains, then say it is for your own good. Are you better off paying the lords, when your babies whimper and starve?'

Petia forgot about her tired legs and sore feet as she listened to the sorceress exhort her followers to what Petia could only call treason. Couched so beautifully in phrases that only one versed in the law might see behind, the sorceress skilfully suggested that the ills of these common folk could be laid at the feet of the powerful, of the lords, of the wealthy merchants. Given the charisma the Flame Sorceress was showing tonight, it would not be long before she revealed to them the holy way of violence and called for open rebellion.

At last, the diatribe masquerading as a sermon ended. Another brief prayer finished the service. Petia gratefully joined the flow leaving.

'Wasn't that a wonderful sermon, so beautiful, so honest?' a sheep Trans walking beside her asked.

'Indeed,' Petia answered, hiding the sarcasm she felt.

The man was garbed entirely in black and appeared to have had too much to drink. He staggered to the bar, waving a goblet from which wine splashed. 'Landlord, his name's Grimsmate. You're sure you don't know him? Fought with him in the War, the bastard. Gonna get even with him.'

Keja sat in the corner of the Maltster's Arms. He had avoided the weaving drunk when he entered. A flagon was a joy to be savoured. Falling down drunk was something Keja thought disgusting. It was only on hearing Giles' name that Keja became alert.

The man continued to wave his goblet and defile Giles' name. Keja watched the man closely; it became clear that the man wasn't as drunk as he pretended to be. He did not have a drunk's glazed eyes. This man's eyes blazed clear and shining, with cunning and intelligence in them, not stupor.

Keja got up to talk with the man in black, only to find him

gone. Keja frowned, finished his ale and left. He would be at the inn when Giles returned and warn him of an enemy.

Giles returned the horses and wagon to the ostler, happy to get away from the hard seat. He started back to the inn when a voice called out, 'Pardon, good sir. Could I trouble you for directions to the Kardavi Theatre?'

Giles turned and stared at the man, then shook his head. 'Sorry. I only recently arrived in Dimly New. You might enquire of the ostler.' He pointed out the man inside the stable.

'Thank you, good sir.' The black-clad man smiled at Giles, turned and walked off, ignoring the ostler. Giles thought that strange, but then the entire city seemed filled with strangeness.

Giles never heard the mocking laughter. He was too intent on returning to the inn with his information.

Thirteen

'I'M CERTAIN that the headquarters for your Flame Sorceress are in the High Forest. When they turned me back, I got the impression there were many guards. I suspect that the entire perimeter is patrolled. We'll have to be careful.'

Giles had recounted his day to Petia and Keja. It was an unsuccessful day for a woodcutter, but successful for their search.

'What do you suppose lies behind the sentries?' Keja asked.

Giles packed his pipe and got it going. 'I have no idea. It could be a castle, a cabin, a mansion, a fort. We'll have to go easy and keep our eyes open.' Giles puffed until his head vanished behind a cloud of blue smoke. 'I doubt those men on the forest road are the only obstacle to finding out. It's going to require all three of us.'

Keja spoke up. 'Giles, you ought to know that a man was asking after you in a tavern this evening. He bore some grudge against you. He pretended to be drunk, but I don't think he was.'

'What man?' Giles asked.

Keja described him as best he could.

Giles frowned. 'I may have seen him outside the stables, though I have no idea who he might be.' He sighed, then pushed it from his mind. They had other things to worry about. 'It might be wise to leave town quickly and quietly. From what Petia says, the sorceress and her temples are likely to stir up trouble soon. Before a civil war breaks out, we want her key.'

'If it even exists,' said Keja.

'It must,' Petia said vehemently. 'That symbol – the Gate! It must be the Gate!'

'I suppose I can accept that, as a place to start,' Keja said, his superior air making Petia want to rip out his throat. Keja smiled and infuriated her further.

By afternoon, they entered the High Forest. Stormclouds had passed during the night and the sun shone down brightly, dappling the mossy undergrowth with the shadows of leaves. The trio moved quietly through the sylvan beauty while keeping a sharp lookout for anyone patrolling.

'How much further were you able to go on the track?' Petia asked.

Giles squinted up at the sun. 'Hard to say. I'd guess another half hour's walk. We should go more slowly from this point on.'

Petia spotted the first sentries where Giles predicted. The trio stopped immediately and crouched. For a quarter of an hour, they watched. The guards were the same as the day before, two men and a young lad. Boredom had worked its stultifying way into their minds, causing them to stretch and yawn loudly from time to time, but never did they move beyond the open forest glade.

Giles pointed back the way they had come. With Keja

leading, they retraced their path through the High Forest until they could talk in guarded tones without being overheard.

When Giles finally halted them, Keja asked, 'What now?'

'We set up a minimal camp. We may have to scout for a couple of days. We need a place to sleep that's dry, build a fire, maybe a source of water.'

They found a perfect spot on the interstice between High Forest and Lesser Green. An old fault line with fallen boulders created a windbreak. Pure, icy cold water bubbled up from a spring nearby.

'Get a fire going, Petia. Keja and I will scout the perimeter to determine what fortifications our flame lady has built. We may be gone for a time.'

'Wait! I'm going, too,' Petia said.

'No, you're not,' said Giles. 'Too dangerous.'

'I'm no Gentian Coast beauty who must be protected. Who went slinking into the inn courtyard to tease those lurchers?'

'That was stupid,' Giles said coldly. 'We have no room for stupidity now. You're not coming with us. No arguments.'

Petia smouldered. 'Damned humans. Don't you think a Trans is good enough to go with you? I've done everything you've done this far.'

'I want to find you here when we return. No matter how long that takes. Do you understand?'

Petia pursed her lips. 'Yes, I understand.' She turned away and stomped off toward the spring.

When she returned, the men had slung their bedrolls, packs and swords against a large boulder. They had left with only their daggers.

Still angry, Petia dug into her pack and brought out a small pot and her mug. Soon, she had a small fire going and boiled water for tea.

Petia slouched against a boulder and sipped the steaming brew. Gradually a calmness settled over her. She would defy Giles' instructions – but unemotionally, utilising those skills that Giles did not seem to want to recognise.

Petia, too, left her sword behind. Quietly, she rinsed her mug in the spring, dried it and put it away. She covered the small fire, letting the simple chores drain away her anger. Petia took one last look at the camp, making certain that all was in

126

order. She fingered her dagger hilt, examined the sky for signs of rain, then melted into the forest.

The men they had first seen in the glade had been replaced by a nearly identical team, no more charmed with their task than the others. Petia spied on them for a short time until she became almost as bored as they were.

A flute sounded its musical note – a signal? Petia slipped away, moving quietly along the forest door, intent on investigating.

Five minutes of careful movement brought her to a different patrol of guards, seated on a log, playing a game with stones on a board drawn in the dirt. Petia wanted to tell the curly-haired one that he had just made a losing move – but he would discover that soon enough.

Petia backtracked cat-soft until she was halfway between the guard stations. She crouched, listening. Not a sound. She moved forward, watching intently. For long minutes she walked, alert for any sound. Although Petia had spent a fair amount of time on the road in the past two years, she still thought of herself as a town dweller. The forest was silent except for an occasional breeze soughing through the tops of the trees, rustling the leaves and sending an occasional one tumbling gently to the ground. The eerie silence made Petia nervous.

She hoped more sentries would appear soon. She knew how to deal with that problem better than with the ominous feeling of the forest giants surrounding her, of unseen and slightly heard beasts stalking about, of things rooting in the soil beneath her feet.

Finally, she saw a clearing ahead. Low to the ground, she crept forward, using the tree trunks to shield her from spying eyes.

A huge ironbeam tree dominated the edge of the clearing, one limb, thick enough to hold her, branching out from the trunk. Its thick, steel-grey foliage would hide her – if she climbed up unseen.

Petia scrambled up the trunk, grasped the branch, and with feline balance, ran along it. She was careful to stop before her weight made the limb bounce and betray her. Cautiously, she parted the leaves and looked down on the clearing.

Beneath her were paths trodden in the grass. They ran through the clearing into the forest. Petia guessed that these were the routes used by the guards to go to their stations.

The paths converged in front of an opening in the side of a forested hill. It was obviously a natural cave, but from her perch there was no way for Petia to tell its extent. She estimated that the entrance was fifteen feet across and nearly ten feet high. Sniffing, Petia detected smoke. Tiny vents lower down the hill, in a deep depression, streamed the fumes from fires hidden in the mountainside. She saw no human activity.

Petia settled down to wait. She concentrated on the cave's mouth. Before long, she saw two men come out of the forest and head straight for the cave. Was there to be no challenge at all?

Petia saw a flickering just inside the entrance. The two guards walked to the cave opening and stopped. Petia's eyes widened as she watched two *things* emerge from the cave. Human in form, they appeared to be made completely of flame. The men backed away as the flame creatures came out into the sunshine. As they walked, dancing fires shimmered about their bodies, masking all but their general shape and making them even more deadly in appearance.

The Flame Sorceress surrounded herself with magical beasts, flame beings. The two creatures carried spears of fire which they crossed in front of the human guards, blocking their way. One guard approached, obviously unwilling. Petia strained to overhear and failed, but a sign or password must have been given. The fiery spears lowered. The men passed between the flame beings, who twisted about searching the clearing, although Petia could not see any eyes. Satisfied, they, too, turned and entered the cave.

Petia studied the paths in relation to the cave mouth, considering how to gain entry. The cave was under a solitary hill, a half mile in circumference and nearly seven hundred feet high. From her vantage, it appeared that the clearing completely surrounded the hill.

How to cross that clearing with nothing to hide her? Other groups of men arrived. Was the guard changing or was this the result of other activities? Had they found Giles and Keja?

When the flurry had passed, Petia took her chance. She left

the security of the ironbeam tree and, staying inside the verge of the wood, crept to a position near a path. She studied the distance and realised that the hill itself was covered in some foliage. Minimal, to be sure, but it would afford some protection for her approach.

Patting her dagger to see that it was secure, she zigzagged across the clearing, keeping low. She continued on for several yards up the hill to a bush ox parsley. Petia paused to catch her breath. Looking up the slope, she was alarmed to see a guard standing several hundred feet above her.

Why had she not seen him from across the way? Too late for self-recrimination. Petia had to be careful to avoid being seen from above or below. She crept along the hillside, and within a few minutes realised that the plumes of smoke rising from the vents had hidden her from the guard above.

Above the cavern entrance, she closed her eyes and concentrated on her cat form, seeking to bring about the most catlike traits possible. Holding her breath, she waited for her eyes to adjust to the darkness. The contrast between the bright sunshine and the interior of the cave made her uneasy.

Flickering light came past a large rock protruding in front of her, and a narrow trail wound to her left around the rock. The guards must still be ahead.

Her breathing normal again, Petia moved forward, staying low to the ground and hugging the stony wall. The path moved forward only a few feet before rounding the rock and doubling back in the opposite direction. For the first time, real fear seized Petia.

'Oh, Giles, Keja, what have I done?' Petia realised they didn't know she was here, that she was truly on her own.

The light became brighter. Petia hesitated, looked behind her, then decided. Curiosity overcame any fear. She crept forward and peered into a small cavern. Several flame beings stood at ease with their backs to her. Bizarre little tongues of flame flickered incessantly along their bodies. Even though they had human shapes, the flames licking their arms and legs, the back of their heads, the brilliance at their crotches, they looked decidedly unhuman – and not in the way the Trans were unhuman.

In the cavern, a dozen Trans worked on making weapons.

They were sharpening swords, spear heads, dagger blades. If the Flame Sorceress brought religion to the cities of Trois Havres, she also brought violence. The cities would have to deal with that. For Petia, the problem was finding the third key to the Gate of Paradise.

She had seen enough; she had news for Giles and Keja.

Silently, Petia turned to head back into the daylight. A shadow fell across the cave entrance. Someone returned from duty outside. Petia sucked in her breath and held it. The shadow remained motionless, the guard waiting to be challenged by the flame beings. Petia was caught between the two.

She desperately hunted for a hiding place in the narrow passageway. None on the ground level. She heard the approaching flame beings. The light grew stronger. The flame creatures came from the depths of the cave.

Above her, Petia spotted a ledge well above the level of a man's head. She leaped for it, scrambling up the slippery stone wall. Tiny bits of displaced rock rattled down. The flame beings turned the corner. Petia crouched, wishing that she could will herself to the size of a kitten.

'What was that?' The voice of the lead flame being was dry and crackled like the kindling of a new fire.

'Bits of rock always falling from above. Pay no attention. Guard waits at entrance,' answered the second. They moved on.

Petia cowered back, petrified. She tried to imagine becoming a piece of rock, of vanishing into the wall. In a few moments, a man passed beneath her, sighing with tiredness. The flame beings trailed behind him and rounded the corner.

Petia let out her pent-up breath and leaped down from her rocky hiding place. The cat Trans breathed silently, holding the image of the flame beings and the guards in her mind, clouding their perceptions, toying with their emotions, so that they would ignore her. Feeling their mental confusion, Petia took a chance and left the cave, then dashed across the clearing and into the relative safety of the forest.

Pausing to catch her breath, she fought to keep from trembling. The emotion-tapping took so much out of her. Petia had bragged about it to Keja and Giles, but there had been little opportunity to practise it. It was definitely not something she did while plying her trade as a thief – she shook too much to rob effectively while altering emotional states.

But she had found the Flame Sorceress' underground head-quarters. And Giles and Keja hadn't! Happily, Petia flitted back into the forest, merging with the shadows and travelling on feet softer than leaves falling on moss.

The expedition went well for Giles and Keja. They stayed outside the perimeter of the sorceress' stronghold, fearing magical wards. From time to time, they saw the usual team of sentries. Giles watched the sun and judged directions from it. The stronghold was guarded by twenty-five teams, if Giles had counted correctly, stationed about five minutes' walk apart. Figuring the distance the sentries covered in the forest growth, the old soldier estimated that the perimeter might be five or six miles in circumference. Seventy-five men on guard at any one time. This gave Giles considerable pause. How many in the stronghold, wherever it might be?

The two men made no attempt to breach the perimeter. It would be enough this afternoon to determine the size of the opposition. As the afternoon wore on, Giles was pleased with their findings.

By late afternoon, they came across a broad, cold, clear stream running south east through the forest. Giles motioned Keja to rest, and pulled a package of dried meat from his pouch, sharing it with him in silence.

The sun slanted down warmly through the trees; the stream burbled merrily; an incautious squirrel sat nearby, openly begging. Giles sat with this back to a log and enjoyed the scene before him. Were it not for their quest for the key, he would be content to homestead in this forest. Not a worry in the world. A nearly perfect life.

Why had he allowed himself to be talked into coming across the Evester to find yet another key? Something to do, an adventure? The War had provided more than enough of that. Adventure had burned out so much inside him – and now he had come along willingly on a new quest. A quest for some-thing that wasn't even real, Giles decided.

He motioned to Keja to follow the stream a way, then doubled around and headed back for camp.

The squirrel chittered angrily at being ignored, puffed out his jowls, then disappeared into the forest.

'You little fool!' Giles raged. 'I *told* you to stay in camp.'

'You're just angry because I found more than you did!' she shot back. Her feline traits were boiling out, both from being practised all afternoon, and due to Giles' response to her scouting the cave and the flame beings within.

Giles simmered.

'Her time does seem to have been better spent than ours,' commented Keja. He winked in Petia's direction. She wasn't sure if she appreciated him being on her side in this or not. She wanted to savour her triumph – alone.

'It leads into the hill?' Giles finally asked.

'Easy to enter, if you're careful. Their security is lax,' Petia said smugly.

'You were just lucky.'

'You're becoming too cautious for your own good – or ours,' she said angrily. 'If we are to steal the key from the Flame Sorceress, we must be bold.'

'We're not even sure she has the key,' said Giles.

'And now you steal arguments from Keja. We *have* to believe the key exists. Otherwise all our efforts are for naught.'

'The cat lady has a point, Giles,' said Keja. All the thief got by way of response from Giles was a sour expression.

The middle of the night seemed the obvious time to make their way into the cave. Petia led two chagrined men between trees that they could hardly see. Her night sight sharpened with every step she took. Petia could hardly contain her excitement. For the first time she had shown her true worth to their venture. Petia nearly purred as she remembered the looks on their faces when she described the cave.

Unerringly, she led them to the ironbeam tree overlooking the clearing. For once, Petia was in command. Silently she motioned Giles and Keja to stay put while she investigated. In the dark, she crossed the clearing and entered the cave. No guards, human, Trans, or flame.

She signalled to Giles and Keja and led them to the cave. It was nearly pitch black in the initial passage, but torches illuminated the walls of the cavern ahead.

'The rock's dirtying my tunic,' complained Keja. 'Should we continue?' He nervously licked dried lips. Petia took special glee at his uneasiness.

'I came this way earlier,' she said with great satisfaction.

'Perhaps one of us should stand as rear guard,' Keja said. 'I will volunteer.'

Across the empty cavern, they saw other passages leading further under the hill. Petia raised her brows. Which one? Keja wanted none of them. Giles shrugged. One was as good as another.

Petia led them across the small cave. Giles stopped and rummaged through the crates he found, surprised at the number of weapons stacked along the walls.

'She is preparing for a war,' he said. 'Our Flame Sorceress grows bolder.'

'Quiet,' Petia said, not wanting to give up her leadership yet. They entered a passage and crept forward, Petia, then Giles, and Keja in the rear.

A jumble of rock filled the next cavern. While the roof arched high, the floor some distance below was small in proportion and was occupied by scores of working humans. Stalagmites had grown from water dripping down across lime-stone spears. Boulders littered the entire area and a narrow rock balcony circled the floor. This small ledge saved them. Sounds of marching men echoed down the corridor behind. Petia gestured for the other two to join her on the balcony. They got there just in time to avoid being seen.

'Give more warning,' said Keja in a choked voice. 'Fear and sweat are going to leave a permanent stain on my fine clothes, if you don't.' He edged away from them and sank down to his hands and knees, looking pale.

They peered down on the working men and women. The women were involved in mixing ingredients with mortar and pestle. Flame beings brought supplies from another part of the cave system and carried away what the women had finished.

The men were burnishing shields, using a paste that made sparks fly from the shining bronze.

Dust from the powders being ground drifted through the air. A draft from a side passage wafted some towards the trio. Try as she might, Petia could not contain the sneeze. The sound blasted like an explosion. All movement within the cavern ceased.

Six flame beings, all carrying burning swords, trotted to the centre of the chamber. Without a glance at the humans working on the cavern floor, they flowed directly to the spot under the ledge where the intruders pressed hard into the wall, trying not to be seen. Giles pushed Keja flat, motioning him to hide.

Keja stayed on his belly, unseen. Flame spears poked up at both Giles and Petia.

With a loud shout, Giles pulled his dagger and jumped. Petia cast a sidelong glance at Keja, then followed Giles, hissing and spitting as she went.

It was over quickly. Giles shouted, 'It's no use! We can't get close enough to do them any damage.'

Petia had already discovered this. She cringed as a flame being's arm came close to her face.

'Steady,' Giles murmured to Petia. To the flame beings, he said, 'We surrender!'

The spears thrust forward and herded the captives into a side corridor before either could speak again.

Hiding on the rock ledge, Keja held his breath. The human workers began to chatter, and he knew that Giles and Petia had been taken away.

His friends' lives depended on him. He had to rescue them. But how? Keja Tchurak had no idea.

Fourteen

HEMMED IN by the fiery guards, Giles and Petia were herded through one passageway after another. At the end of each succeeding passage, they entered a cavern larger than the one before. Finally, they found themselves in a long stone hall. Flame beings stood along either side, casting an eerie, dancing light across the flagstone floor.

At the far end, steps led to a dais. A woman sat on the throne: the Flame Sorceress. The arms and back of the solid black onyx throne were carved into interlocking flames leaping up toward the ceiling.

To the left of the throne burned a fire trapped in a magnificent brass brazier. The bowl sat on a tripod of carved nepler wood legs. Flames of crimson and green and azure leaped several feet above the hammered rim of the bowl.

The prisoners, still surrounded by the flame guards, were prodded down the middle of the hall toward the dais.

'Keep your head,' Giles warned. 'We don't want to arouse her anger needlessly. There may be a way out of this if we stay calm.' Giles wished that following his glib advice were as easy as giving it. Inside, his belly knotted tightly, and his throat constricted to choke him. Of all the dangers he had faced, few had seemed to hold death so imminently.

'But she's trying to subvert the people of Trois Havres, to start a rebellion!' Petia protested. Clearly indignant at the Flame Sorceress' goals, the Trans had chosen a poor time to make known her objections.

'That's not our problem.'

'It may not be yours, but those are my people, both humans and Trans.'

135

A guard gestured at them to be quiet. Petia flinched away from the fiery arm. She stared with unconcealed hatred at the sorceress upon her fine throne.

'I'll be damned if I grovel before her,' Petia muttered.

'We've no choice,' Giles whispered as he bent to kneel. 'Better to live and fight than to die for nothing.'

Petia resisted only until the flame being by her side reached his burning hand toward her back to push her down. She ducked out of the way and crouched on the floor. The flame being reached again and Petia knelt, seething.

'You cannot resist my flambeaux.' The voice rang out, calm and silky and beguiling.

Petia and Giles looked up at the throne. The Flame Sorceress lounged indolently, one slender, well-turned leg crossed over the other. Her flame-coloured silk gown set off auburn hair that cascaded down her back and framed her white oval face in soft waves. Giles had to admit she was an overpoweringly beautiful woman. Her splendid proportions held only one flaw – her lips pulled into a thin and cruel smile.

'None sneaks into my stronghold,' the sorceress scolded. 'People wishing to join the ranks of my beloved followers do so at one of my many temples. They do not come under cover of darkness, creeping like thieves. Nor do they disguise themselves as woodcutters.' She looked at Giles. 'That surprises you, does it not?'

Giles hid his inner turmoil well. The men who had challenged him had not seemed bright enough to report back so accurately. What else did this lovely, dangerous woman know?

'And our angry young Trans here, part cat, from the eyes. Useful blood, is it not, my dear thief? What did you think to find here? Wealth?'

Petia glared up at her. 'We wondered about this new cult. You've gathered quite a number about you, haven't you? Followers mean power. Power corrupts so easily, doesn't it?' The softness of Petia's voice nearly matched that of the sorceress. Giles tried to silence her but the Trans rushed on. 'Temples where the people nearly swoon with the faith that you've preached to them. You would pervert that faith to lead them in rebellion against their lords. Who would wield the power after a civil war? Why, a natural leader, such as yourself. Is it not so?'

'You do not believe in my teachings? I offer these people a better life than any they will ever have on this world. A life with a glorious hereafter.'

'Oh, yes,' Petia said bitterly. 'A life which can neither be proved nor disproved. In the meanwhile, it is a fertile field that you plough. Hundreds – thousands – of people manipulated, made to spread dissent, sapped of their coin so that you may finance your rebellion. People that can be moulded into an army when the time is ripe.'

The sorceress uncrossed her legs and sat forward, no longer the image of calm. 'I do not need those people. I have unlimited power of my own.

'Enough.' She took a deep breath and composed herself. The sorceress rose from her throne. 'You doubt my powers. You lie to me. You care not a whit for the people of this country. I do.

'What you really came for is a key – supposed to open a gate to Paradise, like the one gracing my temple doors. You'll never find that key, and you'll never get to Paradise. My followers will find Paradise here in my teachings, in their own land, before you find yours.'

Sparks showered from the end of her fingertips, then burst into lambent flame. The fire grew. The sorceress flexed her fingers and drew the image of a human in silvery, shimmering air. Another eye-searing flame materialised before her, still amorphous but rapidly taking form. She gestured grandly, and he flowed away with sinuous grace to stand beside her throne.

'You think me a fool. I see it in your eyes!' She held her hands together, as if moulding clay. With the suddenness of lightning in the twilight, she flung a fire ball over their heads. Giles and Petia turned in time to see it hit the floor, scattering flame in all directions. Gradually, as if it held a life of its own, the flame flowed into a pool.

From the pool arose a monstrous form, towering nine feet tall, with a torso as massive as a tree trunk. Long arms hung from broad shoulders, arms so powerful that they could easily crush a human.

'None stands against the life I create.'

The creature stood, swaying from side to side, not knowing

137

what it was supposed to do. The Flame Sorceress gestured, and the monster melted back into the pool of flame and slowly died away. She flung another ball that turned into a six-foot long lizardlike beast with a flickering tongue of flame. A third blossomed into a small tree with branches that waved, seeking for prey to burn. A fourth became a snorting, pawing beast with horns blazing so brightly that Giles averted his eyes. It bleated plaintively at the sorceress, waiting for her command to charge, to bring the destruction for which it had been created.

'You seek a paltry key while I offer salvation!' A flick of her hand dismissed the fire monsters. She stretched out both hands, and from her fingertips flew lances of lightning that struck the wall near the entrance to the hall. Spears of searing brilliance followed. Next came balls of fire that stuck to whatever they hit, as if they were burning pitch.

The awesome power truly frightened Giles. Neither Giles nor Petia could deny that the sorceress commanded vast magicks. What scared Giles was the way she became more intense with each demonstration. She was caught up in her own power and the pleasure of flaunting it. Her ambition – and viciousness – knew no bounds.

'There, unbelievers! You came seeking a key. Don't deny it. I know. You will never find the key to Paradise. You do not need that key. All you need is to follow me. It is within my grasp to give you all the Paradise you need.

'The key is nothing. A piece of gold said to open the gates. And what will you find behind the gates? No one knows. Hundreds of years have passed since the key was forged. It was nothing more than a symbol of a welding of tribes, primitive peoples with primitive ideas. Do you believe that you will find riches? Ha!'

The Flame Sorceress paced back and forth in front of her throne, breasts heaving in passion, brown eyes blazing, her voice rising. 'Here, here are riches, power. You say I manipulate the people. Yes, I admit it. I manipulate the people to bring them wealth and happiness. Their paradise is here in their own land. I will show it to them, I will lead them. They adore me. Together we will bring the throne out of this underground hall and place it in Dimly New. We will become a proudly united people, human and Trans. Wealth and power will flow to me because of my leadership. Nothing can deny me, nothing can get in my way, not you or the pitiful leaders of the coastal cities.'

'She's raving,' Giles whispered. 'She's going to kill us, no matter what we say.'

'Then let's try to escape!' Petia hissed angrily.

'There's still Keja. Wait. Play for time.'

The sorceress' loud ravings fell to abrupt silence. The change proved as chilling as her insane rage. When the Flame Sorceress spoke again, it was with a quietness that was in nerve-jangling contrast to what had gone before. Delivered in a sibilant, even voice, it sent shivers through Giles' soul.

'Meddlers.' She pointed at Giles and Petia; they both flinched, waiting for the leaping flame sent to devour them. 'A small pile of charred ashes, is that what you bargained for when you sought to rob the Flame Sorceress? You think me mad. I see it in your eyes.

'No, no burning here. I will grant you a brief reprieve. When I have liberated the people of Trois Havres, there will be a celebration. The lords and merchants will be driven forth from their castles and mansions. A pyre is what will satisfy the people. A pyre on which to burn the oppressors. And you two shall join the lords of power and commerce on the pyre.

'No key, Grimsmate and Darya. Only death in purifying flame.'

She gestured to the flame beings. 'Take them away. Be sure that the cell bars are close enough that our little cat cannot slip between them.'

The Flame Sorceress sat down heavily, one slender leg draping over the other in what might have been a seductive display had not her clouded face shown only darkness and death. Giles and Petia marched the length of the hall and out of the door, their flame guards close enough to make their skin prickle.

'She didn't kill us outright,' said Petia. 'For only ten seconds alone with her!' Claws sprang forth; the flame beings moved nearer, their body heat effectively preventing an escape.

'Just because she didn't kill us doesn't mean it's still not within her power,' said Giles. He wondered how acute the senses of the flame beings were. Everything said to Petia might

139

be reported back to their mistress, he decided. 'Say nothing more.'

Petia nodded glumly.

They moved through one passage after another, crossing smaller caves between. Finally, a flambeau motioned them into a small nook several feet above the floor.

Another of the flambeaux stooped to the floor. With a flourish, he formed a bar of intense flame running from floor to ceiling. He repeated the motion every few inches from one side of the nook's entrance to the other.

The flame creatures turned without a glance and marched away. Giles and Petia were imprisoned behind bars of flame.

'What will we do, Giles?'

Giles put his hand on Petia's arm. 'The first thing is to get a bit of sleep,' he said, giving her a soldier's advice. 'We'll think better when we've rested.'

'But we've got to get out of here!' Petia was near to panic.

'We will, we will.' Giles took her hands, forcing Petia to look into his eyes. 'Stay calm. We're warm, we're dry. Maybe we'll even be fed. We won't be killed for a while. And Keja is somewhere near. Obviously they did not find him. For all her seeming omniscience, the Flame Sorceress missed Keja.'

'You think that Keja can help?' Petia asked. 'I'm not sure he's much good for anything.'

'He is abler than he shows. Underneath the peacock posturing and womanising lies a brave soul.'

Petia grimaced. 'All right. I'll try to be calm.' She flinched away from the flaming bars again. 'I hate fire,' she said, almost too low for the man to hear.

'At least we'll be warm,' Giles said. 'We could be sleeping outside in the cold.'

'Damn you, Giles Grimsmate.' Petia hissed, then curled into a tight ball.

Keja Tchurak entered the cavern, swinging stride confident. He wanted it to appear that he belonged there. The people looked up from their work and automatically gave the ritual sign. Keja returned it, hoping that it was correct.

'Who are you? Where are you going?' one of them asked.

Keja's heart clogged his throat; the sign had been wrong. The cult had put out his description. Something so small that he had missed it gave him away.

His thief's nerves took over. No great outcry had risen. This was only an innocent query, not an accusation.

'I'm fresh in from Dimly New,' Keja replied without so much as a quaver in his voice. 'I've been sent to question the prisoners. Where were they taken?'

'Probably to the cells.' The man who answered gestured to the left with his head.

Three passageways led off from that side of the cave.

'I've been turned around.' Keja laughed at his own supposed stupidity. 'These caves and passages confuse me so easily. Which leads to the cells?'

Two women giggled at Keja's seeming embarrassment. He graced them with a boyish smile and a deep bow. To the more comely one, Keja even ventured a quick wink. The man said, more brusquely now, wanting Keja away from the women, 'The middle one.'

'Thank you,' Keja said. He made the ritual sign again, and for good measure added, 'The Flame keep you.' He disappeared into the centre opening with relief – and some regret. The one woman, girl actually, had been quite pretty and more than a little smitten by his charms. Keja sighed. Giles and Petia needed rescuing. Then he could seek out the lovely girl and assay the limits of her infatuation with him.

He was beginning to enjoy this.

As he neared the other end of the passage, Keja saw light flickering on the floor of the next cave. He entered cautiously. Bars of liquid flame closed off the cell.

He crept silently across the floor. The bars were so closely spaced that he couldn't see any prisoners within. Squinting, he made out dim figures. He put out his hand and nearly burned himself on the bars.

'Giles, is that you?'

Giles stirred in his sleep. Petia was leaning against his shoulder, asleep. She seemed to be purring.

'Giles,' Keja whispered, louder this time.

'Hmmph?' Giles opened his eyes cautiously. 'What?'

'It's me. Keja.'

Giles came awake and put his hand over Petia's mouth. She snorted and nearly bit him as she, too, awakened.

'How'd you get here?'

'How do you suppose? Master thief and sneakiest of sneaks,' Keja bragged. 'How do I open the bars? This is unlike any prison cell I've ever seen, not that I've often been incarcerated.'

'Let me think.' Giles shook the fog from his head. 'Remember the passageway we found yesterday at the back of the hill?'

Keja nodded.

'There was a stream nearby where we rested and ate. If you divert that stream into the cave system, we could drown the flame beings – her flambeaux, as the sorceress calls them.'

'Sounds like a good plan,' Keja said sarcastically.

'Flood the cave,' Giles ordered. 'I have a hunch that the sorceress derives part of her power from all the fires that she keeps around her. Torches burning all over the place, a brazier by her throne. She's mad, absolutely insane.'

'How am I supposed to divert the stream?' Keja asked.

'Dig a ditch into one of those passages, then dam up the stream. Cut some logs, brush, rocks, anything to divert the stream into that passageway. They must all connect and run into the main cavern.'

'What about you?'

'When the water runs in, it will seek the lowest level. We're not far above that. The water will put out these flaming bars when it reaches here. There should be a fair amount of panic. We'll find a way out.'

'But what about the key? Do we even know it's in here?' Keja asked.

'I'd bet my last royal on it, from the way she talked about it. We don't know where, but we'll figure that out after we sweep all these flame things out of the cave. That's first. Go now, or you'll end up in here with us.'

'You're right,' Keja said. 'It looks warm and comfy in there, though. You all right, Petia?'

'I hate fire,' Petia said. 'But we'll be all right. Just do as Giles has suggested. I can't get out of here fast enough.'

Keja started to reach through the bars to touch them, give them encouragement, then thought better of it. The cuff of his jacket started to char. Instead, he raised his hand and gave them the ritual flame sign. 'Don't go anywhere,' he chuckled. 'May the Flame keep you.'

'When I get out of here,' Petia promised, 'you'll pay for that remark.'

'One more thing, Keja,' Giles said. 'Watch out for any line of flame that seems to run across the floor. It might burst into some monster creature.'

'Why don't I bring some dirt and put it on these bars?'

'Do you see any dirt in the caves? It's all rock. You'd have to go outside and come back again. We can't risk it. Divert the stream. We'll worry about the rest of it.'

Keja did wave this time. Cautiously, he made his way out of the cave. Giles watched the wiry thief vanish, hoping his trust in the man wasn't misplaced. The bars of the cell seemed to be getting hotter by the minute.

Fifteen

KEJA PAUSED to wipe away the sweat rolling down his forehead and into his eyes. He didn't remember working this hard in his entire life.

'I know now why I decided the life of a thief was for me,' he complained, his muscles aching abysmally. Manual labour was something he had always tried to avoid.

Boots soaked and feet cold, he cursed the broad stream running down swiftly from the mountains. When he and Giles had camped the day before, they'd thought it rose up from underground; it merely ducked under the surface for a short way. Keja saw no other way for the water to be so crystalline clear and as cold as ice. Twice, Keja stumbled on slippery rocks to catch himself on his hands, but not before the front of his precious tunic was soaked.

''Tis not enough Giles and Petia get themselves into a cage of fire. They demand I ruin my clothing to rescue them. Pah!' This was not all he ruined. Keja examined his sword and dagger. Their edges were nicked and dirty and would require extensive retempering to be usable again. If this crackbrained plan did work, Giles would owe him new weapons. And a new tunic and jacket. And even a chance to rest in Dimly New. One woman in the market *had* looked upon him with real interest.

He stood, rubbing his aching shoulder and viewing what he had accomplished so far. The stream still rushed on by, but his hard work had piled boulders along the shore and a ditch ran in a straight line from the smoke vents in the rocky hill to a spot just short of the stream. It would take Keja only a few minutes to open the intervening space and send the burbling stream directly down into the cave through the vents.

Then the fight would begin in earnest. Keja didn't fool himself that the human guards would allow the water to pour into their cave without blood being spilled.

His rest over, Keja reached for the sword again. His body ached and his joints froze. 'I know what Giles complains about now,' he muttered. Keja never wanted arthritis to seize up his bones permanently. Better to die in some noble venture.

The small thief seized a boulder and wrestled it into position along the stream's bottom. Standing knee deep in the water, he placed the stones with all the care of an uplands beaver. Side by side, he nestled stones of all sizes, then dabbed in mud. When he reached the opposite side of the stream, he was pleased with the first layer of foundation. Keja struggled on, placing another row parallel with the first.

He placed a third row on top of and between the two foundation layers. Some of the rocks now stuck out above the surface of the water. The water flowed between the rocks, seeking a way through, trying to continue its way downstream.

Keja noticed that the water now rose to his thighs. He looked along the bank and saw that the water was rising nicely behind his makeshift dam. He tested the stones for solidity, then began laying cut ironbeam branches along the upstream side, blocking the dam more effectively. He was so pleased with his engineering feat that he no longer cared that he was shivering cold and wet nearly to his waist.

For another hour he laboured, pausing only occasionally to attempt to relieve the pain in his lower back. When he had finished, Keja panted in exhaustion. But he felt that the ditch was adequate to channel most of the water into the cave system.

'Better than any dozen men might have done,' he said with pride. 'Even if they did know what they were doing, this is better.' Here and there rocks tumbled from his dam and let tiny rivulets through. The lifetime of the dam would have to be measured in hours – or even minutes.

'No reason to wait,' he said, wiping his hands on his trousers. Keja winced at the sight; streaks left by his dirty fingers turned the once fine trousers into a striped mess.

Ignoring the filth and damage done to his clothing, Keja tore into the few remaining feet between the ditch and the stream. Churning, eager water helped him eat away the dirt as it found its way into the virgin path. The pressure behind the dam now had a new outlet and took it with a startlingly loud rush.

Keja leaped for the bank. It collapsed under his feet, and he went down with a windmilling of arms and legs. For one last time, the cold clear water won. Helplessly flailing, Keja was swept along by the powerful force. Even as he foundered, sputtering, he laughed out loud at his success. Eventually he found his feet and staggered out of the ditch, dripping mud and water and laughing insanely. He had done what Giles had asked. The water poured forth and blasted its way down into the cavern through the smoke vents.

All he had to do now was to stop the guards trying to redivert the stream. Keja hefted his nicked and battered sword and sloshed forward.

'What if Keja succeeds? What will I do?'

Giles looked at Petia. She trembled, and clutched herself as if freezing.

'What do you mean? You'll follow me and we'll get out of here, one way or the other.'

'Giles, the fire bars are bad enough. I hate them. Water will be even worse.'

'Listen, young lady,' Giles said sternly. 'You've done splendidly up to this point. Whatever happens, you'll do fine. I have a great deal of faith in you. I may not trust you with the keys, but I have no doubt about your abilities. Keja's, either.' Giles warmed inside. It had been a long while since he'd had to give such a speech. He remembered the new recruits, just before going into battle. All had required some small encouragement – it varied from soldier to soldier.

Some needed to believe they were invincible, that nothing could harm them. They usually fought with reckless abandon and survived. The ones, like Petia, who doubted their own abilities, even for an instant, died. Giles had tried not to become attached to those under his command in the War. Too often, he had, and it gnawed at his guts when they died.

Petia dying would end this crazy quest for the key, whether he lived or not.

A flambeau entered the cavern from a passageway across from their prison. A woman carrying a bowl followed three paces behind it. From the haunted expression on her face, she feared the flame being.

The flambeau stooped before the burning bars. It placed its hand at the juncture of floor and bar. The flaming bar shimmered and went out like a candle flame in a high wind. The creature did it again to the next bar, then stood back and motioned impatiently to the woman.

She hurried forward, stepping cautiously past the flaming form and pushed the bowl through the empty space between the bars.

'Food,' she said, and backed away fearfully.

With two quick gestures, the flambeau set the bars back in place. He turned and marched away, leaving the woman to find her own way back to whatever section of the caves she had come from. The woman cast a fleeting glance at the two prisoners, then disappeared.

'It looks as if we going to eat,' Giles said, sniffing the odours coming from the covered bowl. 'The sorceress doesn't want us to starve to death, at least.'

'Do you really believe she intends to burn us on a pyre?'

146

'She meant it when she said it.' Giles moved the bowls to a spot between them on the ledge. 'Her madness reminds me of a lieutenant I served under during the War. He never understood why the enemy refused to fall into his little traps.'

'What happened to him?'

Giles looked sadly at Petia. 'He died.'

Petia paled. 'You mean his own troops killed him? That's awful!'

'The captain replacing him gave a commendation to the one who drove the dagger into the lieutenant's kidney.' Giles chuckled. 'I still have the medal, somewhere.' Petia just stared at him. Giles sobered and said, 'Given another rage like the one we witnessed, the Flame Sorceress will order us to be burned – with no remorse.'

Petia shuddered.

'Don't worry about it. Let's see what we have to eat. We'll need strength if – when – Keja is successful.'

The stew did not look appetising, but they both ate hungrily. Petia ignored the grease floating on top and dug in. There was little meat, but potatoes, carrots and turnips made it wholesome enough, even if she did prefer rare steak to vegetables.

'A loaf of bread would have rounded it out,' Giles said. 'But complaining to the management will do us little good.'

He set the bowl down and took out his pipe. When he had it nicely packed, he looked around the floor for a twig or a sliver of wood. Finding none, he looked at the flaming bars. 'All this fire, and I don't think I can light my damned smokepot.'

'Couldn't you hold your head sideways and . . .'

They were interrupted by shouts echoing through the tunnels.

'I wonder what that is. You don't suppose . . . Keja?'

The shouting became louder. Footsteps resounded from the walls. People were running in all directions, panicky. Voices died away and then came closer again. Neither Petia nor Giles could tell whether the shouting was near or far away.

Like cannonade, one word came through clearly.

Water!

'He's done it! Keja's diverted the stream into the cave. I'm sure of it.' Giles swung around, ready for instant response.

'What do we do now?' Petia asked.

'Wait. We can't get through these bars. We have to wait until Keja comes to rescue us or the water reaches the bottom of the bars and extinguishes them.'

Petia shuddered and sucked in her breath. 'I hate water as much as I do fire.'

'We'll make it,' Giles said.

They sat, listening to the shouts continuing to reverberate through the caves.

'Look.' Giles pointed to the passageway across from their prison. Water was seeping from the entrance and spreading across the cavern floor. 'I think that this is the lowest level of the caves. I don't know if there's enough water there to do us any good. It's coming in too slowly. It's got to rise faster than that.' Giles rocked forward to grip the bars and shake them. Only Petia's restraining hand kept him from nasty burns.

They heard feet sloshing through a tunnel somewhere. Nearby?

Filthy and mud-splashed, Keja staggered out of a passageway. 'Thanks be to Dismatis and the other poxy gods. I didn't think I'd make it.'

Keja collapsed outside the burning bars. 'I've run most of the way. Except when I was staggering and falling. I don't know if this is doing any good or not, Giles. It's not filling the caves fast enough.'

'Never mind that. Get us out of here. Throw water at the base of these bars.'

Keja crawled over to a small pool of water puddled in a cavity in the floor. He cupped his hands and tried to crawl back on his knees. The water dribbled through his hands.

'Keja! Stand up and do it properly,' Petia cried, almost mad with anguish.

'So say you, lady. You haven't just run a couple of miles.' He propped himself up and struggled to his feet. Carefully this time, he cupped his hands and staggered back to the bars. He lowered his fingers and let the water run out onto the base of one bar. The flame sputtered but did not go out.

'Need more water.' He staggered back to the pool and emptied his leather pouch onto the floor. He filled the pouch with water and came back. The water poured out in a tiny stream. The flame sputtered and winked out.

'One more bar, Keja, and we're free.'

After three trips and what seemed a thousand gallons of water, a second bar was extinguished. Giles guided Petia between the remaining burning bars, then stepped after her.

'You've got to go back, Keja. I hate to ask it of you. You've done a marvellous job so far, but it's not enough.'

Keja looked at Giles, despair in his eyes. After a moment, he nodded and said grimly, 'Yes, I know you're right. If it's going to do any good, there has to be more water. I don't know what happened. I was sure I had the entire stream blocked off. Probably didn't do it well enough – or I didn't kill enough guards trying to undo all my handiwork.' Seven human guards lay dead from Keja's battered blade. 'What are you two going to do?'

'Go and look for the key,' Petia said. 'It's here, and my guess is that it's in the throne room.'

'Where?' Keja asked.

Giles described where they had been taken when they were captured. 'When you've finished diverting all the stream, come back here. Try to find us. We'll be looking for you – and we'll probably need your help.'

'Good luck in finding the key. I'd hate to have ruined a perfectly good suit of clothes only to find the key didn't exist.' Keja stumbled once crossing the cavern, then his spirits seemed to lift. His body straightened. He hurried into a passageway and was gone.

'Which way?' Giles asked. 'Do you remember?'

'I think so,' Petia said. She pointed down a passage. 'Follow me.'

Water bubbled up everywhere. But Giles had been right in his assessment of its volume. Petia and Giles waded through it up to their ankles. At the moment, however, it was flowing downward, seeking the lowest levels of the cavern system.

'At this rate, it will take forever to fill the damned place,' Giles muttered.

Petia looked back at him. 'Let's not worry about it. It caused a furore and got us out of our cage and people are too busy to notice us. I hope Keja got out.'

'So do I,' Giles agreed. 'If he can divert more water, there's a good chance to flood this place right out of existence.'

149

'We've got to find the key before we do that.' Petia pressed on. She had a good memory for the route along which they had been herded and unerringly found the right turnings.

'Look,' Petia pointed. Ahead of them a flambeau came out of a passageway. Seeing the water streaming across the floor, it turned and fled.

'They won't get in our way,' she said.

'The only problem is that they'll seek the higher caverns where it's dry. That means they'll be gathered around the sorceress.'

To their right, another flambeau appeared at the tunnel entrance. It looked at the cavern floor, awash with water, and began to retreat. From behind it, water rushed down the passage. The water hit its feet, and the flame being literally flickered out of existence. Feet, ankles. As each limb was extinguished, the being sank lower to the floor. Knees, waist. The torso steamed and hissed as water splashed upward. Its mouth opened in a crackling scream as the water washed over its head. Then it was . . . gone.

Giles and Petia looked at each other. Their emotions were in tumult. On the one hand, the enemy was dead and legions more would surely follow. Yet, watching even a flame creature meet its inexorable demise in such a fashion was horrible. Giles shuddered as the image of a butcher disjointing a beef flashed through his mind.

'On, go on.' He gave Petia a shove to cover his thoughts. There was no need to express them.

Petia hurried through a passage and into the next cavern. Humans and Trans were gathering goods helter skelter and streaming in the direction Giles remembered as the entrance to the cave system. They paid no heed to the pair.

'Up there.' Giles grabbed Petia's arm and spun her around. 'That way to the hall.'

A scream ripped through the cavern and echoed around the dripping grey limestone walls. They heard the Flame Sorceress taking out her frustrations on any unfortunate enough to be within her sight.

'Idiots, cretins. We will drown! Do something!'

Giles and Petia drew near to the cavern containing the throne and watched. The Flame Sorceress paced back and forth, gesturing wildly at the flambeaux surrounding her. She shouted orders at her flaming soldiers; no human guards were in sight.

'Where is the human captain of the guard?' she screamed. 'Get him here at once. We must move the gold.'

The madwoman had not yet realised that her flambeaux would be extinguished the instant water flowed into the cavern.

Giles murmured, 'Hurry, Keja.' The old warrior stepped out into the cave.

'There are no humans, sorceress,' he yelled. 'They are deserting your caverns, trying to save themselves from drowning.'

The sorceress stopped at the sound of Giles' voice. 'You!' she screamed. 'You and that cat woman. You're responsible for this.'

She flung out her hand and a sparare flashed from the end of her fingertips. The flaming arrow hurtled across the cavern, striking Giles in the left shoulder and piercing the flesh just below his clavicle. It hung there, burning.

Petia leaped to his side. She grabbed the burning shaft and pulled, wincing as it burned her hand. She flung the arrow away. It was consumed before it hit the floor.

Giles clapped his hand to the wound. A small flame still burned where the sparare had entered, searing the open wound. Immense pain clouded his senses with a red veil of agony, and he slumped to the floor.

The Flame Sorceress seemed to dismiss the pair. She did not even deign to acknowledge Petia. She turned to her soldiers and once again began screaming contradictory orders.

Petia lifted Giles by his good arm and dragged him into the nearest passageway. He slumped once again, sitting in the muddy water running around him. His face mirrored the pain racking his body.

Petia tore the cloth of Giles' tunic away from the wound. The sparare had gone deep, making a red and ugly gouge. With impossible speed, the wound was already festering. The complications this would cause if she did not do something spelled Giles' death. She reached beneath her tunic and tore a piece from her white undershirt.

She made a compress and held it against the wound. There was no way to keep it in place. 'Can you hold it there?' she asked.

Giles nodded, his eyes squeezed shut. He put his right hand to the cloth and weakly clutched it. He realised that he must stop the bleeding, but the mounting pain approached the unbearable.

Giles sat, head bowed, grimacing from time to time. Petia stood over him, watching him suffer, patiently waiting for him to determine that he had the strength to go on. Water continued to flow around them. It was well over Petia's ankles now, and flowed over Giles' thighs.

'Giles. Giles!' Petia had to repeat it. 'We've got to move. There's more water. Can you get up?'

Giles looked up at her, pain dulling his grey eyes. His left arm hung loose, but he pushed his right hand against the floor and managed to get over on his knees. Petia helped him to stand, but she could see that it was taking a great effort on Giles' part. The sparare carried not only the burning but magicks intended to give a slow death.

'I'm sorry,' he said. 'Been wounded worse than this, never felt so weak. Sorry.'

'Let's get out of here.' Petia took his good arm.

Giles shook her hand off. A look of determination came over his face. 'No, we've got this far. We search for the key,' he muttered. 'There's no better time. Confusion everywhere. Where's the audience hall?'

'Dammit, you can hardly stand. Don't shake my hand off again. Let me help.'

With Giles staggering by her side, Petia crossed the cavern. They came out of the passageway facing the entrance to the sorceress' grand hall. Giles seemed to gain strength when he saw the black onyx throne.

He removed Petia's helping hand and said, 'I'll be all right. Let's search that hall.'

The water was rising faster now. It washed around their calves as they entered the hall. The dais still stood above the water, but not for long. They forced themselves through the water, each step an effort. Behind them they felt a new surge. The level began to rise rapidly.

'Keja's done it,' Giles said, smiling for the first time since the sparare had injured him.

They had gone only a few steps further when they saw the brazier toppled by a cresting wave. The flame went out with a loud sizzling audible throughout the cavern. The tide ebbed, then surged once more as the pressure behind it mounted. The throne was picked up and floated off the dais, as if it were little more than a child's toy boat.

'Giles, we can't find anything now. It's getting dangerous. We've got to get out. If we stay here, we'll drown.'

'So close.' Tears came to his eyes. From pain? Or frustration at being so close, so damned close? 'But you're right.'

Together they waded from the hall, feeling their way with their feet. They could not see the cavern floor beneath the water. One of them would surely have fallen without the other's support.

As they left the Flame Sorceress' audience hall, they saw the water littered with objects floating through the caverns. Wooden cases. Tables and chairs. Bodies face down. Even small stone implements caught in the maelstrom.

Giles held the cloth to his wound again, depending on Petia to take the lead and find a way out of the aqueous nightmare the caves had become.

'Damned key,' he muttered. 'Who started this? Where's Keja?'

'Let's hope he didn't make it back,' Petia said in a choked voice.

Giles staggered, light-headed, when he saw the wall of water rushing across the cavern toward them. Trapped – and unless they could hold their breath for hours, dead.

Sixteen

'How do we get out of here?' Giles called. The water swirled around their knees and the massive tidal wave blasting toward them spelled certain doom. People struggled through the water from passage to cavern to passage, seeking to save their own lives. Flotsam floated on the water, bobbing and tossing higher and higher, with some of the bigger pieces jamming into the exits and creating barriers.

And the wall of water rose, seemed to pause, then rumbled like a thunderstorm as it washed away all life before it.

Petia pointed, the roar too loud to shout over. Giles never hesitated; to do so meant instant death. They flung themselves into the side passage. Giles felt a giant, watery hand grip at his body, squeeze with cruel intent, lift. They were swept through the tunnel by the force of the water. Trying to cling to one another, they bounced off first one wall and then the other down the entire length of the corridor and came through dazed but unscathed. The force of the water diminished when it spat them into a larger cavern.

'We're getting close,' Petia shouted in Giles' ear. 'This is the second cavern from the entrance.'

It was a large cavern, and Giles expected the water level to be lower – perversely, it filled rapidly. They found themselves struggling in swirling water up to their chests.

'What's happening?' Petia shouted. The panic returned to her eyes. She hated water but had managed to cope with it. The mental image of herself drowning proved almost overpowering. No longer did simple discomfort and her feline aversion to water dominate – Petia now feared death.

'Don't worry, Petia. I'll get you out. There's got to be another way.'

Another surge entered the cave and swept them away. Turbulent water kept them off their feet.

'Do you know how to swim?' Giles asked.

Petia sputtered and blew water out of her mouth. 'Just barely,' she whimpered. 'Cat paddle and float.'

Giles swam to her, trying to use his wounded arm as little as possible. The pain gnawed deeper into the bone, burning as if the flame arrow was still stuck in his flesh. Pushing away his own discomfort, he tried to calm her.

'You know the directions, and I know how to get you out of here alive. Believe it!'

But Giles was not certain that either was true. He talked Petia into turning onto her back. As she floated, he encouraged her to breathe regularly and calm herself.

'Giles, help!' At first, Giles angrily started to tell Petia she was safe. Then he saw the startled expression on her face. The cry had taken her by surprise, too.

The call reverberated around the walls of the cave, camouflaged by the roaring water, seeming to come at Giles from every direction, then echoed back again. But the voice was unmistakable: Keja.

Giles trod water, peering across the boiling surface to find their companion. He failed to locate him anywhere.

'Up! Look up.' Petia thrashed around, pointing. He calmed her, then scanned the walls, turning his body in the water with small strokes of his right hand. Finally, he spotted Keja. He was crouched on a spur of limestone near the ceiling.

'Get down, damn your eyes, and help me get Petia out of the caves!' Giles' mood darkened, and he had little time for Keja's games. With every new buffeting from the incoming water, Giles weakened just a bit more.

Keja clung to the rock, almost in tears. 'I can't. I can't swim.'

'O sweet gods,' Giles muttered. 'One can barely swim, one can't swim at all, and me with a lame arm.' He scissored to the cave wall and found a spot to grab onto a stalactite. Anchoring himself, he called out to Petia, 'Stay here. Keep calm and stay afloat. I've got to help Keja.' He waited until she nodded before proceeding.

Giles tried to keep his injured arm immobile as he used his right arm to begin the swim across the inundated cavern — impossible. Every stroke brought another sharp pang to the wound. Sometimes the pain was so intense that Giles floundered and found himself sucking in water. Each time he roused himself, spat water, and took another stroke.

Each minor recovery took that much more of a toll on his strength. He was fading rapidly.

The surface was awash with sticks, rags, clothing, wooden furniture, and twice Giles bumped his head against heavy objects, further sapping his endurance.

Halfway across the cavern, a wave of nausea swept over him. His body twisted with spasms. He vomited once, then fainted, his head dipping underwater. The wound from the sparare had taken its toll.

Petia floated, consciously willing her panic to subside. The Trans found herself trapped between her fear and loathing of water and seeing her friend vanish beneath the churning, white-crested watery death. Afraid to breathe, she forced herself to inhale calmly and evenly. Her fear began to lessen.

With tentative strokes, Petia turned herself around in spite of the turbulence. Craning her head, she tried to find Giles. Only one or two torches guttered near the ceiling, making it difficult to see.

She peered through the dusky light and found Giles, low in the water, making each one-armed stroke look like his ultimate effort. Glancing upward, she tried to make out Keja, perched somewhere in the top of the cave. She couldn't see him.

Petia turned her full attention again to Giles and his slow progress through the treacherous whirl of water. She watched helplessly as a spasm seized him. Petia did not hear the racking gasps or see him vomit, but she was aware of the sudden cessation of his struggles.

Face down in the water — he'd drown!

'Giles!' she shrieked. No response. He bobbed like a corpse. Petia gave a small moan that echoed back, mocking her. Forgetting her fear of the water, the cat Trans rolled over and began stroking clumsily but fervently. Her hands came down in front of her automatically, and paddled to the inert figure, barely keeping her mouth above water. Her breathing gusted in quick and erratic spurts, but need drove her. Giles would die unless she reached him.

She thought that she'd never reach the floating figure. Determinedly, she kept on. Giles' body slammed against hers, driven by unseen currents, and Petia nearly succumbed. Fear came to her aid now, flooding her body with adrenaline.

'Giles!' she called. No response. 'Don't be dead! Don't you dare!' She reached up with one hand and grasped his hair, pulling his head out of the water. His eyes were closed and blood trickled from his nose. Keeping his head elevated, she nudged his body with her chest. One hand in constant motion, Petia pushed him toward the edge of the cave. Luck favoured her. A careless wave tossed them both high up. Giles slumped over a rock ledge, arms outstretched. Petia clung to his legs until her strength returned sufficiently to pull herself up alongside him.

'Giles,' she yelled in his ear. 'Giles, wake up! I can't swim out with you. You've got to help yourself.' Tears mingled with the fine spray constantly drenching them. Petia shook him as she cried and swore.

From somewhere in the distance, Giles heard Petia calling his name. Why was she cursing him? So tired. Never before had he felt this exhausted. Why wouldn't they let him be? So damned tired.

'Go away,' he muttered. Water rose in his throat, choking him. He vomited, losing both the meal and the filthy water he had swallowed. Panting, fighting to breathe, he slowly realised where he was, what had happened.

'Giles, wake up. Don't fall off the ledge. Hang on, Dismatis take you!'

'I'll hold you up. Won't drown. But so tired . . .'

Petia let go of Giles' thinning hair, and his head fell forward into the water once again.

The water seemed fresh and cool this time. But not in his nose. He lifted his head and snorted like a cetacean clearing its blow hole. His grey eyes opened and gradually focused. He shook his head to clear the hair from obscuring his vision.

'Giles, we've got to get out of here. The water's still rising.'

Giles looked at Petia as if she were some apparition come to haunt his dreams – his nightmares.

157

'Come on. Snap to, soldier.' She slapped him as hard as she could. A kitten's paw held more force than her hand. 'Come to. We've got to get out of here!'

'We've still got to rescue Keja.' Old habits reasserted themselves. Soldiers did not abandon comrades. Petia's invocation of 'soldier' gave him the needed impetus to carry on. He didn't have to think; he had experience to draw on. He pointed at the water washing over the ledge. 'Find something floating. Maybe we could get him out on it.'

Petia stood precariously on the slippery ledge and scanned the surface of the water. 'There's a table. Would that work?'

'Perfect,' Giles said. 'I'll get it.'

'You stay here and rest,' Petia said. She slid into the water, more confident now, and paddled away towards the wood. She got behind it, grabbed the edge of the table and kicked her way back to the ledge, using the table for buoyancy.

'Sure you feel ready to tackle this, Giles? I don't want you fainting on me again.'

'We don't have any choice. The water's going to fill this cave in a few minutes, and we'll all drown. Let's get Keja and then get out of here.'

Giles scooted forward and lowered himself over the ledge. He floated for a moment, testing himself. Then, taking his place alongside Petia, he began to kick. The flow of water made it difficult to keep the table moving in the correct direction.

Keja crouched just above the water level, a stricken look on his face. 'We'll never find the entrance.'

'Calm down,' Petia said. 'Trust my sense of direction.'

'Keja,' Giles warned, 'if you struggle, we'll have to leave you.'

Keja's face went white as Giles explained how they intended to get out of the flooded cave. 'Isn't there any other way?' he pleaded.

'None that I know of,' Giles replied. 'Now get on this table.'

Keja slipped into the water and immediately sank.

Giles had anticipated it and grabbed his arm. Keja came up sputtering, beginning to fight blindly. Giles cuffed him enough to get his attention.

'Hook your elbow over the edge of the table, then stop struggling or I'll knock you inside out!'

The warning had its effect on the frightened thief. Keja had to try twice, but finally he lay prone on the table. Giles smiled to himself when he saw Keja's white knuckles gripping the edges. Afraid, yes, but not out of control. Giles admired that. Everyone who didn't have sand for brains was afraid at one time or another – true bravery lay in overcoming that fear rather than succumbing to it.

Keja and Petia had both displayed real valour.

Giles looked at Petia to see if she was ready. She nodded, still frightened, and they began to kick, guiding the table before them. The churning water formed a vortex that tried to pull them off their support and down to the cave floor a dozen feet under the surface. Giles hung on grimly, dizziness hitting him again as the wound in his arm sent wave after wave of pain hammering into his mind.

'You're the guide, Petia. Wherever you say. I can't tell where the entrance is now. Cave's filling up. Water's coming in faster than I dreamed.'

Petia cocked her head in what she hoped was the right direction, then started kicking.

It took several minutes to cross the cave, pushing the table before them. Keja wasn't a heavy man, but battling the turbulent water made the short swim frighteningly dangerous. Several times the table bumped into other large floating objects. Only constant encouragement from Giles convinced Keja to let go with one hand and guide the pieces out of the way.

When they smashed hard against the far wall, Giles shouted over the roaring water, 'The entrance? Where?'

'Directly below us,' Petia said in a choked voice. Her eyes widened when she understood what had to be done next. From the expression on Keja's face, he didn't understand.

'You can make it,' Giles said. 'Only a little bit more.'

He turned his attention to Keja. 'I can get you out of here, but not unless you cooperate. Understand? We don't have time for arguing.' The pain in Giles' shoulder sapped him of strength, but he had to go on. He reached inside and found reserves he'd thought were lost with his youth.

159

'Maybe we should wait until you've rested,' Petia said, concerned at his pinched expression.

'No! Water's still rising. The sooner we do it, the sooner we'll be out. Then I can collapse.' Giles tried for a lighter tone to reassure them. He failed.

'What do I do?' asked Petia.

'Hang onto my tunic, and I'll do the rest. Do you think you can do that?'

'Yes.'

'That's it. Keja, listen carefully. We've got to dive down and find the cave entrance. The water flowing out of the mouth should sweep us right along. You've got to remember two things. Keja, are you listening to me?'

Giles got no response. Keja lay inert on the floating table, fingers white with the strain of gripping the edges.

Giles reached up and grabbed Keja's foot. 'Keja, listen to me. Turn your head around so I know you hear me.'

Keja's head came around slowly, as if he feared that any sudden movement would deposit him in the water.

'By the gods, I'll leave you here if you don't cooperate.'

Keja's head nodded vigorously, and Giles relaxed a tiny bit.

'Two things. First, before we dive you have to fill your lungs with air, take a deep breath. Second, I'm going to have my arm around your neck and you can't struggle. If you struggle, I'll let you go and you're on your own. I'm not going to drown for you. The going's hard enough without that.'

Keja's eyes were round, but he nodded again.

'A deep breath for you, too, Petia, before we dive.'

Petia nodded.

'All right, Keja. Into the water. Come on, just slide off and I'll hold you up.'

Giles manoeuvered himself behind Keja and kept him from going completely under as he left the security of the table. Giles felt a piercing pain and another wave of nausea. With his injured arm, he reached up around Keja's neck and gripped the collar of the thief's once fancy jacket. He glanced at Petia. 'Feel down until you've got the edge of my tunic,' he told her.

Petia's head bobbed just above the surface of the water when she said, 'I've got it.'

160

'Everybody get ready.' Giles pushed away from the table, caught in the turbulent water like a leaf in a millrace.

The waves closed over their heads. He turned underwater, looking frantically for the cave entrance. Some light would be showing, he knew. So far, neither of his companions had made a move. That was just what Giles wanted. He would need every bit of his strength.

Giles strained to keep his eyes open and find the cave mouth. As he searched, he weakened. Giles had over-estimated his strength. The water tugged more insistently at him, preventing him from surfacing. More from weakness than design, he let it flow and tried to turn his body in the same direction. Lungs filled with liquid fire, at bursting point, more pain than Giles could endure.

The water became a swirling current that turned the three of them completely around. It caught Petia's body and lifted it above Giles. Keja still hung in Giles' feeble grasp. All were tumbled about like stones in a lapidary's polishing drum.

Giles banged into the wall of the cave and tried to kick against it to propel himself to the surface. The current caught them and carried them even further down.

Giles had no more air in his lungs. Fat bubbles escaped from his nose and lips. Life faded from his body, even as he fought against it.

No! he railed. Not only did his own life depend on his abilities, but also those of Petia and Keja. Giles could die, he had lived a full life, but he could not take them with him. They'd trusted him, as so many soldiers had trusted him during the War.

He had failed many of them, but he had always given it every ounce of his soul, his very life in effort.

Once again Giles felt the flow of the water against his face. He edged into the main current, life departing his limbs faster and faster. Each movement became weaker than the one preceeding it.

Giles Grimsmate was dying.

Light shone wanly through the water. At first, Giles thought it was a death apparition, a visitation to prepare him for the gods.

More bubbles erupted from his lips as he tried to cry out in joy as he realised the cave entrance lay ahead!

He struck out with his good arm, fighting the current that swirled in crazy eddies away from the wall and tried to turn them back. Stroking desperately, he edged nearer the centre of the flow. He felt less of the turbulence. He avoided the caressing hands inviting him to relax and give himself up to the currents.

No! Giles Grimsmate would not die this day! No!

The light became brighter, and Giles struggled to stay centred in the strong flow. He fought, but he had reached the limits of his endurance. With safety – and life! – scant yards in front of him, his tortured body rebelled.

Giles kicked feebly, then slumped in the water, the dim circle of light tormentingly close. The last thing he remembered before darkness constricted his senses was the burning inrush of water to his lungs.

Seventeen

THE GODS prepared him for death. Giles Grimsmate had eluded them for too many years. Now, they claimed their due.

'Not so hard,' he mumbled, then choked. Harsh hands plopped him onto his belly and slammed into his spine. He coughed up water and choked again.

Was this what it was like meeting the gods in death?

'Giles,' he heard a death messenger call. The gods wanted to be sure they had the right man.

'Here,' he said weakly. 'Hurry. I don't like it. Feels awful.'

Another fit of choking seized him. Again the hard slaps to his back. Giles forced open his eyes, hardly daring to look into the face of death. All he saw was Petia on her knees behind him and holding him up.

'You, too?' he said, almost sorrowfully. Death claimed all eventually, but Giles had hoped Petia might escape.

'Welcome back,' she said. 'Are you going to be all right?'

'What?' Giles murmured. It took several seconds for him to comprehend his error. He still lived, and so did Petia. 'Keja?' he asked. 'What . . . ?'

'He'll be all right. Coughing his guts up right now. And probably praying to all the gods.' Petia squeezed Giles' arm. 'We made it. And mainly because of Keja. Without his aid, I would never have got you out of the water. He saved both of us, Giles.'

'Yes.' Giles fainted again.

The next time he came to, Keja was standing over him. The small thief's clothing hung in tatters and he looked drained, but otherwise seemed to be none the worse for the narrow escape. If anything, he seemed pleased with himself.

'We made it,' Keja said proudly. 'I actually swam ahead and pulled you and Petia free of the current.'

'Not bad for someone who can't swim,' Giles said, trying to sit up. Lightheadedness assailed him.

'Well,' Keja said, eyes on the ground, 'the currents favoured me. They catapulted me past, and I just grabbed hold.'

'Thank you,' Giles said. The smaller man beamed.

'Do you think you can stand?' Keja knelt and put his arm around Giles' shoulder to aid him in what proved to be an insurmountable effort.

Both Keja and Petia had to support Giles underneath the arms to get him erect.

Water washed around their feet. The grass around them now lay flat and sodden. Giles saw the bodies of several drowned humans who had been swept out of the cave. He didn't want to think of how many might have been trapped in there.

Nearly carrying Giles, Petia and Keja made for a part of the forest where the ground rose. They found a dry spot and lowered Giles gently.

'Any sign of the sorceress?' Giles asked after he leaned back against a large tree bole.

'We didn't see her, but I wasn't looking, either. Too many other things happening. Like staying alive.' Petia knelt to check Giles when she saw his eyelids drop shut. He had slumped

163

over and fallen into a deep sleep, so deep she couldn't rouse him.

Petia made a small fire while Keja retrieved their belongings from their original campsite some distance away. He strutted back, loudly proclaiming, 'By the gods, I did it. By the gods!

'Saved you two, flooded the cave, and defeated the Flame Sorceress.' Keja leaned back on his hands and sighed deeply, a sigh of self-satisfaction.

Petia aroused from her own deep thoughts. 'What? What did you say?'

'I was just congratulating myself on what a good job I did of saving you two and defeating the cult. I've performed some daring exploits in my life, but this is the greatest. The stuff of legends. Don't you agree?'

Petia turned her head. She stared at Keja, not completely certain that he was being serious. He appeared to be.

'All the work I did on diverting the stream into their air vents, entering the cave and getting you out of that flaming prison, then going back and getting an even bigger flow of water into the cave by digging open the vents – and killing another four or five guards. Finally, I returned to that dangerous den of devilment one more time.' He smiled in contentment, the telling increasing his gloating. 'The stuff of legends, or at least a folk tale.'

'You're not joking, are you?' Petia asked in a quiet voice.

'No! Absolutely not. Danger everywhere. Daring rescue. I had to avoid hundreds of the human and Trans guards and also those flame things. I had to dig a ditch to get that water to the cave. All by myself.' Keja should have recognised the quiet anger in Petia's question. He didn't.

'You take the credit for all that? Giles is lying near death with a wound in his shoulder, tossing between chills and fever, and you brag about what a wonderful job you did?'

Keja looked at her as if he didn't believe what he was hearing.

'Where would you be if Giles hadn't risked his life for you? Perched up on some stone in the top of the cave? Oh, yes. You diverted the water into the cave, and it would have been your death, wouldn't it, if Giles hadn't saved your scrawny ass? You don't swim, remember? The gods ought to brand "braggart" on your forehead, Keja. No air, the water rising, and poor little Keja crying out for help, and at the very last, with the water pouring into your mouth and nose, a whimpering child, a mere baby about to die.' Petia stopped, out of breath from her speech.

She put some more sticks into the fire. 'You're not alone in this, Keja. Yes, you did a good job. But you didn't save us. Giles saved us. With a wound in his arm, he took two people with him rather than abandon either of us. One can't swim well and hates water. The other can't swim at all. Think about that for a while, Keja. Giles risked his life. If it hadn't worked, we'd all three be dead. Now, just how wonderful are you?'

'I did get us out of the water,' Keja said lamely.

Petia turned and walked off into the dark forest, disgust showing in her every movement.

Giles moaned in his sleep. One arm thrashed out and he threw the blankets away from his neck again.

Keja looked after Petia, torn between following her and staying to tend Giles. Keja was stunned by her verbal attack. He had seen her angry only once before, the night he had caught her in his room at the Leather Bottle. But that was different. Keja didn't really understand her attitude. He *had* saved them, when both she and Giles were too weak to do more than let the undertow pull them down to watery death. And he *had* diverted the stream, an engineering feat second to none.

Keja thought about what she had said, then shook it off. Women. Trans women. He snorted, leaned back and tried to sleep.

When Petia returned, she boiled some water and dumped leaves from the forest into it. She poured a mug and gave it to Keja. 'Drink this. It's medicinal.' Then she sat quietly by the fire without another word. Yawning, she rose, unrolled her blankets, and lay down to sleep.

Keja blinked in surprise at her actions. The tea tasted minty and soothed his throat. It seemed to help his stomach as well. Silently, he thanked Petia. She was a good woman, even if she didn't appreciate his finer points.

165

While Petia tended Giles' wound, Keja returned to the cave to seek out some sign of the key. Much of the clearing in front of the cave entrance lay covered with water several inches deep. The stream still poured out of the cave mouth with the same force as when they had made their somewhat fortuitous escape.

Keja snorted in disgust as he sloshed around in the water. He saw no way to search the cave – not while the water was still gushing out with such a vengeance.

He wandered around the clearing, poking under the surface of the water with a long stick. Several human bodies had been washed out of the cave and lay with contorted limbs and bloated features, turning them into something less than human.

'Poor, disillusioned fools,' Keja said. 'Dupes. Deluded fools following a false dream, unlike the one I . . .' He cut off the beginning of another fine tale when he glimpsed a streamer of orange tangled around a tree trunk.

He waded across the clearing to find the body of a woman clothed in rich orange. Her auburn hair floated in disarray on the muddy water, straggling across her face. Keja reached down and brushed away the stringy hair.

'You must be the Flame Sorceress,' he said to the corpse. Her lips were pulled back in the agony of her last minutes. She had drowned, just as many of her followers had drowned. She must have floated and been caught in the swirling currents within the cave. Finally, she had been thrown out of the entrance. But even battered, her beauty lingered.

'Thus ended her dreams of power, rebellion, conquest. Here in the forest clearing, water running around her. Twigs and bits of bark cling to her hair, washed down inside her gown. Food for water bugs. No longer will her demented screams be heard through the caverns, ordering about her minions. Like her flame beings, her fire has been extinguished.' Keja allowed himself a thin smile.

'Not too bad. Think I'll tell some bard to include that in the telling of how I defeated the Flame Sorceress. Very poetic, very dramatic.'

The Flame Sorceress lay on her side, one arm flung up. Keja

turned her body onto its back. Open eyes stared up at him. He shuddered.

Avoiding her unseeing eyes, Keja searched her gown for pockets. He found none. He pulled the neck of her gown open, hoping to find a golden key on a chain or necklace. None.

He sighed. The chance had been a slim one. They now knew that the sorceress was dead and that the key was not on her body. He looked at her one last time. 'A lesson in mortality for the masses here,' Keja said. 'Greed and power seeking, vanity . . .' His voice trailed off. All that struck too close to his own motives.

'We've got to search the cave,' Giles said. His fever had broken, and the wound slowly healed. Petia's healing magicks with natural herbs had finally turned the tide against the Flame Sorceress' killing magicks infecting the shoulder wound.

'But it's full of water, flooded,' Keja protested. 'When I explored there earlier, the water was still gushing out, with no sign of stopping.'

'How did it get that way, Keja?'

'Giles,' Keja said in surprise. 'The fever has burned overlong in your head. You know I stopped up the stream on the other side of . . .' A sheepish grin came over Keja's face. 'We need to divert the stream back. Or I will. You're not fit to do any work.'

'We'll have to make it soon, too,' Giles said. 'The cult members from Dimly New and the other temples will be coming on pilgrimages, to get their orders, for many other matters. Some guards outside the caves might have escaped. I don't want to explain to them how their sorceress died.'

'I still think the key is in that throne room,' Petia said. 'It's just a hunch, but we saw several caves that seemed to be her home – unless she had sleeping quarters somewhere else.'

'One step at a time,' Giles said. 'First, we'll get the water out of the cave. Then we'll have a little time to search. But not a lot. I keep thinking of all the cultists in Dimly New. The Flame Sorceress had them all primed for revolution. With her gone, they might take it out on us.'

Keja had done a good job on the dam. Only a small trickle escaped downstream; nearly all the water had been diverted through the cave's smoke vents.

'I'll bet the farmers downstream are wondering what happened to their water supply,' Giles said.

'They'll be up here investigating, too,' said Keja. 'I'd better get at it.'

'We'll just roll a couple of those stones out of the way,' Giles went on. 'The force of the water should help push the others.'

The first stones came loose with difficulty. Keja struggled, pulling loose the branches and throwing them aside. Straddling the upstream row of rocks, he used his foot to shove more stones free. The water sucked greedily at the underpinning of the other rocks. Soon the force of the water assisted Keja in moving the debris to the original side of the stream bed.

'That's fine,' Giles said. 'There's so little that it won't matter. We'll just have to wait until the cave empties now. It will probably take a day or so.'

The dank cave smelled like the inside of an oft-worn boot. Water seeped from cracks and crevices and ran in rivulets along the cave floor, and everywhere they found rotting flotsam. Petia wrinkled her nose disdainfully.

'It smells awful. I don't remember these odours from before.'

'The water has released minerals from the stone. It will smell like this for months,' Giles said. 'The torch doesn't help, either.' The guttering torch spat forth sparks as Giles held it high over his head. The strain tugged at his wound, but the others needed their hands free for the search. His strength had still not returned fully, and lowly torchbearer best fitted his abilities for the moment.

They sloshed through pools of water, stepped over bodies and saw dozens of burned spots on the walls – the only remnants of the flambeaux.

They pressed onward to the great hall. Giles' torch cast a wan light that disappeared halfway down the hall. Along the walls the torches, now only soggy wicks, dripped waxy puddles on the floor. Black streaks, a mixture of ash and oil, ran down the walls.

An eerie feeling held the trio in thrall. Unconscious of their action, they pressed closer and proceeded down the hall, walking in almost reverent silence. The black onyx throne had floated free, only to be dumped unceremoniously upside down in the centre of the room. The back had been broken. The beautiful flame carving was gouged and a large crack ran from top to bottom.

'Fitting,' Giles remarked in a whisper.

They stepped around it and went on. The dais was covered with grime. A thin layer of slimy mud lay across the flooring, mixed with leaves and twigs left behind by the receding water. To one side they noticed a curtain hanging limp and soggy. Petia looked behind it.

'Her sleeping quarters. A bed, nothing much else,' she reported. 'What sort of personal life did she lead?'

'She certainly missed a woman's greatest thrill — me,' said Keja. Both Giles and Petia ignored him. They searched for another hour, growing increasingly dispirited.

'Is this the brazier you mentioned?' Keja pointed to the large brass urn, tipped on its side and barely visible, buried under a veritable mountain of mud and separated from the carved wooden tripod which had once held it. 'The stand must have floated away somewhere.'

Petia walked carefully across the platform, the footing slippery. She studied the overturned bowl. The curvature of the interior still trapped some water. She reached down and tipped the water out.

Frowning, she picked up the large bowl. The sound of metal on metal echoed through the stillness.

'What have you found?' asked Giles. He brought the torch closer.

'I don't know.' Again, Petia rattled the bowl. It appeared empty but the metal on metal sound was distinctive. Holding it up, she saw fine lines at the bottom of the bowl. Cat claws slipped from protective sheaths and pried upon the false bottom.

Lying in a tiny puddle of muddy water gleamed a golden key.

'The key!' she cried. It slid down the curve of the bowl and fell onto the dais. Petia stooped and picked it up. She held it up to the light. Giles and Keja looked at the object of their quest in awed silence. All the death and destruction had netted them only this slender gold key. Giles let a moment's giddiness pass. The key hardly seemed worth the effort.

'Why didn't it melt?' Petia asked. 'It was in the bottom of the brazier. The coals would have melted it!'

'Perhaps not,' said Keja. 'One lord I, uh, came into contact with in a professional pursuit, hid valuables in a similar fashion. Did the brazier burn wood or oil?'

'I thought wood,' said Petia.

'Oil,' Giles insisted. 'The coloured flame came from different oils floating on the surface of coal oil.'

'That's it, then,' said Keja, crossing his arms and looking insufferably smug.

'What is?' Petia demanded, angry.

'The Flame Sorceress placed water in the bottom, then floated the lighter oil on top of it. The combustion occurred in the air *above* the oil, so that the key never got hot.'

'Why put in water at all, if the flames stayed above the oil?'

Keja looked bemused. Giles cut in, 'The bowl rim heated from the flames. The water insulated the key from the brass walls. What a perfect place to hide the key. Who would think to reach into a flaming bowl? What a devious woman she was!'

'Can we get out of here now?' Petia asked.

Giles laughed. It echoed hollowly around the haunted, darkened audience hall.

'Don't you want to stay in this wondrous place?'

'Don't make fun of me, Giles,' Petia said quietly. 'We've found what we came for. Let's go.'

Giles sighed deeply, and winced as the movement of his body tugged at his wound. 'You're right, Petia. There's no reason to stay here.'

No reason to stay, amid the death and the suffering this religion had brought to Trois Havres, with ghosts flittering up and down the dank corridors. Like so much else in Giles' life, he sought life and found death. They had found the key. But the price . . .

They left the hall and threaded their way out of the caves into the bright sunlight.

Eighteen

'THERE'S NOTHING like a little sunshine to dry us out from our marvellous adventure, eh?' Keja almost skipped along the road leading from the forest back to Dimly New.

'You're acting like a little boy,' Petia said.

'Why shouldn't I be happy?' Keja's grin and the slight duck of his head brought a smile to Petia's mouth. 'Haven't we achieved all we set out to do? We've avoided the few survivors from the cave, haven't we? They are such a dispirited lot now. Don't care a fig for us. We have three of the five keys to the Gate, don't we? Let me revel in it! Rich! We're going to be rich!'

'You're forgetting, Keja,' the Trans said, 'that we still lack two keys.'

'Spoilsport,' Keja grumbled, but his mood wasn't diminished by Petia pointing out their need for two more keys.

'How are you doing, Giles?' she asked, looking over at the grizzled veteran.

'I'll make it.' His shoulder was healing slowly, but it would be some time before it regained full power. The triangular scar that had formed would be a reminder, until he died, of the pain given by the Flame Sorceress' magical spear.

The trio emerged from the forest and walked slowly along the main road. The afternoon sunshine struck them directly now that they no longer walked beneath the shade-giving trees. The distance back to the city melted away beneath their feet, in spite of Giles requiring several rest stops. He pushed harder than necessary, a vague sense of uneasiness nagging at him. It was too nebulous for him to trouble Keja and Petia with, but still it drove him with almost desperate fury.

He wanted to be free of Trois Havres as quickly as possible.

As they came into Dimly New, Giles' disquiet turned to something akin to fear. In front of the Temple of Flame a large crowd had gathered. Their mood was nasty, and Giles thought he knew why.

'Let's not look for trouble,' Giles said. 'We'll stay on the opposite side of the square and pass quietly.'

'Do they know our part in their sorceress' death?' asked Keja. His earlier cheerfulness evaporated like mist in the sun.

'There's no need to stop and hear what they're saying,' Giles said softly. 'But it makes me think more than ever that we should just pack up and move on.'

They edged toward the opposite side of the square. The man on the front steps of the temple was yelling loudly enough for a deaf man to hear.

'I was there,' he shouted. 'I saw it all. The stronghold of the Flame Sorceress is no more. It was flooded. Scores of humans and Trans drowned in the caves. The flambeaux have gone — there are no more sacred flame beings! They were extinguished by the water.'

Someone in the crowd wailed. 'The flame in the temple has gone out.'

'Our beloved sorceress,' the man went on, 'has not been seen in two days.'

The crowd's murmurs denied any possible demise.

'She took two prisoners — they must have had something to do with the destruction I witnessed. I recognised one of the prisoners as a woodcutter we stopped a few days ago.'

The man clenched his fists as he looked out over the crowd. His eyes flashed in anger. Suddenly, he stopped his haranguing and stared across the square.

'That one! There he is now. The one who said he was a woodcutter and was later taken prisoner.' He pointed a finger at Giles. 'What do you say, unbeliever? What did you have to do with the flooding?'

'Nothing,' Giles called back. 'I escaped the flooding.'

'How is it that you escaped and our people did not? What evil aided you? You're responsible for bringing an end to our hopes and dreams! What have you done with our beautiful

Flame Sorceress? She would have led us out of our oppression. Answer that, unbeliever.'

'She was leading you into a new oppression,' Giles shouted back. 'You were duped. Power was all she cared about. She held you in a grasp firmer than you know.'

'Liar! Desecrator of all that is holy! Destroyer of the Flame and the beautiful woman who showed us a way out of our miseries.'

'Miseries be damned,' Giles shouted. 'Go back to work and fulfil your own promise. Work for your own betterment, don't depend on false promises. You were more slaves to her than you are to the city.'

Petia plucked at Giles' sleeve. 'Giles, please. Don't behave like Keja. You can't win a crowd over, not with a trained rabblerouser like that whipping them into a frenzy. It's going to turn ugly, and I'd prefer to be somewhere else.'

Petia was right. The crowd turned and began to edge across the square. Some stopped to pick up loose bits of brick and cobble.

'Come on, Giles,' Keja yelled tugging at the older man's arm.

Keja pulled him off balance as the first bricks began to fall around them. One stone barely missed Giles' head.

'Split up,' Giles ordered. 'You two run for the older part of town. Find an old warehouse to hide in. Petia, take our belongings. I'll meet you with horses outside the walls after dark. On the side that leads to Sanustell.'

'Will you be all right?' the Trans asked.

'Yes! Now run!'

Giles saw Petia take off at a dead run in the opposite direction. He started to dodge, but his weakness betrayed him. He stumbled and fell. To his surprise, a strong arm circled his waist and pulled him upright.

'Keja, I told you to go with Petia!'

'She's too much the cat for me to match. You're more my speed.' Keja's aid helped Giles until he got his balance back and stumbled along, the screaming crowd at their heels.

'This way,' Keja said. He turned the corner and ran toward the old part of town.

173

'Know where you're going?' Giles grunted with exertion. The sparare wound throbbed as if it were freshly inflicted.

'I know this part of the city from my tour of the taverns while you were up in the forest.' Keja ran even faster, forcing Giles to a pace he could barely maintain.

The mob howled behind them. Keja ducked down an alleyway, then turned right when they came out of the other end.

Giles tried to keep up with Keja. His shoulder hurt more and more; his breathing was laboured. 'Got to stop soon,' he gasped out. 'Shoulder hurts.'

'Just a little more,' Keja urged. 'You can make it.'

Giles almost laughed as they stumbled on. Their roles had now reversed from their flight from the water-filled caverns. After another five minutes of running, they no longer heard the crowd following them.

'In here.' Keja stood at an open doorway, motioning for Giles to hurry.

Giles tried to speed up, but his body didn't want to cooperate. He staggered the last few steps.

Keja grabbed him and helped him across the sill of the door. He turned and closed the door just as Giles slumped down. Giles lifted himself up and looked around the interior of the room. Dust everywhere. Bales wrapped in burlap along one wall, untouched for years. Cobwebs in the corners and hanging from the rafters.

'How did you find this place?' Giles whispered.

Keja held a finger to his lips as he put his ear to the door, listening. He motioned to Giles that they were leaving.

Keja shook his head and grimaced. 'You think I was only drinking in taverns when you were gone up in the forests? There was this lass, you see, and . . .'

'Never mind,' Giles said tiredly. Then, 'I don't see any marks in the dust.'

'You think you can make it up those stairs? There's a loft above. It's a place where I can keep watch.' Keja reached down for Giles' arm.

Together, they climbed the stairs. In one corner lay a mattress filled with straw. Above it a shelf held a hairbrush and small bowls of cosmetics.

'I think your lass has been here more than once.'

'No doubt,' Keja said tartly.

He went to the far end of the loft and carefully peered out of the dusty window. 'No sign of any of them. I don't think the crowd can find us in here.'

During the afternoon Giles slept. The wound bothered him more than he liked to admit, but it wasn't his first injury and it might not be his last. As with all the others, it would heal, leaving behind a triangular scar and a twinge when rainy weather threatened.

When Giles awoke, they told each other stories of their lives to pass the time. Giles was fascinated with incidents from Keja's life of roguery and theft. Keja was equally taken with stories of battles and raids during the Trans War.

When the moonlight slanted silver beams across the loft, Giles said, 'Time to be on our way. I had hoped it might be cloudy tonight. It looks too bright out for my taste.'

'We'll be careful,' Keja replied. 'I can get us to where we shouldn't see many people.' He went to the front window to take one last look at the street. 'There are city guards roaming around down there. Should we wait them out?'

'I think we ought to be moving,' Giles said. 'I'd intended to get the horses by now. And I'm getting a little anxious about Petia.'

'You said yourself that she could take care of herself.'

'Yes, I know. Still.'

'We can go down into the alley by rope,' said Keja. 'What about your shoulder?'

'Let's look.'

The pulleys and rope swung in place, a gentle night breeze teasing them.

'Can you lower me first?' Giles asked.

Keja grabbed the rope and snubbed it around his wrist. Giles grasped the rope with his right hand, then wrapped his ankle around it. Keja lowered him gently to the ground.

Giles ran the rope around his back and leaned into it, again using his right hand to grasp it. Keja descended a bit more quickly, but landed safely. He took the lead and soon they left the alley.

'If we go by way of the waterfront, we'll probably have an easier time of it,' Keja said.

For the most part, they were disturbed only by barking dogs along the route. The moon lit their way. In one section of narrow streets, where the moonlight failed to penetrate, they crept from window to window. The lamps inside cast a dim light, but it was enough to see by.

They passed through the harbour area without incident. Giles wished that they could have simply taken ship from here; there was no chance of that now, since Petia was still waiting for them outside the city walls.

Keja began to curve inland again. Giles worried about how he would be able to get over the wall. They had agreed not to try the city gates, which closed at nightfall. Guards asked too many questions, and the last thing they needed was to be confronted by one who had become a convert to the Flame.

Keja began unwrapping a rope from around his waist.

'Where did you get that?' Giles asked.

'In the market, while you were asleep.' Keja reached into his pouch and pulled out an iron hook sporting three nasty prongs. As they walked along, Keja bent to the task of fastening hook and rope. When he had finished, he showed it to Giles. 'Thieves' knot,' he said proudly. 'Very handy.'

Keja turned toward the wall. They came out of a dark street running perpendicular to the cracking stone wall. In front of them, Giles saw a long row of hut-like sheds, with fronts that seemed to have no doors.

'The Market of the Poor,' Keja whispered. 'Dealers in junk, cast-off clothes, vegetables and fruit that are thrown away in the big market. I knew you would have trouble getting over the wall, but if we can use the roof of one of those hovels, and if it doesn't cave in, you'll be halfway to the top.'

They crossed the open street and Keja pulled himself up onto the shed roof. He tested its strength, then reached down to assist Giles up. He coiled his rope carefully, stepped back a foot and twirled the hook around his head. A slight clink echoed through the night as the grappling hook sailed over the top of the wall.

Keja pulled cautiously until the hook caught on the outer

edge. Using his weight, he tested it to make sure that it was anchored securely against the stone.

Giles watched in dismay as Keja leaned back into the rope and walked up the wall, more like a fly than a human. Giles peered up and down the dim street. If anyone was watching, he couldn't see them.

The rope dangled loosely. Giles looked at the top of the wall. Keja straddled it and waved down.

'Build a foot loop,' Keja called down. 'I'll haul you up.'

'You can't. I'm too heavy.'

'Don't argue. Just do it.'

Giles fashioned a loop of rope, using knots he had learned long ago. Even that small effort hurt his aching shoulder. He planted one foot carefully into it, then signalled Keja.

The loop tightened over his ankle as Keja began to pull. Giles hoped the rogue knew what he was doing. Unless he knew some trick, he'd never be able to lift Giles.

Giles grunted in surprise when he realised that he was no longer on the roof. He had been tugged a few inches into the air. He put out a hand and steadied himself against the wall. Again an upward tug, another foot gained. Slowly, a few inches at a time, he was being pulled up the wall. He glanced down at the street again. At one end he saw a guard with a lantern turn the corner.

'Keja. A lantern.'

'I see. Just remain still against the wall.'

Giles felt as if he dangled over the edge of the world, certain that he'd be seen. The lantern moved closer. Giles saw the guard more clearly, holding it before him and poking between the huts. Giles held his breath as the sentry passed by without raising his head.

For fully five minutes, Giles hung there. The light from the lantern eventually disappeared. Keja made no move to continue pulling Giles up.

'Are you there, Keja?'

'Just being careful. Ready to get over the top?'

Again the lifting started. Giles tried to estimate how many more feet it was to the top. Giles was surprised. He realised that he was at the top of the wall.

Once Giles had a purchase on the top of the wall, Keja

reached over and grabbed his belt. He hauled on it, and Giles found himself lying on top, gasping for breath.

'No time for that,' Keja told him. 'We've got to hurry now. The guard's going to change soon.'

Getting down the other side was easy. Keja lowered Giles down, using his back and shoulders to take the weight. When Giles reached the bottom, Keja set the hook and walked backward down the wall, using the rope expertly. With a whip of the rope, he loosened the hook and ducked out of the way as it came flying down.

'I think I'll keep one of these with me from now on,' Keja said, wrapping the rope around his waist. 'I wonder where Petia is?'

'You don't suppose she left without us?' Giles said.

'I wouldn't think so. She's only got one key.'

'She might not think it's worth the effort, after all we've been through getting this one.'

'Don't think so, Giles. You're the one who said there is more to her than meets the eye. Unless I misread her, that little cat has enjoyed this more than either of us.'

'You're right. There she is now.' Giles pointed down the road running just outside the wall. 'And she's got horses!'

Petia rode a horse and led two more, their packs neatly tied behind the saddles. She waved to them.

'What took you so long?' she asked, smiling wickedly. The moonlight caught her teeth and turned them into little fangs. 'I've been waiting for over two hours.'

'Wanted one last look at the city,' said Keja. 'So many lovely wenches.' The small thief's eyes sparkled as he added, 'Are you sure this is your home? You hardly seem to fit in with them.'

'Ride,' Giles commanded. 'Ride, both of you!'

Laughing, the trio rode through the moonlight, each with a key to the Gate to Paradise.

Keja broke into a bawdy song in a voice that made the others wince.

> 'Then the mistress of the house
> Said, "My husband is a louse.
> Since the day that we were wed
> He's not taken me to bed.

Won't you come along with me?
I've some things for you to see.''
Then she took me by the hand,
Took me to the starry land.'

At an inn along the city wall, a portly man rose from a table in his soaring tower room. His dark clothes went well with his swarthy visage. He peered down at the letter he had been composing, dropped his quill, and moved restlessly to the window.

The full moon illuminated the entire countryside beyond the city walls. He saw the Ahrome River valley sweeping down to the coast. A road crossed it and continued into the mountains; another road followed the river to join the coast road to Sanustell.

The dark man squinted when he made out three riders coming over a rise in the road. For a moment, he watched them without recognition. Then realisation of the identities of those distant figures came to him.

The dark man called for a servant and gave him rapid instructions. In a few minutes, he threw his pack across the cantle of his saddle and stepped up into the stirrups. His servant was still struggling with his own horse's bridle as the dark man rode off.

The man paused at the crest of the hill. Keja Tchurak's cracked voice raised in song echoed back to him through the still night. The dark man pursed his lips, then emitted a shrill whistle.

From aloft came an answering cry. He held out a gloved left hand and whistled a second time. A black form plummeted downward, landing heavily on the glove. The dark man gentled the hawk as it tensed and relaxed its talons on his leather-covered wrist.

'We'll keep our eyes on those three, won't we, my beauty? They'll have little enough to sing about before we're through. We'll see to that.'

Keja's bawdy song faded as the three adventurers rode on, but the dark man and his hawk followed them easily.

Soon. The dark man's time would come soon.

Book Two

The Skeleton Lord's Key

To Tim, Sean and Shannon –
Scattered but still together

One

'THERE'S NO honour among thieves, and you two are thieves by trade. How else do you expect me to react?'

Giles Grimsmate studied his two companions. They averted their eyes and didn't return his hard look. Keja Tchurak seldom looked Giles in the eye when speaking. The grizzled old veteran had come to expect nothing but subterfuge and excuses from the light-fingered, fair-haired Keja. But from the cat Trans he expected more. Petia Darya lacked Keja's long years of experience at filching anything not securely guarded, but she more than made up for it with her earnest ambition to be like him.

Such a pair they were, Giles reflected. The old man shook his head. How they had ever come together in this mad scheme seemed almost a dream to him – or was it a nightmare? After returning from the Trans War, all he'd wanted to do was find a bit of solace in his old village. That had lasted only a few months. The village had changed; Giles had changed even more. Not for the first time he cursed his craving for action, for just one more grand adventure before dying. Then he cursed Keja and Petia for holding out such hope to him. Hope was for the young, not the old and cynical.

Still, life was not so bad at the moment, Giles decided. The three rode sturdy horses that Petia Darya had acquired in Dimly New. The morning sky was resplendent as the sun glanced off feathery ice clouds and cast down a shower of warmth and promise. Giles couldn't even complain about his arthritic joints since the sun had soaked up moisture from the night's rain. The land sparkled and the day was off to a fine start – except for the argument.

Keja Tchurak looked up, brushed back a lock of hair with a quick, nervous gesture and said, 'Look, Giles. After all we've been through, I fail to see why you don't trust us. Petia nursed you after our escape from the cave. We could have stolen your key then and left you to die in the woods.'

'I've wondered about that,' Giles said. 'But I think you draw a line between taking people's property and people's lives. I'll grant you this, you've done your share in keeping me alive and getting us out of Dimly New, but now that I've healed, I think my key is fair game again.' Giles noted that Keja was trying to look innocent. A hunting eagle had a better chance of convincing a rabbit it wasn't hungry. 'I don't believe you trust each other, either.'

They rode in glum, suspicious silence. The argument had begun immediately after they had escaped from Dimly New. In a short few days, the three had overturned a cult led by the Flame Sorceress, flooded her cavern stronghold, drowning the woman and most of her followers, and found the third key to the Gate of Paradise.

The search for the keys had thrown them together, and the possession of the keys now threatened their tenuous alliance.

'Look,' said Giles. 'If we're going on with this crackbrained quest, we'd better make a decision right now. Three keys won't get us any closer to opening the Gate of Paradise than one did. And I don't think we should keep the keys with us. We could lose one or more of them, or have them stolen. Who knows what might happen? They'd be a lot safer left here.'

'How do we know that?' Petia threw a dark glance at Giles. Her cat nature had come to the forefront, and her eyes slitted like a feline's while she made unconscious preening gestures over nonexistent whiskers.

'Don't you know anything about mercantile houses?'

The Trans indicated that she didn't.

'They act as clearing houses for the business of many countries. They are the banks for commercial accounts. And they are safer than any other place I know to leave valuable property. They have an excellent reputation that they work hard to keep. If you two don't want to leave your keys safely in Sanustell, I'll say goodbye now and be on my way. I don't think I'd want to go on. Or you can make me an offer for my key.'

Both Petia and Keja turned in their saddles and stared at Giles in astonishment. 'You don't mean that, do you?'

'I do. I don't feel like waking up one day to find myself abandoned and my key missing. Either we put the keys in safekeeping, or I'm off.'

Silence descended again like a heavy, cloaking fog. Giles had made his final statement. He was tired to the centre of his soul. His shoulder still ached from the flaming arrow the sorceress had flung at him, and he didn't care whether he continued or not. Foolhardy quests were not his style when the lovely city of Sanustell offered so many immediate comforts for an old warrior.

Sunlight played on the high walls of Sanustell. Morning traffic streamed through the gates. Patiently the three joined the line and passed into the city, receiving only a slight nod from the guard.

'Where are we going to stay?' asked Petia.

'I don't care where you stay,' Giles answered. He had received no answer from Keja or Petia and presumed that they were finished with him. 'I'm going to find an inn, have a bath and a good meal, and spend the evening drinking, in the hope that I'll sleep well.'

'What do you mean, you don't care where we stay?' Keja asked, aggrieved.

'Just that. You obviously don't want to give up the keys, so I'm finished with it. You're on your own. It's been a pleasure knowing you.'

'Wait, Giles! You can't go off like this.'

Giles had already turned his horse toward an alley that led to the quarter of the city where the inns were clustered. He waved tiredly, without looking back.

Petia and Keja stared at each other. 'What do you think?' Petia asked.

Keja shrugged. 'I think we need him, though it galls me to say it. It's even worse admitting that we'd better give in.'

They trotted after the receding figure.

The stately room radiated warmth from the rich tones of ironbeam wood. Candles cast their glow along the panelling, and a polished table of the same wood dominated the middle of the room. Silver candelabra held candles of pure beeswax to illuminate the business transactions made here.

A door at one end of the room opened and a man made his grand entrance, befitting to a member of the mercantile elite. He was slender, and though his clothes were cut stylishly, they were of a sombre grey. He paused for a moment, examining his would-be clients. 'Welcome to Callant Hanse,' he said, as though coming to a conclusion of vast importance. He strode down the length of the room to take his place at the head of the table.

'I am Simon Callant. What may I do for you?'

Giles sat back in his chair and waited for the others to answer for him. He was so tired. When no one responded, he roused himself and looked at Petia and Keja.

'You tell him, Giles,' Keja said. Petia nodded.

Giles sighed. Why couldn't someone else take the lead just for once? Too worn out to waste time, Giles spoke up. 'We have three keys to the Gate of Paradise which we wish to leave in your safekeeping.'

'I see,' Callant said with a slightly raised eyebrow. 'Could I examine them?'

The three reached inside their tunics and each pulled forth a string. From each cord dangled a golden key.

Giles handed his over to Callant. He watched as the man looked at it, and was amused to see the banker's eyebrows arch higher with each passing second.

'Amazing,' whispered Callant. 'Is this truly the key to the Gate of Paradise? I've heard the legend, of course, but never dreamed there was any truth in it.'

'*A* key to the Gate of Paradise,' Giles corrected him. 'That key opens only one lock. There are five on the Gate. And this is one legend with more than a hint of truth to it. We know that already.'

'You want Callant Hanse to safeguard the keys?'

'Yes. We have two more keys to collect and we . . .' He glanced at Keja and Petia, 'I thought it would be best if we left them in your hands. We don't want to risk losing what we have gained.'

'No doubt.' Simon Callant rose and shook a bell pull. A

servant silently entered with wine and cheese. 'Please help yourselves.'

Keja didn't need a second invitation, not having eaten since the night before. Petia poured out small glasses of a rich, red wine. Giles declined the food but took the wine, sipping it in appreciation. Callant Hanse did not serve the swill he usually got at inns.

'Would you tell me how you came by these keys?' Callant asked.

'I think not,' said Giles. 'I thought it was a policy of your hanse not to ask questions.'

'My apologies,' he said. 'It's just that I am so fascinated by your discovery that I have allowed my curiosity to best me.' Giles wondered at that. Simon Callant did not appear to be a man who ever let emotion rule him. 'The keys to the Gate of Paradise. Imagine that. But you are absolutely right. We do not ask questions. There is one thing I must know, however, before we can agree to this commission. You say that you search for the final two keys to the Gate. What is Callant Hanse to do with the keys if you do not return for them? I presume there is a certain amount of danger in such a venture.'

'No need to worry about that,' Keja said, his mouth full of thin wheat flatbread. 'We will return.'

'And if you don't?' Callant persisted. 'The hanse must know your wishes if these keys are not claimed.'

'All three of us must claim the keys — or none gets them,' Giles said. 'Is there something we should sign?' Both Petia and Keja started to protest, but the cold look Giles shot them kept them silent.

Callant saw that the ex-soldier did not want to waste any more time. He summoned the scribe. In seconds, the man was seated with his pen poised, ready to write.

The form was simple and quickly done. All three signed. When Callant had affixed his signature as officer of the hanse, he held out his hand for the keys.

Reluctantly, Keja and Petia passed them over.

'Remember,' Callant said. 'All three of you must be present when you collect the keys.'

'You're certain they will be safe here?' Keja asked, still not sure of what he'd just done.

'We have never had anything stolen or missing from valuables left in our care,' Simon Callant replied haughtily. 'They will be locked in a strongbox in a room which is guarded at all times. You have nothing to fear.'

Wearily, Giles rose from the table and motioned the others to the door. 'We thank you for your assistance. I am sure we will all sleep the better knowing that the keys are safe.'

'Would it be possible to see where . . .' Keja cut short his question when he saw the look in Giles' eye. 'No, I suppose not.' He turned back to the door.

'I thought you hated water,' Keja said. 'You've been extolling the luxuries of that hot bath for the last half hour.'

'There's a difference between icy cold mountain water coming up around your neck and threatening to drown you and hot, steamy, bath water you sink down to your neck in and inhale the fine, subtle fragrance of beldon leaves.' Petia sipped from her glass of light wine, swallowed and smiled wickedly at Keja.

'If I recall rightly,' she added, 'wasn't it you who was perched on top of a rocky outcrop like a gargoyle? You don't swim at all, so you must hate water as much as I do. Don't tell me you didn't enjoy a hot bath, too?'

Keja laughed. 'You're right. Cold water from a mountain stream; there's nothing better to drink. And a hot bath, yes. But I was terrified in the cave,' he said in a low voice. 'Thank the gods for Giles.'

'That's not what you were saying a few hours ago.'

Petia and Keja looked up at the sound of Giles' voice. Keja pulled a chair up to the table, gesturing to it.

Giles sat and called over a serving maid. His hair was still dripping from his bath. He wiped perspiration from his forehead. 'Maybe that bath will sweat some of the poisons out of this old body. We used to do that when I was soldiering. A kind of sweat bath that the men from the north country said was common to their people.'

The maid brought a goblet filled with the golden wine.

'What next, Giles?' Keja made small, wet circles on the table with the base of his goblet.

Giles shook his head. 'I don't want to think about it. Let's not even talk about it. We'll enjoy our dinner and then while away the evening with drink and good talk. Talk about anything but those thrice-damned keys. All right?'

'I just thought . . .'

Petia laid a finger on Keja's wrist. She shook her head and mouthed 'no' at him.

All three fell silent, wrapped in their own thoughts. Perhaps Giles did not want to talk about the keys, but this was what occupied their minds. Finally, Giles stirred. He tipped his empty goblet, and Petia filled it again for him.

'Have you found out what there is for dinner?' Giles asked.

'Too busy drinking,' Keja said.

'Well, let's dine, shall we? I'm starved. And I don't care what they charge. I'm eating 'til I've doubled my waistline!'

The meal was sumptuous. The first course was a thick stew of crab, mussels, a local white bottom fish and potatoes, served with loaves of brown bread direct from the oven. Thick slabs of meat followed, cut from a roast hindquarter of delaine ox which had been turning on a spit since morning. A bread pudding laced with dried hurryberries and spiced delicately with casticon finished off the meal.

Giles ate everything before him, and asked for a second helping of the dessert, with a double portion of thick cream poured over it.

Conversation ceased during the meal. When the dishes were cleared, Giles asked for brandy. He filled his pipe and lit it, puffing silently, nearly hidden by the wreaths of pungent blue smoke around his head.

Keja and Petia made small talk and left Giles to his own thoughts. Petia watched the other people in the room, interested in the patrons attracted by this inn. She watched a dark man dressed in black take a seat at the table behind Keja and Giles. He turned his head to eavesdrop every time she or Keja said anything. She had never seen him before, but the Trans dismissed him out of hand. City people always enjoyed spying on their neighbours.

The brandy finally loosened Giles' tongue. He talked about his life, his war years, the family he had lost. Petia sensed somehow that he needed to get it all out. She prodded him when he slowed, poured more brandy when he emptied his glass.

Three pipes and six glasses later, Giles had told his story and was nodding off. 'We'd better get him up to bed,' Petia said.

Keja managed to get Giles on his feet.

'Careful with his shoulder,' Petia cautioned.

They made it up the stairs without falling over the bannister and got him onto the bed. 'That's all he gets,' Petia said. She felt none too steady herself. They threw a blanket over Giles and left.

'Petia?' Keja said softly. 'The nights have been long – and lonely. Would you share my bed tonight?' The small thief's eyes gleamed with an inner light that was more feral than human.

For all they meant to one another as comrades in arms, Petia wanted nothing to do with Keja as a lover. Better Giles.

She swallowed and rubbed one hand across her forehead. Too much brandy, she decided, to even think of such a thing. She was Trans; Giles was human. There were laws. And he was more like a father to her. Yes, a father.

'You remember what I said to you last time you asked that? The answer hasn't changed. You sleep alone tonight. There may come a day, but don't whistle until it happens, or you'll wear out your lips puckering.'

Petia turned, lost her balance and put her head on the wall to catch herself. Then she straightened and staggered down the hall to her room.

Keja looked after her dolefully. 'Good night, cat lady,' he whispered with more feeling than was his wont.

The night was colder than Petia had anticipated. She pulled her cloak more closely about her shoulders and tried to balance on the gable. Her foot slipped and she barely caught herself.

She looked out across the city, trying to find a route over the rooftops. She could not see an obvious one. She sighed and decided that she would be better off on the ground. Finally in the street, she backed away from the building, memorising it so that she would recognise it when she returned.

Petia closed her eyes and let the part of her that was cat take over, then made her way across the eastern quarter of the city until she reached Callant Hanse. She crouched quietly in the deep shadows, watching the square and the building for any sign of activity. There was none.

She edged around the square until she stood beneath the elegant gold-chased sign that read simply, 'Callant Hanse'. She saw no easy access to its roof. A balcony extended out at the third level, but otherwise the building displayed a bluntly plain front.

Petia changed tactics and scouted the back of the building. From there she could see light inside the building. The guard, of course, wouldn't stand watch in the dark. She purred without even realising it.

She crept over to the adjoining building and swung up onto a loading dock. From there she gripped a window sill and pulled herself up to the lip which protruded only inches out from a double door. A projecting beam for pulleys was the last step up to the roof.

She crossed swiftly to the hanse and made her way to the front. She stepped down easily to the balcony. Once there, she hunched over, quietly catching her breath.

Petia faced a double door. She slid the blade of her knife into the slight space where the two halves joined. She lifted it upward. The knife encountered metal. Petia exerted her strength and felt the metal bar give. Carefully, she lifted it only far enough to get it out of its catch. She did not want it to swing free and clatter. With her clawlike fingernails, she pulled one door.

The guard standing just inside had his three-pronged spear at her throat in an instant. His comrade reached for her hands and clamped metal bracelets on them. A length of chain swung between.

Petia sobered at the ease with which they'd captured her. She should have known better than to try a burglary after drinking so much. Giles and Keja would be furious, and she could imagine the disapproving look on Simon Callant's arrogant face.

The guards dragged her down a hallway and threw her into a windowless room. She fell onto the wooden floor as the doors closed behind her. The key turned with grim finality in the lock.

The grey envelope was embossed with the coat-of-arms of Callant Hanse. The note inside carried Simon Callant's seal. 'At your earliest convenience,' it read, 'Callant Hanse requests the presence of Giles Grimsmate and Keja Tchurak.'

'Should I wake Petia?' Keja asked.

'Let her sleep. Callant didn't ask for her, though I don't know why not. Shall we be on our way?'

Keja quaffed the last of his breakfast ale, stuck a hard-boiled egg in his pocket and followed Giles out of the door.

'I can't imagine what they want with us so early in the morning. I thought we had taken care of everything yesterday.'

Giles snorted. 'Probably some small detail, although Simon Callant didn't seem like a man to forget details, nor to admit it if he had.'

The streets sparkled with early morning dew, but the day promised much. The sun slanted into dusty corners of the marketplace, and the metal workers' quarter was already cloudy with smoke from their forges.

A servant awaited them at the door of Callant Hanse and ushered them to the room where they had met the previous day.

Simon Callant sat uneasily at the end of the table. Petia Darya stood between two guards to his side.

'What's this?' Giles cried angrily. His hand flashed to his sword.

Simon gestured for the Trans woman to explain.

Petia hung her head. 'I'm sorry, Giles. I've become rusty.'

'You tried to steal the keys?' Giles stood in open-mouthed surprise at this turn of events. His hand dropped away from his sword hilt.

Keja shook his head in dismay. 'After what we've been through, you tried to grab all three keys? Giles is right. We can't trust each other.' He slumped into a chair.

'You deserve a good whipping.'

Simon Callant broke in. 'She deserved much more than that. If I turn her over to the city guard for attempted theft, she will be

192

indentured for ten years. I nearly sent for the guard, but thought that I should inform you first.'

Giles looked at Callant. 'Are you saying it's up to us? We decide what happens to Petia?'

'Let me explain our position,' Simon sipped from a cup of tea. 'The Callant Hanse has a reputation to maintain. We are a trustworthy commercial concern of high standing. We would not like it known that a theft was even attempted here. We can send for the city guard and have her taken away, or we can turn her over to you and you may do with her as you like.'

'Why should we want her?' Keja muttered.

'Yes, a good question, Keja.' Giles looked at Callant for permission to help himself to the tea. He poured one for himself and one for Keja. 'We have three keys, no thanks to Petia. We don't need a woman whom we can't even trust accompanying us. We'd be well rid of her. With all due respect, Callant, she is in your hands now. Your house is responsible. We might do well to leave her with you. The theft was attempted against you, not us.'

'That's so. However,' said Callant, 'the agreement signed yesterday cannot be abrogated or abridged. If she is indentured, the keys must remain in the possession of Callant Hanse until all three of you can sign for them.'

'There are some aspects to this woman's character which are attractive, however,' Giles continued, seeing the difficulty pointed out by Callant. 'We might consider them.'

'The keys, lost,' grumbled Keja. 'Knew this was a bad idea.'

Simon Callant sat back and listened to Giles and Keja debate Petia's fate, enjoying the Trans woman's embarrassment. He knew nothing of the strange relationship between the three. He couldn't tell if the two men were being serious or not, but if they arrived at a conclusion which would take her off his hands, he would be pleased. If not, he would have to proceed with formal charges.

'Perhaps we could allow her to work herself back into our good graces,' Giles said.

Keja rubbed his hand across his face. 'That's a possibility. There are some things she could do for us. At least, I can think of one.'

Petia grew more, embarrassed – and angrier – with each passing moment.

Giles put down his cup and looked at Petia. 'What do you have to say for yourself?'

'I say damn the both of you. If you don't care about me any more than that, I'll take indentures.'

'You would. Callant, we will take Petia. We have our reasons, which we need not share with you. If your guards would unlock her bracelets, please.'

As they left the room, Petia murmured, 'I'll get even with you two for making me endure that.'

Giles only shook his head, but Keja laughed loudly. Their lot had been cast. The keys – and each other – meant more to them than any cared to admit.

Two

'I DON'T know what we can do now,' Giles said. 'We've spent all our money.' He whittled at a piece of wood with his dagger.

'We'll think of something,' said Keja. 'Something always blows our way, doesn't it, Petia?'

Petia sat in the corner. She hadn't said a word since leaving Callant Hanse. The two men had embarrassed her. Chastened, she seethed. As much as the Trans hated to admit it, they had been right; she was even angrier at herself for turning a burglary into a blunder.

She sat with her back against the wall, knees drawn up and clasped in her arms, head down.

Giles saw that she was feeling sorry for herself. He had no sympathy for such petulance. It had been stupid trying to rob a well-guarded mercantile house.

'It's like the morning after the battle in here,' Keja commented. 'Why don't we go to the marketplace?'

'Leave me alone.'

'Come on, stop your sulking, Petia.' He flung her cloak over her head, forcing her to come up for air. He grabbed Giles' jacket and his own and opened the door. 'Let's go, you two. Fresh air and fresh outlooks are what you both need.' He herded them out of the inn.

The marketplace sparkled in the sunshine. Vendors displayed their goods under brightly striped awnings that shaded them from the sun and sheltered them from the rain that often swept in from the Evester Sea.

'I'm going to wander around,' said Keja, 'and see if any opportunities arise.' He flexed his fingers to show what he meant. 'You have anything special you need me for, Giles?'

'No. We'll see you back at the inn.'

'Yes, later.' Keja waved and walked off into the crowd.

'I don't know the markets of Trois Havres,' said Giles. 'Is there likely to be a mapmaker or a dealer in maps?'

'There should be,' Petia said listlessly. 'Probably someone who doesn't deal exclusively in maps. Books and paper and such.' She looked around and finally asked a fruit seller. With much arm waving, the merchant directed them to the far end of the marketplace.

They found a man sitting on a low stool, hands folded on his ample stomach, complacently watching the market-goers. Behind him were spread parchments, maps, illustrations, bound books, paper, pens and ink.

'Good day to you, sir and madam. What can I interest you in?'

Giles nodded. 'A map of Bandanarra, if you have one.'

'Ah, Bandanarra, is it now? An inhospitable continent, with an abominably hot climate, peopled by the uncivilised and unenlightened. A truly dreadful place.' He sighed and got to his feet.

'You've been there?' Giles asked. He could not let the opportunity pass if there was information to be obtained.

Petia raised her eyebrows. 'Bandanarra? The continent far to the south? Do you know something you have not told us, Giles?'

195

'Later,' Giles replied. If he feared Keja and Petia stealing his key, he also feared them appropriating his information before he wanted to reveal it. He turned to the seller. 'Have you been there?'

'Ah, no.' The huge man heaved a sigh. 'In all my life I have gone no further than half a league from Sanustell. But I have read of the world, and of Bandanarra, and twice I have talked with sailors who have sailed along the coast. They tell awesome tales.'

Giles laughed. 'Don't all sailors? But do you have a map?'

The man rummaged through stacks of maps and finally pulled one from the bottom. He handed it to Giles. Brown with age, it showed crease marks from many foldings.

Giles spread it over a heap of dusty books. The coastline was well mapped and showed numerous ports along the ocean, but the interior was blank save for a few scattered – and indecipherable – notations.

Giles looked up at the bookseller. 'There's no detail for the interior. Surely there is more to Bandanarra than a coastline with a few towns scattered along it.'

The merchant shrugged. 'Wastes, deserts, nomadic tribes, perhaps. You wouldn't want to go there. The asshole of the world, I have heard it called. With some justice, by all accounts.'

Giles handed the map back to the seller. 'It's of no use to me. I need a more current map, much more detail.'

As they walked away, Petia asked. 'Do you want me to steal it for you?'

'It's not a very good map. And I don't like you stealing needlessly. I've done it, of course, when I was forced to. For food, wine sometimes, but I'm never comfortable with it. I grew sick of the looting and theft during the War. The key I won was probably looted.' He laughed. 'I suppose I do have a conscience, after all. It's a warped one, but it's there just the same.'

'What do you mean, "warped"?' Petia asked.

'It doesn't bother me unduly that you and Keja are thieves. I can't say I was happy that you tried to burgle the keys, but otherwise I'm not bothered when you steal. Don't ask me why. I won't steal unless I have to, or unless it suits my purpose, but

I'll let you. By the way, I need some paper, pen and ink. Your skills need sharpening, if last night was any indication.'

'Oh, Giles, I was just a bit drunk. I should never have attempted it. It was stupid. I'm not even sure why I thought of doing it.'

'It's over. I'm going back to the inn. My shoulder is bothering me. You stay and enjoy yourself. Don't forget the paper and pen.' He waved and walked off in the direction of their inn. Petia licked her lips. This was more like it! She went off whistling a lilting tune, eyes sharp on possible booths laden with too many pens and parchment that would not be missed.

Keja Tchurak found the stall of a swordmaker. He nodded his greetings and bent to inspect the weapons. They looked different to the potmetal blades he wouldn't even deign to steal that were so prevalent in Sanustell. The workmanship of these weapons was nothing less than superb. Picturesque scenes had been engraved on the blades and hilts, turning them into works of art.

'May I examine these?' he asked. Giles still owed him a new sword and dagger after losing his in the cavern of the Flame Sorceress. Of course, he had also mentioned this morning that they were paupers again.

'There is a space at the back where you can swing it without taking anyone's head off.'

Keja found that the swords had a different heft and feel from those he was accustomed to. He tried several swords, but none felt like his old sword. He balanced them across his forefinger and discovered a balance point greatly shifted toward the tip.

He stretched, then shook his arms and hands before picking up one particular sword. Given time, he was certain it would feel comfortable. He set them back in their case. 'Beautiful workmanship,' he told the swordmaker. 'Where did you learn your skill?'

The bearded face turned up to Keja. 'Not here, sir. The local swords here are pieces of shit. No balance, no edge, no spine to them. There are several swordmakers on Bericlere who make an adequate weapon. I learned my art on Nerulta, sir. Not a craft, no. An art, sir. My weapons are an extension of my life, the steel quenched in my very own life's blood. These people in Trois Havres don't know a good sword when they see one.'

'They don't feel the same as mine.'

'You are from?'

'From Bericlere,' Keja replied.

'No, they would not. Bericlere swords have soft edges which nick easily. And they balance further back, so that more effort is needed to wield them. Yes, these may seem strange to you, but in a short while you would not regret having purchased one.'

Keja shrugged and lifted his palms. 'No money.'

'I knew that,' the old man said. 'You will get the money if you want one of my swords. A small warning, though. Do not attempt to steal one. A stolen sword will turn on the thief — always. A sword must be purchased or received as a gift. Never steal a sword, thief.'

'How do you know?'

'I know many things besides the art of making swords. I keep these things to myself, and when I am not busy, I ruminate on them. You are young. I think you will not always be a thief. But for now, remember, do not steal one of my swords. Come back with money, and we will deal.'

Keja grinned.

'I am serious, my friend.'

'I know you are. Forgive my nature. I will remember, you need not worry.' Keja nodded to the man and turned from beneath the awning.

He walked directly into a woman. She lost her balance and would have fallen if he had not caught her by the arm. When she was standing again, Keja took off his cap and bowed to her.

An older woman stepped forward. 'What do you mean by assaulting my lady?' she demanded in a strident voice.

Ah, a chaperone, Keja thought. He bowed to her. 'My deepest pardons, madam. Please forgive me. It was entirely my fault. I turned and should have paid more attention to where I was going. Are you hurt, madame?'

While the chaperone blustered and fumbled, complaining about rude young men, Keja turned to the young woman and looked into the deepest brown eyes he had ever beheld.

She held her hand over her bosom and dainty red spots

appeared on her cheeks. Her breath quickened and the pink tip of her tongue made a slow circuit of her lips. 'You startled me, sir. I thank you for catching me before I fell.'

'My apologies,' Keja said. 'Had I not been so clumsy. But . . .' He looked around the marketplace. 'I'm sorry, I am unfamiliar with your marketplace, being a traveller from Bericlere. Would you accept tea or some other refreshment? I have always found tea to speed recovery remarkably.'

'That won't be necessary,' the chaperone cut in. 'We have many things to attend to.'

'Oh, but we have all afternoon,' the young lady interposed. 'Here is my chance to learn about another continent. You are always saying that my geography is bad.' Her brown eyes darted to Keja, who smiled even more broadly. He'd be willing to share lessons in geography with this lovely lady any day.

'But we do not know this young man,' the older woman said.

'We know his manners. Did you not tell me that one could perceive the difference between a knave and a gentleman by his manners?'

The chaperone mumbled something to herself, but the younger lady had already turned to Keja. 'I am Lady Vaiso. My father owns a small estate on the edge of the town. We are rather minor nobles in Trois Havres, I fear, and are not financially well enough off to travel extensively. And you, sir?'

'Thuse Mabein,' came the facile lie. 'I hail from the seaport of Klepht on the south coast of Bericlere.' Keja bowed again. 'And now, shall we find that tea?'

The Lady Vaiso took Keja's arm and pointed across the square. They walked away, the chaperone in tow and muttering about impropriety. The swordmaker watched with a smile on his face. Soon, very soon, Keja would return with the price of a fine sword.

Petia found Giles resting on his bed. She sat her shawl on the table and flipped open the edges.

Giles sat up and watched. 'You weren't wearing a shawl, were you?'

'How observant, sir,' Petia replied. 'You sent me on a small quest, but it expanded. By the way, I don't think we should expect Keja back this evening. When I last saw him, he was walking arm in arm with an attractive young lady, being followed by a chaperone.'

'Ho-ho. Chaperones are worse than mythological beasts. And their tongues are sharper.' Giles rose and came to the table. 'What have you brought?'

Petia spread the shawl. She placed paper, pen and ink in front of Giles. She fetched a plate from a cupboard and arranged stolen fruit, pastries and cheese on it. 'Just a little something to dull the appetite,' she said. She swirled the shawl around her head and settled it over her shoulders. 'Pretty?'

'Very,' Giles said, shaking his head. 'I beg your pardon, you have not lost all your skills.'

He took a bite of cheese, wiped his hand on his trousers, and picked up the pen to examine it. 'Good quality paper.'

'Only the best for you. A small token of my appreciation for not sending me off to indentures. I am truly sorry, Giles. Brandy can get me into trouble.'

'Indeed.' Giles opened the bottle of ink and dipped the pen into it. With careful strokes and great concentration, he began to draw. Petia stood behind him, watching over his shoulder.

'Why, it's the map of Bandanarra,' she said.

'At least the coastline. This is a skill I learned during the War. No need to buy or steal the map. Just a good memory and a steady hand. That map was not useful, anyway. This will do until we find something better.'

'Why Bandanarra?'

'That's where the next key is.'

'You never said you knew.'

'No, I'm not sure that I did know when we first met. I've had some time to think. It goes back to the notation in the holy book I found in the Glanport temple. I just didn't understand what I saw at the time.'

'Why didn't you tell us?'

'I wanted to see how well we got along, how well the search for the first key went. I'm cautious by nature, Petia.'

Keja did not return to the inn for the evening meal. After his second after-dinner pipe, Giles asked of Petia, 'Care for a walk along the waterfront? It's time to look for passage.'

'Wait until I fetch my knife. It can get rough in waterfront inns.'

The harbour was quiet. Light from the dockside buildings reflected in broken shards across the flat water. A few sailors sat on pilings whittling and sharing chanties, or perched along the edge of the wharf, fishing. One old sailor was having great success. A tidy string of four fish stared up sightlessly at Giles.

'Any of these ships leaving for Bandanarra soon?' Giles asked after exchanging small talk with the sailor.

'One, I believe, Cap'n.' The sailor pointed across to a wharf that jutted into the harbour. 'That's the *Raven*. Captain Obidiah. Yer likely to catch him at the Flying Eel.' He pointed in the opposite direction down the docks.

'Thank you, and good luck with your fishing,' Giles said.

'Ain't nothin' like these and eggs for breakfast. G'night, Cap'n, ma'am.'

The Flying Eel was full of boisterous sailors, but Giles sensed that the landlord brooked no rowdiness. Men sat at their ease; they could relax here without worrying about a fight.

'Captain Obidiah?' Giles asked. The landlord pointed to a corner where an older, grizzled man sat with a younger one.

Giles addressed the older man. 'Captain Obidiah?'

The grizzled man grinned, and thumbed at the younger man.

'Your pardon, Captain. A natural mistake, I think you'd agree.'

'Happens all the time. What can I do for you?'

'We understand that the *Raven* may be leaving soon for Bandanarra. We're looking for passage.'

'That's right. Slow passage it will be. Stopping at Bericlere and Nerulta before we proceed on to Bandanarra. Not in a hurry, are you?'

'No. I would guess that there is no swift passage to Bandanarra.'

'You'd guess right. Just the two of you?'

'No, one more besides.' Giles pulled his pipe out and loaded it.

'Sit down and share an ale. I talk better with a wet whistle. I'll bet you do, too. Ma'am, a spot of wine, perhaps?'

201

Giles and Petia drew up chairs and sat opposite Captain Obidiah. The older man was introduced as Raoul, his mate.

'There is one slight problem, Captain,' Giles said. 'We don't have passage money. Might we be able to work our passage? We're not able-bodied seamen, but we are all hard workers, we learn quickly, and we'll give you good measure.'

Obidiah rubbed his hand along his chin. 'I'm not too keen on that,' he said. 'Two men I could probably put to work, but, beggin' your pardon, ma'am, I don't know about takin' a lady. That way lies treacherous shoals, if you catch my drift.'

Petia bristled. 'I've worked ashore in the kitchens of inns. I can peel potatoes, if nothing else. I wouldn't be surprised if I could teach your cook a thing or two. I know rope making, and I'll bet you've got coils that need repairing. I'm not afraid of heights. Send me up in the crow's nest to stand watch. I'm as dependable as any man, and I can hold my own with a weapon.'

'Ho, steady now. I didn't mean to offend.' Obidiah lifted his tankard to Petia.

The conversation turned to Giles. The captain wanted to know his background, and was impressed with what he learned of Giles' war years. He asked about the third man and listened to Giles and Petia describe Keja.

'What do you think, Raoul?'

'We are short-handed, Captain. We had one leave ship last port, and the cook's stump had been bothering him. I know, I know. He's an old mate of yours for years, but with that wooden leg of his, he could do with some help. You don't have much to lose taking them on, Captain. Working passage don't cost you nothing. And if they can't pull their weight, you can pack them off in Bericlere.'

Giles chimed in. 'No more than fair, Captain. If we don't work as well as you think we should, off we go. Anywhere along your route.'

Obidiah nodded and took a pull from his tankard. He wiped the foam from his mouth and nodded again, having made up his mind. 'The *Raven* sails on the turn of the tide tomorrow evening. Be on her.' He held out his hand. It was all the agreement needed.

Keja did not return at all that evening. At mid-morning he entered their room and dumped a handful of jewellery on the wooden table. 'There's our passage,' he said, beaming.

'There's our quick way to get shortened a head, you idiot,' Giles snarled, drawing a finger across his throat. 'If you had come back last night, you'd know that Petia and I arranged to work our passage. What are going to do with this? You won't have time to find a buyer. The young lady, whoever she is, will find her baubles missing, and her father, no doubt a man of considerable power and greater wrath, will have the guard on you in a flash.'

Petia had never heard such exasperation in Giles' voice. Keja's smile faded, and his abject posture proclaimed his misery.

'I'm sorry, Giles. I was only trying to help. And it was so easy! The gems were just begging to be taken!'

'Maybe I can find someone among the Trans to buy them,' Petia said.

'We ought to just leave them, dump them down a sewer.'

'No!' protested Keja. 'I worked hard for those!'

Giles frowned. 'A burglary is one thing, but to steal from the house where you are a guest is asking for a hanging. They've seen their robber, after all. Get your belongings together. The guard will be here soon and it must look as though you've packed up and gone.'

Giles spoke briefly to the thief, then canted his head as the sounds of heavy bootsteps reached his ears. He shoved Keja over to the window. Keja had barely slipped out when a pounding on the door echoed through the room. 'City guard,' a voice growled.

'Come in,' Petia said, hunching over as if her belly troubled her.

'We're looking for Thuse Mabein. We know he's in your party, although the innkeeper does not recognise that name.'

'Nor do we,' Giles said. 'We travelled from Dimly New with a fellow named Keja Tchurak, the one the innkeeper no doubt mentioned. We are awaiting passage to Bericlere.'

'Is this true, lady?' the older of the two guards asked of Petia. He looked at her odd posture and shook his head. She saw the slight drawing forth of the face, the oversized teeth, the round eyes and guessed the guard might also be a Trans. Petia played on this common bond.

'Yes, would you care to see our papers?' She moved as if seriously injured and elicited some small sympathy from the older guard.

The two examined the papers, whispering and nodding behind their hands. 'And the papers of your companion?'

Giles shrugged. 'We are not certain. When we came from the marketplace this morning, his things were gone. He left no note, so we cannot say whether he will return.'

'You don't know where he went?'

'We have no idea,' Petia replied. 'Why do you seek him?'

The older guard scowled. 'A criminal matter.' As he talked, he poked about the room, sharp eyes missing nothing. Obviously not satisfied, the guard said, 'The sooner you're gone from Sanustell, the better off you will be.'

'What?' Giles exclaimed. 'Guilt by association?'

'A warning – your only warning.' The guards left.

Petia crept to the door and listened to the receding footsteps. 'They're gone,' she whispered finally.

'What did you do with the jewellery?' asked Giles.

Petia straightened. She had clutched the pouch to her body; the hunched-over posture had hidden it. Giles let out a low whistle. Such audacity he had seldom seen.

'I told Keja to hide under the wharves. I think you'd better join him while I distract the guardsmen.'

'But the jewels,' protested Petia. 'We can't let them just go to waste.'

Giles saw that Keja and Petia were cut from the same cloth. Their devious minds trod the same illicit paths.

'Do as you please with the gems. Just don't get caught. And be there when the *Raven* sails at dusk.' Petia's answering smile was more animal than human. Giles shook his head. With companions like these, he need never want for diversion.

But just once, how he longed for some peace and quiet!

Petia spotted the city guardsman following her instantly. Although he wasn't in uniform, his stiff manner gave him away.

She ambled about the marketplace, amusing herself for a time by losing the guard, then letting him find her again. All the while, Petia was alert for anyone careless enough to leave their money pouch outside their clothing.

Lifting a pouch from a roly-poly rug merchant was an easy matter. Letting him know it was more difficult. But a second tug on his belt produced the desired result. His yell could be heard from one end of the market to the other.

'It's him, that one over there,' Petia yelled, pointing to the man who had been following her. 'Grab him before he gets away.'

Several other merchants pinned the man to the ground even as he struggled and proclaimed loudly that he was a guardsman. No one believed him. A crowd gathered around, yanked him to his feet and searched him roughly. Petia seized the opportunity and slipped quietly away. The small pouch of gold would serve them well. As for the merchant, if he did not eat so well, his physique might improve.

A Trans beggar sat on one wall, blind eyes staring up whitely. Petia deftly tossed one of the rug merchant's golden coins slightly to the left of the man's container. He grinned. 'Thank you, lady.' He scrabbled in the dust, but his hand knew exactly where the coin had landed.

Petia squatted down in front of him. She watched him hide the coin in the folds of his tattered robe.

'My pardon,' she said. 'I gave you the wrong coin. That was a gold coin. I meant to give only a copper.'

'Oh, no, lady. It was a copper, indeed it was. You see?' The beggar pulled a copper coin from the same place where he had spirited Petia's offering.

'So I see,' Petia answered. 'I see a blind man who has a good trade. A blind man who sees as well as I do. Someone who will give me information. Is that not so?'

The milky eyes did not move, but the lips did. 'The War solved nothing for the likes of us, did it, lady?'

'I seek a customer to buy some jewellery. A Trans perhaps, no questions.'

Two more gold coins exchanged hands, directions were given and Petia left the marketplace. She knew she'd have to be quick about this. The guard would soon find the beggar.

205

Even though he was a Trans, he'd show her no loyalty. The guard would be on her in a shake unless she kept ahead. Petia hastened on, seeing that the guardsman who had been following her had finally convinced the crowd that he had had nothing to do with the theft of the rug merchant's pouch. Petia ducked down a side alley, got her bearings and began the search for the one named by the Trans beggar.

She stopped outside a fortune teller's tent and simply stared. This had to be the place, but it was not as Petia had imagined. The tent flap fluttered in the light noonday breeze, and odours both pleasing and oddly intoxicating came to her sensitive nostrils. Almost as if she were drawn forward, Petia entered the tent.

Dimness caused her cat-eyes no trouble. She saw the old woman sitting behind a table, cards spread in front of her. The old woman made a show of moving one card to the far side of the table. Petia knew she had seen her enter; she sensed that nothing got past this one unseen.

'I seek Martka,' she said in a sibilant whisper.

'Nothing is as it seems in this place,' the old woman said. 'Why does Petia Darya seek Martka of Farplace?' The words boomed forth, frightening Petia.

Petia started to ask how the old woman knew her name, then bit back the question. This was the stock in trade of a fortune teller. And she had to know what brought Petia here.

'My business is private,' she said. This time the words seemed smothered in her mouth. Petia preferred this to the former unexpected loudness.

The old woman moved a final card, then sat back, satisfied. 'No danger is close at hand,' she said. 'I will look at the jewellery taken from the fair Lady Vaiso. Her father will ransom it at a good price.' The old woman held out a wrinkled hand for the merchandise.

Petia silently handed over the pouch containing the jewellery. In the wink of an eye, gold coins dropped onto the table and the jewels had vanished. Petia rubbed her eyes and turned. She stood outside the tent with its odd acoustics and odder odours. Petia swallowed hard when she spun, looked around and glanced back.

The tent with the old woman had totally vanished, as if it had never existed. Only the hard gold of the coins in her hand convinced Petia she had not dreamed it all. As though wings had sprouted on her heels, she hastened back to the inn to tell Giles of her strange encounter.

Three

THE RAVEN coasted along the vast continent of Bericlere, stopping briefly at Neelarna. Giles had to talk Keja out of hunting down the street urchins who had robbed him when the small thief had last occasioned by the city. Only loud argument and the captain assigning – at Giles' insistence – Keja to stand watch while in port forestalled a confrontation with the younglings.

The coast of Nerulta was new territory to all three of the companions. As they sailed south, the weather grew warmer, cloudless skies smiled down, and they left green coastal forests behind to look shoreward at golden hills. In the ports they found the people darker, the food and articles for sale unfamiliar. 'The Gentian Coast,' sighed Petia. 'Here lies real wealth for the plucking.' Giles let her and Keja pine over the lost opportunities in the rich area and contented himself with watching the showy blue flowers that grew wild everywhere.

Further south they left the continent and set course across the Strait of Dunar. At Kasha, the first port of call on Bandanarra, the three bade their farewells to the captain.

'We appreciate you letting us work our way,' Giles said.

'You gave good work for your passage. If you ever need a steady job at sea, you look for me and the *Raven*.'

Giles paid his respects to those who had become friends

aboard ship. He threw his bag over his shoulder and led the others down to the wharf.

'I'll have to learn to walk all over again,' Petia said. 'My knees don't want to work and the ground surges constantly.'

'It'll come back,' Giles said. 'Let's find an inn.'

The room they rented for the night was spare of furniture, but the thick walls brought a surprising coolness to it. They dumped their belongings on the floor and sat on cotton mats that also served as bedding.

'What now, Giles?'

'The same things we always do. For you, the marketplace for information. Just a general lay of the land, keep your ears open, find out what these people are like. Be careful about picking pockets. It's said that these people could give lessons to a master. I'll look through their temples. The holy book I saw in Glanport led us this far. Maybe another here will hand us the key.'

Petia and Keja walked down to the marketplace. If they thought that the ports along the Gentian Coast were unusual, they found Kasha even stranger. The people wore long, loose black garments that looked intolerably hot in the pounding sun. Yet the native population seemed comfortable, while Keja and Petia perspired copiously, even when they stayed in the shaded areas.

The bazaar proved little more than a street lined with shops huddled under tent-like awnings to shelter from the sun. Petia browsed from merchant to merchant, interested in the unique wares displayed. She learned that the heavy clothing really was cool and was advised that they should purchase similar garments if they intended journeying into the desert. Keja, juice running down his chin, motioned for her to sample a fruit sweeter than any he had ever tasted. At a swordmaker's tent, he lingered and cursed his fate that he had not been able to purchase the sword in Sanustell. He regretted passing up such a fine weapon, but vowed that Giles would buy him a new sword. Debts ought to be paid, no matter who owed them.

'Look.' Petia pointed down the street to the end of the bazaar where cubical cages leaned against the outside wall of a building. 'I wonder what those are?'

'Probably some sort of animal. Let's go and see. You learn much when you find out what pets people keep.'

As they neared the end of the street, they heard piteous cries reverberate from the wall.

'Keja, there are people in those cages!'

Keja squinted against the glaring desert sun. 'You're right.' He turned to a nearby merchant and caught him by a flowing sleeve. 'Why are those people in cages?'

The gaunt man turned and looked as if he had never seen the cages before. 'Slaves,' he said. 'Ready to be sold.'

'How awful,' said Petia. She had spent too much of her life as a slave to put this out of her mind. The mere thought of her keeper, Lord Ambrose and his evil son Segrinn, made her cringe involuntarily.

They continued from stall to stall, but Petia would lift her head at the sound of each cry. Keja saw abject pain showing in her face. He reached out and touched her arm to reassure her, but the Trans woman pulled away, hissing and clawing at him.

As they came closer to the end of the market, Petia went over to the cages and the people held prisoner within them. Keja spoke and, hearing no response, turned to see Petia gazing at the cages at the end of the street.

Petia jerked around and pulled at Keja's sleeve. 'There's a Trans in there, I know it. Come on.'

'What can you do about it, Petia? It will only upset you.' Keja looked around nervously. In cities where slaves were used, they tended to put thieves onto the auction block rather than imprisoning them. He had no desire to find out if Kasha followed this practice.

Petia glared at him. 'I've got to see.'

As they neared the cages, an obese man with blubbery lips moved to intercept them. 'A slave for my lady?' he asked obsequiously. He bowed, his chins bouncing, then took a quick swipe at his sweaty forehead with a dingy towel.

'How can you keep these people caged up like animals?' Petia pulled free of Keja's restraining hand and shoved her face up close to the merchant's.

The fat merchant spread his hands. 'It's business, my lady. For sale, all them. Perhaps a nice young boy for you? Or an old woman to sweep and cook? The old one will go cheap due to age, but she has many years left in her, perhaps as many as five.'

'Come on, Petia. You can't even talk to him about it. He doesn't understand.' Keja took her firmly by the elbow to lead her away.

'Wait,' she pointed. 'Look over there.'

Keja followed her finger to a cage stacked four tiers up. A boy was huddled in the back, knees drawn up in a way that reminded Keja of Petia when she sulked. The lean, filthy slave toyed with the end of a rope fastened around his waist. His hair hung in greasy strands, making it difficult to tell his age from a distance. 'By the gods, he's a Trans!' Keja looked at Petia.

Tears streamed down her face. Her voice choked. 'More than that. He's like me, part cat.'

The boy heard the word 'Trans'. He scooted to the front of the cage and squatted, hanging on to the vertical bars. 'Buy me, lady,' he shouted down to Petia.

Petia confronted the slave dealer. 'How much for the Trans boy?' she questioned.

'Auction, my lady. Public auction tomorrow. Come back then. No private sales allowed. Only by bid.'

Petia stood before the cage again. She signalled to the boy and hoped he understood her dilemma. Then she could not look at him any longer. She turned to Keja and whispered hoarsely, 'Take me away from here.'

Keja saw the devastation in her eyes. He said nothing for a long while. Gently he assisted her through the market. He bought a hot, black cup of tiffa, turned tar-thick with sugar. He made her sit in a shaded spot along the wall to drink the potent beverage.

'I must get that boy out of there. I'll buy him if I have to.' The quiet desperation in her voice told Keja that the boy's rescue had become more significant than anything else. Neither the quest for the key nor even her friendship with Giles and Keja were as important.

When they stood, Petia cast a despairing look towards the slave cages.

'We'll be back, Petia. I'll help. So will Giles. He won't let the boy stay here.'

Petia walked along in a daze, her mind turning back to the

Trans boy. Keya worried about her, but kept his eyes open for what Giles had sent them to find. They came to the stall of a dealer in scrolls and maps. For a few moments, Keja turned over the man's maps. He soon realised, however, that he had no idea of what Giles sought. He heaved a sigh of relief when he saw Giles making his way across the crowded street. He waved and attracted Giles' attention, making gestures about the stall. Giles gave a curt nod and came up. His quick eyes scanned the display of maps.

'Your maps are of high quality,' Giles said, fingering one. 'Good parchment.' He frowned and shook his head, 'But what use is good material if the map isn't accurate?'

'Sir!' the vendor protested. 'These charts are the finest in all Bandanarra!'

'They show the caravan ways, perhaps?' Giles gestured to a stack of maps laying on a table.

'It is so. The desert to the south is the Dus 'i Abat, "The Desert of Skeletons." Many people have died in that desert. You are thinking of journeying there? You will not find a better map for such a venture.'

'I am not certain,' Giles said. 'I wish to study such a map before I make any decision.'

'You lead a caravan? There are spices from the cities on the southern edge of the desert. See? The locations are clearly marked on this fine map. Transporting them north can bring immense wealth.'

'Spices hold no appeal,' Giles said.

'Aaah.' The sigh said much and little. 'Perhaps you would share with me?' Giles studied the map seller. He made a quick gesture, silencing Keja's protest about divulging any of their mission. Giles had come to the conclusion this man could help them. He had a look of knowledge about him – and betrayal, also? That, too, but Giles risked it.

'A gold key. It is said that perhaps it is in the desert.' Giles watched for any sign that the man might know what he was talking about. He was surprised at the answer.

First came another long sigh. 'The key to the Gate of Paradise. It would not be wise to search for it. No, not wise,' the map seller mused. 'It is said that it lies hidden in the desert, and over the years many have come to seek it. But there is a

211

religion in Kasha which believes devoutly that it is sacrilege to hunt for the key. It is sacred to their tenets and, it is rumoured, they have slain many of the impetuous who sought such a key.'

He fell silent and straightened a pile of maps already arranged in near-perfect order.

Giles wondered what had brought about this sudden change from affability to silence. A hush settled over all the nearby stalls. Giles turned to look onto the street. Both Keja and Petia had also spotted the cause.

Two tall, lanky, cadaverous men approached. Cloths wrapping their heads came down almost to their eyebrows. Eyes like burning coals stared out, spreading an aura of contempt, as if the people of the bazaar were mere animals and not worthy of notice. Most of those nearby had turned their backs rather than look upon the two. The men walked on with stiff, unnatural strides, their heads turning from side to side, disdaining all that came within their sight, human or material.

Giles watched until they disappeared around a corner. 'Who are they?' he whispered, struck by the unnatural silence lingering in their wake.

'They are not truly human, or so the people think,' the map merchant said, shuddering in spite of the heat. 'They are of the desert. A good reason for not venturing there.'

'You spoke of a key,' Giles reminded him.

'No. No more. If you want to learn about the key, ask Pessein, the scribe. He knows more than I. And he is a foolish man, unafraid to talk. It will bring his death one day. Tell him that Ryilla, the map seller, sent you.'

'Thank you,' Giles said. 'I'll be back for a map.' Giles saw that the man couldn't have cared less and showed only relief at being free of Giles.

'Giles, I . . .' began Petia.

'Later,' Giles interrupted. 'I must find this Pessein. I don't like the looks of those two who went by. They seemed to be searching for . . . something.' He couldn't put his uneasiness into words, but he felt the pressure of time mounting.

'But Giles,' said Keja, 'Petia's got to . . .'

'Later. See you later at the inn.' Giles had no further time to spend dawdling. He hurried off, leaving Petia and Keja in the bazaar. Giles found the scribe with little effort and Pessein welcomed Giles, inviting him to share tea. He started a pot of water boiling and gestured to a seat. Giles sat, happy to be out of the sun.

While the tea brewed, the scribe straightened his writing materials and made small talk. Only when he had poured out the tea did he settle down to more serious matters. He obviously followed a ritual and would not be hurried through it.

'So. Ryilla sent you to me. There is something you wish to have written?'

'No,' Giles answered, anxious to get to the heart of the matter. 'It is information I seek, information that Ryilla said you may have, and that he was afraid to talk about. I wish to learn about the key to the Gate of Paradise.'

'You seek it?' At Giles' nod, Pessein pulled at his lower lip. 'It is dangerous. Not the story. I care nothing about telling you the story and what I know. But to seek it is foolhardy.' He sipped from his bowl.

'My companions and I have journeyed far and have fought to gain what little we have. We know the risks.'

'You know nothing,' the scribe scoffed. 'The key is sacred to the Harifim. Do you know the Harifim?'

Giles shook his head.

'They are a desert tribe, although some live in the towns. They say that the key keeps the Gate of Paradise locked. They believe that when they die, a secret way through the Gate will be revealed to them. They are extremely jealous of the key, although I am not certain that even they know where it is hidden. For a non-Harifim to open the Gate is sacrilege and will deny them their eternal salvation.'

'They guard a key whose location is a mystery?' Giles asked.

'The Harifim point off vaguely towards the desert, but they never go beyond that. Why should they aid in their own damnation by helping another through the Gate?'

Giles sipped his tea. 'Then you don't know the location of the key.'

Pessein laughed. 'Oh, no. I don't want to know. I scribble and I tell stories to pass the time, but I have little desire to know anything that might get me killed.'

'Do you fear them? Are they so dangerous?'

Pessein looked at Giles for a long moment. 'Did you think it would not be difficult finding your mystical key? The Harifim are a hard desert people. They make enemies easily and friends with difficulty. They do not want anybody else to be interested in the key. Be careful whom you ask about it. I am a garrulous fool who seeks only a modest living.' He arched one eyebrow. Giles took the hint and dropped several gold pieces onto the table.

Giles stiffened when a shadow glanced across the wall. 'How will we learn if we do not ask questions?' He stood. 'Thank you for your hospitality,' he said.

Pessein smiled. 'Be careful, my friend. And,' he added wistfully, 'if you do enter the Gate of Paradise, think of me.' Pessein sighed and Giles recognised in him a kindred spirit.

Giles returned to the stall of Ryilla, keeping a sharp eye out for any who might be following him. The shadow in Pessein's shop had not been that of a casual passer-by. Someone had stood listening at the window – and had been careless for a brief instant.

The map seller looked up with surprise. 'I did not expect to see you again.'

'I still need a map,' Giles said. 'The desert.'

Petia and Keja entered the stall a few minutes later and found Giles poring over a stack of maps Ryilla had laid out for him. Giles looked up, wondering that they hadn't returned to the inn.

'Have you found what you were looking for?' Keja asked.

'Not yet, but I know it's in the desert somewhere.' Giles shifted a map and bent to study the one beneath. Without looking up, he asked, 'Has something brought you back? You were going to the inn.'

'Giles,' blurted Petia, 'there's a matter we have to discuss immediately. We have to . . .'

Giles silenced her when the map merchant came to sit cross-legged in front of Giles. 'You're going to look for it, aren't you?' Ryilla asked, his dark eyes blazing.

'We will go into the desert.' Giles moved another map.

'Did not Pessein warn you? There is great danger.'

'We don't warn off easily.'

'Giles, a word,' begged Petia.

'Later.' Giles spoke sharply and gestured to the map seller.

'Then let me show you the maps with the caravan routes.' Ryilla quickly sorted through the stack of maps, pulling out those with routes currently being used. He tossed the others to one side.

Giles immediately moved to a back table where Ryilla had thrown the older maps. A man perusing various scrolls moved out of his way, and then, nodding to the vendor, left the stall. Some of the maps Giles had already examined, but others he looked at carefully, laying some aside for later scrutiny.

'But,' Ryilla insisted, 'these are the maps you will need. Is everyone from your country as mad as you? These are fine maps!'

Giles looked up and laughed. 'We have a saying in our country. "Madness lies easily upon the back of the hand, and may be seen in the eyes."'

'I believe that. It must be a good saying because it certainly applies to you.' Ryilla shook his head and gestured to Keja and Petia to help themselves to fruit from a nearby bowl. Petia only fumed, but Keja took several of the offered fruits.

'Humour him,' Keja said. 'He will buy. You need not worry which map it is.'

Keja and Ryilla made small talk while Giles continued his search through the old maps. After half an hour, he carried a map to where the three were seated. He laid it down. 'Your price?'

Ryilla looked at the map and frowned. 'This one?' he asked.

Giles nodded.

'It's over a hundred years old. Routes no longer used. Pictures of mythic creatures along the sides. Useless.' Ryilla made it clear by his tone that he thought Giles a little strange. 'Look.' He pointed, a stubby finger grinding into the parchment. 'Cities long abandoned, empty husks of their former glory. Who knows what dwells there now?'

Giles peeled the skin from a strange purple fruit and sucked the juice running down his fingers. 'How much?' he repeated.

'One darhim to the mad foreigner,' Ryilla said in disgust. 'But don't blame me when you get lost. This map is far superior to the one you chose.' Ryilla held up the one he had originally shown to Giles.

Giles paid for the old map. They left Ryilla shaking his head and muttering about demented northerners.

'Where to now?' Keja asked. 'Petia's got something to say to you.'

'The lirjan market,' Giles said, not hearing more than Keja's question. 'We need transport. That's what we're going to buy, and supplies, and clothing for the desert.' Giles finished rolling the map and strode off, leaving the others to catch up.

The beasts looked awkward and gangling, but Giles knew that for the desert the lirjan were infinitely better than horses. Their large, spatulate hooves had evolved to travel easily over the sand. They were only slightly taller than a horse, but were able to survive for long distances in the heat with little water. They could carry two people for short distances but were much happier with only one.

The market roar deafened Giles as he pushed through the crowd. Vendors shouted that they offered the best beasts. Beneath that were the hoarse, husky grumblings of the animals' voices.

The first broker's smile revealed a mouth full of broken teeth. His obsequious manner made Giles move off to seek another. The manner of the second was better, forthright, if not any more honest.

'You must realise, sirs and lady, that I will receive shaharm when you buy. A fee from each side of the transaction, if you will. But I will try to recommend animals who are healthy and strong and can be obtained for a reasonable price. Gashmeen is renowned for his services, his fine animals provided to discerning travellers such as yourselves.' Giles saw that this amounted to little more than bragging, but Gashmeen appeared to do a thriving business. This, if nothing else, recommended him.

'We ask no more,' Giles said, handing over the gold equivalent of the five darhim required.

It was an exhausting, time-consuming task. Long before it was finished, Giles knew that Gashmeen had earned his money. The broker examined the animals from a distance at first, looking at their conformation and their stance. When he had selected some to examine more closely, he found out the price being asked. If it was within the range that Giles had suggested, he continued with his examination. Teeth, nostrils, legs, coat, all were examined carefully. He would even lift their tails and examine the anus.

'I'm glad he's not examining me,' Keja said.

Evening was upon them before the beasts were selected and the bargaining done. For an additional two darhim the broker arranged for care of the animals until they were ready to leave.

'It's too late now,' Giles said, acknowledging the evening dusk. 'But tomorrow we must get our clothing and supplies.'

'Thank the gods,' Keja exclaimed. 'I'm for a flagon. It's not the same fine ale as at home, but it'll do. Moistens the throat well enough.'

'A bowl of fruit for me,' Petia said, resigned to speaking to Giles later about the slave boy. 'I've never tasted so many different fruits with such delicate flavours.'

As they entered the inn, Giles again saw a shadow on the wall. He spun round, then shouted, 'Down!' His quick reflexes saved Keja from a knife in the back. A heavy-bladed hunting knife cartwheeled through the air and loudly *thunked*! into the wooden door.

'We're being warned off,' said Petia, pointing to the knife. She indicated the scrap of paper impaled by it.

Giles took the paper and read the inscribed message, then handed it to Keja. 'The scribe warned me that the Harifim don't like people asking about the key. We'll have to be more careful.'

During the evening a man, old and grizzled, entered the inn. His hunched back seemed bent under the woes of a world. He rubbed his hands as if they were cold, although the sun had set only an hour before. The innkeeper intercepted him as he walked across the common room and started to turn him out. Petia sat lost in her own thoughts while Giles and Keja discussed their trip into the desert. She saw the old man's plight and felt sorry for him. She rose from the table and motioned to the landlord.

She took the old one by the arm and invited him to have a cup of mint tea laced with beldon leaves. The man nodded eagerly. 'Tea in exchange for a story. I give you a story.'

'We are newly arrived in Kasha,' Petia told him. 'Perhaps you can tell us a story about your city or the desert.' She tried to forget the slave pens and the Trans boy. Somehow, Petia thought, by showing kindness to the old man, she might take her mind far away.

His grin was toothless but endearing. His ragged clothing seemed clean, and quick eyes darted around the table, taking in the map Giles poured over. The man took a sip of tea and sighed. He wiped his mouth with the back of his hand and looked around the table. 'What stories would you have me tell?' he asked.

Giles put away the map and drew a coin from his pouch and laid it on the table. The old man's eyes gleamed, and he smiled. 'A tale of the desert, perhaps,' Giles said. 'A tale concerning a key many centuries old – a key sacred to the Harifim.'

A frown crossed the leathery face, adding creases to the creases. 'Dangerous. It is dangerous to talk about the key. You speak of the Harifim. A fierce, unforgiving people. It is better to avoid them. Even those who have come to live in the city; they retain their ways. A savage people, warlike, very dangerous.' The old man shook his head. 'It would be better to avoid them,' he repeated.

Giles took up his pipe and loaded it with tobacco. The man's eyes watched him, birdlike. His eyes pleaded that he be allowed to tell a different story.

Giles lit his pipe, and spoke between puffs. 'The Harifim believe that the key is an important part of their religion. Do they have a temple in the city?'

The old man looked down at the table and then sipped from his mug. He could play the game nearly as well as Giles.

'It is said that the key keeps the Gate of Paradise locked. Only the Harifim find a secret entrance when they die. They believe that the key is in the safekeeping of the Skeleton Lord, who lives in an abandoned city in the desert.'

'And where is this city?' asked Keja.

'I do not know, but you must have seen the Lord's creatures in the city. They are so lean, they look like skeletons. Their eyes are sunk so deep in their sockets that one can never see them, can never read anything but death in them. People are afraid of them. Merchants deal with them quickly and with great courtesy so that they may be rid of them. The Harifim fear them, also, if they are afraid of anyone.'

Giles puffed thoughtfully. 'Tell me about the skeleton men. Where do they come from?'

'The desert.' The old man's hands encompassed the width and breadth of the desert outside the city. 'They could be from anywhere. There are many lost cities out there. Dead for hundreds of years. The Skeleton Lord lives in one such, or so it is said. The desert is their world.' He rubbed his forefinger through some spilled tea and made circles on the table.

He stood up. 'That is all that I know. Please do not say that I have told you these things. Leave the desert alone. I have said too much just for a cup of tea.' The old man bowed and left.

'What do you make of that?' asked Keja.

'Another warning for us,' said Giles, puffing thoughtfully on his pipe. 'Less emphatic than the knife, but still a warning.'

'A warning? Sent by whom?' asked Petia, pulled out of her worry over the boy.

'That is something we'll find out,' Giles Grimsmate said. 'Soon.'

Four

'THEY CAN'T get away with that!' Keja said hotly. 'We can't let them – whoever "they" are – come in here any time they want and rummage through our belongings.'

'Listen to who's talking. The old master thief himself. Now you know what it's like to be robbed.' Giles lounged back and studied the small, slightly disordered room. He suspected those responsible for stealing what little they had of value to be the Harifim. But to prove it? Impossible. 'All we're out are a few coins – and the map.'

'Why would they steal it?' asked Petia. 'Surely they know their way through the desert?'

'It's to keep us from finding the key,' said Keja, still angered by the intrusion into the room. 'I, for one, am not going to let them get away with it! We'll steal their damned key and spit in their eyes doing it! Wait and see!'

'It's off to the marketplace,' Giles said. 'I didn't study that map enough to be able to duplicate it.' He frowned and scratched his head.

'What is it, Giles?' Keja paced furiously. 'Something occur to you?'

'Just trying to think of those who knew I had the map.' The old man Petia had offered the tea to had known – but Giles decided the old man was only a minion of another who already knew.

He left to question Ryilla about the stolen map.

On the way, he passed a second-hand shop, saw the clutter inside, and on impulse entered to look over the old carpets, leather tent flaps, brass utensils, broken swords and other unidentifiable items littering the floor. In a few minutes he had found a pile of old maps. One showed old caravan routes across the desert.

Giles studied it carefully. Drawings of beasts from some ancient desert mythology adorned the map along its edges. The portraits appealed to Giles' sense of humour. He compared the map with his memory of the maps examined the previous day. These routes differed from the ones on Ryilla's more recent maps.

He paid a shambling old woman who appeared from behind a curtain at the back of the room. She examined him with rheumy eyes and bit the coin he handed her. 'Thank you, mother,' he said as she relinquished her hold on the map. Giles didn't see her grin as he left the shop.

He continued up the street, intent on talking to Ryilla once more. Before he reached the marketplace he tucked his recent purchase inside his tunic. The map vendor did not need to know that he had replaced the map with one better suited for his purposes.

When Giles reached the small shop, the dealer was all smiles. 'Ah, good sir. Back to buy another map?'

'Back to find out who you told about selling me the map yesterday.' Giles' face was stern. He dropped a canvas flap over the door and put out the small brass pot indicating that the shop was closed. He had reached the end of his patience with the grinning Ryilla.

'Surely there is a mistake,' Ryilla said, his grin hollow now. His dark eyes darted about, seeking an escape route. Giles was no man to argue with. 'Why would I want to do such a thing? Not for the sake of selling you another map for a darhim or two.'

'Then you know it was stolen.' Giles pinned the man against a wall.

Colour drained from the already grey face. 'I know nothing of the sort. I would not have someone steal it back to sell again.'

'I don't think you would,' Giles replied. 'But I think you would tell the Harifim that a stranger had been asking too many questions. I wonder if you're not of the Harifim yourself.'

'And if I were?' Ryilla looked toward a torn corner of the tent. Giles turned to see eyes staring back at him. 'I would warn you away from the desert. The key is sacred to my people. The faithful are lent the key when they die so that they may enter Paradise. You put yourself in grave danger if you try to steal it!'

Perspiration beaded the map seller's forehead. 'You would do well to go home.'

'Not likely,' Giles said. 'One key would not do you or your friends a bit of good. It takes five to open the Gate.'

Ryilla's mouth hardened into a line and his eyes blazed. 'Heresy! There is only one key.'

'There are five locks, each requiring a separate key. I know. I've seen the Gate.'

'Liar,' Ryilla roared. 'You cannot have seen. Only the Harifim are allowed. Our key alone will open the Gate.'

'I don't think you even know where this key is, this single key you speak of,' Giles said softly.

Ryilla waved his hand and men poured into the tent. Giles had wondered how long it would be before those he had seen spying entered. If all went well, he might learn something of value now.

'This man is blaspheming against our faith,' Ryilla said angrily, grinding his teeth. 'Take him to the temple and lock him in the cell. You need not be careful of how you treat him.'

Giles did not see the haft of the dagger flash toward the back of his head. Nor did he feel the pain from the blow. He was unconscious before the message reached his brain.

Keja had vanished, but Petia paid no heed. She stared up at the young boy in the wooden cage. He knelt at the front, hanging onto the crude bars, looking down imploringly at her.

His clothes hung in tatters, and Petia saw ribs sticking out of his scrawny chest. She wondered how he had got into this situation. Where were his parents? Dead? Brothers and sisters? Perhaps he had none. Petia swallowed hard. Was she in any better condition? Her family had died during the Trans War – and Segrinn. How could she forget his brutalities, the way he hunted her down even now, the punishments in store for her if he caught her?

The slave dealer walked towards Petia, rubbing his hands unctuously. 'My lady is interested in the boy, yes?'

For a brief moment Petia thought to rip out his throat with her claws, but she quieted her rampaging emotions. 'Yes,' she answered. 'He is a Trans, like myself.'

'The auction will begin in half an hour. There are others who are interested in slaves that will sell for much more money than he. He won't come to the block until late in the afternoon.'

Petia stared into the slave dealer's eyes. He averted his. 'That's all right,' Petia said. 'I have a great deal of patience and nothing else to do.'

'As my lady wishes.' The man turned and waddled off, glad to be away from the crazy Trans.

Petia settled gracefully to the ground, hardly stirring the dust beneath her. She would have the boy. Nothing would deter her from purchasing him – or stealing him, if that proved necessary. Giles would be furious and it might mean the end of her part in their quest. She did not care. Giles had ignored her the day before to the point that she had given up trying to mention it. He seemed too wrapped up in the intrigue surrounding the map and its theft to bother about freeing a poor Trans boy.

Patiently she watched cages being unlocked, and humans pulled onto the raised stage and displayed like livestock. Many seemed relieved when they were sold; their waiting was over. No matter the situation they might be entering, at least it would be stable and a known quantity.

The sun beat down with increasing ferocity as Petia waited, signalling to the boy to be patient. She watched as nubile young girls, men shrunken with age, haggard old women and other young boys were led to the block. She heard the eager shouts of various bidders, 'Five darhim, ten darhim, twenty darhim.' And she looked elsewhere when the sale consummated so that she wouldn't see how new owners treated their purchases.

After long hours of waiting, the Trans boy's cage opened. The slavemaster's assistant gestured for him to come down from the fourth tier. The boy scrambled down, using his arms while his legs dangled free. When he reached the bottom, Petia saw that he walked with one leg twisted awkwardly. He limped to the block.

'A healthy Trans boy,' the slave master shouted. 'He limps only because he has been crowded into the cage. The kinks will work themselves out. His legs are as sound as my own.'

The boy shook his head negatively from his crouched position.

'What am I bid for this fine boy, only eleven years of age? Unwanted by his parents but strong and with many good years of service in him.'

Petia's voice rang clearly over the heads of the crowd in front of her. 'Fifty darhim.' The crowd hushed, then gabbling broke out over so high a starting bid. It was traditional to start with five or less darhim.

'Five darhim has been bid,' the slavemaster shouted. 'The lady begins the bidding at five darhim.'

'No, greasy one. Fifty darhim.' Petia's gaze did not waver as the crowd turned to examine her. She heard people near her exclaiming. 'She must really want the boy.' 'It's too bad he is a cripple.' 'No one will bid that high for him.' 'She could have had him cheaper.'

The slavemaster wiped his forehead. 'Fifty darhim,' he shouted, 'for this excellent boy. He is Trans, part-cat. Do I hear fifty-five? Fifty-five darhim, going once.'

Petia's voice rose once again. 'A trick one might expect from such as you, fat-as-a-sow. My bid was fifty darhim, not fifty-five. Shall we now say "fifty darhim, going twice?"'

The crowd laughed at the slavemaster. He shouted, 'Fifty darhim, three times.' The crowd continued to chuckle at his discomfiture. 'Sold for fifty darhim. Take the accursed cripple.' He pushed the boy off the stage. The boy turned and bowed to the slavemaster, then raised his arms and did a dance step on perfectly straight legs. When he had finished, he bowed to the slavemaster again, then turned to greet Petia.

Petia touched her empty pouch – the intruders had stolen her money – but still she smiled. The woman stepped forward, pushing through the crowd. Her nimble fingers worked and purses opened at her passing. By the time she reached the slavemaster, she had more than the fifty darhim required – and it had all been supplied by the very people she hated most.

'Stand up, boy,' she said when he tried to pay her obeisance. 'Such behaviour offends me.'

'Mistress, let me kiss your feet. I would do anything for you.'

'If that is so, then stand up and don't embarrass me. Why did you pretend to be a cripple?'

The boy rose from the dust and looked up into Petia's face. 'I hoped you would buy me. I wanted to go cheaply so that you would not be angry. I was trying to save you money.'

'You are a rascal. What is your name?'

'Anji, my lady.'

'All right, Anji. First we see about something to eat, then some decent clothing for you.'

'But these clothes will be all right. The Mistress has paid good money for me. I am content just to be out of the cage. I will work hard for you, you will see. And I eat little.'

'You will eat what I tell you. You're scrawny. Your ribs stick out. Now be quiet for a moment while I think where to take you for food.'

The boy's eyes widened when he saw that Petia meant to take him to a cafe. 'I have never eaten in one of those, Mistress. I would not know what to do.'

'Then it is time for you to learn, is it not?' Petia took his hand and pulled him along behind her.

She ordered plain food and when it came, Petia leaned back. She enjoyed the sight of the near-starving boy as he wolfed down the food. After a few minutes, she made him slow down. She showed him how to use the table implements, the spoon for the soups and stews, the fork for vegetables and meat, and the knife for cutting.

She sensed that the boy felt awkward and she encouraged him. 'You'll do fine with practice.'

At last Anji sat back, groaning. His stomach hurt from so much food after existing on bare rations for such a long time. He put his hands on his belly and said, 'It hurts.'

'You've gone hungry for a long time, then?' Petia asked.

'Since I was sold to the slavemaster.'

'When was that?'

'A long time ago, Mistress. I was sold once before, but I didn't work hard enough, and my master sold me back to the slavemaster. But I will work hard for you, Mistress. I will do whatever you command.'

'I didn't buy you to be my slave,' Petia said. 'I bought you to set you free. After I get you some decent clothing, you can go wherever you want. Do you understand? You are free.'

The boy's eyes opened wide. He shook his head. 'Do you mean that I am to go away. Where will I go? I want to stay with you, Mistress.'

'I'm not sure that you can do that, Anji. I have obligations to other people. I'm not certain that they would allow you to accompany us. It would be best if you went your own way.' Petia's heart dropped as she said the words; she found the boy appealing. He was a Trans, part-cat as she was, alone in the world. She knew the feeling.

'Where are your parents?' she asked.

Anji turned sullen. 'I don't know. I don't care, either. They sold me to the slavemaster. They didn't want me.'

Petia closed her eyes. Anji had also been rejected by his parents. Petia's own father was long dead, but it was her mother who had indentured her to Lord Ambrose. She took the boy by the hand and went in search of a clothing shop.

A much more presentable Anji followed Petia into the room at the inn. Petia didn't know which of them was the more nervous. Anji had never been allowed inside an inn before, and Petia was unsure of Giles' reaction to the foundling. Of Giles she saw no sign, but she found Keja staring out of the window. He whirled as she and Anji entered.

'Where have you been?' he asked. A worried look creased his brow.

'I'd like you to meet Anji.' The boy peered up at Keja, although there wasn't that much difference in their height.

'The slave boy,' Keja said, finally recognising the youth. 'Hello, Anji. You haven't seen Giles, have you?' Keja asked.

'No. Why? You look worried.'

'He said he'd be back early this afternoon. He hasn't returned or sent any message. You didn't see him in the market?' Keja persisted.

'I don't think there's anything to worry about. Giles knows his way about, and he looked as if he had a lot to do when he left this morning. He'll show up.'

'I'm going out to look for him. Don't you go wandering off.' He almost ran out of the room. Petia barely had time to relax over a cup of scented tea when Keja returned, downcast.

'Did you speak to the map seller?' Petia asked.

'He admitted that Giles had been there and had looked at some more maps. Giles asked about temples, and the map seller, Ryilla, I think his name is, said that he directed him to several around Kasha.'

'Ryilla,' Anji said. 'That is the map seller's name. A Harifim. Be careful of him.'

'How do you know that?' Petia asked.

'My previous owner was of the Harifim. Bad people, he beat me. Ryilla is Harifim, also.'

Keja sighed. 'And the Harifim have warned us not to search for the key. Not in so many words, but a knife in the back can say more than words alone.'

'And Giles has gone to the Harifim temple to see what he can uncover,' Petia concluded.

'They are fanatics,' said Anji. 'They would capture your friend, about whom you worry, and hold him at the temple if they thought that he was trying to get information about their cult. This Ryilla is the guilty one. He gave your friend over to the Harifim. He is one of them!'

'We'd better go and see if Giles is in trouble,' Keja said. 'If he is, we can break into the place and get him away.'

'You do not know the Harifim, sir,' Anji said. 'They are savage. They have guards in their temple. It would be best to wait until nightfall. At vespers their ceremony will be at a point where most of them will be in a trance from a drug they use. You will have a much better chance of getting in then.'

The waiting was unbearable. Keja and Petia hoped to see Giles walk in the door at any moment, but as the dinner hour passed and the sun sank into the hot desert sands and promised a little coolness, Keja became more nervous. Finally he reached into his pack and took out a rope. He wound it carefully around his waist, then flung on his cloak. Petia took her cloak from the hook by the door.

'You stay in the room, Anji, until we get back. Do not go anywhere, do you understand?'

'Yes, Mistress.' The boy's eyes gleamed with excitement, but he sat meekly with his hands folded in his lap. 'You do not know where the temple is,' he said calmly.

Petia muttered in exasperation 'No, but you'll tell us how to reach it, and then you will stay here,' Petia said.

Using Anji's somewhat muddled directions, they found the Harifim temple. The building stood stark against the low desert moon, casting elongated shadows across the square. The building was plain, only two stories high, with a flat roof. There was no dome or tower or other rooftop ornamentation. Neither had ever seen a temple like it.

'Catch the lip of the roof with your hook,' Petia whispered. 'You stand watch while I take a look up there.'

Keja knew better than to argue and unwound the rope from his waist. He attached a triple hook to one end and tied the knot carefully. It caught the ledge on the first try; he tested it with his weight before stepping back.

Petia flexed her fingers, grabbed the rope and paused, concentrating. Mentally she shifted herself to a more feline state, becoming more agile, quicker, her body turning sleeker.

227

She pulled the rope taut and scurried up the wall to the roof. Keja watched in open admiration.

She paused briefly at the edge of the roof, and Keja saw her crouch and peer into the darkness. The Trans turned and signalled that she would leave the hook and rope in place.

Her first glance suggested that there would be no way into the temple from the flat roof, but previous experiences at thievery cautioned her that first impressions were not always true. She circled and, finding nothing, crossed the roof from side to side, studying and feeling its surface with preternaturally sensitive fingers. At the halfway point she felt the roof give slightly. Petia knelt and discovered a trap door, flush with the roof. Her claws slid under the edge of the door; she lifted carefully.

A ladder led down into the Harifim stronghold. Petia went down, head and hands first, and came out in a narrow passage. She lifted her head and tried to identify the strange scent permeating the air. Spicy and pungent, it was unlike anything she had smelled before. The first sniff cleared her head, as if she had been suffering from a cold. The second made her giddy.

The sound of drums, beating softly but with rhythmic intensity, came from beyond the wall. Then she felt that peculiar vibration of people dancing.

Petia moved cautiously down the bare-walled passage until she came to an open archway. She peered around the corner into the room, keeping her head low. Several men stood watching, intent on the scene before them.

There were no women in the room. Except for a few guards, all the men were involved in the dance. Some had reached a trance stage and fallen to the floor. It was evidently the duty of the non-participants to drag the entranced ones out of the way of the dancers. The men still on their feet went through the peculiar dance steps with their eyes closed. They held their arms out at the side as if they were wings, and dipped and glided for a few beats of the drum, a parody of some great bird of prey. Then, in a great flurry, they whirled five or six times. The motion was repeated again and again.

Petia did not worry about the trance dancers. Only the watchers worried her. She backed away from the arch and crept down the passage. At each doorway she peered in cautiously, but found only empty rooms. Petia eventually came to a set of stairs leading downward.

She descended into the main body of the temple. An altar stood near one end of the room, and intricately woven prayer mats covered the floor. No guards, no supplicants, no one.

She saw only two doorways. One led from the front of the temple and was the main entrance from the street. The other she stood in.

Petia started to leave, then stopped, a strangeness to the room making her uneasy. Petia wrinkled her nose. It was not quite a musty smell, not the odour of a building dried and desiccated by the sun-beaten desert. A humid, almost cool feeling to this room reached out and touched her face, her hands. Petia repressed a shiver. She walked quietly up to the altar.

A simple desert cloth adorned it. Behind the altar table a tapestry bright with geometric patterns of talismanic significance stretched across one wall. Petia studied the eye-confusing pattern and decided that it certainly did not depict a scene on this world. She felt the heavy desert cloth and, on impulse, flicked back one edge.

Behind it a narrow passage meandered off to end at a hole in the floor. Narrow treads led down into a subterranean passage. Thanking the gods for feline vision, she descended. Moist, earthen walls immediately answered the question of the strangely humid smell.

Petia closed her eyes and listened intently. She heard disturbed breathing and ventured a quiet call. 'Giles?'

A groan sounded in response. She followed the faint cries of pain and found a rough door, barred on the outside. She called again, but no answer came, not even a moan.

She lifted the bar, set it carefully along the wall and opened the cell door.

Giles Grimsmate lay in a crumpled heap in one corner of the room. She went to him, her heart in her throat. He had been beaten until he was almost unrecognisable. His breath rattled in his throat.

Petia put her hands on his forehead. 'Giles, can you move?'

Even with her superior night vision, Petia could barely see in the dark cell. She tried to rouse Giles, but could get nothing more from him than the intake of a short breath which set him coughing. She could not even tell if he was conscious.

'Giles, wake up.' No response.

Petia grimaced. She needed help, but Keja was still outside on the roof. She would have to go all the way up to the roof to signal him, and the gods knew how they would get Giles out.

Not liking the idea of traversing the Harifim temple, but seeing no way around it, Petia made her way quickly and silently to the roof. In a few minutes she had found Keja and explained the situation.

'We're wasting time,' he told her. 'The sooner we get back to the basement and rescue Giles, the sooner we can be gone from this accursed place.' They retraced Petia's earlier route past the guards and dancers, into the nave and the passage and down to the cell.

Keja gathered the older man and lifted him to his shoulders. 'If we get him out of here without arousing those acolytes, it will be a miracle,' he said. 'Giles is heavier than I expected. Lead on.'

Keja staggered under Giles' weight, but they reached the temple's main floor without incident. Keja leaned against the wall to catch his breath without putting Giles down.

'The next part is going to be tricky,' Petia whispered. 'Try not to breathe too loudly. There are four guards. If we get past them, we have a chance of getting out of here. If we can't . . .' Petia left the sentence unfinished.

The narrow, steep steps forced Keja to struggle for balance. The inert Giles was a dead weight, arms dangling and sometimes swinging from the motion. Keja reached the top of the stairs and concentrated on breathing quietly, almost an impossibility.

Petia motioned for Keja not to rest – too much danger. She pointed to the room where fewer feet could be heard dancing. More of the men had succumbed to the drugs and spin dancing.

Keja heaved a deep breath and moved to the ladder leading to the roof. He raised his right foot and placed it on the first rung. Against his shoulder he felt Giles take a deep breath.

When the unconscious man let out the air, a deep moan echoed down the passageway.

Keja looked at Petia apprehensively. She motioned him on up the ladder. They heard a short exclamation in the desert language, followed all too quickly by the sound of feet rushing toward them. Four acolytes rushed round the corner of the archway.

Petia drew her sword and shouted over her shoulder at Keja. 'Hurry. I'll hold them off.'

She crouched, sword at the ready. The men advanced, although they were unarmed. They obviously intended to bowl her over with their sheer numbers, even though she might kill or injure a couple.

They were still several feet away from her when a yell echoed from the temple room below. 'Hadrani! Arifa! Hadrani!'

Several voices came from below. Petia couldn't understand the language, but the emotion was clearly one of panic. 'Hadrani!' the voices repeated. The men confronting Petia exchanged frowns. One shook his head and took another step towards her. A second man stopped, sniffing the air. 'Hadrani,' he growled, and sniffed again. The others sniffed, then rushed at Petia. To her amazement, they went right past her and disappeared down the stairway to the main temple room.

'Up the ladder quickly,' Keja shouted. 'Pull it up behind you.'

They staggered to the edge of the temple roof. 'You first,' Keja said. 'Then I'll lower Giles.'

In only moments, Keja reached the ground and shouldered Giles again. As they melted into the shadows playing along the street opposite the temple, Anji joined them. 'Did I do good?' he asked.

Petia grabbed the boy's arm. 'What are you doing here? I told you to stay in the room.'

The boy's eyes sparkled as the small band entered the moon-soaked square. 'Hadrani. Hadrani,' he said in a deep voice not his own. 'That is "flee!" in the language of the desert.'

'You? Downstairs in the temple?'

Anji nodded. 'I set a small fire with paper. Lots of smoke.

231

Lots of voices, too. I did three or four men from different corners. I followed you. It is not good to go against the Harifim without someone at your back.'

Petia tried to be angry with the boy and failed. 'We'll talk about this later. Keja, hurry. They'll be after us for certain now. We'd better tend to Giles, then gather our belongings and leave the inn.'

'Where will we hide at this time of night? We don't know the city.'

'Anji does. We'll find a place.'

They entered the inn through the kitchen and hurried up the back stairs to their room. They stripped Giles and Petia tended the bloody abrasions on his body with a clean cloth dipped in wine. He regained consciousness briefly, but his eyes never focused and he closed them again.

'Anji, think of somewhere we can hide.' Petia wiped the cloth across a cut in Giles' forehead.

'Where are you going next?' the boy asked. 'You are obviously travellers from another country.'

'We were going into the desert. We've bought supplies and several lirjan.'

'Where are the lirjan?' asked Anji.

When he heard Petia's answer, he said, 'So. Hide in the caravanserai among the lirjan. They won't find us there. The Harifim come from the desert where they prey on caravans. They are not at all welcome among other travellers.'

Petia found that Giles had no broken bones, but he sucked in his breath noisily when she touched his ribs. She bound them tightly, hoping that none was cracked. A sip of wine forced into his mouth seemed to revive him a bit. He started to talk, but Petia shushed him.

'We've got to leave right now, Giles. Can you walk?'

'Dunno,' he mumbled. With Keja on one side and Petia on the other, he managed to get to his feet. They walked him across the room and back.

'He'll make it if he can lean on both of us and we go slowly,' Keja said. 'What about our belongings?'

'I'll carry them,' Anji spoke up. He gathered the packs together and slung them over his skinny shoulder.

Keja raised his eyebrows at the boy's strength, but shook his head ever so slightly at Petia, warning her to let Anji have his own way. The boy had a great deal of pride and had helped them immensely tonight.

They left the inn quietly and let Anji lead them. Through deserted back streets they reached the carvanserai. The tent guard grumbled at the lateness, but Keja slipped him a coin to quiet him.

They found a place in the middle of the gathering, and lowered Giles to the ground, placing a pack beneath his head. His eyes opened briefly. 'Thank you, friends,' he whispered. 'The map,' he mumbled. He lifted his hand and pointed at the back of his trousers.

'But it was taken,' Keja said, frowning. When Giles motioned again, Keja rolled Giles over and groped inside. When his hand came out, the folded map was between his fingers. Keja frowned even more when he saw the map. 'Not the same one,' he said.

'Giles found a better one,' Petia said with confidence.

Keja tucked the map out of sight in his own tunic, then asked, 'Now, what do we do with the boy?'

Anji knelt in front of Petia, his eyes imploring her. She looked from Anji to Keja and back again. 'If we don't take him with us, he's dead. The Harifim will see to it.'

'He'll only be in the way if he comes with us. Giles will be furious.'

'He wasn't in our way earlier this evening, Keja. Either he goes with us, or I don't go. And don't put words in Giles' mouth.' She glared at Keja.

Keja muttered for a moment, then subsided, shaking his head. 'All right, but he's your responsibility. And you can explain it to Giles.'

'Yes, he is, and I will.' Petia gestured to a space on the ground. 'We'll sleep there.' She lay down and threw her cloak over the boy and herself. They listened briefly to the night noises of the lirjan before they slept, Petia's dreams troubled with visions of drug-crazed Harifim pouncing on her from the darkness.

233

Five

'CARAVANERS FOR Kuilla, rise up, rise up! Kuilla only. Line up your lirjan against the south wall.' The cry rang through the caravanserai. The lirjan grunted as drivers prodded them to their feet.

Petia blinked open her eyes and for an instant thought she'd gone blind. The blackness of the sky above was relieved by only one or two twinkling stars. She stretched and got circulation flowing through tired veins, then roused Anji and kicked Keja to get him awake. 'Up, sleepy head, the day's half gone,' she said with feigned exuberance.

She knelt by Giles. 'How are you feeling? The caravan for Kuilla is preparing to leave.'

'Kuilla? Help me up, will you?'

Petia assisted him. Giles winced at the pain in his ribs. 'You and Keja take care of getting us a spot in the caravan line.'

Giles struggled to get their packs buckled up while the others took care of their duties. He rubbed his side and decided the injury wasn't too bad. He cursed himself for being so stupid and thinking he could learn of the key by allowing himself to be kidnapped by the Harifim. If it hadn't been for his friends, he would have died in the Harifim prison – and to make matters even worse, he had gained no new knowledge for his pains.

He swung the pack up and settled it into a comfortable spot on his back when a boy ran up to him. 'Master Giles, Petia says that the lirjan are in line. We can pack them there.'

'Thank you, boy. This is for your trouble.' He spun a coin into the air.

The boy caught it deftly and tossed it back. 'I cannot take it,

234

Master Giles. Come, this way. I show you.' He pulled at Giles' sleeve.

'Where did you get this little charmer to help you?' Giles asked as he joined the others by their animals.

'I bought him yesterday at the slave market. He is mine,' Petia replied.

'What?' Giles exploded.

'I offered him his freedom, but he wants to stay with me. I can't turn him down. He goes with us.'

'We can't take a child with us,' Giles said. 'We don't have any idea what's ahead – except for more trouble. Who's going to be responsible for him? We don't have enough supplies. He'll be in the way. He could get sick. He doesn't have a lirjan to ride.' Giles paused for breath and finally added, 'And you shouldn't have bought him. Never give so much as a fart to those who deal in human flesh and misery.'

Petia let Giles run through the litany of reasons the boy shouldn't accompany them. When he stopped, she said quietly, 'Anji goes with me, or I don't go.'

'No, Petia. We cannot afford someone who will be in the way.'

'He wasn't in the way last night when Keja and I pulled you out of the Harifim temple. If it hadn't been for him, all three of us would be in that cell right now, instead of getting ready to leave Kasha.' Petia turned and looked back at the city. 'He stays with me,' she said again, returning an unblinking gaze to Giles.

'Hummph! On your head, then!' Giles grumbled before he busied himself with unnecessary repacking.

The half-dark of false dawn still clung tenaciously to the desert when the last lirjan cleared the city gates. For a time the caravan followed a well-beaten track that led past a series of wells outside Kasha's walls. Gradually the path dwindled to a single rut stretching into the desert.

'I had hoped that we would group up and be shielded from prying eyes,' Giles said. 'The Harifim know what we are seeking. They'll be after us, I fear. Keep a careful watch.'

They soon fell into the rolling, awkward gait of the lirjan, although Giles winced with pain at every misstep the animal made. Seeing that the caravan made good time and that the

Harifim would be unable to approach without being seen first, Giles reached for the map.

'Gone!' he cried. 'They got the map!'

Keja put his heels to his animal's flanks and trotted up beside Giles. 'Here. Took it to make sure it wasn't lost. Didn't want you bleeding on it.'

Giles heaved a sigh of relief. He'd been through too much to get this map to have it lost due to his own miscalculations. He didn't bother with the ancient caravan routes; he examined the map's illuminated borders. Around the perimeter cavorted mythical beasts of fantastic proportion and viciousness.

Giles squinted into the morning sun at the long string of lirjan stretching out into the desert. He turned on his mount to look back at a line nearly as long before scanning the desert on both sides for any hint that the Harifim pursued them. He heaved a sigh of relief when he found no trace of the fanatical cultists. Giles decided he might be overestimating the Harifim devotion to protecting their key to the Gate of Paradise.

He returned his attention to the beasts inked onto the map and wondered how a scribe would dream up such creatures. In the upper right hand corner glowered an upright creature, standing on two ponderous legs and covered in tiny scales. The slim torso widened to a mighty chest and shoulders. Eyes looked out from beneath a bony, protruding brow, giving the effect of gloom and brooding.

Beneath it writhed a four-legged reptilian beast, long and sinuous, its hind legs stretched out behind it. Its beaked mouth opened as if it were part bird of prey.

At the bottom the artist had drawn in another physical anomaly. The body of this third animal was covered with a shell, but unlike any turtle Giles had ever seen. The legs were long and slender, the body stout, the head similar to that of a dog, with large round ears pricked up as if listening to the susurration of desert wind against heated sand.

Giles tucked the map away. He would examine the other beasts later. Now all he wanted to do was try to doze off as his lirjan perversely sought the rockiest part of the track.

The day wore on – and the desert stretched forever. Kasha disappeared behind the caravan, taking the ocean with it. For miles around Giles saw only hard, flat soil. He supposed that the sand would come later. Surely, if this is a desert, then there must be sand.

He shaded his eyes with one hand to see into the heat-shimmered distance. Something broke the monotonous flatness through which the caravan passed. Small hills, eroded cliffs, perhaps. But the heat radiating off the land erased any detail. Giles could neither see clearly nor determine distances. It might be one league or ten to the cliffs.

Giles rocked back and forth on his lirjan, watching the bobbing heads of Keja and Petia ahead of him, falling into an almost hypnotic trance. The boy, Anji, was seated in front of Petia out of Giles' line of sight. He wondered idly if their backs ached as badly as his did. He was grateful when the caravan leader called a halt at midday.

Anji nimbly dropped to the hard ground to aid Petia, then hurried back to Keja's mount and helped the small thief. Giles was damned if a mere child was going to help him. After all, he was a veteran of twenty years in the Trans War and had seen and done everything – twice. He threw his foot over the lirjan's withers and slid off. Pain shot through his legs. First the ankles, then the knee, and finally it reached his hips. He staggered back against the animal and heard it grumble. He turned and grabbed a pack rope, hanging on while feeling slowly came back into his legs. Foolish, Giles, he thought. Next time he'd let the boy help.

The afternoon was much the same, although to the west Giles spied the mounded hills of sand dunes. The midday meal sat uneasily on his stomach as Giles endured the lirjan's punishment well beyond the normal dinner time when the caravan master finally called a halt. Giles wanted only a light meal before the sandy horizon swallowed the sun.

Small fires burned around the perimeter of the camp, the lirjan tethered inside the circle of humans. The caravan master insisted on posting guards to watch for brigands; Giles said nothing about the Harifim. As nervous as the master appeared, he might put them out of the caravan at the slightest hint of impropriety on their part.

'Are you all right, Giles?' Petia asked.

'Just tired, Petia. I'm getting too old to take a beating. I'll be

237

all right, unless I get any more bright ideas.' Giles snorted. 'Can't imagine why I tried to take on all the Harifim by myself.' But he did know why and it irritated him even more than the beating. Keja and Petia were so young, so agile. What did an old and tired soldier like himself have to offer? He remembered younger days and all he'd done then. There had been some good times interspersed with the stretches of bad, and he had tried to bring back those with a bit of derring-do. He had known Ryilla's men watched him; he had seen the eyes peeking through the tent. But he'd thought he could conquer them all.

Just as Petia and Keja thought they could.

'My hip joints will never be the same,' Petia laughed. 'Want some tiffa? With sugar?'

'I've had enough for now. I'll just lie here and tell my ribs to stop hurting.'

Petia returned to the small blaze and sat cross-legged in front of it. 'Petia?' Keja looked at her for a time. 'Why are you so aloof? We've been together for quite a while now, and you must know what sort of fellow I am. I need more than just simple companionship. I think you do, too.'

Petia stared at him over the rim of her cup. 'You've known too many others. I don't look forward to being cast off like an unwanted garment. You see, Keja, I don't trust you. We are both thieves, but I don't think we have the same ethic.'

'Who are you to talk of ethic? Thieves have no ethic.'

'Perhaps not. But this thief knows better than to become involved with another thief. And a Trans must be careful with humans. Do you think we have forgotten the Trans War? That any of us can?'

'I don't care about the Trans War,' said Keja. 'I care about you. And I care that at night my blankets are lonely.'

'Ah, yes,' Petia said. 'Creature comforts. There's more to it than a moment's pleasure. But you wouldn't know that, would you?'

Keja lowered his head and glowered at the flames. His mouth was set. He knew that if he spoke he would say something for which he would be sorry.

Anji snuggled next to Petia and pointed away to his left. A figure moved along the perimeter of the camp. Petia looked up from her cup. The caravan master strolled along, making small talk with the caravaners.

Petia nudged Giles, who groaned and rubbed his eyes. 'The caravan master?' he whispered. Anji nodded. Louder, Giles called, 'Good evening, Master. A cup of tiffa at our fire?'

'What strange land do you hail from? I am the dhouti. No one calls me Master. That is blasphemy against . . .' The dhouti's voice trailed off. With an abrupt change of topic, he said, 'I would like the tiffa. All well here?' The dhouti sank to his haunches and accepted a cup from Petia.

'As well as one might expect after a day of torture astride a lirjan, a beast unknown in our country.'

The dhouti laughed and sipped loudly from his cup. 'A ride one must be born to, I fear. You may become accustomed to it, but you will never be comfortable. You must be born of the desert.'

'Then we have a long journey before us. Can you offer advice?' Giles pulled the map from his tunic and spread it out before the dhouti.

'I bought this in a shop in Kasha. The shopkeeper said that the routes shown are no longer used.'

The dhouti leaned forward and studied the map, frowning. 'Yes, that is true. An old map.' He lifted his head and looked out into the desert night. 'Forgotten cities there and there.' He pointed to either side, but his fingers conveyed distances of many days' journey.

'I'm curious about the old roads and the lost cities. Why are they no longer used?'

'Ahh.' A long sigh from the dhouti. 'Dangerous. Dead cities inhabited by who knows what. Ghosts? Spirits? Nothing along those routes but abandoned cities, windows like empty sockets looking out at nothing.' He shook his head. 'Great cities once. Long, long ago. Nothing there now.'

'What of these beasts illuminating the edge of the map? Are there any stories about them? Legends?'

The dhouti pointed at the pictures with the short stick he carried for authority. 'These? Yes, beasts of the desert. They exist out there in the places where men no longer travel.'

Giles laughed. 'We might be strangers to your land, but we know a joke.'

239

'No jest. In the desert –' he flicked the tip of his stick over one shoulder '– beasts such as these still exist. Perhaps they live in the forgotten cities. Good night, sirs and lady.' He rose and thumped his thigh with the riding crop, then continued his rounds of the encampment.

For a long time Giles stared at the map with the animals marching in bizarre ranks around its borders. Finally he snorted, 'Nonsense,' and put the map away.

The days settled into a routine that consisted of endless sun, an endless track, the endless rocking of the lirjan beneath them. If the days were dull, the nights were even more boringly identical. A plain meal, innumerable cups of strong tiffa, reading and writing lessons for Anji, Keja sulking, the dhouti making his rounds. The only positive change was that Giles recovered from his beating more each day.

For five days the lirjan followed one another like animals performing at a fair. Desert heat and the rocking motion and the animal's anus in front was all they could look forward to. Giles finally understood the importance of much that the lirjan broker had insisted upon. If he had to ride along peering up an animal's backside, it had best be in good condition.

Keja became even more sullen. He spoke little and seemed only to be enduring the journey, withdrawing into himself, cutting himself off from those around him. One evening Petia tried to speak to him, but he turned away and walked into the desert. Giles grumbled about this, wishing he could have chosen his travelling companions as he had the lirjan.

Then Giles wished Keja's petulance and Petia's anger at the small thief was all that he had to worry about. The attack came at mid-morning of the sixth day. The dhouti's sharp eyes centred on a swirl of dust on the horizon. How he could distinguish the dust raised by riders from that of a small dust devil Giles would never know. Orders were yelled from the front of the caravan to form a circle as they did for the evening camp. Initial confusion gave way to a methodical plan to defend the caravan. It didn't surprise Giles that the caravaners had experienced such attacks before. They stayed on their animals, facing outward, to allow each rider enough space to wield his sword.

Keja and Giles drew up on either side of Petia. 'Get the boy down,' Giles yelled. 'You need to be able to swing your sword unhindered.'

Anji slid off without a word and ducked behind the circle of lirjan.

Keja pulled back the sleeve of his sword arm, and, throwing back his hood, tied a scarf around his head to keep his hair out of his eyes. Petia shifted nervously, obviously worried about Anji. Giles said nothing. He had faced too many battles not to know how to prepare himself mentally. The old doubts rose; he forced them away. His hand was gripped firmly on the hilt of his sword.

The dust cloud moved closer, an inexorable advance dictated by fate. They saw the horses and their riders when they came within half a league. At one hundred yards they saw the drawn swords. The desert men swept by at fifty yards, brandishing weapons and yelling vile insults. They made no move to attack. They rode the complete circle once, showing their force to all sides of the caravan.

Petia muttered, 'Why don't they attack? What are they waiting for?'

'You've never been in a battle before,' Giles said grimly. 'There's always a little game that takes place first. They're showing us how many they number, how swift they are, how well mounted. They keep outside the distance of a spear thrust or an arrow's flight, although these people don't seem to use bows and arrows. So they are safe. They have the advantage and can take their time.'

'And we just wait?'

'We can't attack. The lirjan are loaded down, and aren't fast enough to catch their horses. So, yes, we wait. We have no choice.'

Keja shifted in his seat. 'Wouldn't it be better if you got behind us, Giles? You're not well enough to fight. You're still not healed.'

'I've fought in worse shape than this.'

The riders continued to circle, their cloaks flowing behind them like giant bats. They brandished their swords and howled

241

maniacally in their desert tongue. It added to the eerie tension of the waiting.

One raider slowed his horse, certain of his own safety surrounded by his comrades. He studied each potential opponent as his mount danced daintily, paws raking the air.

The rider – Giles decided he had to be the brigands' leader – stopped opposite them, made his decision and raised a long ululating call. Immediately the other riders wheeled and gathered behind for the attack.

The dhouti watched impassively from his lirjan. When he heard the call, he raised his own cry and pointed. Giles and the others found themselves on a wedge pointing at the attackers.

'Wait,' Giles protested, not wanting to be used as a shock troop against the brigands.

'Attack or die, cowards!' came the warning from a grizzled old caravaner.

The riders moved forward slowly, gathering momentum like a boulder rolling downhill, then broke into a trot.

Giles turned to Keja and Petia. 'Go with the attack,' he called. 'If we break ranks now the entire caravan will be laid open.' Giles saw Petia's lips move in the single name, 'Anji.' Then the Trans let out a feline howl of rage and kicked her animal forward. Keja found himself hard pressed to stay with her, and Giles led the way on the right side of the wedge.

The leader of the raiders stood in his stirrups. He searched for something. When he couldn't find it, he veered off, racing at a tangent to the caravan circle. His men swept after him and circled into the desert. They slowed and the leader once again stared at the caravan, searching.

Finally he halted, and shouted, 'Dhouti.' There followed a long statement directed to the caravan leader in the desert language. When he had finished, the leader brandished his sword once more and turned away, leading his band of raiders into the desert.

The dhouti shouted, 'Halt the attack! Halt, all halt!' Giles reined in swiftly, but Keja had to grab Petia's sleeve and almost tug her from the back of her animal before her bloodlust quieted. She couldn't attack the brigands alone.

The defenders broke into a gabble as if they could not believe their good fortune. They slapped one another on the back and let out a shrill, rising cry that made Giles wince. It was their way of proclaiming victory.

The dhouti rode slowly to where Giles and the others stood beside their mounts. He slid to the ground and beckoned them to come over to him.

'What are you to the men of the desert?' he asked, gazing coldly at Giles.

Giles lowered himself to sit cross-legged opposite the dhouti. 'We are nothing to them, as far as I know. We arrived in Karsh less than two weeks ago. This is our first trip into the desert, as you can tell.'

The dhouti's hand waved toward the vanishing cloud of dust. 'That is not what Seifal says. He says you seek something in the desert that is not yours, that it will bring your death. This foray was a warning. He could have cut my caravan to bits. What do you seek that upsets them so?' His face came nearer to Giles until they were eye-to-eye. 'Do not lie to me. I will have your head if you do. I will send it to Seifal as a gift.' His dark eyes did not blink.

Around him, Giles could hear the caravaners pulling the lirjan into position in the caravan once again, preparing to continue along their way.

'We look for the forgotten cities,' Giles answered.

'And then?'

'We may find things discarded when the inhabitants left. Things that will be worth much in the markets of Kasha.' Giles' eyes met the dhouti's unwaveringly. Keja and Petia stood to one side, listening.

'You lie,' the dhouti said, with emotion. 'You seek a single object, yes? What is it? You may as well say, because I'm going to abandon you here in any case.'

Giles looked up at Keja and Petia. He turned back to the dhouti. 'We seek the key to the Gate of Paradise.'

'So. It is no wonder the Harifim attack. You walk into danger stupidly and with your eyes open. My caravan will not be a part of it. We seek only safe passage to Kuilla. You will leave here and now. I will give you some water and a compass. You have your own map. I wish you luck. Not in finding the key, may you be cursed eternally, but in keeping your lives.' The dhouti rose and walked away.

By consigning them to the desert, he had sentenced them to a painful death.

Six

'At least that mouse turd left us a waterskin.' Giles made a quick inventory of their supplies. He finally shook his head and heaved a deep sigh. 'It could have been worse. We won't starve or die of thirst yet.'

'Always the optimist, eh, Giles?' Keja bounced around, filled with nervous energy. 'What are we going to do in the middle of the desert? We don't know where we are, we have no protection. What if those raiders come back?'

'We do know where we are.' Giles pointed to the track. It had been worn smooth by thousands of lirjan passing along it for more than a hundred years. 'We can follow it back to Kasha or ahead to Kuilla. There is danger in staying on the caravan track, but probably less than if we take off across the desert. At least we won't get lost.'

Petia sat down on the ground and Anji squatted beside her. She looked at the two men. 'We all might as well sit down. It's time to make another decision. Do we go ahead or do we return to Kasha and give up the search for the key?' She handed the compass to Giles.

Giles sat down; Keja continued to pace.

'Giles, I didn't expect to be abandoned in the middle of a desert.'

'Neither did I.' Giles looked from Anji to Petia. 'And you have the boy to think of, too.'

'The boy will be all right,' Petia said defensively. 'He knows more about this country than we do. I'm more concerned with us. Can we survive out here?'

'We survived near drowning in the Flame Sorceress' cave in Trois Havres,' Giles said. 'Can we survive this heat? We have supplies for ourselves and the animals. We have water, thanks to the dhouti. How long it will last is hard to say. The central question is: How badly do we want the key?'

'I'm not ready to give up yet,' Petia said quietly.

'Nor I. How about you, Keja?'

Keja stared up at the glowing sun and shook his fist. He looked at the other two. 'You're going to have to blame quitting on someone else. I'll stay.' He grinned, teeth flashing in the sunlight. 'But I reserve the right to grumble.'

'All right.' Giles pulled out the map. 'Let's see if we can work out where we are.'

An hour later, Giles felt more confident. He knew approximately where they were. If they continued along the caravan track for several more days, they should arrive at the place where Giles had planned to leave the caravan – the crossroads of an eastern caravan road to Masser.

When they gathered the reins of their lirjan, they could still see evidence of the caravan ahead of them. To either side the desert was empty, but ahead of them the dust drifted upward and to the east.

'Anyone averse to walking?' Giles asked. 'It'll be easier on the animals and may save water. We're not in a hurry, are we?'

The track was wide enough for two animals, and at first Giles and Keja walked together, Petia and Anji behind. They talked little, reserving their strength. Still, it felt good having someone to walk with. For Giles it brought back the days during the Trans War and the comradeship in the ranks.

His mouth turned even drier when he remembered that, with the camaraderie, had come sudden, messy death.

The days settled into the monotony of rising with the sun, walking with animals and camping in the evening. They conserved their supplies, became accustomed to the heat, and began to feel more comfortable with the desert. But occasional strange occurrences kept them on edge. At times during the day they heard eerie, unidentifiable sounds. 'There, there it is again!' Keja grated out. He wiped sand off his chapped lips. 'That sound.' He shuddered.

'It's just wind whistling through the rocks,' Petia said. No one contradicted her, but the air was deathly still.

At night the sounds came more frequently. Even Giles began to fidget and glance over his shoulder – only to see the same barren expanse that lay in front. Empty, silent, giving no clue to the source of the sounds. At times the moans were like human voices, lost souls, tormented beasts. At other times, they were unlike any sound produced by dead or undead that they had ever heard. 'What can we do about it?' Petia asked.

'I don't know. Nothing. We're committed to going on,' Giles replied.

Anji spoke up. 'Why not travel to one side of the caravan track? The going will not be so easy, but if the Harifim raiders came again they will expect to find you on the track.'

'We'll have to go far off it,' Giles said, considering the idea. He had wanted to stay with the path, but if the Harifim were responsible for the eerie sounds echoing across the bleak desert, leaving the track might confuse them. 'We don't want to get lost, but it's worth a try.' Even though Giles didn't admit it, he wanted to be free of the mournful sighs as much as Keja.

Giles scouted ahead, keeping to one side of the track. The small company followed, feeling more secure – and free of the inhuman cries for the moment.

The terrain changed and forced them back to the beaten track, sand dunes stretching like chains across the desert. They stood at the top of a tall dune, an immense bleak plain, too long and wide to be called a canyon, stretching as far as the eye could see. Columns of jagged stone thrust up from the floor like tributes to long-dead heroes, and boulders the size of small sailing ships littered the plain, turning sleek, wind-driven sand into a virtually impassable expanse.

In its grim fashion, the scene inspired wonder – and fear. It nearly broke the travellers' courage.

Anji spoke. 'It is said that the gods made the desert for

themselves. No one else could love it, so they alone could frolic here.'

To that, not even Keja had a comment.

Evening was upon them by the time they reached the rocky floor of the plain. It had become hotter as they descended and the boulders which littered the plain were immense, towering over them. Tired in body and numbed in soul by the over-powering landscape, they tethered the lirjan and dropped thankfully into the shade. Night was spent listening apprehensively for distant howls and moans.

The cries came just before sunrise, then died out, vanishing in the forlorn distance.

Just after the sun poked its diffuse, red eye over the rocky horizon, they encountered cold even more severe than they had felt in the high desert. They ate quickly, stamping their feet about the fire, anxious to be on their way and to have their blood circulating once again through sluggish veins.

Keja let out a roar when he went to pack his lirjan. 'Who's the prankster?' he demanded, dark eyes darting from Giles to Petia and Anji.

Supplies were strewn over a thirty feet circle. Keja's belongings had been dumped on the ground, his bag empty near the head of his somnolent lirjan.

'We wouldn't do anything like that, Keja. This journey is difficult enough without causing trouble for each other.' Petia looked at the scattered goods, then at Anji. 'You didn't do this, did you?'

'Oh, no, Mistress. It is the djinn's handiwork.'

'You don't believe in those tales, do you, Anji?' Giles said.

'Oh, yes. There are djinn in the desert. Ifrit, too. But the djinn are the ones who would do this. They like to make tricks. I have heard so many times.'

'Who are the djinn?' Keja asked, puzzled. 'Not more of the Harifim?'

'They are spirits,' Anji said, his voice taking on a reverent tone. 'They live in the rocks. Up in the hill. They frighten people. And they would think this a funny prank. It makes extra work for you. They watch – and laugh to themselves while you curse.'

247

'I don't believe that. I don't believe in spirits. Come on, help me get this stuff packed.'

Anji bobbed his head and ran off to begin gathering the grain sacks and other items scattered about. Petia shook her head and went to fetch her own pack. Her cry of dismay brought the others at a run. They stared at the pack ropes.

The previous evening she had coiled them carefully and set them on an outcropping of a boulder where they would be near to hand. Instead of a neat coil, the ropes were now tied in knot after knot, more than a hundred knots in the thirty-foot length. While they were simple overhand knots, not difficult to untie, the chore proved time-consuming and frustrating.

Giles looked at Anji. The boy solemnly said, 'Djinn. They are very good at this sort of devilment. There are many stories. Some must hold kernels of truth.'

Giles searched his own gear, expecting to find that some trick had also been played on him. He found nothing amiss, but he had the feeling that it was only a matter of time before his turn came.

When they were finally able to begin picking their way through the rocky plains, Giles called Anji to his side. 'Is there anything we can do to placate the djinn?' he asked.

Anji looked up at him. 'I do not know what "placate" means,' he said.

'Is there anything we can do so the djinn won't play these tricks? Can we leave something for them? Some food, water, a present? If they do this every night, we'll be ripping out each other's throats.'

'The stories don't say anything about how to satisfy the djinn,' the boy said. 'It is their sense of humour. They do it for fun, not for gain.' Anji's foot scuffed at a rock in the middle of a faint track. 'Maybe we will get beyond where they live,' he said.

'If they really are spirits,' Giles said, 'distance won't make any difference. They can come and go as they wish. I hope they tire of this quickly.'

Anji said nothing more, drifting back to walk beside Petia and leaving Giles to worry about the djinn. He hardly noticed the strange electric tension in the air, the odd stillness or the

248

reddening of the sky until in mid-afternoon the first sand storm struck with paralysing virulence.

'Hurry,' Giles yelled as the first touch of the storm cut at his face. 'Cover the animals' heads with your cloaks so they can breathe, then pull your own cowls up over your heads and get down behind your lirjan on the side opposite the storm.'

The wind blew stronger, the slashing sand hit with the impact of a hammer blow, stinging their bare hands and faces by the time they had the animals down. Anji was everywhere, encouraging the animals in his soft voice, as if he had dealt with them all his young life.

They had barely crawled behind the lirjan, hiding their heads, when the storm hit with its full force. The sky filled with red sand and choking dust, blowing northward across the plain. Keja winced as it filtered into the folds of his garment, piling up in a small, irritating ridge along his neck. He wanted desperately to raise his head and shake the dirt off, but he knew the penalty if he did. He kept his head down and his eyes squeezed tightly shut.

They heard the wind blowing, the heavier grains of sand hitting against their cowls. Petia felt sorry for the animals, even though she knew that their shaggy coats and thick skins probably felt little of the storm. As long as their eyes and noses were covered, they would come through the storm unscathed.

After more than an hour, the storm passed. At first, they hardly ventured a glance out for fear that it was a trick of the storm designed to lure them from safety, but cramped muscles and burning, reddened skin finally forced them to take a peek.

'We got through it,' Petia said, amazed, 'and it's over.' Then despair took control. 'Everything is against us. Even the weather. We can't go on. We'll die!' Her body sleekened as she unconsciously adopted catlike features to combat the danger she faced.

'Please,' Keja said. 'Let's not get hysterical.' His own voice carried a brittle edge of terror that Giles had heard before. Soldiers nearing the limits of their endurance struck out at others, just as Keja was doing with Petia.

'Petia, tend the lirjan. Keja, check to see if any of the ropes have loosened. We don't want our supplies left over half the

desert. You, Anji. Scout the ridge. Tell me of the storm's track.'
His firmness and no-nonsense commands broke the impending flare-ups. They shook their clothing out, uncovered the animals' heads and helped them onto their feet. They were soon laughing aloud as they watched the lirjan make their skin quiver from head to tail. The fine, gritty dust billowed out of their coats, forcing the humans to back away before it got into their eyes.

Their mood lighter, they started once more along the compass heading dictated by Giles. The faint signs of a track beneath their animals' hooves spurred them on; even the diabolical storm and its load of dust hadn't been able to obliterate the path.

But their lightheartedness didn't endure long. The storm was only the first of many – and the ones following were even more brutal. For the next four days they were harried by dust devils, whirlwinds, and two more savage sand storms.

'Someone wants us to turn back,' Petia said. 'They are sending the storms to kill us.'

'Nonsense. It's just the seasonal weather in this lovely desert,' Keja said, his tone mocking. 'These things would occur whether we were here or not.'

They travelled cautiously, eyes darting back and forth along the rocky horizon, seeking out new indications of storm. They saw nothing. Keja even managed to drift off to a fitful sleep astride his lirjan. Only when a rock grazed his forehead did Keja come awake again.

His hand shot up to a spot just under his sandy hairline and came away bloody. Keja's eyes hardened as he twisted around to confront his attacker.

'By all the gods,' Keja muttered.

Giles looked up sharply from his position at the head of the ragged column. 'What did you say?'

'A djinn just attacked me.'

Giles studied Keja's face for a moment. 'Tell us about it,' he said.

'Not much to tell. I was dozing and he threw a stone at me.' Keja held up his stained fingers; the scalp wound had already clotted over. 'He must have followed us for quite a distance, off to one side, to our left. After he threw the rock, he pranced

along, making faces at me, then made an obscene gesture and disappeared.'

'I see,' Giles said carefully. 'Did you take your ration of water or did you leave it for Petia?'

'Giles,' Keja said in exasperation. 'I'm all right. I . . . never mind. I should have known you wouldn't believe me. The sun *hasn't* got to me.'

Petia broke in. 'Don't be stupid, Keja. Giles just wanted to make sure . . .'

'So now I'm stupid. First I'm a liar, and now I'm stupid.' Keja yanked the halter of his lirjan and stalked ahead of the others.

Giles bent over and took Petia's upper arm and squeezed, cautioning her to silence. 'It's the heat,' he told her. 'I saw it during the War. Stress, hardship, they do strange things to the mind. When we rest, Keja will be fine.'

'Giles!' protested the woman. 'I believe Keja. I think he saw a djinn, if he says so.' She snapped the reins and rode off in unconscious mimicry of Keja. Giles stopped and stared, not knowing what to make of it. They were all going crazy from the heat. All of them, including himself.

Keja stayed ahead until Giles called for him to halt for a rest. He accepted the cup of water from Petia without looking at her. He sipped, staring off into the distance, and handed it back to her.

'Look, Keja. I'm sorry. It slipped out. I didn't mean it that way.'

'Yes, everything just seems to slip out and not be meant lately,' Keja sneered. 'I'm tired of always being the dolt. In the Flame Sorceress' cave it was me who had to be rescued. It's foolish Keja Tchurak who thinks he sees rock-throwing djinn. I should forget this insane quest and go back to Kasha.'

Giles settled to the ground in the shade of a large boulder. He wiped the perspiration from his forehead. 'I think it's time to talk this out,' he said. He gestured for the others to sit.

He gazed up at the cloudless azure sky while Petia and Keja settled down. Anji sat to one side, his back against a boulder, and closed his eyes. Giles decided Anji neither cared not understood what was going on. To the slave boy, nothing mattered.

'It's the heat,' Giles said. 'Sand storms, whirlwinds. It's

getting on everyone's nerves. Petia's remark wasn't intentional, but we're all starting to bicker.' He studied Petia and Keja to see how they were taking this. Not well, he decided. 'It's getting to us. We are in an unfamiliar land, alone. We're our own company, our only company – and it will get worse if we don't take care. We need to remind ourselves why we're here. We didn't have any problems getting the third key. Maybe it was too easy.'

'It wasn't that easy,' Petia said. 'But it only took a few days, once we found the sorceress' cave. We've been on the road too long, and it's dusty,' she finished with distaste. Petia made unconscious preening motions on whiskers that weren't there.

'That's it,' Giles agreed. 'We're almost at the crossroad where the old track heads east for Masser. We'd better decide now if we want to go on with this. Once we turn east,' he warned, 'we're committed. Why don't we find a good place to camp near here and rest for a day? Then we can talk about it again. Meanwhile, each of us should think about it. We'll decide later, after we've rested.'

'We know the track back to Kasha,' Petia said, glancing over to where Anji slept. 'We don't know what's ahead.'

'You want to quit?' Keja asked. 'Is that what you want?'

'No, it was only something to think about.' Petia folded her arms tightly around herself, withdrawing.

The djinn had not given up. Now that the four travellers had settled down to sleep, the djinn cavorted and danced in tight, vaporous circles; the humans had arrived for their entertainment. When slow, deep snores reached the djinn, they locked thin arms and drifted downward into the camp, misty fingers trailing over Keja's forehead wound, into Giles' nose, making him sneeze, to Petia's more intimate spots and provoking a nasty hiss more feline than human. The djinn even fastened insubstantial fingers around Anji's wrists, pinning him and bringing back memories of chains and cages.

But these were only fleeting amusements. Barely able to contain their mirth, they whispered off to put out the fire which Giles had carefully built, threw sand in the barley soup, untied

252

one lirjan and hid it among the boulders, and finally, as the crowning insult, spilled the contents of Giles' pack.

They had saved him to build the apprehension; now he became the victim of the same pranks that Keja and Petia had suffered earlier.

Only then did they retreat to congregate along one rocky ridge and discuss further pranks and relive the marvellous ones they had just perpetrated.

Giles sneezed again and peered out through one bleary eye when laughter floated down to him. Groaning, he sat up and fixed the fire, wondering how it had gone out. He fell back to sleep, even louder laughter echoing in his head, as much dreamlike as real.

'Now do you believe me?' Keja asked smugly.

'We believe, we believe,' Giles said, pushing the dried dung back into the fire. 'Malicious, aren't they?'

Petia spat out the first mouthful of barley soup she tried. 'Will we ever be rid of them? Or will they only get worse?'

Giles leaned forward, pulling out the map and fixing the corners with small rocks. His expression made Petia ask, 'What's wrong, Giles?'

'Maybe nothing. I just wondered, since the djinn are real, if the rest of these creatures might not be real, too? After all, the dhouti did warn us about them.'

The rest, in spite of the djinns' pranks, did them all good. After they packed the animals on the second morning, Giles said, 'It's time for decisions. Are we going forward or back? Into more djinn — and other beasts — or do we retreat?'

The way Giles spoke told of his decision: push on. They didn't even bother to sit down for the last round of discussion. Petia tugged at a pack knot to make certain that it was tight. She cupped her hands for Anji's foot to heft him onto the lirjan. 'Might as well go on,' she said without turning her head.

Keja looked briefly at Giles. 'Any second thoughts?' he asked. 'Is the key to the Gate of Paradise worth the risk?'

Giles' weathered face turned impassive and hid his true

thoughts. For a man whose joints ached more every day, passing through that Gate and into Paradise was worth any risk. So what if he died trying to retrieve the keys? He had no life other than the quest. Giles allowed himself a small smile now. If anything, this hunt gave purpose to his life, and being with Petia and Keja wasn't too bad.

Even watching after the boy hadn't proved as onerous as he'd thought it would be. Giles Grimsmate was enjoying life more now than he had since the end of the War.

Giles shook his head. 'What about you, Keja?'

'Doesn't make any difference, does it? Two for going on.'

Petia scowled. 'That's not fair, Keja. We want your decision. We don't want to hear later how you were outvoted. Tell us what you think.'

'I think we should go on, too. I think the only ones having any fun on this trip are the djinn. And maybe Anji, who seems to have more energy than the rest of us put together.' He winked at the boy, who blushed and averted his eyes.

'I am enjoying this trip very much, Master Keja. I have regular meals, new clothes, an adventure in the desert where I have never been, and a new mistress who is most kind and who pretends she has freed me. I will go where she goes.' He looked shyly at Petia.

'We'll have no more "master" and "mistress", Anji. I am Petia and they are Giles and Keja. Call us by those names. We are not your owners. You are free, you may leave us whenever you wish. I told you that in Kasha.' She turned toward Giles. 'Are we going to stay here all day?'

They had decided. The four gathered their reins and headed into the sun, which rose as hot as on previous days, the dust as dry and the effort as tiring. But somehow the mood of the small company had lifted. They found the energy to make small talk and to joke.

The caravan road that had once crossed the track from Kasha to Kuilla was marked by a tall cairn looming in the shimmering distance. When they arrived they found that the spire towered several times the height of a person. On top sat four lirjan skulls, bleached by the sun, staring sightlessly in the four directions of the compass.

'Someone's idea of grim humour,' Keja muttered.

'Just the reality of the desert,' said Giles.

They paused only briefly at the cairn. There were no signposts, and they turned eastward after Giles had examined his map once again.

'For someone who could memorise a map of the coast of Bandanarra, you certainly refer to that map a lot,' Petia said, the heat beginning to wear on her again.

'Into the unknown,' Giles said, folding the map. 'Can you imagine how your homeland has changed in a hundred years?'

'A lot more than this country has changed, you can be sure,' Petia replied. 'The Trans War made sure of that.'

A sombre mood settled on them as they turned east from the main track. More than once they turned to look back at the cairn dwindling from their sight. When they could no longer see it, they faced steadily eastward, and settled into their own thoughts. Giles nervously fingered the cloth beneath which the map rode easily. They had left the only place where any possibility of seeing humans existed. They had made the turn, the decision.

They were truly alone in the desert.

Seven

THE TERRAIN began to change within a few miles as they proceeded down the Track of Fourteen indicated on Giles' map. Their Iirjans' hooves crunched differently, revealing more solid ground. Before they knew it, they were walking on a wasteland of solid granite. The large boulders that had plagued their passage gave way to fantastic formations of wind-carved rock looming above them. Shadows created canyons of dancing darkness and light, yet the coolness they expected never quite made its presence known. If anything, this bizarre land of lacy rock sculptures and impossibly hard ground was hotter than the desert sand ever had been.

'Look,' said Giles, pointing. Petia and Keja said nothing. Anji still rode a pack animal, sleeping fitfully. Giles decided it was just as well that the child would not see the corpses of lirjan. They lay, desiccated vestiges of failed caravans long past. Occasionally Giles saw packs and other remnants of baggage that had been transported great distances to end up at this lonely, death-filled spot, but most were empty, shells from which the goods had long been removed. Perhaps the caravaners had redistributed the goods, or animals had carried off foodstuffs, leaving only empty cloth.

Probably they had died and desert scavengers had done the looting.

Through the morning, the companions kept a sharp lookout. By the midday break, their eyes ached from sand, heat and the twisting patterns of light and darkness playing against the rock formations. They sat, knuckling their eyes.

Keja was the first to put his feelings into words. 'I don't care if we're attacked or not, I'm closing my eyes. The glare is killing them.'

'Put some water on a cloth and hold it against them,' Giles said. 'That will help. I'll keep watch.'

Giles wandered away, hoping to find some small oasis of coolness. He knew it had to be cooler in the shadows, but it was not a noticeable difference from the heat reflected off the stony sculptings.

Ahead Giles saw more lirjan corpses. He had become accustomed to finding them along the Track of Fourteen. Lying beside the bleached bones were two humans, dead for many years, preserved by the dry heat. The packs still roped to the lirjan, caught Giles' eye. They contained the caravaners' cargo.

Giles bent over the dead animal and cut the ropes with his dagger. The pack rolled slightly, allowing him to pull open the cover and reveal a mound of desert garments, of fine quality and unravaged by Time's hot, groping fingers. A long, slender bundle, wrapped in canvas and tied with dried tendons, attracted his attention. He lifted it from the pack and cut the ties. The stiff canvas fought back as he unwrapped the heavy bundle.

He let out a low whistle of appreciation at the swords he found. The highly polished blades betrayed not a speck of rust. The hilts were of beautiful workmanship, joining the blades as if forged from a single piece of the finest steel Giles had ever seen.

'Amazing workmanship,' he said, allowing himself nothing more than a reverent whisper. 'And there are five! Never have I seen one sword this fine, and now I stumble across five!'

Giles picked them up one by one and examined them. Four were nearly identical, the only difference being in the decoration adorning the hilts. The fifth sword had a florid inscription beautifully engraved on the blade near the hilt. Giles brought the sword closer, attempting to read the script. The language was not familiar.

He rewrapped the swords and pawed through the pack, but found only more clothing. The others could look at it before they went on. He carried the swords back to his lirjan and slid them under the ropes holding his supplies.

'What did you find, Giles?' asked Petia. 'Anything to make the glare go away?'

'Intriguing goods on that pack animal,' he said. 'Good clothing in the pack farthest from here. Go and see if you want anything from it while I take care of this blinding light.'

'The glare first, then the looting,' said Keja, squinting. Giles nodded and began carving a slit in a small, flat piece of bone he'd picked up from the lirjan skeleton. He unravelled some thread and tied it to the pair of bones with the thin slits carved in them. He tossed one set over to Keja.

'Try these.' Giles watched as Keja fastened the thread around his head. His eyesockets took on the aspect of a death skull, showing only bone-white with a tiny black slit running the length. 'Well? Do they work?'

'I can't see too well,' Keja said, 'but they do reduce the glare.'

'In a few days your eyes will adjust to the narrow field of vision – and with the glare cut down, you won't be complaining so much.' Giles went ahead and fashioned the sun-slits for Petia and Anji, then finished with a set for himself.

They looked like eerie, blind creatures risen from the grave, but their vision cleared. Before the end of the day, they discovered one additional benefit. The slit prevented dust from caking their eyelids shut.

That evening Giles piled dried animal dung on the fire and huddled closer. Coming with the typical desert cold was a strong, gusty wind.

Across his lap he held the wrapped bundle of swords. 'A present for you,' he said to the others.

'I wondered if you were going to share this fine booty, whatever it is,' Keja said. 'I saw you hide the package on your lirjan. No holding back, remember? We're partners, even if we don't trust one another all that much.'

Giles began to unwrap the bundle. Petia and Anji moved closer to him in anticipation. Giles enjoyed the suspense. It reminded him of the solstice celebrations in his village, the gifts, the anticipation of youth for what they might receive.

When he revealed the blades, flashing in the firelight, the others murmured in appreciation. Anji caught his breath. 'The swordmakers of Hamri,' he breathed.

'Who are they, Anji?' Giles asked.

'I have seen two such swords in the market in Kasha. One cannot mistake the workmanship, Master Giles. They are most expensive. Hamri was a place far to the east, on the coast, I think. Very famous swordmakers. But the town is gone, destroyed because of the evil that lived there, it is said. There are no more swords of this quality. See.' He pointed at a small mark below the hilt. 'The mark of the Hamri swordmakers. The little symbol to the right is the signature of the master craftsman who made the sword. Very expensive, priceless! They are said to be brave in battle, such swords.'

Giles lifted one sword and handed it to Keja. He gave a second to Petia. 'See how they feel.'

The two rose and hefted the weight of the new weapons, going through both offensive and defensive movements with them, parrying, lunging, twisting and turning in mock battle. The ring of steel on steel was more than musical – it created a symphony that brought tears to Giles' eyes. Never had he heard or seen such perfection. Keja was the first to say anything.

'Incredible, Giles. It's as if it had been made for me. Beautifully balanced.'

Petia handed her sword back to Giles. 'May I try another? This one is too heavy.'

Giles handed her the shortest of the five. It took only a moment for Petia to know that this sword was better for her. She smiled and ran her fingers along the blade. 'A nice find, Giles. Thank you.'

'I've reserved one for myself.' He lifted the sword with the intricate inscription on the blade. 'I don't know if it's right for my style or not, but such beauty appeals to me.' He rose to test it. Never had the old warrior experienced such fluidity with a blade; it made him feel years younger wielding such a finely tempered weapon.

He, too, rubbed his thumb along the edge of the blade, testing its sharpness. Giles bent closer, examining the delicate script near the hilt, fingertip tracing the fine engraving.

The blade leaped in his hand as if the sword assumed a life of its own. Giles felt a vibration of energy run through his hand and up his arm, giving a power he had not felt even during his prime. He staggered to his feet, clutching at the sword as if it might escape. An aura of the purest blue surrounded the blade, shimmering as if heat radiated from the steel.

Giles stood, wondering if he should throw down the sword. He moved his left hand toward the blade and felt the energy. Then his common sense took hold and he touched the script once more with his forefinger. The sword's radiance vanished instantly. For a brief moment, it lingered in his hand and arm, then it, too, was gone. All that was left was a slight odour of ozone.

Giles sat down by the fire once again. The others stared at him curiously.

'What was it, Giles?' Keja asked. 'Did you hear something?' He leaned forward, a look of concern on his face.

'You couldn't see it?' Giles asked. Their puzzled expressions gave him answer enough. 'The blade came alive when I touched the script. Let me try it again, now that I'm prepared.'

Giles held the sword in his right hand and touched the script once more. Again he felt the vibration, heard the angry buzz.

259

He held the sword in front of Petia and Keja. 'Can't you see the energy shimmering off the edge of the blade?'

'No.'

He thumbed the script again, then held the sword out to Petia. 'Feel normal?'

'Yes, a little heavier than I like,' she answered.

'All right, now touch the script with your finger.'

Petia touched the letters, stared uncomprehendingly at the blade, then touched them again. Worldlessly, she handed the sword on to Keja. His reaction was much the same.

'Did you feel it?' Giles asked. 'It's like a . . . it's magic! You can feel the energy of the sword. I have no idea what it will do in combat, but it makes me want to find out.' Giles sobered and shook his head. 'It's been years since I said anything like that. Wanting to go into battle.' He shivered, but the feeling lingered within his breast. The sword *was* magical. He knew it.

'Keep that sword for yourself,' Keja said. 'I don't like the feel of it, not at all.'

'I'll be careful until I find out exactly what it can do,' Giles said, placing it back into the bundle. He had been brought up on stories of young men stumbling across weapons too powerful for their hands, and the dire consequences of their misuse. Being too cautious with this fine sword didn't seem possible.

Giles drifted off to sleep, his hand resting on the wrapped sword.

The days marched on stolidly, one after another. The Track of Fourteen wound its way out of the monstrous sandstone formations and into another plain, this one dotted with boulders and raska bushes which provided their lirjan with succulent great leaves.

Almost hypnotised by the terrain, it took several seconds for any of them to realise that the odd noises carrying over the plain had to be running footsteps. By the time they had turned on their mounts, a beast had reached the rearmost lirjan. Twisting its tail, it pulled the caravan animal off its feet, spilling Petia and Anji to the ground. The slavering, long-fanged beast loomed over them, taloned claws groping for the helpless pair.

Without bothering to stop his mount, Giles slid to the

ground. He ran, tugging at the new sword which now hung in the scabbard at his side. It slid forth easily. He thumbed the inscription, feeling the throb of energy.

The beast's taloned paws flashed down toward Petia and Anji. It stood on legs massive as stumps, planted wide apart. A mane of red hair flowed down its back.

Giles saw he would be too late; his legs couldn't pump fast enough to give him the speed needed. 'Aieeee!' he shrieked, the old battle-lust rising within him. All thought of personal injury, of aching joints, of anything but saving Petia and Anji, fled his mind.

The beast turned and faced the oncoming man. It was weaponless; with those teeth and talons it didn't need more.

Giles raised the sword and swept forward like a human tornado swathed in steel. Keja followed a dozen steps behind, approaching cautiously, waiting to see what developed between Giles and the beast.

The beast backed away from Giles' insane, blood-crazed rush. As Giles slashed, it dodged to one side with a speed that belied its size. It scrabbled in the sand as though searching for something. It picked up a stone, then stood, facing Giles.

Giles dropped *en garde*. 'Come and throw yourself on my sword tip, monster,' Giles snarled. He didn't care if it understood him or not. The beast backed away, glancing to see where the others were. Without warning, it raised the jagged stone and charged at Giles. Giles extended the sword and waited for the charging creature to run onto it. As the beast reached Giles, it skipped athletically to one side and threw the stone at Giles.

Giles was caught by surprise. In his experience, no animal save man could move with such quickness. The stone grazed his head, staggering him. He saw that the beast had already stooped to pick up another stone. He charged when the hairy creature bent over.

Giles' sword caught the beast in the shoulder as it straightened, a new stone in its clawed hand. The beast staggered. Blood oozed from the wound, and its thick body trembled. It shivered, tried to clap a hand to the wound, and fell to knobby knees.

Petia had struggled to her feet and reached Giles' side, her sword at the ready. They stood, waiting for a new attack, but the beast sagged. It attempted to stand, lifted one knee off the ground but wasn't able to get any further. Tremors ran through its body.

'It's had it,' Keja cried, taking his place by the other two. Anji had gathered an armload of lirjan sods, and danced around, pelting the kneeling beast.

Keja started forward to administer the killing thrust when the beast muttered, 'I surrender.' One hand lifted weakly as if to ward Keja off. 'I surrender.'

'It can talk,' Keja whispered. The small thief took a step backward, lowering the tip of his sword.

'So it seems.' Giles went to the beast, put his hand under its elbow, and helped the creature to its feet. 'Keja, get a fire started so we can boil some water. Petia, something for bandages. We can't let him bleed to death.'

'Why not?' demanded Keja. 'He tried to kill you and Petia. Slay him now!' But Giles grabbed Keja's wrist and stopped the lunge.

'Let's talk to him first, and then decide,' Giles said, the snap of command in his words. Reluctantly, Keja backed away.

When the beast's wound had been tended and mugs of tea had been made from the last of the boiling water, Giles lowered himself to the ground, facing the beast. 'Now, tell us who you are and why you attacked us.'

The beast peered at them near-sightedly. 'I thought you were skeleton men. I hate the skeleton men and their Lord.'

'Do you mean that skeleton men come out here into the desert?' Giles and the others exchanged puzzled looks.

'You know of the skeleton men, too?' the beast asked.

'Two were pointed out to us in Kasha. Do they live out here?'

The beast nodded. 'In Shahal.' He gestured to the east with his head.

'What is Shahal?' Petia asked.

Anji spoke up. 'A lost city in the desert.'

'It's not lost,' the beast said, looking oddly docile now. 'I know exactly where it is.'

Anji drew himself up proudly. 'In Kasha they say that Shahal is a lost city.'

The beast stared at the boy. His myopic, unwavering eyes disconcerted Anji. Then he looked away into the dust.

'The city is not lost. How can it be when I know it is many days' travel to the east. It was my home. Once.' The beast paused and stared off into the distance, remembering better days. 'It was the home of many beasts, a magnificent rock city, Shahal. Cool during the day, pleasant in the evening when we could look across the desert from our balconies, watching the setting sun.' Sadness and nostalgia tinged his voice – and bitterness.

'You said it was your home,' said Keja. 'Why isn't it your home any longer?'

'The Skeleton Lord stole it from us. He and his army of skeleton warriors. They outnumbered us, and the skeleton beings are difficult to kill. They have no blood, so they did not bleed when we fought them; they kept coming. We were driven out and the Skeleton Lord took our city for his own evil purposes.'

'What did you do then?' Giles asked.

'We scattered into the desert. When we tried to go back, we were turned away by the skeleton men.'

Giles pulled the map from his tunic. 'There is no city named Shahal on this map.'

Giles leaned forward and put his finger on the map. 'This is where we are now.'

The beast grabbed the map away and held it closer to his face. 'Look, look,' he cried. 'My friends. See, these are my friends!'

The three bent forward to look. The beast's head came up and he looked from one to another. 'These are all my friends. We lived together in Shahal.' He rocked back and forth with obvious delight.

Keja nodded his head. 'So much for your imaginary beasts, Giles. Just legends, isn't that what you said?'

Giles grimaced.

'These beasts are all your friends?' Giles asked. 'You know them?' He pointed to the edge of the map.

'Yes, I know them all. There are others. But nobody believes in us any more.' Giles thought the beast was going to cry, but the red-haired monstrosity stopped just short of it.

'Do you know where the others are?' asked Petia. 'Where you can find them?'

The beast turned his hands palm up and gestured into the desert. 'They live many places. Like me. In the desert.'

Petia turned to Giles and Keja. 'Perhaps we could make an alliance with them. We'll need help if we are going up against this Skeleton Lord.'

'Of course,' Keja said. 'We've been attacked by one of these beasts. Now you want them for friends. Sometimes I don't understand you, Petia.'

'I don't understand you, either. Look, the beast thought we were the Skeleton Lord's minions. Is it any wonder he attacked us? You remember what the skeleton men were like.' She turned to the beast, putting her hand on its forearm. 'Could you find your friends and bring them to us?'

'Petia, I think we ought to consider what you're suggesting.'

'Really, Giles, what is there to consider? If we are going to Shahal, we are going to have to fight the skeleton men and their lord. We are going to need help. The beasts can help. Perhaps we can even get them back their city.' Petia concentrated, sweat shining on her face. At times she could touch the thoughts – the emotions – of others. She did so now, linking lightly with the beast. Only honesty and a simple-minded friendliness came forth.

If nothing else, Petia felt a bond with the beast, her own Trans nature being closer to that of the creature than either Giles' or Keja's.

A frown wrinkled the beast's face as he listened. It vanished slowly as the impact of what Petia had said became clear to him. 'Give us our city back?' he said, obviously startled at this new idea.

'No promises,' Giles said hastily. 'We don't even know if we can get to the city. Would the beasts be willing to help?'

'Oh, yes, I'm certain of it. I'll go now and bring them.' The beast started to rise.

Petia held him back. 'You are wounded. You need a day of rest before you go. There's no hurry.'

The beast lay back, beaming in satisfaction. That pleased Petia – she felt vindicated in her judgment of the beast.

'Again?' asked Petia, frustration at a peak. She vowed to pronounce the beast's name, but when he had voiced it for what must have been the hundredth time, Petia knew she'd never be able to repeat it.

'Red Mane will have to do,' said Giles. To Red Mane, he said, 'You're healed enough to fetch the others.' He ventured a small pat on the beast's hairy shoulder. Red Mane smiled, fangs gleaming in the sunlight. The beast spun round and ran, massive legs driving him across the desert; quickly he disappeared from view.

'Think we'll ever see him again?' asked Keja.

'Not for a while,' Giles answered. Whether or not Red Mane returned, they had done what they could to get closer to the city.

They did not expect to see anything of him or the other beasts for several more days and were shocked when a shaggy creature entered the camp in mid-afternoon. It said nothing, but seated itself to one side and waited, tiny eyes darting to and fro.

As the day wore on, other beasts arrived. At nightfall Petia and Keja prepared a large kettle of barley soup, flavoured with spindly herbs Anji had found nearby. They took it to the beasts and set it before them.

'None of them has spoken a word to us,' Keja said. His uneasiness had grown as more and more of the beasts came into their camp. 'It's as if they are waiting for our red-headed friend to return.'

'They probably are,' Petia replied. 'He might have warned them not to talk with us. Cautious, I suppose.'

They built a fire against the inky night; soon after, the red-maned one and another beast appeared out of the dark. 'That is all us,' he said.

Giles saw how weary Red Mane was. 'I didn't expect you to return so soon. We will talk in the morning after you've rested. Eat now, and talk to your friends.'

The following morning, the humans and the beasts sat down to a long discussion.

'Shahal,' Red Mane said, 'was once the jewel of the desert, a vital stopping place on the caravan road. We were well known to human caravaners. Trade prospered for all.'

Red Mane let out a low howl of anguish, then shook his head so hard that dust flew in all directions from his thick mop.

'The caravans began to dwindle, and eventually disappeared. Finally the Skeleton Lord and his minions came. We thought they were only odd humans, but they were the ones choking off the trade – trade Shahal needed.' Red Mane made a curious gesture, tugging at the back of his hair as he shook his head.

'Let me guess,' Petia said. 'The Skeleton Lord moved in and tossed you out.'

Red Mane nodded sadly. 'Since then we have lived an aimless existence in the desert.'

'Why didn't you try to build a new city?' asked Keja. 'If you couldn't fight this Skeleton Lord, you could at least made another home.'

'We tried, a few times we tried. He destroys all we attempt. We live in the dunes, scrabbling out a pitiful existence. No caravans, no trade, no Shahal.'

Red Mane came to the end of the tale. 'Will you help us to recover our Shahal? There is great wealth there, a fabulous room of treasure gathered during the trade years. We do not want it; we have no use for it. It is yours if you help us to win back the city.'

Giles answered with his own question. 'Do you know anything about a key belonging to the Skeleton Lord? A gold key that has something to do with the Harifim religion?'

'We do not know of religion. The Harifim are desert people. We think that the skeleton men come from the Harifim. But it is not their choice.'

'So we still don't know if the key is in Shahal,' Petia said in exasperation. 'We could be following a feral slug.'

'A feral slug?' Keja asked. 'That sounds disgusting.'

'I mean not finding anything at all after a great deal of effort.'

'I understand.' Keja raised his eyes to the sky. 'A feral slug,' he muttered as he sat down.

Giles pulled out his map again. 'Do you know Makar, or Lis Abem, or Calaret, or Darestra?'

'All were cities on the old caravan track,' Red Mane said, squinting. 'Darestra was on the coast, the others scattered along the route.'

266

'All of them are on the map,' Giles muttered, 'except Shahal. I wonder why? Not just a deserted city, but a lost city, begging your pardon, Red Mane. And the domain of the Skeleton Lord.' Giles folded the map and said with conviction. 'The best place I can think of to look for the key.'

'We want the key; they want their city back. We could all be in trouble,' Keja said.

'No doubt,' Giles said. He reached over and touched Red Mane's arm. 'We will help you, and you will help us. Agreed?'

Red Mane nodded and rose to his feet. He faced the other beasts and spoke in his tongue-tangling language. The beasts stood and growled.

Giles tensed, but Petia sensed the true emotional current. She laid a calming hand on his arm.

Red Mane turned to the humans, eyes moist. 'They are happy,' he said. 'The caravaners stopped believing in us. It has been a long time. We will return to Shahal!'

Giles hoped it would be so – and then the fourth key to the Gate of Paradise would be his reward.

Eight

THE BEASTS distanced themselves from the humans, too long in the desert to easily consort with others. Red Mane became their spokesman, but even he showed signs of uneasiness around the humans.

Giles, knowing the Petia's ability to touch emotion, spoke to her about it. 'We don't know what they are thinking. We know only what Red Mane decides to tell us. I might be too suspicious, but I wonder if the beasts aren't just using us.'

267

'As we're using them,' Petia said.

Giles only nodded.

'Don't you trust them?' Petia asked.

'I don't distrust them, at least not at the moment. We just don't know enough about them. I believe what Red Mane told us about Shahal and that they once lived there, but how will they react when we get to the city or confront the Skeleton Lord's men? How will they do in a fight? Red Mane certainly didn't show much bravery. One cut and he surrendered.'

'I'll see what I can do,' Petia said. 'I haven't used it much lately, and I get out of practice. Maybe I should have been practising on you and Keja.' Her eyes gleamed impishly.

'Don't let me catch you doing that,' Giles said. 'My thoughts and emotions are private.' The old soldier in him valued his privacy more than anything else – it was in too short a supply under normal circumstances. Giles wanted to be free to feel as his nature dictated.

But it wasn't too much to ask the Trans to spy on Red Mane and the others. Giles counted that as part of their 'war' to win the key to Paradise.

'Oh, so now you want me to trust you and Keja. That's not what you were saying a few weeks ago. I remember the very words: "I still don't trust you two." You don't trust me, but I'm supposed to trust you. You can't have it both ways, Giles. Remember that.'

Giles heaved a deep sigh as Petia stalked off. What bothered him most was that she had cut to the heart of the problem. Travelling with a pair of thieves had done little to instil trust in him.

Giles went to muster the ragtag band and get them moving. This, at least, was something he did well and without upsetting anyone.

The company now looked like a troop of soldiers as they followed the Track of Fourteen. The four humans walked most of the time, leading their lirjan. The beasts ambled along behind. At times Red Mane joined Giles and the others, but mostly he stayed with the other beasts, chattering away in their incomprehensible tongue.

The sun beat down fiercely on the Track as it stretched across the desert, and occasionally they were beset by sand storms.

Sudden winds filled the air with stinging particles that forced the company to wait for calm before moving on. And through the heat and dust and wind they continued on, knowing that the elements were the least part of their ordeal – Shahal and the Skeleton Lord lay ahead.

'I don't understand this land,' Keja mumbled. 'Not a cloud in the sky, the sun blazing down. Then the wind comes up, blows everything into obscurity, and goes away just as quickly. It's not a pleasant place to live in.'

'The gods created the desert for themselves, Anji told us,' Giles replied. 'Red Mane calls it the garden of the gods.'

'They can have it. Once we find that key, we leave.'

'There'll be no reason for staying then,' Giles agreed.

The heat and constant scorching from the sun sapped the humans' strength. They required more water than the beasts, and the goatskin became dangerously lean. When they stopped for the evening, Giles brought up the matter with Red Mane.

'Our water is running low. We don't know where to find it, but you or one of the other beasts must know. You need water too, don't you?'

'We know where to find water.' Red Mane frowned and tugged at his knotted hair as if he had never considered such a request. Finally, as if coming to a momentous conclusion, he said, 'There is a spot, a good place. There are trees and plants. The animals come to drink where the water bubbles up from beneath the ground and makes a small lake.'

'An oasis,' said Giles. 'Could you find it and fill the water-skins for us? Keja and Petia and the boy are losing their strength, and I'm in none too good a condition.'

Red Mane looked at Giles. 'Yes. Water is important in the desert. There is some danger, but I will get someone to go. They will be careful.'

'How dangerous?'

'Only a little. The animals only share grudgingly. We all depend on the same water. Still, it is good to be careful, especially if the Skeleton Lord stirs.'

Giles didn't even want to consider that possibility. Did the Skeleton Lord know they were coming? To regain Shahal? To take away the key?

The party chosen by Red Mane returned two days later to great celebration. Giles watched uneasily as the beasts clawed and tore at each other, growling and gnashing teeth. In spite of this wildness, everyone in the party was careful not to waste any of the hard-won, precious water.

'They do carry on, don't they,' said Keja. The thief's uneasiness was greater than Giles'. Keja's hand never strayed far from his sword hilt.

'They gave us the water we needed. Apparently, they don't require anywhere near as much as we do. We're going to have to ration it.'

'No more cat baths,' Keja said, loud enough for Petia to hear. The Trans woman sniffed and turned away, pointedly ignoring him. Giles started to reprimand Keja; keeping the peace in the party was difficult enough without adding new fuel to the fires of animosity and distrust. Still, Giles didn't think Keja meant his words. This was his way of joking. It fell flat, but he intended no harm. If anything, Giles saw something more between Keja and Petia – though they would be the last ones to admit it.

The party continued along the Track of Fourteen. Each evening Giles pulled out the map and attempted to determine their location. Sometimes he smiled confidently as he put the map away. Other times he finished with a scowl. They were approaching an area marked as the Calabrashio Seas. This worried Giles; they trod across bone-dry desert.

One evening, as Giles finished studying the map, Red Mane asked, 'May I show this wonder to my friends?' Without comment, Giles handed over the map. The humans watched, amused at the joking comments the beasts made about the portraits of their friends on the map. Giles retrieved the map and looked at the illuminations more carefully, then frowned. If he didn't know this map was centuries old, he'd think the artist had used Red Mane and several others in the band as subjects.

When they reached the Calabrashio Seas, Giles could do no more than stare numbly.

'I've never seen anything like this,' Petia muttered.

'I've never even heard of anything like it,' said Keja. He lifted the bone sun-slit Giles had fashioned for him so that it rested on the top of his head. He wiped sand and sweat away, then spat. 'We can't cross *that*.'

Giles almost agreed with him. The sand seas undulated with the motions of enormous waves in constant motion. It was as if they stood on an ocean strand watching the endless incoming tide.

The Track of Fourteen disappeared under the lapping waves of gritty brown sand. No matter how they strained their eyes, there was no evidence of an end to the Calabrashio, or of a road continuing onward.

They drew back, irrationally fearful that the lapping waves would rush forward and swallow them.

'Let's get out of sight,' said Petia. 'Of the waves. They . . . they make me seasick.'

'Yes, let's humour her,' Keja spoke up, but he obviously shared her affliction.

Giles nodded. 'This area is marked on the map, but not as sand. I anticipated something, but I didn't expect this.' His face had lost some of its colour, even under his suntanned, leathery skin.

'We can make our way around it,' Petia said. 'Surely there is an edge to it? What does the map show?'

'We camp,' Giles said forcefully. 'I want to ask Red Mane why he didn't warn us of this.'

When Giles did talk with Red Mane, he was not encouraged. 'I'm sorry,' Red Mane said. 'We thought you knew. The sand seas are huge, no way around them unless you spend many dangerous, waterless weeks. The seas stretch across to the Cliffs of Agrib where the waves of sand break upon the rocks. It is dangerous there. We would be buried immediately.'

The idea that Red Mane considered the end of their journey more dangerous than what Giles saw now tested his determination to pursue the fourth key to the Gate of Paradise. But retreating hardly seemed preferable to continuing on. He knew what lay behind. Perhaps it wasn't so dangerous ahead.

'How can we get through, Red Mane?' Giles stared blankly at the map before him.

'It is dangerous and one must be careful. But it has been done. In the old days, even the caravans crossed it.'

'How? The sand shifts all the time, sliding up and down in waves and troughs.'

Red Mane stared down at the shifting mass, as if he could see through the dark. 'There are places where it is bare and not all one sea of sand. There are many seas. Sometimes you can find your way between them.' He looked at Giles. 'It is the only way across.'

'You know the way, then?' Giles asked, encouraged.

'No. When we were driven out of Shahal, we were harried by the skeleton warriors, herded into the seas. Those of us you see survived. We wandered for days in the seas. Some of us were separated and we never saw each other again.'

Giles rummaged in his pack for the compass the dhouti had given him. In the firelight he studied compass and map, wondering if he could – if he should – lead this small company through the treacherous terrain ahead. Did he want to be responsible for their safety, for their very lives?

'There's no choice,' Giles said, his mind made up. 'We've got to wade through the Calabrashio. Once into it, we'll have to keep going, no stopping. We may find places to rest, but not to sleep. It must be thirty miles wide. We'll start in the morning.'

The sand shifted beneath the travellers' feet, and dust blew off the top of the waves like spray from ocean waves. They found it impossible to keep the sifting sand from their mouths and noses, no matter how tightly they covered them. Even through the thin slits in the sun-slits fine dust seeped, more like water than sand.

Sand got into their boots and found its way into the cracks and crevices of their clothing. Water became even more precious now, and they drank only a little at midday. Both humans and beasts suffered severe dehydration, the water they did allow themselves causing stomach cramps.

The sand ebbed and flowed before them. Giles kept his compass handy, protected from the sand. During lulls in the wind's savage assault, he would pull it out quickly and try to focus on a landmark ahead.

But no true reference points existed. Sand dunes thirty yards ahead would disappear without trace, sinking down into the brown, heat-soaked death of the sand sea. If he tried to follow such ghosts, they veered off course.

Giles tried to keep his eyes straight ahead on the compass setting. He began counting steps, even though this served little purpose. The others staggered behind him, trying to maintain a straight line and ignore the ever-changing terrain.

Even Anji, who was more accustomed to the heat than the other humans, suffered from the lack of water and sleep. He rubbed his eyes frequently, faltered more and more often, but never complained. Petia looked imploringly at Giles, but the bone goggles hid any hint of sympathy. She finally got a piece of rope from Keja, looped one end around Anji's waist and tied the other to her belt. This way, if Anji stumbled and fell, she would know.

Occasionally they found a clear and quiet place to rest for a while. No speech was possible; their mouths had turned to sand and their throats closed. Giles would wait until the restless dust rolled towards them again, then he'd urge the group to their feet and onward. Hunger attacked them, but there was no place to prepare a meal. Thirst was a constant companion. Worst of all, they began to drift alone, each lost in the closed prison of his own mind.

At sunset the wind died slightly and the sand shifted less; tide had begun to ebb.

By the end of the first day, most staggered rather than walked. Giles urged them on into the night. To stop was to die. When the sun went down, the Calabrashio became freezing.

'How can it be so hot during the day and turn so cold at night?' Keja asked.

Giles pointed at the sky. Thousands of stars littered the heartless black expanse. 'No cloud cover. Nothing to hold the heat in. It dissipates rapidly from sand.'

They paused, retied the packs on their lirjan, and wondered if even these hardy animals might survive. After their brief rest, the sands began to move again. Giles found a constellation on

273

which to concentrate and followed it, plodding on through the night.

When first light came, Giles pulled out his compass again. Petia saw him clasping his forehead.

'What's wrong, Giles?' she asked.

'I forgot that the sky turns during the night. I followed that cluster of stars and we've curved south. What a fool!'

'Don't be so hard on yourself,' Petia said. 'We're all tired – dazed. You as well.'

'But I ought to have known better.'

'What will that do? How far are we off course?'

'The gods only know. We may have made some progress east, but probably an equal distance south. When we do get through the Calabrashio, we'll be well south of the Track.'

'Can't we change now to correct our course?' Petia asked.

Giles sighed. 'I can try. Don't tell the others. We have problems enough without them knowing that I've blundered so.'

Petia nodded. Doubt was dangerous and dissension now would kill them. She put her hand on Giles' arm in understanding and encouragement. 'We'll make it,' she said.

Giles shook his head and grimaced, but gratitude shone in his eyes.

While they walked, Giles berated himself for the error of the night before. Finally he realised that what was done was done. Giles convinced himself that he wasn't made of iron, that he alone of the party was indestructible and infallible. Even worse, Giles came to the conclusion that, while he had experience in such forced marches from the twenty years spent during the Trans War, this meant nothing compared to the fact he had aged.

'Old man, keep moving,' he said to himself. The words barely left his gummy mouth, but they had their effect. So what if he had grown old? He wasn't ready for the grave yet – and the Gate beckoned.

If Giles pushed himself, he demanded no less of the others. He drove and harried until they got moving again whenever their determination flagged. He took advantage of every lull in the undulating sand; he knew it was the only way to achieve victory over the Calabrashio.

Keja grumbled that they needed the rest.

'We can't afford to, Keja. We could be lost in here forever if we don't keep moving.'

'I don't think a rest would hurt,' Keja responded. 'I can hardly put one foot after the other. Don't let being leader go to your head.'

'I never asked for the position,' Giles replied. He held the compass for Keja. 'Here. You lead for a while. I'll be happy to follow, as long as you keep walking east.'

Keja turned away, spat, and walked off.

'What was that about?' Petia asked.

'I'm not sure,' Giles said. 'Keja's unhappy because I'm the leader, but it might be more than that. Try to find out what's bothering him.'

After the next short rest, Keja placed himself at the back of the beasts, disassociating himself from Giles, Petia and Anji. Giles knew the signs of mutiny brewing, and he didn't know the reason.

The long, hot afternoon wore into evening, then the sudden darkening into night. Giles, staggering drunkenly, again made the rounds, encouraging beasts and humans alike – except Keja, who remained distant. During the rest, Giles looked at the map and made calculations. If the map was accurate, they should be near the eastern edge of the sand seas by morning, but Giles dared not tell the party. He feared that the map might not be accurate or his calculations wrong. Such disappointment might mark the end of their fragile alliance.

When morning came and they were still staggering through the waves of sand, Giles nearly despaired. It was all he could do to force himself to his feet and urge the others on.

They had been walking for only an hour after the morning rest when Anji cried out. 'The edge!'

Ahead of them lay the flat plain, looking almost the same as it had three days ago when they found the Calabrashio Sea blocking their way. The mid-morning heat shimmered off its surface, but to the party, weary of waves and troughs of sand, the unmoving surface looked like an oasis. Boulders and sandstone columns offered shade.

They staggered forward, stumbling like sailors newly ashore when they reached the solid, unshifting ground. The beasts broke into a lope, heading for the nearest available shade. The humans shuffled after them, with only enough energy left to move one foot in front of the other.

When they reached the shade, they dropped, exhausted. Red Mane came to take the waterskin and share out the water. Giles had only enough energy to pour some water for the lirjan and caution Red Mane that it was still rationed.

But inside himself Giles exulted. They had conquered the treacherous Calabrashio. He lay back and closed his eyes.

Once he had seen that everyone had water, Red Mane collapsed with his back against the stone. No one moved for a long time. When the sun moved around to glare into Giles' face, he roused himself from his exhausted stupor. He stood and Petia opened one eye to look at him.

'What are you doing?' she asked.

'We've got to eat. We haven't had a decent meal in three days.'

Before Giles could get the food started, the beasts cried out in agitation. Giles looked over to the boulder where they were still huddled in the shade. 'I wonder what's wrong?' he said to Petia.

Then he heard Red Mane shout, 'Djinn, djinn!'

Giles saw a swirling dust devil moving across the plain. 'Quick, find shelter,' he yelled at Petia. But she was already running toward Anji, shouting as she went.

Giles' mind snapped from its fatigue-induced lethargy and he saw the danger. The man ran after Petia, shouting, 'Wait, come back!'

The dust devil swerved, aimed itself at the woman and boy. Giles stopped, watching in mute horror as it surrounded them and obscured them from his sight.

The dust cleared for a few seconds, and he saw Petia grab the boy. Almost instantly the swirling wind caught her and hurled her to the ground. Giles stumbled towards them. The wind stopped its lateral movement, intent on playing with the two humans caught in the vortex.

Giles plunged into the whirling brown mass. One groping hand found a leg, grabbed and hung on. From the size, he knew it was Anji. He pulled the boy close to him and staggered out of the small tornado. He set the boy down and shouted in his ear, 'Run! Run to the boulders and hang on to Keja.'

Giles spun, intending to rescue Petia, but he saw nothing. The thick wall of whirling dust had become impenetrable, the sand able to strip the flesh from his bones.

Giles heard a cry – Petia? Then nothing. He stood facing the deadly column of sand, torn between suicide and facing the knowledge he had not tried to save Petia. Or her lifeless body.

Nine

GILES STARED, caught up in the agony of indecision. To plunge into that maelstrom of cutting sand would mean his death, too, but to leave Petia? He didn't think she could have survived.

The indecision vanished when he heard the djinn's mocking laugh. Without hesitation, Giles fought his way into the leaping, cutting pillar of dust, searching for Petia. His lips thinned to a line; he dared not let the sand fill his mouth and choke him. Blindly he flailed about, seeking her. The flesh dissolved from his hands, his face. Red agony burned in his veins now. The bone goggles he wore blinded him in the darkness of the djinn's mischief and did little to hold back the dust.

He fought against the buffeting winds – and he found her. Giles almost fell over the writhing woman but managed to keep his balance. He grabbed Petia's shoulders and pulled her to her feet. When she was standing, he put one arm around her waist and drew his sword, awkwardly thumbing the inscription and feeling the blaze of energy. The enemy might be only a mass of swirling dust, but Giles' anger knew no bounds. If the power of the sword allowed them to fight their way out, he'd use it!

Barely had he levelled the sword when a corridor through the shroud of brown opened before them. Giles held the sword before him and half-carried Petia to the perimeter of the dust storm. As they cleared the edge of the whirlwind and stumbled into the hot desert sun, Giles swung his blade mightily at the axis of the vortex. He knew it was an empty gesture, but his anger at the djinn was great.

Giles heard a howl from the miniature tornado's core. The whirling dust stilled and fell to the desert floor, revealing an immense djinn in human guise who made an obscene gesture and disappeared.

Giles sheathed his sword and assisted Petia, lowering her to the ground to examine the scratches she had suffered.

'You're not too bad,' he said. 'No, don't try to talk.' He wiped away a gooey mixture of spittle and sand from her lips. 'You must rest now.' She tried to speak again but he silenced her, knowing what she wanted. 'Anji is fine. Now sleep.'

This time, Petia did relax. Whether she slept or not, Giles didn't know, but she was safe. That was all that mattered.

Keja dropped down beside Giles, face strained. 'The djinn is gone. I tried to reach you but the dust . . .'

'We'll be all right,' Giles said. Whether Keja had tried to reach him was a moot point. He laughed harshly. 'We survive a sea of moving sand and yet a prankster spirit almost kills us.'

'I will stand guard,' Keja declared, hand on sword.

'Do as you wish. I just want to rest.' Giles curled up in a shady spot, not noticing the hard rocks beneath him. As tired as he was, he might have lain on a bed of flower petals. Giles came groggily awake when he heard Anji cry out.

'We're trapped inside a bottle,' the boy shouted.

Giles wiped his eyes again and looked around. Most of the beasts still slept. He gazed about him, unbelieving. Shards of light splintered against a translucent surface and reflected painfully bright rays into his eyes.

A glass wall encircled them. Giles strode across the enclosure and reached out to assure himself that this was not a nightmare. The hot glass caused him to jerk away his hand – the clear prison wall was all too real.

The others had roused and came to Giles' side with a barrage of questions. No matter what happened, Giles thought, they looked to him for answers. Like it or not, he was the leader.

'I don't know what's happened,' he said. 'Anji discovered it. The djinn, probably. Angry at being driven off.'

Red Mane shook his head. 'Not the djinn. The Skeleton Lord.'

'How do we get out of this one, Giles?' Keja asked, standing back and looking upward.

In the marketplace the rough glass would have been called poor, but it imprisoned them effectively and grew hotter by the minute. Giles wrapped his hand in a fold of his robe and tapped on the thick surface. It wouldn't break easily.

The beasts gibbered among themselves. Red Mane tried to calm them, but their panic grew. 'It will bring death,' one of them said. Giles' anger rose at being penned like this, and he called to Red Mane.

'Can you see through it? Is there anyone outside?'

Red Mane walked around the circle of glass, stopping to peer. 'I can't see anyone out there. If the Skeleton Lord did it, he wouldn't leave anyone on guard. He knows we can't escape.'

'Don't give up so easily,' Giles snapped. He tried to force calmness on himself and his thoughts, but it wasn't easy. In all his years of soldiering, nothing like this had ever happened to him. Facing a drawn sword was one thing, magic another.

Giles knelt where the glass met the desert. He took his dagger and dug into the soil. 'Perhaps we can dig under the glass.'

Willing hands came to his assistance. As he loosened the hard-packed desert soil, others scooped it away. His blade dug deeper and deeper, but always it met the glass wall; the bottle plunged deep into the earth. The perspiration rolled off Giles' forehead, stinging his eyes. Dig as he might, he couldn't reach the bottom of the glass. At last he sat back, looked at his helpers, and shook his head.

'It's no good,' he said. 'I don't think we'll ever dig under it.'

The beasts moaned. 'Die here,' one said.

'No, we won't die here. We *will* get out.' Giles detested this self-pity and wondered if recruiting the beasts had been such a good idea. Give him a small squad of determined volunteers over recruits any day.

Keja moved to the centre of the bottle, looking up. He could see the top of glass enclosure yawning open like a chimney. Because of the sun's glare, the small thief couldn't estimate its height. Slowly he unwound the rope around his waist.

He found his triple hook and attached it to the end of the rope. 'Everyone stand to one side. I'll see if I can hook the top.'

He swung the hook in an ever-widening arc, dipping it low to the ground and then up into the air. The hook swung up, but struck the glass about twenty feet above their heads and tumbled back down.

'Wrong approach,' Keja muttered. He coiled the rope carefully at his feet. This time he swung the hook faster and faster in a vertical circle. When he had the hook travelling at a good speed, he released it upward.

The hook flew true, arching from the centre of the circle and reaching for the top of the glass wall. The rope played out of its circle, reached its end, and continued to fly upward. But once again the hook did not reach the top of the glass enclosure.

He tried over and over, but each time the hook fell back, once nearly hitting a beast. Finally, weary and frustrated, Keja gave up.

'What now?' he said to Giles.

'Let me try my sword. It worked getting rid of the djinn's dust devil.' He widened his stance and pulled the weapon from its scabbard. 'Stand back everyone. We don't want anyone hit by splintering glass.'

Giles selected a spot on the clear wall, thumbed the inscription and felt the sword's energy in his hand and arm. He placed the sword point against the glass and pushed. Nothing. He stepped back a step and swung a weak blow. A tingle rushed up his arm, but the glass held.

He took the sword in both hands and swung with all his might. Energy flowed from the sword and the glass shuddered, but did not break.

'I don't think that's going to do it,' he said, examining the spot he'd struck and noting he hadn't even scratched the glass.

Anji let out a wordless cry of amazement. Giles squinted through the glass and saw the outline of a beast outside their enclosure, trying to peer in.

280

'I forgot about her,' Red Mane cried. 'I exiled her for two days for defecating in my presence. She's caught up with us at last.'

'Shout to her,' Petia said. 'If we can talk, I have an idea.'

Red Mane stood nose to nose with the beast outside the glass and bellowed in his strange tongue.

The beast outside made movements with her mouth, but those inside heard nothing.

Red Mane walked to the middle of the circle and bellowed again. Then he cupped his ear and listened. The others held their breath, not wishing to interfere. No sound came back. Red Mane's voice disappeared into the bright blue sky.

'She cannot hear us,' Red Mane said.

'Petia, can you communicate with her?' Giles asked. 'With your mind?'

'I can try.' Petia sat opposite the beast, seeing only distorted images through the glass. She gathered herself, concentrating. Giles had told her to practise, to learn to tap the beasts' emotions. Her success so far had been limited. Now their lives depended on her feeble Trans ability. The perspiration dripped from her forehead, but she ignored it. If she failed, they would all soon bake to death inside the glass.

She opened her mind, concentrating on the simple, emotion-laden message she wished to send:

Beast, free us! With this went her fears, her hopes, her overpowering need to ensure Anji's safety.

The beast outside became agitated, looking up at the sky and then out into the desert. Petia experienced the panic as if it were her own. Vague pictures formed, confusing ones. She tried to sort them out to use them.

Sleek, Petia sent, knowing the beast's name, at least within her own mind. *Fire!*

Petia shook with the exertion. So much effort for so little information. And Petia didn't even know if this simple plan might work, if Sleek would understand.

The female beast hesitantly piled dried branches against one side of the bottle. Her movements, the way her shadow bobbed across the translucence of the bottle-prison, showed her confusion. But she obeyed the commands Petia arrowed in her direction.

'Sit quietly,' Petia cautioned the others. 'The storm of emotion confuses me, and I might need to reach her again.'

'What's happening?' demanded Keja. Giles silenced him with a curt gesture. Keja fell into a sullen silence.

Sitting quietly by the glass, Petia closed her eyes. She tried to follow Sleek's movements, occasionally encouraging her with mind-murmuring, *yes*! and *good*! Petia tried to remain relaxed when she sniffed – when Sleek sniffed! – the first curl of smoke.

The brush outside burst into flame, visible through their glass confinement. Giles had to motion Keja to silence; he saw Petia's difficulty in keeping contact with the beast outside.

Petia urged Sleek to pile on more brush, to keep adding to the fire until it was so hot that she could not come near enough to throw more wood on. Finally, Petia received a blast of outright fear of the flames from the beast.

Petia collapsed in a limp heap. 'There's nothing I can do until the fire burns down. Let's hope that the heat crystallises the glass enough for your sword to do its work.'

They sat in silence, watching the flames leaping outside the glass. When the piled brush became ashes, Petia nodded to Giles. He pulled his sword again and approached the glass. Weak as he was from the heat, he walked with firm stride and confidence.

Petia's eyes glowed when she lightly brushed across his emotions. Giles put on no act; he radiated confidence and this buoyed her own sagging spirits.

Giles thumbed the sword's inscription and placed its tip against the glass. It quivered and hummed, then broke through. A small triangular piece of glass fell to the sand. A second blow caused larger pieces to break off. Within a few minutes he had made a hole large enough for the beasts and humans to crawl through.

Petia was the first one out. She dashed to Sleek. Petia threw her arms around the beast and cried, 'Sleek, you were wonderful!'

The others poured out of the glass enclosure into the high sun. By comparison with their bottle prison, the desert seemed cool.

'Keja, see to the water. Everyone must be nearly dehydrated. Careful with it, but a double ration for all.'

When everyone had drunk their fill, found shade wherever they could, and regained some measure of strength, Giles called Red Mane and the humans together. 'We can't stay on the Track any longer. The djinn were bad enough. If Red Mane is correct, the Skeleton Lord knows about us, and wants us dead. We must be careful from now on. We have to anticipate another attack, or we won't be so lucky.'

It took a good deal of urging to get the group moving after their ordeal. They understood, but were weary and thirsty and not inclined to go on. It took Giles some time to convince Red Mane that his only hope of regaining Shahal was to attack, not to retreat.

Giles wondered if he believed that himself. But it got the beasts back onto the Track. For the key, Giles would do anything—or almost anything. Where would he draw the line?

When they first saw the oasis shimmering on the horizon, they thought it was a mirage, but the beast who had scouted assured Red Mane that it was real. As eager as the party was for water, their strength had neared its end. They could only struggle on until they reached the promised cool, green place.

Adrenaline pumped through their veins as they reached the rim dividing desert from oasis and sent them rushing forward to plunge their faces into the pool. Giles ran among them, cautioning them not to drink too much or they would be sick.

'Giles,' shouted Petia, 'you are like an old woman, a nanny!' She threw water at him. For a moment, Giles bristled, then relaxed and joined in the play. The water felt good against his skin.

Anji took a small drink, then led the lirjan to one end of the pool. The pack animals drank noisily, but in a moment he pulled them away from the pool and tethered them to a tree nearby.

Anji started back to the pool, then froze, eyes wide. The boy swallowed, then called out in a voice almost too low to be heard, 'Master Giles. A djinn!'

Giles swung around, hand on his sword. Anji pointed to the pool. Only a small swirl of bubbles rose from the depths.

'Master Giles, truly I saw a djinn. He came from beneath the water and looked around as if he didn't believe what he was seeing.'

'Quiet,' Giles ordered. He stood, watching. The bubbles surged to the surface at a quicker rate now.

'The djinn are not usually harmful,' Red Mane said, sidling up next to Giles. 'I truly believe that the one who swept up Petia and Anji in the dust devil did not know that they would be injured. Their fun is a bit malicious, but they are only playing. Perhaps you can trick this one in return, and he will leave us alone.'

'How do we do that?' Giles asked.

'We must lay a trap for him. He is a shy one, to disappear like that.'

Anji kept his eyes on the pool, hoping to see the djinn again. Keja and Giles sat with him, wondering what they could do to disarm the djinn. Otherwise they were certain to suffer some indignity from the creature.

'I wonder if djinn like wine?' Keja mused. 'Or maybe ale. What I wouldn't give for a flagon now.'

'Yes, wine.' The voice ebbed across the water from the centre of the pool.

'Do we have a djinn who talks?' asked Giles.

'You were speaking of wine?' The djinn rose from the water, torso visible. His arms were folded across his chest and the muscles in his brown shoulders rippled.

'Good evening,' Giles said, more calmly than he felt.

'Good evening. You mentioned wine? A good one, I trust, of fine vintage – and not too dry. I loathe dry wines. Comes from being in the desert for so long, I suppose.'

'Yes. A splendid drink, is it not?' Giles agreed, relaxing now. It was difficult to feel menaced by a creature who prattled on at such lengths. 'Warms the stomach and is good for the constitution.'

'You have some, then?' the djinn asked.

Forever after, Giles would not know what prompted him. 'Yes, we do. Would you like some?'

No answer came. The djinn seemed to dissolve. The next moment it appeared, dry, in front of Giles.

'Where is it?' the djinn asked eagerly.

'Wait,' Giles said. 'Just a minute now. We can't afford to let

284

you have the entire wineskin.' He motioned to Keja behind his back. 'You seem anxious. We can't let you drink it all. And we expect something in exchange. Wine is not easy to obtain out here in the desert. You, of all, uh, people, must realise that.'

'Oh, it's been so long since I've had a drink of wine,' the djinn moaned.

Keja turned and walked away. 'Careful with that skin now, Keja,' Giles called after him. 'There's only a little left.'

'Where? Where is it?' the djinn cried.

'In a moment. What do we get in return?'

'Anything, what would you like?'

'I don't know what you can give us,' Giles said. 'Food, perhaps. Directions to Shahal. Something to protect us from the sun. I don't know. You tell me.'

'Yes, yes,' the djinn replied anxiously. 'All those. Now the wine, please.'

'It's over this way. Follow me. There's a slit in the skin, though. You must be careful. You'll have to crawl in. That should be no problem.'

The djinn drew himself up, disappeared into a vaporous puff, then appeared again. 'Of course not.'

The goatskin lay flat on its side. Keja had emptied the last of the water from it.

'Just crawl in there,' Giles said. 'But be sure to leave some for the rest of us.'

The djinn disappeared again. All that could be seen was a slight puffing of the goatskin.

'Quick, the stopper,' Giles whispered.

Keja thrust the stopper into the mouth of the goatskin.

'There's no wine in here.' The anguished cry was muffled by the goatskin.

Giles knelt by the skin. 'What a shame. I seem to have made a mistake in hinting some might be found there,' he answered.

'You will suffer for the indignity you heap upon me!' shouted the djinn. 'I promise eternal vengeance!'

'We've had enough of your tricks. We don't want any more. We've captured you.'

'You can't do that. I haven't harmed you. I never wanted to be a djinn. The Skeleton Lord did this to me as a punishment. I'm really a man.'

'We don't believe you,' Giles said. 'Djinn tell lies, too.'

Petia came to kneel by Giles and Keja. 'What are you going to do?' she whispered.

'Worry him a bit, then strike a bargain.' He held his finger to his lips while the djinn continued to plead. They listened as the creature alternately begged and threatened, grinning at having turned the tables on a djinn.

'Please let me out,' the djinn pleaded. 'I was a caravaner once, a scout and a guard. I know this area well. I can help you on your travels. Is there anyone out there? Oh, no, don't abandon me here forever! Not in a smelly goatskin! How degrading!'

Giles spoke up as if he had been away. 'Are you still shouting in there, djinn? I thought you might be asleep by now. We were getting ready to bed down for the night.'

'Please. Please let me out. It's stuffy in here – awful. I will help you, I promise. I really am a human. I was cruelly turned into a djinn by the evil Skeleton Lord.'

'We can't keep him in there forever, Giles,' Keja whispered. 'We need the goatskin. It's the best water bag we have.'

'I know,' Giles said. 'I just want to scare him a little. Maybe he'll be useful to us. If not . . .' He shrugged.

'How did you get changed into a djinn?' Giles asked, lifting his voice so the trapped djinn could hear.

'I told you. The Skeleton Lord. He turned me into one. He used a spell from a big book.'

'A likely story,' Giles said, beginning to enjoy this. He couldn't forget that a djinn – maybe even this one – had threatened Anji and Petia with the whirlwind. 'I think we're going to leave you inside the goatskin.'

'Wait!' the djinn cried. 'Wait, please, I beg you.'

'Beg me to do what?' Giles goaded.

'I . . . I have many powers, having once been human and now trapped in this djinn form.' The goatskin rippled with agitation. Giles shoved the toe of his boot into the side and watched the side jerk back. 'I hate the Skeleton Lord for what he's done to me. And you must, also. You must!'

'Why?'

'He imprisoned you in the glass bottle. I saw!'

Giles said nothing. The djinn had witnessed their imprisonment but had done nothing to help them. He didn't feel inclined to aid the creature now.

'Together,' the djinn cried, 'together we can defeat the Skeleton Lord. He is not invincible.'

'And you are?'

'Together we can defeat him. I know it. You . . . you can help me return to human form. And I can help you find something worth more than gold!'

'Water is more precious than gold in the desert,' said Giles. 'We have all the water we need. What is it you're referring to?'

'A key. The Skeleton Lord has a special key!'

Keja started to shout out for joy, but Giles restrained him. Hardly able to contain his own excitement, he kept his voice calm when he said, 'A key? We have no need of a key – but perhaps we can strike a deal. You sound contrite.'

'I am!'

Giles motioned for Keja to uncork the goatskin. A wisp of smoke gushed out, then hardened and rose into a column. And the column didn't stop growing until the powerfully muscled djinn loomed a fully twenty feet over their heads.

With a single twitch of his massive hand, the djinn could kill them all. He reached down for Giles.

Ten

GILES GRIMSMATE'S sword whirred as it slid from his sheath – but the movement came too late. The djinn's immense hand scooped Giles up and held the man dangling and kicking helplessly a dozen feet above the ground.

'Stop him!' Giles heard Petia shriek. From Red Mane came a

287

frightened growl. Of Keja, Giles saw and heard nothing. And he had no time to wonder about the small thief. Giles was staring directly into an unwinking, dinner-plate-huge, blood-shot eye. Arms trapped at his sides by vaporous fingers turned iron-hard, Giles felt the life fleeing his body. Every breath was harder to suck in than the last.

As he began to pass out, he heard the djinn's plaintive voice. 'Are you all right?'

Giles couldn't answer, but faintly, as if from a great distance, he heard the sounds of a sword hacking at flesh.

As suddenly as the djinn had picked him up, the creature released him. Giles fell to the ground, shaken and not sure what had happened. When his eyes focused he saw Keja clinging to the side of the giant djinn, slashing away with his sword.

'Stop him, please, oh please, stop him. That *hurts*!'

'Keja,' Giles croaked out. 'Get away.'

The thief obeyed, but warily. They all expected further mischief from the oversized djinn.

'I was overcome with joy at being released. I meant only to thank you,' the djinn said with hurt dignity. 'I did nothing to inspire such an attack.' The djinn smoothed away wrinkles in the magical substance of his body and began to shrink until he was hardly taller than Giles.

Petia shook her head. Keja glowered. They didn't know whether this djinn would continue to be peaceable.

'What is your name?' Petia asked. 'It's difficult to talk to you when I don't know your name.'

The djinn hung his head. 'I'd rather you didn't use it. I have shamed myself before you, and for that I must do penance. If you must address me, just call me Djinn. When I have my own body back, then I'll give voice to my name.'

Petia nodded with understanding. Her Trans talent tapped into the djinn's flow of emotions and almost staggered her with contriteness.

'Have you lived here long?' she asked.

'What is time to a discorporated soul? I don't even know how long ago it was that the Skeleton Lord placed this curse upon me.' Giles thought the djinn held back misty tears only through extreme effort. 'The other djinn won't play with me – they go

288

and do their pranks by themselves. Even among other djinn, I am an outcast.'

'What do you do?'

'I sit, I watch the strange happenings in the desert. Little else amuses me.'

'What strange occurrences are these?' Petia prompted.

'Like a man who has appeared in the desert. He is white, like the two men with you, lovely lady. He dresses in black and rides an immense black horse. I went to see him because he is not of the desert and therefore an amusing curiosity for one such as myself who grows bored with this disembodied existence. I never found out what he seeks.' Djinn crossed arms only slightly less muscular than his larger form as he went on. 'And the desert tribesmen move west, about a day's journey north of here. I don't think they will visit this oasis. There is another closer to their path.'

Petia turned to Giles and asked, 'This man in black Djinn saw. Could he be the same man we encountered in Dimly New?'

Giles frowned and did not answer.

'I see there are beasts with you. I leave them alone. Smelly, awful creatures, though I must admit that this form does not permit me the sense of smell. Damn you, Lord! Why did you have to rob me of my own body?'

The beasts slowly gathered around, staring at Djinn. Giles guessed this was their first opportunity to see one of the spirits without also being on the receiving end of a prank.

'Will this one help us regain our home?' Red Mane asked. The doubt in his voice radiated for all to hear. The beasts began muttering among themselves.

'Shahal?' Djinn asked. 'I know the place. Used to trade there until the Skeleton Lord . . .' Djinn's voice trailed off. 'If it is your will – and if I can regain my body – I'll help you into Shahal.'

'A fair enough trade,' Giles said. Keeping his voice level, he added, as if making a last-minute comment, 'That key you mentioned. Perhaps it would look nice around the lady's neck.' Giles nodded at Petia.

'Yes, a token of esteem!' Djinn cried.

'Such a fine token,' muttered Keja.

Giles ignored Keja's snide remark and continued to delve into Djinn's story, intent on finding out as much about Shahal and the surrounding countryside, the Skeleton Lord, and what they could expect when they arrived there, as possible.

'Are there other humans who were changed into djinn?' he asked.

'I doubt it. I think the Skeleton Lord did it on a whim, just to see if the spell worked. I've met other djinn in the desert, but they were real djinn and always had been.'

Red Mane summoned up enough courage to ask about the desert traveller in black. 'What do you know of him?' Giles and the others listened with interest.

'Nothing, really,' Djinn replied. 'He looked fearsome. I followed him for a while, but I didn't materialise to him. He wasn't travelling fast; he seemed to be searching for something – or someone.'

'Giles,' Red Mane said slowly, 'I think I will send one of my people out to see if he is still in the area. No one rides for pleasure in this desert. He might be a minion of the Skeleton Lord.'

Giles agreed that it would be a good idea to find this mysterious stranger, but ventured no opinion on the man's allegiance. He doubted the Skeleton Lord and this man in black shared similar goals – or if they did, they each wanted the reward for himself.

But what was the reward? The key to the Gate of Paradise? Giles decided to ponder this at greater length later. Red Mane withdrew into his own thoughts, trying to determine who would be the best of the beasts for the job. He went to a younger beast, Torn Ear. The youngster rose and disappeared into the night.

Red Mane returned to his place by the fire. 'It is done,' he said simply. Giles asked Djinn to tell them more.

'When the Skeleton Lord came to power in Shahal, he drove the beasts out. They hounded you from the city like beaten curs, is that not right?' Djinn looked at Red Mane, who had to agree with this shameful appraisal.

'I scouted for the next caravan to call at Shahal. We didn't know that the Skeleton Lord had taken over. His soldiers surprised the caravan and captured us. For a time we were kept together, but gradually one after another of us disappeared. I'm not sure what happened to them. Possibly other experiments.'

'Is this where the skeleton men come from?' Petia asked.

'Yes, I'm certain that they are the Skeleton Lord's one successful experiment. Once he found that he could turn the men into walking skeletons, he concentrated on that. They became his servants, his army, all he needed for his conquests. Several more caravans were captured. Then the caravans stopped using that route. The dhouti must have decided that it was no longer safe to take the Track of Fourteen. No one has crossed it for years, I think. But years have no meaning for me any more.' Djinn gusted a weighty sigh.

'What was his object?' Giles asked. 'What is he after?'

'Power. He wants to extend his power across the desert, then to the cities, Kasha in the north and Kuilla in the south. He already controls the Harifim.'

Giles' eyes lit up. 'That explains a lot. It explains their religion, their belief in the key. And I think it helps to confirm my belief that the key is at Shahal.'

'Ah,' said the djinn, 'the key is important to you. I thought so!'

'What sort of force does he have? What can you tell us about his skeleton men?' Giles still did not trust the djinn and wanted to avoid discussing the key.

'I do not know. In the desert it is said that the original skeleton men captured many Harifim and they, in turn, became skeleton men. It continues. So I do not know how many there are. Very many, to be sure, And there may be other humans who were not transformed.'

'Could we expect any help from those inside?' Keja asked.

Djinn thought about it. 'I cannot tell. I haven't been inside for a long time. There is so little for one such as I to do within the walls of Shahal. The Skeleton Lord changed me into a djinn for his own entertainment. It took me a long time to discover that I could become invisible. I wonder if real djinn come into existence knowing all these things, or if they have to be taught? A manual would have been most helpful to me. When I found out how to do the invisibility, I simply left Shahal to live by myself in the desrt. A lonely, tiresome existence.'

'I can see why,' noted Keja, 'if you have only yourself to listen to.'

'The Skeleton Lord could not see me any better than you can.'

'So you don't know if the skeleton men are unhappy with their lot?' Giles asked.

'I don't think they have any feelings. I was bitterly unhappy and expect them to be, also. If they have any brain left to think with, that is. Perhaps they don't,' Djinn mused. 'My own brain became addled for quite some time. Perhaps they no longer think, only obey.'

'I think the Lord is quite mad. I think he was mad when he came to Shahal. The silence of the desert has been known to touch men like that, though as a human I rather enjoyed it. Away from the grind of big cities.'

To this, Giles had nothing to reply.

The next morning Torn Ear appeared, exhausted after having run a long distance. Red Mane brought him to Giles and the others so he would not have to repeat his story.

'The stranger in black travels with desert tribesmen not of the Harifim. He is not their captive. I tried to spy on them, but they discovered me and chased me.'

'What?' Red Mane stormed. 'Then they will come here.'

'No,' Torn Ear said. 'I led them in a different direction. I may not have your immense experience, Ancient One, but I am not stupid.'

'Don't let your mouth run away with you,' Red Mane warned. He turned and showed the youngling his hind-quarters. When Red Mane's anger had subsided, he asked, 'Where did you last see them?'

'They were heading due west. I led them that way, toward the oasis at Dorassa. Then I went north into the rocks and doubled back, leaving no trail.

'Well done.' Red Man turned to Giles. 'What do we do now?'

Djinn spoke up. 'We are between the Track and the tribes-men. I do not think it wise to stay here much longer.'

'I suppose you are right. It has been so pleasant here that it is

292

hard to move on.' Leaving the tiny pool of water seemed like abandoning an old friend.

'Travel at night,' Djinn said. 'There is enough light to see by, and I can guide you. It will be safer.' Giles looked at Djinn, but the spirit appeared sincere. Petia shrugged, indicating she received no contrary indications from the djinn, but who could say what a disembodied spirit's emotions were like? Still, Giles had little choice but to follow Djinn.

They waited until dark, listening to the silence of the desert and wondering where – and what – the black stranger might be. When they finally left the oasis, Giles had decided they faced two enemies: The Skeleton Lord and this man in black.

They travelled a score of miles through the night. The days of rest had refreshed them. By morning, however, they felt the effort of the night's travel and sighed with relief when Giles called a halt.

Djinn scouted for a place that would keep them out of the sun for most of the day.

'What are we going to do when we reach Shahal?' Petia asked when they had settled down. 'How are we going to get inside?'

'We can't attack,' Keja said. 'That's too obvious. Perhaps there will be some unguarded entrances, those the beasts have spoken of. No lord guards every entrance, at least not so well that a clever thief could not find a way in.'

'Don't be surprised if Shahal is well patrolled,' said Giles. 'We'll scout carefully when we get there. Maybe that will give us some ideas.'

The early false dawn found them in a valley shaped like a shallow bowl. The sun rose and they shaded their eyes to look across the landscape. Shahal, carved centuries before from solid rock, rose from the plain, immense and silent in the dawn. Giles was speechless, not expecting this. He had built an image of a city spread out across the plain. What else had he assumed wrongly?

A tower of rock rising vertically from the desert floor. Many levels were evident from the balconies outlined by the morning light.

'It's huge,' Petia sighed. 'If it does hold the key, how will we ever locate it?'

'The first step is to get in. One thing at a time,' Giles said.

Red Mane came up to his side. 'We had better find somewhere to hide during the day. We can be seen too easily here in the middle of the plain, and the skeleton men patrol ceaselessly.'

'You're right.' Giles looked at the sides of the valley, several miles away. 'Do you have any idea of the best place to conceal ourselves?'

'There is a small cave along that side that would be cool and keep us out of . . .' A murmur rose behind them, and Giles turned to see the cause of it.

The beasts pointed down the valley. The sun glinted off two gates at the foot of the rock city. Slowly, they swung open, as if these might be the real Gate of Paradise. Giles listened for the expected rumble but heard nothing.

The company watched as a troop of soldiers marched in trim ranks from the dark cavern behind the gates. Old habits died hard; Giles estimated that the contingent numbered one hundred by the number of officers decked out with gold rank stripes. Four squads formed and wheeled into the desert with a precision Giles both envied and feared.

'They're well trained,' Giles said. 'Too well trained for my taste. Discipline's good, which is bad for us.'

He glanced at Red Mane. 'How far is it to the cave you mentioned? Can we get there before they see us?'

'I think, perhaps, they have already seen us. We had better run for it.'

'You lead, we'll follow.' Giles felt his heart accelerating. Before battle it was always like this. As much as he hated it, he also needed it. Battle vindicated his existence; he was more than good at it. He survived.

'Hurry,' Giles shouted after Red Mane as the beast loped off. Giles waved to Petia and Keja, who had been tying down their packs in preparation for flight.

He ran to help Anji with the lirjan. The sudden activity had frightened the animals.

'Quietly,' Anji breathed. 'Easy, my lovely ones. It will be all right.' He handed one rope to Giles and kept the other two himself. 'Come, my sweets.' He urged the two lirjan into motion and gestured with his head for Giles to fall in behind, knowing that the single animal would follow its two companions.

'How you can seduce those smelly creatures, I'll never know.' Giles laughed at a sudden thought. When Anji grew older, what would he be like with women? If the boy could gentle odorous, bad-tempered lirjan this easily, he'd have his way with just about any woman.

His mind turning to more immediate problems, Giles estimated the distance separating them from the troop – his practised eye claimed three miles. The disciplined troop would make good time. An individual could outrun a troop of soldiers, but Giles had doubts about his own people and the beasts.

He looked at the side of the valley. Even if they reached it, the soldiers would know where they had gone. And his group was outnumbered. However, they would put up a fight. They had no other choice; retreating into the desert was out of the question.

'What's happening?' Giles asked Anji.

'Another troop.' Anji pointed at the rock city.

A second gate swung open on the western side of Shahal. Soldiers marched smartly out of the shadow. They were near to the valley edge and quick-stepped.

'They'll cut us off,' Giles muttered. 'We're going to be captured unless we think of something fast.'

He watched in dismay as one squad of the original troop separated from the main body, breaking into a trot. The squad outnumbered them two to one.

The beasts cowered together, all confidence gone as they watched the military precision of the men advancing toward them.

'Run!' Giles shouted. 'Back the way we came.' As treacherous as the desert was, it was their only hope to avoid capture.

Petia and Keja ran back to where Giles and Anji stood with the lirjan.

'Red Mane,' Giles shouted again. 'Make them understand. We've got to run.'

The beast stood, a look of sadness on his face, and shook his head. The beasts had given up; in their minds they had already been captured.

'We've got to leave the lirjan, Giles,' Keja said. 'We'll never get away if we try to take them. They'll be able to spot us from miles off.'

'But our supplies,' Petia said. 'We won't survive in the desert without food and water.'

'Keja's right. Use them as a diversion.' Giles pointed and Anji went to each of the animals and patted it on the nose before turning and kicking the animal on the rump. The offended lirjan ambled off.

'Now, hurry.' Giles loosened his sword in its scabbard, then ran westward. The others followed.

In the end, the escape attempt proved fruitless. The humans ran until their lungs strained and every drop of water drained from their bodies. The sun rose higher and the desert shimmered in the heat. The troop pursued them tirelessly.

'Where's that miserable djinn?' gasped out Keja. 'He brought the soldiers down on our necks! He did it!'

Giles had no time to debate the point. Keja might be right. A more immediate problem faced them, though. Skeleton men surrounded them as they lay gasping in the shade of a boulder. Emotionless, white bones, impervious to the burning sun, the skeletal warriors pulled the humans to their feet and bound their hands, not even bothering to take their weapons. To Giles, this amounted to humiliation exceeding any he had ever known. The skeleton troops thought his sword and skill trivial.

They prodded Giles and the others silently toward Shahal.

'Been nice knowing you,' Keja said as they neared the towering, ornately wrought gate into Shahal.

'We're not dead yet,' Giles said, but he shared Keja's feelings. Dread filled him as the gates swung open like a brass-toothed mouth to swallow them.

Eleven

'WE SHOULD have fought,' grumbled Keja.

'They outnumbered us,' said Petia, 'and they weren't tired from travelling all night. We would have been killed.'

'Can skeletons get tired?' asked Keja. 'Bone tired?' He snorted and leaned back against the cold stone wall.

Giles didn't blame the man for his attitude. As a leader, he hadn't done too well. They had been herded into Shahal and thrown into these poxy cells, the likes of which Giles had seldom seen. Even during the Trans War, when he'd spent a short stretch as prisoner of war, he had not endured conditions like these. Even worse, the old gaoler hadn't allowed them to keep their weapons as the skeleton warriors had. He had a fine sense of fear about him and hung their swords in a neat row along one wall of the dungeon.

He looked around to see how the others were. Their arms were tied behind their backs. They lay where they had been pushed, recovering slowly. Giles got his knees under him, pushing with his head and shoulders. He steadied himself, then staggered to his feet. With his hands behind him, he had difficulty helping the others. He moved among them, encouraging them to their feet. Keja was the last, his face ashen.

They lowered themselves gingerly onto a bench running along one wall. The gaoler muttered to himself in one corner of the room. He wiped his nose with the back of his hand, rose from his chair at a small table, and came toward them.

He bent down and stared at each of them. Giles realised then that he had only one eye, his left. Blinking and muttering, he turned away and opened the door of another cage in the corner opposite that of the beasts. The humans saw that he was hunchbacked. He returned to the humans, shuffling and digging inside his dirty robe. His hand finally emerged, bringing with it a knife.

'What are you doing, old man?' Giles asked.

'Cage,' the old man answered, gesturing with the knife to the other side of the room. 'You.' He pointed the blade at Giles' chest.

Giles obeyed, the man using the knifepoint to prod him into the cage. He locked the door with a simple shuttle catch, then returned to the others.

One by one he escorted them into the cage. When he had locked the door for the last time, he stood outside and said, 'Hands.'

'What?' Keja said.

'Hands.' He made a cutting gesture with the knife. Giles understood and backed up to the cage bars. The old man reached through and cut the Giles' bindings, then did the same for the others.

The old man shuffled away to resume his seat at the table.

'I don't think he's very bright,' Keja said. 'One eye, hunchbacked, filthy misshapen pig.'

'He may not be bright, but he's obviously our gaoler,' Petia said. 'He got us into the cage quickly enough.'

'If we're careful and don't anger him, we may be able to talk ourselves back out of the cage.'

'You may be right, Keja,' Giles said. 'But out of the cage isn't out of the dungeon.'

'But it's the first step.'

'I wonder why we weren't taken to the Skeleton Lord?' Petia mused. 'We're probably not important to him, but you'd think he'd be interested in where we've come from and what we're doing in the middle of the desert.'

'Don't be in too much of a hurry to meet the Skeleton Lord,' Giles advised. 'I doubt it will be much fun.'

A bang sounded on the dungeon door. The old hunchback shuffled to unlock it, then stood back, cowering, shielding his good eye with his hand.

A corpulent man dressed in grey and hugging a fur cloak about him came into the room. Behind him stood a tall, emaciated man, dressed in maroon velvet robes. His face was shrivelled, as if the dryness of the desert had removed all the moisture from it. He stepped past the fat man, saying, 'It's all right, Leaal, they've been caged.'

He advanced across the room to stand before the beasts' cage. 'What have we here? The beasts have returned.' He smirked – it turned his skeletal face even uglier. 'Not content with their freedom in the desert, they've returned to offer allegiance to their lord. How discerning of them to wish to serve the one who will soon be master of the entire continent!'

The beasts cowered to the back of the cage. Red Mane was nearest the Skeleton Lord. He glanced at the man, but even he did not have enough courage to face him directly.

The Skeleton Lord stood watching, savouring the fear that the beasts so obviously showed. Then, with a swish of his elegant robe, he turned his attention to the opposite corner of the room.

The four stood, their hands gripping the bars, staring back at the Skeleton Lord. Even Anji dared to stare, unafraid, into the sardonic eyes.

'So, these are the new ones.' The voice echoed silky and sibilant off the dungeon walls. 'Including a Trans woman and a mere child.' He turned to Leaal. 'Why do you suppose they wandered about without permission in my desert? Just curious, or ulterior motives?'

'I'm not a child,' Anji said. 'I'm a young man.' He glared at the Skeleton Lord.

'Ah, a spark of courage,' the Skeleton Lord lisped. 'I hate courage. He will be interesting when we break him.'

'Leave the boy alone,' Petia said hotly.

'Another ember there, my goodness. We do have a lively group here. Entertaining times are in store for us, Leaal.'

Keja rattled the bars. 'Just let us out of here, and we'll show you how entertaining.'

The Skeleton Lord merely raised his thin, darkly arched eyebrows. He turned his attention to Giles. 'And a quiet one. In my experience, I find the quiet ones . . . disquieting. He may be the most dangerous of all. We shall see. Enough, Leaal. I must return to my work. I will question them later. Personally.'

He turned back to the door. The hunchback pulled it open on squeaking hinges, bowing low to the Skeleton Lord. Leaal gave one last glance at the prisoners, whispered something to the gaoler, and followed his master out of the door.

A day passed before the Skeleton Lord's counsellor arrived at the dungeon, accompanied by six guards. He strode up and down the room, smiling as the beasts cowered in one corner of the cage. Leaal stood before them, enjoying the fear his mere presence could inspire. Finally, he turned his attention to the humans.

Giles watched him suspiciously. The man had not come to the dungeon for petty maliciousness.

'Which of you is the leader?' Leaal asked.

'We have no leader,' Keja said. 'We consult the gods and let them choose our course.'

Leaal's lip curled in disdain. 'Do not tell me lies. It will do you no good. One of you is the leader. It is not the Trans bitch or the child. It must be one of you men. But which?'

'Go play with the hunchback,' Giles said. He knew he risked much by angering Leaal, but he had to see how the man would respond. Only by probing for weaknesses might they all escape.

A tremor ran through Leaal's body. The blood rushed to his face. 'You are the leader.'

He stepped back from the cage, ordering the gaoler to open it. The six guards stood with their spears ready. When the cage door swung open, Leaal pointed at Giles. 'You, the old one, come out.'

Giles had no choice but to obey. Petia reached up and touched his arm in reassurance. He ducked under the low door; immediately the skeleton men surrounded him.

Leaal marched out of the dungeon. One skeleton guard prodded Giles with a spear, and he followed. Giles wondered if he would ever see his friends again.

Once out of the subterranean level, they entered wide, well lit hallways. The narrow stairways, however, gave no chance to escape. In a fight, Giles thought, only two guards would be able to control the stairwell. Giles smiled. That reduced the odds facing him, too.

The route twisted and turned. They climbed so many stairs

300

that Giles soon lost track of how many levels they had climbed – seven?

At last, Leaal paused in front of a leather-covered door and then entered. Giles found himself in a large chamber. To his right was an archway, and through it a smaller room. Glassware, candles, elaborate paraphernalia, bound books and loose parchments covered two large tables.

It was exactly as Giles had envisioned an alchemist's laboratory. What experiments did the Skeleton Lord do here? What did he search for? Some hidden knowledge that would add to his power? Wealth? Perhaps he, like other alchemists the world over, was attempting to develop the elixir of flight.

Leaal approached the archway and bowed slightly. 'Lord, the leader of the prisoners begs an audience.'

The Skeleton Lord came through the archway, wiping bony fingers on a white linen cloth. When he had finished his minor ablutions, he flung the rag negligently back into the workroom. The rolled-up sleeves of his gown revealed blue stains on the underside of his arms.

Giles took the opportunity to study the desert lord more closely. When he had first heard of the Skeleton Lord, he had anticipated a skeletal being. The man was tall and slender almost to the point of emaciation, but the frame held firm human flesh and muscle. The face was wrinkled, the cheeks sunken. Thin wisps of white hair escaped from beneath his hood. Dark eyes with a bright madness in them stared out from sunken sockets.

The Skeleton Lord walked past Giles to take his seat on an elaborately carved wooden throne. He pointed to the floor in front of him, and Giles found himself thrust onto his knees before the ruler.

'Why are you here?' The Lord's cruel, thin voice grated on Giles' very soul.

'Because your men captured me and brought me here.'

'Do not be clever, white-skinned one. My men will flay you alive if I so much as lift my finger. What are you and your party doing in my desert?'

Giles had had a day to think of the answer to this inevitable question. 'In my land, we heard that immense riches could be gained from trading in the desert countries. We had thought to

301

re-open the old caravan way, the Track of Fourteen, for trade between Kasha and Kuilla and the cities of the eastern coast, Hamri and Masser.'

'Did no one tell you that this territory is forbidden? Did you not find dead caravaners along the way? I am the lord of all the desert between the coast and the caravan road, between Kasha and Kuilla. The old road will not be re-opened. I do not wish it.'

'But, of course, I am prepared to pay a tariff to the city of Shahal,' Giles said. 'It would be a good place for the caravan to rest.'

'I do not believe you. You have come to spy on me, to steal my secrets. I wield the power here. My warriors obey me, and through them, the tribes of the desert. Why have you stirred up the beasts against me?'

'I met them in the desert. They told me that they could guide me to Shahal. I am unfamiliar with the area, so I accepted their help.'

The Skeleton Lord leaned forward. 'They roam the desert because I will it. They did not deserve so fine a city; I banished them from it. They know better than to come back to Shahal.'

'They did not tell me that.' Giles tried to look confused and appalled at his breach of etiquette.

'Lies! You tell one lie on top of another. I will turn you and all your party into djinn and let you roam the desert with the beasts. But torture first. You must be punished so that you will not repeat the same stupid mistake – and to serve as an example to others of your ilk. When I am finished with you, you will know who is lord.' The Skeleton Lord pointed his finger at Giles.

'But we have done nothing . . .'

'Silence! I have work to do. I have gathered the power of the desert to me. But there are other cities that will come under my power. Eventually, the entire continent. All Bandanarra will be mine. Nobody will interfere with my plan.'

Giles glanced toward the archway into the smaller room. 'You intend to use magic to do that?'

'Take a closer look at my guards, foreign fool,' the Skeleton Lord said. 'Once, they were men like you, but I have transformed them into invincible skeletons with my magic. They require no water or food, need no sleep and can fight harder than a dozen men! And my armies will grow!'

Giles watched as the madness surfaced in the Skeleton Lord. The pupils of his eyes grew larger and his hands shook as he gestured.

'Be careful, animal lover, or you will find yourself and your friends in my skeleton army. As a djinn you will be free to roam the desert. If you do not cooperate, you will become a part of my army, without eyes or flesh or emotion.'

Giles bowed his head, placating the lord with false obeisance. The time for open rebellion had not yet come.

'Take him away. I will deal with him later.'

The cacophony of thoughts disturbed Petia. She used her empathic talent sparingly, projecting only when she needed to, and even then at great mental and physical cost. Contacting Sleek had exhausted her; Giles' request to study Djinn had been virtually impossible except for the strongest of emotions.

But she knew now that it was the gaoler's mind that interfered with her thoughts. The poor old man had been in this dungeon for too long, and had not seen a woman in years. Even in his youth, his misshapen body had left him without voluntary female companionship. Now he lived in this dungeon, as much a prisoner as those he watched, merely a vassal of the Skeleton Lord. He found no joy in his work. He was hated by those he kept, abused by the guards he saw occasionally, despised by Leaal, ignored by the Skeleton Lord.

She read his emotions easily. The old man lusted to touch her. At first, Petia was embarrassed, but gradually she realised there was nothing sexual in his thoughts about her. To him she was so beautiful that simply to touch her hand or face would be enough. While she felt sorry for him, Petia knew that she might be able to use the old man.

Carefully, slowly, so as not to disturb the old man, at great emotional cost to herself, Petia implanted simple thoughts into his mind; primitive emotions into his soul. The gaoler's befuddled mind followed her reasoning easily: These prisoners are not a danger and have not screamed filth at him.

Petia quaked and turned deathly pale as she erased fear from the man's brain and tried to keep her own desperation from intruding.

He had no reason to believe they would do him harm if he let them out for just a little while, Petia instructed. He could easily put them back in their cage when the guards come to check the dungeon each morning and night. The Skeleton Lord would praise him for the good job he was doing.

Petia gently urged the gaoler over to the cage. Hesitantly, he approached and looked at the four prisoners. Petia smiled.

'There is so little room in this cage,' she said. 'It would feel so good to stretch.'

'I . . . Teloq, let you out for a short time,' the gaoler said. 'But you have to go back in when I say. If the guards find you, I will be whipped. You must promise Teloq.'

'We don't want you to get into trouble,' Petia purred, her catlike eyes gleaming with triumph. 'You have been so kind to us. You are our friend. We promise you.' She looked sternly at Giles and Keja, even as she supported herself against the bars.

'Friend,' Teloq the gaoler repeated. 'I am your friend.' He reached for the keys to the door of the cage. Before he got the key into the lock, the click of boots against stone echoed through the passageway. The gaoler jerked back, the tenuous spell Petia held over him broken.

The hunchback bowed low as Leaal strode into the dungeon and silently pointed at Keja. Skeleton warriors pulled the small thief from the cell and jerked him around, holding him easily, no matter how hard he struggled.

When Keja returned, his anger boiled over. 'Giles, you bastard! You've deserted to the enemy!' He turned to Petia. 'Don't believe a thing he says. I don't know what the Skeleton Lord has promised him, but he has sold us out.'

'What are you talking about?' A dangerous softness edged in Giles' voice.

'You said that you didn't trust us,' Keja went on. 'We're the ones who shouldn't have trusted you. The Skeleton Lord has bought you. At what price?'

Petia intervened. 'What do you mean? What has Giles done? Stop talking in circles.'

Keja seethed. 'Giles promised to help him in his experiments. That's what the Skeleton Lord told me. He's searching for greater magicks. What did he offer you, Giles?'

'Don't be a bigger fool than you have to be, Keja.' Giles forced calmness upon himself. 'It must be true,' he finally said.

'What?' demanded Keja. 'What's true?'

'That it's easy to dupe a thief. The Skeleton Lord sucked you in completely with his lies.'

Petia stepped between the two men. 'It's what the Skeleton Lord wanted, Keja. He told you lies, then sent you back here so enraged at Giles that you're ready to fight. It's the oldest ploy in the world.' She took hold of Keja's wrists. 'Sit down and be still. Then we'll listen to what the Skeleton Lord told you.'

'What could he offer me, Keja? The key? We've travelled thousands of miles to find the next key. Do you think I told him about the Gate of Paradise? "Just give me the key and I'll help you with your magicks?" Sometimes you don't think any better than he does.' Giles jerked his head at the hunchback.

'I told you last night what he said. All threats. He didn't even want to bargain for our help. He promised torture, transformation into a djinn, banishment into the desert. I don't know what he's trying to do to us, but Petia's right. It's a stratagem that's been used since the world began.'

Keja said nothing, glaring at Giles.

'This goes deeper than the Lord's lies. You *wanted* to believe him, Keja. Why? You've been sullen and withdrawn for a long time. Since out in the desert.'

For a long while Keja sat alone, stewing. 'I resent you always telling us what to do,' he said. 'Even worse, you're usually right. No one's ever told me what to do in my life.'

'Always the lone warrior,' said Giles, sighing. 'You'll either come to trust the rest of us or we're going to die. The only way we can escape is together. Individual effort won't do it for us.'

'Petia's emotion-tapping . . .' Keja began. Petia put her hand over his mouth to keep the gaoler from overhearing. Teloq shuffled around, glancing in occasionally, his attention mostly on Petia.

'It exhausted her,' Giles said. 'We would have to carry her from the cell if she succeeded. Forcing ideas into *that* head isn't easy for her.' Giles sighed. 'Forcing ideas into *your* head's no easier.'

'The Lord made it sound so plausible,' Keja said.

'He's a good liar,' observed Giles.

From across the corridor came Red Mane's mournful howling. 'He speaks the truth, human. The Skeleton Lord talked us out of our home. Shahal is rightfully ours!'

The brief outburst brought the gaoler back. He prodded Red Mane until the beast subsided, to huddle in the rear of his cell.

'Try it again,' Keja urged Petia. 'Make him let us out.'

Before Petia could answer, the sound of marching soldiers filled the dungeon. Leaal came in, a sneer on his face.

'The Lord has no more use for them. Take them all out – for the experiment!'

Skeletal hands grabbed Giles and the others and pulled them out of their cell. What little time they'd thought remained had now gone.

Twelve

GILES GRIMSMATE would not go to his death at the hands of an alchemist and torturer this easily. He jerked free of the skeletal hands gripping his arm and struck out. Bones rattled and pulled back, but the powerful hold on his arm remained.

'Fight, Keja!' he called. 'You wanted to before. Do it now!' The memory of the Skeleton Lord's laboratory burned too brightly in Giles' brain for him to do anything but struggle now. Still, the bony warriors proved their worth; they overwhelmed him.

As they began to drag him from the chamber, Leaal called

out in a choked voice, 'Stop. I . . . I am wrong. The Lord doesn't want them. None of them.'

Giles wrenched around and saw the expression on Leaal's face. Never had he seen a man more frightened. But of what? This time Giles did not protest as the skeleton warriors thrust him back into the cage. If anything, he felt as if he'd come home safely.

Keja clung to the bars, glaring. The troops marched smartly from the dungeon, Leaal following. Sweat beaded the counsellor's forehead and his eyes darted wildly, seeking ghosts that never appeared to any save himself.

'I don't know what happened, but something changed his mind,' said Giles. He heard a whimpering noise and turned to find Anji huddled beside Petia. The Trans boy shook Petia, who sat with unseeing eyes.

'Petia!' Giles cried.

'I'm all right, Giles. So weak. Head spins. Dark, too. But it worked! I convinced Leaal that taking us signed his death warrant, too.'

Petia's strength returned slowly after her ordeal. Somehow, using her emotion-tapping talents, she had ignited true fear in Leaal and frightened the man away. What awful terrors had she unleashed in the maggoty pit of his mind? Giles shuddered, not wanting to know.

'Then our reprieve is only temporary. When the Lord doesn't find us staked out for his experiment, he'll send Leaal back – or Leaal's replacement.'

'How will we escape now? Can you persuade the gaoler?' asked Keja. He stared down at Petia with concern.

'I . . . I don't think so. My head feels as if it will explode. Just moving about makes me giddy. To touch Teloq so soon after Leaal? No.' Petia turned paler still at the thought.

'There's a chance we can trick him without using Petia,' Giles said. 'If we get out, shall we free the beasts, too?'

Keja looked across to where Red Mane and the other beasts still cowered. 'They are no help to us. How I wish we could turn into puffs of mist like Djinn. Then we could slip through the bars and be off in a flash.'

'By the way, where is Djinn? I haven't seen him since the

troops got us in the valley.' Giles jumped a foot when the voice came next to his ear.

'Right here.' Gradually the djinn materialised. 'I told you that you have to call for me, or I go back to my ethereal state. I've been here all along, listening to your discussion. Just being quiet and awaiting your call. This is a fine dilemma facing you, if I may say so.'

'Is your material body as strong as it looks?' Petia asked, eyeing the bulging shoulders and biceps.

'I don't have anything to compare it to, and I haven't done any real work for untold years, not that I did much while in real human form. But the muscles seem to stay the same, whether I exercise or not.'

'Can you do anything to help us out of here, Djinn?' Keja asked.

'I could put the old fellow in a trance. His mind's none too sharp, or so it seems from here.'

Four voices raised in incredulous unison. 'You could?'

'Easily. His mind is so simple. Not with the Skeleton Lord, though. Nor the skeleton guards. They're mindless.'

Giles rubbed his forehead. 'If you could do that, why didn't you do it to us when we let you out of the goatskin?'

'Djinn lose their power when entirely enclosed. Why? I can't really say, because I have never considered the point overly important. Crawling into a bottle, then pulling in the plug behind you isn't something you do by accident every day.'

Giles said, 'If we can reach the Skeleton Lord's chambers and destroy his grimoires, perhaps even his experiments, we might weaken his magical powers. I think that's what we should attempt first.'

'It's the key we're after,' Keja said. 'Let's just find it and get out.'

'We ought to let the beasts out,' Petia said. 'We can't leave them caged up like that.'

'Why not?' Giles scowled. 'They haven't done a thing for us. All those promises out in the desert and their talk about wanting their city back. We don't have time – and as poorly as they fight, it'd be dangerous for us.'

'While you lot argue it out, do you want me to open the door?' Djinn asked. Giles made an impatient gesture. Djinn made an elegant wave of his hand. Across the room, Teloq put his head to the table and snored loudly. Djinn flowed through the bars, rematerialised and picked up the cage key. In the wink of an eye, he had freed the four.

Suddenly the old man sat up on his bench, staring straight ahead of him. Djinn frowned and shrugged, saying, 'Losing my touch. Been a long time since I had a mind to work with.'

'We noticed,' grumbled Keja. But the djinn put the gaoler back into the trance. Before Teloq's old head touched the table again, Giles had retrieved their weapons from the wall racks.

Armed again, they felt ready to face whatever they might find outside. Keja pulled the door leading out of the dungeon. In spite of his care, it creaked and groaned. Keja grimaced, but Giles laid a hand on his arm in reassurance.

'Wait,' came Red Mane's plaintive cry. 'You can't leave us behind!'

'We're going scouting,' Keja said. 'You'll be safe here.'

'But . . .'

Giles and Keja didn't look back at the beasts, and Petia only glanced at Red Mane. Keja was right in thinking the beasts were less likely to meet danger here than if they blundered about.

Steps led up directly from the dungeon. The companions paused at the bottom, listening intently. Giles tried desperately to remember what the hallway above looked like, but nothing came. He and Keja started up the stairs, but Keja signed for Giles to wait. He closed the dungeon door and locked it behind him.

They advanced to the first turn and paused. Nothing appeared ahead of them. They moved to the top of the stairs. Giles cautioned them with a hand signal, then peered around the corner and down the hallway. Guards stood motionless at each end.

'Can we get around the corner into the next stairway?' Petia whispered from behind.

'No, the stairs don't go on up from here,' Giles answered. 'They are further down the hall. Djinn, can't you put them in a trance?' Giles whispered.

'No. They are already locked in one more powerful than I can cast. When they were transformed, they lost the power to think for themselves. They respond automatically to signals known only to the Lord. I can't put them to sleep.'

'Then we'll have to fight our way through?'

'Yes. And be on the watch for other beings that the Lord has. There are ghouls, seirim and dakari. Ghouls you must run from. The seirim are big, hairy creatures, but they are slow of foot and hand. Cut them in the legs, but be wary of their blood – it burns human flesh. The dakari are hideous females who roam the city at night, crying for their infants that the Lord killed.'

'Thanks for the warning,' Giles said. With such a panoply arrayed against them, simply getting out of Shahal presented insurmountable problems. How were they to find the key they so desired? 'Ready?'

The four took a breath, then stepped in unison into the hall. They walked quietly, hoping to cover some ground between the two guards and themselves before they were discovered.

They nearly made it. Giles was only ten feet away when the first guard turned. In complete and eerie silence, the guard raised his spear. Giles covered the ten feet separating them in two strides, thumbing his sword. The blade took the guard in the spinal column before the spear levelled. Keja bowled the second guard over with his shoulder, then ran his blade through him. The guard paused, unsure of what had happened, then continued his attack. Keja had to cut the legs from under the skeleton warrior, then sever head from torso before it stopped fighting.

Giles gave Keja no time to catch his breath. Giles motioned Petia and Anji up the stairwell. Petia stooped and picked up a short, curved sword. It felt heavier than her own sword, so she let it fall. Pulling Anji's arm, she scurried up the stairwell. Giles and Keja followed closely behind. More guards from the far end of the hall were coming to investigate. By the time they found the two dead skeleton men, the humans had reached the next floor.

They paused briefly to see where the guards were stationed, then dashed around the corner and up another flight. It seemed wiser to elude the guards than to fight from floor to floor. Sooner or later the guards would catch up with them.

The third level was empty. 'Where are the guards?' Petia

whispered. They saw none in front of them or at the far end of the corridor.

Giles stepped gingerly into the hallway. He cupped his ear and listened intently. Quiet. He was turning to signal to the others when he heard a clicking sound on the floor behind him. He spun around with an oath and brought up his sword.

Keja stepped up the last stair and into the hall, ready to face the implacable skeleton guards coming from their right. He blanched.

'What did we do to deserve this?' he gasped.

A mass of scorpions scuttled down the short corridor towards them. Their bodies stood two feet tall, with tails curling wickedly above their backs that added another foot. The carapaces of their segmented bodies gleamed like lacquered boxes and were spotted with glistening fluid that sizzled and popped – poison dripping from the tail barb. And those tails! They weaved from side to side, ready to strike.

Petia came up into the hall and gasped. She pushed Anji to one side and took a position on Giles' left, her sword at the ready.

The eerie clicking sound made it hard to estimate how many of the arachnids were approaching. The tight mass of deadly creatures flowed like a living carpet, and Giles counted at least ten deadly, waving tails.

'Remember,' Giles yelled. 'Watch their tails. Slice them off. By all the gods, don't let them get you with that stinger.'

'Stay behind me, Anji,' Petia yelled over her shoulder.

'Give me your sword, Mistress.'

'No, stay back.'

Then the scorpions erupted over them. Giles thrust at the beady black eye of the centre one, and it backed away. Petia swung her sword in an arc, cutting through the tail of one scorpion and followed down to slice through the carapace. The scorpion was driven to the floor and lay dying, feebly waving its front legs. Petia had to struggle to free her blade from the carcase.

Keja stamped on the floor, momentarily startling the arachnids, then leaped forward, extending one leg and his sword arm. The sword tip slid between the eye and the middle of the scorpion's head. He pulled it out with a vicious twisting motion as he jumped back. He did not have time to watch the ichorous matter oozing from its head, nor to see it drop, twitching, to the floor. Already another was attacking, demanding his full attention.

'Don't these things ever die?' Petia cried. Her blade glanced off armoured carapace as she spoke. Giles grasped his sword in both hands, feeling the energy emanating from it. He leaped forward, swinging it like a broadsword. The sword lopped a scorpion's tail cleanly. It fell with a rattle against the wall, saving Petia from a nasty wound.

'That's three,' he murmured grimly.

Petia started to thank Giles, then heard Anji cry out. While she had been busy with one arachnid, another had scuttled past her. It headed straight for Anji, who backed away. Petia spun and leaped after it. With frenzied energy, she swung the sword in two connected arcs, the first severing the tail and the second decapitating the creature. Without looking, she swung around again to face another scurrying towards her.

Gingerly, Anji picked up the severed tail. It dripped with the venom that had been intended for him. A grim smile crossed his lips. If Petia would not give him a sword, he'd use the severed tail and join the battle.

He ran forward, focusing clearly on one scorpion sidling over to Giles. With an audible cry, he plunged the stinger into the unsuspecting scorpion's eye. It turned quickly, tail wavering, and collapsed at Anji's feet.

'Anji!' Petia cried. 'Get back. That's an order.'

Five scorpions remained. The ugly creatures scurried from side to side, looking for a chance to strike. Giles drew back, taking the opportunity to catch his breath. The danger would not be over until the scorpions retreated or were killed.

And even then . . .

For a moment, the scorpions seemed to hesitate, then rose on short back legs, front feet wavering. They behaved as if they were awaiting instructions.

Keja yelled, 'Now!' He rushed forward, sword aimed low. He thrust upwards into the brittle underbelly, raising his sword as he withdrew it. Giles and Petia took his meaning instantly, and followed. Petia pulled her sword from the scorpion, already thinking of her next move. Without stopping, she slashed to her left and right. The scorpion backed away, but it was too late. The tip of the sword swept across its eyes. It scuttled blindly into the wall, then turned sightlessly. Keja neatly severed its tail, then sliced it in two.

Keja feinted at the single remaining scorpion, got its attention with a second feint, and withdrew. As the arachnid followed, Giles chopped its head off from the side.

'That's all?' Giles asked, still stunned by the horrifying attackers. He thumbed the inscription and relaxed as the energy drained from his sword. They leaned on their weapons, breathing deeply and examining the carnage in front of them. Two of the scorpions still twitched feebly. Petia made a gagging sound and leaned against the wall.

Giles looked down the empty hall and decided they had time to rest. He put his arm on Petia's shoulder. 'She'll be all right in a moment,' he said to Anji. He looked around to congratulate Keja.

Keja had vanished.

Petia ran her hand through her tangled, filthy hair, pushing it out of her eyes. She wiped the perspiration from her forehead. 'That was horrible,' she said, 'but we did it. Can we get out of here? The sight of those awful creatures makes me sick.'

Giles nodded and motioned for her to stay back a pace while he scouted the stairs. They were half a flight up when Petia stumbled and fell.

'Giles, it's Keja. I heard him.'

'I heard nothing,' Giles said, thinking she had lost her mind. If anything, the terrible silence gnawed at his courage.

'I heard Keja with my mind. He let out an emotional cry for help. He's frightened, Giles. Scared out of his mind. I can *feel* it!'

'Keja in trouble is nothing new,' said Giles. 'He knew better than to run off by himself.'

'He's found a treasure room, but he's trapped by a giant snake. Hurry. The images are clouded by his fear.' Petia turned paler by the instant.

'The fool. Why didn't he stay with us?' Giles scowled. He turned the corner of the landing and halted, stumbling back into Petia and Anji. Two guards, spears aimed, came down the steps. Giles thumbed the sword. 'If we're to reach Keja, we must fight,' he said.

Petia took her stance besides Giles, sword at the ready.

Again, Keja's mental shout came to her. She trembled visibly, then thrust it away to concentrate on the enemy ahead. Keja would have to act on his own, but he intruded so in her mind!

The skeleton men advanced with measured steps. When their spears were just in front of the humans, Petia swept her sword to the left, engaging the shaft of one spear and driving it aside. On her return swing, she slashed the guard's legs. His legs buckled, and Giles stepped up to drive his sword through the man. This only slowed the skeleton warrior; Giles recovered and decapitated the guard.

The second guard had time to sweep down at Giles with his spear. Petia stepped inside the blow and deflected it, giving Giles an opportunity to cleave the head from the torso – the only sure way of stopping the skeleton warriors.

The skeleton dropped the spear and put his hands to his neck, then seemed to decide the fight had ended. He twisted around and crashed noisily to the floor.

Keja's cries were audible to Giles when they got to the top of the stairs. Petia pointed down the corridor. A doorway some way down the long hall stood open.

A seething mass of adders filled the doorway. Petia glanced beyond and saw Keja standing on top of a mound of treasure. A huge viper slid towards him.

Giles skidded to a stop beside her. The adders were between them and the interior of the room. They unwound themselves and quickly formed ranks, threatening to encircle them.

'Get me out of here!' screamed Keja. 'I hate snakes!' His sword thrusts were erratic and driven by fear, not skill. Giles saw that Keja would soon perish unless they could reach him.

But how? Killing all the snakes looked an impossible task. For every one that vanished behind a gaudy trinket, two more appeared from chests or from small holes in the walls.

The tip of Giles' sword wavered. 'First scorpions, now adders. The Skeleton Lord has more in his arsenal than just skeleton men, doesn't he?'

Giles gathered his wits, ready to make the run through the

snakes. If he could join Keja, together they might fight their way free.

Maybe. Giles doubted it. There were too many adders.

But he had to try. He let out a loud cry and rushed forward, sword swinging this way and that, slashing through yielding snake parts.

Thirteen

THE FIRST adder struck and missed. Giles jumped, bumping into Petia. 'Sorry,' he said. 'We've got to work together; forge a trail. You and Anji take the right, I'll take the left. Go!'

His sword slashed back and forth, inches above the floor, dealing death with every swing. He severed heads and cut bodies in half until the floor was littered with writhing segments of adder. The reptiles didn't realise that they were dead, and continued to strike.

Giles forged forward powerfully – and the living snakes began retreating. He yelled in triumph, 'Keja! Hurry! We've made a path for you!'

Slipping and sliding over the mound of jewels, Keja faced a viper so large it paralysed the thief with fear. The enormous snake measured fully a sword's width across the mouth and its fangs rivalled Keja's sword for length and sharpness. As the man backed off, the reptile wove its way ponderously among the treasures. Keja had no means of escape. Inexorably, the snake forced him to the wall.

He took a step backwards, and slipped on a chest. The box tipped and Keja sat down in the midst of a king's ransom.

The snake reared, preparing for the death stroke. Keja's eyes

315

widened and fear locked any but the smallest of cries deep in his throat. But when death came, it was to the snake and not the man.

Giles' glowing sword met one fang and chipped it off. Another powerful swing engaged the second fang. By the time the ponderous reptile swung round to see who dared attack it, Giles had found the spot, and he thrust true. The giant viper jerked about the sword, spitting at it, the huge, writhing length smashing priceless artwork to dust.

By the time Giles had pulled his sword free, Keja had recovered. Ashen-faced, he simply stared at the remains.

'Come on!' cried Petia. 'Guards!' She paused at the door of the room. Mounds of treasure winked out at her. Jewels sparkled, reflecting the dim light from the corridor. Goblets of gold, ropes of chalcedony and pearl, pendants of sapphire and emerald tempted her. But Petia left the treasure alone. Too much weight to carry.

Anji repeated Petia's warning: 'Guards, they're coming down the hall.'

Petia sprang to the boy's side. She saw skeleton warriors advancing on them, and for a moment she felt relieved. These were known dangers, not immense snakes or hideous scorpions. Anji now clutched a ceremonial short sword he had recovered from the treasure trove.

The guards walked stiffly down the hall, automatons obeying unheard orders. Petia held her sword and another one she'd picked up. 'Anji, you stay out of this.'

'No, Mistress.'

'And I freed you. Don't call me "Mistress".'

Anji did not move from her side. Four skeleton men advanced. Behind them, four more stood ready.

Giles sprang to the door and thrust Anji back. 'Where's that djinn?' he muttered to himself.

'Here, Giles,' Djinn responded. 'What a noble battle. Reminds me of the old days when I sported a body. We had great fun then, yes, great fun.'

Giles kept his eyes on the skeleton men, but out of the side of his mouth he said. 'Where have you been?'

'I've been here. You've got to remember to call me. Otherwise I vanish. It's the way of djinn.'

'We've got to find a place to hide, somewhere to rest. Find it, then report back to me.'

Djinn bowed. 'I hear and obey, O Master.'

Djinn disappeared, and Giles yelled, 'Keja, where are you? We've got eight guards out here.'

'I lost my sword,' came the answer.

'Hurry up!' Giles sprang at the skeleton man nearest Petia, giving her precious seconds to ready herself. Petia parried a spear thrust, letting it slide by her. She swung her sword hard and low. Her blade caught the warrior just below the knee. He stumbled and fell, blood oozing feebly from the desiccated leg bone. She forgot about him and went on to the next skeleton man.

Giles slashed at the first one and was surprised when the guard dodged to avoid the blade. Never before had he seen one retreat, so little did their ersatz lives mean to them – and so strong was the Skeleton Lord's spell.

Giles felt someone approaching from the rear and spun to meet the aggressor. Keja, still pale from his ordeal, staggered away from the doorway. He carried a gaudy, jewel-encrusted sword, but it looked sturdy enough for a fight. 'The small snakes have returned to the treasure room,' he said.

Then Keja screamed and leaped between Petia and Giles, smashing his sword against a spear. Before the skeleton man could recover, Keja lifted his sword above his head and sliced down on the exposed head. The sword rebounded from hard bone. The guard brought his spear back and thrust at Keja. He spun to the right and the spear grazed the side of his body.

'That does it,' Keja muttered.

He waded in, slicing right and left, making contact with every swing. He didn't care what he hit. Arms, legs, rib cages felt the force of his blows. The dull sword broke bones. Keja paid no attention and hacked away like a demon.

Giles and Petia ducked away from Keja's maddened, wild swings, taking care not to be caught by an errant blow. They found themselves behind the second rank of guards. Petia raised her sword with both hands and angled it down against a neck. The guard dropped, his spear clattering against the wall. Giles thrust through a spine, feeling the hum of his sword destroy the skeletal being.

317

When they looked up, there were no guards left to fight. Keja leaned on his sword, puffing and blowing. The anger left his face, to be replaced by a childlike smile. 'Bring me some more,' he said.

'No,' Giles replied. 'We need to rest. Djinn, where are you?'

Halfway down the hall, Djinn materialised, beckoning to them. Petia pushed Anji ahead of her down the corridor. Giles gripped Keja's shoulder. 'Come on.'

Keja sucked in a deep breath. 'Got to get my own sword. Are you sure that big snake is dead?' He peered cautiously into the room. The viper's tail still writhed feebly. He edged past it and retrieved his weapon. Then he fled after his companions.

'There are nooks and crannies everywhere,' Djinn said. 'What a delightful place to play at scavenger hunt. Guards come by occasionally. They'll be poking their noses in all over soon, but I found a room that looks as though it hasn't been used for a long time.'

He turned a corner, took a few steps and opened a door. It groaned, but opened wide enough for the four to enter. Giles leaned his weight against it and closed it.

Light filtered into the room from an embrasure far above. Giles narrowed his eyes to examine the interior. Some sacking lay against one wall, but otherwise the room was empty.

'I wish we had a candle,' Petia whispered in the dim light. I've had enough of snakes for one day.'

Giles held his sword up and made a tour around the room. He found nothing. He congratulated Djinn on his fine work.

'At last we can relax,' said Keja. He lowered himself onto the sacking and rested his head against the wall. He closed his eyes and murmured, 'I didn't realise how tired I was.'

'That comes from going berserk,' said Giles. He had never seen Keja in such a rage before, and wondered what had really powered the sudden fury.

'Djinn?'

The djinn took form with a loud *pop*! behind Giles.

'I wish you'd stop doing that. It gives me the shivers. I want you to go to the dungeon and release the beasts. Send them back into the desert. They aren't going to be of any help to us, but there's no sense in leaving them to rot away down there.

318

Then come back here. If you ever hope to be changed back into a human, you've got to help us.'

'Ah,' he said knowingly, 'the key, is it? But then, I would do anything to regain my human body.' The djinn disappeared instantly.

Petia slumped to the floor, waving to Anji to sit beside her. She was worried. She had expected skeleton men, but not the slithering and chittering creatures that the Skeleton Lord flung against them. She hadn't worried about Anji during their trip through the desert; that had been his home as a slave. But she had not counted on the dangers confronting them now. She liked the boy and the awesome responsibility for him had finally hit her. He wasn't her own son – but he could have been. Petia wouldn't be able to bear seeing Anji hurt, much less killed.

Giles paced the room for a time, thinking. He glanced at Keja: fast asleep. Petia and Anji talked quietly, but with great emotion. The responsibility of command fell heavily on Giles. It was hard enough with two thieves like Petia and Keja – they didn't need an eleven-year-old to watch. He settled down across from Keja and stretched out. Gradually his heart slowed. The images of scorpions and snakes dimmed. He and the others would stay here, getting needed sleep and regaining their strength. Then . . .

Giles slept.

Djinn made his way down to the dungeon, glancing down the hallway of each floor. Already the bodies of skeleton men, snakes, and scorpions had been removed.

When he reached the large iron door, he became a mere wisp and drifted through the spy hole. Teloq still sat in a stupor behind his table.

Djinn glanced across the room. The beasts were in their cage in one corner. They looked despondent, as if all hope had fled.

The old gaoler reached to a corner of the table and picked up a bottle, unsteady hand pouring into a battered cup. Djinn felt sorry for him. Teloq didn't have much of a life. Even less now that he had let prisoners escape. Solace from a bottle. Djinn understood.

Djinn drifted over and saw how the old man had drunk himself into senselessness. In his condition, the gaoler posed no threat.

Djinn floated to the beast's cage and materialised. 'Red Mane,' he whispered.

'Who's there?' The tawny beast came to the front of the cage.

'I've come to free you. Giles says that I'm to get you out of Shahal and back into the desert. Then you're on your own.'

Red Mane growled. 'What do you mean, back to the desert?' The other beasts crowded around him. He rubbed his hind-quarters until they quieted.

'Giles says you're better off out there than in a cage. He doesn't think you'll help. At first he was angry, but he decided not to let you languish down here. He told me to set you free.'

'Why does he think we can't help?'

Djinn considered for a moment, then blurted, 'The word he used was "cowardice".'

'What?' bellowed Red Mane. He spun and exposed his rump to Djinn in his anger. 'We want our city back, and we will fight! We aren't going back to the desert. We'd rather die first. We swore an oath on it. Let us out of here and take us to Giles.'

Djinn considered this for a moment. 'He didn't say anything about that.'

'Never mind,' Red Mane growled. 'Just release us.'

'You're going to need weapons,' Djinn said. 'I'll unlock the cage, but stay here until I return. I'm going to check the treasure room and see if I can find any decent weapons.'

Red Mane waited impatiently. He turned to the other beasts. 'Just remember what you promised. "Cowards" he called us. If we want our city back, we've got to fight. Do you understand?'

All the beasts nodded.

Djinn returned and checked on poor old Teloq. He snored peacefully, head on the table.

Djinn opened the heavy iron door to the beasts' cage. He whispered in Red Mane's ear, 'The halls are empty, but I don't know how long they'll stay that way. There are weapons, not the best, but serviceable. Quickly now, follow me.'

In minutes they reached the stairs, then slipped into the room Djinn had found for a hiding place.

Giles looked up, surprised at the number of beings entering the room. 'I told you to turn them loose.'

Djinn, halfway changed to a vaporous wisp, lifted nearly immaterial hands in a gesture of futility.

Giles looked hard at Red Mane. 'By the gods, you'd better fight this time. No more cowering in corners. It's side by side with us, or we'll turn on you ourselves.'

Red Mane glared back. 'Don't think you have all the courage, human. We're determined. We want Shahal back and we mean to get it.'

Petia held up her hand. 'Shh. Someone's outside,' she whispered.

Maniacal shouting carried down the corridor. 'Find them, you scum. You've got to find them. Don't let them get away. Kill every last one of them.'

'It's the Skeleton Lord's advisor,' Anji whispered.

They heard the slow tread of the skeleton warriors marching past, with Leaal's voice hounding them mercilessly. 'Onward, you dolts. Find them and bring me their still-beating hearts!' The voice faded down the corridor.

Then the storeroom door burst open.

Fourteen

GILES BLASTED to his feet, sword drawn. The beasts cowered – but Red Mane pressed close to Giles to lend aid against the intruder.

'The door,' Petia started. Her voice died down.

Giles turned red with rage when he saw Djinn pushing

against the door. The spirit creature laughed, trying to hide the sound behind a vaporous hand. 'Oh, that was a good prank, so good!' he chortled. 'The other djinn would approve. You were terribly scared, weren't you?'

'Did any of the guards see you?' demanded Giles, his anger still not fully under control. He forced calmness on himself, but Djinn was making it almost impossible.

'You worry too much,' Djinn said. 'They went off down the corridor to search the far parts of Shahal.' Djinn floated in front of Giles. 'You are mad,' he said, as if he'd never considered this possibility.

'For someone who depends on our aid, you are treading on dangerous ground,' Giles said between clenched teeth.

Djinn looked confused and drifted to the side of the storeroom, then slowly faded to nothingness. Giles indicated that the others should rest. He settled down, arms crossed. Soon the tension fled his body and he, too, was asleep again.

Petia awoke to sunlight warming her face. She rolled over sleepily, then came fully alert when she couldn't find Anji. Petia's quick eyes took a poll of both humans and beasts – Anji and Sleek were both missing.

She jerked to her feet and went to the door, peering out. Where had the boy gone? Giles would be furious at him for wandering off. *She* was angry with him, too!

Petia slipped into the corridor to find the youth. He couldn't have gone far.

Giles awoke to murmurs of concern from the beasts. He sat up, rubbing his eyes, pulling the tangles from his greying hair, wondering what had caused the stir among them. It took him only seconds to discover three missing from the rank.

'When did they go?' Giles demanded.

'I don't know,' Red Mane replied. 'They were gone when we awoke.'

'Sometime during the night, probably,' he mused. 'And who had the idea first, I wonder?' He pulled himself to his feet to face the beasts. 'I'm going to look for them. I want you all to stay here. We won't have any chance if we keep splitting up and going off by ourselves.'

Giles checked the hall and slipped out. At the end of the corridor another hallway crossed at right angles. He looked carefully around the corner – emtpy, stairs on either end.

He took them two at a time, stopping to check the hall on the next level. The passageway was empty. Giles hurried up another flight, straight into the arms of four skeleton men. He reached for his sword – too late. One guard gripped his forearm. The bony body had enormous strength in its arms and hands. Giles struggled, but the grip grew tighter.

In eerie silence, they carried him roughly up a flight of stairs to the Skeleton Lord's chamber. As they entered, the Skeleton Lord looked up, unsurprised, from his reeking flasks.

'Over there,' He pointed to the corner. 'Hold him firmly.'

Burners and candles stood beneath some of the flasks. Liquids of various colours bubbled and simmered, but many of them were shades of red. Insidious odours permeated the room, tormenting his nose. Wisps of vapor rose toward the discoloured ceiling. Gases had condensed to liquid and streaked the wall with ugly blotches.

But it was the Skeleton Lord's attitude that startled Giles the most. The Lord took scarce note of his presence, as though he were little more than a bug that had crawled into the laboratory. Giles watched the Skeleton Lord bend over a table to examine the contents of a beaker. It bubbled merrily, sending an occasional droplet into the air. When they hit the table, they sizzled and then vanished in a wisp of acrid smoke. Giles hoped one would hit the man in the eye.

The Skeleton Lord continued down the table, examining the contents of his glassware. Occasionally he sniffed the contents, and once he dipped an elongated forefinger into the beaker, then tasted the liquid.

When he had finished, he looked at Giles, as if wondering why the man stood there. Finally his eyes cleared and he said, 'Guards. Stand to one side, but be ready. If he tries to attack, kill him.'

One gestured to another. The skeleton man shuffled forward, pulled a knife from his belt, and waited, ready.

The Skeleton Lord came round the table, pulling a stool with him. He perched upon it to confront Giles.

He's nearly as thin as the men he has created, Giles thought. His eyes were sunken, the skin on his face unnaturally pale. It pulled over the cheekbones like a thin layer of parchment. His robes hung loose, and Giles saw a scrawny portion of one leg. For all his power and abilities, the man had wasted away to nothing. A good desert wind would pick him up and bury him in the Calabrashio Seas.

'Well?' The thin, reedy voice puzzled Giles. When he had been questioned only a few days before, the voice had been strong and unwavering. What it meant, Giles feared he would find out all too soon.

'Escaped from my cells, did you? And where are the rest of them? Even the beasts are gone. Poor dumb things.

'You are the leader, even though you deny it,' the Lord continued, his voice still weak. 'The rest of them have no chance without you.' Giles remained quiet, waiting for some clue to the Skeleton Lord's plan.

The Lord leaned forward, rheumy eyes studying Giles. 'A military man, aren't you? It shows in your bearing. And a leader, too. I could use you.'

Giles remained silent.

'Yes, I have need of a man like you,' he mused. 'My skeleton men need leadership. The Harifim are mine, but there is word of a black-robed stranger. Gathering men from the other tribes. I don't know what his intentions are, but I would rather be prepared.'

Giles waited for his chance. It had to come. It had to.

'Those companions of yours,' the Lord continued. 'An unusual lot; unworthy of you. How did you come to throw in with them? Not the key, certainly.' He looked slyly at Giles.

Giles blinked, his first defeat. How did he know they sought the key to the Gate of Paradise?

'I know,' he said confidently. 'And I'll find your companions before long and kill them. But you could be useful to me. You would share power, a great deal of power, with me. With your military experience, I can take over the entire continent more quickly. You will lead the Harifim, be the tactician. They fight well, but they are undisciplined children. With me to make the plans and you to lead them, we will sweep the desert! Then the towns. The continent will be ours!'

'I won't abandon my companions as easily as you think,' Giles muttered. 'And you'll never conquer the continent.'

'You may not like it much,' the reedy voice said. 'But if you care so deeply for your friends, you will want to save their skins.' His eyes cleared for a moment, and Giles was surprised at the intensity shining forth. 'For I will have your help, whether you want to or not.

'As for the key, it is useless without the others. Ah, you look surprised. Yes, there are others. The Gate of Paradise cannot be opened without them all.'

Giles thought he hid his surprise well – and that he had kept the Lord from guessing that the companions already had three keys in safekeeping.

'The Gate of Paradise,' the Lord continued. 'A tale, an old legend. There is no wealth or power there. I will have both, here, on Bandanarra. Do you wish to share it with me?'

'Not especially,' Giles answered. 'I've had enough of war. I've killed enough people. I don't want to kill any more.' The skeleton men moved forward with their spears, pricking Giles in the chest.

'Sick of killing?' The Skeleton Lord looked surprised. 'Why is that? Do you think there is any worth in a human life? There is, as a matter of fact.' He pointed at the beakers on the table. 'Blood. Blood for my experiments. Human blood and animal blood. I have worked long to find its essence.

'When I succeed, I will be able to make my skeleton men live for ever. I will make them more than the shambling beings they have become. They will be the scourge of the desert, élite troops, leaders of the desert tribes. But I need more blood for my experiments. Even yours, if you don't cooperate.'

'How long have you been holed up in this city of rock, working on your insane schemes, changing tribesmen into walking skeletons, seeking the power to rule the entire continent?' Giles hadn't meant to speak; the words spilled out before he could stop them.

The Skeleton Lord held up a beaker containing a viscous red substance. He dipped his finger into it, then licked it with his tongue. Disgusted, Giles averted his eyes.

'This is the essence of life,' the Lord continued. 'This is what will give me great power.'

Giles stirred. 'It doesn't give power when it drains away from men's bodies. I've watched it too many times. The slice of a sword and a man in great pain, watching himself die by inches. It's the same with your soldiers as it has been with soldiers all over the world.'

'The blood of my men will be different!' the Skeleton Lord raged. 'It will not seep away. It will stay within them, rebuilding the tissues, closing the wound.'

'Your men will die exactly like any other men. Your wonderful blood will not prevent that.'

'No!' the Lord screamed. 'Not so. This blood is different.' He dipped his hand into the beaker again. It came out red and dripping. 'This is a fluid that will make men immortal. They will never die. You are wrong!'

Giles leaned back against the wall and watched the Skeleton Lord pace back and forth, mouthing his beliefs in his experiments. Giles wondered if there was any way to calm the man — or if he even wanted to try.

Keja waited anxiously. He wished he had some way of knowing how long Giles had been gone. The shaft of light from the high window had moved several feet up the wall.

'Pacing like that won't bring them back any sooner,' said Red Mane. He patted the floor beside him.

Keja slumped down with a sigh. 'I know, but night is coming, and Giles has been gone all day. If he's not back by dark, I'm going to look for him.'

'Would that be wise?' asked Red Mane. 'He told us to stay here until he came back.'

'We can't stay here until we're skeletons ourselves,' Keja said. 'Are you afraid again? With you or without you, I'm leaving when it's dark.'

'We're not afraid,' Red Mane said, scowling. 'We'll go with you, we'll fight, whether or not it's wise. We know the city and you don't.'

Keja sat in silence for a while longer, then called, 'Djinn.' Once again Keja was disconcerted by the gradual materialisation from spirit to flesh 'I'll never get used to that,' he said.

'How do you think I've felt all these years?' Djinn replied. 'What can I do for you?' He knelt on the floor, facing Keja and Red Mane.

'We need a scout,' Keja said. 'I should have thought of it sooner. If only you'd stick around so we could see you, we wouldn't forget you're here.'

'Sorry, it can't be helped,' Djinn said. 'It's the way djinn are. We have to be called.'

'I want you to find Giles. Or any of the others. Petia, Anji and Sleek are out there, too. I want you to go to the Skeleton Lord's chambers and find out what he's doing.'

'You're taking your life in your hands, Keja. At night the pazuzi, the wind demons, come out of the cliffs along the edge of the plain. They roam the halls and corridors. It's a game to them, but they are dangerous.'

'We'll have to risk it,' Keja said. 'We can't sit here for ever. If the others are alive, they need our help. If they're dead, we need to get out of Shahal. It's that simple.'

Djinn faded and the wisp disappeared beneath the door. 'I hope we can change him back into a human one day,' he said with a shudder.

Djinn returned after an hour and did not bring good news. 'I found no trace of Petia, Anji, or Sleek. Giles is a captive in the Skeleton Lord's chambers. I tried to speak to him, but the Lord was raving. I had no opportunity to free Giles. He's unbound, but his sword is gone.'

'We've got to attempt a rescue,' Keja said. 'What about the hallways?'

'Empty,' replied Djinn. 'The skeleton men leave the halls before the wind demons come. Otherwise they'd be swept right over the edge of Shahal's balconies.'

'Then now is the time to move,' Keja said decisively. 'Listen everybody, we're going to attack the Skeleton Lord's chambers and try to free Giles. Capture the Skeleton Lord, too, if we can.'

Keja and the beasts moved quickly into the corridor. Keja gestured for Red Mane to take the lead. 'You know the way,' he whispered.

Red Mane led the way up the stairs. They reached the next

floor without incident. Red Mane hesitated, checked the corridor, and whispered to Keja, 'Nothing in this hallway. Shall we go up? There are two more floors to the Lord's chambers.'

'Pause when you get up there. We'll need a moment to ready ourselves.' Keja rubbed his hand nervously over his sword hilt. He felt as if he stalked his first victim. He forced himself to be calm by thinking about what Giles might do in this situation — and it bothered him that Giles probably wouldn't be in it at all.

Rapidly they ascended the stairway. Keja stopped at the top. 'This is the floor. We're attacking the Skeleton Lord's chamber. Djinn?'

'Here.'

'Check how many guards are in the chamber and how are they armed? I'm going to mutter your name until you get back, so I can see you.'

Djinn disappeared before Keja could even begin. The spirit returned in a short time, appearing as he came within the sound of Keja's voice.

'Four guards armed with spears,' he reported. 'One commanding; he has a short sword.'

Keja turned to the beasts. 'Then we outnumber them. I'll take care of Giles. You attack the guards, but be careful of the Lord. There's no way of knowing if he can use his magicks against us quickly enough to matter.'

Keja and the others started down the corridor at a trot. Suddenly, Red Mane put out his hand and stopped. Keja halted beside him.

'What is it?' he asked.

Then he heard the whisper of wind. It began softly, like someone blowing across the mouth of a jug. The tone sharpened. At the far end of the hall tapestries curled slightly at the edges, the fringes ruffling. The wind grew and the tapestries billowed out. The sound increased and then the wall hangings whipped about violently.

Behind him Keja heard a beast gasp, 'Pazuzi!'

Fifteen

THE WIND demons roared down the corridor towards Keja. Air compressed ahead of the pazuzi and pushed powerfully at him. His eardrums almost exploded and his eyes began to water.

'Where are they?' he yelled at Red Mane over the deafening rush.

'You can't see them,' Red Mane answered. 'They are only wind. You see their effects, not their bodies.'

'How do we fight them? How can we defend ourselves?' shouted Keja.

'You can't.' Red Mane gestured to the other beasts. 'We will protect you.'

The force of a pazuzi staggered Keja. Recovering, he leaned into the gale, covering his eyes with his forearm. He yelled at Red Mane, but the wind ripped the words from his mouth. He could only hear a hurricane's roar. Red Mane put a finger to his ear and shook his head, but Keja could not see; his eyes poured tears.

A second wind demon hit Keja and whirled him in a circle. He spun like a child's top, crashing into the wall and spinning down the corridor. Keja screamed when he saw that only a low balustrade at the end of the hall protected him from falling five stories to the desert floor.

Red Mane made a circling gesture and one shaggy, long-limbed beast dropped to his hands and knees by the wall, directly in Keja's path. When Keja came within reach, the beast clasped him around the waist. Two others grabbed the small thief's arms and pulled him to the centre of the hall. Red Mane loomed over him to protect him from the wind demons' depradations.

The pazuzi screeched angrily, thwarted of their prey. Dozens of them roared down the hall, buffeting the circle of beasts. The creatures calmly turned their backs to the fierce winds. The force and the chill of the pazuzi did not approach that of the desert.

'Feel that?' Red Mane roared. 'Is this our city? Do you remember?' He faced the pazuzi, raising his hands in a gesture both welcoming and challenging of the battle. A howl of acceptance came from the demons. They remembered the beasts. Gale forces whipped down the hall, creating turbulences deadly to creatures less powerful than the beasts. Had Keja's eyes been open he would have been dumbfounded at the grins which creased their mouths. They were enjoying the contest.

Tornadoes spun around the cluster of beasts, forcing some to huddle against the wind. Others stretched their claws against the invisible enemy.

The demons roared away, having again met their match after so many years.

Keja brushed his watering eyes. 'Is it over?' he asked.

'For tonight,' the shaggy beast answered, smiling broadly. 'I think they enjoyed that. They don't get adequate opposition from the skeleton men.'

Red Mane beckoned to the other beasts. They reached the stairway and began the ascent. The battle with the wind demons had lasted only a short while, but Keja sent Djinn to check the Skeleton Lord's chambers once more.

Giles watched the Skeleton Lord pacing back and forth, muttering, lifting a beaker now and again to sniff it.

'Why is that blood so important?' he asked.

The Skeleton Lord peered at Giles over the beakers and flasks. 'It's the fluid of life, of power.'

'But it's only useful inside a body. Once it has drained away, there is no life force, no power. I've fought against men who thought it contained the strength and cunningness of their enemies, who drank it after battle.' Giles chuckled. 'We defeated them time and again. The blood did them no good.'

The Skeleton Lord glared at Giles. 'No, another reason.

330

Their gods abandoned them, or they were outnumbered. Blood is powerful, even animal blood. In the desert there are great cats, strong and cunning.' He lifted a flask and held it toward Giles. 'See. This is blood from one of them. I will find the essence of those qualities in their blood. Then my skeleton men will be even more powerful, more deceptive!'

He gestured at the array of equipment on the tables. 'All my labours are towards better warriors, leaders; not followers like these slow-wits.'

'You can't give men what they don't already have,' Giles reasoned. 'If they are not courageous, not leaders, or can't think for themselves, no amount of human or animal blood will change them. I once saw a hunter who killed a deer. When he had butchered it, he pulled out its heart and ate it raw. He said it gave him great skill in the forest, the same skill as the deer once possessed. I told him that the deer did not have any great skill or it would not have been killed. The hunter got angry at that.'

'The hunter was right,' the Skeleton Lord said. 'You are wrong.'

'So he told me. He tried to force me to eat some of the heart. I fought him and he lost. I buried the remains of the heart in the grave with him and went away.'

'But a deer is not strong,' the Lord replied. 'It lives by its wits. It lies low during the day, feeds only in the morning and evening, is cautious of its enemies. It runs from danger. Deer are cowardly animals.'

'Not cowardly – cautious. Have you ever seen stags fighting during rutting time? You cannot call them cowardly. They fight to the death.' The Skeleton Lord made an obscene gesture. 'That is what the animal will do for sex,' he said, dismissing Giles' argument.

'Humans are no better, then,' Giles replied with a smile. 'Sex is a strong drive, but your skeleton men don't even have that drive any longer. You took it away from them. Is that not so?'

'They do not need it. There are no women here.'

'Give your warriors back their sex, and allow them to take wives, concubines, lovers. You will have stronger soldiers. They will have something to fight for.'

'No!' An anguished roar came from the Skeleton Lord, his voice no longer weak. 'They need fight only for *me*!'

331

A commotion in the outer chamber interrupted them. The heavy tread of skeleton men was nearly obscured by Anji's sharp voice shouting, 'No, no.'

Guards held the boy's arms on either side, nearly lifting him off his feet.

The Skeleton Lord stared thoughtfully at Anji. 'Put him down. He can do no harm.' He waved his hand at the guards. 'You're dismissed.'

The Skeleton Lord rubbed his hands together and looked at Giles. 'One of your party, I see. We'll have them all before long. You'll get no further on your quest than when you were locked in the dungeon. And, you, young one. Where have you been these past hours?'

Anji looked at the Skeleton Lord and then to Giles. 'I was just trying to help. We thought we could find . . . it.'

He flung himself at Giles, threw his arms around the man's neck, and wept. Giles murmured, 'It's all right, it will be all right.'

'You have affection for the boy?' The Skeleton Lord looked bemused. This was an entirely new idea. He bent forward to examine the boy more closely, expecting to find some quality that caused the emotion in Giles. 'Amazing,' he muttered. 'Looks like an ordinary Trans to me.'

He called the guards. They pulled Anji away from Giles, twisting his arms behind him. 'Put him over in the corner,' the Skeleton Lord said.

'There's no need to be rough with the boy,' Giles said.

'He means that much to you?' the Skeleton Lord asked. 'Perhaps we can bargain. You'd like me to turn the boy loose, wouldn't you?'

'He can't do any harm. Let him go. He's only a youngster.'

'If you tell the others to surrender, and take my guards to their hiding place, then I think it could be arranged.'

'And what would you do with him? Cast him out into the desert to die?'

The Skeleton Lord laughed. 'You have no trust, warrior. No trust. We would take him to join the caravan to Kasha. He would be safe.'

Giles wondered if he could trust the insane man. Keja would certainly be angry with him, but the boy had to be freed. In that instant Giles felt a hundred years older and tireder – all the more reason for him to make the decision. Anji deserved the chance to grow up and live his own life.

'I'll tell you where they are and convince them to surrender if you guarantee the boy will be treated well and taken to the caravan.'

The Skeleton Lord threw back his head and laughed so hard that he choked. When he had caught his breath again, he wiped his eyes and shook his head at Giles. 'What a fool you are. You have no power to bargain. You sit there, a wild pig in a pen, talking as if we were merchants signing a contract. You have no wealth, no army, no power. You are nothing.'

The Lord waved his arms and stomped back and forth in front of Giles. 'You think I am mad. You and the boy are mere midges flying about, thinking to disturb my great work. And your companions are gnats.' His arm swept over the tables where his experiments bubbled.

'I'll have the boy's blood for my work. It will bubble merrily, don't you think? Perhaps it is younger blood that I need. A perfect opportunity to find out.'

'The boy's blood will do you no good,' Giles said. 'You're looking for strength, courage, decisiveness, qualities that will make a stronger soldier. You won't find those things in a boy of this age. He's gained no experience yet to have the characteristics you seek.' Giles spat. 'Foolish, a waste of time. I have gained those experiences. If you must, take my blood.

'Twenty years at war,' he boasted. 'Leading men, killing my enemies, crazy with the smell of battle, wading in when we were outnumbered. That is the blood you want. A more than fair trade for the boy.'

The Skeleton Lord perched upon a stool; watching a simmering jar. Giles knew he was considering the offer.

'You have a point,' the Lord said. 'But I have both of you. Why not experiment on *both* your bloods?' The cackle chilled Giles to the core.

Petia hunted, but had seen nothing of Anji or Sleek. A short while ago she had felt an empathic tug that told her Anji was in trouble, but she had no idea on which level to look.

Earlier she had paused at the end of one corridor, frightened by a loud roaring. It sounded like a storm blowing nearby. Before she could investigate, the sound had disappeared.

Petia crept to the corner and stretched out along the floor. Edging forward slowly, she could look down the adjoining hall. Sleek backed towards her.

'Sleek,' she whispered. The young female beast leaped and twisted, eyes wide with fear. Sleek released her pent-up breath when she recognised Petia.

'Where's Anji?' Petia asked. 'Wasn't he with you?'

'He was, but we got separated. I don't know where he is now.' The young beast was desolate.

'He's been captured,' Petia said. 'I can feel it. What did you two think you were doing?'

Sleek's eyes filled with tears. 'He said he could find the key you seek. I just wanted to prove that not all of us beasts are cowards, like Giles said.'

'Don't worry about it now. We've got to find Anji. If he's been captured, he would have been taken to the Skeleton Lord's chambers.'

Sleek shivered, but Petia put a hand on her shoulder and squeezed, showing her confidence in the beast. The two set off down the hall.

'Djinn? Where is he? It shouldn't take this long,' Keja fumed, standing with one foot on the top step waiting for the djinn to return.

'Patience,' Red Mane said. 'Or are you in a hurry to do battle? Giles would tell you that if there is a possibility of knowing your enemy's strength, it is to wait and find that out first.'

'You're right,' Keja muttered, not liking it when the beast was right and he was wrong. He didn't know where any of his companions were, and it wouldn't help them if he now rushed into a trap. If they had been captured, he would rescue them.

'Djinn!'

'I'm back.'

The voice whispered in Keja's ear and he jumped. 'Djinn! What did you find?'

'Giles is there. Anji, too, but neither one is tied. They're

334

being held at spear point. They don't think Anji is any threat to them.'

'How many guards are there?'

'Five in the chambers,' Djinn replied. 'Eight outside in the corridor. We outnumber them.'

'We must be careful. Even if we capture the Skeleton Lord, we don't know how many troops are scattered around this city, or what they'll do.' He turned to the beasts behind him. 'Everybody ready?'

'Wait, Keja. There's more. I heard a noise in another corridor. I found Petia and Sleek.'

'Where? Can you stay visible long enough to lead us to them?'

'Down this corridor and around the corner. Follow me.'

'There's no sense for all us to go there and then come back. Just this once, stay visible. Go and get them, and bring them here. Can you do that?'

Djinn winked and was gone. In a few minutes he returned with Petia and Sleek in tow.

Keja immediately harangued Petia. 'What made you go off like that? Giles went off to look for you, and now he's been captured. They got Anji, too.'

Petia's eyes flashed. 'I had to look for the boy. I'm the only one who cares about him.'

Red Mane growled deep in his throat. The two stopped and looked at him. 'You can argue all you want when this is done. We must hurry if we are going to get on with it.'

'All right,' said Keja. 'Djinn, where are you? Fade away now; you will be more useful if they can't see you.' Keja turned to the Trans woman. 'We're going to attack the chambers and release Giles and Anji. Keep your weapons ready.'

Djinn appeared again. 'I've checked again. There are more guards in the hall now. Reinforcements.'

'We'll have to fight our way in. I don't think we can plan any further than a battle in the passageway. After that, we'll do whatever we can. I still think we can win, even if we are outnumbered.'

He lifted his hand and motioned the beasts forward. They moved up the final stairway to the level which held the Skeleton Lord's chambers and death.

Sixteen

'A WARRIOR's blood, yes. And a young boy's blood, too.' The Skeleton Lord cackled. 'I will have both. It will be an interesting experiment. The alchemy of youth and courage might be the answer.'

'Damn your lying eyes,' Giles shouted. 'You promised to exchange the boy for me. You said he could go free.'

The Skeleton Lord's eyes narrowed to dagger points, threatening to pierce Giles' very soul. 'Who are you to bargain with me? A vagabond appearing out of the desert. I am the power here. You are only so much sand, blowing into cracks and crevices. Nothing, you are nothing!' His voice rose to a scream with his final words.

'Guards, bring him to my work table. No, you idiots, the big one.'

Giles struggled ineffectually against the skeleton men. The Lord held a short blade in his hands. He stropped it on a leather strap. 'I'll take only a little now, but I'll keep you around, taking a few drops more each time.'

The Skeleton Lord steadied Giles' arm, turning the wrist to expose the veins. He touched the spot where Giles' exertions had caused the blood vessels to stand out and carefully lowered his knife.

'Now!' Keja shouted. Ahead he saw skeleton men standing at ease before the Lord's chamber door. Four of them turned towards the advancing beast throng, and there were at least a dozen more standing further down the hall.

Red Mane threw back his head and roared, and immediately the other beasts took up the call. The guards hesitated for a brief instant. It gave the attackers a small advantage. Keja raised his sword to slash, picked out a target and ran.

The leading skeleton warrior attempted to back away from Keja so that he could use his spear. Other guards crowded behind. He reached deliberately for a short dagger at his hip.

Keja raised his sword waist high. Gripping the edge of the blade below the hilt with his left hand, he drove the blade with both hands into the guard's ribcage, smashing bones and destroying the warrior. Keja stepped back, pulled the weapon loose and watched the guard rattle to the floor.

Petia and Sleek attacked side by side. Petia slashed hard with her short sword, aiming for her opponent's eyes. As the guard retreated, Sleek rushed in, clawing at unprotected legs.

Red Mane became a fury, roaring encouragement to the other beasts. He burst through the first line of guards and attacked those further down the hall. Several beasts followed him through the break, one beast leaping five feet onto the chest of a guard, taking him and several others down to the ground. With savage fangs, he broke exposed bones and left the skeleton warriors helpless.

Giles heard the fighting outside and struggled harder against the hands holding his wrist steady for the Skeleton Lord's knife.

'They want their city back,' he shouted, 'and I don't think either you or your guards will keep them from it.'

The blade trembled in the Skeleton Lord's hand. 'Leaal!' he screamed. Giles had forgotten the advisor and looked for the man. Giles did not see him, so he dismissed him. Then he, yelled. 'Djinn!'

The blade flashed down and slashed Giles' wrist. He looked at the Skeleton Lord, surprised at his presence of mind. Sounds of the fierce fighting echoed from the corridor. The Skeleton Lord bent over, intent on licking the blood which dripped from Giles's wrist.

Giles brought his knee up and caught the Skeleton Lord in the groin; Giles grimaced when he felt little more than bone, but the Lord rocked back against the table, gasping for breath.

'Djinn!' Giles shouted again.

Keja appeared in the doorway and diverted the guards' attention. Giles ripped free of their grasp. He swung his fist at the Skeleton Lord's face.

Djinn finally appeared, smiling. 'You called?' he asked pleasantly, as though the carnage around him meant nothing.

'You took your time,' Giles snarled. 'Destroy everything on the tables.'

Djinn grinned wickedly. The alchemical glassware was the symbol of all that he had suffered. He thrust out one muscular arm and swept down one side of the table. Jars and bottles clattered over the end and smashed on the stone floor. He turned down the aisle between the two tables, an arm on either side, sweeping beakers, vials and other containers before him. Reeking pools of liquid and glass spattered the floor.

The Skeleton Lord stood transfixed as the apparatus crashed down from the tables. He saw all his work being destroyed. Chemicals, tinctures, amalgams and bloods mixed haphazardly on the smooth alabaster work surface. He sagged.

Giles snatched up a sword and went to help the others. He saw the strength ebb out of the Skeleton Lord; he was defeated. A fierce cry behind Giles startled him. The sorceror threw back his head. His back arched as he screamed, 'Leaal!'

Petia glanced up from the skeleton man she had killed. Racing forward from the end of the corridor she saw the Lord's advisor running pell-mell, gesturing to the guards behind him. 'Hurry, you fools. Kill them. Kill them all!' he screamed. The guards broke into a travesty of a run, their feet pounding flatly on the stone.

'Red Mane,' she shouted. 'We need reinforcements.' The shaggy beast motioned to those not fighting. Red Mane's eyes gleamed as they fastened on the advisor.

Red Mane struck Leaal across the face, and the advisor sank to the floor. A second slash left him bleeding and already near death. For a moment Red Mane felt pleasure in his revenge, then pity. He glanced up, seeking another opponent. There was none. The skeleton men stumbled down the hall away from them. 'After them!' Red Mane shouted.

'No,' Petia yelled. Emphatically she knew that the skeleton men were beaten, confused. Without a leader, they were like lost children. 'We'll capture them later.'

In the Lord's chamber, liquids dripped to the floor, a thin spiral of smoke floating upward from one of the mixtures. Flames leaped upwards and spread rapidly across the chamber to lick at the fringes of tapestries hanging on the walls.

Giles felt the heat on his back. He swung at the skeleton man before him, forcing him back. He turned to find sheets of flame already covering two walls. An ominous thought ran through his mind.

The key might be hidden here! He snatched at a burning tapestry, tearing it from the wall and flinging it to the floor. It landed in a pool of liquid and Giles stamped on it, trying to put the fire out. Flame shot up Giles' leg. He leaped away, grabbed a cloak from a hook and attempted to beat out the fire.

Despite Giles' efforts the Skeleton Lord's volatile reagents spread the fire; the wooden legs of the alabaster tables burned like kindling. One table crashed, spilling more liquids. Chemicals and flame raced across the floor, spreading to the outer room.

The fire intensified. How hot must it get before gold melted? he wondered. Their quest might well end in this blazing room.

He heard a muttering behind him and turned to find the Skeleton Lord staggering toward him, hands outstretched. One bony finger pointed at Giles and the reedy voice rose, mouthing a spell. The language was not familiar to Giles, but the spell's impact shook him. A tingling ran through Giles' chest; his arms felt leaden, as if he had been lifting hundredweights of flour; he couldn't move his feet.

Djinn entered the blazing outer chamber beside Keja. He gasped in Keja's ear, 'It's a spell to freeze Giles. Don't let him finish it.'

Keja dashed across the room and caught the Skeleton Lord's arm, twisting it behind him. The sorceror yelled in pain, and Keja clamped a hand over his mouth.

'Some rags, stuff something in his mouth.' Djinn floated toward him with several scarves he had snatched from a shelf. Keja shoved two of them into the Skeleton Lord's mouth.

Rushing to Giles, he asked, 'Are you all right?'

Giles rubbed his arms and stamped his legs. 'Thanks,' he said. 'A few more words and he would have had me. A powerful spell. I'm glad you got here in time.'

Djinn said, 'I've seen him use that spell before. It would have frozen you like a statue.'

Petia cried out from the corridor. 'More guards; human, I

think. Not skeleton men. And the beasts are gone.'

Keja and Djinn headed for the doorway. Giles paused to look for his magical sword, but couldn't find it. He hated to lose it, but he had no time to search further. He kicked at a burning spot and swore, then realised that Anji stood by his side. He shoved the boy ahead of him. 'Don't you have any sense at all? Stay out of the way.'

Giles looked about frantically for his sword until the heat drove him from the chamber. He pulled a spear from the hands of a dead skeleton man and reluctantly joined his companions. Out in the corridor men rushed towards them. As they drew closer, he recognised them as Harifim, the desert tribesmen. He had heard tales of their ferocity in Kasha. Now he would test it.

Keja, Petia, and Giles ranged themselves across the hallway, on the defensive. They fought well, but the Harifim forced them back with a fierce attack. Giles found the spear a clumsy weapon. He could do little more than defend himself.

Petia heard a cry from inside the chamber. 'Anji,' she yelled, and drove two opponents away with a maniacal attack. She reached the doorway and rushed inside, leaving Giles and Keja to fight on.

Anji stood, his arms loaded with bound volumes from the sorceror's shelves. The Skeleton Lord, his body on fire, burned like tinder. Petia watched as the body wrenched once, twice, then fell limp. What life had been in the demented mind and twisted soul now ended in fire. Flames fully enveloped the room. Petia thrust the boy behind her.

'We've got to get out or we'll suffocate,' she yelled. 'Follow me.'

Petia halted at the doorway. The beasts had returned and attacked the Harifim from the rear, giving Giles and Keja a chance to take the offensive. Harifim began dying; others fought on, but the beasts had taken the fight out of them. One gestured with his free hand and laid down his sword. Giles and Keja drew back, waiting to see what the others would do. The fight quickly ended. Seven men surrendered, two were wounded, two lay dead.

'Djinn, find something to bind them with.' Giles kicked the swords across the corridor. 'Is everyone accounted for?' He counted his own party and caught Red Mane's nod.

340

He ran back into the blazing room. Petia called after him that the Skeleton Lord was dead, but he didn't hear her.

The Lord's blackened bones were sprawled on the floor. The desiccated flesh had burned completely. The Skeleton Lord was not only dead, but truly a skeleton. Shielding his eyes with one arm, Giles tried vainly to find his sword. Smoke billowed and hung thickly in the room. A shelf crashed to the floor, spilling charts and showering sparks. Intense heat forced him back. Rivulets of sweat stung Giles' eyes. When he couldn't hold his breath any longer, he stumbled from the room.

In the hallway, he sucked in great drafts of fresh air. Petia wiped his face. 'I called to you that he was dead. Didn't you hear me?'

'My sword, I couldn't find it,' he gasped. A blinding flash illuminated the room, reflecting off the corridor walls. 'I think that was it. The end of a wonderful weapon.'

Giles straightened. 'Djinn, lock these men in the dungeon. Let them carry their own wounded. Then accompany Red Mane and the beasts and search the entire city. Round up any skeleton men. See that our old friend Teloq locks them in the cages.'

'Giles, I'm starving,' Keja moaned. 'Couldn't Djinn find something for us to eat first? If there are men here –' he gestured at the Harifim '– there must be food, a pantry, something. And something to drink. By the gods, even water will do.'

'All right. That first, Djinn. Then we'll round up any who are left.'

Djinn herded the Harifim down the passage, followed by two beasts Red Mane had singled out. He wanted to be sure that these ancient enemies had no opportunity for further mischief. When the men had been locked in an empty room, the beasts returned. Djinn drifted away to disappear down a stairway.

'Let's get away from the smoke,' Petia suggested. 'The city can't catch fire. It's solid rock. When the furnishings have all burned, the fire will go out.'

Giles peered through the doorway. Nothing could be retrieved from the chamber now. Everything was burning. Smoke and scorch marks covered the white walls. He nodded. 'Good idea. Let's go where we can breathe fresh air.'

The company trooped down one level and collapsed along the walls. For a long time no one spoke. Sighs of contentment came from the beasts. They had proven themselves and the city was theirs once more.

Giles reached over and tousled Anji's hair. The boy leaned on one elbow on the stack of books he had rescued from the Skeleton Lord's shelves. 'You're the only one with any sense,' Giles said. 'We promised Djinn that we'd try to change him back into a human. Without these books, we wouldn't have had a chance. I hope you got the right ones.'

Anji grinned. 'Are you glad that I came along? I'm good for some things. I'm good with the lirjan. But I didn't find your key, and sometimes I get in the way, don't I?'

Giles smiled and nodded. He had probably been in someone's way when he was eleven. That was an ancient time for him, beyond remembrance. The faces of his own parents had blurred with the years. Even his wife, Leorra, and his sons, dimmed. Too tired. He'd try again this evening when he went to sleep. Maybe he'd dream of them.

'I've found the kitchen,' Djinn announced. 'There's plenty of food. Follow me.'

Plain food, washed down with a fruity wine, raised the spirits of the company. With full stomachs, they wanted nothing more than to sleep, but Red Mane and Giles roused them. They swept through the city in an organised manner. Djinn ferreted out all the hiding Harifim and skeleton men. The older beasts delighted in finding long-forgotten passageways and rooms, many of which were closed. Parts of Shahal had not been used for decades.

Giles climbed wearily to the seventh level. The Skeleton Lord's chambers were scorched ruins. Ash swirled in the evening breezes. Perhaps the pazuzi would blow it all away during their nightly foray. They had little hope of finding his sword or the key, Giles thought grimly. But tomorrow they would search.

The key to the Gate of Paradise might not have been destroyed.

Seventeen

THE ODOUR of death still hung in the Skeleton Lord's rooms, but it no longer overpowered them. Petia rolled up the sleeves of her robe to begin sifting through the debris for the key to the Gate of Paradise. 'What do you want us to do, Giles?'

Giles stared at the piles of ash-covered rubbish. Molten glass was stuck to the floor in the inner chamber. Charred paper and portions of books lay at one edge of the outer room. Giles picked up a small piece of metal, its twisted shape testifying to the fire's immense heat. Relief replaced worry; for a heart-wrenching moment he thought it might have once been a key.

He threw it down in disgust. 'We've got to sift through all this stuff. There are two things I'm looking for. One is the key, although I'm afraid that if it was here, it would be as twisted as that piece of brass. The other is my sword. I don't have much hope for it, either.'

The three set about the task. They plunged their arms into the mess, moving methodically from one side of the room to the other. They found many metal objects, but none made of gold.

It took an hour to sift through the detritus of the outer room. When they reached the inner chamber, Giles hurried on. 'This is where the sword should be, or what's left of it.' He scrabbled through the ashes on the side of the room where he had lain trussed the evening before. 'Ah,' he said. 'I can feel the hilt.' He tugged and his hand came away with the twisted pommel, hilt and crossbar of the sword – but no blade.

Disappointment clouded Giles' face. 'So much for my wonderful sword. I suspected this last night when I saw the light flash. Whatever magicks were contained in its steel were released in one quick lightning bolt.'

Searching the rest of the chamber took much less time. They searched carefully, but found nothing but misshapen glass-ware, stained by the substances they had once contained. Keja and Giles struggled to move the alabaster tables, but found nothing beneath them.

'I'm now sure the key wasn't in these rooms,' Giles said. 'It'll turn up somewhere else. Let's clean up and see if there is any ale in the pantry. We deserve it.' He tried to sound cheerful, but Petia knew that he was disconsolate about the sword.

Over cheese and ale, Petia said dreamily, 'It might be worth our while to stay here for a few months. We could help the beasts make plans for restoring the city. And take our time searching for the key. And,' she said in a lower voice, 'lead a more normal life.'

'First, we've got to do something about all the Harifim prisoners we've taken,' Giles said. 'We can't keep them locked up for ever. They'll starve.'

'No loss,' said Keja, stuffing a large hunk of coarse bread into his mouth and washing it down with a healthy swig of ale.

Sleek and some of the other beasts entered the room, grinning. They had been wandering up and down the levels, rediscovering their city.

'Glad to see someone's happy,' Giles said. 'Is Shahal all you expected it to be?'

'Yes, dirty and dusty from neglect, but we'll soon set that right,' Sleek said. The other beasts chorused their pleasure with the rock city. 'Red Mane will be here soon. He's climbed several levels higher to look out over the desert. He wanted to be alone, but I don't think he really wants us to see how pleased he is to be home again.'

'Bring us a couple of the skeleton men,' Giles asked the beasts. 'We're going to have to do something with them sooner or later. It might as well be done now.' Torn Ear and several of the younger beasts trotted off to comply.

The two skeleton men they brought stared into space, sunken eyesockets showing no emotion. Giles forced himself to peer closer at them. There *were* eyes there – they had just become minuscule through the Skeleton Lord's magicks. Giles ran his hand down the man's arm. 'Bony, but there is still some flesh there,' he observed. He put his hand to the man's hollow chest and was surprised to feel a regular heart beat.

He peered into the man's almost-invisible eyes. They stared, trance-like, and didn't focus on Giles or follow him when he moved. He waved his hand in front of the skeleton man's face. No reaction. He pushed one man ahead of him across the floor, receiving no resistance. 'It's almost as if they were drugged.'

'Definitely a spell,' Petia said. 'Ever since I've been trying to tap into the emotions of others, I've felt the use of magic around me. Not much, maybe not enough to be useful, but I've sensed it. These men are not permanently changed,' she finished with finality.

'Do you think you can touch them emotionally?' Giles asked. He saw Petia's distaste at the idea. But she had another idea.

'I'm no sorceror, but what about those books Anji rescued? Perhaps I can use some of my skill to make them humans again.' Petia didn't speak with great conviction, but Giles saw that she was willing to try. He beckoned a young beast, who brought the rescued grimoires to the table.

Petia turned the spines of the stack toward her. Alchemical symbols of unknown meaning adorned each back. Petia pulled the top book over and opened the cover, hoping to find a clue to the contents.

There was nothing. Petia sighed and settled in for a long search. 'Giles, you can read. Go through another volume. A binding spell might have the counter-spell added on at the end.'

Together they pored over page after dusty page. Petia found some works in strange, unreadable languages. As the morning wore on, the two lost themselves in the fascination of what they read in the books. Occasionally Petia shuddered and hurriedly turned the page. 'There's some unsavoury stuff in here,' she muttered.

'I've noticed,' Giles replied.

Giles was ready to suggest a break when Petia exclaimed, 'I've found it!'

Giles read over her shoulder. When he finished, he asked, 'Are you willing to try it?'

'I suppose I'm ready.' She sounded uncertain.

Giles brought a skeleton man to stand in front of her. Petia lifted the book and read the words aloud. She went slowly, pausing to watch for any reaction. When Petia had finished the spell she set the book down. For long seconds there was no response. Giles grabbed the man when he began to shiver, as if his bones had caught cold. Giles pulled away – flesh formed under his very fingers. The man's eyes grew to human proportion, cleared and focused. Facial skin and flesh puffed up to give definition to the angularity of his bony structure. Faster and faster the transformation ran until a swarthy, normal human being stood before them, looking bewildered.

He turned his head and gazed about him, obviously confused.

'Do you know where you are?' Petia asked.

'No.' The word came like a key turning in a rusty lock.

'Does the name "Shahal" mean anything to you? Or "The Skeleton Lord"?'

'I remember being captured in the desert. By magic! There were fourteen of my clan with me. We were brought to the rock. There was a man called the Skeleton Lord, yes, that I remember – but nothing more.'

He looked around the room, and tensed defensively when he saw the beasts. He pointed a finger at them and said, 'Don't let them harm me!'

'Are you afraid of them?' Giles asked quietly.

'Yes, they are powerful. They roam the desert. We . . .' He paused, as if a new thought had come to him. 'We leave them alone.'

'Who is we?' Giles prodded.

'The Harifim, the people of the desert.'

Red Mane walked over and stood in front of the man. 'Do you remember when this city, Shahal, was on the trade route?' The man did not.

'So much has been lost.' Red Mane sighed gustily.

'What do you mean?' Giles asked.

'Masser is an important port and trade centre on Banda-narra's eastern coast. Galhib was an inland centre, a transfer point for caravans between Kasha and Kuilla. Shahal is half-way between Galhib and Masser, on the Track of Fourteen. The route was so called because it took fourteen days to travel from Galhib to Masser. All the caravans stopped here for a day's rest.' Red Mane straightened. 'Perhaps we can build it up again. We have to try.'

Giles recognised the despair in Red Mane's voice. He would encourage the beasts as much as possible, but there was much left to do.

'There are stories in my clan,' the skeleton man said, 'that we were once wealthy and traded throughout the desert. But that was long before my memory.'

'It can be like that again,' Giles said. 'If you work together with the beasts of Shahal.' He turned to Petia. 'Try the other one.'

Petia read the spell more easily this time; the second skeleton man regained his bodily contours and looked around apprehensively. Giles examined both of the men. They appeared to be in good health, although thinner than any of the tough desert men he had seen. Regular meals would change that, he was convinced.

Keja entered the room. 'I can't believe this place. It's incredible. The Skeleton Lord ruined a perfectly fine city, but that'll change soon enough.' His enthusiasm blazed through the room.

While Giles elicited the aid of the two freed Harifim, Petia tried to release two skeleton men with one reading but found that it did not work. 'I hope there aren't too many of them,' she said, as she prepared to begin again.

'The Skeleton Lord had many of them. I'm surprised that there are any Harifim left in the desert. It seems as if they are all in Shahal.'

Red Mane came over to where Giles and the two Harifim spoke quietly. The beast had obviously steeled himself for what he had to say. 'We have agreed to share in the profits from trade if we can sign a treaty with the Harifim leaders. We can send these two back as emissaries to show our good intentions. Too many have suffered at the Lord's hand. We must work together to regain what we lost so long ago.'

'Excellent,' Giles said. 'Have you thought about the Calabrashio Seas? You're going to have to find another route.'

'We'll find one. One step at a time.'

As Petia released the skeleton men one by one, the room

347

became crowded. Petia grew weary during the afternoon. She rested briefly and Giles hovered over her, making sure that she took some hot broth. She had memorised the spell and spoke it easily now, but each repetition took a bit more out of her. By the time she had finished, Petia collapsed in exhaustion.

During the evening, Petia sat quietly while the others discussed the day's events. Anji found a brush and sat running it through Petia's hair, draining away her tension. Occasionally Petia's eyes closed and she nodded, but she forced herself awake to listen to the conversation. Even though she was tired, she caught snippets of emotion rolling through the room like waves against a sandy shore.

'We have to begin searching for the key,' Keja said. 'I don't intend to spend all my time feeding the prisoners and making sure they don't turn on us.'

'We won't spend all our time on them,' Giles said. 'Today was different, releasing them from the spell. Beginning tomorrow, we will search.'

Red Mane spoke up. 'We'll all help. We owe it to you.' Giles started to protest, but Red Mane stopped him. 'You have helped us to regain our city. We will help you. If Djinn were here he could lend his assistance, too.'

Djinn slowly materialised at Giles' elbow. He scowled and crossed his massive arms.

'What's the matter with you?' Giles asked.

'Petia has released all the skeleton men. What about our bargain? You said you'd change me back into human form.' Djinn glowered at them.

'If you'd stay in sight, we wouldn't forget about you so easily,' Giles remonstrated. 'Petia, loose this fellow so he gets that ugly frown off his face. I'll bet he's good-looking when he's in a better humour.'

Petia stirred. She recited the words slowly, looking at Djinn and wondering what transformation he would go through. When she finished the unbinding magicks, she stood back, waiting.

Djinn floated several inches off the floor. He watched Petia as she said the words, then looked down at his body, waiting for the changes. Nothing happened.

Djinn frowned. 'I feel just the same,' he said.

'I'm sorry, Djinn,' Petia said. 'I'm so tired. I must have forgotten some of the words. Let me get the book.'

Anji ran to the table and came back with the grimoire. Petia opened it to the proper page and intoned the spell carefully, looking at each word as she said it aloud. When she had finished she closed the book and waited. Again there was no change in the djinn. Stunned, Petia stared from the book to Djinn and back.

'You promised . . .' Djinn began. Vaporous tears formed in his eyes.

'I know we did, Djinn.' Petia reached out to him. 'It must be a different spell. I'll try tomorrow; I'm exhausted tonight. But I'll find it, I promise I will.' Petia realised that she was speaking to empty air. Djinn had disappeared.

'It's not fair,' Petia said. 'He's given us so much help, while the skeleton men were our enemies. They've been released, and he's still a captive of the Lord's magicks.'

Giles put his hand on Petia's shoulder. 'Get some sleep. Tomorrow, when you're fresh, you'll have a clear head to find the proper spell.'

Petia nodded. 'If it's here. I don't think I will be able to face Djinn if it's not.' She rose wearily and, leaning on Anji, left the room.

In the morning, Petia leafed through the books looking for a spell to release Djinn. She found neither a spell for turning a human into a djinn nor for releasing one. Giles sat on one side of her and Keja on the other, helping in the search. They found nothing.

'What are we going to do?' Petia asked.

'We're going to search for the key,' Giles replied. 'This evening we'll go through the spell book again. Try not to think about it during the day. We'll tackle it again this evening.'

The beasts helped to make the search much easier. Giles described the size and shape of the key, and told them that it was crafted of gold. The beasts understood and knew the kind of places it might be hidden. They worked in pairs and started at the lowest level of the city.

When they stopped for the noon meal, they had explored the first six floors. Their spirits were high and they wagered good-naturedly on who would be the one to find the key.

Petia took her cup of tea to a separate table and leafed through the spell books once more. In spite of what Giles had said, her inability to release Djinn preyed on her mind. She studied the pages more carefully until it was time to take up the search for the key to Paradise once again.

The seventh floor brought memories of the battle with the Skeleton Lord. Having searched the lord's chambers, they concentrated on the other rooms. They found nothing and moved on to the upper floors.

By late afternoon Giles wondered if he should call off the search. Fatigue might cause them to miss an important clue. Yet they were nearing the top of Shahal and he was anxious. If they did not find the key, they must begin again and search more carefully.

Giles walked to the end of an open corridor and leaned against the balustrade, staring out over the desert. The sun was sinking and he shielded his eyes from the red glare. Dry and desolate as the terrain was, it had its own beauty.

Gleaming rock cliffs stood like fortresses at the edge of the plain. Streaks of colour cascaded down their faces. Giles caught the scent of water wafted from some distant oasis. He would be happy to leave, but he was not displeased that he had come here. After all, had he not wanted to explore the world and wash away the filth of war? To give purpose once again to a life that had turned into pointless drifting? He had explored more of the world than most. Joining company with those two rogues, Keja and Petia, had led him far from the place of his birth – but that wasn't home. Home no longer existed for him. Maybe it didn't matter whether they found the key or not. Being with good companions held its own rewards.

'Giles, come quickly.' He turned to Petia and, feeling tired, he ambled to the end of the corridor. Nothing, not even the key, could make him hurry.

Petia bounced up and down. 'She's found it. Sleek's found it.'

'Where?'

'Down here. Follow me.'

Giles paused at the threshold to a room that had been sealed shut and hidden by clever plastering. Was it really over? He stepped into the room and stood transfixed. On the far side stood a huge throne, its arms and high back decorated with strangely unsettling symbols. Seated on it was the chalky white skeleton of a giant. Giles swallowed hard. It looked as though some ancient king had seated himself and died, left foot forward, right elbow resting on the throne's arm, skull tipped forward and eyeless sockets studying something in his lap.

Giles followed the gaze. In one outstretched skeletal hand rested a golden key. In the other was a scroll.

'Aren't you going to pick it up?' Petia asked eagerly.

Giles advanced almost reverently to the throne. The others crowded behind him. He picked up the key and examined it briefly. 'This is it,' he said, holding it aloft. He handed it to Petia, and the key was passed around the people and beasts in the room.

Slowly, Giles unrolled the scroll. The map drawn on it was a work of art. Lettering of exquisite calligraphy decorated the upper left-hand corner and told of the Gate of Paradise. The body of the scroll portrayed an unknown country with mountains, forests, and a sea coast coloured in delicate paints. In the lower right-hand corner a key was depicted in gold leaf. The key's shank was set with a green gemstone, possibly an emerald. Large, ornate letters sprawled across the main body of the map. 'Khelora,' it read.

'The location of the final key,' Giles said, his voice hardly more than a husky whisper.

Eighteen

'WE'LL STAY for a while and help you get started,' Giles said. 'It's only fair since you found the key for us.'

'You don't have to stay,' Red Mane said. 'We're grateful to

you, also. We've derived more benefit than you have, to my way of thinking. We have regained our city – and our self-esteem.'

Giles laughed. 'If we keep on congratulating each other, nothing will get done. Now, it seems to me that this wing will provide the immediate housing you need, with easy access to the pantry, scullery, and dining hall.' Soon they were engrossed in the plans.

Keja sat, bemused at the evening's activities. He felt left out, as usual, but he had much to ponder. They would be leaving soon, and they no longer had any animals. The lirjan would have wandered away. Supplies were needed. Those problems would have to be solved.

And the keys. He thought of the keys. Four of them now. One more to go.

He leaned back and watched Petia with Anji. She had become domesticated, at least in her quiet moments. She could still fight right alongside himself and Giles, but the boy had brought about a change in her. Still, she looked lovely. Her cat features only heightened her beauty, lending an exotic quality to her. Keja tried to work out what he really felt for her. He failed.

He yawned and went to his bedroll, still mulling over the key, Petia, Giles, and what might be in store for them in Khelora. His dreams were of the final key, the Gate of Paradise, what he would find beyond the Gate – and through them all ran a frolicking, smiling Petia.

The following morning, Keja approached Giles about new pack animals for their journey. With Red Mane, they interviewed the Harifim and selected two to carry the offer of a truce back to their people. The beasts hoped that this would be the beginning of negotiations with the peoples of all the desert tribes.

Giles and Keja hoped that the men would return with lirjan or horses they could buy. They watched the recovered skeleton men set off across the desert plain and returned to the work at hand.

'Take whatever you want from the treasure room. You

will need money for your passage home,' Red Mane offered.

'You are too generous,' said Giles. Rather than hunting for gold, Giles took the opportunity to search for a new sword. He regretted the loss of the beautiful sword. Eventually he found a serviceable sword, but one which he'd replace at the first opportunity. He left the choosing of jewels and coin to Petia, Keja and Anji.

Surrounded by the immense wealth of the treasure room, they played with the fortune, running ropes of pearls through their fingers, scooping up gold and silver coins and flinging them into the air, whooping with delight as they jangled together.

'It's funny,' Petia said. 'We seek out the five keys that will give us untold wealth, and here we sit like children. We could take enough to keep us comfortably for the rest of our lives, and just forget about the last key.'

Keja whooped. 'We're all mad.' In the end, however, they took only a modest amount, this being all they could carry safely across the desert.

'The beasts will need it to begin their trade again,' Petia said. She gazed wistfully at the ruby brooch in her hand, then gently placed it back on the pile. 'Let's get out of here. It's depressing to think of leaving anything.'

Keja laughed. 'What is even more depressing is that Red Mane is giving all this to us. There's no challenge. I wish I could steal it!'

Petia continued her search through the spell books. She turned every leaf and studied the many volumes Anji had rescued, but to no avail. She could find nothing about turning a human into a djinn – or a djinn into a human.

Djinn remained invisible, angry. Petia ached for him. She knew how he must feel, watching the skeleton men regain their humanity, putting on weight and looking normal again. They had been the enemy.

Petia opened the cover of a book and began again. If it was not possible to change Djinn, it would be no fault of hers. She pushed her hair back from her eyes with quick, preening gestures, and settled down to the task. Anji stood at her side and read over her shoulder.

Petia turned to him. 'Don't you have anything to do?' she asked.

'Giles and Keja say I keep getting in the way,' he answered with a frown. 'Sometimes I don't like them very much.'

'They have a lot to do before we leave Shahal,' Petia said. 'It's too bad you can't read, Anji. I need some help.'

'Will you teach me to read one day? Can I watch?'

'Of course, but you must be quiet, please. I've got to find a way to free Djinn from his spell.'

Petia concentrated on the words. The letters on the page fascinated Anji. Petia had told him that the letters made words and he knew that words had meaning. Still, he did not understand it. He studied the illuminations of the capital letters and the illustrations that appeared at the top of some pages. Some were gory, but others had been drawn by someone with a sense of humour.

Petia reached to turn a page, when something caught Anji's attention. 'Wait,' he cried.

'What is it?' she said, concerned he had seen something that had upset him.

He pointed to the illustration at the top of the left-hand page. 'That's not our Djinn, but it's like the djinn in the stories I heard when I was little.'

Petia laughed. 'You're still only little,' she said, tousling his hair.

'But it is, Mistress,' the boy pleaded. Again he pointed at the drawing. 'See, the muscles in his arms and the scimitar pointing. And he's wearing a vest, but no tunic underneath. And baggy pantalons. It's a djinn, Petia, like in the stories. Perhaps this is the page for the spell.'

Petia examined the page once more. She read the title at the top of the sheet. 'For making the eyes of an enemy weep as if there were grains of sand in them.' She shook her head. 'This has nothing to do with djinn.'

Crestfallen, the boy scowled. 'That's a djinn,' he insisted. 'I know a picture of a djinn when I see one.' He crossed his arms in disgust. 'What's he pointing his scimitar at?'

Petia looked back at the figure. The djinn was pointing his scimitar. She followed the direction across the page, but nothing unusual appeared on the right-hand page. She read the title once more. Its meaning was veiled. At the top, in tiny print by another hand, a one-word warning read: *Cautiously!*

She studied the title, puzzled about the meaning: For XXXXX.

In a flash of inspiration, all became clear to her. She looked at the bottom of the page. A shaft with spearheads pointing in both directions gave her the clue. The spell recited backwards would undo whatever it had done in the first place. She began to read the words softly to herself, then realised that she might accidentally turn Anji into a djinn.

When she had finished reading it, Petia felt uncertain that it was the correct spell. The word 'djinn' did not appear in the spell, but references to a being who would serve, would do one's bidding, were abundant. She sucked in her breath. There was only one way to find out if this would work.

'Djinn, are you here?' she called.

The spirit materialised and glared at her. 'What do you want?' he said sullenly.

'I think I have the spell of unbinding.' She almost laughed at the change of expression on Djinn's face. Petia explained that she was willing to try the unknown spell, but the final decision had to rest with Djinn.

'I'll try every spell in every book,' he promised.

'No, you won't. Unless you want to be changed into something worse than a djinn. Now, compose yourself.'

Petia took a deep breath and tried to follow her own advice. She said the words evenly. Afraid to look up at Djinn, fearing that the spell would not work, she concentrated on the words.

As she finished the last word, she closed her eyes. She felt hands pulling her up from the bench and nearly panicked.

Arms swirled Petia off her feet, and she found herself being danced around the room by a handsome young man.

'You did it, you did it!' The young man so much like Djinn, but not the spirit, set Petia down, hugged her, then dabbed at his eyes.

Anji tugged at his arm. 'Is that you, Djinn?'

'Yes, no. I mean, yes, I was Djinn, but now I'm me. I'm again Hassan, prince of the Mullaheed Harifim!'

'I'm so pleased, Djinn – Hassan,' Petia said. 'I didn't want to give up, but I was getting discouraged.'

Word spread through Shahal and soon another celebration was under way that lasted long into the night. By the time it ended and everyone staggered off to bed, a pact between Hassan and the beasts had been made. He would stay in Shahal and act as a mediator between the beasts and the Harifim.

The humans began their preparations for leaving. The two Harifim who had been sent back to the tribes reappeared and conferred at great length with Hassan. The first step towards a lasting truce between desert clans and the beasts had been taken – and Hassan delivered to Giles five strong desert steeds as payment for all they'd done.

'It's time for us to leave,' Giles said to Petia and Keja. 'The beasts are preoccupied with repairing Shahal, and the Harifim have brought horses for us. We've got no excuse to stay now. We'll head south and find a ship there. There's no sense in going back to Kasha and asking for trouble.'

Petia hoisted Anji up into his saddle. The boy leaned forward and whispered into the horse's ear. It flicked in understanding.

Hassan came to Petia and folded her hands in his, then bowed until his forehead touched her hands. 'Thank you, good lady. I'll always remember you.' Petia blushed.

Hassan clasped hands with Giles and Keja, then stepped back. He watched them ride off into the fading light. 'May the gods guide you and keep you safe,' he called after them. Red Mane and the other beasts watched silently as they put the spurs to their mounts.

Giles laughed and let the wind rush past his face. 'Freedom!' he cried, 'To Khelora!' and the others joined him in the chant.

From the cliffs behind Shahal, a man robed in black threw his hood back. He watched the four horses separate from the Harifim encampment near Shahal and proceed toward a break in the hills to the south.

'Good, very good,' he said softly. 'They have now four keys. And I hold the fifth. The Gate of Paradise will open soon – for me!' Mocking laughter drifted across the desert, and, swallowed up by the distance, died away.

Book Three

The Key of Ice and Steel

For those printing fools from
Stayton, Oregon
Dale and Ginny Goble
Mike and Susie Horvat

One

RAIN PATTERED against the sodden leaves arching like green umbrellas above the four riders. Fat drops fell into the puddles dotting the forest trail even as distant thunder rumbled with the promise of a more vigorous storm. Even though the trees protected the riders from a direct onslaught, they sat astride their horses soggy and miserable.

Keja Tchurak raised his hand and wiped drops from the end of his straight, aristocratic nose. 'Can't we stop and set up camp soon?' he whined.

Giles Grimsmate turned in his saddle and stared with flinty grey eyes until Keja became uncomfortable. He looked away, again feeling that he slowed them, that he kept them from their fabulous quest because he disliked being cold and wet and uncomfortable.

'You do well to look away, Keja. Look around you, man.' Giles swept his heavily muscled arm in an arc encompassing both sides of the trail. The low ground ran with water, which gathered into pools, then burst through dams of leaves and twigs to run away in rivulets to even lower ground. 'If you want to build camp in this swamp, you're welcome. I'm as eager as you are to climb down and find shelter, but not so stupid to want to spend the night up to my arse in water. When I find some high ground, we'll stop.'

Giles stretched his arthritic, tired limbs and looked at the others slumped in their saddles, soaked blankets over their heads lending little protection. Petia Darya and Anji, the two Trans who made up half of the company, said nothing. Miserable, hissing like the part feline that she was, Petia barely guided her horse. Young Anji let his plod behind. Both seemed content to let the more experienced Giles make such decisions.

Giles looked ahead into the dripping forest and muttered a small prayer that they would find high ground soon. He wanted out of the wet as much as anyone, even the catlike Trans. He hoped that the foul weather was not an omen of things to come on this, their last adventure.

They travelled two miles before the track began to rise. Giles sat erect in his saddle and peered into the rain, finding a knoll worthy of a campsite. He called back to the others.

'That ought to do.' He swung down from his horse, tying it loosely to a nearby tree.

Keja slid from his mount, also. His foot landed in a puddle of water and slipped on the leaf mould beneath it. He sprawled, cursing all the gods supposedly protecting thieves from such ignominy. Petia foresaw Anji's laugh and motioned quickly with her hand, cutting him off before he began. The trail had been long and tempers frayed. Anji's mirth would only provoke an angry outburst from Keja.

She dismounted, grabbed Keja's arm and assisted him to his feet. Then she turned quickly to Giles before Keja could mutter that he didn't need any help from a woman.

'We'll need to build shelter,' Giles said. 'Branches from those conifers will shed the rain. I'll cut some small limbs for the framework.'

They worked silently, their mood so depressed by the weather that they didn't dare talk to each other. Giles' long years as a sergeant during the Trans War enabled him to build a shelter quickly. The others simply cut and carried and let him work. The sooner the shelter was built, the sooner they had a chance of finding a modicum of comfort.

By the time Anji had found the first dry wood, a lean-to shelter offered protection from the storm. Anji arranged the stacks carefully, making sure that there would be enough wood to last through the night. Assured of adequate – and dry – fuel, he went to bring the horses into the woods and find the best shelter possible for them. The animals were Anji's special love. Giles paused in his work and watched the boy. At times he wondered if the Trans could speak with the horses. He shook his head and sent droplets flying from his thinning grey hair and returned to his work.

Keja warmed with the activity and his mood improved. He silently helped Anji unsaddle and remove packs and wipe the water from the animals as best they could. When they returned to the shelter a small fire blazed into life, Petia carefully encouraging it.

'Make you wish you were back in the desert, Keja?' Giles grinned at the small thief.

'The next quest we go on, let me choose the place,' Keja said. His tone came lighter and joking. 'Somewhere moderate, balmy days, cloudless nights, and no snakes, please. And women. Lots of willing wanton women eager for a passionate night with one such as myself.'

'Impossible,' scoffed Petia. 'Not even passing through the Gate of Paradise will give you all that.'

She ducked when Keja tossed a pinecone at her.

'What do you think lies behind the Gate?' he asked. '*I* think it is riches and leisure.'

'At the moment, all I want is dry and warm,' muttered Petia.

As the fire burned higher, the companions spread their blankets and cloaks to dry, and Giles and Petia tended the kettle of stew.

The sound of rain and the occasional stamping of the animals disturbed their meal. Each kept to his own thoughts. Only when Giles stuffed and lit his pipe did they stir from wild dreams of what finding the fifth and final key to the Gate of Paradise would grant each of them.

'I told you we should have waited until spring,' Keja said. 'We could be sitting around a warm fire in the inn at Sanustell. And keeping an eye on those people at Callant Hanse. I don't trust them.'

Giles chuckled. 'The keys were still there, weren't they? You insisted on seeing the other three when we deposited the fourth. They brought the box out and we all had to sign before they opened it, just as we agreed. What makes you think that they'd risk a two-hundred-year-old reputation to steal our keys? Especially when those four keys to the Gate are worthless without the fifth?'

'Yes, but these are keys to the Gate of Paradise. They're not just your everyday keys, you might say,' Keja said. 'I sweated rivers in the Bandanarra desert and faced a snake as big as a room and hungrier than a beggar to get that last key. And I say that the closer we are to having all five keys, the bigger the risk leaving them there.'

'You have no faith, Keja,' Petia said. 'Giles is right. A mercantile house like the Callant Hanse isn't going to throw over a reputation it took centuries to build, even for keys to the Gate of Paradise. It's only fools like us who do such things.'

Giles laughed and tamped more tobacco into his pipe. 'They don't even know what those keys open,' he pointed out. 'If I hadn't thought the keys were safe, I'd never have left them, now would I? We've suffered too much to casually lose them.'

Anji pulled the blanket closer about his shoulders. 'I'd rather be back in Bandanarra than in this miserable dripping forest,' he said.

Giles looked at the boy, kindness in his eyes. 'Desert heat is normal to you. We were all born here in the north and are used to cooler weather. But even I could do with a little less of this autumn rain.' He peered out from beneath the edge of the lean-to. Clouds obscured the stars and he saw no moon. 'I don't think it's going to stop.'

'Does it ever quit?' The boy looked plaintively at Petia.

She reached out and tousled his wet hair. 'You've forgotten already how beautiful it was on Bericlere when we first arrived. We have seasons here. Autumn begins with the summer heat still in it and slowly gives way to the cold of winter. You'll become accustomed to the diversity it lends to our lives. It's not like the desert where each day is like every other, the entire year round.'

'That's not true!' The boy pulled his head back angrily from beneath Petia's hand. 'It rains in the desert,' he said. 'Just because you never saw it . . .' He lowered his head and sulked, trying to feel more sorry for himself than he actually was.

Petia stared at the two men and shook her head. They understood and fell silent. Anji had been through much – more than any of them. Petia had rescued him from slavers. She knew, in part, the prejudices the boy had endured because of his Trans heritage, but she came from Trois Havres where most

362

were Trans. Petia stroked Anji's head until the boy's tenseness faded.

Keja poked at the fire with a stick, then rose to fetch a piece of rope from his pack. He settled again and worked at binding the frayed ends.

The boy's voice broke the silence again. 'We were followed today.'

Keja's fingers grew still. Giles leaned forward, his eyes searching the boy's face. Petia drew a breath.

'By whom?' Giles asked.

'I don't know,' Anji said. 'Maybe the man in black we heard about in Bandanarra. The desert people knew nothing of him, but I think he was there to watch us.'

Petia nodded. 'I felt the mind of a catamount today. It was upset, but I thought that we intruded on its territory. I didn't give it a second thought, except to make sure that it kept its distance. But there might well have been someone else.'

Giles shook his head and reached for a fire brand. Between puffs of relighting his pipe he said, 'It's a reminder that we need to be on guard.' He turned to Anji. 'How do you know we were followed?'

Anji looked at Petia. 'She's been teaching me to use my Trans senses. Nobody ever did that before. When my mother sold me into slavery I was a dumb fetch-and-carry servant. So I've been practising hard. I heard the catamount, too.' He avoided Petia's eyes. 'But I tried to go beyond the big cat. There were several horses and I caught the barest sense of men. They were quite a ways behind us, I'm sure.'

'I'll backtrack in the morning,' Giles said, venting a huge sigh. The old soldier wondered if he would spend the rest of his life looking over his shoulder, waiting for the knife to descend. 'Thank you, Anji. I had hoped we wouldn't need to do this so soon. Let's set the watches.'

Even when the others stood watch, Giles lay awake, listening hard and worrying. He knew they had been lucky thus far — in spite of their travails, they had been lucky. With the man in black actively following, if it even was the mysterious stranger in the desert, danger mounted for all four of them.

When the wet, grey morning came, Giles ached in every joint. He ordered the others on ahead, then went tracking.

The following evening they sat in the common room of a rustic mountain inn nestled in the foothills of the Adversaries, a mountain range stretching several hundred miles towards the even colder northlands. Giles, bone-tired, wanted to retire early. Petia pressed him for what he had learned.

With some trepidation over worrying them needlessly, Giles said, 'I found hoofprints all right. But they turned east, forded a stream, and continued into the forest.

'So they don't appear to be following us. It goes to show, however, we must keep a sharp eye out for the unusual. Keep your senses alert, Anji.' The boy grinned. 'You too, Petia. We're too near success to be beaten now.'

'What success can that be, I ask you?' a man spoke up from across the room. 'There's naught to be done in this forsaken wasteland.'

Giles sucked on his pipe and nodded to the man who had interrupted. He offered him his tobacco pouch when the man's pipe sputtered and went out. 'Do you know this area well?' Giles asked.

The man puffed solemnly for a moment, tamping his pipe to make certain that it burned evenly. 'You might say so.' He nodded in emphasis. 'I'm a peddler by trade. Been travelling these parts for a good many years.'

Giles motioned for Petia, Anji and Keja to be silent, then pulled a map from his tunic. 'Maybe you can tell what we have ahead of us. We're travelling through these parts for the first time.'

The peddler hunched forward over the map, one grubby finger tracing familiar routes until he had found the inn. 'Which way do you travel from here?' he asked.

'North,' Giles answered.

The peddler's eyes widened. 'Arrgh, it's a bad time of the year you've chosen,' he said. 'Snow coming any time now. Even in the best of times it's not a pleasant place you're heading into. Mountains and secluded valleys and the people most inhospitable. They tolerate me for my goods, but not much more. I wouldn't care to be snowed in there for the winter. I'm heading for the coast where it's warmer and the ale isn't bitter.'

'Tell us about the snow,' Giles said.

'I can only tell you what I've heard from others,' the peddler

364

replied puffing blue clouds of smoke that veiled his weathered face. 'I don't take any chances. I make certain that I've finished my rounds and am well away before the winter comes hard. The people tell stories of immense storms, of being snowed in for weeks. They may be exaggerating, but they make it sound as if you shouldn't be caught out in the open.'

Petia leaned forward. 'I don't like this, Giles. We can take the wet, but snow is different.'

'It's cold *and* wet,' grumbled Keja, used to city amenities.

Giles leaned back, puffing thoughtfully on his pipe.

The peddler bowed towards Petia. 'Good evening, miss. We don't see many Trans in these parts, not since they came runnin' in this direction during the War, beggin' your pardon. Understand, I don't have any problems with your people. I've traded in the Trois Havres and have always been treated honestly.'

Petia sat back, steeling herself to hear how he wasn't prejudiced against the Trans. She watched the peddler as he swallowed half a tankard of ale before returning to the pipe fuelled by Giles' tobacco.

'You and the boy had best be careful, though. These mountain people are strange. They don't like outsiders of any persuasion much, and I'm not sure how they'll react to a pair of Trans. Some of them are all right, I guess. They're honest folk, but they have some funny ideas. I'd keep a sharp eye out.'

Petia tensed. Giles rested a hand on hers, cautioning her to silence. Giles didn't need Petia's emotion-sensing talents to see that the peddler wondered how he could use information about the four to his own advantage.

Giles rose from the table, yawning and stretching. He picked up his pipe and tobacco pouch. 'We've had a long day on the road. I hope you'll excuse us if we retire.'

The others followed him after curt 'Good nights' to the peddler. At the top of the stairs, Giles paused and whispered. 'We'll discuss it in the morning. Let's sleep late and take our time in the morning.' He grinned wryly. 'It might be the last time we sleep warm and dry for a while.'

In the morning they ate a leisurely breakfast, much to Keja's delight. Not only the food pleased him, but he couldn't keep his eyes off the serving maid. When the maid had cleared their bowls, Giles said, 'I think we ought to stay here another day and talk this out. The peddler's news last night wasn't particularly encouraging. We should consider whether to continue or leave this venture until spring.'

'I agree, Giles. You're right. Very right.' Keja smiled broadly and winked at the maid, who seemed inclined toward the small man.

'No! I, for one . . .' Petia was stilled by Giles' huge hand.

'Let's enjoy the morning. With no pressure just to survive, we can think more clearly about continuing or waiting. Another day isn't going to hurt our plans, one way or the other.'

Giles rose from the table and went to the window, peering out. 'It's clear at the moment. I'm going for a walk. Fresh air helps my thinking.' He slung his cloak around him and left the inn, closing the door carefully behind him.

Keja stared after him, as if unable to believe his good fortune. 'I guess he means it. I'll be damned.' He stood, straightened his tunic and announced, 'I do my best thinking in bed.' He disappeared up the stairway.

Anji looked questioningly at Petia, who glumly nodded. 'The maid went upstairs after she took our dishes. I think Keja will be well occupied for the rest of the day. Are you up for a game of Threes and Fours?'

'What's that?' the boy asked. Petia got a leather cup filled with dice from the innkeeper and spent the day showing Anji how to play.

At dinner, Petia was nearly ready to burst. The inactivity had worn on her, as much as she enjoyed the time with Anji. Giles was not to be hurried, however, and only when his pipe was lit did he begin.

Keja, sated after a day with the winsome maid, felt magnanimous and allowed Petia to speak first. He leaned back, hiked booted feet to the table and laced his nimble fingers behind his head.

'Spending the winter in one of the cities of Trois Havres would make me crazy,' she said. 'I can't stand inactivity. I want to push on. I have Anji to think about and the sooner we get the final key and pick up the treasure behind the Gate, the sooner Anji and I can get on with our lives.'

Petia's speech came out in a rush and was the closest she had ever come to saying how much the boy she had purchased at the slave market meant to her. The boy from Bandanarra had become a part of her life – a significant part.

Keja smiled to himself. The boy was changing Petia, and not in subtle ways. He imagined her as a middle-aged homebody, having supper ready when Anji returned from schooling. The thought amused him. In five or six years the boy would be old enough to go out on his own. What then for Petia? He wondered if she had thought of that.

What then for Keja Tchuark? The thief scowled now as he realised how much Petia meant to him. He tried to shrug off the feelings. It'd never do for him to be tied down like that. A home? Petia and Anji? Keja snorted and shook his head at the insane idea.

'So you're for going on?' Giles nodded. 'Let's hear what Keja has to say, and then Anji.'

Keja brought his feet to the floor and leaned forward. 'I'm still wanted, so to speak. I saw some old handbills while we were in Sanustell. They were faded, of course, but the reward is real. I imagine it's the father of my one-time paramour from whom I stole the first key who is responsible. And back on Bericlere there was a trivial matter of the theft of that overly endowed woman's jewels. What was her name, anyway? I'm good at figures, but I never was good with names.' He grinned. 'I could find someplace to hide out over the winter, I'm sure, but you know me. I'd just get into more trouble.' He put his feet up again, finished.

'Anji, you may be the youngest, but still you're part of our pleasant little band. What do you say?'

The boy looked at Petia, but she simply nodded as if to say, 'Go ahead, say what you think.'

'I don't like the rain, and I don't think I'll like snow, although I've never seen any before. Petia says it can get bitterly cold. I don't see how I can get any colder than I already am, but I trust Petia.' The boy paused, gathering his thoughts. 'She wants to go on and get it over. When she bought me in the slave market, I promised I'd follow her anywhere. She wanted to set me free, and I guess I am, but I'm going to stay with her. If she goes on, I'll go, even if it means freezing to death.'

'That leaves you, Giles,' Petia prodded. 'Your turn.'

'Yes, my turn. Anji is the only one who has spoken of the hardship from the cold and snow. I'm an old man . . .' He held up his hand to stop the protests forming. 'You know how many years I spent fighting in the Trans War. Twenty years took a lot out of me. I'd be a lot more comfortable holed up in some inn for the winter, toasting my bones in front of the fire. But I'm a bit like Keja. No posters out for my head, but I'm not well liked among the Flame Sorceress' worshippers in Sanustell. Not after I killed her to get the flame key. So none of the Trois Havres towns for me, either.

'But let's get down to cases. Do we have enough warm clothing to make it? The horses are in good shape, well fed, capable of getting through the winter, I'd say.' He saw Anji nod vigorously, eyes shining. 'The people we can ignore. Nothing can be more hostile than the Bandanarra desert, and we survived that. We should be able to cope with these hill folk, even if they prove surly.'

Petia spoke up. 'We packed woollen cloaks. If it's as harsh as the peddler said, we need skins and furs. But I think we'll make out all right. We won't freeze, Anji.'

The boy smiled at her, adoration in his eyes. He would follow her anywhere, even if he had no clear idea about her need to find this fifth key to what the boy believed to be only a legend.

'No strong arguments for going back, then,' Giles said. 'We'll continue in the morning.'

'I'll see to our gear,' said Keja. 'The serving wench hinted that she might have a special waterproofing for our cloaks.'

'I'm sure,' Petia said sourly.

Keja looked at her curiously, wondering what bothered her. Whistling he set off to find the maid and attend to their cloaks.

'Anji, go see to the horses. We want them ready for a long ride tomorrow,' said Giles. 'And Petia. I want you to memorise this map. I've opened and closed it so many times, the paper wears thin. I'd not like to be the only one knowing the terrain.'

She nodded, knowing what was on the man's mind. If anything happened to him, Giles wanted the others to be able to return. Giles and Petia bent over his map, looking up only when Anji rushed back in.

Anji burst into the inn's common room, shouting, 'Giles, Petia, someone's cut open the saddles and the bags.'

Giles shot to his feet and nearly ran Anji down getting out the door. Petia ran a pace behind him.

They found the riding equipment exactly as Anji had said. Their gear had been scattered about the stables, each piece tossed aside after close scrutiny. Someone had made a thorough job of it. The seams of the saddle skirts were split, as was the joint between cantle and skirts. The cloth linings had been ripped free and now hung in tatters. Saddlebags had been emptied, and spare clothing and blankets thrown aside to drape over the bales of straw in one corner.

'Somebody's searched thoroughly,' Giles said, collapsing onto a pile of loose hay. 'It looks as if they hunted for something very small – and we know what that means. Someone knows we have the keys.' He picked up a saddlebag, turning it over to see what damage had been done.

Anji checked the horses carefully, crooning to them. He lifted each leg, checking their hooves to see that no injury had been done to them. He saw Giles' questioning look, and said, 'In Bandanarra the desert raiders often damage the hooves of their enemies' horses. I have to make sure we will not ride out only to become stranded in a way or two.'

Giles sighed. He rose and began to gather the pieces. 'Help me sort this out. Petia. We no longer have a quiet evening before us. Everything needs repair. Anji, when you've finished with the horses, fetch Keja. He can repair a saddle as easily as I can. A catastrophe here, danger behind, and . . . what ahead?'

Giles shook his head. 'It looks as if we're in for more trouble.'

He hoped that the final key to Paradise would be worth the effort.

Two

AT BREAKFAST, Giles glowered as the others took their places at the table, muttering a barely sociable 'Good morning,' Keja started to tell him that their position wasn't too bad, but Petia nudged him in the ribs and silenced him. The small thief subsided, seeing she had more accurately gauged Giles' mood. Any talk now would turn bitter.

They had dragged the saddles into the inn after supper and worked late into the night repairing them. The longer they had worked the more angry Giles had become, and it was apparent that the night's sleep had not brought any change.

Finished with breakfast, Giles growled, 'Someone is after us, that's certain. I thought everything would be safe at an inn. We should have set watches. And from now on we will. These saddles are almost worthless. Maybe we should turn back.'

'Not on your life!' Petia exclaimed. 'We made the decision to go on and we're going to. We'll ride on saddle blankets if we have to. You just didn't get enough sleep last night. You're acting like an old grump.'

Keja turned away and stared at the fire, hiding his grin. Petia could get away with that: he couldn't. If he had said anything like that to Giles, he would have had a fight on his hands.

'I didn't want to go on this crazy treasure hunt in the first place,' Giles muttered. 'Even before I met up with you two I got hit on the head and accused of murdering a priest in a temple. Then I nearly drowned saving you two in the Flame Sorceress' cave. Then some mysterious stranger followed us all the way to Bandanarra, as if we didn't have our hands full with the Skeleton Lord and his snakes.'

370

He headed towards the door. 'Why can't we just this once retrieve the key without somebody harrying us all the way? I'm fed up to here with this.' He gestured against his throat with the side of his hand and went out, slamming the door.

'Let's give him a few minutes to simmer down,' Petia said. 'Anji, check our room to see that we didn't leave anything.'

The boy, whose eyes had widened at Giles' outburst, nodded. 'I've never heard Giles like that before,' he said. 'I didn't know he had a temper.'

'He doesn't usually,' Petia said. 'He'll come out of it once we're on our way. It's always the start of a journey that's the hardest. Now, get on with you. Check the room.'

When they reached the stable, Giles was still muttering, but he had two horses saddled. The saddles were no longer things of beauty but the repairs looked as if they would hold. Anji went to each of the horses, greeting them in a soft voice. Keja and Petia saw to the packs and saddlebags, while Giles completed the saddling.

When he had pulled tight the last cinch, he stepped away from his horse, craning his neck to scan the sky. 'Looks like the day won't be too bad,' he said, and stepped up into his stirrup. The others hastily mounted and trailed behind him as Giles rode from the stableyard.

For an hour the track remained level. Wispy, rainless clouds came and went, turning the day grey, but if it got no worse than this, it would be pleasant enough. By mid-morning the road began to turn upward into the Adversaries. Giles pulled the map from inside his tunic and halted to scan it.

'The road rises to Honiton Pass,' he said. 'The map seems accurate. I was afraid that it might not be.'

'It's the map we found in Shahal, isn't it?' Keja asked. 'The one in the giant skeleton's hands?'

'It's a copy I made,' Giles answered. 'There was some information on the original that I've left out, just in case it falls into other hands. Some notes nobody else needs to know about, if you take my meaning.'

'You think it will take us to the last key?'

Giles clucked up his horse. 'If it continues to be as accurate as it has been up to now,' he said.

They rested at noon and ate a sparse lunch, taking the

371

opportunity to water and feed their horses. The companions had not resumed their journey for long before Keja remarked on the number of tree branches scattered along the road. 'There must have been a big storm through here recently,' the small thief said. 'Those weren't cut, they were blown off the trees.'

It wasn't long before they found the road completely blocked by a fallen tree. They rounded a bend and found an ironhorn lying aslant the road. To their right gaped a hole in the earth and the massive root system jutted up, exposed. The trunk was several times the thickness of Giles' waist and crushed into the ground. There was no room to lead the horses through.

They dismounted and surveyed the tree. 'There's a giant for you,' Giles commented. 'And we had been making such good time, too.'

He strode to the left side of the road, following the length of the tree into the forest. 'It must be over a hundred feet tall,' he said. 'The underbrush is thick on both sides of the road, but the shortest way around is past the roots. He gestured to the right, and began to tug his sword free from its scabbard. 'Tie the horses, Anji, and we'll start hacking a path through the under-growth. Time to work up a sweat, my friends.'

Anji tended the horses while Keja and Petia pulled their swords and began helping Giles hack through the thick foliage. Anji tethered the horses and watched as the three cleared ferns and the sturdier salal and tamra grape. Anji tested the reins, took a deep breath and then slipped into the forest.

The Trans boy moved through the underbrush swiftly and silently. He did not return to the road until he came to the other side of the bend. When he emerged, he stayed close to the verge, looking behind him. The road stretched empty and uninviting. Anji broke into a trot, watching carefully as far as he could see up the road. He had sensed something when they had stopped for their midday meal. He hadn't heard it, just sensed it. He was sure that someone – or something – followed. Giles may have found tracks leading off in another direction, but they were still followed, Anji was certain. He'd prove his worth to them by discovering the identity of that persistent tracker.

Petia paused to wipe a drop of perspiration from the tip of her pert, upturned nose. She picked up a clump of brush and threw it behind her. 'Anji!' she called. 'Come and clear the cut brush.' She moved forward and hacked at the bottom of a particularly rugged salal bush that blocked their progress.

Keja straightened to stretch cramped muscles. 'Damnable stuff, isn't it?' He massaged the small of his back and together they bent again, his eyes on Petia. Although she had ignored him, he felt her nearness and thrilled to it. His attraction for her had grown from simple physical desire to something more complicated, unlike anything he'd experienced before.

He snorted and redoubled his efforts, forcing such thoughts from his mind. So what if he found himself actually admiring her tenacity and courage? She had rebuffed his advances over and over. And weren't there enough serving wenches and maids such as the one at the inn for him?

The next time Petia paused for a breath, she looked back to see what progress they had made. The clump which she had asked Anji to clear away still blocked the trail. She raised her voice. 'Anji.' No answer. 'Where did he go?' she muttered, planting her sword in the soil.

Petia made her way back to the road. The tethered horses grazed contendedly, but of Anji she saw no trace.

'Anji!' she shouted, but the sound was muffled by the massive trunks of the ironhorn. She ran back along the road, rounded the bend and saw – nothing. She called again, but received no reply.

Petia hurried up the track. 'Giles, Keja! Anji's gone.'

Giles emerged from the brush, wiping his forehead. 'What?' Keja stumbled after him and sat on a stump to catch his breath. Petia arrived breathless, her heart pounding. Between gasps she managed to get out, 'Anji . . . he's gone . . . I called . . . he's not here.'

'Easy, now, lass,' Giles said. 'Catch your breath and then start over.' He guided Petia to a place where she could sit. 'Now what's this all about?'

Petia gestured weakly. 'Anji. He's gone. I asked him to clear some of the brush we'd cut. He didn't come. I went to look and he's gone. He tied the horses up neat as you please and then slipped off. He must have. There's no sign of anyone else.'

Giles gestured at Keja to go look, then returned his attention to Petia. 'Maybe he's just gone off to play and didn't hear you. He's still a boy, remember.'

Petia looked up at him, despair in her eyes. 'He's a boy with experiences that turn young men grey. In eleven years he's lived forty.' Petia took a deep, calming breath. 'He's not playing, Giles. He's gone. He said that someone was trailing us the other day. He's gone back to find out. I know it! You backtracked the other day and said that everything was fine. Then our saddles and packs were ripped open. Anji must still think someone's behind us. He knew I wouldn't let him go if he asked, so he's slipped away when our backs were turned. He's got courage, but I'll tan his hide when I catch him.'

'You're not going to catch him,' Giles said. 'You're going to wait right here until he comes back.' He looked up at Keja's return.

'No sign of him,' Keja said. 'But Petia's right. No sign of a struggle with anyone, either.'

'I'm going after him,' Petia said. 'There's no telling what might happen to him.' She started to get up, but Giles pushed her back.

'Wait a moment, before you go running off. Never mount a campaign without planning. And sustenance in the belly. Keja, fetch some water from the packs.'

When they finished drinking, Giles settled cross-legged on the ground. 'Keja says no struggle. You say the boy has gone off to find out if we're being followed. Could well be. Both you and he have senses that Keja and I don't. It seems like this would be a good time to use yours.'

Petia stared at Giles for a moment. 'I'm sorry, Giles. Worry wins out over common sense every time, I guess. Be still while I concentrate.'

She composed herself, closed her eyes, and began to drift mentally. She sensed animals scurrying through forest and open country; Petia had known of the roving catamount for days. She let her mind relax even more, then reached out along the track they had travelled, exploring both sides of the road, attempting to soak up any trace of animal or human.

'Getting anything?' Keja asked, but Giles silenced him with a wave of his hand.

Impressions came to Petia of tiny animals, shrews and voles, and once a stoat. In a moment, as she stretched her mind even further, a deer and fawn made their way cautiously to a secret watering place. But no indication of the boy came, not the slightest clue to show where he had gone.

Petia raised quivering fingertips to her temples and rocked back and forth, attempting to intensify her empathy with Anji. Nothing. At last she opened her eyes and looked at Giles in quiet desperation. 'I can't find him. I don't *feel* him anywhere.'

Giles touched her shoulder reassuringly. 'That doesn't mean he's not there, Petia. You've been training the boy, teaching him how to use his Trans senses. Perhaps you've taught too well. The boy may have more natural talent than you know. He may have found a way to conceal his presence from your mind.'

Fear seized Petia. 'Why would he do that?'

Giles laughed. 'Didn't you ever do anything you didn't want your mother to know about? He knows you'll be angry with him and will come after him if you find out where he is. It's just self-preservation.'

'I've got to go after him, find him and bring him back. He may be in danger.'

'You'd be the one in danger,' Keja observed. 'If you can't reach him, *feel* him, you'll never find him. You'll walk right on past him and be the one stumbling into something. If Anji is right and we're being tracked, he'll return to tell us.' Keja shrugged. 'For that matter, he'll come back anyway.'

'Keja's right,' Giles said. 'Anji will come back. I have no doubt. You told me, Petia, that he's crammed forty years into his eleven-year life. He knows how to be wary. I don't like the idea of him going off alone, but we're not dividing forces further to look for him. Meanwhile, we still have to get around this fallen tree. The best thing we can do is keep working and be ready to continue when Anji returns.'

Petia saw the wisdom in what Giles and Keja said. Anji was no ordinary boy. He had lived by his wits and knew better than to tangle with whomever followed. But she was still angry with Anji, and he'd know it when she got him alone. The two men had convinced her that it was foolish to look for him, but she still worried, and would until he returned. Petia took out her frustration by hacking away at the brush.

They worked steadily for more than half an hour before taking another break. They had barely sat down to rest when Petia jerked upright and twisted, looking back towards the road. 'Anji!' she called.

The boy stumbled towards them, out of breath. Giles passed him the waterskin. When Anji had recovered, he grinned at the three adults.

'I told you someone trailed us.' He saw the anger on Petia's face. 'I had to go. I heard something earlier when we stopped to eat. Didn't you hear or sense it, Petia? It wasn't really a sound, I don't think, but I was sure something was back there.'

'Well?' Giles asked, impatient.

'I didn't go far enough to see them, just far enough to use my senses, like you've been teaching me, Petia.' He looked to her for approval. She signalled for him to continue.

'Somebody *is* following us. I got the impression of five men, mounted on horseback, and a pack of dogs, about ten of them, I think.'

'What sort of men?' Giles lightly fingered his sword. That many men – and dogs – boded ill for them.

'I don't know, exactly. I wanted to get close enough for a good look, and I would have, too, if it wasn't for the dogs. They would have caught my scent. The men wouldn't have ever known I was there. I could have hid from them easy. But I was afraid of the dogs.'

'Describe the men,' Giles ordered.

'One of them was huge, and fat, and sweaty, I could tell that,' Anji answered. Keja and Giles exchanged glances. 'Another gave off a feeling of power, but I couldn't tell anything else. The others were just servants, obeying orders and hating it.'

'What about the dogs? What kind?''

'Big, hunting types. In Bandanarra we call them felji.'

Petia's eyes grew large. 'Segrinn! He's found me again!'

'Don't worry,' Giles said. 'If it is, we'll deal with him. People like him need to be taken care of. Permanently.'

Anji stared at Petia. Fear haunted her eyes. Something he

had never seen before. Petia was strong. Petia had bought him in a slave market and set him free. Petia wasn't afraid of anything. He knelt by her knee, his eyes searching hers, looking for reassurance. 'Who is this Segrinn?' he asked.

Petia smoothed Anji's hair. Her anger at him for running off had drained out of her the moment she realised whom Anji described. 'He's a bad man,' she told him. 'My mother indentured me to Lord Ambrose, his father, something like your mother sold you into slavery. Segrinn wanted me to sleep with him. I ran away, and he's never forgiven me. He caught me once before but I escaped. It looks like he's never going to give up.'

'We'll stop him this time,' Keja said with bravado.

'If it is Segrinn, we had better finish cutting this trail through and be on our way.' Giles picked up his sword and walked away.

Keja laid a hand on Petia's shoulder. 'It will be all right. Come on. Neither Giles nor I will let anything happen to you or Anji.'

She looked at him strangely, then nodded. They returned to their task, hacking away with renewed energy, uneasy about enemies at their backs. They finished the job quickly, not caring that it was untidily done. Anji fetched the horses and they mounted and were on their way.

The road continued to rise steadily towards the haze-hidden pass. Ahead the sky gradually turned grey, the clouds lowering, until by mid-afternoon the light shone more like dusk.

Giles shook his head. 'It's going to snow,' he said. 'I can feel it in the air. Maybe we can get through the pass before it gets too bad.' He pulled his cloak closer about his shoulders.

Giles' prediction came true. Small flakes began to fall and grew larger the farther they went. Anji stared at the white, fluttering crystals in fascination, not knowing whether to rejoice in seeing his first snow or to worry. By good fortune they found a shelter as the snow began to drift knee-high along the trail.

To the right of the road, they found a tiny log hut with a sturdy roof and thick door. Keja pulled the door open onto a sparse interior. Four ledges along the wall provided sleeping space and a small firepit had been dug in the centre of the earthen floor. A small protected vent hole in the roof allowed the smoke to escape.

They made a meagre supper and ate with no real appetite, their minds on Segrinn. The companions settled down to sleep soon after with little conversation. None slept easily.

In the morning they awoke to the baleful whine of wind blowing dry snow against the shelter. They didn't bother with a fire, eating the cold remains of last night's supper.

'Enough of this place,' Giles said. 'I want to make the pass before mid-day.' Giles stuffed his bowl into his pack and went to open the hut's only door. It wouldn't budge. He put his shoulder agains it. 'Snow's piled up against the outside,' he said. 'C'mon, Keja, lend me your body.'

They pushed the door open enough to allow Anji to slip out. He cleared away enough snow for the door to swing open, and stood, his hands clasped between his legs, as the adults sidled out through the opening. 'Is snow always this cold?' he asked, and didn't think it funny when the others laughed.

Giles gazed at the obscured road. It was covered with drifted snow which provided beautiful scenery, but a barely distinguishable track. 'We've got to get through the pass.' He stared up at the sky. 'It could snow again at any time. See where the snow falls away at the side of the road? Keep several feet away from that and we should be all right. I don't want anyone going over the side. Do you understand. Anji?'

'Yes, Giles,' the boy said as he swung up onto his horse. 'Just don't forget who got us out of our temporary prison.' His eyes twinkled.

Giles snorted and watched the silvery plumes hover in front of his face. He mounted and led the way.

They found the going slippery and the road indistinct. At times one or another of them would dismount and feel along the road, picking a safe path for the others to follow. Fog cloaked their progress until the road began to descend, with only an occasional rise in the ground. They had passed the summit. Elated, but tired, they guided their horses through snow deeper than their horses' hocks. Light snow began to fall again.

'We'd best find shelter.' Giles said. 'I don't want to be on the trail in a blizzard.'

'You feel such a storm coming, Giles? What does it feel like?'' Anji wanted to know. Even though the boy's nose had turned to a cherry-red button, he still stared in wide-eyed awe at the snow.

'Can't tell you,' Giles said. 'Might just be my joints stiffening on me.' Anji looked disappointed. Not for the first time, Giles envied the Trans their powers. But he knew others found nothing to envy in unknown power — they hated what they didn't understand. The Trans War had been fuelled by such prejudices.

'Giles. There,' came Keja's voice. The small man shivered with the cold. 'Through the snow to the left. A light. Fire! A farmhouse!'

Giles motioned for Petia and Anji to follow. Keja surged on ahead, eager for the warmth promised by the farm.

The reception they received reminded them of their conversation with the peddler. The stout woman who came out to confront them in the barnyard wiped her hands on a greasy apron. She squinted at them and asked in a gravelly voice, 'What do you want?' She didn't wait for an answer. She called her husband from the barn. Silently the pair faced the travellers.

Giles pulled the hood back from his face and tried to smile. His lips cracked from the cold. Wincing at the small pain, he said, 'We're looking for a place to stay for the night. We've just come over the pass, and we've spent the last two days battling the snow. We thought you might have a place for us to spend the night. A place to sleep. And perhaps a meal.'

'This ain't no inn,' the wife said.

Keja took a step forward, but Giles gestured him back. 'We knew you weren't an inn, madam,' he said smoothly. 'If there were an inn, we would have continued on to it. We'll pay for accommodations. We understand that it will make extra work for you.'

The farmer's eyes glinted. 'Mother, they could sleep in the barn. And we might find some bread and cheese for their supper, eh?'

Giles suppressed his smile at the greed written upon the dirty face. 'Bread and cheese and fresh straw will do us just fine,' he said, dismounting. 'If you'll just show us the way, please.'

There were no stalls for the horses, but they were inside and protected from the snow. The travellers had tasted better than the mouldy bread and bitter cheese, but at least they didn't go hungry. 'We know now,' Keja said, as they wrapped themselves in their cloaks. 'Strangers are not welcome here, just as the peddler said.'

Three

IN THE morning, the farmer, with a vicious, snapping barnyard dog at his heel, came to the gate and leaned on it, watching them go. The dog barked at the horses, making them skittish, but the farmer silenced it with several strokes using a gnarled stick.

'What an awful place,' Petia said when they got out of earshot along the snowpacked road. 'And despicable people. I don't think they've ever learned to smile. Last night the woman acted as if she were giving away the last morsel of food for their winter, even when they were well paid for it. The man had only money on his mind. And making us sleep in the barn.' Petia snorted derisively.

'Did you sleep well?' Giles asked. He remembered all too well the times he'd slept in freezing mud and was glad for even that. 'Believe me, you slept better than if we'd been in the house. Unless you like flea bites. I think the man was jealous of us, too.'

'Jealous?' Petia said, eyes widening in disbelief. 'He hated us!'

'See the way he stared when we rode off? He'd love the freedom we have. There was real envy in his eyes.'

Petia shuddered. 'Shall we try for an inn tonight? I'd like to wash the straw out of my hair.'

'The map shows a village called Malor still a good day's travel ahead,' Giles said. 'Any village ought to have an inn, but I make no promise on that score. The map doesn't show such detail.'

The day turned clear and crisp, with the snap of real winter in it. The snow on the road had crusted from an overnight freeze. The horses' hooves broke through, making the going difficult until the sun softened the surface and turned the road to muddy slush. Even so, Giles and Anji dismounted periodically to examine the horses' hooves and fetlocks for ice cuts.

When the road widened, Giles beckoned Anji forward to ride beside him. He questioned him closely about what he had sensed as he backtracked at the fallen ironhorn tree.

'How far did you go?' he asked.

'I don't know, Giles,' the boy answered. 'I can't tell distances with all these tall trees. If we were in my desert, I could have told you.'

Giles stared at the sharp azure sky, trying to remember how long the rascal had been gone, and doing sums of the distance in his head. 'You couldn't have gone more than a couple of miles in the time you were gone,' he said. 'Do you have any sense of them still following?'

'No,' Anji answered. 'I've been staying alert. They seem to have disappeared, or at least are beyond my range.'

Giles called back to Petia. She shook her bridle and trotted up to ride on Giles' other side.

'Can anyone block you from sensing them?' Giles asked.

'I don't know. Another Trans might. If you're thinking about those who were following us the day before yesterday, Anji is certain that it wasn't a Trans.'

'Have you been listening?' Giles asked. 'Sensing?'

Petia nodded, her expression grim. 'My mind seeks constantly now. If it is Segrinn back there, I'll know it.'

'Sing out the instant you know anything,' Giles said.

In late afternoon they rode into Malor, which proved a larger village than Giles had expected, but certainly not a town. Winter had shut down any industry that might have flourished during warmer months, but Giles doubted Malor prospered even then. The entire village had a curious, dead feeling about it.

'You, good sir,' he called to a man standing in the road silently watching them. 'Is there an inn nearby?' The answer was nothing more than a vague wave of the hand. The man turned and walked off in sullen silence.

'What wonderful hospitality,' grumbled Keja, who had complained of the cold all day. 'We'll find this inn and discover it closed. Wait and see.'

He shivered and wrapped his arms around himself for the scant added warmth this provided. Giles shook his head. Anji ought to be the one suffering. The boy seemed to enjoy the novelty of the cold. But Keja? Giles pushed the small thief from his mind. If Keja wasn't griping about something, then Giles would worry.

The sign hanging over the inn door needed repainting, but the quartet made out the name, The Bread and Water. A plain loaf of bread, no butter, and a tin cup only half full of water portrayed the words.

'If this is someone's idea of a joke,' Keja said, 'we might be better off in their gaol.'

No ostler ran out to help with the horses, and Anji and Keja were left to hold the reins while Giles and Petia went to see about rooms. They were aware of surly glances from heavily dressed men standing nearby, but amused themselves by whistling an old folk song in two-part harmony. 'That ought to cheer the old place up,' Keja said. 'It certainly looks as if it needs it.'

The onlookers silently left, as if Keja and Anji's tune offended them.

When Giles and Petia returned, Giles said, 'The colour of our money seems good. We have rooms and a meal, but don't expect much else. I've never seen anything like this.' He took his horse's reins from Anji's hand. 'The stable is around in back, and we take care of our own horses.' Giles looked around the glum village, then added, 'We set watches tonight.' The others nodded, remembering all too well their problems at the last inn.

The meal had been edible, but not much more could be said for it except that it proved better than the mouldy bread and bitter cheese of the previous night. Giles and Keja ordered mulled wine after dinner. The wine was poor but tolerable because of the spice stick overpowering the taste.

Just as they settled down comfortably by the large fireplace, the inn door swung open and a guard officer entered. He ordered an ale from the innkeeper, then turned to survey the room. Keja watched his eyes light up as he saw them. 'Here it comes,' he whispered to the others. He loosened his dagger in its sheath, waiting for the inevitable.

'Let me tell our story,' Giles whispered back.

The officer seemed content to leave them alone. But Giles had served in the military long enough to know the type. While Giles fought in the Trans War this overdressed upstart of an officer was probably hiding beneath a haystack, only coming out to boast of his noble exploits. The companions sat quietly, chatting, and ignored the officer.

When he swaggered over to their table, Keja finished telling the story he had begun and paid no attention to the man. Everyone chuckled at the end of the story, and Giles poured more wine into Keja's cup. At last, settled again, he looked up as if he was noticing the man for the first time.

'Good evening, sir. Would you care for a cup of our mulled wine?'

The officer leaned back against the neighbouring table, knowing full well that he had been purposely ignored. 'Strangers here, aren't you?' Keja snorted in disgust at such an obvious question. Petia restrained him before he made a flip reply.

'Just passing through,' Giles answered mildly. 'On our way north.'

'North?' The officer's voice was tinged with sarcasm. 'At this time of year? What would you be going north for?'

Keja leaned forward, but Giles spoke before a single sarcastic word left Keja's mouth.

'We've heard, on good authority, that a great deal of mineral wealth in the north country offers itself to the bold. We're going exploring.' He leaned back and took a sip of his wine. 'Sure you won't have some?' he asked. The story was a poor one, but the officer might not care. He might be content with running them out of town in the morning, claiming to have done his duty. What worried Giles the most, the officer was entirely right when he mentioned that, with winter coming on, it was the worst time of the year for prospecting.

Keja spoke up now, but Giles thought that he would follow his lead.

'Actually,' Keja said, voice dropping low, 'we're looking for gold. A source we can't name, a noted explorer from Bericlere, told us where we might find it in the northlands.'

Giles marvelled at Keja's skill. He made the tall tale sound plausible. Giles had to admit that Keja performed his chosen profession well.

The officer turned his head enquiringly. 'Where might that be?'

Keja leaned back and chuckled. 'Now, you don't really think we'd tell you, do you? We may look stupid, but we aren't going to give away that kind of secret.'

The officer gestured at Petia and Anji. 'Your wife and son?'

'No,' Keja said. 'Although . . .'

Giles broke in. 'Partners in our venture. We've travelled a good bit together. This isn't the first time that we've joined up.'

'Trans, aren't they?' The man said it as if his mouth filled with muck. 'Why'd you pick up with Trans?'

Petia flushed. Her anger made the veins along her temple jump. She opened her mouth to answer, but Giles touched her knee under the table, signalling for her silence.

'These two are good at prospecting. They have the knack of finding all that's worth finding.' He touched Petia with his knee again, pleading silently with her to hold her temper and let him and Keja do the talking. Giles decided to see if he could elicit some pity. 'Petia's husband was killed during the War.'

'Your choice,' the officer said, not bothering to hide his contempt. 'We don't like Trans much here. Don't like strangers, either. I'm going to have to report your arrival to my superiors. Meanwhile, stay close to the inn. No telling what might happen if you get to wandering around the village.'

'That's no problem,' Keja said. 'We're only staying the night. We'll be on our way in the morning.'

'You'll need a pass to continue. Meanwhile,' he said, painfully drawing his seal on the bottom of a tattered sheet of paper, 'here's a temporary authorisation to be in Malor. Don't go anywhere until you see me again – and don't leave Malor.' He laid the authorisation on the table. 'See that you keep that with you and show it whenever you are asked by any of the uniformed soldiers.'

He swaggered to the door, made an obviously rude remark about the quartet to the men sitting nearby. He raised a loud guffaw for his efforts. He winked at the innkeeper and left.

'Nice people,' Keja commented. 'We haven't even done anything and they hate us.'

'Unusual, indeed,' Giles murmured. 'I wonder how they feel about each other. Are they ever happy? Well, drink up.' He poured into Keja's cup again. 'Petia, would you like a small glass? It will make you sleep better.'

Giles frowned when he saw that she had turned sombre, melancholy written all over her face. Giles reached out and touched her hand. 'Petia, what's the matter? Don't worry about that guardsman. They're all alike, all wanting to make their power known.'

Petia raised her head. Twin tears ran down her face. 'What you said to him was true. I *did* have a husband, and he *was* killed in the War. I never told you before. I thought I was over it. I . . . I'm not.'

'I'm sorry. I would never have said that if I had the slightest notion it might be true. I was simply making up a story to satisfy that oaf. I truly am sorry.'

Petia dabbed at her eyes. 'It's all right, Giles. It seems like such a long time ago. Being indentured by my mother, escaping from Segrinn, being married, the war. Do things ever settle down? Is there ever any peace in life? When this is all over, I don't think I want to see either of you ever again.'

Giles and Keja were stunned by Petia's words. Unsure what to do or say, both turned back to their mulled wine. The silence between them became oppressive.

'You can come up for air now,' she said after staring into the dancing flames in the fireplace. 'I apologise. I shouldn't take out my feelings on you. It must be this place. I'm starting to be as inhospitable as the villagers.'

Keja stretched. 'It's not the friendliest place I've ever visited.' He picked up the pass. 'What a regimented country. I wonder if the locals are allowed to move around without a pass? Maybe they don't want to. Can you imagine being stuck in one place all your life? Not me.'

'The only reason,' Giles said, 'you've moved around so much is because someone is always after your thieving hide. You'd probably love to settle down in one place, but you won't admit it.'

'Not true, Giles. I could have stayed with l'Karm's daughter. I thought about it.'

'Except you thought about the gold key more,' Giles said. 'And ended up stealing it. Her father's men are still after you for that. Face it, Keja, you'll never settle down.'

Keja tried to work up a scowl, but his face broke into a crooked smile. 'If I did, I wouldn't pick Malor. Unfriendly people, tin soldiers marching around, snide remarks about visitors, terrible ale, ugly women. I wonder what other problems we'll have.'

'Giles, I would like a small glass of your wine, after all.'

Giles gestured to the innkeeper. 'And a glass for the lady, please.' He heard a snicker from the nearby table, but when he turned a cold eye in that direction, the men fell silent. They read danger – and death – in that unwavering look.

The innkeeper brought more wine and the extra glass. Giles gestured for him to sit and share a cup with them. The man nodded and fetched his own mug. When he had poured the wine, Petia continued. 'Having to carry a pass is absurd.'

The innkeeper's voice rang out deep and robust. 'Everyone needs a pass here, even the people who live here.' He pulled a brass sliver from his apron pocket and waved it.

'What sort of place is this?' Keja asked. 'Not even the citizens are trusted.'

'It's getting so we don't even trust each other, much less strangers. It wasn't always like this.' The man drained his mug and set it down with a loud, empty click.

Giles moved forward and refilled the innkeeper's cup. 'Tell us about it,' he said.

'We're a good people, but lately there's been a big change.' Even this obvious statement caused the innkeeper to drain another mug. Giles obliged, refilling silently. 'Simple folk, living here in the foothills of the mountains. We used to help each other out. Then the soldiers came. Said we couldn't go anywhere without a damned pass. Threw people in gaol if they didn't have one. Scared us good, they did.'

'Aren't they your own soldiers?'

The innkeeper paused and thought on this. 'Guess we had soldiers of our own, once,' he said. 'But we never saw them, except once in a while when a troop would march through. We might have to billet them for a night. Never came back after the War, not a one of them. But now we've got a contingent of *them* here all the time, struttin' around, askin' to see our passes.'

'Who's your ruler?' Keja asked.

'Lord Onyx,' the innkeeper said. 'We've never seen him. He wasn't the ruler before the Trans War, but now he is, it seems. Nobody knows how that happened, but we've got new laws. And the soldiers.' He sighed. 'Ain't much we can do about it, but it grates on you after a while, the way people have shut up and keep secretive all the time. People just ain't the same as they used to be.'

'We're going north,' Keja said. 'Can we expect the same treatment all the way?'

'I'd think it likely. We ain't allowed to travel much, as you probably can tell. People is keepin' things close to themselves. They's bein' especially careful around strangers. No, you ain't got much welcome to look forward to. Not from the people or the land. You're goin' deep into the Adversaries and in the winter time they ain't very forgivin'.'

'I thought we were already into the mountains,' Giles said.

The innkeeper leaned forward and looked at Giles as if to see if he was making a joke. 'You're only in the foothills. If the weather would clear a little you could stand in the middle of the street and see the mountains up ahead of you. I wouldn't care to be heading that way, not at this time of year.'

'The weather?'

'Oh, that, too, I reckon. I was thinkin' about the ice demons and the snow demons. We don't see them much. They've only attacked a couple of times in the last five years. But that's because Malor is so far away from their lairs. The closer you get to them mountains, the more likely you are to be attacked. The ice demons live in ice caves, so don't go takin' no shelter in them. The snow demons, well, I guess they build caves, too.'

'You believe in spirits?' Keja asked. He licked suddenly dry lips at the idea of meeting such beings.

'Oh, yes. You'd better, too. I could take you down to the end of the road near here and show you a log cabin with the sides ripped right out. You'd believe me then. Tell you what, son. You go on up to them mountains and keep them demons busy. Then they'll leave *us* alone this winter.' The innkeeper sighed and swallowed the last of his wine. 'Don't want to tell me what you're going after, I suppose?'

Giles stuck to the story he had told the guard officer. 'Doing a little prospecting, looking for gold, mostly, but anything else we might find, silver, lead, iron.'

'Bad time of year for doin' that.' The innkeeper gazed vaguely at a ceiling beam. 'I don't believe you for a minute, but you stick with your story.' He winked at Petia, put his hand on Anji's shoulder. 'Back to work. Thank you for the wine and the talk.' With that he wandered off to take care of the other guests.

The companions sat quietly, pondering what the innkeeper had said. Giles drew circles with the drops of wine which had spilled onto the table. Petia studied her fingers.

At last Keja broke the silence. 'It doesn't sound good, Giles. Ice and snow demons and the winter coming on.'

'No.' Giles' statement was more of a long sigh than a response. 'Maybe we ought to sleep on this.' He rose and walked away, deep in thought over how far they had come, how close they were to success. The fifth and final key that opened the Gate of Paradise lay ahead. Could an old man with sparse years remaining pass up such a tasty morsel as Paradise?

The gods insisted that it wasn't going to be an easy decision.

The innkeeper served them a big breakfast. Giles deciphered the man's expression as a nostalgic remembrance of older times when people had been friendlier to strangers – and one another. A loaf of fresh brown bread, a platter of scrambled eggs and salted fish, and mugs of tea brewed from the leaves of a native bush were set before the four. Anji's eyes sparkled as he dug in. The others ate stolidly, knowing that a decision must be reached whether to go on or to return to warmer climes. If they ventured deeper into the mountains, there'd be no turning back.

When they were finished, Keja moved the platters aside and folded his hands on the table. 'Well, Giles?'

Before Giles could respond, the door opened and the guard officer of the evening before stalked into the room. Two soldiers accompanied him. Petia saw others outside. 'Trouble,' she whispered.

The officer strutted over to the table. 'I see that you didn't sneak off in the middle of the night,' he said.

'Why should we do that?' Giles asked. 'We're simply travelling through.'

'Your pass.' He thrust out his hand for the scrap of paper. A frown came over his face as he stared at it. 'This won't do.'

'I don't understand. Are you revoking our pass through this country? What's the reason?'

'Place them under arrest!' Those with the guardsman moved to obey. The officer smirked.

Giles and Keja sprang to their feet. 'Why? What's the reason?'

The two soldiers stopped, tugging at their swords. The officer held them back with a wave of his hand.

'Be careful, you two. There are more soldiers in the street outside, if needed.' He sneered openly.

'We haven't done anything!' protested Keja.

'This pass is invalid.'

'But you gave it us!' cried Petia, outraged.

'I'm only following orders,' he said, with obvious enthusiasm. 'All with revoked or out-of-date passes are to be arrested.'

'We don't understand,' Giles said patiently. 'You've got to give us an explanation.'

'I don't have to give you anything,' the officer snarled. 'I have my orders and I carry them out. That is all you need to know. Now get your belongings.'

'I'm sure there's some mistake,' Giles said. 'I'd like to see your superior. Then we can straighten this out.'

The gleam in the man's eye told Giles that he'd get no more satisfaction from the higher ranks that he got from this lowly officer.

It took only a few minutes to gather their packs and re-assemble downstairs. The innkeeper stood silently. He gave a minute shrug that told the four he was sorry for them. The officer gestured grandly and followed them into the bright sun.

'Run for it?' Keja whispered.

Giles shook his head. 'No good. We need the horses, and they'll have someone posted at the stables.' He looked at the troop standing at ease in the street.

The officer slammed the inn door behind him and commanded the party to step down from the plank porch. Four soldiers led their horses from around the corner of the building. They were saddled, but their bridles were tied loosely to the back of the saddles.

'We'll bring your horses, but you'll walk. Since my men don't have horses, I see no reason that you should be allowed to ride.'

Anji went to the horses and spoke softly to them, rubbing each of them on the nose. A soldier jerked him away and shoved him back toward the others.

Townspeople lined the street, gathered to see what had caused the commotion. The officer pushed the four into the street, and soldiers formed around them. He gave the orders to march. Cheers followed them, punctuated with jeers at the strangers. 'Stay out of Malor. We don't want strangers here.' 'Get out, dirty Trans.' 'Kill them all!'

Giles squeezed Petia's shoulder. 'It's all right.'

Petia nodded, but her face showed that it wasn't.

Four

'WHERE ARE you taking us?' asked Giles Grimsmate.

The soldiers surrounded the party and stood awaiting orders from their officer. Giles received no answer, nor had he expected one. He took the opportunity to examine the troop. An old soldier's habits die hard. Giles had commanded his own men for far too many years not to deduce a great deal about the men who hemmed them in – and about their officer.

He found them to be a slovenly bunch. If they had been in his company, he would have given them extra duty until they turned as old and grey as Giles himself. With snow on the ground, he expected their boots to be dirty, but the snow did not reach to their belts or to the brass buttons on the front of their coats. Leather belts hung in untended tatters, the buckles hadn't been polished in months, and tarnish had accumulated so thick on the buttons that Giles began to wonder if they were brass.

Giles turned in disgust from these so-called military men and took a step towards the officer. Several soldiers tensed at the movement and prepared to seize him. A single cold stare froze them in their tracks.

He again demanded, 'Where are you taking us?'

'He won't answer,' Petia said. The cat Trans hissed in disgust. 'He's having too much fun lording it over us and playing to the crowd. One such as he wouldn't know, anyway. He has to wait. He has to be told. He's only someone else's lackey.' She put her arm around Anji and looked to see how he was taking their arrest. The boy looked up and winked. He wasn't afraid and seemed to be enjoying himself.

Giles wished the boy showed more sense in this. These men might not be good soldiers, but they were soldiers.

Keja stayed aloof, not deigning to acknowledge the soldiers. He looked past them to the jeering crowd standing along the road. The small thief elevated his nose and tried to look as haughty as possible. Giles gave him a quick nod. Only by maintaining their aloofness and superiority over these country yokels would they escape. Keep the enemy off balance and wondering what he'd done wrong. And never show fear. Never.

Giles looked at Petia and tapped his forehead with his finger. She frowned, but the silent instruction became clear when he nodded slightly at the officer.

She paused, collecting her mind, and sent it searching for the slightest clue in the man's brain. The officer's thoughts swirled in confusing eddies devoid of any real content. He worried about promotion, his wife, something about blackness. The Trans scowled, angry at her inability to figure out what tore so at the officer's emotions. Petia couldn't read minds, but her skills in empathic communication allowed her to discern more than was carried by simple words. Usually. This wasn't one of those times, however, and she shook her head at Giles and shrugged.

The officer argued, gesturing wildly, but the innkeeper remained adamant. About what? Giles tried to edge closer to hear more distinctly but one guard drove a hard elbow into his side. Giles avoided the worst of the blow and glowered at the soldier. The man turned pale and stepped away from Giles.

'You *will* pay, by all that's holy,' the innkeeper said, loud enough for all along the street to hear. 'You take them before they pay, fine. That's your business, Brellon. But I will get my money for their board and room.'

'This is none of your concern,' the officer said, licking his lips nervously at the crowd forming around them. It became increasingly obvious this arrest wouldn't be done quietly.

'Then let me collect from them. They're retrieved their belongings. They have the coin.' The innkeeper tried to shove past the officer, only to be knocked to the ground.

'Stay away from them. They're prisoners.'

Giles saw a chance for sowing even more discord in their

captors' ranks. 'You won't even allow your poor citizenry to receive their rightful pay? This country is worse than I had imagined!' He took a large coin from his pouch and flung it towards the innkeeper, aiming in such a way that the man missed it by an arm's length.

A scramble of children pouncing for the coin ensued. They ended in a pile, arms and legs going every direction until one boy came up with the coin. He took it to the innkeeper, and Giles saw the man pull a smaller coin from his pocket and present it to the boy. Perhaps a little good and truth and justice lived in the town, but it was very little.

In spite of the moment's inattention, none of the companions had a chance to slip away from their guards. Giles' action effectively ended the argument, but the officer realised that the jeering crowd become increasingly restless.

'Get moving,' Brellon ordered. 'Now!' He kicked several of his soldiers to make them obey. Giles heaved a sigh and shook his head.

Just give me these churls for a month, no, two weeks, and I'd turn them into real soldiers, he thought. Still, their slovenliness afforded a chance for escape at some time in the future. All Giles and the others had to do was wait, no matter how difficult that proved.

They moved off, boots scuffing through the snow. The jeers faded as the people realised that, with the entertainment over, their feet were cold. The town fell away behind them and, when they rounded a corner in the road, vanished completely.

'We're well away from there,' the pudgy officer said. 'March easy, men.'

Their display for the townspeople, such as it had been, was finished.

The ranks opened and stragglers slowed their pace. Some of the men pulled pipes and tobacco from their pockets. The officer fell back from his position at the front of his squad, and walked beside the four prisoners.

'A beautiful day,' he said squinting in the reflected sun. 'Not bad for marching, since it's marching we must do.'

'*Now* will you tell us where you're taking us?' Giles asked in exasperation.

'Can't do that. I have my orders,' Brellon said. 'But there's no need for us to be uncouth about it. I haven't had anyone new to talk to for a long time. These louts –' he waved a pudgy hand at his squadron '– can't talk about anything but drinking, gambling and women. I hope we can pass the time with more interesting talk than that. Don't you?'

'What else is there but . . .' began Keja. He subsided when he saw that the officer continued his little talk without waiting for an answer.

Keja raised his eyebrows, with a suggestion of resignation. The man was garrulous, no doubt about it. Maybe Brellon would stumble upon an interesting topic, but for the moment the officer seemed intent on bragging about his importance.

Giles silenced the others and allowed the officer to ramble on while they settled into a steady pace. The officer didn't seem to notice that they were not taking part in the dreary monologue of his tedious life, his tepid loves, his insignificant travels, the places he had been, the dull people he had met.

Brellon still flowed over with the verbal diarrhoea at mid-morning, when he realised that he had not given his men a rest. He halted the troop, split it into groups to relieve themselves, and allowed the prisoners the same privilege, but under close supervision.

'You will *not* assign a man to watch me at my toilet!' the Trans snapped. She hissed and raked at the air in front of his nose. The officer stepped away, wide-eyed.

'But you're my prisoner, and I'm responsible for your well-being,' he said, befuddled. A smile slowly crossed Brellon's face as the dilemma worked itself out. 'You can go alone, if you promise not to attempt escape.'

'I give you my word,' Petia said with ill grace.

Giles almost wished Petia would vanish over the low rise and keep going, but he knew she wouldn't. She'd given her bond – and Anji had stayed behind. The officer apparently missed the closeness between the Trans. For that Giles heaved a sigh of relief. Until they discovered more about their destination – and the one ordering them arrested – he wanted only physical impediments to their escape. If the officer discovered he could use the boy as leverage, he might do something they'd all regret.

Giles had seen Petia angry. Her cat nature rose to the surface and turned her more animal than human. Even the bovine officer didn't deserve such a fate.

'Come on, you slugs,' the officer shouted at his squad. 'There's ale for you at the day's end and billeting in the inn, but not if we don't arrive there. You'll be sleeping under a sword tree tonight if you don't crook a leg.'

'We travel for more than one day, then?' Keja asked.

'That's more than I care to tell,' the officer said slyly. 'Might that not be your destination? The end of your road, so to speak?'

'We,' cut in Giles, 'are simple prospectors, nothing more. We stay at inns for the time being, looking for the right place to sally forth and stake our claims in the mountains.'

Keja bit his tongue. He had almost answered the officer that they went farther than any mere country tavern in their search for the fifth key to the Gate of Paradise. He resolved for the thirtieth time to think before he spouted off.

At the rest for the noon meal the prisoners had their first chance to talk with each other. The officer went off to inspect his men. He ended up examining the horses enviously.

'He's certainly not opening up, is he?' Petia said, eyeing Brellon. 'We don't know any more about our destination than when we left this morning.'

'I'm sorry I said anything to him,' Keja said. 'He thought he was being terribly clever when he concluded that this was the way we had been travelling. I didn't want to give him any information at all.'

'Yes, I know,' Giles said. 'Any fool could have figured out that we were travelling north — even *that* fool. In fact, we told him so last evening. I worry that he's taking us in the direction we wanted to go.'

'We can get away. Giles. I know it.' Keja's eyes darted from one soldier to the next. 'Look at them. Lazy, inattentive.'

'Like you, eh?' Petia said. Before Keja responded angrily, she rushed on. 'We don't know whether we're going to march for a day or a week. I say we should watch for any opportunity to get away.'

'I'd hate to leave the horses,' Giles said.

'Don't forget the equipment and supplies and our weapons,' Petia said. 'We can't leave all that behind.'

'We could, but it'd make things more difficult than I want in the midst of winter-wracked mountains,' Giles replied.

'Why not just be agreeable and find out where we're being taken?' Keja asked. 'After all, we head in the proper direction, don't we?'

Giles grimaced. He stared at Keja as if he were a small child asking a stupid question, then turned away. The idea of being anyone's prisoner tore at Giles' sense of honour. He hadn't fought against the slavery imposed on the Trans out of repugnance at what was done to them – at first. He had been drafted and fought because his lord commanded it. But over the years he had come loathe slavery in all its forms. Every grey hair on his head marked a new promise to fight against such oppression.

While they weren't slaves, Giles cared little more for being subject to another's whim.

The rest came to an end and the officer prodded his troops into a semblance of formation. The four companions took their places and set off. The officer seemed to have talked himself out; their only accompaniment was the scrunch of boots through the dry snow. Even the wind took a rest from its mournful howling between mountain peaks. Giles marched along as if in a soundless bubble, lost in his own thoughts. Keja might be right about going along with their captor – but deep in his heart he knew Petia spoke the truth.

At the first opportunity they'd have to make a break for freedom.

Later in the afternoon the squad tired of shuffling through the snow and began to complain bitterly to their leader. Brellon had to encourage them with promises of billeting and beer. Grumblers, Giles thought. And probably insubordinate when the going got tough. Certainly not men he wanted at his back in battle.

In spite of the discord, Giles saw no good chance for escape. They arrived at a small village as the day turned to dusk.

'Trenora, isn't it?' Giles asked. He remembered that much from his map. Instinctively, he touched the spot where the map lay beneath his tunic, hidden. At first, he'd been surprised that he hadn't been searched when arrested. In his day they stripped prisoners and looked for messages, briefs and maps.

But he had come to know how poorly planned their arrest had been and how little the officer knew of his job. One more indication of sloppy soldiering.

'That it is,' Brellon responded, not even wondering how Giles had known. He spat into the snowy street as a crowd began to form around them. The people here did not even have the energy to jeer. They stood and stared with dull eyes.

The four companions were taken to the inn and, with a great deal of fussing, the officer obtained billeting for his men and a room where his prisoners could be held. When a meal of sorts was brought to Giles and the others, they saw that two guards lounged outside their door. When the dishes were taken away, they found that the guard had been increased to four. In spite of being weaponless, they might have overpowered two guards, but four guaranteed the failure of any escape attempt.

'We'd best settle down and rest. This is becoming tedious,' Giles said.

Their travels became even more tedious; for two more days and part of a third they continued marching north. Mornings found Brellon talkative and gregarious. And boring.

The days continued mild and indistinguishable from one another. Each night a trace of light, dry snow fell. The mornings were crisp and the weak afternoon sun brought little real warmth. At times the companions wondered how long this would go on, whether they had died and marched to the lowest regions of Hell.

Giles' impression of the officer was raised a notch when he realised that no circumstances developed in which they might escape. With the soldiers often edging perilously close to insurrection, Giles found this startling.

Even more puzzling to him than the undercurrent of discipline in an otherwise outwardly slovenly squad, which became the topic of whispered discussion among the four companions.

Keja expressed it best that night when they stopped at another inn. 'How did they send the message so fast? On one night we were given a pass, and the following morning it was revoked and we were arrested. We've been on the road for two days already and haven't reached the place where the message must have come from. What manner of sending must they have?'

'Perhaps we'll find out when we arrive there, if we ever do,' Giles said. 'We certainly haven't had any chance to escape yet, so just keep trudging along and keep your eyes and ears open.'

'The order for our arrest might have come from some place different than our destination,' Petia said. 'That indicates a control over the country tighter than any I've seen, even in Trois Havres.'

'Time will tell, I suppose,' Giles answered. 'Do we believe in magic?'

'After Bandanarra, yes,' Keja said emphatically. 'I also believe in sleep, prisoner or not.' He stretched out on the hard wooden floor, pulled his cloak around him, and gave up thinking about the mysterious sending of messages.

On the third day, the road began to climb and they moaned at the strain in their leg muscles. When they entered a pass at midday and saw the mountains ahead, the towering peaks seemed close enough to touch. Anji's eyes widened. 'Are we going to climb over them?' he asked as the road straightened out and appeared to be heading directly towards them.

Giles laughed. 'Let's hope not. We're hardly dressed for a climbing expedition.'

On the morning of the fourth day they came over a small rise and looked out across a high meadow that stretched for miles. In spite of their predicament, the companions paused and marvelled at the purple-hazed mountains rising from their base at the far side.

'No time for gawking,' the officer said. He prodded at them and kept them moving, pressing hard throughout the morning. He gave the impression that their journey neared its end. Their noonday stop was short and he hurried them along. Within an hour the outline of a citadel sharpened and became more distinct through the distance haze.

'It looks as if it grew from the mountain's base,' said Keja, awed in spite of his best intentions to let nothing impress him.

'It also looks to be our destination,' Giles said. Giles gave himself over to introspection. He didn't know what to expect when they arrived at the prodigious pile of stone. He ran through the possibilities. They should stick to their story of searching for minerals. But they must also agree on their backgrounds. If they were given the chance to talk, they dared not contradict one another.

As they drew nearer, they were overwhelmed by the size of the citadel. 'It's as big as Shahal,' Anji breathed.

'Yes, nearly so,' Petia agreed. 'Except that Shahal is vertical and this hugs the base of the mountain and stretches out. It doesn't have as many floors as Shahal.'

'It is huge, big enough to have dungeons.' Anji voiced a concern no one had yet spoken aloud, the possibility that they would be imprisoned, for whatever reasons the ruler of this sorry country might have.

The high cirrus clouds parted and the wan sun lit the sides of the citadel. Huge blocks of a grey stone rose in tier after sloping tier. In some respects it reminded Giles of a story he had once heard about a structure built by the gods and called a pyramid, although he recalled that the mythical pyramid continued upward until it ended in a sharp point.

This building rose from a base stretching along the mountains to a height of more than two hundred feet. Crenellations decorated the top of the wall, and Giles suspected that behind it stretched a broad walkway, perfect for sentry duty and defence. From its battlements, guards would be able to look across the grassy high meadow for miles. Capturing such a fortress would be a difficult task.

But even as the thought crossed his mind, Giles began formulating ways to do so. He cursed this futile activity, but recognised it as part of his training.

'To conquer *that*!' he said with a gusty sigh.

As they drew closer, they saw the huge ironwood gate built into the wall. The road ended there, swallowed by the structure. Giles saw sentries walking their stations along the wall and knew that the arrival of their little band would have been announced long ago. As if in response to his thoughts, the doors of the gate swung open. Their thickness confirmed Giles' suspicions that, no matter his feelings about the soldiers who had arrested them, this was a well-built fortress. Inside he anticipated finding well-drilled troops under the command of tough, demanding officers.

And in supreme command would be, ironically, a military man whom he might respect – and who had ordered them imprisoned.

Now within sight of their destination, Brellon showed his nervousness. It was obvious that they were being watched and he wished to present a troop of something besides stragglers. He tried desperately to form his men into reasonable ranks, to bring them to a semblance of a squad in fighting trim, ready and eager to take orders.

Giles nudged Keja and nodded towards the ineffectual officer. They enjoyed the look of embarrassment and dismay on his face. It might be their last bit of entertainment for a while.

Giles sobered when he realised that any chance for escape had evaporated upon their arrival at the citadel. This had to be the ruler's fortress. No one else in a country would be allowed to possess such a powerful base.

What had the innkeeper called him? Lord Onyx? Giles straightened as he came to the decision that they had been summoned by Lord Onyx.

An officer and troop of guards awaited their arrival at the gate. The solid door was even more impressive at close quarters. The soldiers stood at ease in an orderly fashion, alert and awaiting commands. Their officer stepped forward and said, 'I'll take command of the prisoners, Brellon. Take your men to the lower level barracks, and by the gods, see that they bathe and clean their uniforms and weapons. They look disgraceful. I will personally conduct inspection in the morning.'

He forced away the look of disgust at Brellon's soldiers, then commanded his guard to attention and form ranks behind the prisoners. Two men broke rank and took the animals to stables within the citadel. Then in a calm voice the officer ordered the companions to follow him.

Keja tensed, but Petia restrained him. It was not good to fight now. They all realised that their chance for freedom lay behind them. They could only go along with their captors and confront the man who commanded such grand forces in the otherwise miserable mountain kingdom. They trudged up wide granite stairs lighted by torches placed in twisted wrought-iron brackets along the wall.

Ever the soldier, Giles paid close attention to the route. They climbed several flights of stairs, each ascending in a different direction. They took the left, the left, two rights and a final left staircase before entering a broad hall.

The officer turned smartly and said, 'Remain here. You may warm yourselves at the fire until I return. You shan't be waiting long.' His guard efficiently fell in behind as the officer walked away.

'What do you make of that?' Keja asked.

'We do as he says,' Petia replied, shivering. 'He doesn't look like Brellon. He'd kill and never miss a night's sleep over it.'

'He's a soldier.' Giles counted that as the highest compliment he could give. He gestured to the others and they took advantage of a roaring fire in a fireplace along one wall. Four-foot-long logs sent waves of heat out into the room from the massive head-high fireplace. Having marched through the snow for four days, all four eagerly crowded close, hands extended, feeling warmth crawl back into them.

'What next?' Keja asked. Already the small thief moved from the fire and appraised the room's furnishings. Back in Neelarna the solid gold candlesticks would bring a small fortune to anyone bold enough to offer them to the right buyer. He saw no way of slipping even the smallest candlestick into his tunic without being obvious.

'We'll soon find out,' Giles replied. 'This is the end of the track in this snowbound country.'

Doors burst open at the far end of the long hall. The companions turned at the sound and saw guards bring their halberds to attention. A rustle of activity made Giles uneasy for no reason. Then he saw a small hunchback man – a dwarf? – bustle about, shooing people out of his way. Giles jumped when a robust laugh echoed throughout the huge room. A rotund man, magnificently dressed, strutted through the door, stopped and struck a pose.

He threw his arms wide in greeting, and his voice boomed down the hallway. 'Welcome, my friends.'

Anji gasped. The boy's eyes widened and he exclaimed. 'The mysterious stranger! The one who has followed us for so long!'

Five

A CHUCKLE came from the man's huge frame, then grew into a hearty laugh. He threw his entire body into the effort, holding his sides and tossing his head back. When the laugh finally subsided, his baritone voice rolled like thunder down the hall.

'This room has excellent acoustics. I could hear your young friend's whisper all the way from where you stand. Remarkable, is it not?'

The four stood, transfixed by the booming voice. Its owner was dressed in knee breeches of burgundy velvet with a rose brocade coat with a white linen shirt underneath. Gold braid decorated his shoulders, and his shoes bore massive gold buckles. His stockings were tinted a delicate pink.

The man walked towards them, the dwarf preceding him with hands fluttering right and left to clear the way.

'So you call me the "mysterious stranger", do you? I like that. I had not thought you would notice me, but it's obvious that you did.'

'We only knew that a man in black has been following us,' Giles said, frowning. This might be the man he had run into so long ago before confronting the Flame Sorceress. 'You followed us on Milbante, too. Why have you been spying on us?'

'Let us say that it was enlightened self-interest, keeping apprised of a situation which interests me greatly.'

'And what would that be?' Keja asked.

'There will be time for discussion later, my friend. You must be tired from your long journey. Please, follow me.' He turned and led the way back along the hall. At the doorway, he beckoned to the dwarf. They were amused to see the mis-shapen creature stand on tiptoe and cup one ear to hear his master's orders. They could hear them well.

'Get rid of these other people. They bore me. And close the doors after us. See that refreshments are brought.' The man backed away and began to turn. 'And be sure to bring that wine from Albiado,' the huge man roared after him.

He led them into a sumptuously furnished room. Another fireplace burned with the same vigour they had witnessed in the outer hall. A long table covered with a linen cloth ranged along one wall, candelabra spaced evenly along it. Chairs upholstered in brocade faced the fire.

The huge man gestured. 'Sit, sit, my friends. There will be food soon. After your meal, you will be shown to your suite. No, no.' He held up his hands. 'No questions now. Tomorrow. Tomorrow we will talk. In the meantime, please do not consider yourselves as prisoners. Rather, consider yourselves the guests of Lord Onyx.'

Giles and the others exchanged glances. This *was* the lord of the region, the Lord Onyx mentioned by the innkeeper.

'Serve them,' Lord Onyx ordered as a silent servant entered. 'The fire warms without and the wine warms within. Don't be afraid, my friends. It's not poison. I have much to talk about with you and the dead hold little converse. Ah, the lady and the boy grow tired.'

Petia stifled a yawn behind her hand, but Anji's yawn was audible and his eyelids drooping.

Onyx rose and pulled at a tasseled rope near the fireplace. A meticulously groomed major-domo appeared.

'Their room is prepared? Then escort them to it. We shall talk later. In the meantime, be comfortable, my friends, enjoy the delicate fruits, the wholesome meats, the vintage wines. Food, a hot bath and a good sleep is what you need. You have journeyed long and will find the beds most comfortable here.'

They followed the silent major-domo, constantly aware of their escort – a half-dozen soldiers trailed behind. They climbed stairs, walked down long hallways, and rounded corners. Anji's legs began to fold as he was nearly asleep on his feet. Keja scooped him up and carried him in his arms, and Petia gave him a grateful look. Her own arms lacked strength to hold even one as small as Anji.

At last the servant stopped at a doorway. Two guards stood outside. The servant opened the door to a suite unlike any the companions had ever seen. No common hostelry this, the rooms were large and appointed with rich furniture and draperies. A table set with silver goblets and decorated china, platters of meat and cheese, and bowls filled with ripe fruits ranged along one wall. A loaf of bread, neatly sliced, was arranged artistically on a board of polished ironhorn.

The major-domo turned, inclined his head towards a woman standing in a doorway leading deeper into the suite of rooms. Without a word, he left.

'Is the water drawn?' she asked.

'Yes, Mistress Oa,' four voices rang in unison. Giles jumped at the answer. He hadn't seen the other servants when he'd entered the room. He had been too engrossed in the luxurious settings. The four bowed and silently left, just as the major-domo had. This time Giles paid more attention.

The door closed softly behind them. Giles listened closely for the click of a lock. He heard none.

'All has been readied for you,' Mistress Oa said. 'If there is anything more you require, please ring. I shall be in attendance.' She bowed slightly and floated from the room as if she had clouds instead of feet.

'What do you think of all this, Giles?' Keja said when the door closed.

Giles put a finger to his lips and led the way to the fire. Beckoning them close, he whispered, 'Let's leave talk until later tonight. Someone is undoubtedly listening. You heard the acoustics in the main hall. I don't trust these rooms – or Lord Onyx.'

Keja raised his eyes in exasperation, but complied. 'Something to eat,' he said. 'There's a feast over there.'

When he had filled a plate, he wandered into the adjoining room to test the beds. When Giles and Petia had finished eating a light meal, they found him fast asleep, his plate resting on his stomach.

'Not a bad idea,' Giles said. He stretched out on another bed, wrapped a blanket around himself and closed his eyes.

The sun was slanting through the windows when they awoke. Giles noticed instantly that their clothes had been cleaned and returned. Giles went to the door and opened it. Soldiers stood guard outside. One looked balefully at him but uttered no word. Everyone but Onyx seemed taciturn here. With a shrug, Giles turned back and closed the door.

'"Guests", he said. "My friends. You're not prisoners, but of course, you can't leave."' Giles strode to the fire and heaved another log on to it, watching the sparks and ashes whirl upward.

When Anji finally awakened Giles asked, 'I want you to think carefully before you answer, Anji. Is the man downstairs, the one calling himself Lord Onyx, the man whom you sensed when we first reached Khelora? Is he the one who followed us on the road?'

'I think so, Giles, but I can't be sure,' the boy replied. 'I never did see him, but I *know* he's the one in Bandanarra.'

'What do you suppose he intends to do with us?' Petia asked.

'I don't even want to guess,' Giles replied. He walked to the window and stared out over the meadow. 'Sloping walls a couple of hundred feet down. We're not likely to get out that way.'

'You can be sure that friendliness is only an act,' Keja said. 'A façade as big as his belly.'

Giles nodded, stuffing his pipe. When he had it going, he let wreaths of smoke envelop his head while he thought.

'Everything we saw as we travelled here indicates a ruler who brooks no opposition. A ruler who expects to be obeyed, who totally dominates his subjects and turns them unfriendly and suspicious. I fear that our next conversation with him will not be so pleasant.'

Giles pointed his pipe stem at the others. 'Whatever happens, stick to our story. We're simply looking for minerals, gold specifically.'

'But if he's been following us, Giles,' said Keja, 'he knows that's a lie.'

Giles nodded glumly. 'Onyx obviously knows more of us than we do of him. We have no choice but to play a waiting game. We'll see what the fat man has to say and then go from there. Meantime, we scout ways out of this place.'

He walked to the windows again. Two hundred feet below pale sunlight bathed the snow-covered meadow. The windows were hinged and Giles tested a fastening. To his surprise, it released easily. He swung the window outward, and the cold night air gusted into the room.

Giles bent outward over the sill, carefully examining the sloping wall. The stonework was magnificent, the joining of stones nearly imperceptible. Petia, Anji and Keja came to stand at his back, eager to see if they could hope for escape in that direction.

Giles shook his head. 'Nothing, not the slightest toehold. It would be a long slide, probably exhilarating. But the stop at the bottom would be abrupt – and deadly.' He sighed. 'Hang onto my feet.' He stepped onto the still, holding on to the opened window and bracing against the frame. When he had gained his balance, Keja held him by the ankles.

Giles found a new grip and leaned out as far as he dared. Immediately above him he found the upper window casement mounted flush with the wall, joined smoothly with the stones. No hand or foothold there, either. Above him stretched more floors of the citadel, some identifiable by windows. Giles could not see the battlements along the top.

He swung back into the room. 'It's a marvellous piece of architecture,' he said. 'It must take an enormous base to support a building like this. If you were to drop a line straight down from the battlements. I'll wager you'd find that the base is over a hundred feet thick.'

'Wonderful, Giles,' Keja said. 'A lesson in architecture is what we need right now. So how do we escape?'

'That's what I like about you, Keja. You go right to the heart of the matter. I don't know how we get out of here. Not by windows and wall, I can assure you. Even if they hadn't taken away our ropes, I don't think they'd be long enough to reach the bottom.' Giles glanced out of the window again. 'And it looks as if there'd be a welcoming committee if you made it.'

The others crowded around Giles and looked down. Two

guards marched along a wide pathway on the south side of the citadel, their heads swaying alertly from side to side as they patrolled. The companions watched the guards until they disappeared around the corner. Giles caught movement to his right, and said, 'Look, here come another pair.'

'How can they circle the citadel?' Keja asked, perplexed. 'It's built right into the mountains, isn't it?'

'Inside passage,' Giles muttered, his mind elsewhere.

The soft rustle of silk skirts caused them to turn. Mistress Oa stood in the doorway, a frown on her face.

'Lord Onyx has summoned you,' she said. 'Please follow me to the audience chamber.'

'But . . .'

Keja tried to engage the woman in conversation. She turned and left, as if he didn't exist. Giles slapped Keja on the shoulder, then made a mocking bow in the direction of the open door. Few were the women not responding to Keja Tchurak's charms.

They were led once again down the long corridors and wide stairways to the chamber in which they had first met Lord Onyx. The portly man stared at them with cold eyes.

'I see you are rested, my friends,' Onyx said. 'You seem to find my hospitality agreeable and know I am a caring ruler.'

'Why are you holding us?' Keja interrupted. 'We were simply travelling through this country —'

He was cut off by Onyx's voice, as angry as a growling bear. 'Don't give me any of your tall tales. I know who and what you are. Keja Tchurak, petty thief. Petia Darya, good over the roofs, but there her thieving skills end. Also rescuer of Anji, no last name, Trans boy bought in a slave market on Bandanarra. Anji, clever boy, learning quickly what Petia has to teach.' He turned away and paced in the front of the fireplace. When he turned back, his anger had abated. 'Giles Grimsmate, the only one for whom I have any respect. Twenty years in the Trans War, able fighter, well-liked sergeant, cynical, wearied by witnessing too much death.'

Onyx shook his leonine head. 'What an unlikely partnership! Searching for minerals, especially gold. An even more unlikely story.'

'But it's tr—' Keja began.

Onyx turned fiercely on him. 'Remain silent or I'll have your flapping tongue cut out. I don't need your lies, Tchurak. Instead I will tell you some truths. Do you remember being hit on the head in the Temple of Welcome in Glanport, Giles? You three came together at the Gate of Paradise and couldn't open it, is that not so? Two keys for five locks. Somehow you defeated the Flame Sorceress — I watched you leave Sanustell. Were you cold hiding underneath the docks, Tchurak? I hoped you would drown with the high tide. And you, Darya Trans-woman. The Callant Hanse should have demanded your death for trying to rob them. Sloppy work, but then, all your thieving has been sloppy.'

He paused to take a ripe plum from the bowl on the table. 'Bandanarra almost finished your adventures, didn't it?' he resumed. 'The Seas of Calabrashio, the Skeleton Lord and his men? I do hope the poor beasts can revive the caravan trade to Shahal and along the Track of Fourteen.'

Giles and the others were overwhelmed by Onyx's detailed knowledge of their adventures over the past two years.

'So please humour me, and don't attempt that sorry story of prospecting,' Onyx said, his lips curling into a slight sneer. 'It's the final key you're after. I know it, and you know it. There are five keys, one for each lock on the Gate of Paradise. Four of them sit safely in the vaults of the Callant Hanse. An admirable choice, by the way. A well-respected merchant house, eminently trustworthy. Much more than I can say for the four of you. Now, you will excuse me for a moment, while I let you digest this information. Please be seated.'

Onyx strode away to the opposite end of the room where the grey-clad dwarf huddled over a stack of papers. The companions sank into chairs and sat quietly, each absorbed in his own thoughts. Remembrances of their adventures bombarded them, and behind each image was the thought that they had been watched. This elegantly dressed man *was* the man in black, the mysterious stranger, as Anji had named him. He had watched and chuckled at their struggles, sometimes intervening.

Damn, damn him! Giles thought. They had been used. Onyx wanted the keys and had let them take the risks obtaining the other four. Giles had no doubt that Lord Onyx held the fifth and final key to the Gate.

Onyx strode back to the shocked companions. As he reached them, the doors of the chamber swung open and a figure entered. If Onyx could be described as stout, this man was obese. Petia stared and then gasped in recognition. 'Segrinn,' she sobbed. The Trans seemed to shrink in size, cowering down in her chair.

Giles and Keja turned to her. 'What? Him?'

'You know him, my dear?' Onyx asked, ingratiatingly. 'An old friend of yours, no doubt.'

Petia's hands knotted in her lap. The man waddled down the centre of the room, his eyes fixed on the Trans woman. 'You've done it, my Lord Onyx,' he bellowed. 'You've found my luscious Petia.'

Petia shook free of her shock and sprang to her feet, baring her teeth and snarling. 'Keep that swine away from me, or I'll tear his throat out. I'm not his and never will be.'

Anji stared at her, this woman who had rescued him. She had turned into a feral cat cornered by a hunting dog and determined to fight to the death. He had seen Petia fight before and knew that she could be fierce and relentless, but never had he seen such savagery. It frightened him; a small sound came from his throat.

'It gives one pause, does it not, my dear?' Onyx said. He turned to Segrinn. 'No further, good sire. You may return to your rooms.'

'But I wish to . . .' Segrinn began. His voice trailed off when he saw Onyx's expression.

'Go. Now.' Onyx's bellow echoed around the room.

Segrinn blanched and glanced at Petia. He reached a tentative hand towards her, looked at Lord Onyx, and turned on his heel. His shoulders sagged as he left the room.

'You see, many reins of power rest in my hand,' Lord Onyx said as he settled himself in a comfortable chair facing the four. 'Now, let us get down to some simple bargaining.'

'Our four keys in exchange for our lives,' said Keja.

'What else?' answered Onyx, smiling wickedly. 'You think, no doubt, that you know the location of the final key. That is why you came to Khelora, not for such a ridiculous reason as prospecting in the winter-cloaked Adversaries. You came for gold, that much is true. The gold key.'

He paused, as if waiting for a response. None came. Onyx continued. 'The key is not where you suppose it to be. Oh yes, I have the final key, but you would never find it, even if I stood aside and watched, with a great deal of amusement, I might add, while you searched for it.'

'Why do you want the keys?' Giles spoke up. 'You appear to have all a man could want. Wealth, power, a country of your own. What can the Gate of Paradise mean to you?'

Onyx looked at Giles as if he were insane, turned to the fireplace, warming his hands and staring into the leaping flames. At last he turned back.

'You truly don't know, do you?' He searched each face in turn, finding nothing but puzzlement at his question. Then he threw his head back and laughed.

'What's so funny?' Keja muttered.

'You're looking at a god, and you don't realise it. A minor one in the pantheon, as such things go, but a god, none the less. I watched the Gate of Paradise being built, or rather, *placed* on this miserable world. It was no engineering feat, no architectural wonder. It was merely the thought in the mind of one more powerful than I.

'I battled another god. A decree came from an even higher, more potent god that we were to desist. I did not. As punishment I was cast from what you mortals call Paradise. Exiled on the Hawk's Prairie, I saw the Gate set in place, and listened to the locks click shut. My powers were stripped from me, and I was told that when I found the five gold keys unlocking the Gate, I would be allowed to return to Paradise. You don't know how many centuries it has taken to come this far, nor would you believe the hardships I have suffered. I have not always been as you see me now.'

'You want us to hand over our four keys?' Giles asked.

'It is a hard command, is it not?' Lord Onyx's voice hinted at sympathy, but his eyes were colder than steel. 'Return to your suite and consider the consequences. For three of you, the alternative is death. And for Petia, my dear Trans, a living death with that odious pig, Segrinn. You may go now.'

Onyx lunged out of the chair and tugged on the bell cord.

410

The door opened and Mistress Oa entered, with her escort of guards, to lead them back to their room.

Onyx seemed in no hurry. For two days the companions stewed over the dilemma facing them. At first Giles, Petia and Keja despaired. There followed a period of anger, then at last a quieter discussion of their plight. They knew that they were being given time to come to a decision, and that the only decision acceptable to Onyx was for them to hand over the keys.

But their anger sustained them. They had been through much, perhaps not as much as Onyx had hinted of his own tenure on this world, but they were determined not to give in easily.

'We must escape, Giles,' Keja said. Petia nodded and Keja went on. 'If he calls for us again, it may well be the last time. If we refuse to give up the keys . . .' He drew a finger across his throat. 'And Petia is turned over to that waddling beast again.'

'I know, Keja, but how do you propose to get out of here? We've examined the wall again. It is not a route to escape, but to death.'

'Maybe better death trying to escape than the kind that will greet us when Onyx calls again.'

Anji had been listening to the conversation flow around him. He had heard the despair, the anger, the abortive thoughts of escape. He understood the danger, but for a boy just turned twelve, he had faced more danger than most grown men.

Suddenly he gasped, clutched at his stomach, and staggered from his couch to fall, writhing, to the floor.

Petia jumped to her feet and knelt at his side. 'Anji, what is it? What's wrong?'

The boy turned his head and looked up at her. His brown eyes shone like a deep dew pond from which devilment bubbled up.

Petia looked up at Giles, who slowly nodded. Keja was slower to understand, but when he did, he couldn't keep from smiling broadly.

Petia opened the door and darted into the hallway. The guards jumped alertly.

'The boy, the boy,' Petia shouted, gesturing for the guards.

411

'Come quickly. He's got the falling sickness.' She wrung her hands. 'He's writhing on the floor. I think he's dying.'

The two guards rushed into the room, seeing only the boy in convulsions on the floor. One laid his halberd down and turned the boy over.

Keja stood nearby, looking distraught and yelling. 'Do something for him. Don't let him die!'

The guard still holding his weapon turned to tell Keja to calm down. Keja seized the guard's wrist and twisted the man's arm behind him. The guard yelled in pain. The second guard looked up to see what was happening just as Giles hammered a blow to the small of his back with two closed fists. The breath went out of the soldier with a whoosh, and he slumped over Anji's body.

'Move carefully and don't make any noise,' Keja said as he forced his prisoner to his feet. Giles tied the arms of his man with strips of cloth torn from the window drapes. Petia stuffed the bound guard's mouth with more of the material. When the first guard was secure, they tied the second, then dragged both to the interior room.

For a moment, they stopped and drew a breath. When their hearts had slowed, Giles nodded. Petia pulled on the rope pull which would summon a woman servant. They captured her with little effort.

Petia slipped the outer garment from the servant and put it on over her own clothing. Giles and Keja took the guards' jackets and boots, tucking their own trousers into the boot tops, to look as much like guards as possible.

Keja stood at the door, while Giles and Petia questioned the servingwoman about the layout of the citadel.

'Is there a way out of here besides the main doors?' Giles prodded.

The woman shook her head, fear in her eyes.

Giles put a sword he had taken from a guard to her throat. She saw her death written on the grizzled man's face.

'Yes, yes,' she stammered. 'Don't kill me. I'll tell.'

'If you lie, we will come back and kill you,' Giles threatened when she had told them. They tied and gagged the woman and put her in the room with the guards.

They opened the door quietly and slipped into the corridor.

Empty. They went swiftly and silently along it, pausing only at the corners of stairways to check the floors below. Once, they heard voices and waited for a small knot of servants to pass. Petia counted each floor on their way to the lowest floor. At last she touched Giles on the arm and nodded.

'This level?' he whispered. 'You're sure?'

Petia nodded again, and Anji nodded, too, verifying it.

Keja cupped his ear, and they fell silent, listening. The sound of boots echoed somewhere, but from which direction, they could not tell. They were certain, however, that guards patrolled nearby.

Had the alarm been put out for them yet? Did those guards already seek them?

Giles peered around the stair railing, searching for the doorway marking the exit. He spotted it and pointed to it. The boot echoes sounded closer. The guards were certain to round the corner soon.

'Come on, let's run for it.' He swung around the banister and broke into a run, the others at his heels. Behind them they heard a voice. 'Halt! Stop where you are! Stop by the command of Lord Onyx!'

Keja glanced over his shoulder to see how close the pursuit might be. Four guards lumbered along nearly a hundred feet behind them. 'Keep going,' he yelled at the others. 'We can beat them.'

When next he glanced at the guards he saw that they had not broken into a run. They walked no faster than they had when he had first spotted them.

Giles reached the archway the servant had told them about. Inside it stood a small round door of solid iron with a large ring for a handle. Breathing a prayer, Giles pulled. The door swung open. He motioned the others to hurry through.

Glancing back he saw the guards standing in the corridor, hands on hips. They made no effort to pursue them.

One was laughing and beating a fellow guard on the back. Another cupped his hand around his mouth and shouted. 'Go ahead, take the tunnel. Feed the ice demons!'

Giles hesitated as he looked after the others, then ducked his head and stepped through the door. It clanged shut behind him with a peal like that of a death bell.

413

Six

'Hurry!' Giles urged, pushing Keja by the shoulder. Herding the others ahead of him, Giles pelted down the tunnel, expecting at any moment to hear boots pounding after him.

Only the words of the guards chased him. 'Go on, that's right, run. We don't need to pursue you. We'll leave you for the ice demons, demons, demons . . .'

The words echoed down the corridor, turning him increasingly fearful with every step. Had they entered the home of the ferocious ice creatures they had heard about earlier?

Giles skidded to a stop and turned to see if the guards were loosing any hounds, but in the dim light of the tunnel all he saw was the huge iron door, a closed, baleful eye. He jumped when metal slammed against metal. Giles realised that the guards had dropped an iron bar across the other side of the door. Entry back through the citadel had been effectively denied them by that simple act.

'You can slow down,' Giles shouted after his retreating companions. 'We need to take stock. They've closed and barred the door behind us.'

A pale blue light filtered back to them from somewhere ahead, giving adequate light for them to make their way. Even though the tunnel proved wide enough to walk abreast, they continued to walk in single file, with Keja in the lead. Walls of dark grey granite glistened with seeping water that puddled in little pools on the uneven floor. Giles' feet grew wetter and colder by the minute.

Adding to their discomfort, the underground coldness began to work its insidious fingers through their clothing.

'Giles,' Petia said. 'Let's stop for a minute. I want to fasten

414

the blankets.' They all threw the blankets Petia had brought around their shoulders as cloaks. 'When we have time, I'll try to make clasps.' Petia seemed dissatisfied with the way the knotted blankets kept coming loose from around her neck.

Giles nodded, pulling his blanket closer and enjoying the warmth. But it would get worse, he knew. If the tunnel led farther into the mountain, the air could only become colder. He had taken a squad of men into a mine once, searching for the enemy rumoured to be hiding there. They weren't, but the experience wasn't among his favourites of the war years. He had lost six good soldiers, to cold and gas.

His greatest desire now was that a tunnel would lead off in a direction other than north. He preferred angling to the north-west, in hopes of finding a way out of the underground. If they couldn't, they might come crawling back to scratch feebly at the iron door – only to find that Lord Onyx no longer cared.

Giles almost screamed at the idea of them dying in the closed-in tunnels, tons of rock on all sides. A premature burial. Their own crypt, with them still living.

Morbid thoughts, Giles told himself. He had never liked confined rooms. Surviving the Flame Sorceress' cave had been easy enough – it had been vaster than many cathedrals. In Shahal he'd had no trouble, either. But here? Too tight, too damned tight around him!

'Best we find the source of that light, no matter how feeble,' he said, more to hear his own voice than to tell the others something they already knew.

Keja turned and beckoned to Giles. 'Tunnels lead off on both sides. Which way do we go?'

Giles entered a tunnel that branched off to his left. Within a few feet, the light dimmed drastically. If they continued, they would soon be groping in total darkness. He came out of the tunnel.

'Without candles, there's no way we can make our way. We'll have to keep going towards that light ahead.'

They proceeded down the tunnel, sometimes stumbling on the rough floor, often wading through shallow pools of frigid water they couldn't avoid. From time to time they investigated other tunnels leading off at angles but always found impenetrable darkness.

Time became meaningless. The tunnel stretched forward but the light at the end never changed intensity. Giles wondered if they were getting any closer to it. They plodded onward, heading north directly into the mountain, Giles feared.

When they stopped to rest, Petia took some fruit from her pouch and shared it with them. She was the only one with the presence of mind to gather some food before they left the chamber. And without the blankets she had scooped from the beds before they left, their escape would have already ended in freezing death.

Cold and stiff when they resumed their walk, they were glad to be moving again. Giles wondered how they would sleep when their bodies could no longer go on. The prospect of freezing loomed larger and larger to the veteran soldier.

And the walls! They closed in on Giles so much that he often had to shut his eyes and imagine himself on a vast prairie just to keep his sanity.

Gradually, those tunnel walls turned from hard granite to slick ice. At first it had been a thin coating but thickened until the rock vanished beneath it.

Just as Giles thought the tunnel would never end, an exit appeared in the blue ice. Giles restrained himself from racing forward.

'Caution,' he muttered to himself. To his surprise he had broken out in a sweat from the ordeal of trooping along the tight, suffocating tunnel. 'Let me scout ahead,' he told the others.

He slipped forward and gazed out into a large ice cavern, illuminated by no discernible source. It was empty, but he spied tunnels leading off in a dozen directions.

'What now?' asked Keja, crowding beside Giles.

Giles lined himself up with the tunnel back to the citadel and then said, 'That one,' indicating the largest tunnel to their left.

'As good as any,' the small thief said, shrugging. The tunnel was much like the earlier one, with icy walls, sometimes slippery patches of ice. Anji, unable to contain himself, ran at one particularly long stretch and slid the length of it. He would have done it again had not Petia chastised him.

For the others, it was an episode they wished to be quickly

over and as quickly forgotten. They plodded on, silent and alert. The sameness bored them and they prayed for escape from this underground of ice. For Giles, it was the worst experience of his life. He had to continually fight the feelings of suffocation, of having the walls close in on him. All his life had been spent on open ranges, in the mountains where he viewed thousands of square miles. Being able to reach out and touch the limits of his cold world wore heavily on him.

Hour followed hour, the monotony broken only by finding another empty cavern. There was no way to tell time, and at last, staggering with fatigue, Petie said, 'Giles, we've got to stop. I don't know if it's night or not. Anji is out on his feet, and I'm not much better.'

'When we reach the next cavern,' Giles replied. He didn't want to share his fears. If they kept moving, he could convince himself the ice walls wouldn't crush him. But to stop? He shivered. 'I keep hoping we'll find a stick of wood, anything to try to make a fire, but from what we've seen so far, that's only wishful thinking.'

When at last they reached a cavern, Petia sagged to the floor. 'We've got to keep each other warm,' she said.

Keja laughed. 'I've been trying to tell you that for ages, but you've always rebuffed me.'

Petia scowled at him as she lowered Anji to the floor. She fussed with his blanket, making sure that he was not sitting on the bare earth. She turned to find Keja sitting beside her, and said quietly, 'It would be best to have the boy between us so that he can draw warmth from both of us.' She moved to the opposite side of the boy, pulling her blanket around herself and Anji. She leaned wearily against the wall.

Giles checked the tunnels leading from this cavern before he, too, settled against the wall. He rested his head on his knees for a moment. It had been a tiring escape. No longer on the move, he felt the cold more keenly now – and his fears. If they got any sleep at all, it would be a restless one. He knew that they should keep watches, and started to say something. The others were already asleep, exhausted. Giles gave himself into the hands of the gods and closed his eyes.

He had no idea how long they slept. When they awoke, limbs stiff and knee joints protesting, it took several minutes to

417

orient themselves. Petia pulled out a few pitiful remnants of fruit, saying the words none wanted to hear. 'It's the only food we have.'

The Trans woman offered it to Giles, who refused. Keja looked at the rinds with some longing, then declined the offer, also. Anji ate what remained.

Giles grew restive. The claustrophobia began to work its terror on him once more. They moved on into the next tunnel and found it led to the inevitable empty cavern. Giles shook his head. 'I've lost my sense of direction. Might as well toss a coin, unless any of you has a better idea.' No one answered as Giles went to examine the tunnels leading onward.

A sudden, bitter wind issued forth from a tunnel to his left. Shards of icy crystals blew out into the room and swirled around the walls.

'Get your cloaks over your faces,' Petia yelled. 'The ice will slice our flesh to bloody ribbons.' She grabbed the edge of the blanket and flung her arm up to protect herself.

'At least someone has blood left. More than I can say for myself,' grumbled Keja.

Squinting, Giles tried to find the wind's source. For a moment, he saw nothing but the eddying ice. As it fell towards the floor, four creatures stepped out of the tunnel mouth.

'Ice demons!' Keja shouted.

Taller than humans and more massive, the creatures stood with icy legs planted firmly. They ranged themselves across the cavern. Their frozen torsos presented an excellent target, but long arms holding swords of ice told of their fighting prowess.

Giles drew his sword and handed it to Petia. 'Give me the halberd,' he yelled.

The monstrous creatures stood gazing at them from sockets without eyes. Although Giles knew sight was impossible, it was obvious that the demons knew exactly where the humans stood. Giles waded in.

The demons moved slowly but with a power no human could match. A blow from an ice sword would kill, but Giles easily avoided them. He swung the halberd at one demon's arm. The creature tried to pull the arm back, but Giles' shaft caught the ice sword and shattered it. Shards of ice dropped to the floor, but already Giles was swinging back the other way.

The shaft caught the demon's right arm below the shoulder. Giles watched in fascination as the arm fell to the floor and shattered. The creature plodded on, oblivious of missing sword and arm. Giles swept the halberd shaft low, catching the demon at the knee. He jerked hard; the leg came off. The demon toppled heavily to the floor and lay, scratching feebly with his remaining hand.

Keja, meantime, put his sword skills to good use. He ducked the swing of an ice sword and drove his sword point upward into the centre of the torso, aiming for what should have been a breastbone on a human opponent. A thin line started where the sword point hit, and quickly streaked down the centre of the demon's body from throat to groin. The creature took a step forward, but only half of its body moved. One side of the torso sheared neatly from the other and both sides crashed to the cavern floor.

Giles and Keja combined to slay the third ice demon while Petia raised her sword high and brought it down on the remaining ice demon's crown. The battle was over. The cavern floor was littered with blocks of ice, sparkling travesties of bodies which shed no blood.

'It feels good to be warm again,' Giles said, wiping sweat from his forehead.

'Giles, come here.' Anji had retreated across the cavern when the ice demons had appeared. Now he beckoned to Giles and the others. 'Come here, quick. Feel.'

'What are you talking about, Anji?' Giles asked.

'It's warm down this tunnel,' the boy said, pointing.

Giles held his palm out, but shook his head. 'I can't feel it, but then I'm sweating. You try, Petia.'

'Some warmth, but not much,' Petia said. 'What do you think is causing it?'

'I have no idea. It could be –' Swirling ice cut off Giles' words. Across the tunnel he saw the vortex created at the tunnel mouth. Hailstones filled the air. They flung their cloaks across their eyes for protection. The ice whipped the cavern once again, and Giles tried to shout against the rattle it created as it hit walls and floor.

'More ice demons,' he shouted. 'Quick. Down the tunnel. Petia and Anji first. Keja and I will hold them off.'

'No,' Petia shouted. 'I can fight, too.'

Giles spun her by the shoulder and shoved her down the tunnel. 'There will be more of them this time.'

Giles shuddered when he realised how right he was. Four shambled out, then four more, and a final four. They stood as if awaiting even more to bolster their ranks.

'Stay close to the tunnel mouth,' Giles yelled into Keja's ear. 'If they're too much for us, we retreat. There's only room for two side by side in there.'

The great creatures shuffled towards them. Giles shifted the halberd and charged. Keja followed immediately, aiming for the demon's sword arm.

Soon, shards of ice littered the floor and made their footing treacherously slippery. Giles put his years of combat experience to good use. First he used the haft to break the ice sword off, then swung quickly to fracture the creature's leg. Finally, a thrust would split the demon in two. Giles fell into fighting rhythm and, for him, the most dangerous part became getting out of the way when his opponent toppled. The ice demons backed away, giving Giles time to see how Keja fared.

The demons had forced the small man away from the tunnel mouth and backed him against the cavern wall. Two ice demons closed in for the kill, Keja swinging wildly in an attempt to slow them.

Giles attacked from behind. Against humans he might have shouted a warning, but against these moving blocks of magically animated ice he had no such compunction.

Keja, relieved of one opponent, dealt with the other. Splinters of ice showered the room as he hacked at any limbs he could reach. Pieces of the demon fell to the floor as Keja whittled him down to size.

The ice demons retreated from such ferocity. Giles gave a battle cry and brandished his weapon at them. They moved even further away. But he became too cocky. He slipped on the icy floor and yelped in pain as he pulled a muscle in his groin. Gritting his teeth, Giles planted the halberd and pulled himself erect. The creatures sensed weakness and closed in again.

'Keja, can you take over?' Giles shouted.

Keja slipped and slid to Giles' side. 'What's the matter?' he yelled, as he slashed at the oncoming ice demon.

'Hurt. Better retreat into the tunnel,' he said. 'There isn't as much room to move around, but they'll only be able to attack us two at a time.'

Giles limped towards the tunnel entrance.

Keja slashed once more at the oncoming creature, then followed into the tunnel.

The ice demons hesitated, then two lumbered forward. The sword tip of the leading ice demon found its mark, scoring Keja's left shoulder. The young thief leaped backward, clapping a hand to the injured spot.

Behind him, Giles massaged the aching groin muscle, willing it to stop hurting. He realised he'd have to fight wounded or they'd both die.

Lifting his weapon, he said to Keja, 'Step behind me.'

Keja retreated, moving around Giles in the narrow passage. He massaged the shoulder, which burned like fire.

The ice demons plodded after them. Giles rushed forward to meet another demon, holding his halberd high to strike with the cutting edge. Before the creature could recover, Giles thrust three times at the crystal blue neck. Ice chips flew back in his eyes, but he kept thrusting until the creature's head fell from its shoulders. It stumbled blindly into the wall and collapsed.

Another took its place, but Giles and Keja retreated fifty feet down the tunnel. Petia and Anji had rounded a corner and were safely beyond their sight. The two men watched in silence, catching their breaths as the demon lumbered forward. Just as they prepared for another fight, it stopped and looked from side to side.

Giles leaned on his halberd, watching in bewilderment.

Water dripped from the creature's arms and body, puddling on to the floor. The demon looked at its feet, perplexed. It turned slowly and made its way back along the tunnel.

Giles and Keja heaved sighs of relief.

But why had the ice demon started to melt? They hurried down the tunnel to find the answer to this unexpected rescue.

Seven

GILES CLAPPED Keja on the shoulder. 'We've done it, they're going for good.'

Keja fingered the sore spot on his shoulder. 'I don't think it was us so much as the warmth of the tunnel,' he said.

They found Petia and Anji crouched around a corner, awaiting the outcome of the encounter. 'Did you kill them?' Anji asked, eyes shining with excitement.

'The heat did it,' Giles answered. 'Let's find where it's coming from. If it's a volcanic firepit under the mountains, we might be worse off than fighting ice demons.'

The tunnel became warmer as they walked along. Eventually they removed their blanket cloaks. The ice walls dripped and refroze, creating a clear, glazed surface that glistened in the wan light.

The tunnel sloped downward and Keja commented on it. 'We won't find a way out if we're heading for some volcanic centre,' he said.

'At the moment I don't care,' Giles replied. 'I want to find the source of the heat and get thoroughly warm. If we have to turn around later, then we will. And we need to look at your shoulder. Your tunic is ugly where the demon's sword touched you. I'm almost afraid to see what's under your shirt.'

At last they stopped for a rest. Petia sagged to the floor on one side of the tunnel and Anji collapsed beside her.

'What's that?' Anji asked, cupping his ear with a hand.

'I don't hear anything,' Giles replied. He looked at Petia to see if she sensed danger. Petia shook her head.

'What do you think it is, Anji?' Giles asked. 'Your hearing must be better than ours.'

'I don't know. Just a noise. It's a faint and a long way off. I can't make it out.'

Giles looked around and shivered – and not from the cold. His fear of enclosed places heightened again. The idea of some unknown beast lurking in a dark side tunnel filled him with almost uncontrollable fear. The old veteran fought this inner battle and won, more for the sake of the others than himself.

They depended on his coolness in combat. He didn't dare let them down now.

'Let's go on – cautiously.' He motioned and they rose to continue.

In a short while they turned a corner and they all heard the sound. They continued on, stopping from time to time to listen intently.

Giles looked puzzled. 'There's the sound of metal,' he said, shaking his head. 'But something else, too.'

Anji looked up with a grin. 'It's singing – or someone trying to sing.'

As they moved closer, the sounds became louder and clearer. Giles made out the melody of a song which had been popular during the War, a song not about war, but about the ladies. He smiled as he remembered some of the words. Whoever was singing did not remember the words, only the melody, and that not very well. They would hear a phrase, then a pause and the clang of metal, then the singing would resume for another half line.

'It's a smith. I'd bet my life,' Giles said.

'What do we do now?' asked Keja.

'We can go on and discover who this fellow is or we can turn and retreat,' Giles answered. 'I'm for finding out, and for getting warm. This is the source of the heat that held back the ice demons. Maybe we can even talk the smith out of a meal.'

'What if it's not human?' Petia asked. 'Have you considered that it might be a dwarf? They're as famous for mining and smithing as they are for hating humans – and Trans. We might be in greater danger than we were back in Onyx's citadel.'

'Caution is the word, Petia,' Giles said, feeling as if he wanted to throw all caution to the gods and rush out of the tunnel. 'With all the noise the fellow is making, we should be able to get a peek at him without him seeing us. If it's a dwarf, we'll turn back.'

They crept along, making as little noise as possible. The tunnel widened, and they felt the force of the heat from the forge fire. They hesitated. The anvil seemed to be around the corner to the right, unless the acoustics of the place played strange tricks.

They moved forward again, and at last looked down a circular staircase. Giles gestured for silence and placed each foot carefully as he negotiated the metal stairs.

The smith was human, tall and well proportioned with muscles that rippled and sweaty arms like the trunks of small trees. Long, grey hair that had once been black hung down his back.

He lifted the hammer and brought it down on the sword blade he fashioned. Sparks flew from the red-hot piece; the smith raised the hammer and struck again. Between blows his voice rang out, sometimes grunting, sometimes repeating a few bars of the song. At every blow the man changed key, as if he had never learned to carry a tune properly. Tone deaf, from the noise of his trade perhaps, Giles thought.

Keja, Petia and Anji followed Giles down the hand-crafted stairs and now peered around him to see into the smithy.

The smith held up the ragged blade and studied it, plunged it into the coals of the fire, then returned it to his anvil. Again the hammer rose and fell, shaping the metal, thinning its edge, working in the essence of sharpness that would later be honed into perfection.

There was beauty in the man's work and his own satisfaction with it. Occasionally, his face turned to the side so that the companions could see it. They saw delight in the smith's creation, a bit of smugness that things went well, and above all, contentment.

For a final time, the smith held the blade aloft and examined it critically. He held it out from him and sighted down its fiery length. He gave two final taps of the hammer, almost love taps, and plunged the blade into a barrel of water. Steam billowed into the room as the smith placed his hammer atop the anvil and picked up a towel begrimed with charcoal.

From behind the towel, his deep voice growled at them.

424

'Well, don't just stand there, come in and keep me company the while.'

Giles stepped into the room. 'How did you know we were here? You never turned around.' Perhaps the man's hearing wasn't as bad as Giles had suspected.

'When you've spent as much time alone as I have, you can always tell when someone else is near,' the smith replied. His huge hands cleared shavings of metal from a bench and several tools. He gestured. 'Sit, sit. You must be tired. You've come a long way from the citadel.'

While the four of them sat, turning to the forge fire and soaking up its warmth, the smith bustled around the room. He hung his worn leather apron from a hook on the wall, and wandered out of the room.

Giles watched him go. A puzzled expression crossed his face. 'I know this man,' Giles said. 'I feel I've seen him somewhere in my wanderings. Can't remember where.'

Several minutes later the smith returned, carrying a board covered with apples and cheese, a thick, round loaf of bread, and bowls of steaming stew.

Using one foot, he pulled a stool over and placed the banquet board down on it. 'Eat, eat,' he said. 'There's plenty of time for talk later.'

When they had finished their first real meal in what had to be two days, the smith cleared it away and returned with goblets and a pitcher of wine. He poured, sprinkled spice, then thrust a poker into the fire and quickly mulled each of the goblets.

Giles settled back and lit his pipe. Wreathed in a cloud of smoke he waited for the inevitable questions.

'You've escaped from my Lord Onyx, then?' the smith began. 'He's a cruel one, my lord is. By the way, I'm Bellisar.'

Giles introduced Petia, Anji and Keja, then sat back to let Bellisar continue.

'It's a favourite trick of his, you know, to let prisoners escape down the tunnel. He lets the ice demons do his dirty work for him. The tunnels are tricky, as you no doubt learned. It's only sheer luck you've found me.'

'We were attacked by ice demons twice,' Giles said. 'We fought them off, and Anji found the tunnel leading here. But I don't think we were *allowed* to escape, we worked hard at it.

Onyx won't be pleased since we still have something he wants.'

'Ah,' the huge man sighed. 'You were something more than criminals exiled into the tunnels, then. Well, you can thank the lad for discovering the warm tunnel. Smart boy. Got your wits about you, haven't you?' He beamed at Anji, and the boy responded in kind.

'But what of you?' Giles asked. 'I've heard of communities of dwarves living underground, mining, smelting, smithing. But you were a surprise. When we saw a human pounding away, we thought our senses had left us.'

The smith looked keenly from face to face. 'You three certainly were caught up in the Trans War. Perhaps not the boy. Giles, you would have been involved longest. Beggin' your pardon, Petia and Keja, but you're too young to have endured it for many years. The gods be thanked it finally ended.'

'Not so,' Petia interrupted. 'You have no idea. I was only a five-year-old Trans kid when the War broke out. I may not have fought, but that doesn't mean I escaped the War. I'd rather not talk about it. You wouldn't like the stories.'

A look of anguish crossed Bellisar's face. 'My apologies, lady. Those of us who went off to fight came home with a peculiar view of what happened elsewhere. I'm sincerely sorry.'

He paused, gazing into the fire, then went on. 'I don't like to talk about it, either. I was sick of it by the time the War ended. There were battles – Kelter Plain, Malden, Chevin – where I saw men die by the hundreds, bodies piled up, and a stench you could smell for miles. I reeled away, retching, more than once. Never got used to it.

'When it was over, I tried to settle down. Various places along the Nerulta coast. All I found was the constant pettiness of man. Lord Onyx saw my work and liked it. He's an evil man, no question of that, but insidiously perceptive. He examined my soul, so to speak, and offered me the only position I couldn't refuse: all my needs taken care of and a place where I no longer had to deal with people. I didn't even stop to consider.'

'And now you spend your time hidden underground, forging

426

more weapons,' Giles mused. 'Weapons kill people, or have you forgotten already, Bellisar?'

Bellisar gave Giles a black look. 'Don't preach to me, old man. I know what I do, but I'm beyond caring. If I don't provide a sword, someone else will. My pleasure lies in creating works of functional art.'

Bellisar reached behind him and took from the wall a polished sword. He placed a cloth across his lap and laid the weapon reverently on it. The guard was of filigreed silver and the hilt intricately engraved. The pommel had been fashioned in the figure of a raven's head. Along the blade in Granarian script ran the quotation from Tenera I, judged guilty by his court and sentenced to death: 'Is this justice, and in a rightful cause? Then I answer, yes.'

Cryptic questions, Giles thought. I hope that whoever owns the sword thinks on them before using the weapon.

'Onyx's invitation allows me to create. No one has been given such time and materials as I have. I've perfected a new steel process, and I make weapons that are *art*. It is my hope that they will live after me. Be not so harsh on me, old man. It tells too much of your own thoughts.'

Silence filled the room. Was this smith, Bellisar, the enemy? Or had he only taken the first opportunity to escape from a world he no longer fitted into?

He's right. Who am I, Giles thought, to question him? But since Bellisar was Onyx's man, could they expect any help from him, even the barest information?

The smith refilled their goblets. Giles returned from his thoughts when Bellisar resumed his seat and said. 'Now it's your turn. Tell me of yourselves.'

They took turns giving him their backgrounds. Bellisar nodded often as Giles told of his long years at war. He understood. His eyes held true sadness when Petia related how the War had affected her, the loss of her husband, her indenture by her mother for a paltry few coins, her escape from Segrinn's father, Ambrose, and turning to thievery.

Keja actually made him laugh a time or two with tales of his roguery, but afterwards Bellisar realised that the man had revealed nothing of his own ancestry or childhood. He simply nodded as Anji told about his life as a Bandanarran slave until his rescue by Petia. 'Exactly,' Bellisar murmured. 'From people like these I am able to exclude myself.

'Why did you come to Khelora?' he asked when they had finished.

Giles looked from one to the other. Petia frowned and shook her head negatively. Keja shrugged and studied the weapons hung about the wall.

'Have you heard of the Gate of Paradise?' Giles asked, making the final decision. They had revealed much of themselves to this solitary man. Giles had the gut feeling that they would not go wrong revealing their quest, too.

'Of course. You're after the key.' The big smith brought his palm down on his knee. 'I should have guessed.'

Jaws dropped and they stared at Bellisar in amazement.

'The key,' Bellisar mused. 'You're as discontented as I was before coming into the tunnels. Can't any of you find peace in your lives? Do you think you'll find peace behind those gates? I doubt you will.'

Petia spoke up. 'Whatever I find behind those gates will be small repayment for what has been done to me. I'll find a better life for Anji and myself. The War may be over but we Trans are still treated like garbage. Money will buy us respect. It may be only to our faces, but I don't care what happens behind our backs. Anji will have an education and I'll have some security for what remains of my life.'

'Let us hope,' Bellisar murmured.

'I like the challenge,' Keja said. 'I've seen more in the last couple of years than I ever dreamed of. I've stayed out of gaol, thanks to Giles more than anyone. But this is not thievery for small coin. The reward is immense and the adventure, while it hasn't always been fun, will be something to tell my grandchildren about.' He laughed quietly. 'Providing I ever stand still long enough to find a wife and have the luck to sire a child. They say that children have to come before you can have grandchildren.

'If I have none, then I will spin tall tales in taverns and live to the end of my days a hero!'

Giles listened with as much interest as Bellisar did. They had started the quest for the keys two years ago with little discussion. They had neither found the time nor had the inclination to discuss their reasons since then. They had simply plunged on, with only the keys as a goal. Interesting answers, Giles thought. Revealing. He would have to think about this some more. But now it was his turn, he realised, as Bellisar turned towards him.

'I'm somewhat like Keja,' he said. He skipped over his military career, relating only a few of his experiences, told of the death of his wife and children, and his own dissatisfaction with life after the War. 'This has become a quest, and I'm afraid that the quest has become more important than the result. Truth to tell, I don't know what will happen when we find the final key and go to open the Gate.'

Giles puffed thoughtfully. 'It will be all over, won't it?' He asked the question as if only now realising the answer. And what then?

'I think I understand,' Bellisar said. 'Probably better than you. In your own way you're doing the same thing I am: turning your back on society. I've hidden, you've run off on the great adventure. A boy again, playing a more dangerous game. Do you have any of the other keys?'

'Four of them. This is the final one,' Keja blurted, and blanched at Giles' scowl.

'What if I told you that the final gold key had been melted down? That I did it myself?'

'Nooo!' Keja wailed.

'You're lying,' Giles said. 'Onyx told us that he had the final key. He wanted us to exchange our four for our lives. That's why we ran.'

Bellisar held his right hand in the air. 'I swear. I melted it down right there.' He pointed at the forge fire. 'Later I made it into the medallion Onyx wears around his neck. You must have seen it. It's his little joke, tells you something about his humour.'

Giles jumped up and paced. 'It can't be. We've come too far. No, I won't believe it. If it were true, why would Onyx want our keys? They'd be no good to him without the fifth one.'

He stopped and stared at the others. Their eyes held a stricken look, and Giles knew that they did not want to believe any more than he did. They had been through so much together.

Maybe too much.

Then he clapped his hands together. 'Of course!' he cried. 'You're a devil, Bellisar. You made a copy of the key before melting the gold one down. Come on, confess.'

The smith threw back his head and roared with laughter. When he could breathe again, he gasped, 'You're a clever one, old man. I wish I had known you during the War. Indeed, that's exactly what happened. The gold key is now Onyx's medallion. But he took a steel key of my own making, a duplicate of the golden one.'

'So, in spite of all, there is a final key.'

'Yes,' Bellisar replied. 'For all the good that does you. Are you happy now?'

'We're happier now than we were a few minutes ago,' Giles said. 'At least there's still hope of finding it – if we ever find our way out of this forsaken mountain.'

'It's not so bad,' said Bellisar.

'How you can stand it down here?' Keja asked. 'Alone, no one to talk to. If I were in your place, my own thoughts would drive me crazy.'

'I'm content. Must every man be alike? Then it would be a dull world. Besides, I sing the old songs. I love to sing.'

'Yes, we know,' Petia murmured, but Bellisar went on, not hearing her.

'I have much to think on. I packed more into my life than it would seem from my age. I am grateful to be away from people, although I must say I am enjoying your visit. It's been years since I had unannounced visitors, other than a few criminals and the occasional foolish ice demon. Neither lasts for long near my forge.'

Giles sat down again. 'We can hope again. But the map is no good now. The duplicate key is obviously no longer where the map shows it.'

'May I see it?' Bellisar asked. Giles pulled it from his tunic and handed it to the burly smith.

He unfolded it carefully and laid it across his lap. With a grimy finger he traced places that he had nearly forgotten from his days on the surface of the land. The thick finger edged up the page, stopping for a moment here and there as Bellisar smiled at some remembered incident. At last he

430

stopped. 'I don't see any mark. Where do you think the key is hidden?'

Giles pointed to a spot north of the Adversary Mountains.

Bellisar thought, looking up from time to time to stare into space, then returning to the spot. Finally he shook his head. 'The key is not there, I can guarantee that. I heard Lord Onyx murmur something about the Mountains of the Lions. And this' – he jabbed it with his finger for emphasis – 'is nowhere near the Mountains of the Lions.'

'Where are these mountains?' Giles asked, not expecting an answer.

'Somewhere in this area.' The finger jabbed again. 'There are two immense peaks. If viewed from the right spot, you can see the outline of two lions, lying down and facing each other. I'm told it is a magnificent sight. The mountains go up and up and your eye follows them. And there on the heights, splendid in their majesty, are two lions couchant.' Bellisar sighed, as if considering how isolated his life had become. 'It would be like Onyx to hide the key there, guarded by two such regal animals. It would appeal to his twisted sense of humour.'

'You don't know the exact area, then?' Petia prompted.

'No, only what I heard Onyx say. For all I know it could lie between the paws of one or the other. And there is a pass between them. Now, don't go running off all excited. I only said that by way of example. I truly don't know, my lady.'

'Onyx may have said that in your hearing only to conceal the real hiding place, so that even you, should you decide to go looking, wouldn't know where it was truly hidden.'

'Yes, I suppose that's so,' Bellisar replied, rubbing the harsh stubble on his chin. 'Never gave it much thought. What good would only one key do? Even if I were interested?'

Bellisar glanced at an hour candle burning in one corner of the room. 'Ah, best we be making some preparations. Up with you.'

The companions stared at him for a moment, but he heaved himself from his chair. 'Come on, come on, they'll be here shortly.'

Shock struck the four. 'Who?' they echoed with one voice.

'Guards. Every week they bring supplies. Today is the day, this is the hour, and you wouldn't want to be found, would

431

you? You'd be dragged back to Onyx. I gather that's one thing you wouldn't like.'

The four shot out of their chairs. 'Where can we hide?'

'Don't get upset,' Bellisar cautioned. 'There's no problem, if you can stay quiet. No sneezes now.' He pointed towards a ladder made of small tree trunks. The limbs had been trimmed, but the bark had been left. It led upward onto a platform in one corner of the cavern.

'I like to sleep there, near my forge fire. Keeps me warm. You just climb up there, crawl under the skins I use for covers and try not to sneeze. And no giggling, either, young man.' He mussed Anji's hair and swatted him on the bottom to hurry him along. 'I'll call you after they've gone.'

As he waited at the bottom of the ladder, Giles watched Bellisar pull the skin curtain aside and leave the room. He wondered what lay beyond this room, and, not for the first time, whether the man could be trusted. Their lives were now in his hands.

There were skins aplenty on the platform, and more than enough room for the four of them. They pulled the skins over them, and immediately realised that they were going to have a sweaty time of it. The heat and smoke from the forge fire rose to the ceiling of the cavernous room and hung there, dissipating slowly through a tiny vent hole.

'Petia, I'm hot,' Anji whispered.

'Quiet. A day back you were complaining of the cold. And remember, no sneezes.'

Giles heard Bellisar's voice from beyond the curtain. 'Come in and sit where it's warm.' Had they been lulled into a false sense of security by the smith? Were they about to be sold out? After all, Lord Onyx had brought Bellisar here and was, nominally at least, his ruler. What loyalties did Bellisar have to the man in black?

From all Giles could discern, Bellisar owed his very existence to Onyx.

Giles' pounding heart slowed when he heard the guards speak. They sounded like the lowliest recruits, assigned to the job because of their newness. They told Bellisar the latest news from the citadel and warned him to watch for a group of four 'very dangerous' people who had escaped into the ice tunnels.

432

When the guards had gone, Bellisar called the four down, and laid out more food and drink for them. He laughed when Giles told him that he had suspected that they were about to be turned over to the guards.

'Why should I do that?' Bellisar asked. 'I care nothing about what Onyx does, or you four, either, for that matter. I am my own man, doing what I enjoy doing.'

'For your sake, I hope that it always remains so. I trust Onyx no farther than I could throw him.'

'Then you might look over your shoulder for his guards when you leave my forge,' Bellisar said, walking to his anvil and picking up the heavy hammer. Giles jumped a foot when the smith smashed it down onto the hard surface.

Eight

'ARE YOU saying we'll be going into a trap?' asked Giles Grimsmate.

Bellisar shrugged. He pumped the bellows a few times, and watched the coals come to life. 'Nothing's safe within these ice caves. You know that. All I want's to be left alone.' He thrust a bar of metal into it, then turned to Anji. 'How'd you like a knife all your own, young fellow?' he asked, and nodded at the smile that lit the boy's face.

Giles studied the smith and wondered at his intentions. Then the grey-haired man's thoughts turned gloomier still. He had to face the end of their quest. Only he knew that only one would be allowed through the Gate of Paradise; the runic inscription on it told this. What of Keja and Petia and Anji then? Giles felt a dozen years older in that instant, almost unwilling to continue the path he now followed. When he had told

Bellisar that the road meant more than the goal, he'd meant it.

Life, since the War, since the death of his beloved wife and children, had been a concatenation of barely endurable days. Seeking the keys to the Gate had brought back a vitality to his arthritic limbs. Giles didn't kid himself into believing he felt as good as he had twenty years earlier, but he felt a little better than he had for some time.

The final key would rob him of even this. The thrill of the hunt would be gone. And a decision had to be made concerning entry into Paradise. The weight of years slumped his shoulders even more with that thought.

'Giles, look!' exclaimed Anji, holding the shiny blade forged by Bellisar. 'Never have I seen one so fine.'

'Nor I,' said Giles, looking at the knife but not taking it from the boy. He remembered his own first knife and knew Anji would be loath to part with it for even an instant. 'Best get some hide to wrap the handle.'

'A moment, then,' said Bellisar. Bellisar bustled through the curtain and returned with his arms full. He tossed Anji a cut strip of hide. The boy sank down and began winding it about the knife handle. To Giles, Bellisar said, 'You can't stay here, but I can't send you off without food.'

'It's time for us to go,' Giles agreed. 'But we can't take the food. It will leave you short of supplies for the coming week.'

Bellisar dumped the food on the table. 'Nonsense,' he bellowed. 'You ever hear of fasting? It's good for one with a bloated belly like mine. The body gets too accustomed to being filled. Deprive it once in a while, show it who's boss.'

Giles looked at the smith and failed to find even a hint of fat anywhere on his muscular body.

'We'd be grateful,' Petia said, shooting a dark look at Giles. She fetched her pouch and began to pack the food.

'Thank you, Bellisar. But even more than the food, we could use directions out of this godforsaken mountain.'

Bellisar fetched a piece of paper and the stub of a crude pencil. On one side of the paper was a drawing of a beautiful weapon. Bellisar drew a large X across it. 'It wasn't a good design,' he said. He closed his eyes for a second and his head bobbed and turned as he mentally traced a route through the complicated tunnel system.

Finally satisfied, he opened his eyes and began to draw. 'This will get you to an exit on the west of the mountain. But there are several tricky parts. See here . . .' For the next fifteen minutes he went over his drawing, describing certain places carefully, and occasionally writing notes with arrows drawn to the points where special care must be taken. Finished, he looked to Giles for any questions. Seeing none, he rose and tugged on the bellows rope, bringing the forge fire to life and preparing for another day at his solitary craft.

Giles rose and fetched his pouch. Keja nodded behind Bellisar's back and mouthed, 'I don't trust him. It's too easy. Why should he give us a route away from our enemy, who also happens to be his lord?'

Giles shrugged and touched Petia's arm. He nodded toward Bellisar.

Petia closed her eyes, concentrating on any emotions emanating from the smith. She found only delight at beginning a day's work at a task the man truly enjoyed. Bellisar had already dismissed them from his thoughts. His work, whether craft or art, was all that was on his mind.

Petia shook her head at Giles and motioned that they should depart.

The twisting tunnels and dim light had long ago confused them. They gave their trust to the map and Bellisar's notes and only once did they come to a juncture which gave them pause. They debated the meaning of the note, and finally agreed which tunnel to follow. Keja, only partly trusting the map, made a large X on the cavern wall in case they had to retrace their steps.

When they grew tired, they slept, keeping watches. But time ceased to have meaning. For Giles, after it became apparent that Bellisar's route avoided the ice demons' lairs, all that existed was the gnawing fear of the tight tunnels. At last the light became brighter, the tunnel walls changed gradually from ice to solid rock, and they knew that they were nearing the exit. They emerged blinking into a mid-morning sun reflecting from a valley. Immediately below them the snow slope was darkened by the shadow cast from the mountain at their backs.

Giles muttered, 'At last.' He didn't quite run out into the freedom offered by the valley, but the pressure lifted from him and he allowed himself to relax for the first time in what seemed an eternity.

Three days later the companions followed a rapidly descending river valley to a broad plain. They saw the river rushing in many directions and finding its own pleasure in carving myriad paths through the gravel surface. It was a strange delta-like vista, several miles across, and Giles wondered how close they were to the coast.

They staggered, leg-weary, onto the river bed. Logs lay scattered, torn up by the roots and brought down from the slopes above by previous spring floods. They sat and rested.

Giles pulled out his maps. He folded the sketchy map that Bellisar had drawn and was about to toss it away when he thought better of it and slipped it back inside his tunic. The other he flattened onto his lap.

'Is this where we turn north?' Keja asked.

'I've been giving that some thought. I wonder if we should reconsider,' Giles said.

'What? Give up?' Petia glared at Giles, and Keja leaped to his feet.

'You misunderstand. The more I think about it, the more I'm convinced that the key isn't in the Mountains of the Lions. We know that Onyx retrieved the original, the one Bellisar melted down. Now, I believe Bellisar when he says he made a duplicate. I don't think Onyx would take that back to the mountains.'

'Why wouldn't he?' Keja asked, finally sitting down again.

'He obviously knew that we had the other keys. He told us so and wanted to bargain our lives in exchange for them. He knew about the Callant Hanse, Bandanarra, everything. I don't know if he's a god or not, even a minor one. But he has immense powers. That is unquestionable.'

'So?' A 'prove it' tone tinged Petia's question. 'Why does this convince you that the final key isn't where Bellisar says?'

'Think about it,' Giles said. 'If you had found the key, would you put it back in the same place? Might not someone have a map, like we do, and come looking for it? I'd hide it somewhere else so nobody could find it if they had the map.'

'So where would he hide it?' Keja asked.

'Ah, good question, Keja. Where would he hide it? He knew that we would come looking for it. He intended to capture us and bargain for our four keys. He knew we'd all have to travel to Callant Hanse if we agreed. He'd have his own key, the fifth, somewhere close by.'

'At Callant Hanse?' asked Keja.

'Somewhere in the citadel?' Petia suggested.

'Exactly,' Giles said. 'At least, that's what I think. Why don't we stop here for the rest of today and tonight? You three think about it and see if you can tell me where I'm wrong. If you persuade me I am, we head north. Otherwise, we have to head back to the citadel.'

The others agreed and each of them spent the afternoon alone. Keja and Anji had their knives out, Keja whittling sticks away to nothingness, and Anji concentrating on his first attempt to carve with his new knife. Petia, tired of sitting, paced along one path of the river. She threw rocks, trying to fathom answers in the showers of water that splashed up.

By morning they had come to agree with Giles. Keja glanced at Petia, who nodded. 'You're right, Giles. Nothing else makes sense. But what do we do now?'

'Follow the river. Down to the delta, find a boat and sail to a sea town and do our planning there. Even with the map, I'm not absolutely sure I know where we are.'

They set off, braving the frigid spray from the river. Only when night fell did they stop to rest. Warmed by the fire and with food in their stomachs, all felt better.

'Petia,' Anji said nervously. 'Are there huge dogs over there?' He gestured with his head.

'Wolves,' she told him. 'I sensed them earlier today, but now it looks like they're getting bolder. We'll have to be careful tonight.' She raised her voice. 'Giles, wolves approach.'

Giles looked up from staring into the fire and brooding. 'They won't give us any trouble if we have the fire and keep watches. They're interesting animals, have a society of their

437

own. Look at them pacing back and forth. They're curious, but unless they're absolutely ravenous, they won't attack us.'

'What makes you think so?' Keja asked. He moved closer to the fire, hand on his knife. Keja preferred the city – and its human wolves.

'I've had some experience with them. On Bericlere during the War.'

'By the gods, is there anything you haven't done or experienced?' Keja asked. 'You must be a thousand years old.'

'I feel like it,' Giles said glumly. 'I'm getting too old for these adventures. I wish they'd end. It's too late now, but I could give you a good argument for leaving this search for the last key until spring.'

'That doesn't sound like the Giles we know,' Petia said. 'What's bothering you?'

'Sorry, Petia. I'm tired and getting old, and I don't feel like wandering any more. What are we doing out here, anyway? Wading through water, fighting ice demons, running from some black lord. For what? Some wealth hidden behind gates on another continent. Why don't we just go home and take up thievery with style?' Giles hunkered down before the fire and warmed his hands.

'You don't mean that,' Keja said. 'Tell me you don't. Not after everything we've gone through to come this far.'

Giles sighed. 'I don't know, Keja. Ask me again in the morning.' He turned to warm his backside.

Petia looked at Keja and shook her head. Turning to Giles, she said, 'Meantime, O downcast one, what are we going to do about the wolves? It's too dark to see them any longer, but they're prowling out there. You may have had some experience with them, but I haven't. And remember, Anji and I are part cat. They make us uncomfortable.'

'How many are there?' Giles asked.

'About a dozen, I think. Four or five big ones and some smaller ones.'

'Probably two families running together, with cubs. We'll watch tonight and keep the fire built up. No sleeping, not even nodding off. Wolves are discerning. They know when you're not on watch and they can attack swiftly. Keep a burning brand close to hand. They don't like fire. Not at all.'

'Something else's out there,' Anji said. 'To the left and upstream.'

Petia looked at him, disconcerted that he was aware of something she had missed. Her thoughts had been elsewhere. Now she concentrated, facing upstream and closing her eyes. 'Anji's right,' she said. 'There are deer grazing up along the bank. They've come out of the forest into a clearing.'

'Can you influence them?' Giles asked. 'If you can steer them down to where the wolves can pick up their scent, we wouldn't have to worry about ending up as wolf meat.'

'I can't communicate with animals, but I'll try, no guarantees.'

The others remained silent while Petia put her empathic powers to work. Giles and the others watched, wondering what went on in Petia's mind at a time like this. They were puzzled when, after a long time, Petia turned her face in an entirely different direction. At last her body relaxed, her rigid concentration ebbing away.

'Well?' Keja asked.

'I don't know. At first the deer became uneasy when my emotions empathically touched theirs, but soon they settled back to browsing. I think they may be heading this way, but I can't tell whether they'll come within scent of the wolves. We'd better post watches to be safe, Giles.'

Giles nodded. 'What else is out there, Petia? We saw your head turn and look in a different direction.'

'I don't know. I can't tell if it's human or animal, if it's intelligent or not. Something's out there, but it's not moving. But not thinking, almost as if it can't.'

'Another good reason for keeping watch. Is it moving?'

'It's not doing anything. Or they aren't, oh, it's all confusing. I can't tell if it's one or a dozen.' Petia shook her head in desperation.

'Don't worry about it,' Giles said. 'We know it's out there, whatever it is. We'll be extra careful.' He turned and checked the wood supply that Keja had gathered. 'Looks like plenty for the night. Wolves still pacing?'

Petia peered off into the dark, as if trying to penetrate the blackness that lay outside the firelight. In a moment, she nodded. 'Yes, although one has gone off. Let's hope it's to investigate some faint scent. Like deer, maybe. I've always said that venison is much tastier than human flesh.'

Keja made a disgusting face. 'Petia, do you have to?'

Giles chuckled. 'Don't you agree with her, Keja? I do.' He threw a few more sticks of wood onto the fire, and laid one stick carefully so that only one end would burn. It was a brand to pick up quickly in case of attack. 'I'm for sleep. Keja, take the first watch.'

For once in his life, Keja stayed fully alert during his watch. Sometimes he had been known to nod off, but tonight he determined that wolves and some other unknown were enough to keep him alert. He tended the fire and thought about Giles, how the man seemed to be growing older and tireder with every passing day. He wondered if they would ever collect all the keys. Keja snorted. Beyond that, he didn't want to think about the Gate of Paradise and the hardships of reaching it.

These thoughts disturbed him, and he turned to daydreaming of settling down with his hard-earned wealth and entertaining the ladies in a respectable manner. He'd own his own house, dress fashionably, serve special wines and rare viands. A stable with beautiful horses, perhaps even a carriage. A respected gentleman of the town, that's what he'd be.

He added wood to the fire and stepped beyond its light to peer into the darkness. Staring upstream, he saw nothing but the blackness of the sky and a star or two where the clouds parted. He turned and cupped his ears in the direction of the wolves. He heard nothing.

Turning downstream, he was startled to see dancing light motes against the night sky. A column of sparks erupted skyward, and Keja knew a fire similar to their own burned. He grew uneasy and spent the rest of his watch staring downstream. He still faced that direction when Petia relieved him.

She came up to him and touched his arm. Keja pointed and Petia hoisted herself up on the log for a better look. 'I don't feel any danger in that direction. Probably natives. They're not hostile, I'm sure.'

'Should we wake Giles?' Keja asked.

'I don't think so. He was so tired tonight. And depressed. I'm worried about him, Keja.'

'I was thinking about that earlier tonight. Maybe we should wait until spring.'

'No matter, for the moment,' Petia said. 'Let's not wake him. Soon enough when he takes his watch. I don't think we're in any danger. But we'd better be on our way again in the morning.' She shuddered. 'Wolves, and humans, and something else. How do we get into these situations?'

But Keja was already wrapped in his cloak. Within minutes Petia heard his snores. She sat staring, wondering, beginning to fear what lay out there awaiting them.

Nine

DAYLIGHT CLIMBED slowly over the mountains they had left several days before. The dawn showed little of the alluvial plain, but to the west Giles saw morning light reflecting from the sea.

Petia had told him about the fires farther downstream, but he saw no sign now.

'Giles, I'm not easy with this place. Let's go now.' Petia's earnestness convinced Giles.

As Giles turned, four tall, young men stood with drawn bows in their hands and four arrows aimed directly at Giles' chest. He turned to grab the halberd stuck in the river's sand and saw four more of the natives standing to his left. On his right were four more.

Giles dropped his hands and said, 'Wake up, Keja. Petia.' He kicked them. 'Come up easy. We have company.'

Keja rolled, caught in his cloak, straining his neck, and saw

441

the natives and their weapons. He waved half-heartedly, hoping the men would not take his gesture as threatening. He disentangled himself and sat up.

'I didn't do a very good job of standing watch,' Giles said. 'Or these people are good stalkers. I didn't hear a thing. Better wake Anji.'

A middle-aged man stepped forward, motioning them to stand in a line facing him so that they would have their backs to the arrows. The natives had the advantage, Giles admitted ruefully. He still didn't understand how they had been able to sneak up without his hearing. 'You *are* getting old,' he muttered to himself.

The older man spoke. 'So Lord Onyx now sends spies to dog the Brada. Do the steel warriors follow in your footsteps?'

Keja, always quick to take offence, stepped forward. 'We weren't sent by Onyx. We're not spies and we don't know anything about any steel warriors.'

The man gestured slightly; Keja winced at the arrowpoint in the middle of his back. He stepped away cautiously.

Giles warned him to control his tongue, and said to the leader. 'We're not from Onyx. In fact, we escaped from him and fled through the ice tunnels.'

'You lie!' the man snapped. 'No one escaped from Lord Onyx – not through the ice tunnels. The ice demons would get you.'

'But we did escape,' Giles said. He was determined to keep secret Bellisar's assistance. 'What are Brada?'

The man drew himself up, and Giles saw that the others stiffened as well. 'We are Brada,' the leader hit his chest with a closed fist. 'We will not be harassed by Onyx. You will come with us, but first we will tie your hands. You must not escape and tell Lord Onyx of us.'

He gestured to the four young men on his right. They stepped forward, pulled the arms of the companions behind them and bound them with rawhide thongs. When they were bound, the leader pointed for others to pick up the captives' packs. They set off at a brisk pace.

'What are we going to do, Giles?' Petia asked between breaths.

'Wait. They're obviously taking us to their leader. We've got

442

to convince him that we weren't sent by Onyx. If we can do that, we might find some valuable allies.'

For two hours they marched, with only one rest. Giles tried to wriggle loose from his bonds but found them too tight. Neither asking for them to be loosened nor promising that they would not attempt escape brought the slightest response.

They had not yet reached the seacoast when the leader led them up the south river bank and into a forest of scrubby, wind-blown conifers. A trail led south and skirted a salt marsh. As they passed it, Giles saw long-legged birds, frightened by their appearance, explode upwards and wing their way north across the river.

At last they stopped. The leader yelped several times like a wolf cub, then repeated it. When he heard an answering call, he urged them over a rise and down into a village. It was a temporary affair, Giles saw, with the dwellings made of beach driftwood, their roofs of tree boughs.

Giles and his companions were hustled to an open shelter in the village square. People dropped their tasks and came to stare at the prisoners. An older man sat on a stool in the centre of the building, and the war party leader shoved Giles forward until he faced the man. The man examined Giles silently, before turning to Petia, Keja, and Anji.

Finally he turned to the man who had led their capture. 'Who are these?' he asked.

'We took them prisoner along the river. They are spies sent by Lord Onyx to scout for the steel ones.'

'We are *not* spies,' Giles interrupted. 'We tried to explain, but he wouldn't listen.'

Keja said, 'We were prisoners in the citadel. We escaped down the ice tunnels and don't like Onyx any better than you do.'

The man looked at Keja with expressionless eyes. 'The older one only will speak.'

'We're equals; he's not our leader.'

Keja's words were cut short. The sitting man made a small gesture, and a native seized Keja from behind, thrust a piece of leather into his mouth and tied a thong behind his head. He hauled Keja away and threw him into a nearby hut.

Petia started to protest, but a look from Giles stopped her.

Petia hissed, angry at their captors and at Giles, but she held her tongue.

Giles faced the village leader. How could he convince the older man that they were not spies for Onyx? Would the leader believe him if Giles told the truth? When at last Giles spoke, he told their story carefully, leaving nothing out except their assistance from Bellisar.

There were many questions, and Giles answered them truthfully. He was pleased that the questioning never got around to their reason for being in Khelora. When the questioning got to Petia, she answered for herself. She wasn't surprised that most of the questioning involved the feline qualities the Trans blood gave her and Anji.

At last the leader held a conference with other village elders. They spoke rapidly in their native language and Giles had no idea how the discussion was going. The leader smiled at Giles.

'We hear truth in your words,' he said. 'Excuse our caution. We have been harried ever since Onyx came to our land and captured many of our people for slaves. Many died during the construction of his citadel.'

The old man straightened proudly. 'Khelora is Brada land. The Brada have always been here in peace with those who farmed the valleys. We are a simple people, hunting, fishing, doing some small agriculture. Onyx does not even allow us to do that. His soldiers and his steel beings push us from place to place.

'Now we hide our villages, but when we are putting in our supplies for the winter, we live in these temporary huts. We build these huts knowing that they will be destroyed whenever we are found.'

'We know of Onyx's cruelty,' Petia said.

'He tries to beat us down,' the old man replied. 'But Brada were here before he came and we will be here after.' A rustling sound caused Petia to look up and see the natives slapping their right hands on the knuckles of their left hand. It was a curious applause, but she knew that his people agreed with the old leader.

'Then we are of one mind,' Giles said. 'He has hounded us, too, even in other countries. We did not always know it, but we have found that he has injured us more than once. We intend to pay him back and to get something from him which we need badly.' Giles did not intend to relate the story of the Gate of Paradise and the five keys. The old man's next question surprised him.

'What can we do to help? We have offended you by doubting your honesty. We must repay this debt.'

'I don't know,' Giles replied, taken aback. 'Maybe nothing more than food and drink. Perhaps you would release our companion now?'

Keja cursed loudly when he was brought from the hut and his bindings cut. He spit the taste of leather and then scowled at the serene old man, ready to charge him. It was all Giles could do to restrain him. 'Easy does it, Keja. We've found allies. Don't do anything to upset that.'

'They had no right to . . .'

'Neither did Onyx.'

Keja turned red, then scowled at the old man once more and turned away.

A scout ran into the village, came up and bowed to the old man, who signed to him to speak. 'The steel ones have been seen. They march along the river plain.' He described the location to the elders, who nodded.

So did Petia. 'Giles,' she whispered, 'that's where we were when we camped. Before we were captured. The steel ones must be what I sensed in the dark. Find out what they are.'

Giles waited patiently while the discussion went on around him. When they paused, he asked, 'What are the steel ones?'

The leader's eyebrows shot up in surprise at Giles' ignorance. 'Special troops of Onyx made of steel, but they look like men. They walk upright and cannot be killed. Sometimes they do not move at all, as if they sleep on their feet. We think that they have no minds of their own, or perhaps only tiny ones. They do not have a leader but get orders during combat. We do not know how.'

'If they are Onyx's creatures. I say attack,' Keja said. 'I'm tired of being hounded.'

Giles was cautious. 'We haven't seen these creatures. We don't know what we're up against. Petia, can you sense them?' Petia shook her head. 'Well,' Giles continued, 'this poses a problem.'

'And I don't think that we'll get back to the citadel until we remove these steel ones, whatever they are,' Keja snorted. 'Caution is the hallmark of old age, I'm told. You said you were getting old, and I'm beginning to believe it.'

Giles frowned, but Keja continued. 'This whole trip, ever since we left Bericlere, you've been holding me back. I'm getting tired of it. You don't seem to have the drive any more. Perhaps you don't want to see our adventure end. Are you afraid of being wealthy, is that it? Or don't you want to lose the only friends you've got? Damn, Giles, I say *let's get on with it*. Get what we came for, and if it's where you think it is, then the steel ones are going to be in our way.' He stopped finally, breathing hard, pleased that he had finally expressed his feelings.

Giles stared at the small thief, taken aback by what Keja had said. He would mull it over when there was time. Before he could respond, a Brada ran into the village shouting, 'They come! They come!'

'Do you not stand and fight?' Giles asked when he saw the Brada beginning to flee. 'Are there so many of them?'

'We move away,' an elder said. 'They are slower and cannot catch us.'

'Would you give us some help?' Giles asked the leader. 'Would you lend us some of your bravest young men? We wish to go and take a closer look at these steel ones.'

'I don't know.' The leader rubbed his chin.

'Please, Father.' The voice came from a young man standing to the rear of the shelter. He was tall and slender, well-muscled. The old man stared at his son. He saw eyes pleading for a chance to go with the strangers against the steel ones. 'We will take great care, Father. I will not endanger lives without need.'

The leader turned questioningly. Giles nodded approval. 'We would welcome his assistance, and four more young men of his choosing.'

Keja was still muttering to himself, and Petia was attempting to mollify him. Giles went to the leader's son.

'Giles Grimsmate,' he introduced himself.

'I am Natabor, son of Veldon.' Pride rang in the young man's voice, pride of self, of father, of the Brada.

446

'Choose well, as your father directed,' Giles said. 'There must be a way to fight these steel creatures, rather than running away. If so, we'll find it.'

Natabor's eyes narrowed, and for a moment Giles thought that he had offended the young man. 'For long years we have sought a way – and failed. Yet there is something about you that inspires faith.'

'I've seen a considerable number of good men die,' Giles said, his thoughts returning to the war years. 'Choose well, Natabor.'

The leader's son picked four, then motioned to the runner who had brought the warning. Natabor knew the information Giles needed and interrogated the scout. From time to time he made gestures, while the other man nodded. Once they squatted and the scout drew a rudimentary map on the ground. Finally, Natabor, confident that he knew where the beings had been seen, rose and faced Giles. 'We are ready,' he said, simply.

'You might be, but I don't think we are,' Giles replied. 'We had a long run this morning when we were captives, and we need a bit of a rest. Unless those steel beings move fast. I think they can wait. Tell us of them.'

Natabor sent a man to fetch food, and while they ate, Natabor answered questions about the steel ones.

'They are like men, but are not men,' Natabor said. 'While man-shaped they move slowly, as if uncertain of their actions – or have no control of their own bodies. But they are made of steel, and it does no good to fight them. Arrows bounce off their bodies, and a spear will not go through them. We have found no way to kill them.'

'Strange,' Keja said, forgetting his anger in his intensity of listening to the description. 'Do they think? Do they have a leader? How do they attack?'

'They do not appear to have a leader,' Natabor answered. 'They move forward as a group, but not in any formation. Sometimes they change directions together, but sometimes one or two of them continue, as if they didn't hear the order. Then finally they straggle along behind.'

'Mind control,' Petia said. 'Someone tells them what to do. Are they good fighters?'

'We have not fought them. When we found that spears and arrows could not stop them, we always ran from them. When they find out temporary villages, they tear them apart with their hands, tipping over the huts, scattering the wood around.'

'There may be a way to disable them,' Giles said, wiping his hands on his trousers. 'Ready?' As they rose, he touched Natabor's elbow. 'Go slowly or we'll never keep up.'

They skirted the marsh once more, sending up a cloud of wildfowl. Soon they entered the alluvial plain and moved along paths through the trees on the south river bank. Snow covered the tree boughs but for the most part, the path was clear. Giles had to remind Natabor that he and his companions needed to rest occasionally. While the pace was slower than in the morning, it was considerably faster than they were accustomed to.

When Petia sensed the steel ones, she cautioned Giles and he ordered the group to a halt. 'They are near,' he told Natabor, and saw the young man's consternation.

'How do you know?' Natabor asked. 'We have seen no sign.'

'Petia is able to sense people and animals. She is Trans, part cat.'

Natabor nodded, but Giles knew that the young native did not understand. He wasn't sure that he did himself, but he relied on Petia's ability.

'First we'll have a look,' Giles said. 'Then we'll see about setting a trap for them.' He glanced at Petia and she pointed the direction to the steel creatures.

'Quietly now,' Giles cautioned Natabor.

They set off along the path. Natabor ducked to one side and under a bush. They followed and Giles found a hidden path that opened out into a forest clearing. He nodded to himself as he passed under the great trees. 'You've got an idea hatching, haven't you?' Petia asked. Giles only smiled.

Anji, paying close attention to what his senses told him, touched Giles' arm. Giles gave a low whistle and the natives halted. 'They're close now, according to Anji.'

Natabor frowned. 'Him, too?' he whispered.

Giles nodded. 'Let's take a look. Great caution is needed now.'

They crept ahead slowly until the forest ended at the river bank. Lowering themselves onto their stomachs, they peered out between dried grasses with seed heads covered with snow. Keja gave a small cry as snow dropped down his neck, but Giles' angry look made him smother any further sound.

In the centre of the river bed a dozen of the steel beings moved west towards the sea. They seemed oblivious of their surroundings, plodding ahead through water channels and gravel bars alike. They were truly as Natabor had described, creatures of steel, mechanical beings with metal joints instead of knees and elbows. The unclothed structures looked obscene to the humans and Trans.

Their shape was more or less human. They even had a rudimentary head set on a slender neck. Giles looked quizzically at Petia. 'What do you sense?' he mouthed. Petia studied the creatures and opened her mind to them. She shook her head, then held up her hand to forestall interruption.

After a moment, she put her lips close to Giles's ear. 'Someone directs them. Their own minds are so elementary that they merely get by, but they take orders from someone else. It feels like Onyx, or perhaps that dwarf advisor.'

Giles gestured to the others to retreat into the forest. When they reached the clearing, he called them around him. 'Can we lure the steel creatures here?' he asked Petia.

Natabor spoke up. 'They follow easily. Often we send runners out to lead them away, while the villagers escape in a different direction.'

'Can you lead them in here?' Giles gestured at the clearing in which they conferred.

'Yes, but why?' Natabor was clearly puzzled.

'I have an idea,' Giles said. As he outlined it, he saw smiles crease the faces of the Brada. In a half-hour all was ready.

Natabor explained carefully to his companions and cautioned them that they must go slowly to ensure that the steel ones followed.

'Good luck,' Giles whispered and sent them off. He turned to his own companions and they made ready to spring the trap.

They waited silently, hidden so they would not be noticed by the pursuing steel beings, or, Giles hoped, by whomever was directing them. Soon they heard the Brada youths coming noisily along the forest trail. Behind them sounded the rustling of metal against the low bushes. The Brada broke into the clearing, turning as if looking for a way to escape. The steel ones plodded into the clearing after them. For a moment it looked as though all the steel soldiers would follow only one youth. Giles groaned inwardly. Then, haltingly, the steel beings sorted themselves out so that three of them pursued each Brada.

The youths turned and backed slowly across the clearing. The steel creatures plodded after them, raising shining steel swords which Giles recognised as Bellisar's work.

Natabor shot an arm into the air and shouted, 'Now!'

Giles, Keja, and Petia along with Anji, pulled hard on ropes in their hands. Loops enclosed the feet of the steel beings and pulled them off their feet. A loud clang echoed as they fell heavily to the ground. Giles and Keja pulled on their ropes and Natabor and the other Brada rushed to assist them. They hoisted the beings into the air. They wrapped the ropes around the trees and secured them, then ran to help Petia and Anji. The third group of steel soldiers was lifted into the air, twirling upside down at the end of the ropes.

Natabor sent several of the youths to climb the trees and secure the ends of the rope farther up, where they would be more difficult to reach. When done, Giles gestured to Natabor and the party faded back along the path.

'Onyx is not happy,' Petia said. 'I can feel it.'

'I didn't expect him to be, but at least he gets a taste of defeat for a change,' Giles said.

'I think it's all-out war now. Giles,' Petia said. 'I've never felt such rage in my life.' She looked at Anji. The boy felt it so strongly that he put his hands alongside his head to ease the pain.

Lord Onyx would not let them live after this, keys or no keys.

Ten

THE BRADA village rejoiced when their warriors returned with Giles and his companions. Natabor's eyes shone as he told his father about the trap and its success. The young men left behind, though jealous, pounded the backs of the heroes from their village.

The villagers stored their belongings in the huts, and by dusk life had returned to normal. Veldon ordered a feast in celebration. Fish from the sea cooked on planks set around the fire, and waterfowl roasted on spits above. Giles, Petia, Keja and Anji were treated as heroes and allowed to do nothing but enjoy the adulation.

'Quite honestly,' said Giles, 'I'm thankful for a chance to sit. I wonder how many miles we've covered today?'

'I don't ever want to run like we were forced to this morning,' Keja said. 'These people are a marvel when it comes to running. When Natabor sent one with the news of the steel ones, he disappeared down the trail faster than a hare. By the time we returned, the news of our success had spread throughout the village.'

'It's not over, though,' Petia said. 'Onyx will cut the steel men down from the trees. We should have tried to smash their limbs and put them out of commission permanently.' She sipped at a warm drink. 'The Brada are foolish to stay here. Onyx won't accept this easily.'

'I'll talk to Veldon,' Giles said. 'They know where the citadel is and can lead us back. Either the key is there or it isn't. If it isn't, we'll have to find out where Onyx has hidden it.' Giles subsided, the day's events finally enervating him. He slept through most of the festivities and still found it difficult rising at first light.

Veldon embraced each of the companions as they prepared to go, saying, 'You are always welcome at the Brada fire. When your quest is at an end, come and spend time with us. You have given us new hope that we will triumph over the black lord.'

The villagers gathered to watch the strange troop leave. Two humans, two Trans, and five of their own young men against the power of Lord Onyx. They stood quietly, neither waving nor shouting, but Petia and Anji felt the villagers' strength pouring out, wishing further success. Petia shivered, impressed at the power derived from the closeness of these people.

For four days the group marched along coastal paths and secret trails through forests. Often they turned inland to skirt inlets, and once walked carefully through a marsh where a false step into the sucking bottom might have meant disaster. Natabor led and his friends each guided one of the companions, staking reputations – and lives – on their knowledge of the route.

At last Natabor turned inland. On the afternoon of the fourth day they came within view of Onyx's mighty citadel. From the edge of the forest they stared out across the open meadow towards the vast fortress.

'Well, you've brought us here,' Giles said. 'Now it's up to us to get inside. When we were prisoners we examined those walls closely. There's no way to scale them. There might be a foothold here and there, but it's much too smooth to climb.'

'How about another entrance?' Keja asked. 'Another door. Or maybe through an ice tunnel?'

A grimace of exasperation came to Giles' face. 'You liked the cold and the ice demons that much, eh? One of these days you are going to learn to think before you speak. Didn't you hear the iron door clang behind us, or the bar being dropped? No, there's got to be another way in.' Giles cut himself short of mentioning the irrational fear of being crushed within the tunnels. Petia and Keja didn't share that with him.

Natabor hunkered down, eyes narrowing as he studied the

citadel. 'A suggestion?' he asked, with deference. At Giles' nod, the young Brada continued. 'The citadel is supplied from outside. Wagons come from the south. They cross the meadow there.' He pointed. 'They enter the citadel and unload. If we captured a wagon, we might get you inside as part of the delivery crew.'

'Wouldn't they recognise us?' Keja asked.

Giles eyes lit up. 'They might four of us, especially two Trans. But if we captured the wagon, kept the driver who they would recognise, and hid our two Trans friends, we could disguise ourselves. It just might work.'

Watching the sentries parading along the battlements, they withdrew carefully into the forest. Natabor sent one of his men off to scout for the supply wagon along the road, cautioning him to be back by nightfall. The rest settled down to a cold meal and working on a plan.

The scout returned at dusk. 'Did you find the wagon?' Natabor asked. The young Brada shook his head and described in detail how far he had gone. Natabor suggested that the next day they work their way along the road. 'With one scouting in front, we can be ready to ambush them.'

The plan left a lot to chance, Giles thought, but he could think of nothing better. The next morning they followed a path through the forest, finding a perfect place for an ambush within a day's walk from the citadel. There they would wait until the wagon came to them.

An immense boulder, nearly sixteen feet high and twenty feet long, lay on the right-hand side of the road. The opposite side was covered with dense bushes taller than any of the party. They made themselves as comfortable as possible without a fire. Natabor sent another youth to scout and report when the wagon came into view.

A day and a half went by with no news from the scout. When the youth brought word that the wagon was on its way, Giles stopped brooding. He and the others sprang into action. The plan was simple in its concept, and they hoped that it would be as easy to accomplish.

Natabor gestured to one of his friends. 'You know what to do, Jella. Wait for the signal and play your part well.'

The youth trotted away in the direction of the citadel. Giles and the others took their positions. From where Giles hid behind the boulder, he could see two of the Brada youths. One was in the direction from which the wagon would approach and would signal Giles. The other youth had gone in the opposite direction. Each was a carefully stepped off distance from the place where the ambush was set.

When the wagon passed the first Brada, he raised a hand. Giles passed the signal on to the second youth, then lifted his halberd and made ready. Since the battles in the ice caves, he had become fond of the weapon. He let Petia keep the sword. It was a bit heavy for her but she knew how to handle it.

The wagon drew near. Two horses pulled it and the wagoner seemed in no great hurry. Two guards sat idly on the tailgate of the wagon, their feet dangling above the muddy road.

Giles heard the wagoner call his team to a halt. The snuffling and blowing of the horses carried to him easily on the crisp winter air. 'What's this?' the wagoner said. 'A Brada seeks help?'

Keja jumped from the boulder, rushed to the centre of the road and grabbed the horses by their bridles. Giles followed him and placed his halberd at the wagoner's throat.

The two guards, hearing the wagoner halt the team, had turned and climbed to their feet. They were facing forward when they felt sword points in the middle of their backs. The attack lasted only seconds.

The Brada hauled the two guards from the back of the wagon and tied them with ropes of braided rawhide before dragging them behind the huge boulder.

Giles looked at the wagoner, a bearded man getting on in years, the glitter of his eyes showing intelligence. Even with a spearpoint at his throat, he was thinking. 'Don't do anything foolish, old man,' Giles said. 'Follow our orders and you'll get out of this with your life.'

'If it's the supplies you want, take them,' the wagoner said.

'No, it's not the supplies. We want to get into the citadel.'

The wagoner stared. 'You must be mad. Nobody wants to get *into* that awful place. They usually want to get *out*.' He cackled at his own joke. 'But if that's what you really want, it's you who should be worried. You go in there and you'll never come out alive.'

'We think not,' Giles said. 'What you're going to do is deliver your load, just as you always do. You simply will have two new guards. Explain that any way you like, but don't give us away. The Trans woman and boy will be hidden in the load.'

The wagoner turned his head carefully and looked at Petia and Anji standing at the rear of the wagon. His eyes widened. Obviously he had never seen Trans before.

'There will be a knife at your back the entire way,' Giles continued. 'Your life is in your own hands. We don't wish to hurt you. Go gently and you will have no trouble. You can pick up your companions on the way home. We'll leave them secured, but comfortable. A little hunger is all they will suffer.'

Natabor said, 'We'll watch along the way until you come to the meadow. We'll wait at the edge of the forest for two days,' Natabor said. 'I don't know how we could help, but we will wait, just the same.' Giles nodded in appreciation. The Brada youth clasped arms with Giles, then the three melted into the forest, gone.

In a flash, Petia and Anji concealed themselves within the load. Giles and Keja took seats on the wagon, and the wagoner urged his team forward. Keja sat on the tailgate, but Giles sat on the edge of the box, his dagger in his lap, hidden by a cloak. The wagoner had been shown exactly where it was aimed, and hunched his shoulder blades often as if he already felt the sharp tip piercing his flesh.

By mid-afternoon the wagon left the confines of the forest road and followed the road across the long meadow. The citadel loomed larger, and Giles had more than enough time to wonder whether they were making a huge mistake.

The wagon had been sighted by sentries, and as it reached the base of the citadel the huge doors swung open. Only the major-domo and two kitchen servants stood there to welcome them. The steward sniffed when he saw the dirt on the two guards' faces but paid no more attention to them.

With great self-importance he removed a key and chain from around his neck. He unlocked a large storeroom and swung the doors back, motioning for the servants to begin unloading. The wagoner handed him a sheaf of papers, bills of lading for the delivery. The steward glanced at it, then handed it to a menial. He turned without another word and disappeared up the stairway.

Giles motioned for Keja to keep an eye on the wagoner. He stood at the back of the wagon and watched the kitchen servants unload the supplies. One was a Brada youngster, and he touched him lightly on the arm. The Brada looked up, fear in his eyes. Giles smiled and whispered, 'We come from Veldon. Natabor waits in the woods. Can you hide us? Four?' He held up his fingers.

The youth gulped and hefted a sack of barley onto his shoulders. He staggered off under the load, but when he returned his eyes shone. He nodded and smiled, and Giles trusted that the young man had a plan. While the unloading went on, Petia and Anji slipped over the side of the wagon and crouched out of sight.

The Brada's plan was amazingly simple. He timed it so that he was alone with the four while the other servant worked in the storeroom. He pointed to the corner near the huge doors where a guard cell stood empty. They hurried into it and crouched against the wall. The other servant seemed not to notice. When the unloading was finished, he locked the storeroom door and tucked the key inside his shirt. He waited while the wagoner turned his wagon and drove out of the citadel not noticing the absence of the two guards on the tailgate. He and the Brada closed the door and lowered the bars on the inside. Then he hurried up the stairs to report to the major-domo.

The Brada youngster poked his head into the room. 'Stay here until I come for you. It will only be a short while. I'll find a place for you to hide.'

A half an hour later Giles heard stealthy footsteps on the stone stairway. He slid his fingers along the halberd shaft and readied himself for whomever approached. He roused the others from their drowsy mood.

'It's me. Helleon.'

Cautiously Giles rose and edged to the door. The young Brada saw the speartip and gestured with his hands wide. He whispered that the way was clear, but that they must hurry.

'Where are you taking us?' Giles asked.

'Kitchen. No time for talk. Hurry.'

They followed the Brada swiftly and silently up the stairs. He paused briefly at the first landing, then led them up a second flight of steps. At the top he turned left down a hallway, motioning them to be quick.

They slid through an open archway into an enormous kitchen and pantry. Giles took in the entire room at a glance. They saw no servants, yet a huge fire blazed in an open pit, with a quarter of a beef spitted over it. Around the room food being prepared for various dishes awaited chefs. He threw a quizzical look at Helleon.

The young man beckoned. 'No time. I'll explain later.' He led them to a small alcove in the corner of the room. Boxes were stacked helter-skelter, some filled with fruit, others empty. 'Quickly,' Helleon said. 'Move some of the boxes and hide behind them. No one will look in here until tomorrow. We will move you before then. Just be quiet until I come for you again.'

They heard voices in the main kitchen. Helleon held a finger to his lips and disappeared around the corner.

The four companions were alone again, but they knew that they had entered the heart of the citadel and that they had at least one ally there. The boy had said, 'We will move you.' Giles wondered how many other Brada captives in the citadel might be counted upon. Was there a way they could be used? He felt a twinge of conscience. Was there a way to free them?

Silently he and Keja lifted empty boxes and stacked them carefully until they had built a cubby-hole where they could sit with their backs against the wall and their legs stretched out. Warmth from the kitchen seeped into the alcove, and they removed their cloaks to provide padding for the stone floor.

Occasionally, they could hear the major-domo's voice roaring in disapproval at one of the kitchen staff for some misdemeanour. As kitchen noises filtered through to them and preparations for the evening meal went on, Giles and the others began to relax. No one entered the alcove. Through the late afternoon they dozed, warm and comfortable in their hiding place.

They awoke to a great bustle during the serving time for the evening meal. When the noise finally ceased, Giles knew that the meal was over. He heard the servants settle down to their own meal in the kitchen, followed by the desultory conversation of the weary. Then suddenly all was quiet. What now? Where had they all gone? Giles was tempted to investigate, but remembered that Helleon had said that he would return for them.

Petia touched his arm and whispered, 'Someone's coming.'

Giles gripped his spear, but the young Brada's voice spoke. 'Quickly now. There's not much time.'

They rose and came out into the kitchen. 'Where is everyone?' Giles asked.

'They'll be back soon to wash up and start tomorrow morning's meal. But we have a little time to rest after the evening meal. Hurry now.'

'Where are you taking us?' Keja asked.

'A better hiding place,' the youth whispered back. A young Brada woman stood at the door, checking the hallway. 'This is Linnia. She'll lead you, while I bring up the rear.'

The hallway was empty and Linnia led off quickly. Halfway down the hall she unlocked a storeroom door and ushered them in. It was a larger room than the alcove in which they had hidden. Helleon slid into the room behind them and closed the door quietly. He pulled a candle from a pocket of his tunic and lit it, the flame casting eerie shadows on the walls. 'You'll be safe here for tonight. Maybe for a couple of nights.'

'The first thing we want to do,' Giles said, 'is to help you and the other Brada escape. At least as many as we can. Natabor and some others are waiting in the forest across the meadow. We promised him we would try. He said he'd wait for a signal.'

'Why are you here?' Helleon asked. 'Surely not to rescue us.'

Giles shook his head. 'It's too long a story to tell. It has nothing to do with the Brada, except that Veldon helped us. With Natabor and four others we defeated a troop of Onyx's steel men and that has embarrassed him terribly. He's angry and brooding and you Brada will bear the brunt of his wrath if we don't help you to escape.'

Linnia spoke up. 'I can alert the others and bring them to you. But how can we get out? At night guards keep watch at the doors where you entered.'

'Can you get me rope, a lot of rope?' Keja asked. Helleon nodded. 'Good. Is there an open window where we won't be seen? I can lower people down the wall if we can work undisturbed.'

Linnia said, 'There is a storeroom used to –'

Keja cut her off. 'Never mind, if you know where we can do it. Just bring plenty of rope. Enough that it will reach the ground.'

The two Brada left to carry out Keja's instructions. Petia saw that Linnia had provided food for them and, while they waited, they ate their first full meal of the day. When Helleon returned with the rope, Keja put down a drumstick and went to work. He examined each length for weaknesses, then carefully began to knot the lengths together.

Meanwhile, Giles questioned Helleon about the citadel. The youth was unable to describe it to Giles' satisfaction. As a slave who worked in the kitchen, he had access to no more than a few floors and then only at one end of the vast building. But Giles got an accurate enough picture of that part of the citadel and, by patient questioning, learned what Helleon had heard from others. Linnia interrupted at times to add what she knew.

When Giles had finished, he retired to a corner to think about the plan taking shape in his mind. Petia took up where he had left off. 'How many Brada are there?' she asked. Linnia counted them off on her fingers, Helleon nodding in agreement. There were only four others besides themselves. 'Six all told,' Petia said. 'Good. If there were more, it'd be difficult for you to escape without being noticed.'

Giles stirred. 'Can you meet us in the middle of the night when everyone is asleep?' He sketched out the location for the Brada.

'Not everyone sleeps,' Helleon corrected. 'There are guards, always. But we will be there. Linnia will take the others to the place. I will come for you.'

Giles was pleased with the young man's confidence and his own grew with it.

The hall where they met was dark and empty; Helleon led them up two more flights of stairs and down a hall. Flambeaux at each end of the hall cast a sputtering light along the corridor. Helleon scratched at the door, and Linnia, eyes wide, slowly opened it. The companions slipped in and set to work at once.

Keja loosened the rope and cast it through the open window. Slowly he paid it out, watching as it descended the sloping wall. Satisfied that it reached the ground, he retrieved it and tied one end around his waist. He coiled the rest carefully on the floor, tying a loop at the other end. He explained carefully what the Brada must do.

It was a long drop to the ground, nearly eighty feet, but Giles was convinced that these were a brave people. For their own sakes, they would not cry out and alarm the guards.

He lit a candle and moved it across the embrasure three times. He did not expect any answering signal from the Brada in the forest, but he was confident that they waited there.

Keja gripped the rope, passed it around his back and over his shoulder, and placed one foot against the sill of the window to brace himself. 'Ready,' he said quietly.

'They will come after us,' moaned Linnia, eyeing the dark drop to freedom. 'Always before, they have hunted us down with the steel creatures.'

'It'll be different this time,' Giles assured her. 'Natabor and the others will protect you until you rejoin the villagers.'

'But then?' Linnia protested, fright growing.

'Let us worry about that.' Petia's calmness soothed the Brada more than Giles' assurances.

Giles explained how the Brada would be lowered. He scanned the sky. The moon shone clear, but clouds drifted from the west, casting occasional shadows on the wall below and across the meadow. 'When you get to the ground, step out of the loop but stay close to the wall. Make your way to the right until you come to the end of the building. Watch carefully at the west end of the citadel. We don't know if there are any guards there. If not, work your way along the base of the cliff until you are well away. If there are guards, you'll have to run for it across the meadow.' He put a hand on the shoulder of the first Brada woman and said, 'Good luck.' He nodded to Keja, who braced himself to take the weight.

Petia thought the job went slowly and worried that someone would discover them. She whispered to Anji, 'Help me sense if anyone is in the hallway. Turn your back to what's happening and ignore it. Concentrate on the corridor.' But they sensed nothing and the operation behind them continued smoothly.

When Keja had finished lowering two Brada women, he stepped back, flexing his back and shoulders. Giles suggested that he take over, but Keja shook his head. 'I'm always making mistakes, but this is one thing I do right. Me and my ropes.' He grinned and stepped back to the window. The third woman descended the cloud-shadowed wall.

When the last Brada was lowered, Giles gestured to Linnia to go next. She shook her head. Tears glistened in her eyes, but she looked directly at Giles and said, 'Helleon and I are staying. To help you however we can.'

'You can't,' Giles said. Petia's voice was nearly an echo.

'We must. Onyx is our enemy, too, and we don't know exactly why you came here. But we must stay and help you.'

'We can't guarantee that we'll get you out of here if you don't go now,' Giles said. 'We don't even know if we'll get out ourselves. You had better go while you have the chance.'

'We will stay.' Helleon's voice carried such determination that the others knew it was useless to argue. He dug into his tunic pocket and pulled forth a key. He handed it to Giles. 'This is the key to the storeroom. I'll tell them that I lost it. You can't lock the door from the inside, but you can keep it locked while you're gone. It might be useful to you.' He clasped Giles' arm and nodded at Keja.

'You might attract Onyx's wrath – for the others who have already escaped.'

'We've suffered at his hand. We know how to endure the lord's anger.'

Giles went to the window and watched the Brada women make their way along the wall to the end of the building. He saw them hesitate, then turn the corner and disappear. Keja had pulled the rope up and coiled it neatly. He slipped it over his shoulder and said, 'I'm ready.'

Petia looked up with relief on her face. 'I didn't think they could do it. Nothing moving out there.' She nodded toward the hall.

They opened the door and silently left. Linnia and Helleon disappeared around a corner and were gone. Giles and the others moved down halls and stairways until they arrived back at their storeroom hiding place. They collapsed onto the floor, pleased with their double success at getting into the citadel and helping the Brada captives escape. They were well aware, however, that they might have created more trouble for themselves. By morning Lord Onyx would learn of the escape and his rage would be unparalleled. They had to think, also, that Onyx might order a careful search of his fortress for the escaped slaves.

To be found during such a search meant immediate death — or worse. Onyx might carry out his threat to hand Petia over to Segrinn. Giles slumped down, bone-tired. They had only a few hours before they'd pass beyond even the gods' help.

Until then, though, he wanted nothing more than a few hours sleep. He was tired, so tired.

He slept.

Eleven

GILES AWOKE to a strange smell. He sniffed once and remembered that they hid in the kitchen supply room. He opened his eyes and saw cured meats hanging from the ceiling. He glanced at the others, still sleeping.

He sat up, already worrying about their situation. The Brada women would be reported missing this morning, and Onyx would be furious when he found out. But that wouldn't be soon. The major-domo would make every effort to find the escaped slaves before reporting their absence. His head would be on the block.

Giles wanted to act before the guards centred on the kitchen quarters. Until Onyx was certain that the Brada women had escaped the citadel, Giles and his companions were in great danger. He hoped desperately that Helleon or Linnia would come to the storeroom soon. They had to move, and he

462

thought how foolish they had been last night to return
here.

Still, he hadn't been able to act effectively. His body had
betrayed him more and more with tiredness, with aching
joints, with shaking hands and blurring vision. Giles had
needed the rest and that offset the risk.

He roused the others, and they munched on apples which
they found in a nearby barrel. They heard a scratching on the
door and opened it cautiously. Helleon slipped into the room.

'Are we glad to see you!' Giles said. 'Have they discovered
that the women are missing yet?'

'Yes and no,' Helleon replied. 'The major-domo knows that
they didn't appear for morning duty. He sent others to get them
and is threatening extra kitchen duty for not rising on time. It is
only a matter of minutes before he will know.'

'Can you find us another place to hide?' Giles asked.
'Guards will search this area of the citadel as if their lives
depended on it – and they might. Unless you can move us,
we'll be found.'

'I've thought of that,' Helleon replied. 'We talked about it
last night. We chose another storeroom farther away. Linnia is
making sure that the door is unlocked and that it's empty.'

Another scratching came at the door. Petia jumped to her
feet, eyes wide. She strained her senses but heard only footsteps continuing down the hallway.

'It's all right,' Helleon said. 'That was Linnia letting me know
that the room is safe. Now listen carefully.' He described how to
reach the room, and Giles repeated the directions. 'You're on
your own,' Helleon said. 'Linnia and I have a story that we've
found something strange far from here. We'll lead the guards
away, but be careful. When Onyx hears about his missing
slaves, he'll launch a fullscale search. Once you get to the new
room, stay there until we come again. No wandering around.'

'You can depend on that,' Giles said. 'It's going to be
dangerous out there for a while. We'll do our exploring after
things have quieted.'

Helleon slipped out the door and vanished.

The four sat in silence, wrapped in their own concerns. Giles
tried to keep time in his head. Five minutes, Helleon had said.
Finally, he signalled to the others. They opened the door and

463

crept into the hall, making sure to close the door fully behind them. Giles urged the others to follow quickly, then set his mind to remembering Helleon's instructions.

They arrived without event wondering what Helleon and Linnia had done to completely empty the halls of guards. Bright young people, Giles thought. If we ever get out of here alive, we owe them a debt that will be hard to repay.

It was mid-afternoon when they heard a scratching at the door, Helleon's signal.

The young man slipped in and set down a sack.

'What's the news outside?' Giles asked. 'This room was an excellent choice. No one's bothered us.'

'Onyx doesn't think that the four have left the citadel,' Helleon replied. 'He thinks they will still be found inside, but they're not considered very important. He's called off the search for the time being. He thinks they'll get hungry and come out of hiding.'

'Good, they'll be well away,' Giles said. 'What about you and Linnia? Aren't you suspected of helping them?'

'That's what we need to talk about.' Helleon settled to the floor, facing the others. 'Linnia and I discussed that, too, last night. We'll help as best we can, but don't expect too much from us. We're only lowly kitchen help. We'll be watched. Anyway, we don't know what the rest of the citadel is like.'

'Then we're pretty much on our own, Giles,' Keja said.

'Yes,' Giles said, 'but do you realise how much we owe these two? They've done more than enough.'

'There's another thing that you should be aware of. Onyx has a counsellor, a little dwarf of a man. You saw him when you were here the first time?' Giles nodded. 'His name is Ulinek. We hear stories about him in the kitchen. He's said to be a crafty one. And it's rumoured that he has powers of the mind.' Linnia and Helleon glanced from Giles to Petia and Anji.

The Trans became more alert. 'What powers?' Petia asked.

'I'm not sure,' Helleon said. 'I don't know much about that sort of magic. We hear that he can probe minds, sometimes even direct people to work against their wills. He's someone to be extremely careful of. When things are upset, like this morning, it disturbs him. His mind powers fail then, and Onyx shouts at him. That just upsets Ulinek more. It's when things are quiet that he's more dangerous, at least that's what people say.

'He came to the kitchen this morning, poking his nose into everything. Linnia and I were scared to death, but we made ourselves think of home on the coast. He dithered so much that I don't think he could read anything. Anyway, I thought I had better warn you about him.'

'Thank you, Helleon,' Petia said. 'Anji and I are sensitive to such a presence, and we may be able to do something about it. I'm glad you warned us about him. When I first saw him, I sensed something – but mostly I thought him the court fool.'

'I must go or I'll be missed. We'll try to stay in touch with you, but I can't promise.' Helleon left as quietly as he had come.

Late in the afternoon they heard the scratching again. This time Linnia slipped into the storeroom. She brought the news that Onyx had ordered a large detachment of the guard to leave on an expedition to punish the Brada.

'The rumour is that there are only a few guards left in the citadel. Helleon and I don't know what that means, because we don't know how many guards there are altogether.' She wrung her hands and said, 'I just hope that the women are a long way from here.'

'Do Brada women run as fast as the men do?' Giles asked.

'Nearly so,' Linnia said. 'We race with them.' She smiled shyly. Giles guessed that this somehow was part of their mating rituals.

'Then don't worry about the women. They cover twice the ground that poor mortals like us can in the same amount of time. They've been gone since last night. They're probably a day ahead of the guard. They'll get away.' Giles spoke with such assurance that Linnia's face brightened.

Linnia's news lifted the mood of the hiding companions. 'When we go exploring tonight, we'll have fewer guards to avoid,' Giles said. 'But we may as well get used to being the hunted until we get the key.' Giles silently added, even after that. If Onyx were a god, he wouldn't permit them to walk away with the key and not pursue them.

Could a god — even a deposed one — be killed? Giles frowned. They'd have to find out.

'And we have no idea if the key is here or not,' Petia added. She toyed with the end of her belt. 'What if we've made a mistake? What if it really *is* still hidden in the Mountains of the Lions?'

'We can't think that way, Petia,' Giles said. 'It won't be the first time we've made a mistake. I can almost guarantee that it won't be the last.' Giles shrugged. 'If we learn that it's not here, then we get out and go back on our trek. Either way we've got to stay out of Onyx's clutches. That's the most important thing.'

Late in the evening Helleon and Linnia slipped into the room again.

'We didn't think we would see you again today,' Giles said.

'We've brought some paper and a stick of charcoal,' Linnia said. 'We thought it might help if we gave you as much information as we can about the citadel,'

'Indeed, it will,' Giles answered. He took the paper and smoothed it out on the floor, moving a candle closer. For the next half-hour the six of them huddled over the paper, while Giles drew from the directions Helleon and Linia gave him.

When at last Helleon and Linnia had exhausted their knowledge, and Giles, Keja and Petia had asked their last questions, they sat back. 'Any more news about the guards leaving on their expedition?' Keja asked. 'I'd like to know how many we have to avoid in our midnight wanderings.'

'When the major-domo gave orders for preparation of the evening meal, we tried to figure out what it meant in terms of people,' Linnia said. 'There are still plenty of people in the citadel, but many are servants. We don't know how many are guards.'

'The only thing we can say,' Helleon said, 'is that you must take care. The commander of the guards thinks that the women are still inside the citadel, but he's becoming less sure as the day wears on. A lesser officer led the troop to the coast.' Helleon and Linnia exchanged glances. 'We'd better go. They'll check our quarters tonight, and we must not violate

466

curfew. There would be too many questions, and we would be of no further use to you.'

After the two Brada left, Giles studied the map again before folding it up. 'Are we ready to go?' he asked, glancing at the others.

'Off to confront Onyx!' cried Keja.

Petia put up a hand, asking for a moment. She clasped Anji's hand, staring into his eyes, and nodding her head. 'You can do it, you'll see,' she whispered.

Once again Keja felt uncomfortable when Petia concentrated on that part of her which was truly Trans, and took on catlike characteristics. She had been working with Anji, and Keja shuddered as the boy, too, set his mind to becoming cat Trans. Giles simply watched in fascination, knowing that the two would be even more helpful in that guise. He didn't know how they accomplished it any more than Keja did, but he knew that it was a valuable characteristic they would put to excellent use this night.

The hallway was empty, but somewhere ahead Petia picked up the sound of pacing feet. She shot a warning look back at the two men and stalked ahead. The hall stretched for ever. Its sides were resplendent with arrases, and the moonlight occasionally glinted from golden threads. Giles reached for the edge of one tapestry and pulled it away from the wall. He was surprised to find a niche behind it, one large enough to stand in. He hoped that they were all like that, ready-made places to hide.

Giles slid behind the tapestry and examined the niche, expecting to find a spy hole overlooking some interior room. There was none, and he wondered at their purpose. He heard Keja call softly to Petia. 'Giles has disappeared.'

When he stepped back into the hallway, he saw a look of relief flood over Keja's face. 'By the gods, man, don't do that to me!'

'Might come in handy,' Giles replied.

Twice they heard guards, but Petia and Anji warned them in time to elude them. Once they hurried back to an intersection of the hall and hid in a doorway. A second time they slipped into a niche behind a tapestry, and blessed Giles for having discovered it.

The guards patrolled in pairs, rather than standing stationary duty. 'That makes it easier for us to explore,' Giles said. 'Just keep alert and warn us.' He motioned Petia and Anji to a transverse hallway. When they came to the end of it, Giles thought he recognised where he was. They overlooked the main hall. The doors to the room where they had been questioned stood open. A guard slouched before it, leaning on a pike.

'Can you two draw him off while we get inside?' Giles asked. Petia nodded and for a brief second Giles saw the image of two very different cats. One was long and sinuous from Petia's home, while Anji's figure appeared to take on the characteristics of a Bandanarra sand cat.

They began descending the stairway, but Petia turned and hissed Keja and Giles back. Startled, they watched in awe as two phantom cat figures crept through the shadows and crossed the main hall. A yowl sounded and the guard leaped to attention. Two cats scurried past, and the guard lifted his pike and followed.

'Now.' Giles and Keja hurried down the stairs and into the room. 'There'll not be much time,' Giles whispered. 'You take that side. Look for any places Onyx might have hidden the key. And pick up some of the fruit from the table when you pass it.' Without waiting, Giles went to the fireplace, searching the mantle first. He touched anything looking even remotely as if it would reveal a secret hiding place.

There was none, but Giles wasn't discouraged. He knew that their search might prove long and arduous. One look into Keja's eyes when they met at the end of the room told him that the small thief had failed, too. He jerked his head towards the door and they tiptoed down the room. The guard hadn't returned; Keja and Giles ascended the stairway quickly to hide in the shadows and await Petia and Anji.

'How did you get up to this floor?' he whispered when Petia and Anji padded up on silent feet.

'We eluded the guard,' Petia answered. 'Too slow. We took the stairs up, hiding in the shadows, and found our way back here. Cats have a good sense of direction, you know.'

'Did you see anything interesting down that hallway?' Keja asked.

Anji's eyes gleamed. 'There's what looks like a throne room on the lower floor. The door was open as we went past. There's a huge throne and rich tapestries. Maybe the key is hidden in there, Giles.'

'Can we get there without going past the guard again?' Giles asked.

'Yes.' Petia and Anji led off in the direction from which they had come. No guard stood at this end of the long hall, but one passed the foot of the stairs they intended to descend. They waited in the shadows until his footsteps faded. 'Turn right when you get to the bottom. Anji and I will go ahead and see if the way is clear.'

'Spooky!' Keja muttered as the pair vanished from sight.

At the bottom Giles saw no sign of the Trans. He took this as a sign that all was safe. He turned right, came to an intersecting hallway and turned right again. He felt confident that he knew his directions. He saw Anji beckon from a doorway down the hall. With Keja on his heels, he hurried down the hall, making as little noise as possible.

The richness of the room surprised them. The immense throne looked more than capable of holding Onyx's bulk. Carved of an ebony wood, it was inlaid with intricate designs of white birch and *jaffro* pine. The stark white of the inlays contrasted beautifully with the jet black. Each of the arms ended with carvings of lions couchant. Giles prodded Keja. 'Look, lions.'

'Do you suppose . . . ?'

'We'll have to look,' Giles answered. 'I'm past making guesses. It just gets me into trouble.'

They rushed to the far end of the room and examined the throne. Keja ran his hands over every inch of the back, seeking anything that might open to reveal the key. Giles searched the arms, and Petia reached her slender arms under the throne, feeling with sensitive fingers for a hiding place. There was none.

Anji, meantime, looked behind every hanging tapestry. He found nothing but a spy hole which looked into the room where they had first met Lord Onyx. There was little else in the room. Some chairs were scattered around the room, and stools stood along the walls. It was evidently used for ceremonial occasions and would have held a large contingent of the guard, perhaps all who were quartered in the citadel.

Giles shook his head. 'Not here, I'm sure. There must be a treasure room somewhere in the citadel. That would be a more likely place, if we can find it.'

Petia pulled at Giles' arm. 'We're spending too much time searching for the damned key. We intended to make this night an exploration, and we're spending all our time running our hands over things, expecting the key to leap out at us. We're supposed to be scouting the layout of the citadel.'

Giles stepped back and bowed to the Trans lady. 'You're absolutely right. I always jump at opportunities to search when no one is around. I stand corrected. Lead on.'

For the rest of the night they kept to the task they'd set for themselves. Giles grew more confident at every turn of a hallway, every stairway that they ascended. Petia and Anji did an excellent job of alerting them to the roaming guards.

'We couldn't have chosen a better time to explore,' Petia said when they stopped to rest. 'With most of the guard gone, the others are forced to roam around the building. We could never have avoided them if they guarded their regular stations.'

Once, they crouched behind a railing to watch Ulinek pacing a long hallway, muttering to himself. Petia pointed to her forehead in warning that they should block their own thoughts or Ulinek would detect them. They closed their eyes, as Petia had taught them, and thought only of a blank wall. Petia watched as the frowning dwarf paced the length of the hall. He turned, as though he were a citadel guard, rocking on his stubby feet. Then he paced back again. As he neared Petia, he closed his eyes in concentration. Ulinek raised his chin and, had his eyes been open, he would have looked directly at the companions.

Petia closed her own eyes and concentrated on an image of two guards walking down either side of the hall, looking carefully behind each arras. She sensed a mood of security come over the dwarf. She opened her eyes to see him nodding to himself, then he walked away purposefully and disappeared from view.

As morning approached, guard activity died down. The night watch tired of roaming the citadel and occasionally the companions came across guards asleep at their posts. Giles had measured the length of the citadel, and except for the precise configuration of rooms and hallways, he was confident that he knew where they were in the structure as they ascended to each new floor.

'Time to get back to our hidey-hole,' Giles said. His voice, though weary, contained a resonance that showed his pleasure with their success. It had been a night well spent. They had not only learned the plan of the citadel, but had examined two rooms thoroughly.

Petia and Anji led off, taking an unused side staircase which they had discovered earlier. Giles counted the floors as they descended, wanting to verify the number he had arrived at previously. On the fourth floor he paused, and the others went on, not aware that he had stopped.

He looked around, then back up the stairway. He continued down and paused again, puzzled. Something niggled at the back of his mind, something not right. He shook his head and looked over a banister at the open hallway below. Exhausted, he shook his head and hurried to catch the others as they arrived at the storeroom. Something was wrong, but he was much too tired to try to puzzle it out now. Maybe when sleep had refreshed him, he would give it more thought and it would make sense.

Giles Grimsmate fell into a fitful sleep, the stairway haunting his dreams. It ran upward to the sky – and down into a pit filled with leering faces all shouting for his death.

Twelve

GILES AWOKE with a crick in his lower back. He started to turn over and grimaced as the pain shot across his waist. Gingerly, he got to his knees and finally stood, cursing under his breath. 'Too old for this nonsense. Oh, for a bed again.'

The morning he expected was really mid-afternoon. Giles had enjoyed a good sleep except for the pain in his back. He massaged it with one hand and wiped the sand from his eyes with the other. 'Anyone been out?' he asked. The others shook their heads. 'Umm,' he grunted. 'Helleon or Linnia been here?' Again a negative response.

Giles grumbled as he worked out the stiffness in his joints. Petia was explaining to Anji how to improve his ability to turn and to project images misleading to their enemy. The boy concentrated, nodding from time to time as Petia emphasised a specific image which she had found useful.

Keja sat in a corner of the room, his ropes spread out before him. He inspected every inch of them, searching for frayed spots. He wished that he had his triple hooks, wonderful devices for hooking the tops of walls, ledges, window sills and tree branches, but they had been taken away by Onyx's guards. He had been so distrustful of Bellisar that he had not thought to ask him to manufacture some during their stay in the smith's quarters. Now he kicked himself and envied Anji the knife that Bellisar had forged for him.

Giles rubbed his eyes again as he saw the desert of Banda-narra appear where the wall ought to be. The scene changed to a pillar of lirjan skulls that had marked the Track of Fourteen, then shifted to the swirling, moving sands of the Calabrashio Seas. Giles shook his head, wondering if he was becoming ill. He felt his forehead: when he opened his eyes again the wall was solidly back in place.

'It's Anji practising,' Keja said, looking up from his ropes. 'It's been going on all morning – well – afternoon. Since he awoke. The boy is becoming good. Petia won't be able to teach him much more – all she does is sense emotion. Anji can project mental images. I've tried to avoid looking, but I've been treated to the slave cages, the temple in Kasha, and an attack by the desert tribesmen. It's uncanny.'

'Thank the gods,' Giles breathed. 'I thought a fever stole my senses.' He chewed on a piece of meat left over from the day before. 'Petia, have Anji turn down his new-found power. There's something I've got to puzzle out, something that wasn't right last night.'

Still chewing, Giles sank down facing the wall. He closed his eyes, bringing back images of the previous night, all the halls, corridors and stairways they had examined. For a long time he remained lost in his own thoughts. At last he came to the end of their long night of exploration. He remembered that it was only when they were returning to their hiding place that something had felt wrong.

Giles strived to make the picture clear in his mind. They had been on an upper floor when the dawn light began to filter into the citadel. They had hurried down many flights of stairs, but somewhere between the third and fifth floors he had hesitated. The images of stairways came and went. One stairway looked like any other. Walls covered with tapestry on either side, a flight of stairs going down.

Then a thought came to him. The relationship of stairs to the rooms seemed wrong. Giles thought back to the rooms they had been in. The room where they had been questioned, the throne room they had examined last night, the suite where they had been kept when they first arrived. He leaned back and stared at the ceiling of the storeroom. Yes, even this room. All the rooms they had been in were of the same height.

And the staircases they had come down were of the same length. But Giles realised that on the fourth floor there were no doorways into any rooms. Certainly there was a corridor running the length of the building – but not a single doorway along it.

'Something secret there,' Giles muttered. 'Something hidden behind those walls.' He uncrossed his legs and stretched them out before him, moaning as his hip joints protested. Old men should remember not to sit that way, he reminded himself. The pain subsided.

He lay back, staring at the ceiling. Petia threw a cloak over Anji, who, tired from his practice, had closed his eyes and napped. 'Giles,' Petia whispered.

'Hmmm?' His mind still turned over the problem, not content to stop where it had.

'I'm going to slip out and see if I can examine Onyx's bedchamber. It will be empty at this hour, and we don't know when the guards will be coming back. It's an opportune time.' She obviously expected an argument, but all she got was another 'Hmmm.'

She slipped out of the room and Giles returned to his problem.

No guards patrolled in this hall, but when Petia ascended two floors, she saw them standing at either end of the corridor. She crouched down and cast images of a scrawny tabby before and behind. Then, staying close to the wall, she made for Onyx's bedchamber. The guards took no more notice of her than they would have of a servant bearing a message down the hallway.

The door stood ajar, for airing Petia supposed. She slipped inside, and stood in wonder at the sumptuousness of the quarters. The room was dominated by a four-poster bed large enough for a zuulan of the farthermost eastern regions of the world and all his concubines. What a romp that would be, Petia thought. He could chase them all night and never catch a one. A brocade awning stretched between four ornately carved posts. Cushions of silk clustered near the headboard.

Petia scanned the room. One wall held a fireplace large enough to roast an ox. A small fire burned in it now, and she knew that she would have to search quickly. Someone might return to check the fire and add logs.

Wall tapestries depicting gods at play festooned all four walls. Petia wished that she had the time to study the beautifully woven arrases. An extraordinary artist had wrought them.

A voice startled Petia. She looked around, fearful that she had been discovered. The room was still empty. The voice faded away, then came back more strongly. '. . . to the coast. These Brada . . .' Onyx's voice faded in and out, as if he were pacing first one direction, then another.

Petia frowned. She searched for an airshaft or other opening in the wall which might carry the words to her. Then she noticed a door half-hidden behind a tapestry in the wall opposite the fireplace. She walked across the room and tugged gently at the handle. The door did not budge, but Onyx's voice came more clearly once again.

'When they return, we will turn this citadel upside down.' A second voice cut in. 'My lord, it would not be seemly to be overconcerned. The guards will bring back Brada prisoners, be assured. They will compensate for the loss of the Brada women.'

Petia wondered if this was Ulinek, the dwarf counsellor. They're just on the other side of the door, she thought. At the same time, she realised that the two rooms Onyx would most likely occupy during the day, the throne room or the room where she and the others had been interrogated, were a long distance from the bedchamber.

In the next moment, Giles' voice overlaid Onyx's response. She couldn't understand the words of either man, but this was followed by a silence before Keja's voice came through clearly. 'Ho. Anji, did you have a good sleep?'

Confused, Petia stood listening by the door. Voices came from the kitchen, the major-domo's loudest of all. She heard a captain of the guards snapping orders, a woman berating a maid for making up a bed sloppily and not replenishing a fruit bowl with fresh grapes.

Keja's voice came through again. 'What will we do tonight, Giles? Now that we know the layout of the building, will we begin searching in earnest?'

By the gods! Petia thought. Keja's words rang as clear as a bell. They were all in incredible danger if Onyx came to his room and overheard their conversation from the storeroom. She spun to hurry back and warn the others.

Giles' eyes went wider than Petia had ever seen them before. She continued to nod her head vigorously, her lips pursed.

'Yes,' she said. 'When your voices weren't interfered with by others, I heard you as plain as if I were in the same room.'

They whispered now. Giles felt apprehension crawl along his scalp, thinking of how their voices might have trapped them before they got any farther. 'Repeat it again,' he said, gesturing with his hand for her to start all over.

Petia crossed her legs and sketched with a stick on the storeroom floor. She drew the dimensions of the room, then the placement of the fireplace, the bed, and the door through which she heard the voices.

'You didn't hear the voices coming from the fireplace, or some vent near the bed?' Giles asked.

'No,' Petia whispered. 'I heard the voices from other places in the room, but the closer I got to the door, the better I heard.'

'What was on the other side of the door?' Keja asked.

Petia grimaced, exasperated. 'I told you. The door was locked, so I don't know.'

'It fits what I've been thinking since last night,' Giles said. 'Something's funny about this building, and I'm sure it's a room or rooms inside the walls, and probably passages we don't know. The voices certainly could carry through air shafts, but I think there's more to it than that.'

'If that's true,' Petia said, 'how do we find our way in? That's the next step, isn't it?'

'Don't know,' Giles said. 'I hope Helleon or Linnia come before dark. They might know something about it. If there are passages and we can get into them, we should be able to explore at leisure. We still have to be quiet, or Onyx will hear us, but, with any luck, we'd find out whether there is a hidden room.'

'Behind the door in Onyx's room,' Petia said positively.

When the sun set, they prepared to spend another night in exploration. Neither Helleon nor Linnia had come during the late afternoon. Keja was in the process of wrapping one of his ropes around his waist when a scratching came at the door.

When Petia opened the door, both Helleon and Linnia slipped inside, pouches slung over their arms. 'Food,' Helleon said, setting his bag down.

Giles dismissed all thought of food. He took Helleon by the

476

arm and whispered, 'You don't know how badly I wanted you to come today. Are there any passages inside the walls?'

'Passages?'

'Crawl spaces, air vents, even narrow hallways inside the walls, anything like that?'

Giles explained about the voices which Petia had heard and urged them to keep their voices to a murmur.

'Nothing that I'm aware of,' Helleon replied.

The look of disappointment covered Giles' face. It left with the next words.

'Wait!' Linnia said. 'In the cold room!'

Helleon nodded. 'Go ahead, you tell them.'

'There's a small space in the cold room. Some slaves bring ice to keep things cold, and there's a special storeroom set aside to hang whole oxen and pigs. In one corner there's a hole. It lets water run away when the ice melts. That's the only one I know.'

'Describe where it is,' Giles requested. He listened carefully, asking questions when he did not understand. When they had finished, he asked, 'Is it locked?'

They shook their heads. 'There's no reason for it to be. The cooks send people there all day to fetch meat for the spit.'

'Can you leave us some candles there?' Giles asked. 'We've run low.' When they nodded again, he said, 'All right, you'd better go now, before we all get caught.'

When the Brada had left. Giles pointed at the pouches. 'We'd better eat, now that there's food. Then we'll go take a look at this storeroom.'

No one prowled the lower levels of the citadel, not guards, cooks, servants, slaves, or even the bullying major-domo. They made their way swiftly along the halls, Giles feeling more confident with every step of his sense of direction within the vast building.

The ice room door fitted tightly but opened easily. Cold air hit them in the face and Anji pulled his cloak around him. They stepped into a large room filled with hanging meat, skinned and gutted, but not yet quartered. Along the walls stood boxes of fruit, apples, pears, plums, being kept cold to stave off spoilage.

Keja started to pull the door closed behind him and said, 'A joint of roast ox wouldn't taste too . . .'

477

Petia put her hand over his mouth. 'The walls have ears, and maybe eyes, too.'

Giles only glared and motioned for Keja to leave the door open until he found if the Brada had been able to leave candles. He found them between the fruit boxes, a half-dozen long white tapers. He lit one, watched it gutter for a moment before the flame burned steady, then nodded for Keja to close the door.

Quickly, he walked to the four corners of the room. At the corner farthest from the door, he found the space Linnia had spoken of. Water from the blocks of ice ran down to a grating and disappeared beyond the wall. The hole was large enough for them to crawl through on their hands and knees.

'Want me to go through and see where it leads, Giles?' Anji asked, eyes shining. 'I'm the smallest. Maybe it doesn't go anywhere.'

'Only five feet. No farther. Look around, then come out immediately,' Giles whispered in his ear. He handed the candle to the boy. 'Only a quick look,' he repeated.

The boy ducked his head, and took the candle from Giles' hand. He flung the front of his cloak back over his shoulders and, dropping to his knees, disappeared, leaving the cold room in darkness.

Good at his word, and afraid of what Giles might do to him if he disobeyed, he returned almost immediately. 'A passage that leads off in that direction.'' He pointed. 'The water runs off the other way. It's mucky for a few feet. You'll get your hands and knees dirty.'

Giles looked at the others, questioning them with his eyes. 'Let's give it a try,' he said.

Keja shuddered and Petia said, 'I'm the one who's supposed to do that.'

'Not you,' Keja said. 'You're a cat and can see in the dark. I'll bet it's like a tomb in there.'

Anji spoke up. 'It's not bad once you get through the hole. You can stand up and the candle gives a pretty good light. Come on, we're wasting time.'

Giles bowed to Anji, and with an impish grin the boy disappeared through the hole again. The rest of them were left standing in near darkness. Giles stepped towards the feeble candlelight and dropped to his hands and knees. Keja and Petia followed, blinking as they came into the light again.

A passage ran ahead in a westerly direction. Giles had to close his eyes and paused for a few seconds to recoup his courage. This was worse than the ice tunnels. He took the candle from Anji and stepped out ahead of them.

The candle threw its light against crudely finished grey stone. The passage was low, the ceiling only a few inches higher than Keja's head. It was cold, but Giles thought perhaps that came from the ice in the cold room. No water dripped from the walls; their dryness complemented the rough surface.

They walked forty feet to the passage end. The candle showed metal rungs affixed to the wall ahead of them, a ladder which disappeared up into the dark. Giles tested the bottom rung with his foot. It appeared sturdy and he stepped up, putting his weight on it. It was solid and he held the candle in one hand, reaching for the next rung.

'I'm going up. Wait here.' His voice rumbled in the hollow passage, but he was certain that, no matter how stranger the acoustics of the citadel, it would only be one more rumbling voice in the myriad which must reach Onyx's chamber.

The rungs remained firm, and Giles climbed twenty feet into the darkness, the candle showing only the sides of the shaft. At length Giles reached the top and stepped cautiously out onto the floor of another passage. It appeared to be much like the one they had entered: dry grey stone, high enough for the party to walk through. He examined it for several feet, then returned and motioned with the candle for them to come ahead.

When the party had assembled again, they discussed lighting a second candle but decided against it. Giles looked for a second set of rungs to take them to a higher floor, but there was none in sight. He led off down the passageway, intent on exploring to the west.

At the end of the passage they found not only another ladder set in the stone, but a passage leading to the right.

'We haven't gone high enough to be at the level to find any hidden room.' Giles moved the candle about, intently studying the walls and ceiling. He motioned at the rungs. They climbed again. This time finding two passages and a ladder.

Giles felt comfortable that they were now at a proper level to explore seriously. He suggested that they turn right, and with the candle held high to light their way, led off down the passage. They walked quietly but to their own ears their footsteps sounded like the rumble of thunder.

A soft breeze blew through the passages. Sometimes it was in their faces, sometimes behind them. Occasionally a gust made Giles wonder at the cause. They closed their eyes to keep out dust picked up from the floor.

From time to time they heard voices of guards giving the night-time challenges as they made their rounds of the fortress. They sounded edgy tonight, probably from lack of sleep on the previous night, Giles thought. He remembered such nights himself, nights during the War, when everyone knew that men like themselves sat on the opposite side of a meadow or at the edge of a forest, waiting for the dawn. Perhaps the testiness they occasionally heard would be of some assistance to them, though he couldn't conceive how.

They came to a spy hole in the wall. Giles was astonished at the thickness of these interior walls. The spy holes angled downward through the stone, to enable looking down into hallways and passages. Once he watched a young officer in discussion with an even younger guard. The guard's face showed apprehension, if not fright, at having no older companion with which to share his watch. The officer patted him on the shoulder before continuing on his rounds. He'll have enough to do before this night is over, Giles thought. He had done the same to many a young recruit.

They came to the end of yet another passage and halted. Petia pulled a farmer's sausage from her pocket, took a bit, and passed it on. 'Does anyone know where we are?' she asked around a mouthful of the meat.

'I do,' Keja replied, passing the sausage on to Anji. 'We're on the fourth floor, at the intersection of the farthest east hallway and the long main corridor.'

'I don't think so,' Giles said. 'That hallway that we looked down on is not the main hallway.'

'The point I'm trying to make is,' Petia said, 'do we know how to get back to where we entered this maze? We've been turning corners right and left, and I have the feeling that not one of us has been keeping track.'

Giles said, 'I can get us back from here. Don't worry.' But the Trans saw that Giles' attention lay elsewhere.

'I'll be the one responsible from here on. I don't want someone stumbling across our skeletons a hundred years from now.' She pulled out a piece of string from her pocket. 'An old Trans trick.' Petia smiled. 'Nothing to worry about from here on,' she said, as she knotted it once.

Thirteen

THE CITADEL must be honeycombed with the hidden passages, perhaps reaching to the top of the many-storeyed building. More important, might one of them provide a vantage from which to look down into the throne room, the private chamber, or even the bedchamber of Lord Onyx?

The candle had burned to a stub, dripping hot wax onto Giles' fingers. He handed it to Keja and pulled another from his pouch, lighting it. When it was burning well, he blew Keja's out, warning him, 'Keep that stub. We may need it before we're through.'

With the new candle lighted and confidence in Petia's ability to keep tracks of the twists and turns, they pressed on. The bite of sausage had relieved their hunger, but Giles wished they had brought provisions. The gigantic citadel might take days to explore. There was hope now of reaching parts of the complex which they would never have attempted during night-time forays through the main hallways and corridors. They couldn't stay for long, however, without food. They would need to return to the kitchen area during the night to steal provisions. Giles' stomach knotted at the closeness of the passage; while he trusted Petia's skills, he wondered if he would be able to win free of this maze.

481

But for the final key, anything could be endured.

They came to another spy-hole and gathered around it to peer down into a darkened hallway. Light flickered from a flambeau and Giles heard boots echoing, but no guardsman came into view. They moved on, finding more spy holes. This part of the citadel had many spaced evenly along the passage. They looked down from both sides of the passage into both the hallway and the interiors of rooms.

The overall structure of the building was complex, but there was a pattern to it, the genius of a master builder. He might compare with the great Alvarious Teneclif, whose masterpiece, the palace at Yetmifune, Giles had once seen during his wanderings.

Petia looked down into a suite similar to the one in which they had been held when they first arrived. Voices carried on the air, faintly at first, then louder and with a great deal of clarity.

'It's Maida that I want,' a young male voice said. 'Have you watched her hips when she walks away? She holds herself so straight and her figure is delicious. Oh, for just one night with her.'

Petia turned bright crimson. 'That's what I get for spying,' she whispered. 'That's how the sound must travel. Through the spy holes and along these passages. The problem is that you can't tell where it's coming from. But a great deal of it reflects back to Onyx's chamber, at least from what I heard when I was there.'

Giles nodded. 'It's a potent hold to have over his people. He must get great satisfaction out of hearing secrets that no one would suspect him of knowing.'

The four moved on, descending to the level which contained the throne room. They moved quietly, Giles checking through the spy holes to reassure himself of their position. Finally, they looked down into the room. Petia clapped Giles on the arm in appreciation of his growing knowledge of the citadel.

The room stretched empty before them, dimly lit by a torch at either end of the room. In the darkness, the throne stood massive, its intricate designs barely visible. Even the deep lion design of the back was veiled in shadow. They examined the room as well as they could, but inky black hid all but a small portion of it.

Disappointed, Giles slid to the floor and sat, holding his

head. The others sat, too, taking the opportunity to rest. He looked up at them, shaking his head. 'I'm not sure that we're getting anywhere. This place is so vast that we could roam these passageways for ever. They run everywhere, floor after floor of them. We'll need incredible luck to find the key. If we could find a treasure room, perhaps . . .'

He shook his head. 'I don't know. I just don't know.'

'Sometimes you seem to know exactly what you're doing, Giles,' Petia said. 'And other times, you're as confused as the rest of us.'

'I know. I get my bearings when I can look down into a hallway, then we go off at an angle and I'm confident. When we get to the next turning, I find myself lost again, until I find a spy hole that looks out on something I'm familiar with. It's frustrating.'

Keja slapped at his trousers, raising a cloud of dust. 'Thirsty, that's what I am. Confused, tired, and thirsty and hungry. Got any more sausage, Petia?' When she answered negatively, Keja hung his head. A mood of depression settled over the companions.

Giles needed to use his head rather than his feet if they were to find the key. But confusion blurred his thoughts and all he wanted to do was sleep.

Ulinek sat hunched over a stack of papers, muttering as he sorted them into stacks. Being advisor and counsellor to Lord Onyx proved no easy task. So much to attend to, and he was never certain where Onyx wanted him to expend his energy. A secretive man, Ulinek thought, not quiet, but he keeps his plans locked inside him. A hard man to advise.

A hard man to rob.

He moved another piece of paper, placing it onto a stack that did not need his immediate attention. He had learned long ago how to separate the urgent from the less important. A shouting fit from Onyx taught him to be ready with advice of some kind, even if it were never taken.

Never time to do anything right, always time to do it over. Ulinek snorted in disgust at the necessities involved in running the citadel for such a capricious lord.

Candlelight threw shadows of Ulinek's squat figure across the floor and onto the wall. The dwarf measured his age by his service to his lord, and he could hardly remember the time before Onyx. Once, Ulinek had travelled dusty roads from one fair to another, setting up his small booth to tell fortunes in exchange for copper coins. He sighed. Such a fine life it had been — until at a fair in Karlile when a robust man dressed completely in black, and, to Ulinek, huger than life, had sat across from him. He had asked such a simple question that Ulinek nearly laughed out loud and did not answer it. He couldn't remember what had prompted him to give the question more consideration than it deserved, and to answer it seriously. That had changed his life, even though he sometimes wondered at its lack of pleasure. By the standards of most men, he had accumulated enormous wealth, but he found no great joy in it. Putting up with Onyx's frequent rages was what he was paid for, or so it seemed.

Ulinek sighed and climbed down from his tall stool, striding across the floor to arrange the papers on a lower table which he could reach easily. He straightened the stacks and paused, cocking his head to one side. Strange noises in the citadel tonight, he thought.

He had been unsettled these last few days, since the escape of the Brada women. He had told Onyx time and again that he was of much more use to him when things were quiet in the huge building. If Onyx had not immediately summoned the guard and set pursuit in motion, Ulinek might have been able to tell him something substantive about the escape.

'I've got powers, yes I have.' Ulinek muttered to himself. 'If he'd listen to me, there's lots more I could tell him. Quiet is what I need, but he won't remember that. Gets guards running up and down the halls, fetching provisions, readying the horses, breaking out weapons. So much activity, so much noise, I can't think, the brain won't work. If he'd order silence through the citadel, I'd tell him quick. Ferret out those responsible, send my mind searching the rooms and corridors.'

Ulinek brightened. Silence ruled a citadel again bathed in moonlight from clear winter skies. Sleeping, everyone sleeping, and quiet so the mind can once be calm and creep from room to room, testing, searching, probing.

'Give me another day of quiet and I'll hand you the culprit. Already I have suspicions. Two young Brada from the kitchen staff. Oh, yes. Why didn't they escape with the other Brada at the same time? A good question, yes.'

Ulinek paced the floor, stopping to warm his hands at the huge fires burning at each end. Finally, his blood circulating, he reached for a large book, bound in the leather from an unborn calf. He carried it to his work table and climbed the rungs to perch on his stool.

Settled, he turned the vellum pages, pages he had written or transcribed himself. Ulinek chortled. This was the chief work of his life, a work he would finish one day, the gods willing – and Onyx one of them, or so he claimed. Ulinek wrote the record of Onyx's constant quest to return to his rightful place among the gods. It was an important position, so Onyx averred, but Ulinek knew better. If Onyx did not lie, he was a minor god, indeed. Yet powerful enough, don't forget that, old son, the dwarf told himself.

The reward for helping Onyx return to those paradisial fields, however, was enough that Ulinek never spoke of Onyx's rank in the pantheon. If they succeeded, the citadel became Ulinek's – a worthy prize for half a lifetime's work. Meantime Ulinek was warm, dry, well fed and held a position of power in Onyx's earthly realm. He kept his complaints to himself and did whatever he could to keep from upsetting the Black Lord. When he chastised Onyx for the pandemonium he caused, he did so humbly, waiting cautiously for the proper moment.

Ulinek hunched forward and studied his last entry. Complex, he wasn't even sure it applied to Onyx. However, better to write it down and give it some thought than dismiss it out of hand.

He closed his eyes and another image came to him. His eyelids popped open, and he stared into the orange, dancing tongues of fire. His thoughts raced, rejecting, ordering, searching for any flaw in his own abilities.

He let his mind roam the citadel. Yes, they were here. Inside the building. The four escaped prisoners. In spite of the obstacles in their path, all the reasons they should be dead by now, frozen or killed by the ice demons, he had no doubt that

485

they were back in the citadel. Perhaps they had something to do with the escape of the Brada women? Why? What did this gain them in their hunt for Onyx's precious key? Ulinek pushed these questions aside.

He must find them.

It was the sort of task in which Ulinek revelled. A problem with a finite answer and a logical way of exploring it. He had often done it for practice, searching out the guard captain or a pretty serving maid at odd hours. As vast and complex as the building was, patterns existed. He could explore the entire building with his mind, never missing a corner. His mental quest moved to the main gate, and he commenced his exploration.

A half-hour later, perplexed, Ulinek rubbed his eyes and swore. It showed the depth of his frustration. The four hid in the citadel, of that he was convinced. But his probe had failed to locate them. He cursed again and climbed down from the stool. Onyx must be told. Ulinek knew that he would once again bear the Black Lord's wrath because of the failure.

Ulinek dashed water from a basin onto his face and wiped his eyes clear with a towel. Silent halls led to Onyx's bed-chamber. He cast his mind here and there at random, still hoping to find where the companions hid.

Onyx awoke with a start as guards opened the chamber door for the advisor. Ulinek bowed and said, 'My lord.' Onyx sat up, blinking. He looked foolish, coming out of his sleep, Ulinek thought, especially wearing that nightcap with black tassels on the end.

'What is it, dwarf?' Onyx bellowed.

Ulinek bowed again, hiding the hurt that came each time Onyx addressed him in such a slighting manner.

'My Lord Onyx,' he began, 'I have reason to believe that the four prisoners who escaped earlier are back within the citadel.'

'What? You woke me to tell me that four useless Brada women did not leave? I should flay you, dwarf.'

'Not the Brada, my lord.' That's twice he's called me that, Ulinek thought, growing wroth. 'Grimsmate and his companions, the Trans woman and boy, and the thief.'

Onyx's eyes smouldered. 'Where?' His voice filled the room. 'The guards, summon the guard captain!' Onyx tugged at the bell rope beside his bed. 'The hall, the hall, you idiot.

Call for the nearest guard.'

Ulinek shuddered and held up his hands, supplicating Onyx not to destroy everything he had accomplished. 'My lord,' he pleaded, 'please contain yourself and I will find them. I know only that they are within the walls. Excitement and commotion in the citadel counteract my abilities.'

But it was too late. Onyx, in his black silk nightshirt and the tassels of his nightcap flying, plunged across the room. If Ulinek would not summon the guards, he'd do it himself. He flung the door open, bellowing, 'Guard, summon the captain. Tell him to roust the men. Prepare to search the citadel. And send for my valet.' He turned to find Ulinek covering his ears. 'Where are they? Take your damned hands away from your ears and speak, dwarf.'

Giles felt a hand on his sleeve and he awoke with a start. He must have been napping. He closed his eyes again and thought, I must be getting old. Shaking off the sleep, he opened his eyes again and saw Petia, her face close to his ear. 'What is it?' he whispered.

'Someone's probing us. I feel another mind. I'm sure that whoever it is knows that we're here.'

'The dwarf!' Giles said, now fully awake. 'Remember? Helleon and Linnia told us of the rumour. Does he know our exact location?'

'I don't think so.' Petia reached over and shook Anji. The boy shuddered in his sleep, not wanting to wake, fighting as children often do. Petia shook him again.

The boy's eyes opened. He scowled at Petia. 'Leave me alone. I was asleep.'

'I know you were,' Petia said. 'I need your help. Please.'

Anji struggled, rubbing his eyes. He stretched his arms and yawned. 'What do you want?' Indignation still tinged his voice.

Petia, somewhat exasperated herself, took Anji's ear and pulled it close to her mouth. 'Listen carefully, bratling. I think someone probes for us. Trying to find out where we are. Do you feel it, too?'

The boy's eyes opened widely. Awake now, fear showed in

his face. Petia nodded solemnly at him, and urged him to see if he sensed the same thing that she did.

The boy concentrated, then nodded without looking at Petia. He sensed the other's thoughts, but they were unfocused, confused. He turned to Petia. 'He's unsure – he's certain we are here, but his mind looks hard for us. What can we do?' Finally wide awake and eager to help, he was too unskilled to know the next step.

'We've got to create a diversion. He may know we are here, but if we can keep him from finding our exact location, we may be all right.'

'He'll tell Onyx, nevertheless,' Giles broke in. 'There'll be a search, but we may be able to avoid them. Why not imagine a roaring fire in another part of the citadel, Anji? That should create chaos to keep them all busy for a while longer. I'll think of something else as we go along.'

'Wait,' Petia said. 'His probing is all muddled now. His mind runs everywhere, agitated. I have no idea what's happening.' She paused, head cocked to one side, as if listening. Then she said, 'It's gone now. Completely. I don't know what's going on.'

'Stay alert,' Giles pleaded. 'If it happens again, let us know.'

'Believe me, I will,' Petia said. 'You, too, Anji. Keep your mind tuned to anything that doesn't feel right.' The boy nodded.

'Are we going to stay here or go?' Keja asked. 'I'm for moving on. They can't hit a moving target, that's an old motto of mine.'

'I think you're right, Keja,' Giles answered. 'Let's see if we can get up another level.' Giles led off down the passageway, praying that Petia and Anji could give them at least some warning. He wanted his weapons out when the soldiers came for him.

Giles found a stairway, swept cobwebs aside, and peered upward in the dim light. They had blown the candle out when they came to the spy holes, the light filtering through the slits in the stone sufficient for them to make their way. Giles lit the candle again to climb the darkened stairway. He made his way to the top and held the candle high so that the others could see the steps.

At the top, Giles said, 'Petia, describe again Onyx's private chamber.'

Petia knelt and drew a map in the dust of the floor. Giles nodded and blew the candle out, stuffing it under his belt. 'If we cross this passage and turn left at the end, we should come out above it. Let's hope there is a hole we can watch from. Maybe we'll find out something that will help us.'

He turned and led the way down an even narrower passage, then moved into a wider one. Within a few steps Petia caught at his arm. Giles stopped.

'For a moment,' she whispered, 'I thought I felt the probe again, but it's gone. Listen.'

Giles heard shouting ahead. While unable to make out the words, it sounded like Onyx's roaring voice. He put his fingers to his lips and tiptoed towards the sound. Within ten steps, they heard the voice more forcefully and made out the words. 'The guards, call the guards, you idiot.'

They gathered around the stone slit and stared down into Lord Onyx's bedchamber. Anji, the shortest, stood in front, and the others peered over him. He turned with a look of astonishment on his face and pointed at Ulinek. 'What?' he mouthed.

The dwarf sat on the edge of a hassock by Onyx's bed, his hands over his ears, his eyes shut so tightly they crinkled at their corners. Giles shrugged, not understanding either. Petia gestured to her head, waving her hands in circles to communicate Ulinek's confusion. She wasn't sure why, but if it stayed that way she was pleased.

Onyx disappeared from their view; he shouted for guards. He appeared again, shouting at the dwarf to find the intruders. Pain showed on Ulinek's face as he looked up, pleading with the Black Lord to give him the quiet he needed to do his best.

Petia pursed her lips. Now she understood. She touched Anji's arm and said, 'Smoke and fire.' To Giles and Keja she made a singular gesture. She cupped one hand in the other, placed them on her forehead, then slid them outward, trailing her fingers across the skin, telling them to blank their minds.

She pulled Anji away from the hole and sat him on the floor, sinking cross-legged to face him. 'Smoke and fire,' she whispered again, then closed her eyes, conjuring the image in her mind, a roaring fire, flames leaping along the edge of the citadel, thick, black smoke pouring from the windows and down hallways.

Keja fidgeted, trying to blank his mind, but it filled continuously with the scene playing out below them. He saw the dwarf again, pain obvious on his face, the sinister Onyx standing over him, berating him. He shook his head and tried to empty his mind of all thoughts and images. He looked again down into the chamber. He saw the fireplace on one side of the room, the rich tapestries Petia had described to them, the four-poster bed, and the doorway with the mountains carved on it.

Desperately he tried to erase these thoughts from his mind, knowing that he might give away their location and place them all in jeopardy. He closed his eyes, and images came of endless dusty passages and corridors, climbing rungs in stone walls. He pressed his hands to his forehead, trying to push his thoughts away.

The dwarf's cry reached them. Petia and Anji had been sitting motionless, concentrating on smoke and fire. Their thoughts were shattered by the cry.

'They're somewhere in the tunnels!' The shriek was one of desperation, a shrill shout to get Onyx to remain quiet so that Ulinek might pinpoint the intruders.

A sigh of relief came from the mountain of man striding up and down the bedchamber in his black nightclothes. Onyx drew a key from a drawer and walked to the door with the mountains carved upon it. Unlocking it, he flung it open. Giles glimpsed only a shadowy entrance into what he supposed was yet another tunnel.

'I know you're in there, Grimsmate, you and your companions, coughing dust in that honeycomb of tunnels. *I deny you escape!* Before you can retrace your steps, all the entrances will be sealed.' His booming laugh reverberated through the tunnels. It took a long time to fade, and once Giles thought that he heard echoes of the laugh meeting each other from opposite ends of the citadel.

Giles shook his head and pantomimed to them that there was no way that Onyx's men could seal the entrances and close of all passageways. He beckoned to them to leave their vantage point over the bedchamber. He led the way but had to go back when Keja did not follow. He pulled a depressed Keja to his feet and gave him a shove down the hallway.

At the next intersection, Giles turned left to find another

490

spy hole above Onyx's bedchamber – and over the door with the mountains carved on it. He paced off the steps he had calculated, keeping his eyes on the left-hand wall.

When he reached the spot, he ran his hands over the wall but found nothing. Anji, behind him, began to jump up and down. Giles started to curb the boy's enthusiasm; the boy pointed to the opposite wall.

There, at the level of Giles' head, was an ornate bas-relief. A shelf protruded from the wall, and above it was an exact replica of the mountains, the Mountains of the Lions, with their magnificent profiles cleanly etched in the sculpted stone. Giles stared at it, but Anji, delighted in his find, leaped up and curled his fingers over the edge of the shelf.

It fell away, pulled by his weight, and Petia stepped forward to admonish the boy. A section of the wall crumbled with the shelf. At floor level a smaller passageway was revealed.

The entrance was too small for the adults but large enough for the Trans boy to enter.

Fourteen

'I'LL BE careful,' the boy pleaded. 'Just let me go in for a few feet. I'll come right back and tell you what I see. If there's any danger, I'll crawl right back out.'

Petia shook her head, not wanting the boy to put himself in danger. 'We can't let him go in there, Giles. If something happens to him, there's no way we can rescue him. It's not worth it.' She raised her hand for quiet. 'The dwarf still probes for us. I can feel him.'

'What do you think?' Giles whispered, looking at the others. 'Anji is eager to see what's in there.'

Keja shrugged. 'It can't do any harm. I doubt that the key is in there, but we should take a look. Then we'd know for certain.'

'Let's think about this for a minute. There's something that Bellisar told us when we were in his smithy. By the gods, that seems like such a long time ago! Onyx retrieved the key from the mountains, which is where the map placed it. Bellisar melted the gold key but made a duplicate. We've assumed that Onyx wouldn't take the steel key back to the mountains to hide it. We've spent several days inside the citadel, learning the layout, discovering the hidden passages.' He pcked up the bas-relief from where it lay amid a mound of crumbled plaster. 'This may be the best clue we've had. I don't think we should ignore it.'

He looked at Anji. 'Are you sure you want to take the risk?'

Anji lifted his earnest face. 'I'm part of this company, have been ever since Petia rescued me in Bandanarra. I may be only a little boy, but little is what you need right now. You're all too big to get through the tunnel. I'm just the right size to squirm through. I can make the right decisions; I won't do anything stupid.' He turned to Petia and took her hand. 'Please, Petia,' he pleaded.

Petia took Anji's hands in her own and forced him to face her. She looked closely into his eyes and whispered. 'Promise?'

Giles watched as Anji nodded and said, 'Yes.' A single tear threatened to spill from Petia's eye. She was becoming more of a mother and less of a thief every day. It would be good for her when this adventure ended. He didn't intend that Petia would ever reach the Gate of Paradise before him, but he would somehow see to it that she and Anji shared in whatever treasures were there. They could never pass – only one could, and he'd be that one – but there would be enough for them to settle somewhere, buy a dwelling, hire a teacher for Anji, perhaps. By her own admission, Petia had not been a good thief. She got caught too often.

Giles smiled without humour. She hadn't even figured out the runes on the Gate telling that only one could pass.

Petia let go of Anji's hands. The boy turned and dropped to the floor. Giles handed him a newly lighted candle. The hole was too small for Anji to crawl on his hands and knees. Wriggling forward on his chest, he disappeared headfirst into the hole. Almost immediately the tunnel turned to the left and Anji struggled to make his body do the same.

'Anji,' Petia whispered. 'Send back images.'

Giles grinned wryly. She's still afraid for him, he thought. What will it be like when he's a little older?

Giles, Petia and Keja stood alone in the dark. The only sound was their breathing. Then, from Petia, 'He's turned another corner to the right. Wait, the tunnel is getting even smaller.'

Silence descended again as they waited for Anji to send an image back to Petia. 'He's still able to make it, but only by hunching along with his elbows. A tight squeeze.'

Keja folded himself to the floor and made himself comfortable with his back to the wall. He reached idly for something to keep his hands busy and touched the bas-relief. He pulled it onto his lap and ran his fingers over the sculpture, lightly touching both mountains and lions. Somehow it gave him sardonic comfort. The others seemed unaware that he was to blame for the dwarf finding out that they were within the hidden passages.

Time slipped away slowly in the darkness. When Petia received an image she relayed the information. Sometimes she said only. 'He's all right.'

Nearly five minutes had elapsed when a voice booming down the passage startled them. It was unmistakably the voice of Lord Onyx, and Giles sensed the pleasure he took in their predicament.

'Hear me, my friends. Are you enjoying yourselves in the dark passages? A bit dusty, are they not? Forgive me for not knowing that you would be visiting them. I would have had them cleaned for you. But I shall make amends for that. I'm sending something to you now – something which will clean those passages of unwanted filth. It will be there soon, oh, yes. It is deadly and swift, this cleaner of tunnels. And it's coming for you, my friends. You'll not escape me this time.'

The hearty, bellowing laugh that the companions had come to despise followed the message through the hollow passages. It twisted and turned, as their stomachs were beginning to do.

Anji's nose pressed close against the floor, and his elbows ached. He ignored the pain and struggled on. He had the opportunity to prove himself, and he didn't intend to let Giles or the others down. Most of all, he had to prove his capabilities to Petia. He was tougher than she thought, and sometimes she coddled him too much.

He thrust the candle out at arm's length and peered ahead. The restricting tunnel made it difficult to see past the halo of light. There was little headroom, but the tunnel appeared to slope upward. He scrabbled forward a few more feet and felt the surface begin to slant. He drew a deep breath and inched forward. His elbows slipped on the surface, and he put his fingers down to feel a surface different from that which he had been crawling over. That had been rough stone; this gave the impression of polished steel.

From the corner of his eye Anji noticed that the ceiling of the tunnel also appeared to be different. Handholds! He reached up with one hand and cupped his fingers, straining to pull his body along. Then he realised how they were meant to be used.

He relaxed again, thinking it through. The candle posed a problem. He needed to turn onto his back and use both hands. One step at a time, he thought, and began to turn over. Rolling was impossible in the tight quarters, but bit by bit he got onto his back, without losing the candle flame. He thrust the candle ahead of him and tried to make it stick to the polished stone. He puddled a little of the hot wax, then pushed the end of the candle down into it. But the slope of the tunnel defeated him.

Frustrated by the attempt, he took the candle in his teeth, the flame to one side, and reached overhead for the handholds. He pulled himself along the smooth surface with only minuscule effort. When Anji had covered twenty feet, he noticed only emptiness under his head. He reached backward and found that there was no longer a ceiling close above his head. The tunnel ended abruptly.

Anji removed the candle from his mouth and twisted his head to one side. He stared down into an open room. A narrow ledge ran around the edge of the room where Anji had emerged. He stood cautiously, his back against the wall. Holding the candle high and to one side, he saw the ceiling far above him. Below him stood a room empty but for a single

pedestal in the centre. On top of the pedestal lay a steel key.

Anji drew a deep breath and held it. Petia's mind searched for him. But all he could think of was that he had been right! The bas-relief of the mountains was more than a clue. It was the device that revealed the tunnel and led to the key. All he had to do was jump down into the room and retrieve the key. Their quest would be over!

He sent back an image of the room to Petia. The emotion she returned was one of concern. He expected that, and had become accustomed to it. But the concern was not only for him. He wished that they could communicate better. He saw the image of the tunnel where the others waited. Petia and Keja had their swords drawn and Giles stood with the halberd ready to thrust. Then an image of himself, peering cautiously before he jumped down into the room. She was urging him to be careful.

Anji examined the walls of the room as well as he could with the light from the candle. There appeared to be no door to the room, but he realised that one might be concealed. In the dim light, the floor appeared to be covered with a thin layer of white sand. The pedestal itself was of a white stone, perhaps alabaster. It was a simple column, square and unadorned, flat on top. The key rested in the centre of the surface.

Anji searched the room twice. He saw nothing dangerous. He could make the drop to the floor easily. He sat on the ledge, found a place where the candle wax would stick and made sure that the candle was steady and giving adequate light. He pushed off from the ledge and let his knees bend when he hit the floor. The bottoms of his feet stung a bit, but otherwise he had succeeded!

He picked himself up off the floor, dusting his hands of the white sand which covered the floor. Perhaps it had been placed there so that some watcher could see if the room had been disturbed. The gods forbid that anyone should look now, Anji thought. The marks he left were plain to see, even in the dim light.

He walked to the pedestal and, standing on tiptoe, plucked the steel key from the top. Highly polished, it gleamed in the candlelight, sending reflected light dashing around the walls. Anji held it in his hand, admiring the cleanness of Bellisar's

work. The final key, Anji thought, and flashed the image back to Petia.

He was too excited to note that no image came back. He lifted the key, pleased with his achievement. In his glee, he danced about the room, leaving more marks in the sand. He wanted to whoop, but he remembered the need for quiet in time and contained himself.

Finally, his delight exhausted, he tucked the key into his pocket. He checked it three times to be sure it was secure. He walked to the side of the room and looked up at the ledge. Checking the key once more, he bent his legs and sprang into the air, reaching for the ledge. He fell short. When he landed, he slipped on the sand, his feet going out from under him.

A sharp pain shot through his ankle. He rubbed it ruefully and picked himself up from the floor. He brushed away the sand, finding a wooden floor underneath it. When he had a large enough spot cleared so that he would not slip again, he made ready for another try. His ankle still hurt, but he ignored it.

He leaped again and fell short. The ankle protested against the abuse. Anji looked around the room for something to help him. The pedestal! If he could drag it over to the side of the room. He tested it. Whether the stone was too heavy for him or was attached in some way to the floor, Anji could not budge it.

Several more tries convinced him that he was trapped in the room. He was neither tall enough nor strong enough to catch the ledge. He sent as powerful an image as he could to Petia. Then he sat, rubbing his sprained ankle.

Anji went cold all over when he realised that Petia was much too large to come through the tunnel. He was a prisoner in the room and couldn't expect help. With tears in his eyes, he picked up handfuls of sand and flung them in frustration.

Onyx's words froze the three companions. They sounded so close that Petia was sure that he stood next to them. They might have been better off if he had been present. Onyx had loosed some terrible beast into the tunnels, and she had little doubt that it would find them.

'Bluffing,' Giles said. 'Onyx may know that we're in here

somewhere, but I think he's only trying to frighten us. Still, it's always good to be prepared.' He handed the sword to Petia and took a firm grip on his halberd. Keja took the hint and pulled his sword from his belt.

A blood-chilling howl echoed through the passages. It started with a roar, deep and robust, and ended in a high-pitched shriek which set their teeth on edge.

'By the gods,' Petia breathed.

The howl began again, and came at them from every direction. Petia grabbed Giles by the sleeve. 'What about Anji?' she asked.

'We'll have to take one thing at a time,' Giles said. 'Just remember, we defeated the ice demons and Onyx's steel men. Don't lose your courage now. It's only another obstacle to overcome. Whatever this thing is, we'll kill it.'

'You're a mountain of confidence,' Keja said sarcastically.

Giles grinned. 'Why shouldn't I be? With stalwart companions who have been through so much together, what's one more little beastie to worry about?' He turned his head, trying to sort the real voice of the beast from the echoes reverberating through the endless tunnels.

The howls confused them, coming from every direction. Keja turned to face the way they had come, while Giles took several steps forward in the direction they had been walking when they found the bas-relief. In truth, he thought, I don't know if there's one or a dozen nor from what direction they are coming. Where's Anji? If the boy were here we could retreat. In spite of his outward calm, his apprehension mounted.

He glanced at Petia Although she clutched the sword, her mind was on Anji. She crouched by the hole in the wall, shouting his name. She wasn't going to be of much good in the coming battle, with her mind torn between her own preservation and the boy's predicament.

Giles went to her. He had to shout in her ear in order for her to hear over the roaring that surrounded them. 'What of Anji?'

Petia held down panic as pain showed in her eyes. 'I don't know. I don't get any images. I don't know what's happened to him.'

Giles put his hand on her elbow. He glanced back at the passageway. In the distance two red eyes glowed in the dark.

They moved closer, and another roar shook the tunnel. At Keja's end, he saw nothing but Keja's startled face, looking back over his shoulder and staring down the tunnel.

'You've got to reach Anji,' Giles shouted. 'Concentrate.' He turned and gripped his halberd. 'Never mind the battle. Keja and I . . .'

The roaring ceased; all they heard was snorting and pawing. Unseen claws rasped against the stone floor. Keja came to Giles' side and stood, his sword ready.

'Giles. Anji is trapped,' Petia cried. 'He has the key, but he can't get out.' Giles turned one ear to listen, not taking his eyes from the red eyes which glowed ever closer in the darkness. 'He jumped down into a room and now he can't jump high enough to reach the ledge and get back to us.'

Giles cursed beneath his breath. 'Concentrate on Anji. You've got to figure out some way to rescue him. We'll do what we can with Onyx's little friend.' He shook Petia's arm. 'You can do it. Never mind how the fight is going. Just put your mind to getting Anji out of there.'

The sound of claws against stone came closer. The red eyes looked larger than saucers. A deep-throated growl sapped at Giles' faith in defeating this unseen creature.

'Come on, beastie,' he said. 'We're ready for you.'

He hoped that would prove true.

Petia crouched by the hole, ignoring the snorting and pawing from the other end of the passage. She followed Giles' advice and cleared her mind, focusing on Anji and the room into which he had so foolishly jumped. She went back over his route to the room, remembering the pictures he had cast back to her. It was impossible for her to follow him through the twisting tunnel. It had been difficult enough for a skinny cat Trans boy.

'Think, Petia,' she murmured to herself and pounded her fist on her knee. A memory flitted through her mind. She recalled one of her less successful attempts at thievery. She had been careless enough to wake the householder of a house she was burgling and had left hastily through a window. Not hastily enough, as it turned out. She had found herself trapped by the

night watch in a narrow passageway between houses. She had stood frozen, then remembered the feline part of her Trans nature. Catlike, she had escaped while the watch stood scratching their heads.

'Rope, Keja!' Keja's head swivelled. He tugged at a rope around his waist. He pulled the end free and unwound it quickly, handing it to Petia and resuming the grip on his sword.

Quickly Petia rewound it around her own waist so tightly that it hurt to breathe. Then she dropped to the floor, closing her eyes and focusing on the hidden part of her nature. She felt the changes and waited. Patience and impatience warred within her. The rope become looser. Never had Petia gone this far with physical transformation. Always before she had adopted cat traits, but never the full physical aspects of a true feline.

She saw Keja glance at her, close his eyes, and shake his head. Petia knew that he was still uncomfortable with this part of her Trans heritage.

Petia took one last look at Giles and Keja, standing ready for battle, murmured, 'The gods be with you.' and disappeared into the hole, her sleek cat body easily fitting the tunnel.

Ulinek cowered in the corner of Lord Onyx's bedchamber, his head throbbing from his attempt to locate the intruders. An impossible task, he knew, but Onyx insisted that he keep trying.

Soldiers filled the chamber. The guard captain arrived, accompanied by two lesser officers. Young recruits stood ready to act as runners, carrying messages from one end of the citadel to the other. How could he concentrate on a probe with so many people, talking, running here and there, their minds causing a continual buzz? Feet tramped the hallways, adding their hollow echoes to the din.

The ache in Ulinek's head moved up behind his ears; he rubbed his fingers over the heavy mastoid bones, massaging them in a vain attempt to relieve the pain. If only Onyx would provide him with the silence he so badly needed. He switched to rubbing his temples and forehead, then inspired, he sent a recruit for Actina, a serving maid.

When she arrived, Ulinek explained his distress and asked her to rub his neck and head. She had done this many times before and set to work with good will. Ulinek groaned with relief as Actina's soothing fingers massaged the cords at the back of his neck, brushing upward behind his ears. Of all the servants only Actina seemed not to notice his diminutive stature.

At last Onyx issued orders for all who remained in the citadel. Ulinek waited until he subsided, then lifted his hands in a plea for silence. 'Please, my lord. No intrusions for a moment. I beg of you.'

Onyx scowled, then stomped to a chair near his bed. He sat, frowning, chin in his hand, but he remained silent.

The serving woman continued to massage Ulinek's neck, and a measure of tranquillity filled the dwarf. He closed his eyes and probed again, for the first time in nearly an hour able to focus his mind. Up and down the passages, quickly now, before another disturbance.

He found the companions and knew that one of them had the key. 'My lord?'

'What? I thought you wanted quiet.'

'I have found them, my lord. One has the key.'

Onyx threw back his head and laughed. 'Have they found it then? I never would have believed it possible, but never mind. I have sent the beast for them. There will be no escape this time. As for the key, a small enough matter, for a small enough advisor. Is that not right, my dwarfish friend?'

'I do not take your meaning, my lord,' Ulinek said. But already fear of Onyx's next words was upon him. He knew what the Black Lord meant and dreaded what he was about to hear.

'I think you do, Ulinek. You, little one, are small enough to recover the key for me. Is it not so?'

Ulinek fell to his knees, and Actina drew back, embarrassed for the little man. The dwarf touched his forehead to the floor, grovelling towards Onyx. Ulinek's muffled voice pleaded, 'No, my lord. Please. Not the *passages*!'

He looked up to see Onyx's black eyes fixed on him. He found no pity in them. He could plead for ever, but in the end he would be sent into the passages – the *passages* – for the key. He closed his eyes, shuddered once, and collapsed.

Fifteen

GILES HAD time only for a glance at Petia as she disappeared into the hole in the wall of the passageway. The glowing red eyes commanded his full attention. He did not know what foul creature Onyx had sent against them, but he had no doubt that the Black Lord intended that it should rid him of the intruders for ever. He chuckled.

Keja gazed at him in the dim candlelight. 'You're crazy, aren't you? Death stares us in the face and you laugh.'

'Exactly,' Giles answered, continuing to watch the luminous eyes in the dark corridor. 'If we die, Onyx will have an impossible time of it getting the other four keys from the Callant Hanse. He'll never do it without destroying that ancient merchant house. Sometimes our mysterious man in black, god or not, doesn't think too well.'

The beast roared again, then grew quiet. It stopped pawing and scratching at the floor.

'Watch for it, Keja. It will pounce soon.'

Giles heard the sound of the beast churning towards him out of the darkness. The feet drummed faster and faster as they came. The eyes glowed larger and redder. Giles thought fleetingly of runaway wagons. 'Back against the wall, Keja!' he shouted. He flattened himself against the wall as the beast charged past.

The candle-flame wavered in the breeze stirred by the charging beast. Please don't go out, Giles prayed silently. In a pitch-black tunnel, there would be no battle at all.

The beast turned at the end of the tunnel and ambient light from the intersecting tunnel showed Giles and Keja what they fought. It spun on all fours and reared onto its hindlegs, standing as tall as the two men. Lizardlike, with short, massive forelegs and a thick body, it reminded Giles of an ocean amphibian he had seen from the ship that had carried them to Bandanarra. The captain had told him that the beasts were vicious and had been known to kill and eat humans.

Its flat face, long and slender, contained wickedly sharp teeth. A harsh rattle came from the beast's throat. The eyes blinked, then opened to glare at Keja and Giles. It dropped to all fours and pawed once. 'Here it comes again,' Giles warned.

The beast did not charge, however, but lumbered towards them, an unstoppable juggernaut. Giles heard the talons of its claws scratching the stones with every step. Its thick tail, saw-toothed along the edges, lashed back and forth.

He thought quickly. 'Watch the tail and the claws, Keja,' he said quietly. 'Can you build a loop with your rope?'

Keja immediately caught the sense of Giles' question. He loosened a second rope from his waist, and awkwardly worked.

Giles took several steps towards the beast to give Keja the time he needed. He held his halberd ready and watched the lizard creature advance. Several feet away from him, it reared onto its stubby hindlegs. Talons seemed to grow longer before Giles' eyes, and he knew that he faced a dangerous weapon.

He stepped quickly towards the beast, thrusting the axe-edge of the halberd at the palm of one claw. He felt the cutting edge bite into the flesh, and turned the shaft in his hand, withdrawing to use the point. Blood gushed onto the floor. The creature snorted in pain and swung its claws wildly. Giles stepped back quickly and the blow met only air.

The beast gave a hoarse grunt. Giles smelled the beast's foul breath and wrinkled his nose. There was little room for him to move – except back. He stabbed again at Onyx's pet; the creature retreated. Although Giles' weapon did not reach the animal, it gave him time to manoeuvre. He glanced over his shoulder at Keja and saw that the loop was nearly ready.

The beast extended its arms once again and attacked Giles. The man's world filled with the grime of its claws, dirt and filthy decay of meat ground between pad and talon. If those claws drew blood, Giles knew, his death would be a slow one.

He had seen disease run rampant during the War from lack of sanitation.

Keja joined Giles, laying the loop on the ground. The beast balanced on its tail, confused by two people. Its small brain decided both might die as easily as one. It lunged forward. Keja brought the flattened loop up in an overhead gesture. The loop fell short but settled over one outstretched scaly limb. Keja pulled the loop taut and planted his feet solidly on the floor. He leaned back against the rope, straining to contain the beast.

The beast struggled against the rope, then fell to all four feet to pull against the restraint. Its tail lashed from side to side. It opened its mouth, changed direction, and rushed Keja.

The small thief leaped into the air but kept a hold on the rope. He came down on the beast's tail. The tail lashed once and threw Keja against the wall. Stunned, he gripped the rope and staggered aside in time to avoid the tail once again.

'Pull, Keja,' Giles shouted.

His head throbbing, blood running down his side, Keja planted his feet. He pulled the beast's leg off the floor, exposing a soft spot underneath.

The beast turned its head towards Keja; Giles seized the opportunity. He positioned the halberd, and with the force of his entire weight, lunged with all his might. The point disappeared into the fold of flesh and sank several inches up the shaft. Giles shoved hard against the butt of the halberd and saw it sink even deeper into the beast.

The beast roared in pain and struck once again at Giles. He let go his grip on the shaft and backed away, weaponless. He retreated down the hallway with the beast, dripping blood, following after him. Keja was pulled along behind.

'Use your sword!' Giles yelled, searching desperately for something to use as a weapon.

Keja wrapped the rope around his wrist, then used his free hand to pull his sword loose. He took aim at the base of the creature's neck, and thrust. The tip found the spot, but the blade bent and the sword slipped away harmlessly.

But the sword had done its work. Distracted again, the beast twisted its head, looking back at Keja.

Giles leaped towards the huge lizard and grasped the halberd shaft, twisting and turning it as he pulled it loose. The creature snorted and hissed. As it opened its mouth, Giles thrust the point into the back of its throat. The hiss turned to a gurgle and gouts of hot blood rushed from the creature's mouth. Its tail lashed feebly once, but the spear had taken its toll. Bleeding internally from the first thrust and choking on its own blood, the beast's head lowered.

Giles and Keja backed away and let it die. They stood, breathing heavily. Giles moaned, aching all over. His joints seized up on him, even though he had escaped unscathed. Keja's wounds were minor and quickly bound. Only then did Giles turn to the hole in the wall and wonder how Petia was doing. He wiped his face with the back of his sleeve, then froze as Onyx's voice echoed through the tunnels.

'Having fun with my pet? No? Then you can thank me. I have something else. But I won't send it yet. As host, however, I must see that you don't lack for entertainment, am I not right?' The laughter turned Giles' blood into a frigid river.

Petia crept catlike along the tunnel, first to the left and then to the right. Unable to carry a candle, her feral-eyed pupils dilated to capture any available light. The dim light from the candle in the corridor faded within a few feet, and she made her way in total darkness. Every sense alert, she followed the tunnel to the right. Then she saw, many feet away, a faint ray of light.

Realising that the light must be Anji's candle, she crept towards it as quickly as possible. When the tunnel sloped upward and her hands clawed at the slippery stone beneath her, she couldn't find a purchase. There was little need for caution now. Onyx, warned by his dwarfish advisor, knew that they explored the passages.

She called to Anji. 'Are you all right?'

Anji's small voice echoed as if it came from a barrel. 'Yes, Petia, but I can't jump high enough to reach the ledge.'

'I know. I'm at the slippery stone. How did you get through?'

Anji explained about the handgrips in the ceiling of the low tunnel. Petia told him to be patient, turned onto her back and felt along the upper surface until she found the holds. In a few minutes, she looked down into the room and saw a subdued Anji standing morosely on the floor below.

'I'm sorry, Petia. I was so excited about seeing the key that I jumped down before I even thought about how I'd get back.'

'Don't worry, I'll get you out.' She balanced on the narrow ledge and unwound the rope from her waist. She let one end of the rope down into the room. Anji took hold of the end.

'What do I do now?' he asked.

She coiled the extra rope carefully at her feet, then looped the rope over her left shoulder, and took up the slack in her right hand. 'See if you can climb the rope. Try to lean back and walk up the wall.'

The boy looked doubtful, but he grasped the rope and put one foot against the wall. He leaned back and pulled himself up. He managed to gain a couple of feet before his arms weakened and he had to jump back down. 'I'm sorry, Petia, my arms are not strong enough.'

Petia knelt, rubbing the shoulder which had taken the boy's weight. She looked at the leftover length of rope coiled beside her. It was nearly as long as the slippery tunnel she had worked her way through. Quickly she pulled the rope up from the room and knotted a loop in its end. Dropping the loop back to Anji, she said, 'Stand in the loop.' She explained what she was going to do. 'When you get close enough to grab the ledge, try to take your weight on your arms and scramble up.'

Anji stepped into the loop and held onto the rope. Petia removed her tunic and carefully made a pad on the edge of the ledge for the rope to slide over. She wound the rope around her waist again and backed into the tunnel. She turned to lay on her back and immediately felt her body begin to slip on the polished stone surface.

The rope tightened around her waist, but her body continued its slide down the tunnel. She held her breath, knowing that for every foot she slid, Anji was a foot nearer the ledge. She felt the pressure on her stomach ease suddenly. The boy had reached the top of the ledge.

She waited patiently until she heard Anji's voice. 'Petia?'

'I'm here,' she replied. 'I'm not coming back up the tunnel. Coil the rope around your waist and follow me out. But be careful. There might be something waiting outside for us.'

Petia discovered that she could not turn around in the tight quarters. Cursing silently, she backed her way down the tunnel. Before she had gone more than a couple of feet, Anji slid head first down the tunnel. She reached out and tousled his hair. 'You still have the key?'

'I made sure that it was deep in my pocket before I left the room, and I checked again just now.'

The final key was theirs!

Giles and Keja stood over the lifeless beast. Blood still oozed from its side and mouth, but its breath was gone. They leaned heavily on one another, glad of the contact with another human. Giles cleaned his halberd as well as he could on the beast's body.

Keja went to the hole in the wall and leaned his head down to the opening. 'Petia,' he shouted. 'Are you there?'

Petia's voice came from so close that Keja jumped back, startled. 'She's almost back,' he said to Giles. 'I wonder if she has Anji.'

'He's right behind me,' Petia replied. 'We'll be out soon — and he's got the key!'

Petia's legs emerged as she twisted and turned negotiating the tight turn in the tunnel near the entrance. She backed out on her hands and knees and stood, winded from her efforts. She shook all over as her body thickened once more into its normal shape, the cat sleekness leaving her.

Anji's face showed in the opening, a bit grimy, but wearing an angelic smile. He stood and hugged Petia, then dug deep into his pocket and pulled out the steel key, flourishing it dramatically. When he had finished, he held it out to Giles.

Giles examined it briefly, then handed it on to Keja. Keja looked at it and shrugged. 'So that's the last one,' he said, handing it back to Giles. 'Hardly looks worth the effort.'

'I haven't seen it yet,' Petia said, peevishly.

'Sorry, Petia, I thought you had.' Giles handed the key to her, but she gave it only a cursory look before handing it back to Anji. Keja opened his mouth to protest, but Giles warned him with a hard look.

The boy stuffed the key back into his pocket. 'What's next?' he said, finished with his task and looking up at Giles.

'Getting out of here. And getting Helleon and Linnia out with us. I hope you and Petia can produce some incredible images.' Giles leaned back against the wall and drew a long breath. 'Can you project a void at the dwarf? A nothing, no emotion, no action, emptiness?'

'Whatever for?' Petia asked. 'What will that accomplish?'

'I want Onyx to think we've been killed, that the beast has done us in. If he thinks we're dead, he'll forget about us and go on to other things.'

'You forget the key, Giles. He'll send someone for it, a soldier or maybe the dwarf.'

'Yes, but we'll be gone by then,' Giles responded. 'Keja and I will empty our minds. You and Anji project "nothing". Onyx will think he has plenty of time to recover the key.'

Keja's face turned white. 'I can't do it, Giles. I tried before and I couldn't empty my mind. The harder I tried the more thoughts flashed through it. That's how Ulinek found out where we were. I'll give us away again.'

'You can do it, Keja,' Giles said. He stepped forward, and before Keja could react, Giles closed his fist and struck the younger man flush on the chin. He stepped back, rubbing his knuckles, and watched as Keja sagged to the floor.

He turned to Petia. 'Do it. Now.'

'Better than a nothingness,' Petia said, 'how about an image of the lizard-beast devouring our bodies?'

'A great idea. Just don't overdo it.' He motioned with his hand for her to get on with it.

Petia conferred with Anji briefly, then they sat, facing each other. They linked hands. The two Trans stared deeply into each other's eyes, concentrating, fixing the image, agreeing on the details.

Giles realised how much he asked of them. For several minutes, Petia and Anji didn't move. Giles propped Keja up against the wall. He felt secure that Keja wasn't thinking anything that would interfere with the success of the image-makers. Petia released her grip from Anji's hands. She leaned back, sighed, and nodded at Giles.

'Are you all right?' he asked.

Petia stood and helped Anji to his feet. 'Yes,' she whispered, but her voice came out faint and thready.

Giles reached under Keja's arms and lifted him until he was erect and leaning against the wall. He bent and slung him over his back. 'Hang on to me,' he whispered back. 'Both of you.' He staggered under Keja's weight, shrugged once to redistribute it, and began to walk down the passage. Petia bent and picked up the candle. She put an arm around Anji, caught up with Giles and clung to his sleeve.

At the end of the corridor, they turned the corner. Giles made unerringly for the steps that would take them down two levels of the citadel.

Anji tugged at Petia's sleeve and she turned, questioningly. 'Rats,' Anji whispered. Petia paused and concentrated. 'Onyx has turned rats loose in the passage above. They've found the lizard's body and are feasting on it.' She grimaced. 'It's ugly. They're tearing it to shreds.'

'As long as it's not us,' Giles said, turning the corner at the bottom of the stairs and striding off towards the iron ladder.

At last they came to the narrow shaft leading downward to the storeroom where they had begun their night's adventures. Giles lowered Keja to the floor, propping him up, and stood back to flex his back muscles. He was winded from the exertion and stood, breathing heavily, heart triphammering.

'How are you going to get him down?' Petia asked.

'Wake him up. He's going to have do the rest under his own power. Got to rest.' He sat and said, 'Have you got any strength left?'

'Not much,' Petia replied. 'What do you need?'

'We've got to get those two Brada out with us. Can you let them know?'

'I'll try. All I can do is throw images at them and hope they understand.'

'Anything. Show themselves carrying the garbage out.' Giles leaned forward and slapped Keja's cheek, gently at first, and when he got no response, harder. Keja moaned and his eyes fluttered. 'Come on, Keja, time to come back to life.' Giles slapped him again and Keja's arm shot up to grip Giles' wrist. 'Ah, good.' Giles relaxed and let Keja come awake by himself.

'I think I've gotten through. I wish my powers weren't so

simple. I sent them a bit of fear, a need to escape. I'd like to be able to communicate in words instead of hoping that vague emotions will get the message across.'

'Be thankful for what you have,' Giles said. 'It's time to get moving again.' He pulled himself up and went to the shaft, peering down and listening intently for any sounds below. There were none. He motioned Petia to go down first. Anji followed.

'You next, Keja. And I'm sorry about the punch, but I had to make sure you didn't spoil things.'

Keja grunted and made a face that turned into a wry grin. 'I know, but I'll get even with you sometime, just the same.'

'I reckoned you would,' Giles said, slapping him on the shoulder. 'Down you go.'

Two floors below they came to the cold room. As they crawled through the hole into the room, Keja spotted a string cheese hanging from the ceiling. He drew his battered sword, cut it down and sliced the strings. Quickly he knotted several strings together, testing to see that the knots held.

'The key, Anji,' he said, holding out his hand. Reluctantly the boy fished in his pocket and pulled forth the final object of their long quest.

Keja slipped the key onto the string, measured it against Anji's head and tied a final knot. He slipped the loop over Anji's head. 'Tuck that inside your tunic,' he said. 'We're not about to lose that key now.' The boy grinned, happy that they still trusted him with the key.

Giles opened the door a crack, listening cautiously for any sound of guards in the hallway or kitchen area. He closed the door gently. 'I don't hear anything except normal kitchen sounds,' he said. 'Any ideas about how to get out of here?'

'Why not the same way we came in?' Keja asked.

Petia closed her eyes. When she opened them again, she shook her head. 'Guards there. But that's the only doorway on that side of the citadel.'

'We're on a lower level now,' Keja said. 'Can we go out of a window like the Brada women did when we helped them escape?'

'I'd forgotten completely about that,' Giles said. 'It seems like aeons ago, in some past life. Are your ropes in good order?'

He turned to Petia and Anji. 'Can you tell anything about our Brada friends?'

'How long do they need to be?' Keja asked as he unwound his ropes.

'Helleon and Linnia are uneasy, but they're not sure why. They act as if they know we've returned, but they don't know what to do.'

'We can't wait any longer. We'll take them right out of the kitchen. Come on.'

Giles opened the door, checked the hallway and led the others at a run towards the kitchen staff's quarters. Startled faces looked up from their tasks as they rushed into the room. The major-domo rushed towards them to protest, and Keja hit him square on the nose. Blood gushed and the portly man sat down squarely on a sack of potatoes.

'Helleon! Linnia!' Giles shouted. The two came running, Helleon from around the corner and Linnia from the other side of the huge spit.

They left as quickly as they had entered. Keja spotted a meat hook and grabbed it as he flew by. 'Where's a room with a window?' Giles asked as they ran.

'This way,' Linnia said, and shouldered her way to the front.

The furnished room was empty of inhabitants. Giles rushed to the window and found it locked. Grabbing a chair, he smashed at the window, shattering glass and bending the frame. Keja deftly knotted the meat hook to his ropes. When Giles finished, he threw the ropes through the window, hooking the underside of the ledge with the hook.

'Brada first, then Anji, Petia, Keja,' Giles said. 'I'll go last.'

They quickly slid down the rope to the ground thirty feet below. Gathered at the bottom, Keja tried in vain to loosen the hook and retrieve his ropes.

'Leave them,' Giles said. 'They've served their purpose.'

The dash across the meadow to the forest seemed to take for ever. They heard a warning cry from the citadel and saw sentries on the top battlements gesturing. They had been spotted but ran for the protection of the trees and underbrush.

Just inside the forest they stopped to rest.

'Giles, Helleon, Linnia.' Natabor and another young Brada

swung down from a tree above them. 'No time to talk. Follow us.'

They trotted across a clearing, ducked behind a bush and found the Bradas' secret path. Giles silently praised the dedication of the two young Brada who had waited for them. They had promised to wait for two nights. This was the third. He wondered how much longer they would have waited. Good people, he thought, and then set his mind to keeping up with their tireless pace.

But Giles began to tire immediately. Within five minutes, he knew his old body wouldn't be able to maintain the pace. Panting, temples pounding, his breath coming in gasps of liquid fire, he stopped, using a tree for support.

Sixteen

ALONG THE sea's edge, the Brada set up a temporary encampment deep in the forest, surrounded on three sides by brackish marshland filled with potholes and ponds. It was a difficult area to search, and not a likely place for the Brada to have disappeared.

Giles and the others arrived, weary and bone tired. It was a long run with few stops; they had pushed hard to get back to the coast. With every step, Giles was more impressed by the Brada's stamina, intelligence, knowledge of woodlore, and most of all by their determination to hold on to what they considered theirs. But this did nothing to alleviate the pain Giles felt in every muscle in his body.

He was near collapse when he entered the camp. Giles vaguely remembered hearing a hawk screech, as if on the hunt, and realised only later that it was a warning from a perimeter lookout. He slumped to the boggy ground, not caring about the wet and cold.

'A feast tomorrow,' Veldon said. 'Tonight, a nourishing broth and a long sleep.'

Giles nodded wearily and thanked him before Keja and Natabor half-carried him to a temporary hut made of beach driftwood, conifer boughs, and chinks filled with moss. The last thing he remembered was the harsh texture of the blanket with which someone covered him.

The late afternoon sun, glinting wanly through the ocean mist, greeted Giles when he awoke. Although he had slept, he hadn't truly rested. His body ached all over and his vision blurred and cleared. He had about reached the end of his endurance—and yet Giles knew the hardest part still lay ahead.

Giles stirred enough to find Keja and Petia. Anji sat with two village elders, excitedly telling them of the part he had played in stealing the key from the heart of Onyx's citadel. Giles let the boy boast. Little enough reward for the risks taken.

To Veldon, Giles said, 'Lord Onyx won't stop until he punishes all Brada.' He stopped short of mentioning the steel key. Veldon might know of it; whether he did mattered little to Giles. All that counted now was Onyx's wrath and what he'd do to stop them.

'We waited only for you,' Veldon replied. 'We have endured much at Onyx's hand, but as you see, this is a temporary village. Most of the Brada have gone farther south to avoid Onyx's steel warriors. We can now join the others.'

Giles wanted nothing more than to rest but realised the necessity for flight. 'Let's leave now,' he said. 'We may have lingered too long.' Giles had developed a sense for danger over the years. Even through his fatigue, he sensed the nearness of death.

Veldon nodded and motioned to Natabor, who came to them and said that canoes awaited them on the beach.

'We intended to walk,' Giles said. 'You and your people should be on your way.'

'Many left during the night while you slept. Speed is your true ally against Onyx.' Natabor cocked his head to one side but didn't say what he thought: Giles Grimsmate couldn't walk ten feet, much less the many miles required for escape. Instead, Natabor said, 'We'll take you along the coast faster than you could travel on foot. We cannot take you all the way to a port, but we will leave you with others, friends of the Brada, who will take you. From there you must be on your own.'

Giles gripped the young man's arm. 'You have done more than enough. We are grateful.'

Natabor shook his head. 'No, brother, it is we who are grateful.' He shouldered two of the packs and led the way to the beach.

The canoes were long and narrow, only one person wide. Natabor ushered the companions into the slender boat, seating them one behind the other. He pushed the canoe off from the sandy beach, wading through the water to his knees, then leaping aboard to take a seat in the front facing the six paddlers already churning water with their long, powerful strokes.

Natabor grunted once and the six Brada lifted their paddles. He grunted again, and they lowered them into the water. Then he hit the side of the canoe softly with the heel of his hand and the first stroke took them out on the waves. Giles marvelled at the precision and power with which the young men stroked.

Soon, the shoreline disappeared and Natabor turned the canoe southeast and established a tireless rhythm. For two days they stayed beyond sight of land. Occasionally, the Brada exchanged places, each taking a turn at navigating. Sometimes the paddlers would switch sides so that their arms would not tire, but always they moved up and down silently in the waves, with nothing to look at but endless water. The Brada took short naps from time to time, but Giles, feeling more tired than he had since the wars had ended, slept often and long.

At the end of the fourth day, Natabor signalled to the navigator to turn landward. When they came within sight of land, a small fire glowed on the dark beach. The canoe made directly for it.

'Giles,' said Natabor, 'we must leave you now.' He started to say more but emotion choked him. He hugged Giles close, then turned and jumped back into the canoe before the older man could appropriately thank the Brada.

'Some good fella, eh?' said a man lounging near the fire. He coughed and spat into the fire. 'We will set you on a beach near Grifield. From there you are on your own. You have never seen us nor will you recognise us if you see us again. Understood?'

A man of few and direct words, Giles thought. 'Nor do you know us. We are grateful and we thank you.'

'Not for you. For them.' The man indicated the rapidly vanishing Brada canoe. Their packs were taken and stored in a kind of dory, much wider than the canoe, with high bow planks. Six men pulled the oars and they travelled only by night, hugging the coastline. By early morning, the dory slipped into a small cove.

The leader, whose name they never learned, stepped onto a rock ledge and held the dory steady. Giles and the others heaved their packs ashore and followed them.

Immediately the leader stepped back into the boat, and the oarsmen backed out of the narrow channel. As the companions stood, trying to find a path up from the cove in the faint light, a whisper came across the water, 'May the gods speed you.'

The Sea Hag was only one of many taverns with accommodation along the docks. It displayed a shabby exterior, but Giles thought it safer than the fancier inn down the rocky road. Petia vouched that the sheets were clean, and Keja pronounced the smells from the kitchen to be wholesome and appetising.

Giles set off early in the morning to enquire about passage to Trois Havres. When he returned in the mid-afternoon, disappointment showed in his face. 'They tell me that shipping is limited to Grifield during the winter. Ships do call, but they are few and far between. We could wait a month, they say.'

'What will we do, wait?' Petia asked.

'I don't think that would be wise,' Keja said. 'Onyx is looking for us.'

Anji spoke up from the corner where he polished the knife Bellisar had given him. 'I was out in the town this morning and heard people gossiping about Onyx. He is expected. Keja is right. We cannot linger.'

'It's time to move on,' Giles said. 'Just like the old ballad says, "last night she slept in a goosedown bed, tonight she sleeps in the heather." Keja, I'll leave it to you to find horses for us.'

When Keja returned an hour later, he brought more news of Onyx. 'The Black Lord's not here yet, but some of his men are. The ostler took me into the stable, and I saw a row of saddles hanging along one wall in the tack room. They all had Onyx's crest in steel on each side of the cantle. Another little project from the forge of your friend, Bellisar.'

'How many?' Giles asked curtly.

'Six,' Keja replied, 'but the ostler said that he expected to be full by tonight. The ostler's a talkative old man. I played the interested stranger. He told me all about Onyx. He's expected with another dozen men by evening.'

'Did he give you any reason for Onyx coming now, in the dead of winter?' Giles asked.

'He didn't know,' said Keja. 'He said he heard some of the men talking about looking for someone, but he thought they meant some women.'

Petia snorted. 'Men are all alike,' she said, looking scornfully at Keja and Giles.

'How about the horses? Did you get us any?'

'Two was all he had. And jugheads at that. But I figured we couldn't be picky. Anji will have to ride one with you, and Petia and I will ride double on the other.'

'I'll ride double with Anji,' Petia said.

'No,' Giles said more forcefully than he intended. 'Keja and I are too heavy together. We need to make the best time we can, and riding double is going to slow us.' The strain mounted on Giles. He wanted nothing more than to be back on Hawk's Prairie and through the Gate of Paradise.

Without Keja. Without Petia and Anji. Without the continual pressure of pursuit from Onyx and Segrinn.

Petia gave in with obvious reluctance. They hastily packed and got the two horses an hour after sunset. The fog drifted in from the ocean, covering the town. All was quiet and the companions rode along the edges of buildings disturbing the eerie setting as little as possible. They breathed more easily when Grifield lay behind them.

A short way along, the fog thinned and the moon tried valiantly to show them the road. Winter had brought mud-puddles and potholes to the road to Larra. The fog made it difficult to guide the horses, so Giles let his mount pick its own way. No one had told them that the road would dwindle to a mere track within a few miles of Grifield.

Before they had gone a mile on the treacherous path, Keja's horse stumbled. When it recovered balance it began limping. Giles slid off his horse to examine the animal and found that it had an old, uncared for cut behind the fetlock.

'How far to Larra?' Petia asked, her eyes glassy and un-focused.

'About fifteen miles from Grifield, another twelve miles perhaps,' Giles said. 'Why?'

'Because I'm certain that Onyx has found our trail and comes after us. I sense his emotions strongly. Triumph. Hate. It's definitely Onyx.'

'That's just fine,' Keja said. 'We'll never get away from him. He'll hound us the rest of our lives. Or until he gets the keys. How'd he find out about us this time?'

'How does he ever find out about us?' Giles said. 'How has he followed us all over the world? Shall we keep asking ourselves those questions every time we turn around, or shall we do something about it? We have to stop him, once and for all.'

Keja looked up from examining the horse's leg. 'Are you crazy?'

Giles shook his head. 'No, I'm just tired. I'm not getting any younger, and I want to be finished with this whole adventure. We've got the keys, but we also have Onyx after us once again. Until we do something about him, we'll be chevied around the world. He's like a plague. Our lives aren't worth anything until we rid ourselves of him.'

Keja shook his head, obviously concerned about the state of Giles' brain. 'You have a plan?' he asked.

'At the moment, no. We should leave the road, hide some-where until we've had time to think. One horse is lame and even with a head start, they'll catch us if we keep going.'

The fog swirled around them, becoming thicker or thinner with the vagaries of an offshore breeze. They could hardly see

516

their surroundings, making it almost impossible to stay on the track leading along the coast.

'Some things are in our favour,' Giles continued. 'We're ahead of Onyx by a few miles, he'll expect us to continue straight on, and the fog slows him as much as it does us. But we must leave the road and soon.'

He tied the horses to a windblown scrub oak and shouldered his pack. 'Best we walk. The horses are no good to us now,' he said as he strode off.

The others caught up with him in short time, and felt their way along the track. Each time the fog thinned, Giles stopped, hoping to see enough of their surroundings to make a decision. Once he stopped and cupped his ear, listening to an unidentifiable thundering sound.

A short time later it became clear. Ahead a waterfall rushed its way over boulders. The force of its passage created air currents that lifted the fog thirty feet into the air. When they reached a narrow bridge spanning the stream, Giles could see a way up alongside the water.

'If we go up here, the rushing water will drown out any noise we make. It will disturb the dwarf, too, if Onyx brought him along.'

They climbed steadily, and as they gained elevation the fog thinned. At the top of the cliff a long meadow sloped gently upward. The stream running across it burbled less boisterously before it cascaded over the edge of the cliff.

Giles sat, breathing heavily from the climb. When his heart had slowed, he looked at the others. 'Now's the time for thinking. We must rid ourselves of Onyx, once and for all. Tell me everything you think of, no matter how stupid it sounds.'

'We can't fight the entire troop,' Petia said. 'Not with swords. They outnumber us. If what Keja heard is correct, there are at least eighteen of them, plus Onyx.'

'You're right. Eighteen against four. It has to be something that gives us the advantage, something devious.'

Keja stood. 'Excuse me, I've got to relieve myself,' he said, and walked away along the edge of the cliff. When he returned a smile crossed his face.

Petia grinned wryly. 'Feel that much better?' she asked.

'No, it's something I saw. I don't know if this will work,

Giles, but you said to mention everything. When you get to the edge of the cliffs, there is an overhang where the winds have sculpted out the rock. You think you're walking on solid ground, but from the side you can see that there's only about a foot of soil and sod, and nothing but thin air beneath it.'

Giles nodded. 'Go on,' he said.

'Farther down, a huge hunk of cliff has fallen away. It must weigh tons. But it didn't slide far. If we could get it moving again, it might carry right down to the track.'

'And bury Onyx, is that what you're thinking?' Giles asked.

'Keja, that sounds —' Petia began, but Giles stopped her with a gesture.

'Let's take a look. Lead on, Keja.'

When they reached the place, Keja stretched his hand out. 'Stand over here, Giles. See how there's nothing but emptiness under those overhangs? They've got to be dangerous. Now, see where that big piece gave way.'

Giles stared down. Twenty feet below the dawn light limned a chunk of earth, broken away from the top and still wearing its sod and grass crest. Cracks and crevices around the base of the huge hunk showed that its purchase was precarious at best.

'Rope, Keja,' Giles said. He took the rope from the young thief and knotted it around his waist. 'Keep a firm grip on that,' he said as he disappeared over the side of the cliff. Giles made his way down the landslide to the huge chunk of earth. He prodded the hairline cracks and larger crevices with his halberd point, nodding to himself from time to time. He skirted below the fallen segment, and Petia feared that it would choose that moment to release its tentative grip.

When Giles climbed back up, he said wearily, 'It's worth a try. If it lets go, it will be splendid. If it doesn't, let's hope that Onyx doesn't look up and discover us. Keja, we'll have to be roped, and you've got to find something to anchor us. If that goes, the whole cliff could go with it.'

An hour later all was ready. The companions waited nervously. Giles and Keja took the outside places, Petia and Anji, the inside. Giles had probed cautiously again and thought he had found the precise spot that would trigger the avalanche. Anji had gathered some thick lengths of scrub oak branches and Keja had tested them for strength. They had placed boulders to provide leverage, and dug warily to reveal wet clay underneath the base of the cliff segment. Giles showed his first optimism in days.

They squatted patiently behind the fallen segment of the cliff, alert for any sign of travellers along the road. Petia occasionally cast for emotional activity back along the road. She could give them ample warning, but still all were tense. This might be the only opportunity to rid themselves of the Black Lord.

Below, the fog swirled in from the sea, eddying with the breeze. At times they could see the road, and at others it vanished beneath a soft grey layer. Giles worried that the fog might never lift.

Nearly an hour later Petia signalled that she sensed something. 'How far?' Giles mouthed, afraid that even the slightest sound would carry over fog and water to warn their enemy.

Petia shook her head slightly and whispered, 'Can't tell yet.'

Tense now, they waited impatiently, eager for any action. At last the sound of horses snuffling carried faintly to them on the moist morning air. Giles flexed his arms in anticipation, anxiously peering below for sight of the road.

Keja nervously checked the ropes which held them. He had sharpened a branch into a stake and sunk it deep in the ground some distance into the meadow. Each of the companions was held by a rope tied to the stake. If the whole cliff let loose, he was certain they would be safe.

The discipline of Onyx's men was good. They came without a sound. There was no conversation, only the occasional jingle of a snaffle and the creak of leather. Hoofbeats were muffled by the soft winter ground.

Giles stood, hoping for a glimpse of Onyx – and that it would come soon enough for them to set the landslide in motion. In answer to his prayer, the seaborne fog thinned.

Onyx did not ride at the head of his troop. The guard rode single-file on the narrow track, and Giles counted heads as they neared. Another and another, appearing out of the mist, heads down and muffled against the wet chill.

The others had risen, too, and taken their places. Eighteen, Giles counted silently, and hoped once again that Keja had heard the correct number. He caught his breath when the next head coming out of the swirling fog wore a black casque ornamented in gold. Lord Onyx, the Black Lord.

Giles' arm swept down and the others concentrated their energies on the job ahead of them. Giles' halberd prodded deep into a crevice he had discovered earlier. When he had pulled it out, wet clay covered its tip. He hoped that the moisture beneath would provide the slippage they needed. They would give it all the encouragement they could.

Keja threw his weight against the end of a long thrust into a hole they had dug. A boulder several feet in circumference provided a fulcrum for the log. Petia and Anji each had positions where they added their lighter weights to the project.

Giles leaned his weight against the halberd, probing, urging, goading the tons of earth to release its precarious grip. He felt a tremor under his feet, as if the fallen segment could not make up its mind. Again he probed, finding a soft spot through which the speartip cut. Again and again he worked it back and forth, loosening the soil's hold from the more solid earth below it.

Giles felt more than the quivering movement. The entire section began to slide, slowly, and he raised an arm to urge the others to greater effort. Keja jumped up and down, throwing his weight against his prying log, thrusting its end up a fraction of an inch farther each time.

When the earth gave, it did so with silence and great dignity. It gave not so much as a groan but began to slide effortlessly, the top collapsing inward as it went. It gathered momentum, and Giles watched jubilantly.

The section pulled great hunks of earth after it, strata breaking away and following down the slope. Petia felt the earth move beneath her feet and tried to scramble up the slope. Her feet were pulled out from beneath her and she fell – but Keja's rope held. She turned, pulling herself to her feet, and headed for the top of the slope before any more dirt gave way.

Keja felt the slide begin and scrambled to get out of the way. The log, loosed from its mooring, slid off the boulder and banged his ankle. He leaped away to avoid further injury. Anji jumped the other way and scrambled up the slope.

Giles simply stood and watched the results of their efforts. The landslide cut through the fog, swirling it. It gathered in the loose dirt below and grew with every passing moment. A low rumble surrounded them as it gained momentum. He saw guards look up and kick their heels into their horses. Horses plunged at the sound, and their riders attempted to control them. The narrow track between cliff and seashore allowed little room for manoeuvring – and none for escape.

He heard Onyx shout, but the words were meaningless. Riders at the beginning of the file urged their mounts forward. Some of them might make it, Giles knew. For others, escape was impossible.

Giles saw Onyx pull his horse around in a vain attempt to escape in the other direction, but it was too late. The leading edge of the landslide hit the bottom of the cliff and cascaded across the track. Onyx's horse reared, then its hind legs were swept from beneath it. It fell heavily on its side. Onyx lifted one foot from the stirrup.

The earth swept over him. Giles saw one arm raised, the fist clenched, then Onyx disappeared completely, buried under tons of earth.

Giles felt the rope suddenly tighten around his waist. The earth disappeared beneath him, and he swung in empty space along the cliff face. He had been so intent upon the happenings below that he had not felt the ground giving way. He craned his neck and saw Petia and Anji scrambling up the slope.

Keja was already on top, reaching a hand down to assist the others. He called down to Giles, 'Don't do anything. I'll pull you up.'

After what seemed an eternity, Keja pulled Giles far enough to plant his feet and climb to the top. Willing hands pulled him the last few steps. Keja sat, massaging his hands. 'You're a heavy one, aren't you?' he said between gasps. 'Not only are you getting old, you're getting fat.'

'Did it work, Giles?' Petia asked. 'Is Onyx dead?'

'I think so. Nothing would surprise me much with that man, but I saw him buried under the landslide. If he's not dead, then I'll believe his story about being a god.'

Larra was a city of remarkable attractions. A castle and a temple dominated the two hills of the city, commerce the middle slopes and warehouses and dock facilities the level spaces near the ocean. The four companions drew a collective breath as rays of the winter sun reflected from the golden tower of the temple.

The city was clean, the people prosperous, and best of all, several ships had anchored in the harbour. They waited their turn to dock, moorage being at a premium.

Anji touched Giles' arm and pointed. Several of Onyx's guard rode down the street. Their heads were bowed and they slumped in their saddles. They looked neither right nor left. Giles saw that they had nothing to fear from the few battered survivors of Onyx's escort.

Giles felt no sense of triumph at the sight. If anything, the weariness he'd experienced before returned even stronger. Was entry into Paradise worth such death, destruction and hardship? Giles heaved a deep sigh. Soon enough, he'd find out.

And abandon his friends when he did so.

He set his mind to their immediate objectives. A bath, a meal, a bed, a ship. All were easy to find. The *Flying Cloud* sailed to Milbante in two days and the companions were aboard; the voyage not particularly pleasant. Winter winds and weather and an occasional squall made it a trip during which the companions stayed below a good deal of the time, and more than once fought off seasickness.

But in the gods' own time it ended. The ship docked at Dimly New and Giles and the others were mounted once again. Sanustell lay only a few miles down the coast road. The keys, as Giles had to convince Keja once more, rested safely in the vault of the Callant Hanse.

How did Giles tell his small, suspicious friend that he need not fear those of the mercantile house but rather the man who rode beside him?

Seventeen

'AH, NEW clothes!' Keja cried like a child with a new toy. He stuck out one arm to admire the crimson sleeve ribbons and the material blousing from the tight velvet cuff.

'You're incredible, Keja,' Petia said, watching the fashion show. 'I've never seen such vanity.'

'Are you two ready?' Giles asked from across the room. 'Anji and I have been ready to go for the last half-hour.'

Keja turned one last time to see whether his new trousers fitted as well as he had thought when he purchased them. They were tight and Petia admired the curve of his bottom in the mirror once again. She would never let on that she thought so, but Keja did have a wonderful body.

Keja picked up his new cloak, heather blue with two broad grey chevrons, and quite dashing. He twirled it to see how the ends layed out, then stood still to admire its drape.

'Come on, Keja,' Giles ordered. 'The women will all adore you. But they won't have a chance if we don't get out on the street where you can be seen.'

Once Giles got them moving towards the Callant Hanse, he allowed no further delay. On the street he walked determinedly, with Anji trying to match him stride for stride. Petia and Keja walked along behind, but Petia kept the young rogue from stopping to admire the goods in shop windows. When they reached the marketplace, she had a more difficult time. Keja wanted to paw every item laid out in the stalls, his quick glances roving from one table to another. Giles and Anji got farther ahead and Petia pulled Keja by the arm.

At the Callant Hanse they announced themselves and their

business. They were ushered into the consultation room. The young master, Simon Callant, entered and greeted them. 'You're all looking satisfied,' he said. 'I take it you've successfully found the final key.' Giles nodded. 'And now you want the other four?'

'Not yet,' Giles said. 'We think we'll give the final one into your keeping for a while.'

Surprise showed on Callant's face, but he kept his thoughts to himself. He looked at the gaudy Keja Tchurak. 'And you would like to see the other four keys.' It was more statement than question.

Keja reddened. 'Yes.'

Callant pulled the bell rope close to hand. When a young man appeared, he ordered the keys brought from the vault. 'And meantime, refreshments. Jaeger.'

When the servant poured the wine, Simon Callant toasted the end of a successful endeavour, but true to the philosophy of the great merchant house, Callant asked no questions about how they had obtained the key. He talked about the state of the economy, the upcoming goose fair, and the hanging of a rogue several weeks back.

When the keys arrived, the servant presented them on a red velvet pillow. Giles nudged Anji, who removed the cord from around his neck. Giles pulled a small knife from its scabbard at his belt, and snicked the string holding the key. He gestured to Anji, who removed the final key and placed it with the four others.

Giles shivered at the beautiful sight: four gold keys, each with a semi-precious stone in the round flat portion at the end of the shaft. Peridot, ruby, emerald, amethyst. And the final key, which ought to have been gold, a duplicate in steel. The hair on the back of Giles' neck rose at the sight of them.

'May I?' Keja looked at Giles, who nodded. Keja lifted the keys, one by one, and examined them. Then he passed them along to the others. Anji, last in line, replaced them with reverence.

Giles drained the last of his wine and stood. 'Thank you, Master Callant. We will be back.' He led the way out of the room while the young banker stared after them.

The days wore on slowly, but no one seemed to mind. The companions had money from the jewels and gold they had brought back from their adventure in Shahal. Petia spent her time teaching Anji to read and write. Giles took long, pensive walks along the seawall. Keja managed to keep himself occupied with the young ladies of Sanustell's society.

Giles carefully kept a close watch on ship movements into the harbour. Few ships crossed from Bericlere during the winter. Harsh winds threatened when the first one called, and the captain and crew of the second were an ugly lot, whom he did not trust. The third would have done, but it was sailing for the far east of Bericlere, and Giles decided to pass.

In the midst of waiting for the proper ship, Giles worried over the course he must follow. He knew he had to trick his friends and steal the five keys to the Gate of Paradise. Only One May Enter. That inscription haunted him until he lost weight and began to sleep poorly. Petia thought he had an ague; but even self-centred Keja noticed and inquired often.

Giles knew he would have to act soon. But how?

Hints of spring came to trees and shrubs when a fourth vessel called, a clean ship with a wholesome-looking crew. Its next port of call was Arginis, near Klepht where their adventures had begun, although they hadn't known each other at the time. Giles made arrangements with the captain for passage for himself and his three companions. They made a final visit to Callant Hanse and took possession of the five keys.

Simon Callant stared suspiciously at Giles – or did the grizzled old veteran only imagine it? Giles Grimsmate's hand shook as he secured the five keys and bid the mercantile house owner farewell.

The voyage proved calm, in spite of brisk spring winds. The companions walked the deck from bow to stern and back, enjoying the fresh air. On the tenth day the landmass of Bericlere showed on the horizon, and on the eleventh the ship made land and docked at Arginis. The companions said their goodbyes to captain and crew and found an inn for the night.

The Sleeping Kraken was as cosy an inn as they had ever

stayed in. Mistress Allyne hovered about them as if they were the first guests she had had in years. She fussed over the fireplace, rattling it up into a full flame and adding another log. She insisted that they were warm themselves while she mulled wine for them. When they were warm both inside and out, she showed them to their two rooms. Both had fires burning in fireplaces and the sea chill in the previously unoccupied rooms had fled.

Early the next morning, Keja began the accumulation of gear for their trip to Hawk's Prairie – and the Gate.

That evening Keja staggered into the inn with a grinning Anji at his heels. 'Damn the boy,' Keja announced. 'We looked at every horse in town and some outside. "Giles wouldn't like that one," he says. "No, too old, see the teeth. This one's got a nasty temperament. Bowed tendons on this one, look." He wouldn't let me buy even one horse so we could ride. No, we had to walk all over town, and then retrace our steps.'

Giles laughed as Keja recited the litany. Petia smiled, because Giles had not laughed in a long time. She worried about him. Since arriving he had become increasingly withdrawn.

'But we have four good horses, Giles,' Anji said proudly. 'The best I could find. They are strong and well-mannered and will carry us wherever we want to go. Not one of them will go lame, I promise you.'

'I believe you, Anji. You have a gift with horses. Now, you're just in time for supper. Mistress Allyne says that she has something special for us this evening.'

Still they lingered in Arginis. Giles, usually the restive one, found dozens of reasons not to continue. And each day spent at the inn wore him down even more.

Finally, Petia said, 'The weather has turned fine. The trees have blossomed while we've been here, birds are building nests, the spring lambs have been turned out to pasture and still we sit.'

The others did not speak, eyes on Giles. Giles rose and paced the room. 'Well, I'm ready,' he said. 'No more delays. This may be the greatest adventure of them all.' The words caught in his throat. 'We will leave in the morning.' With that he almost ran from the room.

They rode along the coastal road from Arginis to Klepht, the sun shining stronger than it had for days. Evidence of spring was everywhere. To their left the calm ocean waves lapped on a shingle beach. Listening to the riffle of rocks washed back and forth by each wave lulled the riders. They relaxed in their saddles, enjoying the fresh air and the greenery springing forth at every hand.

All, save Giles. Each clop of his horse took him closer to the Gate and the need to betray the others.

'It hardly seems like we're on the last leg,' Petia said, 'When we started this, I was sure that we'd never make it. But it didn't make any difference. I was running away and had nothing better to do.'

'I was running, too, in a sense,' Giles said. 'I didn't think of it that way at the time, but I couldn't stand my own village, its people, and, most of all, its memories. I told myself that I was off to see a bit of the world before I got old. But I was really running.'

Keja laughed out loud. 'You two don't know the first thing about running. I'm not even going to tell you about some of my chases.'

'Speaking of running, Giles, would it be all right if we didn't go through Klepht?' Petia looked concerned. 'I had forgotten until now. I killed a couple of men who followed me out of Klepht, and the city guards' memory is long.'

'And I was so looking forward to the fish stew at the Laughing Cod.' Giles pulled a map from his tunic.

'I'll never think of you without seeing you pulling out a map,' Petia laughed.

'They come in handy,' Giles answered. 'We'll turn off and take to the cliff tops.'

By evening they were northeast of Klepht, sheltered in a vale. They were seated around a campfire, content with full stomachs, reminiscing about their earlier adventures. It was a scene that would repeat itself each evening. They relived the scrapes, the times they had been near death, the good people and the bad whom they had met, and most of all they delighted again in their triumphs.

Petia retired early, snuggling down in her blankets on the opposite side of the fire, with Anji close by. For a while, Giles and Keja talked in a desultory fashion. Giles got up to add wood to the fire, and checked to see if Petia slept soundly.

When he sat down again, he turned, a serious expression on his face. 'I've got to talk with you, Keja. I've been waiting for the proper time.'

Keja's eyebrows lifted. 'What about?'

'The Gate. Specifically, the inscriptions written on the archway above it. Do you remember it?'

'I can't say that I do,' Keja replied. 'I remember that there were runes, but I couldn't read them.'

'I could. They say that only' – Giles swallowed hard at the lie – 'two people can enter the Gate.'

Keja's mouth dropped. 'You mean . . .' Keja pointed helplessly at Petia and Anji sleeping opposite the fire.

'It appears that way to me,' Giles replied. 'Can you imagine what it would be like if all four of us got there and then Petia and Anji discovered that they couldn't enter?'

'What are you proposing, Giles? Come on, spit it out.'

'It's obvious, Keja. We've got to take the keys and leave Petia and Anji.'

Even devious Keja was taken aback at this. 'But after all we've been through, we can't do that!'

'I don't intend to leave them penniless, Keja.' Giles frowned. 'I'm not that mercenary. With all the wealth we'll have when we unlock the Gate of Paradise, we needn't worry about money, or jewels, or gold for ourselves. I intend to leave them my share that we withdrew at the Callant Hanse. They won't suffer. It will be more wealth than Petia has ever dreamed of. She can settle down with Anji, see that he has schooling, own her own dwelling and horses. She'll have enough to last her the rest of her life, and give Anji a good start as well.'

Keja stared into the flames, as if dealing with something he could never have imagined, coming to grips with a new idea. He got up, stirred the fire, added sticks, and poured a cup of tea for himself. When he sat down, a puzzled look crossed his face.

Finally he shook his head. 'I thought I was the one who was underhanded. When will we go?' he asked.

'There's plenty of time yet, but we should pick a time and then stick with it. The keys are no problem; they're all in a sealskin packet. We'll go quietly in the middle of the night. We'll be well away by the time they wake.'

Keja nodded. 'Enough time to reach the Gate with days to spare, so we can take what we want and be away before they catch up with us.'

Giles knew exactly how many days it would take to reach Hawk's Prairie and suggested when they should leave. Having got Keja's agreement, he smoked one last pipe, then stretched out beneath his blankets. For a while, he thought about his betrayal of the Trans woman and her ward. At last he slept, restlessly.

A week later, as he built up the evening fire, Giles signalled Keja that they would leave tonight. Keja nodded. Although there had not been any opportunity to talk about it further, both men had made their preparations. They would leave with a minimum of noise.

After supper Giles asked Keja to help him wash their bowls in a nearby stream. 'Tonight,' he told the small thief, hating himself for it. 'I've got the keys. They'll be asleep soon.' Keja nodded his agreement.

Halfway between midnight and dawn Giles placed his hand over Keja's mouth, and shook his shoulder. The man roused himself quickly, threw his blanket over one shoulder, his pack over the other, and crept away to the place where the horses were tied.

Before leaving, Giles placed his own treasure in Petia's pack. Now he looked sadly at Petia and Anji and whispered an apology to them. He saw Petia's lips turn upward in a smile, as if she had heard him and acknowledged.

Giles turned away, heavy in his heart. He liked Petia and Anji, perhaps even loved them, and would miss them terribly. 'Damn,' he muttered. If there was a way to explain it to her, he would have stayed and done so.

He walked carefully away to the horses. Without a word to Keja, he threw the saddle on his mount, stuffed the bridle into the top of his pack, and loosened the halter rope. He turned and led the way down to the stream, then waded downstream. His face was a stormcloud, and had Keja been able to

529

see, he would have thought twice about accompanying this man.

For a long while Giles waded through the water, seemingly oblivious of its coldness. He hated himself and thought more than once of turning back. But ahead lay the Gate of Paradise and the promise locked behind it. He had pursued that dream for over two years, and he was not to be denied. But he had never betrayed friends, and he knew he must do it once again before passing into Paradise and the obliteration of his bodily aches, pains and increasing old age.

Paradise meant youth to Giles, a removal of pain more valuable than any gold.

At last he turned, dripping, from the stream, and tied his horse to a bush so that he could properly saddle and bridle it. He lashed his pack to the back of the cantle and mounted, waiting impatiently for Keja. When Keja was mounted, he nodded curtly and urged the horse into a canter.

The cool night air did little to erase Giles' intense anger with himself. He raged internally for the remainder of the night, and when Keja essayed conversation, Giles cut him short.

But something more than his betrayal niggled at the edges of Giles' mind. An hour before dawn, he stopped, head cocked to one side as if listening.

'What is it?' asked Keja, hardly any happier than Giles over their perfidy.

'Something's wrong.' Giles' eyes widened. 'Segrinn!' he cried.

'What? What do you mean? He's back in . . .' Keja's voice trailed off. 'Why should he stay at Onyx's citadel,' the small thief said, 'when the Black Lord is dead?'

'He knows where we go and has had a month or more to go directly while we dawdled.'

As one they cried, 'Petia!'

They spun and galloped back towards the camp they'd vacated. As Giles rode, a sense of impending disaster mounted. Just out of earshot of the camp, he halted their rush. They dismounted. He fingered the sword dangling at his belt but did not draw it.

'Giles!' Keja whispered urgently. 'Listen!'

The snuffling of hounds came on the wind. Giles drew his sword; Keja followed his lead. The wind in their face carried wet animal scents. Giles' entire body came alive once again as he prepared for combat.

When one of Segrinn's hell-hounds bounded out of the shadows, Giles reacted instinctively. The sword tip spitted the animal, but the hound's weight carried Giles to the ground. Keja finished the animal with a powerful overhead cut that severed its spine.

Keja started to gloat. Giles silenced him. A dozen feet away stood a large, black figure. The glint of wan firelight reflected off the dagger blade.

Giles moved with purpose — and a silent tread that hadn't been his for twenty years. The sword spun around, edge at the hidden figure's throat.

Segrinn squeaked as the blade bit deeply into his throat. Giles spun him around and Keja kicked the dagger out of the slaver's hand.

'Quiet, or I cut your throat,' Giles whispered hotly into the man's ear. Segrinn's struggles quieted.

'You'll not get away with this,' Segrinn said in low tones. 'You might take care of that fool Onyx, but not the son of Lord Ambrose! The cat Trans will be mine again! I swear it!'

'He's mad, Giles,' Keja said. 'Listen to him. You'd think he had the sword at your throat.'

'Name your price. I want the Trans bitch!'

Keja faded into the dark, returning a few minutes later. 'He's alone. No sign of soldiers. And that was the only hound.'

'Wealth!' cried Segrinn, beginning to froth at the mouth. 'Gold! I want the bitch!'

Giles cut deeper and felt liquid drip down the sword blade and on to his hand. 'Silence!' he hissed.

Segrinn ignored him. 'Onyx was a fool. He wanted only those ridiculous keys. I want Petia Darya!'

'What of your troops?' asked Giles, still worrying.

'Dead, with Onyx. Even his hawk perished with him! You killed the man who bonded you away from murder charges. Ingrate!'

'Onyx killed the priest,' Giles growled. 'He left me to take the blame.' Giles had suspected Onyx had been responsible

531

for his release but hadn't known until this moment. But all that lay in the past – the distant past.

'*I want her!*' Segrinn heaved and tossed Giles over his shoulder. As he swung through the air, Giles jerked hard on his sword. A fountain of blood showered down from Segrinn's severed neck. But the huge man seemed not to notice. Head bobbing at a crazy angle, he lurched towards the camp where Petia still slept peacefully.

Keja moved with lightning speed. His sword cut at Segrinn's legs. Hamstrings slashed, the insane slaver toppled and lay twitching in the mud. Giles and Keja stood, staring at the body.

'He'll never bother her again,' Keja said, shock in his voice.

'Get the horses. We'll drag his carcass away. The hound, too.' Giles peered through the thicket towards the dying campfire. Petia hadn't stirred.

'You're still going on to Hawk's Prairie? Without Petia and Anji?' Keja seemed even more shocked at this.

Giles made an impatient gesture. He had given Petia one final present. But even killing Segrinn and saving her from his insane lust seemed small recompense for stealing Paradise.

Eighteen

THE DAY dawned with clouds in the sky and an occasional shower. Giles rode hunched in the saddle. He was exhausted from the long ride, for he had pushed his horse through the night. Beside him rode Keja Tchurak, a curious expression on his face. Giles interpreted it well – another measure of his growing ability for treachery.

'Giles,' Keja said, 'there's something I don't understand.'

'What?' Giles asked, instantly alert.

'The Gate of Paradise — if we're to believe Onyx — was a form of punishment. He had to recover the five keys before he returned to his pantheon as a god.'

'So?'

'Why should the Gate allow *two* through? Wouldn't it be more reasonable that the gods intended only one, Onyx, to return?'

'Maybe Onyx lied.'

'I've considered that,' Keja said, frowning. 'He might have been as obsessed as Segrinn was, in his own way, but I don't believe he lied.'

'Look!' Giles cried. 'There's the Gate! Out there!'

As Keja turned in the saddle, Giles neatly clipped him on the side of the head. The small thief tumbled from the saddle to lay motionless on the ground. Giles hastened to dismount, checking to be certain Keja wasn't seriously injured. With trembling fingers, Giles used Keja's precious ropes to bind the thief securely to a small tree.

Keja's eyelids trembled, then opened. It took several seconds to focus. Then he asked, 'Why, Giles?'

'Forgive me, Keja. Please.'

'I can hardly believe this is you. Pleading? Begging me?'

'I'm sorry, but what lies on the far side of the Gate is more precious to me than any gold.' He hunkered down, his face close to Keja's. 'Youth, Keja. Vitality! No more will my arthritic joints pain me in the mornings. You can't know how difficult it's been for me to keep up with you and Petia.' His face softened. 'And Anji. I see so much in him that I want again for my own.'

'Why did you bring me this far?'

Giles smiled without humour. 'Divide and conquer. I learned the lesson well during the War. Together with Petia, the pair of you might have stopped me. Now?' Giles shrugged. 'She might not even pursue, thinking us knaves.'

'And you leave me to die of starvation.'

Giles laughed and stood up. 'Hardly. You're a clever one. Those knots won't survive your efforts longer than a few hours. But by then I'll have reached the Gate.'

'Giles?'

'Goodbye, Keja. Please don't think ill of me. You're young and quick and have ample booty.'

Giles turned and left before he relented. He had learned during the War that a friend at your back counted for more than even a full belly and warm bed. And in the past twelve hours he had betrayed three friends.

But the reward! The Gate of Paradise!

Giles mounted and rode full out, mud from Hawk's Prairie rising under his horse's hooves.

Though he had tied Keja well, he knew that the young thief would be free of his bonds in a short time. The track led down, levelling gently as it neared the bottom. Giles Grimsmate looked down, unable to see the Gate from this vantage, but knowing that it was there. When the gods had set it there, they had done a remarkable job of camouflage. Only those with a key in hand might see it.

Giles glanced at the sky; the sun appeared and he saw spring moisture burning off. He urged his horse forward.

When Giles arrived at the spot he remembered so well, he dismounted, tying his horse to a bush. He pulled a leather pouch from his belt and emptied the five keys into his hand.

The Gate of Paradise appeared out of thin air before him. Walking slowly towards the Gate, he smiled mirthlessly as he read the runic inscription: *Only One May Enter.*

The locks were just as he had left them two years earlier. They showed no wear or evidence of exposure to the elements. Indeed, they looked as if the locksmith had just finished burnishing them.

Methodically, hands trembling, Giles inserted the keys into the five locks. He did not unlock any until he was certain that each key was in its own lock. Then, starting at the top, he turned the keys. Each lock snapped open with a loud crack, as if released from long imprisonment. When he had finished with the last one, he tugged at the massive gate and stood back.

It swung open slowly, effortlessly. All his dreams would be realised on the other side.

For a moment Giles stood, holding his breath. Then he edged closer and stared inside. He cried in frustration. There

534

was no wealth visible, no chests overflowing with gold and jewels. A barren chamber stretched before him, walls of unadorned rock. There was no furniture, no tables, chairs, chests, wardrobes. In the distance an object emerged from the floor, but it was too far away to identify.

Hand on sword, Giles took a tentative step into the cool chamber. Quiet, an air of peace, enveloped him. It was as if he had walked into a temple, away from the bustle of life, and found a profound serenity. His anxiety ceased; he knew that he was safe. Assured, he walked to the one visible object.

Closer, Giles saw a stone pedestal which seemed to grow out of the solid stone. When he reached it, he found that it was a crudely carved seat, devoid of marks or inscriptions. He stood, unsure, gazing around the chamber. Suddenly he laughed, a laugh that started deep in his gut and rolled out, echoing from the barren walls around him.

There was no treasure.

Wiping his eyes with the back of his hand, he stumbled backwards and sat on the stone seat. He'd wait for Keja, and they could share the humour of their quest. Truly, the gods played mortals for fools. His laughter finally subsided to a mere chuckle, and he pulled a handkerchief from his sleeve and wiped his eyes again.

He took a deep breath and leaned back.

A voice whispered, 'Be content.'

Giles sat up, alert, wondering if he were hallucinating. Again the voice came, 'Be content.' It was a voice filled with age, wisdom, and great love, and the peace which Giles had felt on first entering the chamber welled up within him.

Giles sat back, savouring the feeling. He began to think about the times of his life when he had been content. There were happy times before the War, his childhood and young manhood. He remembered courting his wife, their marriage and their joy at the births of their sons.

Then the War came, a long, terrible, exhausting struggle. Even then there had been moments of true happiness with good comrades. Men had given of themselves, were always there in times of need, and Giles had enjoyed good times between battles. Giles had counted those men as brothers.

His thoughts turned to the past two years. The quest for the

535

keys had been as difficult a thing as he had ever done, but every step of the way he had been accompanied by two of the closest, staunchest friends he had ever known. Keja, vain, not always the brightest, getting in scrapes and having to be rescued. Giles chuckled at the vision of Keja in the treasure room of Shahal, backed up against the wall by the giant snake. But who had rescued him from the temple in Kasha, carrying him up the stairs? Who had flooded the cave fortress of the Flame Sorceress? A poor thief, a great lover, a man who enjoyed life, a true friend and what more could one ask?

And Petia? He smiled at the image of Petia as mother, for that is what she had become. Another thief, even less skilled than Keja. But she always came through when she was needed, slipping into her cat persona and accomplishing things he and Keja could never do.

They were his two greatest friends: two thieves, one a Trans. And the boy, Anji, also a Trans, a slave when they had met. Giles had opposed bringing the boy along, but Anji had contributed more than his share to the success of their adventures. A bright lad who would grow up to bring some good into the world.

'By the gods, I am content,' Giles said, mood brightening. 'Life has not always treated me kindly, but it has treated me fairly.' He stretched cramped joints. 'There is no treasure here. A legend had promised it, but the legend was false. And whose fault is that? Mine or the legend's?' Giles shook his head. He'd been foolish, believing in Paradise. But he wasted no time castigating himself for it. Without hope what was there in the world?

Giles slid forward to the front of the stone seat. 'Yes,' he whispered back. 'Yes, by the gods, I am content.' He stood, stepped forward and disappeared.

Keja stared at the Gate. He peered from the inscription carved above it to the open locks, to the yawning ironwork gate. He stepped up to the entrance. 'Giles,' he called. 'Giles, answer me!'

Only silence greeted him. He looked furtively behind him. Perhaps Giles had already left and was watching him, laughing himself to death. He saw no one, yet Giles' horse was tethered nearby, and the Gate stood open. He peered into the dark, cool interior and called again.

His voice echoed back from the walls, but no other sound could be heard. Pulling out his sword, Keja passed warily through the Gate. The empty chamber surprised him: had Giles already looted so much treasure? He made his way cautiously, alert, just a little fearful.

He walked uneasily the length of the chamber, more perplexed with each step. No treasure. This was not at all what Keja had been led to expect. The room should be a treasure chamber, piled high with gold, silver, jewels, pieces of art. Only emptiness and silence met him, a cold stone chamber inhabited by echoes that mocked.

Keja approached the stone pedestal silently, anticipating Giles hiding on the opposite side, a big grin on his face, laughing at the joke the gods had played on them. He gave the stone seat a wide berth, in spite of expecting to find Giles there. He had been a thief for too long to let down his guard.

As he rounded the pedestal, he found the seat empty. An object glinted on the floor in front of the seat. It was a sword, and Keja recognised it as the one Giles had purchased in Sanustell.

He picked it up, looking around the chamber, wondering where Giles could be. The chamber was not so large that he could not see to the far end. No one was in sight, not Giles, or anyone else. He examined the sword carefully, then realised how foolish it was to think that it might hold a clue.

Frowning, he sat gingerly on the edge of the stone seat. The words came clearly, repeated three times. 'Be content.'

As Giles had done before him, Keja leaned back, musing about his past deeds. His life had been a short one, so far, but interesting. Inimitably Keja, his first thoughts went to the women he had loved. There had been so many, each with her own special, precious personality. His affairs had been tense, emotional, frenzied, sometimes suspenseful, occasionally peaceful and loving for a short time. He would not have missed a single one.

His childhood he skipped over quickly. It had been unpleasant and the less he thought about it the better. His life as a thief and rogue had been exciting, although not entirely successful. He wondered if there was any other trade he might pursue with more success. Shaking his head wryly, he thought not.

But perhaps he was wrong.

Throwing in with Giles and Petia had been the best thing that had happened in his life, he decided. The last two years had been more exciting than anything he had done previously. They had become deep and true friends, helping each other, living adventures unlike any others in the world, he had no doubt. He was saddened that it was over.

'I can never be content,' Keja said aloud. *Giles* had been content. He, too, must have thought over his life and found it good, as good as might be expected, in these uneasy times with all their upheaval. Giles had admitted that he was content and . . .

. . . had gone beyond.

'I'm not content,' Keja said almost joyously. 'How can I be when all of life lies before me? There's still much to do, women to love, the world to be experienced. I'm young, healthy, have plenty of time. I want to see all the world has to offer. No, I'm *not* content.'

Keja grinned broadly now, happy that it had been Giles who had passed through the Gate first. Keja wasn't content and didn't intend to be! The world offered too much for a rogue!

He stood, laughed and walked from stone seat. He lifted Giles' sword and held it vertically in front of his face in salute to his companion of the last two years.

'Goobye, Giles,' he whispered. 'Be with the gods. I'm off to find Petia and Anji and see what mischief we can get into. If they're willing, there's lots to see before we settle down. I wish that you would be with us, but you've made your decision. I'll miss you, we'll all miss you. But there are still worlds to conquer.'

He saluted again and strode away towards the Gate and the light of day outside. The Gate of Paradise. Keja chuckled and the hollow echoes multiplied until the chamber resounded eerily with the chuckles of a hundred voices. The Gate of Paradise was truly named. Men had searched for it over the centuries, led on by the legend of its treasures.

Five keys, and they had found them all. Keja drew near the Gate and wondered if Giles had left them in the locks. He passed through and turned. From each of them, a key protruded. He pulled the keys from the locks, and, starting at the top, closed each one. The clicks were solid and satisfactory.

He stowed the keys in a soft leather bag and placed the bag in the pouch at his belt, closing the leather-and-bone catch securely. The keys out of his hand, the Gate vanished. Keja stiffened, reached into the pouch and touched the keys. The Gate popped back into sight. He tested the locks one last time, then patted the pouch.

Keja didn't know if the Gate of Paradise would ever allow another through. Giles might be the only mortal ever to pass through, but Keja doubted it. The gods might enjoy a joke, but they occasionally dispensed mercy to mortals.

There might be a time when he would want those keys, a time when he might feel contented with the life he had led. But not yet. When that time came scores of years from now, Keja believed that the Gate would lead him to Paradise, just as it had Giles Grimsmate.

He stepped back; the Gate had once again vanished.

Keja stared through where the Gate stood and spied the top of the hill where he had left his mount tied next to Giles' horse. Petia sat beside the track. Anji knelt beside her, and Petia's arms circled the boy's shoulders. Keja tensed until he saw the smile on Petia's face and the joy mirrored in Anji's.

'Mother and child,' Keja muttered. And that didn't seem bad at all.

'Great treasures?' Petia called down to him.

Keja raised empty hands to her and laughed. 'Take as much as you want,' he called back.

He clambered up the hill towards the two Trans. When he reached them, he stood and surveyed the surroundings, the plain below, and the hilly country to north and south. Unsought and unwanted, the image of Lord Onyx flashed through Keja's mind. He had watched the Black Lord and his horse vanish beneath tons of earth, but the image of one raised fist, a black studded gauntlet surrounding the wrist, shaken in absolute defiance of his death, had invaded Keja's dreams during more than one night's sleep. The Gate of Paradise had been left by the gods. Giles had proved that. He had to believe that Onyx had been a god. Once.

But Onyx had died. And Segrinn, too. Keja's buoyant good spirits pushed them from his thoughts.

Keja collapsed onto the ground beside Petia and Anji. 'No treasure,' he said. 'And no Giles.' He described the chamber and what he had found there. 'We're no richer than we were when we started.'

Petia laughed. 'Yes, we are. Giles left me his share of what we brought back from Bandanarra. You must still have some of yours. Even gaudy clothes such as you're sporting now couldn't have cost *that* much. Anji and I will do well. What about you, dear Keja?'

Keja shrugged, then grinned. 'I've had a wonderful adventure, my Pet. I've enjoyed every second of it. Well, almost. I'm certainly no worse off than I was when I started, and I do have a few coins left. And you have one gift from Giles beyond compare.' Keja told of Segrinn's death. He climbed to his feet and touched Anji's arm. 'Take good care of Petia, Anji,' he said.

Then he turned, collected his horse, and swung himself up into the saddle. He saluted the startled Petia, and swung his mount back onto the trail heading west.

He came to the top of the rise and gave the horse its head as the track descended down into a vale. Springtime, a nice time of the year, new beginnings. For the first time in ages, a ballad sprang to his lips and he sang the words with gusto. He reached the bottom of the track and let his horse drink from the clear stream that ran through it.

Unclear words wafted to him from the top of the hill behind. He saw two horses on the skyline. The words came again, clearer.

'Keja. Wait. Wait for us!'

Keja waited.